UNDER ONE ROOF

Two Historical Novels by Norah Lofts

UNDER ONE ROOF

BLESS THIS HOUSE

Bless This House

This is the story of Merravay, a moderately sized house in South Suffolk which was built in 1577 by men who, though primarily concerned with earning their bread, found in their work the only outlet for their creative instinct. Therefore they made it beautiful, with a beauty to which some of those who came after were susceptible and others immune.

This is the story of those who built it, those who loved it, those who hated it, those who bought it with money, those who paid for it in other coin.

Such a story, spanning the years between the two Elizabeths, if made continuous, would be too long, so here, in a series of significant episodes, in each of which the house itself plays a part, is offered the history of Merravay.

Contents

The Apprentice

WE—that is my Uncle Francis and I—finished the building of Tom Row-hedge's new house at Merravay on the last Sunday in October in the year 1577.

The weather had changed that day and it was bright and clear with a hint of frost in the air. It was still sunny when, at midafternoon, Uncle Francis stepped back to survey the last bit of the work that had fallen to his share, the carving of the great newel post at the stair foot. I knew he had finished although I had my back to him and did not look round. I heard him grunt as he straightened himself; heard his foot on the floor as he stepped back; heard the sound of his horny hands rubbing together with satisfaction. Presently he spoke,

"Well, Jonathan boy, thass done. And though I say it, as sound and pretty a job as any I ever see."

I said, "Umm," behind my teeth. If he wanted praise for his work, I thought, let him look elsewhere. Not that praise would be lacking, for every bit of his skill and craftsmanship had gone into that staircase, and it was a job any man might rightly be proud of. He waited for a moment as though expectant of some further response from me, but I went on with my own last job, the fitting of the wide seat into the space under the big window on the far side of the hall. I hoped that he would go away, go home and leave me in peace. My thoughts, though far from pleasant, were preferable to his company.

He moved over to the place where our rush baskets yawned on the floor. I heard the clank of his tools as he laid them away, and then the gurgle of ale as he drank from the wooden bottle.

"Are you dry?"

"No," I said.

He fumbled about in the bag in which we carried our noon pieces. There was food in it, for he had eaten lightly at noon, being anxious to get back to his newel post, and I, not to be outdone, had also gone back to work with my hunger unsatisfied. I now heard the squeak of a knife against the crisp crust of the loaf, and then the moister sound of an onion being sliced.

"Care for a bite, then?" he asked.

"No."

He chumbled his food in his usual noisy way.

"How long do you reckon it'll take you to finish?"

If I said a short time he would wait for me; if I said a long one he would offer to help me.

"I don't know," I said.

He strolled over towards me, wiping his mouth on the back of his hand.

"You keep on at that rate, boy, and you gotta hour's work. Thass where you're weak, yet, Jonathan—reckoning up a job. You want to be able to cast your eye over a job and reckon exactly how long it'll take; otherwise when a customer say, 'How much,' you'd be all at sea, like. You'll hev to go a bit more careful when you get this end near the brickwork, don't you'll skin your knuckles. And you know I *still* think them pegs is cut a mite short. I quite see there ain't the wear and tear on a window seat that there is on stairs, still you want a job to last. Every peg in them stairs . . ." he turned and looked at his handiwork ". . . is six inches long. Ah, them stairs'll be there, sound as they are today, when your children's children are old 'uns with children of their own."

Wonderful! I thought. Tom Rowhedge's children and theirs, and theirs scampering up and down, all safe and secure because every peg in "them" stairs is six inches long and driven by an honest man. Oh for God's sake go away and leave me alone! With my teeth on edge I waited for him to say that he'd give me a hand. However, when he spoke he said,

"I'll just go and hev a look at that well cover; then there's another little job I wanta do. I'll be back time you're finished. On'y go a bit wary-like when you get to the corner. Once knew a man bark his knuckles on a new wall that hadn't had time to get friendly and a rare lot of trouble he had. His fingers was stiff to the end of his days."

"I'm always careful," I said shortly.

He left me. I heard the big door beyond the screen open and close, sweetly for all it was so newly hung.

Well, God be thanked, I thought, that's over. These last two months when Uncle Francis and I had been working alone in Tom's house had been about as much as I could endure. But it was over; when the last of my too-short, new-fashioned pegs was driven home Tom's house would stand, sound and beautiful, all ready for occupation.

I had only two more to drive when a chance glance through the window showed me Uncle Francis, with a short axe in his hand, striding away across the cleared space which was to be the garden and in which there was already a sundial, like the hub of a wheel, with tiny young box hedges radiating out like spokes, marking off the beds where next year the flowers would bloom. He jumped, nimble as a boy, across the dividing ditch, and set off across the meadow in the direction of Layer Wood. This afternoon the lowering sun shone on the thinned blazing leaves of the beeches, and the contrast between them and the few dark firs that grew amongst them was as startling and lovely as it was in the spring of the year when the firs looked black against the bright translucent young green. Wondering what in the world he was up to now, I drove home my last two pegs and laid my tools away. Then I lifted the ale bottle and shook it. It was empty. Quite reasonably, when I said I wasn't thirsty, Uncle Francis had drained it. I was reminded of one of the hateful old sayings which he quoted at me when I was a child and refused something and then regretted it. "He who will not when he may, when he would he shall have nothing." My uncle was never at a loss for a proverb and he produced every one as though it were mint-new.

Setting the empty bottle back in the basket, I remembered another of his silly sayings, "More ways of killing a cat than choking it with butter." Most applicable in my case because I had just remembered where I could get myself a drink. At Easter time, just before the bricklayers, the tilers, the plasterers, and ordinary carpenters had finished their work and were about to leave, Tom Rowhedge had paid us a day's visit and had stumped about all over the house, laughing and shouting, wildly excited, extremely pleased with all he saw. He had brought food with him, a whole ham, a great silverside of beef, a barrel of ale, a butt of wine, and a little keg of French brandy. There'd been a hilarious feast.

I was sick that day and although I hoped nobody had noticed me when I crept away, Tom had; and next morning, very early on his way back to Bywater, where his ship lay, he had halted his horse by our house and, without dismounting, rapped on the door. I opened it. He looked down at me and said,

"I was sorry you took sick, Jon. You still look a bit green; have a care to yourself. What I came to tell you was—they finished all but the brandy and that I laid by for you when you feel better. It's in the buttery cupboard and the key's under the beam. I must go. God keep you, Jon. I'll see you at Christmas."

He rode off into the mist of the August morning, leaving me with this new bit of his kindness lying like lead in my sick belly.

Now I took from the basket the horn cup which Uncle Francis had not troubled to use when he drank, and I carried it along, through the passage that led to the kitchen quarters, into the buttery, which smelt clean and fresh of new wood and new whitewash. I found the key and opened the cupboard and there was the little keg. I drew myself a cupful of the brandy and sipped it, somewhat disappointed. I had never tasted brandy before; the duty on it was heavy and put it beyond the means of workingmen, but I had heard about it and had expected something wonderful. And plainly Tom had thought he was doing me a special favour when he hid it for me. I thought it lacked the flavour of good ale and it hadn't the same mouth-filling quality; one's thirst didn't leap to welcome it and there was something rather choky about it. However, it was something to drink; and as it went down it was warming. I was grateful for that because I'd been working hard and grown hot, and the buttery, placed on the north side of the house for coolness, struck me with a sudden chill. So I emptied the cup and filled it again. And then, quite suddenly I understood why people who could afford it would buy brandy whatever the duty on it. I felt warm and light and taken out of myself. I could look back and regard all that had happened to me as though it had happened to another person. Nothing hurt any more. Everything was very clear and bright, but it was like a story, or like—if one could imagine such a thing—a series of vivid pictures in which people moved and talked . . . and I watched, understanding, sympathising, one with the person whose story it was, and yet detached and unhurt.

I suppose it was natural, since I was sitting in Tom Rowhedge's house, drinking Tom Rowhedge's brandy, that I should begin my remembering, or my recalling, or my re-seeing, with my first meeting with him. I'd seen him before because we were both at King Edward VI's Grammar School; but he was a lordly great boy of thirteen and I was a lowly worm of eight, so between us there was a great gulf fixed, a gulf wider and deeper and more carefully guarded than any which the adult world knows, a gulf neither of us would have dreamed of crossing even if we had been blood brothers. The sight of him walking with his father into the little apothecary's shop which my father kept in the Friargate, and which I was "minding" on this August morning during my first holiday, covered me with the blushing confusion only experienced by schoolboys. It was made all the worse because I had just then a private and particular reason for trying to appear indispensable to my father but I knew I couldn't serve Mr. Rowhedge nimbly and satisfactorily under Tom's eye, so I weakly rang the bell which summonsed Father. He came and quickly served Mr. Rowhedge with the horse pills he wanted.

"Your boy, Martin?" he asked.

"Aye, and a right helpful little fellow," said Father.

Tom's father eyed me as though I were an animal he thought of purchasing but had doubts about.

"Bit pingling looking, ain't he? Either you work him too hard, Martin, or else you give him the wrong physic." It was understandable that old Rowhedge, accustomed to looking at Tom, and perhaps to catching sight of his own reflection in a polished pan, should think that I looked very small and pale, for their faces—very much alike—were broad and red and shining with health.

"He isn't much of an advertisement for my trade, certainly," said Father in his precise way. "But apart from his little trouble—and that is mending —he's healthy enough. He seldom ails." Please God, I begged, don't let the great oaf ask what is my little trouble! "And he has a head on him," Father went on fatuously. "Doing well up at the school, aren't you, Jon boy?" Oh horror upon horror! In front of a big boy, too.

"Tell you what, Martin," said Mr. Rowhedge, "it'd do him the world of good to come out to Slipwell till th'end of the holiday. Famous good air out at Slipwell. A chestful of that and a bellyful of good farm food'd make a new boy of him."

My face felt redder than a poppy. The man meant well, of course, but I resented his remarks about my appearance and I was embarrassed beyond measure at the suggestion that I should go and stay in Tom Rowhedge's house. Good heavens, he might be obliged to speak to me.

"What d'you say, Jon? Would you like that?" Father was never the man to make up another person's mind for him.

I looked helplessly at Tom; and he was grinning at me.

"You could be my crew," he said. "I want somebody small and light." That was nothing less than an order. So I nodded, being beyond speech.

"You can ride back ahind of Tom," said Mr. Rowhedge. "The cob'll never notice your weight!"

The holiday thus carelessly suggested changed not the course but the flavour of my life. Not because of anything in itself but because it forestalled and prevented me from asking Father to let me leave school. I'd had a half year at King Edward's School and that was quite enough for me. I was almost certain that I had only to tell Father what it was really like and he would not wish me to remain.

But the holiday had slipped away without ever presenting me with the ideal opportunity for stating my case; Father was very busy. He had his shop and his workroom; he had his hobby, which was helping an eccentric old neighbour to set up and work a little printing press upon which they aimed, one day, to print Greaves' Herbal, and he had also to do all that was done on the domestic side. My mother had died when I was very small and Father's experience with hired help had been discouraging. So, being anxious to have his whole attention for my horrifying tale, I had avoided all those occasions when it seemed likely that he would say, "Don't bother me at the moment, Jon boy," or "Oh yes. Yes. Yes, I'm listening," when it was obvious that he was doing nothing of the sort. I had concentrated upon helping him, so earnestly, so devotedly, that he would deem me indispensable. And my reward for that was to be in the shop when the Rowhedges came in, and to be whisked off to Slipwell all in a minute and finally find myself, at the end of the holiday, riding back to school behind Tom. I'd hesitated and I'd lost.

By the time that school closed for Christmas the idea of leaving would have filled me with dismay.

The change was in me, not in the school. The rising bell still clanged at six in the morning; we still washed in cold water, seven or eight to a basin and woe betide him whose ablutions were scamped; we still hurried down to the great cold classroom and did two hours' work before attaining the dubious comfort of breakfast, a hunk of bread thinly smeared with lardy fat and a mug of the sourest flattest liquid ever called ale. No item of the routine varied. After breakfast we were turned into the yard to warm ourselves with rough play, and the bullies were busy, the tricksters played their practical jokes. Then we worked again until midday, each misunderstanding, each mistake, each scrap of detected inattention calling into play the formidable birch that Dr. Trudgett always carried under his left arm, whence it could, in the blink of an eye, be transferred to his right hand, which, for all it looked thin and frail, was as strong as a blacksmith's.

When I had planned my school-leaving campaign I had especially meant to emphasise the difference between the Dr. Trudgett whom my Father knew and liked and the Dr. Trudgett whom the classroom knew and feared. For many years Father had had dealings with the schoolmaster because, when King Edward had established the school on the site of the old Abbey of St. Dunstan, the first headmaster had saved from ruin the little herb garden which the monks had tended. In later days this had become a source of steady income to his successors, for most of the herb gardens attached to the monasteries and nunneries had been allowed to perish through lack of care, and in my day apothecaries and physicians from as far away as London sent to Baildon for their supplies. It was through buying herbs from the school garden that Father first got in touch with Dr. Trudgett, whom he came to admire very much, saying

—and this was high praise—that he was a most enlightened man. And I can believe that, standing in the evening light amongst the sweet-smelling herbs, discoursing upon this subject and that, Dr. Trudgett showed to advantage. Possibly Father showed to advantage too; for when the idea of sending me to school was mooted, Dr. Trudgett welcomed it, despite my disability, which Father in his honest way felt bound to mention.

"I have enough healthy ploughboys," he said. "And more than a few good scholars have been subject to just such fits as you describe in your boy."

He had added that most boys came to school too late and that in his opinion I should begin at once. And so I went to school after the Christmas in the year when I was eight.

But Father had never seen Dr. Trudgett in the classroom. Never heard him say to some pallid, trembling blunderer,

"You cannot reckon seven times eight! That must be mended, sir. Bend over and count aloud."

Seven times eight is fifty-six, and fifty-six strokes from Dr. Trudgett's birch would set the blood running from a boy's breeches.

That was the kind of thing I had intended to tell Father. But I never did. For as soon as I entered upon my second half year, having in the first mastered the painful rudiments, I found that I had the makings of a scholar. There is no vanity in that statement; it is a quotation from Dr. Trudgett's own dictum.

Within a week of our return to school I went to the head of the bench, and I stayed there. Before Michaelmas I moved to the next, where nobody was less than twelve years old. I was fuddled at first but I was so eager, so desperate to get along with this fascinating business of learning, that I even ventured to hold up my arm and ask for enlightenment when I did not understand. And more than once Dr. Trudgett would say, "That is an intelligent question!" and he would explain painstakingly.

Within the classroom all began to go well; and outside, too, in the yard, on the holding of forty acres where we worked for Dr. Trudgett's benefit in the afternoon, and in the big dormitory at night, things were better. I mean for me. And thanks for that were due to Tom Rowhedge. I might now be roaring ahead with the trivium, that is grammar, logic, and rhetoric, and rather more than holding my own with the quadrivium, though my arithmetic was faulty yet, but I was still a small boy, weak-fisted, and a born butt for fools because of my funny fits. But after that holiday, when I had been the meek, easily ordered "crew" of the boat that Tom had built and loved to sail on the river at Slipwell, he had assumed a kind of responsibility for me. By doing so he showed not merely physical courage but a boldness of spirit, a disregard for custom and tradition. He was thirteen years old, very big and strong for his age, but he was not yet amongst the biggest of the boys and he was a lamentably poor scholar. He still had his way to make in his own sphere. Any other big boy would have withdrawn himself and ignored me once we were back at school; but Tom did not. And one day, finding me in trouble, he said, "Leave him alone or you'll have me to reckon with." The boys who were bullying me were bigger than Tom and higher up in the school. But they were taken by surprise at his unorthodoxy, and remembered his reputation as a fighter. They jeered, of course, to cover their discomfiture but they drifted off without having accomplished their purpose, which was to see if I could be teased into having a fit. And after that I noticed a great lessening in the torment to which I had been subjected.

I don't think I could have been teased into a fit. Nobody teased me, that I can remember, when I lived at home with Father, and there I had fits pretty frequently. In those days they took me unaware. There would be a kind of crackling sound, like that of a stick fire newly lighted, in my ears, and a flash or two of light before my eyes. Then the shutter came down, and there was darkness. When I came round I felt a little weak and dizzy, but quite all right, except that once I had almost bitten my tongue through. After that—I suppose I was about six years old then—at the first crackle I used to thrust my thumb into my mouth and wait, looking like a thumb-sucking zany until the shutter fell. And soon I was wary enough to seek privacy at the first warning sign. At school, of course, that wasn't always possible, and to the louts my fits were a source of amusement. Dr. Trudgett, on the other hand, one day when I had one in his presence and came round, dizzy and apologetic, said,

"Don't worry about it, Borage. I've always been inclined to think that the Apostle Paul was similarly afflicted. He speaks often of a bodily weakness and men have been at pains to name it, attributing to him everything from lameness to lung sickness. But I think the clue lies in his experience on the road to Damascus. Tell me, do you see a great light?"

"Not a great light, sir. A feeble flash or two."

"And do you hear voices?"

"No voices, sir. Only a faint crackling."

"Well, you are young. And you are not an apostle. And you are not a saint. And probably I am talking nonsense. I merely wished to point out to you that your ailment is no reason for shame; nor for idleness. . . ."

I certainly was not idle, though that was small credit to me. I learned as naturally, as eagerly, and with as much pleasure as other boys played. When I returned to school after the Christmas when I was ten years old I was placed on the top bench but one and I vowed to myself that by

Easter I would deserve, even though I did not attain, a remove. Tom Rowhedge, who before Christmas had occupied the very seat in which I now sat, did not return to school, having realised his dream of going to sea. His father, with three elder sons to work the farm and share it, was anxious that he should seek a livelihood elsewhere and had sent him to school with the intention of making a merchant of him. But Tom chose for himself and the old man had promised that when he was as much at home on the sea as he was on land, he would buy and fit out a ship for him.

It was February and I was halfway up the bench and with six weeks still to go before Easter when it happened.

The usher, Master Richards, was taking the evening class when the message came for me to go to Dr. Trudgett's room. Boys near me whispered their jibes or their commiserations, according to their nature, and indicated by dumb show what I might expect when I got there. But walking along the dim passage which in the old days had been a cloister, I could not, search my mind as I might, hit upon any fault or any offence serious enough to rate my being called out from evening study. Even my arithmetic—always shaky—had seemed correct when I checked my answers with those of a boy who very seldom made a miscalculation. Still one never knew . . .

Dr. Trudgett was not alone in his grim little room; I was aware of that though I did not look at the visitor. I took a swift glance at my master's face and saw that something had upset him. He had a pale face as a rule, but anger always painted a thin pink glaze over his cheekbones. It was there now, and I dropped my eyes quickly and stood looking down at my own feet while my trepidation mounted. However, Dr. Trudgett spoke kindly,

"Come in, boy." He turned on the stranger and said, "Well, here he is, and you can see for yourself what I said. He's not cut out for manual labour. He has a modicum of brains, though. I had hopes for him."

"Had," not "have"; even then I noticed the tense.

I looked up, this time at the other man. He was a big, thickset fellow, clad in the drab-coloured homespun which workmen wear on Sundays and holidays, when they discard their working clothes. His deeply tanned face was heavily furrowed and wore a brooding look; the frown-scars on his brow, the way the thick eyebrows jutted and knotted, prepared one for a glance of some ferocity, yet his eyes, surprisingly light and blue, had a mild and kindly look.

"I'm your uncle, Francis Sheply," he said, "and I'm afraid I've brung you bad news."

I had never heard of him in my life; I was unaware that I had any relatives at all.

"Yes," said Dr. Trudgett. "Perhaps you'd better sit down, Borage."

More puzzled than ever, I took the chair he indicated and sat down on its edge, glancing from one face to another, waiting for one man or the other to break the bad news whatever it might be. I hadn't a suspicion, even then. "Your father is dead," said my uncle. "It seem he cut his thumb a while back and never heeded it, but it turned to blood poisoning and his end come very sudden. He on'y just had time to send for me and bid me care for you. And that, my boy, I'm right ready to do." He gave me a smile of kind reassurance which lighted his dark face strangely, and then he looked at Dr. Trudgett and added firmly, "According to my lights."

Dr. Trudgett ignored this and came and laid his hand on my shoulder. "You've sustained a heavy loss, Jonathan. You have my sympathy." His hand increased its pressure for a second before it withdrew. "Cry if you want to," he said. "There's easement in tears."

But there were no tears in me just then. I sat there with every feeling in me stunned, save only a half-fearful curiosity. Dr. Trudgett moved towards the window embrasure and with a jerk of his head indicated that my uncle should follow him.

"About this other business," he began in a low voice, "we must beware of making a hasty decision. And one thing to remember is that the lad is subject to fits. It seems to me that your plan for him would offer certain risks."

"He'll be under my eye. And he might well take a fit when he was sharpening a quill! There's another thing, too. For a boy like that a quiet outdoor life might work a cure. Too much striving indoors and fretting his brain may be the root of the trouble."

"Nonsense!" ejaculated Dr. Trudgett. But it seemed to me that even *he* had realised that Uncle Francis Sheply was not a man to be turned by direct opposition. He said more persuasively,

"Let us defer the matter for a while, say until the end of the half year. That can do no harm. And if you are thinking of the cost—as I can well understand you may be—think no more of it. Martin Borage chose to pay the fee but there are provisions in the foundation for poor scholars and there would be no difficulty, no difficulty at all."

" 'Tisn't the cost. The boy is no pauper. Martin Borage had money saved and owned his freehold. There'll be enough to set Jonathan up in business when the time comes."

This simple—and interesting—statement seemed to set fire to Dr. Trudgett's always easily inflammable temper.

"Then in God's name, man, *why* do you suggest taking him away?"

"Because, on his deathbed, Martin Borage sent for me and I gave him my solemn promise to handle the boy as though he was my own. Martin Borage and me was never friends, but the boy is my sister's child and therefore my flesh and blood, halfway at least. So I give my word, and my boy he is from this day forward. And no boy of mine would spend his young years sitting on a school bench."

"Why not?"

"Because I don't hold with it." That was the first time I heard those words fall from my uncle's tongue and I did not understand their deadly significance. I sat there, apparently disregarded, with my head in my hands, listening avidly; and I knew now roughly what the argument was about. I trusted Dr. Trudgett to rout Francis Sheply. I didn't know then that when Francis Sheply said, "I don't hold with it," there was no more to be said.

Dr. Trudgett, equally ignorant, said,

"And what, pray, do you mean by *that*? Why do you not hold with schooling?"

"I never said I didn't hold with schooling. I said I didn't hold with a boy of mine heving schooling. There've been schoolmen since the beginning. But 'tis plain to me that things was better, aye, a far sight better, when learning was kept where it belonged, to the great and the godly that was born to it in the station of life to which God had called them." (The smooth, pat, cultured phrase sounded strange on his rough tongue.) "To my mind things hev gone wrong through them that should be butchers and blacksmiths and shepherds getting a little learning and getting blown up with pride and argufying about what they don't wholly understand nor hev proper respect for."

"I *see*," said Dr. Trudgett drily. So did I. I knew at that moment what my uncle was; a backward-looking, would-be Papist. To him and to his sort Thomas Wolsey was a butcher, Thomas Cromwell a blacksmith. I understood why my uncle and my father had never been friends; I'd heard my father and his crony the printer talk about my uncle's kind; unprogressive, reactionary, people whose cardinal belief was, "As it was in the beginning so it shall be, henceforth and forever more." Years and years ago there'd been a lot of them, thirty thousand of them in the north of England had actually rebelled against the King. The Old Men and the New Men had come to blows and the Old Men had been defeated. But in lonely places, in a few stubborn minds the old fires, carefully hidden, still smouldered.

I waited now for Dr. Trudgett, with his shrewd wit and sharp tongue, to put my uncle in his place. He began with one of those calm, oblique statements which so often presaged devastating rage in the classroom.

"You are indeed a bold man to say that to *me!*"

But before he could proceed my uncle cut in with,

"Aye. And I'm sorry to run down in your hearing the trade you make your bread by. 'Tis as aggravating, I do see, as though somebody should say to me that carpentering and joining was a wicked waste of time. Just the same, feeling and thinking as I do about all this here new learning and the making of bad schoolmen out of what might hev been good workmen, I can on'y do my duty as I see it; and that is to take and make a good craftsman out of Jonathan here, same as I would my own boy."

Afterwards, thinking it over, as I did endlessly, I wondered whether Dr. Trudgett was conscious, as I was, of the blow dealt to his dignity and authority by the opening words of that speech. Without—I am sure—wittingly intending to do so, this rough country carpenter had reduced Dr. Trudgett to his own level, a man with a living to earn. He stripped him of his gown, of his birch, and under cover of a half apology, said, "If everybody thought as I think, you'd starve!" Whether Dr. Trudgett saw it as I saw it I never knew. Certainly he did not turn and rend my uncle as I had expected and hoped he would. He said, still in a reasonable voice.

"But he is not your boy; that must be remembered. His father sent him to school and so far as we can tell intended him to remain there. His wishes should be considered. Also I think, the boy's own. He is very young but his understanding is beyond his years. This is hardly the time perhaps . . . the news has been a blow to him. Really, I do feel that this should all be left for the moment. Why must such an important matter be decided this evening?"

"Thass a full day's walk from Nettleton to Baildon," said my uncle simply. "Altogether, time I see Martin Borage decently buried and get meself home again I'll hev lost five days' work. I don't want to hev to come back in the summer and go on argufying about what to my mind is plain at this minute. As for the dead man's wishes, 'twasn't you he sent hotfoot for as soon as he knew he was dying; 'twas for me. And though, poor man, he was past saying much, maybe sending for me had meaning. There's many a man," said Uncle Francis firmly, "that hev lived in error, die knowing the old ways is best; and maybe Martin Borage at the end knew it too. Otherwise why did he send for me, a day's walk away and no friend of his?"

"He was probably not in his right mind," said Dr. Trudgett sharply.

My uncle swung round; he brought one of his great hands, clenched into a fist, down on the end of the table.

"There you are!" he cried. "Thass the way it go now. Tossing the words hither and thither, spinning a web as sticky as a spider's to catch a man's wits in. He was out of his mind, you say; because when he was dying he saw how he'd been wrong with his pills and his potions and his new learning and his printing and his sending his boy to be stuffed up with pride. With his last breath, with his eyes darkening, a man incline to repentance —else why send for me that was dead set agin all *he* believed in. And so he's out of his mind. That'll do, sir; there's nought more to be said. I see how the wind blow here, and it is as I allust suspected. No fit place for the boy I hev took for my own." He moved around the table and touched my arm. "Come along, Jonathan. Thass time we was moving. Go fetch your duds, if you want 'em. You're coming home to bide with me and your aunt and I promise you it on't be our fault if you ain't happy there."

I moved my arm away from his hand and stood up.

"I don't want to go with you," I said. I turned to my master, "Please, sir, permit me to stay here."

"With the best will in the world, boy," said Dr. Trudgett. He bit his lip and beat his finger tips on the table; he seemed to be thinking deeply and rapidly. My uncle drew back a little. One could see how the deep grooves on each side of his mouth had been carved; his smile, no longer kindly, deepened them.

"As an orphan," said Dr. Trudgett quietly, "Jonathan now falls under the jurisdiction of the Justices. It is too late now, but tomorrow morning I will consult Mr. Aldridge upon this matter. I am prepared to abide by his decision. And you?"

The sardonic smile on my uncle's face deepened.

"That hare on't run, sir. 'Twas Mr. Aldridge himself that Mr. Turnbull the attorney called in to witness the will he'd drawed up in such a hurry. I can give you the wording. 'I appoint the brother of my wife, deceased, Francis Sheply, carpenter, of Nettleton in this county, to act as guardian to my son Jonathan and to hold for him, in trust, for the which he shall answer in the day of Judgement, such property as I die possessed of, until he shall come of age.' Thass plain enough, ain't it? And time the attorney did the writing I said, 'Martin, rest easy about the boy; he shall be to me as my own.' But, of course, if you doubt my word and hev a fancy to waste your time, and mine, we'll beat it out in front of the Justices."

"I hardly think you would have invented that legal phrasing. Well, in the circumstances . . ." He turned to me. "I'm sorry, Jonathan. You have the makings of a scholar and could have been a credit to the school. It's a very great pity." He stood for a moment, looking directly into my eyes with his boring gaze, and when he spoke again it was in his brisk, bracing schoolroom manner. "We mustn't waste energy on idle regrets, my boy. You *can* read, you've had a thorough grounding, such as few people attain. And man who can read has a door open in his mind which no one but himself can close again. Keep yours open. I hope you'll remember something of what you have learned, and I hope too that you will so apply yourself to your new trade that your uncle's prejudice against schooling for common people withers away."

The words were so final, so completely valedictory, that the expostulations and protests forming in my mind died away. There is something frightening in the sight of someone whom one has regarded as omnipotent suddenly yielding to a superior authority.

"I believe you already possess a book of your own. A *printed* book, is it not?"

"Yes, sir. A Gospel of St. Matthew."

Dr. Trudgett went over to the cupboard where his own books, a dozen or so of them, lay, and after some deliberation selected a chunky little book, clumsily bound in a linen cover.

"My father gave me this," said my master. "He wrote it and made it himself. He was bedridden many years. He devised this plan for making me *wish* to read Latin for pleasure. See . . . each story begins in English and then, at the turning point of the tale, goes on in Latin. I hope the day will come, my dear boy, when you will read on and never notice the change of language. And now I see that your uncle is impatient. Go and collect your belongings."

They were few enough. A change of linen, a spare pair of shoes, my printed Testament, and a sea shell given me by Tom Rowhedge as a parting present. I owned a knife, too, and a foot rule, and several quills, and a dozen coloured marbles; but they were in the classroom and I did not intend to risk, for their sake, the open question from Master Richards, "What are you about, Borage?" and the whispered questions of the boys. I laid my spare shirt flat on the floor, piled my goods on it and made a bundle. I remembered my cloak and retrieved it from the pegs in the dormitory passage. All the time something in my mind, relentless and sterile as the knock of a passing bell, kept saying, "This is the end, the end, the end."

On my way back to the room where my uncle waited I passed a little slit window where one June evening, towards the end of my first half year, when I was miserably unhappy and fully determined not to come back after the holidays, I had stood and looked out and seen my father, with his big basket on his arm, going across the yard towards the herb garden to collect his supplies. The sight had called to mind happy summer evenings in the past when I had been with him; and I had cried a few hot tears of homesickness and self-pity which I had imagined came from affection. Now I stood by the same window and suddenly, great boy though I was, I was crying again. And now I was wise enough to realise that I was not weeping for my father, who had always been so kind to me. For that I blamed Francis Sheply. If he had come with his news and gone again without interfering with me . . . then I should have had tears to spare.

II

If, during my first wretched half year at King Edward's, Uncle Francis had arrived and whisked me away, I should probably have settled down in Nettleton and thought myself happy and lucky. My uncle lived very comfortably indeed. The cottage had been built by my grandfather, and stood, with the adjoining workshop, in two acres of ground. We had our own cow, a number of pigs, a good many hens and ducks and geese; the garden produced all, and more, that we needed in the way of fruit and vegetables; and my Aunt Mary devoted her entire life to the management of her household. Except to go to church on Sunday morning she never set foot outside her own domain. She had no contacts with the outer world; Uncle Francis did what little marketing was needed, and even over so personal a matter as a new pair of shoes she would say, "When you pass Jim Farrow's next time, my man, bespeak my winter shoes; and tell him to allow for the growth of my bunion." And presently my uncle or I would fetch home the shoes and she would try them on and say, "They do very well. Thank you." She spoke less than any woman I ever knew; in fact she never made an unnecessary remark and for days on end would only open her mouth to say, "Supper's ready" or "Would you like some more?" On the evening, when we arrived at the cottage, tired and hungry, Uncle Francis said to her,

"Martin Borage is dead. This is his boy, Jonathan. I brung him home to live with us," and she looked at me—quite kindly—and said,

"He's welcome. I'll set another place."

I am not sure that she ever knew my name. She fed me and washed and mended my clothes, looked after me tenderly when I chanced to be sick, addressed me as "you" and referred to me always as "the boy." For all the impact I made on her I might have been a new bit of livestock Uncle Francis had brought home. And at first so far as I was concerned she might have been livestock too, an animal, domesticated, superlatively well trained: later on I found myself wondering about her. Had she once been otherwise? Had she come to this cottage a lively, ordinary, pretty young bride? (That she had, once, been very pretty, was obvious even yet.) And had she perhaps had likes and dislikes, a personality of her own; and had she come up against the deadly, overpowering character of my uncle and suffered a defeat, and retreated and taken refuge in making herself simply another of his tools? Was her silence, her complete negation, a defence? After I had repeatedly battered myself against his never-to-be-shaken, never-to-be-ruffled, so reasonable unreasonableness, I did sometimes wonder. I did sometimes consider following her example. Why speak, for instance, when what you said was without effect? Why not give in, become just another useful, inanimate tool?

It seemed plain to me, from the very first, that I should never be a good carpenter, even with the best will in the world. Material, the dead stuff I worked with, was against me. I might cut two pieces of wood, cut them with the greatest care, each, say, four inches long; when I had them nailed together—not when I measured them tentatively, mind—one would be slightly longer than the other, and the protuberant edge could never be neatly sliced off because it would develop an unsuspected knot, or go splintery. With even so simple a business beyond me, with every tool I handled going blunt or demented or purely vicious, my life was misery; and always there was Uncle Francis looming up, kindly, watchful, determined. "Now look, boy. You wanta take your hammer . . ."—or "your saw" or "your chisel"—"like this and put your hand so . . ."; and I used to think furiously, It isn't *my* hammer; damn you, it's your damned hammer; take your damned hammer, damn you, and do your own damned job. (My repertoire of abuse, even mental abuse, was pretty restricted.)

One day, irritated past caution, I said,

"Now do you see? Can't you realise that never in my life shall I be a good carpenter? I just haven't the aptitude. Please, please, Uncle Francis, let me go back to school and do something I *can* do."

"Don't talk so silly," he said placidly. "Didn't they ever teach you at school—if at first you don't succeed, try, try, agin. If not they oughta. Come on now, you give your mind to it. Thass really the trouble with you, you know. Your heart ain't here, yet. You still would rather be a half-baked clerk going round ready to sell your soul for a bit of scribe-work, than a master carpenter like I mean you to be."

"And what right," I asked hotly, "have *you* to choose what I should be?"

"Every right. You was left to me to bring up as my own."

"That was a mistake," I said, putting into words the certainty which I had fingered over many times. "My father was frightened. He was dying, suddenly, and he wanted to be sure that I had a home and somebody to look after me. That was all he meant. He wanted *you* to take *his* place, not that *I* should take the place of the son *you* never had! Can't you see that? My father cared about people being able to read and write . . . he'd turn in his grave to know that I was wasting my life here banging silly nails into bits of wood."

"Now half you a minute." (That was one of his irritating country expressions, meaning "Wait half a minute.") "You got this all wrong, boy. Look here. As you say I never had no son of me own, and many a time I hev wondered why God should see fit to hev me childless, when I hev a house, and a holding, and a good honest trade to pass on. And many a time I hev thought of taking a boy to rear and bring up in my craft. But something hev allust bin agin that idea. Then suddenly there is my own sister's boy handed to me. And maybe as you say your father was frightened, as well he might be, called to meet his God with all his sins on him; but he was in his right mind; so why, as I said to the man to his face, why didn't he hand you over to your Dr. Trudgett or leave you and his bit of money to the Justices to take care of? I know why. God guided him. God knew that you and me would fit in like a neat bit of dovetail. I saw that plain. And nobody, least of all you, my boy, can tell me any different."

Firm conviction is a contagious thing; and so is . . . well, what can one call it? . . . superstition? I know I stood there with my face still hot with fury and felt a cold finger trail down my spine. Stated with such confidence, the idea was just feasible enough to be uncomfortable.

It made *me* so negligible. Here's a boy for Martin Borage to send to school and take pride in. Right about turn! Here, Francis Sheply, is the boy you always wanted, a boy to train to be a carpenter!

But what about me?

Dr. Trudgett had often pointed out the distinction between the theories that were, as he termed it, "susceptible to proof" and those which were not, and later that day it struck me that Uncle Francis' theory about my destiny fell into the former class. So that evening after supper—it was early summer by this time and the daylight lingered—I stuffed my bilingual *Tales from Boccaccio* into my jerkin and, with my Testament under my arm, strolled out, saying that I was going to Layer Wood to read. To have taken two books would have aroused suspicion but the one visible one under my arm merely provoked Uncle Francis' dry comment that at this rate I should soon know it off by heart.

I walked to the wood, found the path, and started to run. The path was a short cut from Nettleton to Clevely and when I emerged from the wood, close to Rawley's farm, I was near the main road to Baildon. I walked again when I was near enough to Rawley's to be under observation, and then, once on the road, ran again as though the devil were after me. I walked through Minsham, then ran again, and so continued through the thickening darkness. I was more than halfway to Baildon before I was thoroughly exhausted. Then I lay down in a dry ditch and slept until the light of the new day, and the chorus of bird song which greeted it, waked me.

I was in Baildon, washing my hands and face and smoothing my hair over the horse trough in the Friargate just before nine o'clock, and at the school gate as the bell rang for the beginning of the morning class. I couldn't have timed it better. I was in the passage, just outside Dr. Trudgett's study door, when he emerged, settling the birch under his arm, twitching his gown into place, on his way to the classroom.

I said, "Sir."

He halted, looked at me for a second without recognition, and then said, "Ha, Borage! So you've come back, eh?"

"Yes, sir," I gasped; and then, because I knew he was impatient and time was short and this no place for beating about the bush and being diffident and deferential, I gabbled on. I told him that I couldn't bear life at Nettleton, couldn't bear being a carpenter; please, I said, please, couldn't I come back; couldn't he, wouldn't he, take me in and if my uncle came in search of me, say that I wasn't there.

"Dear me," he said, when I had gabbled myself to a standstill, "in one respect you tell the truth, at least. That your mind is withering. In good truth, that is so. I always thought you were a sensible fellow. And now you invite me, *me*, to conspire with you in the telling of a lie, and what is worse a stupid lie! How could I hide you, as you so flippantly suggest? To begin with you would have to re-enter as a poor scholar, and your qualifications for that estate would involve the submittance of your name, your antecedents, and circumstances to the Justices and the Governors. Besides, do you seriously imagine that when your uncle raised the hue and cry for you I should perjure myself on your behalf. Really, Borage, it is a plan of which any intelligent boy on the bottom form would be ashamed!"

"It was all I could think of," I mumbled.

"The obvious thing, I suppose. So obvious that your uncle and guardian is probably at the gate this moment! Come in here a moment." He opened the door of his room. "Now, tell me truly—is it merely that you dislike the work, the way of life, or is he unkind to you? Are you ill fed? Ill treated?"

"Oh no," I said, rather wildly, because his suggestion that my uncle might already be on my trail threw me into a panic. "He's kind to me. It's just that I don't like it there. I don't want to be a carpenter. I want to come back to school. I want to go on learning. I'd rather be here and be beaten every day for misconstruing or miscalculations than do woodwork with my *kind* uncle."

"Few of them," said Dr. Trudgett, jerking his head in the direction of the schoolroom, "would agree with you." He brooded for a moment. "It does all seem a pity, a very great pity indeed. I was grieved at the time, I remember. But your uncle is within his rights and honestly, Borage, there is nothing *I* can do. In Utopia, I suppose, education will be compulsory and men like your uncle will gnash their teeth in vain . . . but this is not Utopia. How old are you, Borage?"

"Thirteen in November."

"Eight years to wait. In eight years you will be of age and your own man." He scowled, trying to remember. "And your uncle mentioned a little property. Look," he said, and his expression lightened, "I do believe that you are one of those rare people who do seek after learning, and wish to pursue it. If you can practise your reading and not let your mind rust, it would not be too late in eight years' time. Come back to me then. You'll be twenty-one in November—providing I am still alive we will spend the Christmas holiday together; we'll work fourteen hours a day. And then you shall go to Cambridge. The Master of Peterhouse is an old friend of mine. . . . It shall be managed, Borage. Tell me, can you remember when you were five . . . anything that happened when you were about that age?"

"Why yes, sir. On the day itself I broke a precious flask in my father's workroom and I remember him saying that were it not my birthday I should go supperless to bed for meddling."

"And that seems long ago?"

"No, sir. When I speak of it, it seems like yesterday."

"Well, that was eight years ago. In a similar length of time you will be free to sate your hunger for learning. And now you must go back and do your duty by your uncle, thanking God that he is, as you say, kind. Many are not. Wait . . . I have another thought. Nettleton . . . of course! Simon Dodson is priest of that parish; a very learned man, though his stutter has prevented his gaining preferment. *He* could help you; he has books, ability . . . and, I doubt not, is lonely and fears as you do the withering of his mind. Have you not become acquainted? I will write to him on your behalf. Two old King Edward's boys in one small parish, and not friends? Strange!"

"But he is married, sir."

"And how should that prevent his noticing a good mind dying for lack of sustenance on his doorstep?"

"My uncle strongly disapproves of married priests, sir. On Sundays we go to church and my uncle pays his dues. But only to escape the penalties. Privately he calls Pastor Dodson 'the leader of the Geneva Jig' and outside the church door has no truck with him."

Dr. Trudgett wrinkled his brow.

"The Geneva Jig; what is that?"

"A derisive term, sir, applied to the Psalms as arranged for congregational singing by a Catholic gentleman—of Cornwall, I believe."

"A man of your uncle's mind?"

I nodded.

"I see. So closer contact with Simon Dodson would be an embarrassment to you. What a pity! Yes, yes. Come in," he cried as a timid knock sounded on the door. And there was a boy, sent by Master Richards, to ask with all respect whether the bell has been rung loud enough . . .

I knew that to the end of my days I should remember the lonely, deserted feeling which came upon me as I saw Dr. Trudgett settle the birch and twitch at his gown as he sent the boy running to say yes, of course he had heard the bell and would be in the classroom in a moment. There was a close organisation, a little society, going its way, and he had his place in it . . . and I had once had mine. But no more! I was outside of it; and I was alone. I had the thought that as I felt then the dying might feel. All this activity, all this routine in which I once had a share, is going on without me. . . . Horrible.

I stood in the yard for quite a long time. I could hear the murmur of voices, and twice the unmistakable smack of the birch. And I looked ahead at eight long years of sawing and planing, hammering and chiseling; eight years of Uncle Francis saying "I don't hold with it" and the subject being closed. I thought, I won't go back. I'll go on and I'll find another school; I'll say my name is Jon Carter or something like that and that I am an orphan. . . . I'll get in somewhere, somehow.

Of course, I was young, immature, and romantic.

I was not yet sure that Uncle Francis' theory had been disproved.

Presently I gave myself a shake and remembered that if Uncle Francis really were looking for me this would be one of the places he would search. So I trotted out of the school gate and away down the hill to the market place, from which roads led off in all directions. I intended to take the one to Colchester, which went on, I knew, to London. But by this time I was extremely hungry. The stomach has its habits and mine was used to being stuffed full of bread and bacon and home-brewed ale at seven o'clock each morning. It was now almost ten. And on the corner of the market place and the road to Colchester there was a baker's shop. A smell to make the hungry mouth water issued from the new loaves which a pleasant-faced, stout woman was taking from a big basket and laying on the shelves. I halted, sniffing. I hadn't a penny in my pocket; yet the idea of begging took a bit of getting used to. While I hesitated, the woman looked out and saw me.

"What do *you* want?" she asked; her voice far less pleasant than her face would have led one to expect.

I would have said, "Nothing," and moved on, but the thought struck me that I must get used to asking for what I wanted, what I needed, what I must have . . . and I might as well start now.

"I want a penny loaf and I have no penny."

"Oh!" she said. "Well, I have a weevilly flour bin that should be emptied and scoured out against the new lot coming in this very morning. If you like to do that for me you can have a loaf . . . when the job's done."

Such a chance might not occur again between here and Colchester, I thought, so I said I would do the job and she led me through the shop into the bakehouse, showed me the bin and the bucket and the scrubbing brush, and then stood and watched while I took off my doublet and laid it, with my books, on another bin.

"Have you run away from school?" she asked.

"No."

"Yet you ain't a Baildon boy; nor you don't look like a beggar," she mused.

"I'm on my way from one school to another, if you must know," I said.

"No need to be rude. And do well into the corners," she said. She went away to the shop; but presently she was back and stood there telling me about the accident which had happened to her husband. "So I'm single-handed," she said. "And before you go you can help me open the yard gate, then it'll be ready for the miller. But you can eat your loaf first." She inspected the bin and seemed pleased, and when she brought me the loaf she had split it and laid a piece of meat within. I wolfed it quickly and then went to help her with the gate, a tall heavy one which had sunk on its hinges and opened with the utmost difficulty. As I tugged it the last stubborn foot the woman said, "Well, ain't that timely. Here is miller." I looked out and saw the wagon; and then the miller—Jacob Woody of Nettleton.

"Well," he exclaimed, "I'll go to sea if it ain't Jon Borage. You wicked little varmint. There's your pore uncle standing at the crossroads asking everybody to cry you . . ."

I had turned as he spoke and was making for the shop, thinking that I could be through it and away up the Colchester road before he had climbed down from the wagon. But the woman had already slammed the door and was standing guard of it, saying,

"There, I knew it. I had a feeling . . ."

"By cock," said the miller, now on his feet in the gateway, "if you was mine, I'd give you a rare walloping. Up all night Francy Sheply was and half a dozen more with him, reckoning you'd took a fit. Hollering and hunting all through Layer with lanterns they was, and down by the river. And now there he stand, wasting a working day, asking everybody

what pass to look out for ye and hev you cried everywhere and pass on
the word. I should hope he'll give you a hiding—and here's one on account." He raised the whip he had in his hand and aimed a blow at me.
Without warning the crackling, flashing darkness whirled down on me,
and when I came to my senses again I was lying on the wagon floor and
the wagon was rumbling into Nettleton. I'd had no time to push my
thumb into my mouth and consequently my tongue was so badly bitten
that I couldn't speak or eat for several days. When I could speak I said to
my uncle, "I'm sorry you were alarmed about me; but I still don't see
that you had the right to have me cried as though I were a stray horse."

"Oh! Well, I shall hev," he answered.

At the end of that week he had me up in front of the Justices and I
was formally apprenticed to him for seven years, with four years of journeyman status to follow. Until I became twenty-three I should be, virtually,
his bondsman. Incongruously enough, at the same time he moved his
order for flour and meal from Jacob Woody and gave it to the miller at
Clevely. Woody, when he brought me home, had said frankly that he had
struck me, and Uncle Francis "didn't hold" with that.

Well, so far as any theory concerning God's intentions and man's destiny was "susceptible to proof," my uncle's idea that he and I were intended to be dovetailed together seemed to have stood the test. Half-
convinced, but even more resentful, I began to settle down.

III

I was fifteen when I made my next, rather less amateur bid for freedom.
By that time I had grown a good deal and my fits came more and more
rarely. Uncle Francis was fond of pointing out that he had been right
about the health-giving effect of manual work. He delighted also in my
increasing handiness and skill, for by this time I had had sense to see that
if I must be a carpenter I might as well be a good one; there had been a
time when I had done slovenly work deliberately, but that became boring
in the end. I might finally have found some pleasure in my work but for
the fact that Tom Rowhedge came home from sea just at the time when
my uncle and I were working on a new barn at Slipwell. There again
the finger of destiny might be perceptible; for Slipwell was eight or nine
miles from Nettleton, and it is unlikely that Tom would ever have known
that I was in Nettleton, or, knowing it, have troubled to seek me out.

Tom was now twenty, an enormous, handsome, swaggering fellow,
with a darkly tanned face and a huge copper-coloured beard and thick
gold rings in his ears. At no time in our lives had the five years' difference
in our ages loomed so large. He had done his five years at sea—and from

things he occasionally let drop in conversation I gathered that they had been years of great hardship; even Tom, who was tough and plucky, confessed that during the first months he had contemplated running away *from* sea more often than when at King Edward's he had dreamed of running away *to* sea. But he had survived and was now to reap his reward; his father was going to fit out a ship of which Tom would be master. Old Rowhedge could afford that—as well as paying other people to build his barns—because he had been made very prosperous through the peculiar thing which was happening at Slipwell. Farther to the north the coast was sinking into the sea, at Dunwich whole streets and great churches were being lost, but at Slipwell the land was rising. There were old men there who could remember their fathers recalling the time when the marshes at Slipwell were useless, wet, and reedy, and actually under water for eight months of the year. Gradually, over the last hundred or hundred and fifty years, the marshes had risen and were now useful grazing ground for sheep. True the animals were scrawny, but old Tom Rowhedge was not interested in the amount or the quality of the mutton they produced; he reared them for their wool, and since wool was in great demand just then, he was making a pretty penny.

I can only suppose that Tom, once the excitement of his home-coming had died down, was lonely and found it easier to talk to someone who had *seen* a globe and knew the difference between America and Africa, even if that someone were only a fifteen-year-old carpenter's apprentice, than to his father and brothers and the men in the village whose idea of a far distant place was Colchester or Dunwich. Whatever the reason, during the weeks when he was at home he seemed to seek my company, and often while I was working he would lounge about and talk, or even lend a hand to the job I was doing. And in the evenings we often walked together. Towards the end of his stay, softened by his friendliness, I spoke of myself and tried to tell him something of my wretched discontent. Tom, like Dr. Trudgett, asked whether my uncle was kind to me.

"Completely, entirely," I said. "But you know, Tom, you can murder a fellow by cracking his skull with an axe, and you can also do it by pushing a featherbed over him and holding it down long enough. That's how his *kindness* feels to me. I'd far rather he fetched me a clout occasionally and gave me a shabby breakfast and let me go and read with Pastor Dodson."

"Don't wish for clouts or bad food," said Tom. "But why shouldn't you read with old Dodson if you want to?"

"Because Uncle Francis doesn't hold with him! I see pretty clearly now what's in his mind. He's absolutely old-fashioned, practically a Papist you know, and he thinks all the new ways are just temporary things. So it's the duty of people who think as he does—and there are more of them than you might think—to rear up a generation of young ones with the same ideas. It'd be such a pity, wouldn't it," I said sourly, "if when the old ideas became fashionable again nobody remembered exactly what they were!"

"I can't exactly see the old ideas coming back," said Tom. "The new 'uns fit far too easy. Married clerics for example. Who'd want to go back to the old ways when it meant giving up a nice little bed-partner like Agnes Dodson. She must be at least twenty years younger than he is, wouldn't you think?"

I'd never noticed Mistress Dodson. My interest in women was still so completely childlike that I still reckoned them adorable if they handed out cake when one worked for them, and detestable if, halfway through a job, they changed their minds and wanted something altered. Also at this moment I was irritated by the switching of the conversation from the general to the particular.

"I don't know how old they are," I said. "I only know he has a lot of books, more even than Dr. Trudgett; and I'm not allowed to do more than answer him civilly if he greets me. That *does* stick in my craw. Together with a lot of other things."

"What things?" Tom asked; accepting my change of subject more good-humouredly than I had accepted his.

"Well, this apprenticeship, for instance. Seven years and then four. Positive slavery, and all over the country the system is on its last legs, and he knows it. Only the old-fashioned people bother nowadays; and a good thing, too. Don't you think it's iniquitous that until I'm twenty-three I can't get a job, or choose where I live, or get married. . . ."

"And are you anxious to get married?" Tom asked with a smile.

"Don't be silly. It's just a rotten system whereby a person who doesn't want to do a job at all is tied to it in such a way that when he gets out of bondage he's too old to do anything else. That's the old way, the good old way!"

"Aye; I can see. It's hard-tack for you. And there ain't much I can do, Jonathan. Now if you had a hankering for the sea . . ."

"But I have," I said, not with complete truth, for until Tom had returned with his wonderful stories and his fine clothes and gold rings I had never actually envied him his trade; his freedom to choose it, yes, I had envied that.

"Well then . . . if you really mean that, boy, maybe we could come to some arrangement with your uncle. It costs a bit to break or transfer indentures I believe . . ." He scowled. "But a handy boy like you,

trained carpenter and all, and light in the rigging would be a very useful thing to have. And I'd see you got your sea legs, Jonathan, a damned
sight easier than I did." His eyes began to sparkle with the old boyish
enthusiasm I remembered.

"It needn't cost you anything," I said proudly. "My father left me fifty
pounds. Uncle Francis has it locked in the chest by his bed; and every
month he adds a shilling to it. It's *just* possible that if I offered him that
for my freedom . . . Oh, Tom, if only he would!" It seemed, for a moment,
almost likely, for Uncle Francis was, within limits, a money-minded
man. He would not put money before his principles, and he was not the
kind of "careful man," of whom there were many in our neighbourhood,
who would live meagrely in order to save a penny, but he would, and
often did, haggle for an hour over the price of a job he was to do, or
of material he had to buy, and I never knew anyone get the better of
him in a bargain.

That evening I suggested to Uncle Francis that he should cancel my
indentures and allow me to go to sea with Tom, and in return take my
fifty pounds for his own.

He laughed his rare laugh.

"You really are a silly young fool, Jon," he said. "The most I ever
heard of paid for indenture breaking was twenty pounds, and that was
a gentleman's son that was apprenticed to the wine trade, and both
his father and two brothers older than him died in one week of the winter
sickness so he must buy himself out and go to look after his manor.
And here's you, my own flesh and blood, offer me fifty to do a thing I
wouldn't do for ten times the money! Where'd you be in a year's time, a
silly great gaby like you. Tom Rowhedge can look on the sea as a playground, soon's he's sick or sorry there's a plough waiting for him at Slipwell. You'd be just a half-timed apprentice, no more use than a half-baked
loaf. You just oughta go down to Bywater one day and take a look at
the old sailormen on the quay there, poor old hulks with one eye, or peg
legs, or empty sleeves. They was all going to make their fortunes, once.
Now they wish they'd stayed at home and learned a craft. And thass what
you're going to do, boy, willy-nilly. And the day you finish, a right craftsman like me, able to hold your own with all comers, with fifty pounds
in your hand, and a bit added, you'll thank me from your heart. Them
that went so fast, with a three-years apprenticeship—they've cut to that
now, God forgive 'em—poor handless critters that couldn't make a kitchen
shelf—they'll look up to you and call you master. Aye, you'll bless the memory of your uncle that wouldn't let you runagate, wasting your substance
or your time. And thass my last word, Jon," he said, his face growing
sombre again.

IV

So Tom Rowhedge sailed away in quest of fortune and I stayed at home, mastering the carpenter's craft and in my spare time reading my two books, trying to keep open that door in my mind of which Dr. Trudgett had spoken, until the rather horrible day came when I realised that I was not *reading* any more; I knew my Gospel and *Tales from Boccaccio* by heart. It was useless to ask Uncle Francis to give me money to buy a new book, he didn't hold with reading. However, I was now well on into my eighteenth year; in fourteen or fifteen months I should be a journeyman, drawing a journeyman's small wage. The first thing I would buy would be a book, I thought.

And then I fell in love.

Her name was Elizabeth—Elizabeth Rawley—and she was the youngest of five pretty girls who owed no part of their charm to their ribbons and laces and such falderals, for their father was an old curmudgeon, noted for his meanness even in our parts, where "carefulness" was regarded with respectful admiration. He was very unneighbourly too, and as his farm lay on the far side of Layer Wood, on the boundary of Nettleton and Clevely, the Rawley girls were hardly known to us by sight until old Rawley fell out with the parson at Clevely over a load of hay. After that he elected to attend our church, as he was entitled to do since he had land in both parishes, though the church at Clevely was much nearer his house. We knew about the dispute concerning the hay because it was the kind of news which Uncle Francis would seize upon and drone on about as another sign of the bad new times; he sided heavily with the parson of Clevely, who, since he was unmarried, was more to his taste than our Pastor Dodson. So we were not surprised one Sunday morning to see old Rawley walk into church, looking like an angry old bear and followed by his wife and four daughters. The eldest girl had been married a year or so previously and the grudging meagre wedding feast had been a matter of gossip ever since.

It was a lovely warm summer morning and all but the elderly women were wearing light-coloured gowns or dull ones brightened by a bit of cambric or ribbon. The Rawley girls wore a kind of uniform, skimpy straight gowns of grey homespun, and plain straw bonnets. But they were young, and they were pretty, and they were new to us, and that morning there was a good deal of fidgeting and head-turning among the younger men—and some no longer young.

It happened that they were just in front of me, so close that I could smell the lavender in which those ugly dresses had been laid; and presently I noticed that although, from the back, they looked so much alike, there were differences in size and shape. And whereas three of the girls had yellow hair, one had black. Little tendrils of it crept out from under the bonnet's edge and lay, soft and curly, like little feathers against the whiteness of her neck. Unfairly, I immediately began to credit her with all the sweet smell of lavender. Then I noticed that she was the smallest and slightest of the four . . . and something began to move in my stomach, which was entirely new and rather painful and yet altogether delightful and exciting.

The moment service ended old Rawley led the way out and they all followed, looking neither right nor left, but I did catch a glimpse of the dark-haired girl's face, and it was, to my mind, the prettiest of all. The others were pink-cheeked and touched by the sun, but she was pale, pale as the windflowers which shimmered through Layer Wood in the spring.

I ceased to look forward to the moment when I should earn a wage and be able to buy a book. My forward-looking narrowed itself down to seven-day stretches between Sunday mornings. The curious feeling in my stomach grew. Presently it no longer depended upon the sight of her; it was there, all aquiver, when I thought about her.

Then there came a memorable evening when I was taking the short cut through Layer Wood. I was alone, for lately Uncle Francis had trusted me with simple jobs, and this one, the building of settles either side a hearth in a house at Clevely, was well within my scope. I was walking along a ride thickly bordered by blackberry bushes when, just ahead of me, I saw my little dark-haired girl. She was jumping and snatching at something in the bushes. I quickened my step and saw what had happened. She had hooked down a branch where the berries grew larger and in greater profusion, and the spray had sprung back, taking her crooked stick with it. As soon as she saw me she desisted from her effort to recover the stick and, turning to a lower bush, began to pick busily. It was a chance not to be missed. Yet I almost passed by because at the idea of speaking to her my heart began to thump so heavily that I went dizzy and a kind of blackness came in front of my eyes. I was reminded of my now all-but-outgrown affliction, and thought with terror—suppose I had a fit now! A thought to remember with irony later on. The dizziness did not crackle, however, nor did the darkness flash, and I finally got back enough breath to say chokingly,

"Let me try."

It was too high even for me; but I had my tools with me and it was the matter of a moment to walk into the wood, find a crooked hazel, and cut another.

"Oh thank you," she said, and smiled, and I saw how sweetly her mouth curved over her small teeth, and how long her eyelashes were. Everything in me moved towards her with pure love.

"Wait a minute," I said, and, taking the stick I had made, I hooked down the one she had lost; then there were two sticks, and two people gathering the berries.

We hardly spoke. I asked her name and she told me, Elizabeth; and the word was full of music and wonder, as though that had been the first time it had ever fallen on human ear. I told her that I had seen her in church, and she said, yes, she knew. My shyness wore off with a rapidity that astonished even me, and when the basket was full to the brim I was bold enough to ask,

"Will you be blackberrying tomorrow?"

"Oh no. Thanks to your help I have enough."

"Let's throw some away."

She was shocked. "Oh no. I couldn't do that."

"Well, what will you be doing tomorrow?"

"Making the jelly, I expect. I have the little jobs while the others help to bring in the corn."

"And what about the next night?"

"Oh . . . well, if the jelly sets I might carry some to my Aunt Thomasin. I usually do and then, later on, she gives us some of her quinces."

I knew where her aunt lived.

"If you could make it about this time on the day after tomorrow, I should be finished work and I could meet you here again. If you like," I added.

"It isn't what I like. It's Father. He'd be very cross. He'd be cross if he knew I was talking to you now."

"Why?"

"We're not allowed to talk to people, well . . . men, or boys. . . ."

"Then he shan't know. I'll meet you here, about this time, the day after tomorrow." Already that moment had a luminous golden haze around it.

"All right," she said dubiously. "But if it rained, or if the jelly didn't set or anything . . ."

I carried the basket to the edge of the wood. She was ill at ease again and finally almost snatched it from me.

The next evening but one was quite fine; but though I waited about in the ride until it was pitch-dark she didn't come; nor did she any evening for the rest of the week. And when on Sunday all the other people stood about after church, greeting one another, gossiping, exchanging the week's news, and making the most of what, for those who lived in outlying places, was the only meeting during the week, old Rawley walked straight past and away and though I was so close to Elizabeth that I could have leaned forward and kissed her, she never even glanced at me.

The next week—though my work at Clevely was done and it was awkward to manage the time—I spent the evenings in the woodland ride; and the next Sunday was as unrewarding as its predecessor. It was plain to me that some action was needed.

The following week was the Harvest Fair in Baildon. Everybody had a holiday on that day. Even Uncle Francis took the day off; not because he approved of the various devices for parting labouring men from their hard-earned coins but because the Fair was one of "the old customs" and mixed up in the merrymaking there were genuine stalls where goods and stores for the winter could be purchased at less-than-market prices. My father, who had never respected anything merely because it was old, had heartily disapproved of the Fair on account of the low prices, which, he held, were unjust to the regular shopkeepers in the town.

However, the Fair gave me an idea, because on that Sunday, staring at the little curls on Elizabeth's neck, I thought how easy it would be, if she were almost any other girl, for me to ask her come with me to the Fair. And so an idea fell into my head.

Some kind of sentiment prevented me from parting with the book Dr. Trudgett had given me; so I sold my Testament back to the printer who had been my father's friend. He scolded me heartily until I said, "But it is useless to me now. I know every word in it by heart."

Then he ruffled the pages and asked, "Is that so, indeed? Tell me then what follows the words, 'This fellow doth not cast out devils but by Beelzebub the prince of devils.' Go on from there."

"'And Jesus knew their thoughts and said unto them, Every kingdom that is divided against itself is brought to desolation; and every city or house divided against itself shall not stand. And if Satan cast out Satan . . .'" I went on, glib and flawless while the printer stared.

"Enough!" he said at last. "As you say, you need this no more. How come you to have such knowledge of it?"

I told him that it, and one other, had been my sole reading for five years.

"Oh then," he said, "you wish another book . . ." and began to gabble about how much he would allow on the Testament against a new one, what new ones he had, and so on.

I was furious with myself not to have thought of making an exchange before; and I was furious with myself because even then, even with my plan in mind, I *was* tempted. I wanted another book, I was hungry for one. So I said gruffly what I wanted was money for the Testament; what would he give me?

I went straight to a stall of trinkets and bought a pair of shoe buckles, very plain, but good of their kind.

Next evening I walked boldly up to Rawley's door. The lower half of it was closed, the upper half open, and when I reached it, angrily and loudly announced by the yard dog, every member of the family seated about the supper table was turned towards the opening. I saw Elizabeth's creamy pallor change to the grey-white of ashes as she recognised me; I hated myself for frightening her; I tried to shoot her a reassuring glance.

Old Matt Rawley was in the process of lifting a thick slice of brawn balanced on a thicker piece of bread towards his mouth. He arrested it just long enough to ask,

"Whadda you want?"

I held out my hand in which lay one of the shoe buckles, now somewhat battered and scratched and far from new-looking.

"On Sunday morning," I said quickly, anxious to put Elizabeth out of her torment, "I picked this up in the aisle just after you'd gone past; and I thought it might belong to one of the young ladies."

One could imagine the flutter of interest and inquiry that such an announcement, made from some distance, would cause in any other family of five women. Around the Rawley table no one said a word. And only Elizabeth moved. She leaned back in her chair with a gesture of relief.

"Whad is it?" Matt Rawley demanded.

I took that as invitation to enter. I'm in, I thought.

"Shoe buckle, ain't it?" he said, as I laid the object beside his plate. "Any of you mawthers hev such a thing?" His fierce little eyes swept round the table, as though daring any daughter of his to admit to the possession of such an ornament. One by one they said, "No, Father." Then Mrs. Rawley said,

"My Sunday shoes have buckles. May I see? No. Mine are quite different."

"Oh well," I said, "I just wondered. I'll give it to Sexton. Whoever lost it will be asking on Sunday."

"It was kind of you," said Mrs. Rawley in her quiet little voice. It was from her that the girls had their prettiness and their gentle ways.

"It was a pleasure," I said. Then I turned about to Matt who was proceeding with his supper.

"By the way," I said, "I suppose you know about your gate at the top there."

"What about it?"

"It's down, post and all. I wondered. I noticed you'd got stock in the field."

He shoved the last piece of brawn into his mouth and jumped up.

"You young fool, why the hell di'n't you say so afore. Stand there blithering about a pack o'nonsense time my cows get out. Come on. You can gimme a hand."

He blundered out into the yard, muttering. "One of them brutes musta rubbed agin it. 'Twasn't very stiddy certainly but 'twas all right last time I hitched it."

And it had been all right, that is no more tumble-down than anything else on the ramshackle place, when I unhitched it. Now it lay flat, with two broken bars; and the post with its rotted end lay beside it. I'd done a thorough job there if I never did another.

"Thass past mending," Matt said. "That musta bin the devil of a shove. I wonder if the brute as did that got out." He turned and stared towards the cattle, shadowy in the gathering dusk. "They seem all right. Eight. D'you make eight? Your eyes is younger'n mine."

I agreed that there were eight. He then began to direct me how to help him prop the gate in such a way that it would form a temporary stop-gap. The broken, sagging thing was difficult to handle, but when I dropped my end and wrecked it still further Matt Rawley's temper gave way,

"You clumsy young b——, you!" he said.

I put up a good show of resentment.

"Can I help it if your gate is so rotten that it falls to pieces in my hand? You should thank me for trying, not call me names. But for my warning you, you'd have your cows in the pound by the morning."

"Thass true. Thass true, too, that but for your help I'd hev propped this up. Broke past mending now, it is, thanks to you."

"It was that before I ever touched it."

"'Twas not. By all rights you oughta make me a new one real cheap."

"Make you a new one!" I said, and laughed.

"Ah, so you should. Call yourself a carpenter don't you? And go round breaking folkses gates!" He was well away now, scenting a shrewd bargain.

"That does sound bad," I admitted. "Well, what would you call cheap?"

"You oughta do it for nowt! I find wood and you do the work. You broke it arter all."

"One bar," I said.

We argued very happily for ten minutes and finally reached an arrangement satisfactory to us both. I was to make him a new gate in my spare time in return for sixpence and my supper. I pointed out firmly that if I came direct from my ordinary work and worked until darkness fell I should miss my meal at home; and he said,

"Damn it, I'll give you some grub."

I think that apart from the Bywater merchant who had married Caroline Rawley I was the only person ever to be invited to sit at the Rawley table. Surely a good augury!

I did not hurry over the gate and managed to spend four evenings at the farm, eating four obviously grudged suppers with Elizabeth just across the table. She never spoke, and hardly looked at me, but it was joy to see her; and on the third evening, by cutting my finger a little and walking up to the house to ask for a bit of bandage I did manage to find her in the kitchen alone; and short and furtive as the meeting was it served my purpose, for we were able to arrange not only our next meeting but a whole series of meetings for the future.

Each Saturday one of the Rawley girls went to Thomasin Griggs' lonely little cottage to clean and cook. The old woman was Matt Rawley's sister and very like him. She was a widow, childless, and possessed considerable property in Baildon. The girls took strict turns because the capricious old creature demanded it, saying that Susan was the best brass cleaner, Ellen the best washerwoman, Emma the best cook, and Elizabeth the best company. They themselves adhered as strictly as possible to the rotation because the three-mile walk through Layer Wood and a hard day's work under a carping old woman was anything but a pleasure, especially in winter. Weather was never allowed to interfere with the routine, for Matt Rawley had great hopes of his sister; hopes never justified, for when she did die she left all her property to found almshouses in Baildon for "poor respectable tradespeople"—presumably those who had paid extortionate rents for the little shops which she had owned.

So every fourth Saturday it would be possible for me to meet Elizabeth and walk home with her. And with that, being young and simple and undemanding, we were, for the moment, quite content.

We did, of course, speak about other meetings, less furtive, less far separated; but the very mention put Elizabeth into a panic. She explained to me the origin of her father's order about not speaking to men.

"He's been strict like that ever since Caroline married."

"But why?" I asked. For everyone agreed that Caroline Rawley had married marvellously well. James Braddock, a well-to-do wool chandler was surely a good match for a girl from an outlying farm, however pretty she was.

"Well, you see; Father and James Braddock had arranged that Caroline should marry him when she was seventeen, and then when the time came Caroline didn't want to. She had got to know somebody else and wanted to marry him instead. She always was headstrong and though Father was mad as a hornet she stuck out a long time. He beat her—real hard, I mean, not just a clout—she was really black and blue; and then he locked her up and every day she had just a crust and a mug of water. So, of course, in

the end she had to give in. But it took a long time. And then Father said
he'd see that none of the rest of us took fancies like that into our heads
and we were never to look at or speak to any man. Truly, Jon dear, when
you came to the door that time I felt quite *sick*. I was so afraid you might
say something and he'd know. Father's beatings are nothing to laugh at."

"I can believe that," I said. "All the same, when the time comes I shall
marry you, you know. It might be quite easy. When I am twenty-three I
shall have a bit of money and a trade to my hand."

"But when you are twenty-three I shall be twenty-two. Father will have
promised me before that!" The thought struck me dumb; and she went on
calmly. "Susan is getting married at Christmas; she's very lucky, her man
is young and cheerful and nice to look at. Ellen is promised, and she's not
much more than a year older than I am, and though her man is old—he's
got children older than Ellen—and he's bald and hasn't got many teeth,
she will be well off and she will get away. Emma now will never be married at all."

"Why not?"

"Well, there are two reasons. Emma isn't . . . well, not very pretty.
I don't know whether you noticed, but she isn't as pretty as Susan or
Ellen. And she is a very good cook. I've never known her spoil a dish,
and whatever she makes, even pease porridge, somehow tastes better than
ours. So Emma is the one who is to stay at home and look after Father
and Mother when they are old."

"He's got it all arranged, hasn't he?" I said savagely.

"Oh yes. Even the farm. Because we have no brother—and do you
know he still throws that at Mother, oh, almost every day—that is why
Susan has such a nice man chosen for her. Robin Fulger has only just a
little farm but it's next to ours, and the two are going to be put together
and when Father is old Robin will work them both. And when they
have a boy he's to be called Rawley!" She made this announcement with
a kind of pride and pleasure and plainly shared her father's satisfaction
over the arrangement. To me it was just one more instance, a particularly
glaring one perhaps, of the dreadful domination of the old over the young.

"What beats me," I said, "is how your father sets about his matchmaking.
Nobody ever sees you except at church."

"There's the stall," she said, as though that explained everything. Seeing
my mystification, she explained that they had a butter stall on Baildon
market place each Friday. It was there that James Braddock had seen Caroline, and the bald, almost toothless man had seen Ellen.

"With Robin, Father just went and arranged with *his* father. He'd
had his eye on Robin for a long time."

"Do you go to tend the stall?"

"Not yet. Ellen and Susan so far, but when Susan marries then I shall go."

"Well, after Christmas I shall play hooky and come and visit the stall sometimes," I said. But that was one of what I called my unacceptable remarks. Elizabeth seemed to fear and dread any reference to the future or to any kind of contact other than these Saturday evening walks through the wood.

"Father is there, and very watchful," she said.

Susan was married at Christmas and *she* had a proper wedding because Robin Fulger's mother insisted on it, saying she wasn't going to have her son married like a hedge tinker. After that Elizabeth went to market every Friday and I had to wait for the third Saturday—Susan's marriage did do that for us—before I could ask my searching questions. Had anyone hung about the stall and then talked to Matt Rawley? Had anyone spoken to Elizabeth, stared at her, bought more butter than seemed normal? Every Friday I could imagine the dreadful thing happening.

One spring day I did as I promised and made an excuse to go into Baildon on a Friday. I did the errands that had been entrusted to me and then went and sat in the church porch, which overlooked the market, and watched. It seemed to me that every man in Baildon that day seemed to linger and stare as he passed the stall where the two pretty girls were selling the butter and the eggs and the little cheeses. And I looked ahead, half in panic, half with assurance. In November I should be nineteen and my apprenticeship would be done. If I could get my uncle's consent to my marriage I could present myself to Matt Rawley as a suitor for Elizabeth's hand. I wasn't rich, but I had more than sixty pounds laid by, for Uncle Francis had been meticulous about adding the shilling to the coffer's store, and I had a trade. I wasn't such a hopeless suitor. What I earned during the next four years would pay for Elizabeth's food and she could share my bed. (God, what that thought called up!) And she would be a help to Aunt Mary in the house. On the other hand, if out of timidity or diffidence I waited, some oaf, some lout, some beastly bald toothless rich old man—or worse, some rich and handsome young one—would step in. And I could not lose Elizabeth now; we'd never done more than kiss one another, or walk handed, but she was part of my very vitals.

The business of speaking to my uncle went badly from the start. The idea agitated me so cruelly that at my first attempt I went down in a fit before I had given him any notion of what I wanted to talk about. It must have been eighteen months at least since I had been so taken, and I was as surprised as he was. He had the sense to push a wad of linen between my teeth, and for that I was grateful. I could at least talk when I came to myself.

I could talk, and I was calm and lucid. I said that I had found the girl I wanted to marry, but that if I waited for four years I was afraid she would be married to someone else, so please would he give me his permission to be married at once. I outlined my plans for the arrangements of bed and board.

"And who is the wench?"

"I'm afraid that there are reasons for not telling you that until I have your consent, sir."

"Somebody you're ashamed of?"

"Not at all."

"Is it Bess Whymark of The Evening Star?"

"Good God no! Never mind the name. I'll tell you when you have said yes or no to the question I asked to begin with. Will you give me your permission to get married before I finish my journeyman's time?"

"I will not."

"Why?"

"I don't hold with married journeymen. For one thing they don't tend their work properly and for another it's awkward. You talk glib as sharing your bed and this house as ain't yours to share. Hev you thought what that means? Hev you thought about your Aunt Mary who's been good to you? Hev you thought about the three young 'uns you might breed in four years? How'd they fit in in a quiet house?"

"All right," I said. "Then will you give me your permission and pay me a proper wage—you could take it out of the money you hold for me. Clapper Green's cottage is empty. I could hire that and live there. Uncle Francis, it's my very life you hold in your hands; I must get married, soon. I can't wait until I'm twenty-three."

"Hev you gone and got a girl into trouble?"

"No. Of course not. What do you think I am? Look, promise on your honour not to tell. It's Elizabeth Rawley, and you know what her father is. He'll marry her off to the first comer who makes a good bid for her. And that mustn't happen."

"Now thass what I tell you about changing times," said my uncle, bringing one hand down on his knee. "When I was young a man got a roof to his head, a bed of his own, a chair and a table, and a few pots and pans and *then* he looked round for a wench to wed. You young 'uns nowadays got no foresight, you go at things like a bull at a gate. Do you really think Matt Rawley'd let his girl marry a fellow with four years still to do at his craft and not so much as a saucepan to his name? He've done well with his wenches, Matt hev, and the one you're sick for is the pick of the bunch, you young fool. He'll hev an alderman for her; don't, I'll go to sea."

"That's just what I'm afraid of," I cried. "If you can see that, you must see why it is essential that I speak for her *now*."

"Well, lucky I'm here and hev a hold on you. I can at least stop you making that much fool of yourself. See here, Jon boy. The best plums come at the top of the tree and to get 'em you hev to hev a ladder. The time'll come maybe, I hope and trust it will, when you'll be a master carpenter with a place and a business and 'prentices of your own . . . that'll be your ladder. *Then* you can look about and pick a wench whose father'll be glad to listen to you, and treat you respectful. And that'll be seemly. But to go to Matt Rawley and ask him to give his girl to come and tuck in *here*, thass just asking him to kick your teeth in, and he *would*."

"I'd risk that. If you would just give me your permission."

"Well, I ain't give it and I shan't. I got my pride like other men; and part of it is to see you a right proper craftsman, finished and set up; not to be kicked on to Matt Rawley's dungheap for a silly handless young fool."

The mention of *his* pride went to my temper like a flame to faggot; I stormed at him, my voice rising shrill and shaky, using abusive terms I hardly knew I knew. But he was not to be moved, and I realised that the noise I was making was no more than the yelping of a newly tethered puppy, half-choked by the chain. And lest, as with a puppy, my rage die down into a whimper of self-pity and my tears come and shame me before my uncle, I was obliged to dash out of the house, leaving him in every way the victor.

V

In the September preceding my nineteenth birthday Tom Rowhedge came home again. He had been away for more than four years; and if his previous absence had changed him from boy to man, the second one had worked an even greater change. Tom came home a rich man and a hero. He'd sailed from Bywater in the ship which his father had fitted out for him and with very little else, save his wits; he came home with money in his pocket, the title deeds of Merravay in his hand, and with his fame running before him like a courier. It is true that he had sailed away a whole and handsome man and returned with a patch over an empty eye socket and an ugly scar seaming one side of his face . . . but most men would have given an eye to have had his story.

He had made two or three modestly profitable voyages to Continental ports, carrying cargoes of wool and bringing back wines and silks and spices; and, but for his kindness of heart and his easily roused enthusiasm, might have continued in that trade, one of a thousand men who followed their bent, made a living, and remained unknown. But one day, in a low tavern in Calais, he fell in with an old English sailor who said he was a Devon man, and dying, and who was trying to beg a passage home because he wanted to be buried in Totnes. Hard drinking, and the new pox which had raged through the seaports ever since the trade with Africa had been established, had made this old man a very repulsive object to look upon; and, as Tom Rowhedge confessed to me, though he felt sorry for him he didn't fancy his company "on my nice clean ship." However, pity won the day and Tom made room for the derelict, who, once aboard and sober, seemed to take a new lease of life; even his horrid sores sloughed off. He began to talk. He said he had once been John Hawkins' gunner and he could give what sounded like a first-hand account of the disaster of San Juan de Ulúa; and he did know about the trade in blackamoors. He knew where they were to be bought, and what one should look for in buying them; he knew where they should be sold, and what prices should be asked. There was, he said, a fortune to be made in the trade because the Spanish colonists in America, having worked and whipped all the Indians to death, were now working and whipping the Negroes at such a rate that the demand was enormous while the supply was small and dwindling since Spain had forbidden the colonists to buy slaves transported by any but Spanish ships, and what with the searching and the fighting that re-sulted, none but the hardiest and bravest of the English would engage in the trade.

"Look what happened to Jack Hawkins hisself back in '68 . . ." The old man told his tale again. But he added that there was fortune to be made even yet by those who had the pluck to take the risk. Tom's ambi-tion and enthusiasm took light; the old man, whose name was Jabez Trengrove, decided to postpone his death for a while and make one more effort to acquire that fortune which had lured him to sea so many years before. In return for showing Tom the ropes of the new trade, and acting as gunner if necessary, he was to have a tenth of the profits. So they made all things ready and set off for Africa.

As Tom told me this story—sitting on the lid of the dower chest on which I was carving a bride's initials and the date—I realised that he com-bined, in an unusual degree, a kind heart and a complete lack of imagina-tion. Brought face to face with any kind of misery, he was moved to immediate pity and to alleviating action, but misery unseen was, for him, non-existent. So he sailed off in the highest spirits in his "nice clean ship," eager to engage in the dirtiest trade on earth. But when Trengrove found the river which he remembered and had led the way ashore and Tom saw the slave stockades for the first time, "Then," he said, "I began to have my doubts." Trengrove talked him out of them. He seems to have had a glib tongue. He said that left to themselves the blackamoors ate one another, or were eaten, either by their human enemies or by crocodiles and lions; their customs were hideous, their diseases innumerable, and their expectation of life practically negligible. In fact, he said, the best thing that could happen to them was to be shipped to America, and nothing but their hopeless ignorance made the slave trade, the stockades, the collars and the bonds necessary. If they had the sense of lice they would swarm aboard and beg to be taken away. Tom let himself be persuaded, the more easily perhaps because he was just falling victim to the fever which attacks every white man on his first visit to these unhealthy places. Trengrove concluded the bargaining, loaded the blacks, and brought the ship out to sea. They were south of the Cape Verde islands, where they meant to water, when Tom was well enough to leave his bunk.

"Most of the time I was sick, Jon, I'd either been building that first little boat of mine—you remember?—or was back at King Edward's; and wherever my mind was, my nose was conscious of a most horrible stink. If I was in my boat I used to think it was the river mud; if I was at school I thought they'd burnt the pease porridge again. But that day I was clear in my mind and knew I was aboard my own ship and what in Hell the stench could be I couldn't think. . . ."

When he knew, when he had traced the dreadful smell to its source and seen in the low, stifling hold, meant for the stowing of wool bales and wine barrels, the black men and women lying closer than salt herrings in a keg, on boards thick with the slime of their own excreta; when he learned that on an average five died each day, and were tossed overboard with no more ceremony than if they were maggoty apples, his horror and indignation knew no bounds.

"But you must of knowed," Trengrove said. "You must allow for half or rather more to die. The Middle Passage sieves them out, see? The good 'uns live and the weak 'uns die and you know them you sell is good stuff. That allust have been that way and allust will."

"Not on *my* ship," Tom said.

Trengrove's one fear was that Tom would allow the slaves out of the hold. He told a terrifying tale about a slave ship where the captain had thought that exercise and fresh air might reduce the death rate. One evening the batch being exercised had turned on the unwary crew and overcome them. They'd spared only the boy who had been in the habit of bringing them water. After that the ship had drifted since there was no one capable of steering her, and finally they'd set her on fire. The boy, and the black woman whom he had been "given" as a sign of favour, had been picked up and told the tale. "You don't want that to happen, do you?" Trengrove asked.

"We'll air them ten at a time then, and have the space where the ten have been swabbed down."

"Well, that'll keep us busy till we get to Curama," Trengrove said, lightly because he was relieved.

"I shan't wait for Curama," said Tom. "I shall unload them at the first place I come to."

"Now, now," said Trengrove. "We agreed on Curama. The prices there are the best in the world."

"B—— the prices!" said Tom.

Notwithstanding the alleviation in their lot the Negroes, homesick and seasick, continued to die. And Tom continued to fret despite Trengrove's repeated assurances that they were making the passage with a phenomenally low death rate. One morning when they were still full ten degrees east of Trinidad, Tom sighted a smear on the horizon.

"Land," he said to Trengrove. "Know anything about it?"

"An island," said Trengrove laconically. "You'll see a lot of them between here and Curama."

"Spanish island?"

"Could I know? There's scores of 'em in these parts. No bigger'n peppercorns lots of 'em. Chaps that ain't got nothing else to do land on 'em sometimes and stamp about and sort of christen 'em, either with their own name or the name of their favourite saint. I daresay that little dot is to let in a manner of speaking and if you were so minded and weren't all sail set for Curama, you could land there and call it Rowhedge Island, or St. Thomas. There'd be nothing to show for it, and the next silly b—— that came along'd give *his* name. See? Islands about here mean nothing till they've been took over and built on. This is the new world, remember."

"I see," Tom said; and turning, he called out to the man at the helm to change course and steer for the smudge on the skyline.

"So you want to discover an island, do you?" asked Trengrove, jibing but good-humoured. "Well, no doubt it's been discovered before and will be again. Islands are difficult to put a mark on."

"If this one is suitable for the purpose I'll put my mark on it," Tom said.

"How?"

"I'm going to chuck the blacks on to it."

And that, despite Trengrove's frenzied protests, was exactly what he did do. He landed himself first on what he described as a dish-shaped island about as big as Nettleton parish. The little peppercorn of an island bore no sign of very recent human occupation, but men had lived there once. He found some ruined huts smothered with creepers; a spring of water with the rock under its lip worn away where at some time women had rested their vessels. The clear water teemed with fish, and there were tall trees bearing bananas—a fruit which Tom tried to describe to me.

"I landed them there, Jon, boatload by boatload, and at first they were puzzled and fearful; but when they began to understand, they were like children let lose in a cherry orchard. It was wonderful. I felt like God! They dashed into the water and splashed about and sang and swam and shouted; they shinned up the trees after the fruit. They gathered flowers and made great wreaths to hang round their necks and my neck. And I stood there and stared at them and realised what they'd cost me! After four years of being my own master I'd got a ship without a cargo, a crew to pay, a savagely angry partner, and not a penny piece in the world."

"So *then* you decided to turn pirate, Tom?"

"Well, not exactly. What I meant to do was to come back to England and either ask Father for a loan, or, if he couldn't manage it, mortgage my ship for three or four voyages. I had to pay the crew, I had to give Trengrove his percentage—he'd have gone stark staring crazy, I reckon, before we got home—he was near to raving then; so when the old *Sancta Theresa* hove in sight, it was like an answer to prayer, Jon."

It was, of course, just Tom's luck that the *Sancta Theresa* was stuffed as full as she could hold without sinking with silver from the mines at Santiago, and with treasures from Cuzco, the Inca capital which the Spaniards had been stripping for nearly twenty years and hadn't yet picked clean. There was more wealth in that one vessel than a hundred small ships like Tom's could have earned by honest trading in a hundred years.

The little *Mermaid* brought the *Sancta Theresa* into port at Plymouth like a small dingy sheep dog bringing a great gilded sheep into the fold, and there were great rejoicings. By law and tradition the greater part of the immense treasure went into the Queen's coffers, but the share which fell to Tom and Trengrove, whom he insisted upon treating as his partner because he said that but for him he would never have done more than ferry across the Channel, was enough to make them moderately rich for the rest of their lives. Nevertheless Tom was astonished and immensely flattered when the Queen sent for him.

I suppose that before he dies Tom will tell the tale of that meeting a thousand times; but I was amongst the first to whom it was told, for Tom rode straight from London to Slipwell afterwards and sought me out on the second day after his arrival in order to give me the present he had bought for me in London. Strange man, he had remembered that on that evening when I poured out my heart of discontent to him, I had mentioned my great dearth of books; and riding out of London, he had stopped in Cheapside and bought me three! Malory's *Morte d'Arthur*,

More's *Utopia,* and Tottel's *Miscellany.* For a moment, with them in my hand, I also felt rich. Perhaps that is why I always think of Tom's interview with the Queen (about which he proceeded to tell me) as taking place in bright sunshine.

"What was she like, Tom?" I asked.

"Not like anything, except maybe the figurehead of a ship." He said that innocently, almost unintentionally, and then, quite suddenly saw the value of it. He slapped his hand on his knee.

"But that's it exactly," he exclaimed, astonished by his own perceptiveness. "That's what she's like—the figurehead of a ship just newly painted."

"Is she beautiful?" I had by that time a measure for beauty; I had my tally stick. *My* Elizabeth was beautiful; I was eager to hear how Tom's Elizabeth stood with that measure.

"Oh no," Tom said. "Not as a woman; but then how could she be? She is old, over forty you know. But nobody in his senses would think of that! I mean . . . who asks the age of a figurehead? If it is significant, and freshly coloured . . ."

I could see that he was still a little dazed by the one leap of imagination he had ever known. So I said invitingly,

"But she was significant then?"

"Oh yes. Not like anybody you ever saw, or thought about. She sat at the end of a big room at Whitehall Palace. That is difficult to describe, too. You see, Jon, it's bigger than Nettleton church, and empty—except for the people, of course. And she sat at the end of it in a chair, with a crowd of people about; all in very bright rich clothes. Well, then somebody said my name very loud; and the lords and ladies drew back a bit, so there was all that big open space for me to walk over; and I felt, Jon, like we used to feel when old Trudgett used to say, 'Come up here, boy,' only worse. The floor seemed to rock, you know. But I got across it and went down on my knee like a fellow outside had told me to . . . and then . . ." He broke off with a laugh in which there was some embarrassment.

"Yes, Tom, then?"

"Well, she patted my head, as though I'd been a good dog that had caught a hare for the pot! And she thanked me and said several pleasant things. Then she said, 'Stand up and let us look at you.' So I stood up, and I felt a thorough fool. And she said something about being handsome and what a pity it was about this. . . ." He laid a finger to the patch and the scar. And then she must have made some sign, though I didn't mark it; for all the people skipped away except for the two guards at the door. And then she said,

" 'I would knight you, Thomas Rowhedge, if I dared, but I dare not. And lest you think me a coward for saying I dare not, I will tell you why.

His Majesty of Spain has a curious habit of misconstruing my actions and chooses to think that I commission my brave men to sack his ships; a thing I have never done, in peace, and never should. It would be so *unnecessary!* You smile—you have, I see, an understanding humour! Then you will understand that to set Sir Thomas Rowhedge on the Rolls would —shall we say?—*remind* those who watch that it was Thomas Rowhedge who brought the *Sancta Theresa* to port? And just at this moment that would be unwise.' I muttered something about not looking for any reward of that nature . . . you know the sort of thing one says at such moments, and then she said, 'But you have lost an eye, my good man, and that is a great pity for your beauty is marred now.' And she stared at me as though the loss of an eye were a very great matter. I mumbled again and what I said was perfectly true, Jon—after a bit you *can* see quite well with one eye. And then she asked me where I came from, and I told her Slipwell, where Essex joins Suffolk; and she asked me what my father did and various other questions which I would have resented from any-one else. Suddenly she snapped her fingers. Her hands are longer and thinner and whiter than anyone else's and she uses them more, Jon. She snapped her fingers and said, 'On that border there is a place called Mer-ravay, is there not?' 'Yes,' I said, 'lying between Slipwell and Nettleton. There is a ruined castle there and some acres of good land gone derelict since my Lord of Norfolk went to the Tower. . . .' I chopped off there, it being a sore subject and verging on the political. But she laughed and said, 'I see you carry your sea eye ashore with you, Tom Rowhedge! Dere-lict it is and that is a pity. Well, since I am reminded of that estate, and since I have it in my gift and can dispose of it without a trumpeting that will sound in the ears of Spain, Merravay is yours!' And even while I was thanking her, you know, it seemed strange that with all she has to think of and to manage and control she should remember Merravay."

"They say she never forgets anything."

Tom gave his old cheerful chuckle. "Well, *that*, as old Trudgett used to say, 'is susceptible to proof,' Jon. Because then she asked me what I should do with Merravay, and I said I should build a house there and get the land under plough again, and make a place to retire to one day. And what do you think she said? 'I shall visit you,' she said. 'Indeed a house in that quarter will be a convenience for me. There is Hengrave, in Suffolk, which is a pleasant place indeed, and Framlingham, which I dislike heart-ily because of its associations; and Essex is thick with great houses; but hitherto on the border accommodation has been meagre. So look for me at Merravay, Tom Rowhedge.' That was her last word, Jon. And next day a pale-faced fellow brought along all the papers, sealed and signed."

"Well," I said; and "Well" again. And then I recovered myself a little and said, "It will have to be a big, grand house, Tom."

"Not too big." He had been sitting on his old accustomed seat—the sawhorse in our workshop; now he rose and began to walk about amongst the shavings and sawdust. "After the open sea, Jon, a man doesn't crave space; he longs for something cosy and close. I'll have a small house, but everything fine in it. After all, I'm the one who has to live in it. Look, this is what I've been thinking . . . tell me what you think of this. . . ." He took a splinter of wood, brushed away the shavings and litter from a space on the floor, and began to draw on the bare earth thus exposed. "Let's say a fair-sized hall—then if she *does* come there'll be room for her, and everything—about what? Fifty feet long by twenty wide; the door coming in here, with a screen, nicely carved to keep the draught out; the stairs going up *here* to the gallery. See? Now on this side a smaller room; twenty by twenty—that's big, isn't it? Big enough for me, anyway; with a huge hearth, and I shall sit at table with my back to it. Then I'll have the kitchens directly to the rear, so that dishes come hot to table; brewhouse, washhouse, storeroom; we needn't bother about them at the moment. Then look. The stairs come up here. Nothing over the hall, I think. People are beginning to floor over the hall nowadays, for economy's sake, but I needn't bother about that. The hall goes to the roof, apart from the gallery, that is. You see I have to bear in mind that she might come, and then we'd need a gallery for the musicians. Gallery along here, and then sleeping chambers could lead off. How many would I need, Jon? Eight? Ten?"

"You couldn't get many over the one chamber and the kitchens," I said. "Unless you had another floor."

"Oh, must I? I fancied a small house."

"Then have another room here," I said, taking the stick from his hand and adding my contribution. "See, that would balance better. The big hall across the front, two rooms, each half as large as the hall, behind, and then kitchens behind them. That way, if you didn't want very big sleeping chambers, you could manage."

"One must be a fair size. Suppose she stayed the night."

"One big one then, running this way, see?" And then I suddenly remembered something which I had heard. "No, Tom," I said. "That won't do at all. This plan is working out square. And I'm told that nowadays all the new houses are being built on an E as a compliment to the Queen. And if there's a likelihood that she will visit and perhaps even spend a night here, and she gave you the land and knows the house is new-built . . . by cock, Tom, if ever a house had to be an E it is this house of yours. Now, let me see." I scrubbed my foot over the lines already drawn and set to work again. I'd never planned a house before, never indeed thought of a house in terms of planning, but it seemed to come easily to me, and in a few minutes I had it drawn out on the floor.

"There you are, Tom," I said, in a voice that betrayed my elation. "There's your E. There you have your big hall, with the gallery above, and the kitchens handy behind it. Rooms to the left and right can be many or few, large or small to suit your fancy, so long as you build forward to make the top leg and the bottom, and set the porch in the centre for the third. Turn the face of the house to the south, lad, so your buttery and larder and storerooms stand cool on the north, and at one end of the gallery above, make a great bedchamber with another window to catch the morning sun—a chamber fit for a queen."

I stared at the lines scratched in the earth and the sawdust, and out of them I saw a stately house, a beautiful house, rear itself. A poem built not with words, but with timber and glass and stone and brick. . . .

"By cock!" said Tom, clapping me on the back, "now I can *see* it. Till now I've been in the dark. I had in mind some snug little place to tuck into when I got too old to go to sea. And when I told the Queen I'd build a house I meant in time to come. But now . . ." His eyes took on a far-away look. "Ah, Jon, I see it, with every timber seasoned oak, and red bricks for the walls. Come along with me, now, and let's go see where we'll set her. . . ."

So I rode pillion behind him again, as in our boyhood days, taking the track out of the village which could only be used in fair weather and which led on through Slipwell to Bywater.

Away back in the time of the Normans there had been a castle at Merravay, and there was an old story which said that in those days the sea had covered all Slipwell and the man who reared the castle had been warned that one day the sea would come up and engulf it; the name "Merravay" was supposed to have its origin in that threat. The castle had been ruined and deserted for many generations and now all that was left was a broken tower, no more than ten feet high. In more recent times, when the land was held by the Duke of Norfolk and tilled on his behalf, labourers had lived in the tower under a roof of reeds laid flat across it. This thatch had rotted and fallen inwards like the crust of an ill-made pie, but inside the thick walls the mark of old ancient fires could still be traced; and somehow that was pitiable. And the whole place had a sad, desolate air, so that even Tom, little fanciful as he was, turned his back on the ruins and said,

"The stones can maybe be used for barn or byre; for the house I'd lief even the foundations were new."

We walked forward and came to a dip in the ground where the moat had been. The water had drained away long since and it was now no moister than a ditch, and like a ditch, was full of ferns and dead meadow-sweet. Beyond, the ground rose gently but surely.

I looked about me, seeking the likeliest site. Then I turned and faced the sad ruins again. Between them and the edge of the moat where we stood were two great trees, unlike any I had ever seen before, very sombre with their almost black foliage. I did not know their name then, but later on, while we were building, I heard somebody say that he had been told that they were cedars, probably brought home as saplings by some owner of the castle who had been on Crusade. And it is true that there was a Crusader's tomb in Nettleton church. That morning, without knowing their value or their history, I could see their virtue in relation to our plans, and I said,

"Tom, if it were my house, I'd set her between those trees. 'Twill be years before any tree you plant is grown high enough to give shade in summer or shelter in winter. And if you put the house there you'll have this space for a garden and the dip will make a boundary between garden and field. . . ."

"If she'll lay there, Jon. Let's pace it out and see. . . ."

The space was exactly right, and the ground was level there.

"But they're melancholy things," said Tom, eyeing the black trees with small favour.

"The whole place has a melancholy air," I agreed, "but that is because it has been long deserted. And when your trees have grown these can come down."

So it was decided. On the way home Tom said he would ride straight on and engage Clem Hubbard, a master mason to do the building; "And you and your uncle must care for all the woodwork, Jon."

"It would please me to have a hand on your house, Tom; but an apprentice can't pledge for his master. You must see *him* about the business."

Privately I entertained a grave doubt as to whether Uncle Francis would take kindly to the idea of working on a house that was to be built with money stolen from the Spaniards who were real Papists, on land given to Tom by a queen in whose authority my uncle barely believed. He might easily not hold with it. I was surprised when, a few days later, he came to me, rubbing his hands and saying gleefully that we had work for two years ahead, building Tom Rowhedge's new house at Merravay. Some nasty carping streak in me made me express my surprise in one of my sweet-sour remarks, and he said,

"Bless the boy, what a simpleton it is! Why even in the good days when Queen Mary sat on the throne, the English hated the Span'ards and robbed 'em whenever they could! Why, if I met a Span'ard I'd rob him myself, if for no other reason than because a Span'ard put an end to the owd ways in England."

"How do you make that out?"

"Plumb easy. 'Twas a Span'ard married Queen Mary and used her so ill that she died broken-hearted. Anybody that was half a man 'ud hev stayed by her and bred a bevy of sons to stand between the throne and the bastard. . . ."

Even for Uncle Francis, in the privacy of his home, that was very plain speaking; he knew it and checked himself and looked, for a moment, ill at ease. Encouraged by the sight of his rare discomfiture I said mercilessly,

"But that is what I meant. If you think *that* of the Queen, you must think also that Merravay was not hers to give, however you skim round the idea of Tom's deserving a reward."

"Nor I do, in a way," he said slowly. "But 'twas wasted as it was, Jon. Been laying waste these many years. Surely 'tis better in Tom's hands." He recovered from the little setback which his slip of the tongue had occasioned and became his usual, ever-right, moralising self.

"You oughta be owd enough now, boy, not to pick holes in your own blanket. Take a look round you. Whass been ordered this month? A dower chest and a coupla milking stools! We ain't had a proper big job for months and with the harvest so bad we ain't likely to get one. We should all go down on our knees and thank God for Tom Rowhedge and the fine big house that'll mean bread for us and a dozen like us for the next coupla years."

As well as being pleased with the prospect of steady work for a long time my uncle was enjoying a sense of importance; for, as Tom had told the Queen, Merravay lay about midway between Nettleton and Slipwell, and so our carpenter's shop made a convenient headquarters for the conferences which were necessary before the house was begun. Tom's loyalty, or his lack of imagination, had led him to make the thing as purely local as possible. Clem Hubbard, the master builder of Baildon had said confidently that he could build a palace or a cathedral so long as he had a free hand and a plan to go by. He put his faith, he said, in a good foundation; building, like gardening, was a matter of digging deep enough; given eight feet of sound foundation underground, you couldn't go wrong. He was exactly like my uncle in his devotion to rule-of-thumb sayings and in his faith in his own ability. My uncle, who to my knowledge had never worked on anything bigger or more important than Rowhedge's new barn, and who really specialised in small, meticulously finished work, was equally confident when he talked about kingpins and beams nine inches square. He pinned his faith in sound wood. If you stuck to oak, well seasoned, and used plenty of it, and didn't scamp your pinning, you couldn't go wrong.

There were several such meetings in the warm, apple-scented evenings of that September before Tom went back to his ship. And they were always held in our shop. Sometimes there were as many as ten of us gathered the bench; for the man who made bricks at Maldon and the man who was supplying the timber and the lead worker from Bywater who was to cast spout heads bearing a Tudor rose, the initials T R, and the date 1577—these and their sons, or their journeymen, must all have a say. And unless it happened to be Elizabeth's Saturday for visiting her aunt, I was there too. Midway through the chatter and the amicable argument we would hear the scream of the well pulley and know that Aunt Mary was hauling the jug of ale from the deeps in which it had been cooling, and presently she would come in, quiet as a ghost, with the ale and the mugs and a plate of saffron cakes and a dish of damsons.

At first, in the centre of the bench there lay the piece of paper bearing the plan which I had drawn on the floor; it was always referred to as "Jon's picture"; presently it was joined by other pictures. Tom said, "I want the bricks laid herringbone fashion, Clem," and it had fallen to me to illustrate what he meant. It was the same with the spout heads. But though they valued the "pictures" as guides in what was—had they admitted it—pretty uncharted territory, they never allowed me to feel in the least important because I had made them. Nothing *really* mattered save good deep foundations, and sound, well-seasoned timber. And as I once said to Tom, "If in the end you get a house that is anything but a glorified barn, you'll have me to thank!"

So, on the first day of October we stood in the mellow sunshine while Tom took spade in hand and cut the first sod. Then Uncle Francis came forward with a handful of salt and gravely sprinkled it in the sign of the cross over the broken soil, and said, "Bless the ground on which we build, and the house that we build." And even those of the company who thought that very old-fashioned said, "Amen." Uncle Francis, though he was a carpenter, a master man, then took spade in hand and began to dig with the best, saying as he did so, "Well begun is half done!"

Then the mass of day labourers whom Clem Hubbard had engaged fell to work and began to dig the foundations along the lines which we had previously pegged out by the plan.

In that same week Tom rode off to Plymouth, where he had left his *Mermaid* for refitting. He was returning to the Continental trade, having had, he said, his bellyful of adventure. He said he intended to crowd in as much trade as he could in the two years while Merravay was building;

"For I doubt, Jon, whether, once the place is finished, I shall ever willingly leave it again."

I said then the thing that had been on the tip of my tongue many times. "When you settle down, Tom, you'll have to get married."

"I know," he said, and laughed. "The trouble with me is I like so many wenches so much! I should have been a Turk!"

"And you never saw one you preferred above all?"

"No."

"You will," I said.

"I hope so," he said quite gravely. "The house will need a mistress."

I think it was then that my feeling for Tom suffered damage. It began like the hairline crack in a plaster wall which, left untended, will widen and let in the frost and the rain until it brings the wall down. And once the thing had happened I was surprised that it hadn't happened before; but it is true that, until he spoke of installing a wife at Merravay, I had not envied him. He had and he was everything that I had not and was not, and during my first wretched year at Nettleton I had often thought, Lucky Tom to be allowed to choose his own trade, but that was all. Nor had I envied him his luck, his money, his fame, his meeting with the Queen; in fact, because he was my friend, and always so kind to me, I had felt a vicarious pleasure in his success. None of it was an encroachment upon *me*. But now I thought, quite bitterly—Yes, *you've* only to look round and wag your finger and you can marry any girl you fancy, whereas I . . .

VI

However I saw him off pleasantly and was flattered because although my uncle and Clem Hubbard set small store by me Tom said openly, "Jon knows what I want the house to be like. We planned it together and he made me see it; so if any question arises he is to decide." And all through the next year I was tolerably happy. The work was far more interesting and absorbing than any I had ever been engaged on before; working with a number of men was a pleasant change, saving my spirit from the constant rub of my uncle's company; now and then I was able to exercise a certain authority in the making of a decision; and so far there had been no mention of anyone "speaking" for Elizabeth. She still stood, each Friday, behind the butter stall, as open for offers, had folks but known it, as the dairy stuff she sold; and I still endured agonies for great stretches of time. I would meet her on a Saturday and walk from Thomasin Griggs' cottage to within sight of Rawley's, and my first question was "Has anything happened?" So far she had always said, "Nothing";

and I could then be happy until the next Friday when she went to the stall again. And that was a childish snatch at consolation, like whistling in the dark, because I knew perfectly well that someone might make approaches to her father at any moment of those six charmed days, even at the moment when we were walking along the woodland ride, telling one another that all might yet come right. Nevertheless I always felt better between the Saturday when I saw her and the following Friday; and then there were fifteen days to wait before I saw her again.

Still, the weeks and the months flew past, all the faster for this constant looking forward, this constant awareness of time; and I was twenty. In three years I should be free. Often we spoke of that. Often Elizabeth said, "I do want to marry you, Jon. I know I like you better than I shall ever like anyone. But I couldn't stand up to Father. Even Caroline couldn't, and she was very brave." And I would remember that she had been only a child when Caroline had defied that dreadful man; the beating, the locking up on bread and water, the final capitulation had all made a deep and lasting impression on her. She couldn't be blamed for that. So I would say, "But you would let me know. I wouldn't just let you go. I'd do something!" And she would say, "Of course, Jon. I'd let you know. And now let's talk about something else."

Generally I then went on to tell her how Merravay was growing.

It grew apace. And it was beautiful. Though I say—I who made the plan and said where the windows should be set and what patterns should be carved over the hearth at which, on cold nights at sea, Tom dreamed of warming his back—it was a beautiful house. I came to love it. There were times when it seemed more mine than Tom's.

He only saw it twice. He came home in the first February, when the walls were about roof-high and the inside no more than a skeleton, and he stamped about a bit and then said to me,

"The old men have done a good job, so far. But it looks raw and kind of lonely. I think I should put the garden in hand." He looked away towards Layer Wood and grinned a little sheepishly. "It sounds a bit lordly, Jon, but I happened to fall in with an old man who had a deal to do with the laying out of the garden at Hampton. He's crippled now . . . in fact he was begging in Plymouth when I found him . . . but if one took the trouble and had him carried about . . . he still *knows* about gardens," he ended almost defiantly.

"And what is lordly about that?" I asked.

"He worked for the Queen, and for the King, Jon."

"And now he begs."

"Yes. Isn't that sad?"

"He was lucky to fall in with you," I said.

They brought the old man in easy stages to Nettleton, where Tom arranged him lodgings at The Evening Star. And my uncle made a little wheeled cart, in which for the next few months the old man sat like a goblin, directing the laying out of the garden. Nobody liked him much, for, though Tom's kindness had brought him up from the gutter, he acted in a very disdainful way towards us all, calling us Johnny Go-to-ploughs, and bumpkins. Also he always held a long staff across his knees and did not hesitate to strike out with it if anyone annoyed him or got in his way. Once he even hit out at Clem Hubbard, who had stepped on a bed of young wallflowers. But he planned a garden such as had never been seen in our parts before, where even quite big houses, such as Mr. Turnbull's at Baildon, had gardens which had grown up haphazard and were more for use than ornament.

Unfortunately for me the more Merravay grew in beauty the more I loved it, and the more I envied Tom. And every time I envied Tom I fell to brooding over what might have been my lot if my uncle had let me buy myself out and go with him to sea when he invited me. I might then have had some money and could have been building a house, nothing like so stately as this one, of course, but a pretty little cottage for Elizabeth. Thoughts like that were hard to bear, and on the day when Tom arrived just at Easter, bringing food and wine and brandy and making an impromptu feast, all my stomach seemed to go sour and I was sick, physically sick. (I'd heard Dr. Trudgett pour scorn upon the theory of the ascendancy of the various humours in man; but a bilious humour certainly had me that day.)

Soon after Easter the bricklayers were paid off; and then the tilers; the lead-beaters came and fixed the handsome waterspouts and the guttering and lounged about waiting for a wet day to test their work and then went away satisfied. Finally only Uncle Francis and I were left at Merravay, putting the finishing touches.

The previous Saturday had been one of those golden-haloed days which came once in three weeks for me, and the fact that it was a drear dismal drizzly day, like so many had been that month, did nothing to lower my spirits. Truth to tell I rather liked a wet Saturday night, for then I could make Elizabeth walk under my cloak for quite a bit of the road—though we must always make sure that she did not arrive home too dry-looking—and now and again when we came to a particularly splashy place in the path I would lift her over. So light and warm and fluttery she was then, like a bird.

The evening promised well. At six o'clock it was almost dark and rain was falling. I waited at my usual place, as near to the old woman's cottage as I could well be and yet remain out of sight should she look from the tiny window; and when Elizabeth, carrying her basket, rounded the corner I opened my cloak and said, "Come under," and put my arm about her as I had done on a dozen similar evenings. But this evening, instead of coming under and nestling up to me like a bird, she said,

"No, thank you, Jon," and began to walk briskly along the path.

"What's the matter?" I asked. "Is anything the matter?"

I thought she shook her head. "Well then, why won't you walk under my cloak? You'll be soaked before you get home."

She walked more quickly until she was almost running. I reached out and took her arm, but my handhold was mostly cloak and she shook me off quite easily.

"Glory to God," I said, "what is wrong with you tonight?"

And then I saw that she was crying. Even that didn't bring me to a sense of disaster, for old Thomasin Griggs took an infernal delight in tormenting her nieces and it was nothing new for Elizabeth to emerge from that cottage in tears; but ordinarily she would run to me and tell me about it and I would kiss her and talk nonsense until she cheered up again.

"Is it the old she-devil?" I asked, hurrying along just behind Elizabeth, for the path was so narrow that two people could only walk abreast if both willed it. "Tell me, honeysweet, it'll be better if you tell me. What did she do to you?" This time I had a firm hold of her arm and pulled her to a standstill, swinging her round so that I could see her face, so small and pale and sweet in her hood, and only just visible, what with the trees' shadow and the early dusk.

"It isn't her," she said in a voice that was a crying voice but still more or less familiar. Then in a wild high one that I never heard before she said, "It's you and me, and Father . . . and Tom Rowhedge."

"Tom Rowhedge," I repeated stupidly. "What's he . . . ?" Then, of course, I knew.

To him that hath shall be given, and from him that hath not shall be taken the one thing that he hath.

"Darling, try to stop crying," I said; for now she was sobbing uncontrollably and I couldn't think as clearly as I needed to.

"When did this happen? When he was home at Easter?"

"I suppose so. I don't know. I do remember that week because we had market on Thursday because of it being Good Friday week. And he came and talked to Father and then he rode beside us as far as Goose Green and Father asked him to supper. And on Easter Sunday he came again. . . ."

"You never told me," I said harshly. For it was that kind of thing which I had dreaded each time I asked her if anything had happened since I saw her last.

"I didn't know. He never said anything. Nor did Father until the night before last when we heard that Chris Huxstable had died when they cut him for the stone."

She was still sobbing wildly and twisting my hands in hers, and her last sentence was the kind of non sequitur that occurs in delirium. I thought for a moment that she was raving.

"Chris Huxstable? What's he got to do with it?"

"Father said . . . oh, Jon, this is horrible, but he said it . . . Chris Huxstable spoke for me as long ago as last Christmas. But he was sick then and didn't want to be married till he was better. If he would have married me out of hand Father said he'd have struck hands on the bargain at once, then I'd be a widow and rich. But Chris said he'd try drinking the Walsingham water, and if that didn't shift his trouble he'd be cut. So you see, Jon, Father couldn't say aye or nay to Tom Rowhedge at Easter, because Chris was still at Walsingham then. But the water didn't work and so he was cut and he died and when Father heard he just said, 'Oh. Well, my girl, you'll have Merravay instead of the tannery; and it smells sweeter.' And that, truly, was the first I knew."

"God!" I said, "I'm glad of Hell! There should be Hell for men like your father. He'd have given *you* to Chris Huxstable, who stank of rotting hides and his own corruption till you could smell him a mile off. Darling, Lisbeth darling . . ." I clutched her to me, shuddering, aghast at the thought of what she had escaped. My mind rocked. "Tom is young and clean," I said. "But he shan't have you! And Tom is my friend . . . he wouldn't want to take my sweetheart." I had a sudden flash of enlightenment. "Honeysweet, I'll wager anything in the world that Tom spoke for you out of kindness. Tom has the kindest heart in the world," I said. "He'd want to save you from Chris Huxstable." I felt her stiffen under my hands.

"Thank you for that, Jon," she said, and pulled herself away and began to walk on.

"Oh, what have I said now? Lisbeth you know I meant no offence; you know, don't you, that I think you so sweet and pretty and altogether desirable that the King—if we had a king—might well seek your favours and count himself lucky if you smiled on him. But what I said about Tom is true . . . he is kind; and I'm quite sure that if I tell him that you are my sweetheart, he will withdraw his offer."

Alas, the further I plunged the deeper I went in the mire.

"You think it was so lightly made?"

"No, no. But Tom would understand. He has so much, Lisbeth. . . . I have so little . . . nothing but my love. . . ."

All wrong, all wrong!

"If you talk him into withdrawing, then it will be another Chris Huxstable for me," she said. "And though I must bear my father's arrangements for me . . . because he is my father . . . I cannot see why you and Tom Rowhedge should bandy me about as though I was a marble. . . ." She spoke angrily and began to walk again with short, sharp steps. Some sort of madness flared in me and I said,

"I'm beginning to think you *want* to marry Tom. Is that it? Maybe you think you're like Susan—lucky?"

"When I think of Chris Huxstable I know I am!" She stopped again, and wiped the back of her hand and the cuff of her sleeve across her face. "Don't be angry, Jon. We knew all along that we could never be married, didn't we? These times together . . . they were very sweet . . . I shall always remember them; but they were like something in a song, or a story, not a bit of real life. . . ."

She sounded very old suddenly, old and wise and calm. An appalling sense of loneliness fastened down on me. She had gone over; she was now on the side of the old men who arranged things without taking any count of human feelings.

"If you're so philosophic and resigned all at once," I said unkindly, "tell me—why were you crying when I met you?"

My bleeding vanity yearned for one word of comfort to staunch its wound; I wanted her to say that she minded, too. She gave me as honest an answer as any man ever had from a woman, I think.

"I was afraid you might be angry with me, Jon. I always cry when I'm frightened."

"And for *me* you have no feeling at all?"

"Oh that isn't true. Honestly, Jon, ever since the night before last I've been thinking . . . I know it sounds a strange thing to say . . . but I wished you'd never sought me out and talked to me and walked with me, because then I should be so glad that it was Tom Rowhedge and not Chris Huxstable that I'd be the happiest girl in the world."

"Oh," I said. I stood for a moment so coldly furious that I wanted to break her in pieces, and then all at once I saw what those words implied; poor little darling! Pity for her, and self-pity, and fury, and my feeling of being deserted all churned together in my mind, and far off, like distant thunder, I heard that warning crackle.

"Run along," I said. "Somebody calling . . . your father! Go! And be happy!"

I did not see her go. I had just time to turn round and thrust my thumb into my mouth when the crackling, flashing dark, saying be happy, be happy, BE HAPPY, closed down on me.

When it cleared the rain had stopped and the moon was high and the mud of the puddle in which I had been lying had soaked to my skin.

VII

Sitting there in the freshly whitewashed buttery of Merravay, I could look back and see all my life up to that point quite clearly, and quite dispassionately. But after that there was a blur. I couldn't eat more than a few mouthfuls without sickening and I learned that there are many levels to sleep. Ordinarily one dives in and is received in the cradling depths, but it is possible to float just under the surface, to be no longer fully wakeful, to be a prey to dreams, and yet not quite asleep. I did that every night; and every day I went to Merravay and worked and sometimes my uncle would say things—like he had just said that about my children's children and the stairs at Merravay—which pressed on my hurt.

But the brandy was good. It seemed to take the place of the food which sickened and the sleep which eluded me. For the first time for a week I felt like myself. I set the cup on the shelf and stood up. I thought, well, this is Merravay, the house which I planned and Tom paid for, the house in which Elizabeth will live. I shall never come here again; so I will look over it now.

This is the hall; fifty feet by twenty as we planned, with the screen to keep out the draught of the door. And, by God, the screen carving is beautiful; solid oak carved to the delicacy of lace; the best job Uncle Francis ever did. And here is the staircase, solid and sound, every peg six inches long, and such a lovely piece of carving on the newel posts: Moses with his staff turning into a snake. . . . I told Uncle Francis that story; he can't read, he doesn't approve of reading, he really wishes back the time when nobody in a village could read except the priest—and that in Latin—and yet he liked that story, and used it; so here is Moses, looking very much like Mr. Aldridge, J.P.; just his beard I swear; and just about the look of surprise that he would wear if his walking stick turned into a snake. But it's a fine piece of work, and I hope when the Queen comes she will notice it. Elizabeth will have to make a curtsey to the Queen. And the Queen, if she is a woman at all, will envy her complexion and probably ask if she uses rose water or witch-hazel for it. And Elizabeth will surely give her an honest answer; she's extremely honest, my Elizabeth, Tom's Elizabeth. . . .

Ah well . . . here's the room Tom dreamed of; a fine square room with a good hearth, the board above it nicely carved too, though not so magnificent a work as the Moses; this is Tudor roses, very right and proper because it was the Tudor Queen who gave Tom Merravay. And who thought of that pretty touch? Jon Borage, bless him! Never at a loss. Tudor roses in this chamber; and in the other, across the hall, there's a sailing ship. And in both rooms there's this big fair window, with a window seat. In the morning Elizabeth can sit here in the sun; and in the evening she can cross the hall and sit in the other and still have the sun. And be happy! be happy! BE HAPPY! Better not think about that.

But you want her to be happy, don't you? Of course I do. She never did me any harm. She was my little honey-sweet love, my darling, my little bird, but the plums worth gathering grow at the top and you have to have a ladder; you have to have a ladder and you haven't got a ladder have you Jon Borage you haven't you have to have a ladder.

Come on now. You're upstairs. Here is the gallery where the musicians will sit, will sit, will sit and play when the Queen comes. Will anyone notice that it is carved in the lacy pattern and matches the screen by the door? At this end of the gallery is the state bedroom. You'd better face it, you know; they'll surely use it on the wedding night. What here? Yes; here. You know, Jon Borage, you are a fool. You could have taken her maidenhead; you know you could. Any night last summer when the hawthorn was in bloom and the cuckoo was calling. What a fool, what a cuckoo you were. There was your chance! She loved you then; she used to cling to you and kiss you and walk under your cloak when it rained. If you'd taken her then . . . and she'd quickened, he'd have been glad, Matt Rawley would have been glad, to have you make an honest woman of her. Oh, but she is honest; she told me why she cried . . . hardly any other woman would have done that. And then when your uncle asked, "Have you gone and got a girl into trouble?" you could have said, "Yes," and then he would have been all agog for you to marry her. Do you see? But she was like a flower, to be handled gently. Oh yes, gently, brought to market with the bloom on her, "Fresh violets!" . . . oh the fool that you were! Cuckoo! Cuckoo!

Pass we on. Here are six bedchambers, all square and sound. There'll be a little boy one day, and his hair will be copper-coloured and his cheeks will be rosy; and there'll be a little girl with black hair and a skin of cream. And maybe Elizabeth will say, "He shall be Thomas Jonathan." Would she dare? Why not? I never did them any harm; I planned this house. He'll say, "Of course, Jonathan, good old Jonathan . . . why does he never come to see us?" And the little girl will be Elizabeth Thomasin. Why Thomasin, darling? Because and because . . . but that is a secret. Because while that cuckoo called and while that hawthorn bloomed something that might have happened didn't happen . . . because life like sleep has different levels and on one level . . . Yes, darling, on one level you belonged to me.

There'll be guests and there'll be servants.

Let's go down again. What a fine kitchen! You could roast an ox by that hearth; doubtless you will. When the Queen comes. And at this end by the little fire . . . blackberry jelly, my sweet. You'll stand here and seal the jars down with a bit of pig's bladder and you'll carry them across here into the storeroom. . . . I shall always see your little purple-stained hands dropping the glossy berries into the basket. Will you see mine? Truly, my dear, I hope not; because you always knew that we had no future. You saw what I refused to see. So make your blackberry jelly, make your curtsey, make your little boy and your little girl and be happy! be happy!

And what of me?

I was back now in the hall, in the place from which I had started, near the window farthest from the stairs. And as clearly as I had seen what life held for Tom and Elizabeth, I saw what was left for me. Nothing. Nothing for my mind, because Uncle Francy didn't hold with book learning; nothing for my heart because he didn't hold with apprentices marrying. . . . I looked down a dark, cold narrow tunnel of years, a slipway to the grave; and despair, the last, the worst, enemy of man, came upon me. I saw myself going on and on through all the changing seasons, empty-minded, empty-hearted, with just my hands busy. Stools and cupboards and coffins. Even Merravay which I had planned with joy was finished now and such a job would never come my way again. I was nothing and had nothing to hope for. . . .

And I saw, with piercing clarity, who was to blame. My uncle had taken me, spoiled and deformed me as surely as though he had sawn off my head, cut out my heart, and used my dead hands for hammers. If he had done that, in a physical sense, they would have hanged him; as it was they praised him for his charity to an orphan! The Bible was wiser . . . it bade us not to fear those who killed the body but to fear those who killed the soul. It also said that man could not live by bread alone . . . bread, years and years of earning bread, eating bread, caring, thinking, knowing nothing of anything but one's bread. It wasn't bearable. . . .

I stood there and I died.

He bustled in, carrying in his hand the lopped-off top of a fir tree.

"Had to go a long way in to get a well-shaped one," he said. His voice rang very loud and clear in my ears, the voice of someone shouting down a well. I saw him clearly too. Every line and furrow in his face and the bits of sawdust on the lock of hair that showed under his white carpenter's hat looked as huge and distinct as cobblestones.

He went over to his tool basket and took out a length of white ribbon, which he folded and hacked into lengths with his knife.

I sat down on the window seat and watched him. He propped up the little tree and began to tie the bits of ribbon to its boughs. "This is for prosperity," he said, "and this for health." He mentioned long life and happiness, fertility and charity. Then he tied the last knot to the topmost bough and said, "God bless this house."

And I sat and watched him.

"In the old days, Jon," he said, straightening himself, "every house that was reared was blessed. And who can deny it, the houses stood better and the folks were happier. You and me are alone now, boy, and there's none to mock; so though I know you don't feel about the old things as I do, we'll go now together and put the Bless-this-house on Tom Rowhedge's roof."

The old things. The old way of thinking that a carpenter's boy must stick to his bench; the old way of apprenticing boys so that the master's will was law; the old way of making girls marry the man their father chose; the old superstitions . . . the idea that an omnipotent, omniscient God would look kindly on a house because of a bit of fir tree and some ribbon knots. Horrible, obscene!

Alive I might have ventured some futile protest. But I was dead. I rose and followed him out of the house and into the yard at the back. The space was paved with stones, even as eggs, so that on wet days no one would need to don clogs to cross it. My uncle took a ladder and reared it against the back porch.

"Now you on'y hev to stand by," he said, "and when I hev it fixed you say 'Bless this House,' and Heaven'll be so pleased to see us holding to the old customs, the blessings'll come tumbling thick and fast."

He climbed up the ladder and gained the roof of the porch. After that it was easy, for the planes had been so set that a man could gain access to inspect the tiles or clear the snow from the gutter between the gables. I saw his long knobbly legs in their coarse grey hose and the seat of his soiled, baggy breeches disappear. I heard the scratch of his nailed shoes on the tiles. Then there was silence, and after a space, his voice.

"God bless this house," he said earnestly.

The stick-crackling sound began in my ears. And this time the voices about which, long ago, Dr. Trudgett had inquired did make themselves heard. First, very faint and far-away the voice of my father saying things about the chains which superstition clamped upon men; then Uncle Francy's voice saying that he didn't hold with schooling and did I think

Matt Rawley would let his daughter marry a fellow with four years still to do at his craft; and then another voice, soft, persuasive, and un-recognised. The voice of hope. . . . Yes, at this moment, when all hope was ended, there was the voice, the indomitable voice, saying to me that Elizabeth and Tom were not married yet, that there was money in the coffer, that death cancelled indentures and the world was wide.

For a moment everything seemed marvellously clear and I thought what a fool I had been not to think of this sooner. Then the darkness and the confusion which I knew so well began to close in. A darkness shot with sparks and flashes of horrid light. In one flash I saw him coming, carefully, spiderlike, along the ridge of the porch and towards the ladder. I put my left thumb in my mouth for I knew what the whirling and the darkness and the lights portended; but at the same time I laid my right hand on the ladder. The sound of its fall came sharp and hard through the crackling noises; the sound of his fall was just a soft thud. The voice in my head began to scream as it drew away into the distance.

And then it was quite dark and very quiet.

Interlude

That autumn was long remembered. Seldom, if ever before in the course of their long history, had the parishes of Nettleton, Clevely, and Slip-well been shaken by such a series of dramatic happenings.

There was first the tragedy—the almost double tragedy—at Merravay. The ladder had slipped under Francy Sheply's feet and cast him to his death; and the boy Jon, finding him thus, had been taken with a fit of such severity and length that he, too, was taken up for dead. Indeed the hastily summoned helpers who lashed planks into rough stretchers and carried them back to Nettleton were convinced that they carried two corpses.

This story, exciting enough in itself, was lent a peculiar embellishment by the behaviour of Mary Sheply, who claimed to have had a warning. Because she was so silent and unobtrusive a woman people tended to believe without question her story of how, just at sunset on the day of the tragedy, she went to fetch a last pail of water from the well, and had "a feeling" that something untoward had happened. She ignored it for a while, but when supper was ready and darkness complete and neither of her men had returned, she—who never ventured forth alone—walked into The Evening Star, looked round, and, not finding what she sought, said,

"Is there a man here who will come with me to Merravay? I have a feeling that something has happened to my husband."

On the way, accompanied by three or four kind-hearted fellows, she spoke again.

"I should have come at first warning, before it was dark."

Afterwards they took pains to assure her that even an earlier arrival could have done nothing for Francy. They said, too, how fortunate it was that she had acted in time to save Jon; for that night brought a sharp frost, and lying there with the life at such low ebb in him, he might have died too. As it was he was up and about again in time to follow his uncle to the graveyard, where the sad rites were considerably enlivened by his falling into another fit.

The account of these disasters had just reached the most outlying farm and cottage when from the centre of Nettleton village a new story began to ripple. The story of Jon Borage's almost inconceivable conduct. After all, said the gossips, he was an orphan, and Francy Sheply had been a father to him, far more dutiful and conscientious than many fathers were in these days. The gossips could name one or two men who had done less for their own children than Francy had done for Jon. And Mary had done her duty by him too. One would have expected that he would now turn about and do his bounden duty, which was obviously to stay in Nettleton and ply the carpenter's trade and keep a roof over Mary's head. But no! A most amazing thing had happened.

Francy Sheply had died on a Saturday and been buried on the following Friday. On that Friday Jon had fallen into a fit and for several days had been carefully and lovingly tended by his aunt. On Saturday he had risen from his bed and staggered to the chest where his uncle had kept his savings. The total sum amounted, they said, to just over one hundred pounds sterling. The boy had claimed fifty.

Mary Sheply, suddenly garrulous, had reported the scene.

"Jon said to me, 'This was what my father left me. Francis Sheply put it away—I hope before your eyes,' and I said, 'That is true. I saw him do it.' And then he said, 'He added a shilling for every week of toil I bore, but that I will not take. That is yours.' And I said, 'But it is yours by right, boy.' But of that he took no notice at all. He took his fifty pounds and said that now he would go to Cambridge. But when he said it he shook and trembled and his face went all awry so that I feared he would be taken with another fit. But he did not. He grew calm and told me the value of the timber and the tools and what I should ask for them; and then he kissed me and thanked me for my care of him.

"And I said, 'Do you go straight to Cambridge?'—because it was in my mind to pack him some food in a poke against the journey. And he said he had something to do first. 'If this thing had come about two years ago,' he said, 'I could have gone straight with a free heart, but now it is late.' And with that he left me."

Sympathetic hearers condoled with her, the victim of such monstrous ingratitude. But she said, "He was always longing to be elsewhere. I knew from the first; but my man was not one to be gainsaid. Now he is gone and it is better so."

This story had not reached the outskirts before another was hard on its heels. And the next happening, because it might have fallen upon any one of the villagers, took pride of place. In order to fall from a ladder one must climb one; in order to be deserted by an ingrate nephew one must adopt one; but anybody, anybody walking in the darkness alone, might be set on as Elizabeth Rawley was. And the thought "That might have been me" lends a sharp edge to one's appreciation of another's narrow escape.

Elizabeth Rawley had left her Aunt Thomasin's cottage at the usual time. As was her custom during winter she carried a small horn lantern as well as her basket. What was unusual—and this gave rise to endless speculation as to whether or not the attacker had had information or motive—was that on this evening the basket, instead of containing some trivial domestic offering, held part of Aunt Thomasin's wedding gift to her niece. Thomasin Griggs was mean and miserly, but Elizabeth was her favourite niece and the cloud of senility was thickening about the old woman's mind. All day, ever since Elizabeth had told her of her betrothal, which she did as soon as she arrived, Aunt Thomasin had been diving into chests and cupboards and bringing out articles, some worthless, some of value and piling them together, saying, "All for you, my dear; all for you." Elizabeth, before she left, had loaded her basket, leaving the rest of the pile to be carried home gradually; and being a shrewd girl, she had selected the most valuable of the goods, since there was considerable likelihood that Aunt Thomasin's mood would change and the articles return to their hiding places. So she had in the basket a fine copper skillet, a pewter meat dish, two silver spoons, a horn mug bound with silver and a three-parts-finished patchwork quilt, work upon which had outlasted the old woman's eyesight. Laden with spoil and in high spirits, she had set out for home.

Two hours later, without lantern, without basket, with her clothing torn and muddied and her mouth bruised and swollen, she staggered into the kitchen at Rawley's in a state of hysterical collapse. It was a long time before any coherent statement could be drawn from her. Questions, cosseting, and hot milk laced with a spoonful of Matt's precious hoarded brandy having failed, the father's temper gave way and he shouted at her to stop that blether and speak or he'd try what a clout would do. And so presently the story came out. A man, a stranger, had jumped out of the bushes, hit her in the mouth, knocked her down in the mud, and run off with her basket.

"And was that all?" Matt demanded.

Elizabeth nodded, putting her hands to her mouth.

"All? And enough, surely," her mother said.

It was Emma who said, "But you're over an hour late, Lisbeth. And this all sounds so quick."

"I lay dazed; and . . . having lost my lantern in the scuffle, I walked slowly," Elizabeth said. And having said that quite calmly, she broke down again; so that they saw that further questioning would be useless. Grieved as they were for the loss of the skillet, the dish, spoons, mug, and quilt, but thankful that the thief had been content with taking what was replaceable, they got her to bed.

With the first light of morning Matt Rawley walked along the woodland ride, intent upon the recovery of the lantern. Elizabeth said that when the man jumped upon her she dropped the lantern and it went out; so there was a chance it had been overlooked; and it was a good lantern, worth fourteen pence.

Such carefulness merits reward. The lantern lay there beside the path, and near by the stiff, bleached grass and some bushes with broken twigs bore out Elizabeth's story of a struggle having taken place. Matt retrieved the lantern, walked on as far as Thomasin Griggs' cottage and told her the tale, briefly, and then returned home. At some point along the path his attention was caught by a gleam of scarlet amongst the dun of the thicket; investigating, he drew out a patchwork quilt. The thief had evidently thought it too bulky, or too recognisable, and had thrown it away. Which proved him a fool; for Elizabeth had prudently rolled the two silver spoons and the mug in its heavy folds.

After that Matt walked slowly, keeping, as he said, his eyes skinned, though hardly expecting to find further treasure. He did not leave the path, or search very thoroughly, which was perhaps a pity; for everything which Elizabeth had lost was there within a stone's throw. The quilt, a bulky bundle, had not made quite such an arching flight as the other things, that was all. And on the other side of the path, in the little hazel coppice from which Jon Borage had once cut a crook for Elizabeth's blackberrying, there was something else which would have interested Matt Rawley very much.

But that lay hidden with its hopes and its despairs, its love and hatred, its frailty and its sins for almost three hundred years.

Through all the dark of that winter women feared to venture out alone and men talked sternly of what measures should be taken to suppress such sturdy beggars and vagabonds as the one whom Elizabeth Rawley had encountered.

At Christmas Tom Rowhedge came home and married Elizabeth Rawley and took up residence in his fine new house, and in the August of the following year Elizabeth, who should have known better than to indulge in such activities when heavily pregnant, slipped from the stool on which she was standing to turn her ripe cheeses on their rack. The fall precipitated the birth, and the child—a boy—was born some six or seven weeks before his time. That, of course, accounted for his frail and delicate appearance.

In June of the next year 1579 Her Majesty the Queen kept her promise to visit Merravay. Tom Rowhedge, honest man, knowing his limitations, forebore to attempt the masques and plays which other of her hosts —often less well founded than Tom—devised for her entertainment. On the lawn, now grown smooth and green, which stretched between the house and the edge of Layer Wood, he set up a Maypole; and there, until sunset, the young people of three parishes performed, under the indulgent royal eye, exactly the same ritual dances, "Gathering Peascods," "Hayman's Hoff," "Granny Go Far," as they ordinarily measured upon the village green. And when the sun was down the rural musicians moved with their fiddles and their horns and their cymbals into the gallery of the great hall and played while a mixed company sat at feast below. Tom made the one courtier speech of his life when he said,

"Your Grace commands even the seasons. Ordinarily such food and such company come together only after harvest; and then we call it a 'horkey.'"

And the Queen said, "I have never been present at a horkey and this pleases me well."

And once she looked round and pressed her long thin hands together and said, "This is the very heart of England. My thanks, Master Rowhedge, for bringing it so close to me."

In the morning, just before she rode off for Framlingham, she brought up, out of that memory of hers where nothing was ever mislaid or mislabelled, the recollection of her half-intent to knight Tom Rowhedge.

"Now I can do it and the Spanish ambassador will feel no prick. I can knight you, Master Rowhedge, for the best hospitality I have known on this journey."

That evening young Thomas Rowhedge, with a good dose of poppyhead syrup soothing his stomach, slept peacefully while in the small west-facing room his father and mother, careful folk, supped upon the remains of the feast of yesterday. Tom Rowhedge, worrying the last fragment from a chicken bone, suddenly paused and stared at the fireless hearth above which wreathed the Tudor roses which Francy Sheply had carved.

"Lisbeth," he said, "I reckon that now we'll rate a crest; and I know what it shall be. My ship is the *Mermaid*, and my Maypole pleased the Queen. We'll have a mermaid with a Maypole behind her. If that is to your fancy."

Elizabeth thought that that would do very well.

And then Tom said,

"You know, all these two days Jon Borage has been in my mind. He it was that planned the house, 'fit for the Queen' as he said. I wish he could have been here to see her in it and to see. . ."

He broke off, astonished, because his wife had begun to cry in a wild, distraught fashion.

Quite understandable, of course; so much strain and excitement, for a woman in her condition. She was carrying her second child, the boy Matthew who was, in looks and liveliness, greatly to surpass his brother. Young Thomas, however, remained his mother's favourite, and largely due to her unremitting care lived to inherit Merravay, to become one of James I's original baronets, to marry late in life and beget one child, unfortunately a girl.

The Witch

YESTERDAY, when I asked Master Turnbull to add to his kindness by sending me some writing materials, he, thinking that I intended to write letters, warned me to be very careful what I wrote. He is sceptical of the charge they have brought against me and hopes for an acquittal. I am less hopeful, perhaps because I am less certain of my innocence.

Most people accused of witchcraft—and the number so charged has greatly increased in the last few years—violently and vehemently repudiate the accusation, but some, whom I privately suspect of being crazy, admit it and go to their doom muttering curses and incantations and expecting, I fear, some magical intervention at the last moment. Even those who proclaim their innocence seem to know about things which mean nothing to me; they speak of incubi, succubi, familiars, midnight brews, sabbaths, and covens; but now and then I have a troubling suspicion that these things are only the rubbish which clutter the edges of that unknown world and that maybe I missed them and went straight to the heart. Perhaps I am the only person who, asked whether she were a witch or not, could truthfully say, "I do not know." I do know that some very strange things have happened to me, or through me.

The first occurred when I was eleven years old. I was then living at Merravay with my father, Sir Thomas Rowhedge, who was almost bedridden, and my grandmother, Dame Elizabeth, who bore me a grudge because, being the only child of my father, I had been born a girl. I was very young indeed when a conversation between my father and grandmother sent me stealing into the kitchen to ask old Annie, my friend and comforter, "What is the difference between a boy and a girl?" Annie said, "They're a different shape, love," and gave me a piece of pork crackling to chew. The untimely gift and the note in her voice convinced me that of the two shapes I was the wrong one.

My grandmother was always busy with the affairs of the estate and the household, and with looking after my father, whom she loved so dearly that she was jealous of the very hound he fondled. He was busy, too, with the books he read and the poems and plays which he wrote; but he was kind and I should have spent more time with him had not my grandmother stood between us. As it was, I sought company in the kitchens and yard, and at the time of which I am writing I had found the—to my mind—perfect friend. His name was Robin and he looked after sheep. His father had been hanged for stealing and his mother had married our shepherd and had three or four children by him; there was little room for Robin in heart or home. Once he was sure that I was friendly and no spy for my grandmother he accepted my company gladly and we had merry times together. Despite his hard life he was cheerful and kind; he knew many songs and old stories; he could make wonderful whistles out of an elder twig, and he could sing like a blackbird.

One October day he told me that on the following morning he was to walk over to Ockley to fetch home two dozen sheep which my grandmother had bought from the Fennel flock. I said I would go with him and take a bag dinner; he was always hungry. I also said I would try to get a horse, then he could ride pillion to Ockley and, coming home, we would ride and tie. I was rather proud of my skill as a sheep drover.

It was a blue and gold morning with a singing wind and I was skipping blithely over the cobbles of the yard on my way to the stables when my grandmother rapped on a window and demanded to know where I was going. She was immensely annoyed. It would look well, would it not, she asked, for me to appear at Ockley as a sheep wench! And what had I in the bag? Annie had seen to it that I had a thoroughly good bag dinner; two crusty loaves, a cold pheasant, a hard Suffolk cheese, six apples, and some walnuts. "A little food," I said. But when I was back in the Ship Chamber and my grandmother took the bag from my hand and swung it so that it caught me a clout on the side of my head it did not seem so little. All day, as I sat by the spinning wheel to which she condemned me, my head rang and throbbed.

I watched Robin go trudging off alone; I knew he would have nothing in his bag but a slab of cold porridge. And he would think me faithless. He should have come back at five and I edged my wheel nearer the window so that when he came I might wave and indicate by grimaces what had happened to me; but dusk came and then full dark and still he had not come. We were at supper when someone ran in from the kitchen to say that Sheep Robin was back and that he had lost four sheep on Strawless Common, where a great dog had run out and scattered the flock. He had searched as long as the light lasted but had only rounded up twenty.

The sheep were of some breed which my grandmother had coveted for a long time and the loss sent her into a screaming fury. Carrying with her the chop bone which she had been picking, she hurried into the yard and shouted to Robin that he must go back and search again and that if he didn't bring back the sheep she would see that he was hanged as his father had been. When she returned to table my father said mildly, "That was a dire threat; the poor boy may have taken it literally."

"I meant it so," she said, and leaned over to hack herself another chop.

I spent most of that night on my knees, praying to God to help Robin to find the sheep.

I was early about, and hopeful, but he had not returned; and shortly before noon my grandmother despatched Robin's stepfather and another man to help with the search. They came back at dusk. They had found no trace of the sheep; but they had found Robin, hanging lifeless from the bough of a tree on the edge of the common.

My father was quite peevish and said, "There, what did I tell you?"

My grandmother said, "I consider it proof of guilt."

I could only think that Robin would never sing or whistle or laugh again. And he'd had such a poor life; even his last day had been darkened by disappointment. It was quite unbearable. I imagined him searching and searching, growing desperate, tired to the bone, cold, hungry, and frightened. . . .

Once safe in my own room I cried and cried. Then, remembering my prayers of the previous night, I grew savagely angry with God. "King of Kings whose power no creature is able to resist," it said; couldn't He have called those sheep back, wherever they were? "Not a sparrow falls," it said, but Robin had dangled, lifeless. And who cared? Nobody but me.

And then there came into my mind, neat and complete as though somebody had spoken it in my ear, the remark, "But you must allow for the Devil!" And then out went my candle.

There was nothing unusual about that; for though we made our own and had great stores of them my grandmother doled them out meanly and I was quite used to undressing in the dark; but the failure of my candle drew my attention to the passing of time for it had been new that night. I hurried into bed and there I began to think about the Devil.

I am trying now to be entirely honest. I did actually find *comfort* in the thought that the Devil had, on Strawless Common, defeated God. I much preferred that thought to the thought that God hadn't cared, hadn't helped Robin. I thought all the way back to the story of Eden. God, all-loving, all-wise, had surely wanted people to be happy and healthy and good; it was the Devil who spoiled it all . . . and since so many people were miserable and sickly and bad the Devil must indeed be very powerful. The lifeless, voiceless thing, lately a singing boy, which they had cut down and put under a sack in the barn to await an unhallowed crossroad grave seemed to me to prove the power of the Devil.

But I must insist that though, at that moment, I was forced to acknowledge his power that was all I did. I did not applaud it; I was indeed sorry. I was on God's side. . . .

Having pursued that line of thought to its conclusion, I began to think more practically. I was quite certain that Robin had neither lost the sheep through carelessness nor connived at their removal from the flock. But I knew how in quiet country districts like ours stories passed down from generation to generation, and I thought that what I wanted now—all I could want for Robin—was that in years to come when men told the story by fire on winter nights they should add, "And after all, those sheep were found."

Suddenly that became a matter of the utmost urgency. It sounds absurd now . . . but at that time I was only a child. . . . I reached out in the dark and took in my hand the last whistle which Robin had made for me. I said, in my mind, "Robin, I swear by this whistle that I will . . . I must prove your innocence." And then it happened. I saw as clearly as I now see this quill and this paper, a disused clay pit, so long abandoned that grass and nettles and willow-herb had grown about its slopes; and seven wind-bent young hawthorns leaned over its edge. I thought, Ah! that is the place, and in the morning I shall go there and find those sheep. And I fell asleep as though I had been poleaxed.

At first light I stole out of the house, saddled a horse, and was away. There had been a light hoarfrost and all the world was webbed over with a grey-white shining veil.

I rode blindly, making for Strawless Common, which I had never seen, but I knew its direction and I had heard it described, and roads in our parts were few. I recognised it when I arrived, a great rough stretch of common land, a space of rabbit-burrowed turf, dotted with gorse bushes, blackberry brambles, heather clumps, and stunted hawthorns. At one edge a few clod cottages stood, and the animals belonging to the cottagers, sharp-boned donkeys and cows and goats, lived on the meagre pasture of the sterile land; and beyond these unsatisfactory grazing places the common stretched away to Ockley. I realised that I might search all day every day for a week without finding what I sought; so I did what I have heard of fogbound travellers doing. I laid the reins on my horse's neck and said, "Now go."

He seemed to pick his way as daintily as a dancer, skirting a heather clump, rounding a bush, avoiding a rabbit hole; and all the time I wondered why, free of guidance, he had not turned and made for home. Certainty mounted in me as he moved, and I was not one mite surprised when at last he checked and there was a row of seven wind-bowed hawthorns, with their berries shining darkly red under the frosty cobwebs. I slipped out of the saddle, said "Stand," and walked forward, passing between the trees.

And there was the pit, full of grass, nettles, and willow-herb, and at its bottom four woolly carcasses, horribly mangled and bloody, and standing guard over them, roused from glutted slumber by my approach, was one of those great fierce herd-hounds which poor men keep . . . and keep hungry to foster their natural fierceness.

I knew with a certainty beyond all doubt that on each woolly, bloodied haunch there would be the Fennel mark, the arrow of red ochre, cancelled out by a tarry stroke . . . but I meant to see. When I faced my grandmother with the truth there must be no undermining shadow of doubt. I began to let myself down into the pit. The dog resented that. As I slid and shuffled along the slope he raised his hackles and began to circle about his kill, and when a final slither brought me to the comparatively level ground of the pit's bottom he came forward menacingly. And all at once I was furious with him. Granted he was hungry . . . he had killed Robin and was now prepared to defeat me in my determination to clear the dead boy's name. Damn him, I thought. I was armed only with a little light switch which I carried more for show than use, for my horse, well fed and well trained, needed neither stimulus nor correction. As a weapon it was negligible and evidently the dog thought so, for as I stepped forward he came on, stiff-legged, his eyes shining green, his muzzle wrinkled back to show his long fangs. And something snapped in my head.

"You devil!" I yelled at him. "I'll kill you. I'll kill you!" I raised the little switch and went forward. I saw the menace in his eyes turn to terror; the wrinkled snarl smoothed out. His tail dropped; he pivoted round on his hind legs and went tearing across the pit's bottom and scrambling up its far side.

I made sure of the marks on the wool and then turned and began to climb back towards the hawthorns. When I was almost at the top the thyme-covered hummock on which my feet were braced gave way and I was left with my hands frenziedly digging into the edge of the pit while my feet sought for hold in the raw clay. And it was then that I called to my horse, as though he were a person. "Come here," I said. And he came. "Nearer, so that I can take hold of the bridle," I said. And when I had gripped the rein I said, "Pull!"

I swear that at that moment there seemed nothing strange or unnatural about it at all. When I mounted and rode back to Merravay to face my grandmother there was nothing in my mind except simple triumph because I had proved Robin's integrity. And later on all the wonder I felt was concerned with the fact that I had had a vision of the place where the sheep lay. That the dog had feared me and the horse obeyed me did not seem strange at all. Yet it is all this talk about animals, horses and dogs, which is to be my undoing. . . . And even as I feel bound to protest that no animal has ever been my "familiar," I know full well that if on any market day I leaned from the little slit of a window which admits light and air to this cell and said to a herd of beasts on their way to the slaughterhouse, "Turn about and face the blows and go the other way," they would do it. I know they would. They would do it because I *know* they would. But does that make me a witch?

II

All through the next year each change of season reminded me of Robin and started the pain anew. I wept for him when the first lambs bleated, when the first hawthorn buds broke white, when the first cuckoo called. Fortunately for me my father, who was not without guile in his own way, countered my grandmother's complaints about what she called my "runagate behaviour" by determining to teach me to read and write. The next few years passed rapidly and without incident, at least so far as this confession is concerned.

There came the harvesttime when my grandmother said, perhaps truly, that I was too big to go and help in the fields; my part in the corngathering was henceforth to be confined to the baking of big flat saffron cakes known as "harvest buns" and the making of the very small smallbeer which was provided for the workers at this season. Working with, and under the eye of, the old woman whose resentment towards me seemed to increase with the years was far from pleasant and I was not wholly sorry—God forgive me—when my father took one of his "summer colds" and needed all her attention. We were all used to his indispositions and the way my grandmother behaved when he was ill; and this time everything followed the ordinary pattern, even to her taking Dido, his favourite hound, by the scruff of her neck and hauling her out from under the bed and shutting her into a shed in the yard. On the third morning of my father's illness my grandmother, coming into the kitchen, reported that he was much better; and later in the day, cheered by this news and knowing that there were buns and beer in plenty, I took advantage of her preoccupation to wander out into the sunshine and presently I found myself in the harvest field. It was at some distance from the house and was part of the land known as New Holding because it had been added to the Merravay estate during the last twenty years. The women, scantily clad and wearing bright sunbonnets, followed with rakes and pitchforks and bundles of twine, shocking and stooking the corn behind the men who wielded the scythes; they laughed and sang as they worked, and almost before I knew what I was about I was amongst them, as busy and as merry as the best of them. And then, all suddenly, through the happy noise, there came the melancholy howling of the hound. I said, "My father is dead!" and, dropping the sheaf I held, I burst into tears.

They crowded about me, asking how I knew, and I must have sobbed out something about the dog. There are those who claim now to have seen a great black dog run through the stubble towards me, but that, I am perfectly sure, is nonsense. I am equally sure that those who say that at that moment they all drew away from me in terror are lying; I can clearly remember how they all crowded about me and how in a cluster we moved back to the house, where we learned that what I had said was dismally true.

There followed some weeks of unrelieved misery. Unostentatious as the bond between me and my father had been, it was real enough and his death was a loss to me in many ways. However, there is no place here for detailed description of my feelings.

Since I was a girl the title passed, naturally, to my cousin Rawley, who was the son of my grandmother's second child. About my uncle Matthew Rowhedge there was some slight mystery, darkly hinted at by Annie, who could now and then say things of startling malignancy about my grandmother. Dame Elizabeth had never been fond of or fair to her second son, though by all accounts he had been a strong, handsome, lusty boy, the sort upon whom any normal woman would have doted; apparently my grandfather had much preferred him to my father, who had been ailing and bookish even as a child. My grandfather had died untimely, gored by a bull, and soon afterwards Matthew had gone to sea and had not been seen at Merravay again. He had died in the Caribbean long ago.

I think—though I have no proof—that it was a shock to my grandmother to learn that my father had willed Merravay to Rawley. The place was not entailed and could have been left to her, or to me, but no doubt my father's sense of seemliness had demanded that the original land should go with the title. The fields and the empty house at New Holding and the recently purchased Slipwell meadows were left to my grandmother for her lifetime, and then to me; and if I married while she was alive she was to provide me with a dowry of five hundred pounds.

I was secretly grieved by the realisation that I should never own Merravay, which had always seemed to me to be the most beautiful house in the world, and I was depressed at the thought of going to live in the New Holding house with my grandmother, who now began to speak openly of the move. Only once did she express any resentment.

"I've slept in that room for fifty years and had a mind to die in it," she said.

"It is possible that Rawley might let us stay here," I said hopefully. "The house is large enough."

"I should never dream of asking a favour of him," she retorted; then she added, "Of course if he asked me to stay that would be another matter."

Rawley was at that moment on the high seas, on his way home from Bermuda. Mr. Turnbull, the attorney who had drawn up Father's will, had sent him news of his inheritance and had also made some half-hearted attempts—easily frustrated by Dame Elizabeth—to assume some authority at Merravay pending the heir's arrival.

"I am capable of continuing the management and am prepared to give an account of my stewardship," she said.

What she was not capable of doing—and vast was her annoyance—was to read the letter which eventually arrived from Rawley. Unwillingly she handed it to me. She could do the most complicated reckonings in her head or with the aid of a tally stick, and she never forgot a fact or a figure, but she had never learned to read.

Now, as I broke the seal and looked with dismay at the vile, almost illegible script, she leaned on my shoulder, breathing audibly and giving me little nips in her impatience.

"Well," she snapped, "in what manner does he write?"

I began to read the letter slowly, word by word as I deciphered it.

"Never mind that. In what *manner*, fool? Civil or cool or what?"

"Very civil, I think. . . . Oh yes, indeed. He says it will be a month or more before he has set his own affairs in order. He says he would be vastly obliged if you would 'see to and handle and manage all things' as he understands you have done in the past."

"Is there mention of Master Turnbull?"

"None."

She straightened herself and I could feel the certainty of present power and the hope of its continuance flow through her, heartening as wine.

"He sounds like a young man of good judgement. Fetch your tools, girl, and write to him straightaway."

When I came back she was holding the letter in her hand, gravely studying the marks which made no sense for her. Then she looked up at me with an expression which I had never seen turned on me before, appraising, as though I were a colt or a heifer whose value she was assessing.

"It is a pity that you are so plain and like a pikestaff," she said. "A young man of good sense might think to marry you and hold the land entire. Here take it. . . ." She pushed the letter into my hand.

"But ma'am," I began.

"I want no buts from you! Sit down and make ready to write. . . ."

For once I was grateful to her for cutting me short, for my sentence would have ended, "Rawley is married already." Then she would have demanded to know how I knew and for that I had no answer, and her suspicion that I had not read the letter properly would have been the least of the unpleasant results. But I did know! What is more I knew that Rawley's wife was in some way strange, was small and pale and beautiful, and that there was a fragrance about her, the scent of some flower I had never smelt.

III

I had seen and smelt aright. Rawley had married a Spanish girl, the daughter of a man with great estates. It had been a runaway match, for Isabella's father had had no intention of allowing his lovely daughter to marry a penniless English sailor.

I was completely enchanted by Isabella from the moment I saw her. I was just at the age when, for all I was so ugly and coltish, I was on the verge of becoming a woman, looking half longingly, half reluctantly, into the world of femininity in which Isabella moved with such grace and assurance. I had never had a sister or a girl friend; I had no memory of my mother; and my grandmother, though Annie swore that she had once been pretty and charming, had long ago put aside all the trappings of sex. So when Isabella allowed me into her room, let me look at and finger her things, let me watch her at her toilet and even brush her long black hair, I was like some earnest young apprentice in the presence of a master craftsman. And she was extravagantly kind to me, partly because she and my grandmother were at loggerheads from the start and took opposite sides in everything. Also, of course, those first months at Merravay were lonely for Isabella. Rawley had much to learn and was out on the land much of the day, spending the evenings with Dame Elizabeth, now his mentor. She had set herself to convince him that she was indispensable, and Rawley, out of his element, easy-going by nature, and, truth to tell, no match for her in wits, seemed content to consult her and lean upon her. There was no more talk of leaving Merravay, and it looked as though the old woman would attain her wish to die in the great room which was always spoken of as the "Queen's Chamber."

Rawley and Isabella came to Merravay in the winter and that year the cold was severe even for our parts. Isabella, huddled in a shawl, went shuddering about as chilled as a butterfly which has outstayed its season. My grandmother, always scant of sympathy and utterly ignorant of warmer climates, attributed Isabella's misery to the fact that she undressed to go to bed and occasionally took a bath. One should, said my grandmother, don a good flannel shift and petticoat at Michaelmas and keep them on, day and night, till Easter; that way one stored up heat.

There came an April morning when the wind veered round and the sun shone. I had been in Isabella's room, fitting on a dress which she was making for me. She sewed beautifully and had taken my wardrobe in hand. Her room was in the west "leg" of the house and at that hour, at that season, was cold and sunless. When we came out on to the gallery we stood warming ourselves in the sun and chatting. Isabella had been telling me about her distant home, which sounded like a palace to me, and I suppose it was pride and loyalty to Merravay which made me say, "You've never seen the best bedchamber here, have you? The Queen once slept in it."

Making sure that my grandmother was downstairs on her rounds of kitchen, dairy, and buttery, I opened the door of the room to which I had so often gone in fear and trembling and the certainty of punishment. I intended now to display to Isabella the grandeur and beauty of the apartment with its two great deep-set windows, its noble fireplace, its walls lined with wood so neatly and finely carved they looked as if they were hung with linen, the little dais on which the vast bed stood. Long familiarity had blinded me to the other aspects of the room. My grandmother used it for other purposes than sleeping. There were tally sticks, samples of wool and seed, specially choice medicines for all ailments, human and animal, great rolls of flannel and print for the servants' annual dole and, besides, a great medley of ill-assorted articles which had been put there to await the moment when my grandmother could give them her leisurely attention The windows had not, I think, been opened during her occupancy and the room stank of wool, of horse liniment, and sheep-dip, and, perhaps, a little of unfastidious old woman. The fire had been allowed to go out but the sun shone in strongly and, as well as lighting up the cobwebs on the scarred old tally sticks and the general disorder, made the room as warm as summer.

"It is the most warm room of the house," Isabella said.

"And it could be beautiful," I felt compelled to add.

"The smell is that of the slave cabins," Isabella said. "Come away!"

But she had made up her mind and within a few hours the war of the Queen's Chamber had begun.

There was more to it than two women fighting for the possession of one room. What they were both after was proof of Rawley's allegiance. He loved Isabella quite fanatically; he wanted her to be warm and comfortable; he recognised her right, as mistress of the house, to the best bedchamber; but somewhere along the road Dame Elizabeth had extorted or tricked out of him a promise that so long as she stayed at Merravay and helped him she should remain in that room; and this was the lambing season, when even the toughest, most knowledgeable old shepherd did not mind asking the dame's advice and would say with topsy-turvy pride, "Ah, her's a masterpiece! 'That'll live,' she say, and live that do though I give it up for dead!"

While the fight raged there came, as there always does as soon as the poor lambs are dropped, a spell of really bitter weather, and one evening Isabella, shivering by the fire, asked me to run up to her room and bring down her little shoulder cape which was made of velvet lined with fur and which had a snug, upstanding collar.

The days were beginning to draw out into those long evenings which are so sad in cold weather and I did not take a candle. I looked into Isabella's clothes closet, sniffing the fragrance, and failed to find the cape on any peg. Then I looked into her chest and was on the point of lighting a candle to aid my search when I thought of the shelf in the closet. I reached up and my fingers touched the fur. Then I realised that something else, something hard, had come down with the cape into my hand. It was a little doll.

My first thought was sentimental and female; Isabella was going to have a baby and had made it a doll already! I knew she wanted a baby more than anything and I was glad for her. With the cape over my arm and the doll in my hand I went towards the window, beyond which the sunset sky, coldly lilac and green, was beginning to darken. Then I wondered why Isabella had made a doll so ugly . . . so exactly like my grandmother.

My grandmother still wore a great wheel ruff in the old style, a ruff which it became more and more difficult to get dressed properly as one after another of the old servants who had learnt the art died off. She also wore the stiff, padded panniers which King James I had forbidden to be worn at court, years ago, because they took up so much room. Old Annie had once told me that the ruff and the panniers were exact copies of those which Queen Elizabeth had worn when she visited Merravay and made my grandfather a knight. Perhaps, I thought, she had also said that to Isabella and perhaps Isabella, much as she disliked my grandmother, had seen the romance of that and had wished her child's first toy to link with the tradition. And then I thought, How careless! For one of Isabella's best brass-headed pins had been left in the doll, stuck in in such a fashion that the point protruded at the back of the bodice. I pulled it out and would have put it in the little pin box where it belonged, and then I remembered that by doing so I should betray the fact that I knew Isabella's secret. I was not supposed to have seen the doll at all. So I pushed the pin back, carefully, into the thickness of the panniered skirt so that the point was hidden and couldn't scratch anyone as it had so nearly scratched me.

Then I realised that the room seemed suddenly darker and colder and that I had an uncomfortable feeling of being alone, a long way from the warm, inhabited part of the house . . . and yet perhaps not quite alone! I hurried back to Isabella.

Two or three days later when my grandmother was coming downstairs she slipped and broke her thigh bone. We carried her to one of the side rooms, and, knowing the seriousness of a broken bone at her age, I felt a little sorry that she was, after all, not to die in her own chamber. However she did not die. The bone knitted, though crookedly so that she was lame and lopsided from that time on. She could no longer walk upstairs and refused to be carried; so the tally sticks and all her other treasures were brought downstairs. On level ground she could move, slowly and awkwardly, but indefatigably, and Jack Lantern made her a little cart, like a chair set on wheels, in which she could be pushed about out of doors.

After a week's scrubbing and polishing and airing the Queen's Chamber was ready for Isabella.

IV

Time passed. The confidence which I awaited from Isabella never came, and beneath all the increasingly gay social life which was beginning to enliven Merravay—for Rawley was convivial and popular—there was just a trace of discontent and anxiety; there was, each month, a day or two when Isabella was gloomy and downcast, and I would think, Poor Isabella, disappointed again!

So we came to my birthday, which was in June, and we must have a party with the Fennels, the Blackwoods, and the Headways to eat supper with us and play hide-and-seek and other merry games in the garden in the warm dusk and afterwards dance in the hall. Lady Fennel, who had a loud, hearty voice, asked me how old I was and when I said, "Sixteen," she said, "How time passes! Think, by Yule I shall be a grand-mother!"

Mrs. Headway said, "Mary has lost no time! Why, she was married only at Candlemas."

"Ah, well," said Lady Fennel, "I always say a good tinder strikes first time and a damp one never will!" They laughed. I happened to look at Isabella and saw her white-rose pallor take on a tallowy hue and the bones showed in her nose.

Two nights later there was a full moon; I had no curtains to my win-dow and the light, falling full on my bed, woke me. After a while I got up and went towards the screen which in winter stood between me and the window to exclude the draught and which in summer leaned, folded, by the wall. It would now serve to shade me from this extraordinarily vivid and strangely melancholy light. Hanging over the screen at that moment was the exquisitely made petticoat which Isabella had sewn and given me for my birthday. I had not laid it away in my press because I was waiting for some rose leaves which I was drying to be ready enough to sprinkle in its folds. It was so lovely with its delicate stitching and fine embroidery that I meant to lay it up with care to await some really special occasion. As I lifted it from the screen I thought about that special occasion . . . for most girls of my age that would mean my wedding day; but I had little hope that anyone would fall in love with me. I was so tall, so thin; and in me the Rowhedge red hair, instead of being dark chestnut, was a pale, very unbecoming russet, and it was short, very curly, and springy, so that even my grandmother had never succeeded in making a parting in it; it grew like a lamb's pelt. Also I had pale green eyes and in summer hundreds of freckles.

I was thinking these purely personal thoughts as I took the petticoat in hand, and then everything rushed out of my mind except terror. Not for myself; for Isabella. I knew in that special way of knowing that she was in danger, horrible danger. How, lying there in her own bedroom with Rawley by her side, she could be in danger of any kind I could not think; but I knew she was. Then I thought that she might be ill. My first impulse was to go running along the gallery, but even under the im-pact of terror some sense remained with me and I thought that if this were all nonsense and they were asleep they would hardly thank me for going to their room. But if she had been taken ill Rawley would have made a light. I ran to my window from which theirs was visible. I looked out. I don't think I even saw their window, for my eye was caught by something which moved, accompanied by a sharp black shadow, across the smooth turf of the lawn. It had almost reached the point where a deep decline separated the garden from the field. There, in old times, when the castle of Merravay was in being, the moat had lain.

The moving figure—and I was almost certain that it was Isabella—disappeared into the dip and then emerged again in the cornfield and began to move towards Layer Wood. It was Isabella, and my first thought was that she was walking in her sleep, for never consciously would *she* leave her warm bed and go wandering in the night. I had been led to believe that nothing untoward ever happened to sleepwalkers; so I wondered again why I should have the certainty that she was in peril. Then I remembered.

Years earlier, when I was very young, I had been a frequent visitor to Layer Wood, going there in search of wild flowers and the very small, very sweet wild strawberries which grew there in profusion; until one day I pushed my way through a little hazel thicket and had been so frightened, of nothing, seized with such sheer reasonless animal terror that I had dropped my basket and run home like a rabbit. Ever since I had avoided that spot, and called it, in my own mind, the Bad Place. Now Isabella was walking straight towards it.

I pushed my bare feet into my shoes and, hitching up my night shift, ran out into the moonlight. I could, at need, run like a stag and if I had stopped to put on my stockings and fasten my shoes I might have saved time. As it was, my feet, slippery with the cold sweat of fear, came out of my shoes at each step until finally I discarded the shoes altogether and ran barefoot over the sharp tufts left from the hay-scything in the field.

Isabella was in the wood when I reached her; and she was wide awake. I gasped out, "What are you doing?"

She said shortly, "A thing of importance. You must help or go away. Better I think you should go."

"I can't leave you here, alone. This is a bad place . . ."

"A right place. Now lend me your hands and stay silent or go. And never speak, never, of what you see."

I stayed; I helped. Does that make me a witch? Does a kitchen slut handing a dish, passing a spoon, thereby become a cook?

I hated it all; I hated it so much that by the time the thing was done I was well on the way to hating Isabella herself. When it was over she sat down exhausted on a fallen tree trunk, and it was I who stamped out the fire and buried the poor drained body of the little white cock who would never greet the sun again. Then I picked up the doubly sullied bowl.

"That must be broken," she said. I hesitated, for it was one of a new set and pretty, yellow with a brown rim. She took it from me and smashed it against the tree trunk. It fell into four almost even pieces. She counted them and then fitted the pieces together as though to make certain that none was missing.

"It is a pity. It will be a girl. But that is the beginning only. I shall call her by your name."

"Do you really believe . . ."

"Oh yes. It is a thing very old, brought by the slave people from Africa, but very sure. And all that was left to do, Alice; marrying Rawley, who is heretic, has made me incommunicate—not even the little saints would ask for me. But by next year this time I shall have a baby. Let us go home now."

In April of the following year the baby was born; and it was a girl. But it was not named for me; for Isabella died within half an hour of its birth and it was left to my grandmother, the only person unaffected by the tragedy, to choose the name. She chose Thomasina.

V

Rawley took refuge in drunkenness.

My grandmother bore with him patiently at first, but as the sum of months mounted she took on a censorious tone. One day she told him that *she* had always found hard work the best cure for heartbreak.

"How could you know? You never loved anything but a tally stick!" he said bitterly.

Another day she suggested—I think with good intent—that he should leave Merravay and return to the sea for a while. She said she would look after his affairs for him.

"I'm damned sure of that!" Rawley said nastily.

Things worsened between them as he grew more and more sottish, and one evening as he slumped over the supper table she snapped out,

"If you are so uxorious that being widowed makes a sot of you, the best thing you can do is to marry again."

Rawley cried out like an animal, a wordless sound of pain; then he picked up his heavy silver tankard and flung it at her. She put up her hand and by the luckiest chance caught the tankard by the handle. Setting it with exaggerated care on the table, she said coldly,

"That is exactly the action of a spoilt child whose toy has been taken away." Then with dignity, despite her limp, she walked away and Rawley lowered his head until it rested on the table.

"She shouldn't say such things to you," I said. Filled with pity I went near and laid my arm across his shoulders. I meant to comfort him as one comforts a child, and like a child he turned to me, making a little muffled sound, half groan, half sob, as he thrust his head against me. I stroked his head and said, "Poor Rawley."

Then all at once it was "Poor Alice"! I began to tremble, sharp pain transfixed me, I was dizzy, I was gasping for breath.

Rawley moved, freeing himself.

"Dear little Alice," he mumbled. "Kind. Mustn't upset yourself. Be all right." He patted me as though I were a dog, and went lurching away not to the Queen's Chamber but to a small bare room which actually *smelt* of his misery.

And that is how I fell in love with Rawley.

The pain continued in me and grew worse and added to it was a terrible shyness. I was so afraid that he might guess what I felt about him that I dared not look him in the face; I could hardly speak to him and avoided seeing him whenever I could.

The slow months passed and there came the time when rumours about Rawley and Phyllis Whymark, the girl from The Evening Star, began to creep about. Strange as it may sound I could see exactly what it was that Rawley sought and found in her; I liked her too. There had been a time when she used to drive geese up to the London market and she would come to Merravay some days before the setting-out day to dip the feet of the geese in tar, which hardened and protected them from the wear and tear of the long journey. I used to steal out to watch this process, to enjoy her easy, wryly humourous conversation and to gaze with admiration upon a girl, not much my senior, who could undertake that long hazardous journey alone. Her mother was a woman of notorious bad character, but though I wouldn't have staked a pin on Phyllis being a virgin, she wasn't a whore either, the respect with which men spoke of and to her proved *that*. With her nimble wit, earthy philosophy, and salty humour she was just the company for Rawley at that moment and she would never in any way remind him of Isabella. But for the fact that I was myself in love with him I should have regarded the affair as a blessing.

Not so my grandmother; she was scornful and furious and in her fury precipitated the very situation she dreaded, for one day she faced Rawley with the rumour, and he whipped round and said that if the idea of his having Phyl Whymark as his mistress was so shocking and repulsive the only way of mending the matter that he could think of would be that he should marry her! And despite the aching of my heart I could not deny that he could have done worse; there was something vital and vigorous about that young woman; if Rawley married her he would never miss his grandmother, for Phyl was capable of running Merravay or anything else. The very way she walked showed that.

Probably the old woman recognised her match; for as soon as she had convinced herself that Rawley meant what he said she began again to make preparations for leaving Merravay and going to New Holding. She took a high-handed attitude towards the affair, an attitude which I could but admire.

"Don't for one moment imagine," she said, "that I shall stay here working myself into my grave to keep that baseborn slut in comfort! I leave you to go to ruin at your own gait."

She began to gather her gear together, and at last there came the—to me—dreadful day when she told Jack Lantern to take out all the sacred tally sticks and burn them. I knew then that there was no hope.

Later that day she told me to make ready anything I wished to take with me to New Holding; the servants would convey the baggage next day, make fires in the house and arrange it, and we should follow on the day after.

I went up to my room feeling that life was over. I must turn my back on the man I loved, the house I loved, and go forward through the joyless days in bleak and bitter company.

Since my grandmother had decided to leave Rawley to his fate she had been less strict about candles and I went to my room with two long new ones.

I had few possessions and I was too wretched to care much what I took or what I left; but at the very bottom of my chest I came upon two things which I had hidden there because the very sight of them gave me pain. One was the petticoat which Isabella had given me on my birthday, the other was the last little whistle that Robin had ever made. I couldn't leave them behind, nor could I take them with me. I thought of the Dame's tally sticks and decided that her action was seemly. I carried my treasures over to the hearth and, taking my candle, tilted the stick so that the flame licked at the fine linen; but before it was smouldering the candle fell out of the stick, rolled away, and went out.

In the dark once more I felt my way to my chest, took up my brush and began to brush my hair; thinking as I did so about the whistle and the clay pit, about the petticoat and that night of full moon.

This is what confuses me. I performed no ritual; I said nothing; but I *thought,* and as I thought I became aware of a kind of power, something welling up in me so that instead of thinking to myself, I wish Rawley would marry me instead of Phyllis Whymark, I was thinking, breathing, willing, *being* to myself, He shan't marry Phyllis Whymark, he must marry me! I will it, it shall happen.

VI

The next day passed without event, save that my grandmother suddenly remembered a couple of silver spoons and a mug.

"They were of small value measured by all that has come into this house since," she said, "but they are mine and must go with me." That sounded reasonable enough. But when the things were found she said, "They are dear to me though I had overlooked them. They were with me in the mud that night. Then I flung them into the bushes and my father found them. A very stern man was my father; he was to blame for everything."

The idea of her ever throwing anything of value into a bush was somewhat startling, but I was too miserable to give it much heed.

Rawley did not come near us that day. Darkness fell and my grandmother and I sat down to our last supper at Merravay. I thought she looked pale and a little tired, which was not to be wondered at. We ate, with small appetite, in silence until she said abruptly,

"Chris Huxstable is dead, you know. He was cut for the stone and died. So now you'll have Merravay, my girl, and that will smell sweeter than the tannery!"

"I beg pardon, ma'am; I don't understand."

"No, well, you're young. But I give you warning. You never *have* anything. Whether it's a stinking tannery or a beautiful estate you don't have it; it has you; and when it has sucked your very marrow they'll cast you on the dung heap. That happened to me, clever as I was. But they didn't have it all their own way, you know. There was a time when I had nothing; and the few things I had I must throw away to make it look like a robbery. And it was so muddy too! But I was so happy. So happy. I've never been happy since."

I was alarmed and shocked to see that tears were running down her face. I had never seen her cry before; even when my father died she had shed her tears behind a closed door.

"I think you are feeling unwell, ma'am," I said, rising from the table and going to where she sat. "Come let me help you to your room."

She took my wrist in her thin hard old hand and I could feel the unnatural heat of it.

"You must decide," she said. "And now; there is no time to waste. Will you come or won't you? Fifty gold pieces will last a long time and I'm not without skill. You'll never lack." Her voice changed, losing its urgency, its curious echo of youth. "That is what he said, you know. And then it was so muddy and I wondered how I could explain. But I did. I fooled them all."

"Of course," I said soothingly. "Come and lie down now."

In the kitchen, whither I went to fetch a hot brick, for the old woman's feet were as cold as her hands were hot, I found Jack Lantern trying to persuade the cook to put two hedgehogs in the oven for him. He had found them on his way back from taking our baggage to New Holding. The cook refused to have anything to do with such uncanny creatures and he went off disgruntedly muttering that he would cook them himself.

Apparently he did so, over a fire made of Dame Elizabeth's tally sticks. Later on he swore that the fire was out before he left it and went to sleep off his orgy, and that may well have been true. A spark may have flown up and started a quiet slow smouldering in the thatch of the stable while he was enjoying his strange repast. It was hours later, hard on midnight, when the glare and crackle of the fire and the screams of the frightened horses trapped in the stable roused the house.

When I reached the yard the roof of the stable was all ablaze, but all the horses save three at the far end, beyond an eight-foot-high partition, had been got out. Just over the partition a portion of the flaming roof had fallen inwards, setting fire to the partition itself. Jack Lantern had actually made one dash past the flames and attempted to drive the three horses out, but they had refused to face the blazing barrier and were now rearing and screaming against the farther wall. I could see instantly that though the partition was aflame there was still a passage between its end and the wall. The opening in normal times was wide enough to admit a man with a forkful of hay, and I knew that I could save the horses if they would just do what I told them. Darting and shrugging away from those who would have restrained me, I ran in through the opening that was arched and bordered with flame and seized the first horse by the mane. My hands were as steady as they ever were at table, my voice as calm as though I were exchanging the time of day with a passer-by. "Steady now," I said. "Trust me; there is room. Steady, you're safe with me." Three times I did it, and as I followed the last horse past the flames and into safety the whole roof, with a snarling roar, caved in. Smoke and flames and bits of blazing débris seemed to reach towards me; I lurched forward and fell into Rawley's arms.

They are saying now, of course, that I went to and fro through the flames, exalting and unhurt. That is hardly true. I suffered no serious damage, but my hair and eyebrows, like the manes and tails of the horses, were singed; and the skin of my face and arms were scorched so that it peeled off like cornhusks and left me painfully raw. They lie who say that, tempered by the fires of Hell, I emerged from a burning stable unscathed. . . .

But . . . but ought I to deny the power of the Power which had come to my aid so timely? In twenty-four hours I should have been at New Holding and Merravay might have burned to the ground without my knowing. I had willed that something should happen to take Rawley from Phyl Whymark and give him to me . . . and what I willed had come to pass.

This is no love story and these things are too intimate to set down here. It suffices to say that while they were larding my raw flesh with goose grease and then powdering over the grease with flour, so that I was most grotesquely masked, and my close pelt of hair, crisped and blackened, was flaking about like ash Rawley came and knelt by my bed and told me how he had felt when he saw that burning stable and heard that I was within. And I shall always cherish the knowledge that he was coming to me through the flames.

VII

And after that, for almost twenty years nothing strange took place. Life proceeded in normal, placid fashion. We were very happy.

I was one of Lady Fennel's "good tinder" kind. Within a year I had borne a child, a boy, whom we called Charles. He was a happy, healthy, handsome little boy and with him and Thomasina, who now seemed like my own, I was well content.

My grandmother lived only a short while after the night of the fire and was never again wholly sound of mind. At the end I had her carried up into the Queen's Chamber so that she might die there as she had wished, but it was a wasted gesture, for she seemed to imagine that she was lying in Layer Wood and complained bitterly about the mud.

Tucked away between the woods, the river, and the sea, we at Merravay led, I can now see, a life that was isolated, self-contained, and perhaps unduly complacent. It was life after the antique fashion, in which a bad batch of butter or a hailstorm that flattened a wheat field seemed of more dire importance than the disputes of bishops or the conferences of kings.

We were warned, of course. As early as the December of 1637, Sir Walter Fennel, sitting at our table, full of our food and wine, suddenly leaned forward and asked Rawley,

"Have you paid your ship-money yet?"

"Some time since. Why?"

"Pity," said Sir Walter, cracking a walnut between his fingers. "I didn't.

And now I see that this Buckinghamshire fellow, Hampden, is refusing to pay and letting his case come into court. And not a penny will they get from me until I see which way the cat jumps."

"I can tell you that now," said Rawley cheerfully. "They'll make him pay—and next year put up his dues!"

"That remains to be seen," said Sir Walter. "After all Hampden rests his case upon an indisputable fact—that ship-money is illegal."

The old sailor in Rawley knew a brief resurrection.

"God above us! We've got to have ships, haven't we? And how can we have ships without money?"

"Taxes should be levied by Parliament," said Sir Walter, something stubborn and pontifical creeping into his voice.

"But we haven't had a parliament for eight years! And when you wail about ship-money you should remember, Walter, what a mass of taxes the Parliament men would have levied if they'd sat there all that time with nothing else to do."

That seemed to me a sound argument; and since Rawley was holding his own so well I forebore to say anything.

"Well . . . of course, if that is the attitude you take . . ." There was something a little ominous about Sir Walter's unfinished sentence, and although for a long time after that conversation our families continued to meet and maintain friendly relationships something sour remained and would reveal itself from time to time in remarks such as "You're a King's man, aren't you, Rawley?" or "Don't say such things in Rowhedge's house, he's Royalist, remember!"

One day Rawley said to me, "I'd give a shilling to know where Fennel gets his information. To my certain knowledge he's not been in London these last three years, yet everything that's said and done there is known at Ockley within a week—if we can believe him."

Next time I saw Lady Fennel I asked her the question and she was pleased to tell me about the weekly *Newsletter* to which Sir Walter, the Headways, and Blackwoods subscribed and shared. An enterprising fellow called Shuttle had started the scheme to supply news to country places, and the service was now so swift that a *Newsletter* sent from London on Wednesday morning reached Ockley on Saturday afternoon. I promptly ordered a copy for us, and then, when I found it to be violently anti-Royalist I also subscribed to another which was equally biassed on the other side; but though we read—or rather I read while Rawley listened, yawning—and talked about what we read the whole business seemed remote, unimportant. So unconcerned were we that when in 1640 the King did call a Parliament which promptly declared ship-money to be illegal, the first thing Rawley said was, "Now Walter will be happy! Let's ask him to supper and see his shining face!"

I also remember, quite clearly, that we were at Ockley when the news came that the Queen had left England and gone to Holland.

"That means war and nothing less," said Sir Walter. "She's off to beg, borrow, or steal money and with the powder and shot and the foreign mercenaries thus provided, the King'll shed our English blood!"

"But the Queen has gone to convey the Princess to her husband, which is reasonable enough," Rawley protested.

"The Princess is a child of ten!" Sir Walter snorted. "It's time you faced facts, Rowhedge; or do you mean to sit on the fence till you're pushed off?"

I suppose that was our intention, if we could have been said to have any at all; but in the end we were forced into taking sides. By our own son.

Charles, then aged seventeen, was at Cambridge; and one day in June we received a letter from him. Instead of the usual rather rambling amusing discourse to which we were accustomed this letter contained some terse instructions.

"Please send as quickly as possible, my mare and a sound pack horse, my warm cloak, my silver cup and ten pounds. Let young Lantern, or Bill Woods, or better still both if you can spare them come to ride with me. I am for Oxford."

"Oxford," said Rawley. "What in the Devil's name does he want with Oxford. Didn't we thrash out the question and settle on Cambridge for his learning?"

"He is going to the King," I said.

"That is nonsense! Now that I will not allow," Rawley spluttered. "This is a grown men's quarrel, whipped up by old fools. If it comes to blows let the old men give and receive them. Sit you down, Alice, and write to him bluntly and say I bid him stay where he is. Or better still, come home. Aye, that is it. If this matter of learning is so light that it can be abandoned to go gallivanting off to Oxford then the boy might just as well . . ."

I never heard the end of that sentence. I stood there with Charles' letter in my hand, and the thing which had not happened for so many years happened again. I saw my son, grown older and thinner and brown of skin, standing in a strange place. He stood between sky and sea, both blue with an intensity of blue that our skies, our seas, never knew. There was fierce, vivid sunlight, and queer trees with feathery foliage which shook out a warm spicy odour. He looked well and prosperous and assured, and something remained of his old boyish merriment, tinged now with bitterness. . . .

"Here," Rawley said, slipping his arm about me. "Bear up, Alice, don't take it so hard. He hasn't gone yet, and, by God, he shall not go! I'll ride myself to Cambridge and knock sense into his head if needs be."

"He'll go if he has set his mind to it," I said; "and if he goes he must go well equipped."

"He won't go," said Rawley stubbornly. "He won't want to go when I've had my say."

"I will come with you," I said, "to take leave of him, in case . . . And we will take what he asks for, in case . . . But of course I hope that you may persuade him."

I knew then that it was a vain hope, and when we reached Cambridge I was more than ever certain. The whole place was in an uproar. The town and the surrounding countryside was strongly Parliamentarian but the Colleges were for the King. Behind the closed gates the young men were making ready, melting down their silverware, gathering their gear, looking to their weapons. They were all in wild, hilarious high spirits, like children about to go on some long-promised treat, and of course poor Rawley's arguments and persuasions were no more than leaves in a wind. In fact there was one moment when it seemed as though the contagious enthusiasm might make a convert of him.

Despite my inner certainty that Charles was not going to his death, that he would live to be at least thirty, I parted with him in agony, for I did not believe that I should ever see him in the flesh again. I was also miserable for Rawley's sake and wished that I could have told him what I *knew*. But that was impossible; for one thing he would have thought me mad; for another there was some deep instinct which informed me that these were not things to speak of.

All I could do as the battles of Edgehill and Newbury and Chalgrove Field followed one another was to say, "I feel in my bones that the boy has taken no harm. I should have known, Rawley. I am his mother."

VIII

At Merravay, through all these troublous times, life went on much as usual. Except for the Hattons at Mortiboys all our neighbours were inclined to the Puritan cause, but there was no fighting in our district. Since we were known to veer the other way and had a son rising rapidly in the Royalist ranks, the worst that befell us was that we were regarded a little askance and avoided, rather as though we had a case of plague in our house. Sir Walter Fennel, most Puritan of our neighbours, foreswore our company, but he still sent his mares to our Barbary stallion. With the Blackwoods we remained on cordial terms because two years before war broke out Thomasina had married young Robert Blackwood. When her first-born was christened Robert Rawley we were asked to the ceremony, and, the Royalist cause being in the ascendant at the time, we were not unwelcome to the other guests. But as time went on matters became more difficult.

For one thing, a Huntingdon squire named Oliver Cromwell came back after the first Battle of Newbury to raise new forces in East Anglia. He had said of the Parliamentarian forces, "Do you think that the spirits of such base fellows will ever be able to encounter gentlemen that have honour and courage and resolution in them," and he had vowed to raise an army of his own from men of honour and courage and resolution. In due time there came to us at Merravay a manifesto, a demand for men and money.

The moment I had it in my hand I saw—just as I had seen the clay pit, and Rawley's wife, and Charles aged thirty in a far place—a really horrid sight, a mass of mouldering bones hanging in chains above the heads of a great crowd of people all jeering and pointing, rejoicing in the grisly sight.

"From whose hand?" I asked. "Who wrote this?"

"The General's own," they told me. I drew Rawley aside and said, "Though it would be expedient now to trim our sails a trifle, have nothing to do with this man. I have a feeling that he will come to a bad end."

Rawley stared at me, astonished. "What could I have to do with him, Alice, even if he were headed for the Throne itself. With Charles on the other side!"

(This incident seems strange to remember now, when Cromwell rides so high and I lie so low. But that "eye in my hand" never saw wrong and the end is not yet!)

One day soon after that Rawley was in Baildon, in the yard of a hostelry called The Hawk In Hand, where he stabled his horse, and one of the hostlers came up and asked rather furtively, "The young master is with the King, ain't he, Sir Rawley?" We had never made a secret of that, so Rawley said, "Yes."

"Well, if ever you want to send him owt, bring it here. We've got ways of managing." And shortly after that we began to receive cryptic little messages from Charles, demanding money. We sent it, cautiously and suspiciously at first, but it always reached its destination and was always acknowledged in terms which made sense to me but would have meant nothing to anyone who had intercepted the letter. One little note, for instance, read, "Who used to be a notorious gambler? Wouldn't he put up a stake?" And that sent Rawley riding to Kit Hatton, who would have bet on which way the wind would blow tomorrow, and Kit raised two hundred pounds which went down "The Tunnel" as we called this line of communication.

Then came the second Battle of Newbury, and next time Rawley visited Baildon he found The Hawk In Hand closed down. For many weeks during that long cold winter we had no news of Charles at all and what other news we received was all discouraging.

One evening Rawley and I were sitting in the Ship Chamber when I heard a stealthy tapping at the window. I thought it might be a gull. In bad weather they came up the river and grew bold, friendly as barnyard fowls, and I often put scraps on the sill for them. I looked and saw something—too large to be a gull—move behind the pane.

"Rawley . . . there is someone by the window."

For the last week or so Rawley had been convinced that he was being watched wherever he went. He rose now in anger and said, "Spying on us at our fireside now, are they?" He went and unlatched the casement and flung it open and then stepped back with a cry. Charles put a leg over the sill.

"Dear hearts," he said, "I hope I did not alarm you." He pulled off the old woollen cap he wore and came to kiss me. All his lovely glossy curls had been shorn, and as soon as I had recovered myself I said, "Oh Charles, you look like a Roundhead."

"That was my intention. I've got so far on my looks but I dared not trust them where I was known. That is why I came to the window. Mother, can I have something to eat, at once? I've a great deal to say and I must be on my way in an hour."

I began to bestir myself. I ran to the kitchen and brought food and the ingredients for mulled wine, for the boy was soaked to the skin. Then I went to his room and picked out the plainest and shabbiest of the clothes he had left behind at the beginning of that Cambridge term which now seemed like a lifetime ago. Old as they were they were too fine to fit the rôle he had chosen, so while he sat by the fire, eating with the voracity of a wolf, talking all the while, and Rawley mulled the wine, I busied myself by cutting off the bits of fur and velvet and the fancy buttons as I listened to his talk.

The King, he said, had men in plenty, for the reverse at Newbury had brought forward many formerly lukewarm; but he was tragically short of arms. However, arrangements had been made; the King of France had no wish to see his brother king defeated and was sending weapons of war.

"To get them in . . . that is the trouble. The Cropheads hold all the ports, and places like Plymouth and Poole where we hold the land inward are too well watched and guarded. So we thought of the east, where they hold both port and land and so feel secure and are less careful. And we hope to land arms at Hull, and Yarmouth . . . and Bywater!" He broke off and eyed us over the bread and bacon which he was stuffing into his mouth.

"A bold scheme," said Rawley thoughtfully. "Under their very bows as it were."

"I'm glad you're in favour of it," Charles said quickly, "because this is what you must do . . ."

It all sounded wildly fantastic, as unreal and unlikely as the games children play or the dramas that unfold themselves on a stage, and when Charles finally stood up, looked at the hat from which I had removed band and buckle, and said, "Still far too jaunty," and pulled on the sodden woollen cap again, I stared at him, feeling that it was all—his visit, his talk, his disguise—part of a dream from which I must surely soon wake.

"There," he said, "now don't I look like Jeremiah Oh-Lord-Arise-Scatter-Thy-Enemies Jones? And now, can you get me a horse? You'll find the one I came on in the Low Meadow. It's foundered but it was a good horse and could be again."

A few minutes later, out in the windy dark, he kissed us and mounted. We said, "Be careful of yourself" and "God keep you."

"And you. And speed you in all you do." Then, raising the old cap, he cried, "God save the King!" softly but as though it were a battle cry. He touched the horse with his heel and in a second the double dark of the night and the avenue's shade had engulfed him.

We never saw him again, but I know he is alive, somewhere.

He left us wholly committed to the King's cause.

IX

It would be tedious to describe in detail the campaign of subterfuges, shifts, and lies upon which we then embarked. What we had to do sounded simple enough. We had only to provide transport for the arms between Bywater and Merravay and warn the innkeeper of The Red Lion at Colchester who would then make the next link in the chain. (Almost without exception the innkeepers were Royalist because they feared that the Puritans, once in power, would close their houses.) Had Rawley and I been a simple farmer and his wife, used to drivng our own teams, it would have been easy enough; as it was it demanded great cunning. We had decided not to involve any one of our servants, not so much because we did not trust them as to avoid the slightest risk of an indiscreet word, an ill-timed significant glance; consequently we were obliged to behave as though these old faithful friends were all enemies. To me fell the task of carrying the warning to the men at The Red Lion and many were the devices to which I was driven to shake off, even for a few minutes, the servant who had for years attended me whenever I rode so far. Twice, I remember, I went so far as to have a tooth drawn by a man who had lately set up as a tooth-dragger in a room behind the inn. Sometimes, too, I chose to ride the Barbary and saw to it that the servant was mounted on a slow-moving horse and I pretended that it was past my power to hold the great black horse to the pace of the plodder.

We tried never to repeat a story or to play the same game twice; and as the weeks mounted into months we had the satisfaction of knowing that the arms had at least reached Colchester safely and been sped on their way. Now and then when the King scored one of his spectacular—but, alas, indecisive—little victories we could look at one another and think that perhaps, with our scheming, hard riding, and sacrifice of sleep, we had contributed a trifle towards it.

One day in May we were notified in the usual manner that a load waited at Bywater. This time we were providing the team and wagon in the least troublesome, though most expensive, way. Rawley was going to Bywater, where he meant to buy the best that the market offered. After nightfall he would drive it to the place where the Colchester men with their vehicle always waited—a lonely place where a tongue of Layer Wood ran down to meet the road to Bywater. There he would stay with it until later next day and then drive it home. Such a procedure would be easily explained in view of the approaching haysel and harvest.

I had decided to use the tooth-dragging again as my excuse for a visit to Colchester, though this time I had decided that I would not carry the pretence quite so far. Rawley and I rode out together as far as the cross-roads and there in the sunshine, under trees where crinkled young leaves were unfolding, we said good-bye to one another.

Colchester, which was a completely Puritan town, was very dull that day and full of soldiers; as soon as my errand was done I started for home, not even bothering to look into the shops, which, if they had anything gay and pretty—which I doubt—kept it well hidden. I decided to ride round and visit Thomasina, who was expecting another child at the time. Truth to tell I always found the day before one of these night ventures intolerably long and trying; I was not cut out for a life of risk and excitement; I could too easily imagine the number of things which might go wrong. I should find Thomasina's company soothing and diverting.

She was, as always, delighted to see me, but I thought that the behaviour of the other members of the family was strikingly cool and formal. The King's cause was no longer flourishing as it had been at the time of the christening of Robert Rawley Blackwood, and Thomasina's mother-in-law, with whom I never had been much of a favourite because long ago she had hoped to marry one of her many daughters to Rawley, said with a dark look that if things went on as they were doing the war would soon be over and there were those who would be sorry for the attitude they had taken. The Blackwoods had recently had soldiers billeted on them and spoke highly of their behaviour. These soldiers of the New Model Army were models indeed; they neither drank nor swore; they did not steal; they left the maids alone. And think of it! When some went to billet on the Hattons at Mortiboys and Mrs. Hatton said, quite untruthfully, that she thought they should move on as they suspected a case of plague in the house, the sergeant in charge had said, "God will take care of His own!" and moved in, uncaring.

Still, even the barbed chatter served its purpose in keeping my mind off the journey which Rawley must soon make with the wagon so heavily loaded that even the best team he might buy could only move slowly through the night. So I stayed on until the shadows were long across the lawn in which Mr. Blackwood took such pride, and it was dusk when I reached Merravay.

The day had been very warm and my sticky clothes were turning chill on me, so I went to my room to wash and change. I was taking my time over it, thinking that in a few minutes Rawley would be setting out; then I could linger over supper, walk in the garden for awhile . . . anything rather than go to bed and lie there thinking about that slow progress through the dark. There was no doubt about it, Rawley was dearer to me than any cause, even though, through Charles I owed it my allegiance.

I was putting on my dress when a servant came to tell me that some soldiers had arrived, seeking accommodation for their horses and themselves. That had happened before, not often because Merravay lay far back from the road, but often enough for us to be used to it and for me to know that all that Mrs. Blackwood had said about Puritan soldiers was quite true. In fact, as I ran down, hastily fastening my dress, I thought it was a pity that soldiers of the New Model Army were so very abstemious. Otherwise I would have opened a cask of good brown ale and made sure that when they lay down they slept soundly. Although the place of rendezvous which we had chosen for our transactions with the Colchester men was at a safe distance from the house, its very existence made me nervous and vulnerable to thoughts of danger.

It was only a small contingent, a captain, a sergeant, and eight troopers; they asked civilly for what they might have demanded or taken without a word. They looked tired, so did their horses, but when I suggested that the animals should be turned loose in the pasture the captain thanked me and said he would make his own arrangements. As I turned away, leaving him to do so, Sir Walter Fennel rode into the yard.

It was months since I had seen him face to face, for since the decline in the social relationship between our families the strictly "farmyard" business which he had had to do with Rawley had been conducted out of doors. He greeted me with surprising cordiality and then, looking towards the open cart-shed where the soldiers were installing themselves, he said,

"Ah, I see you have company. Is Rawley home yet?"

"No. I do not expect him until tomorrow morning."

"But he has only . . . I called this morning and your servants said that he had gone to Bywater. I hoped he'd be back."

I was heartily glad that *this* time there had been no secrecy, no subterfuge, no juggling with means of transport or even with time.

"He could have been, of course. But Rawley is an old sailor, remember, and once he gets to Bywater, where there are ships to look at and sailors to talk to, he likes to take his time." I smiled. "In the meantime, is there anything I could do? I know a little about most things."

"Thank you, Alice; no there is nothing. . . . Unless you cared to invite me to supper. I have been in the saddle all day and it would be late before I reached home."

I managed, with difficulty, to conceal my enormous surprise.

"It would be a pleasure," I said. "It is a long time since you honoured our table."

Fear, or fear's beginning, began to move, cold and slippery, in my stomach. Across the yard the soldiers were watering their horses . . . but they had not unsaddled!

"Since you will stay I think I will invite the captain to join us," I said. I would have him under my eye.

Sir Walter strolled across with me and I thought—I could not be sure, for I distrusted my knowledge-engendered suspicion—that a significant glance, a look of recognition and confirmation, passed between the two men.

The captain accepted my invitation and I led the way into the Ship Chamber, where I excused myself, saying that I must go to the kitchen to speak about extra places at table. I did not close the door and, having gone with a tapping of heels and a rustle of silk across the hall towards the kitchen quarters, I stole back along the wall.

". . . a bigger force," I heard Sir Walter say.

"Others are posted and patrolling. No loophole this time," said the soldier.

Before I had reached the kitchen I had known—and thrust aside—the impulse to do the obvious and dangerous thing. My first thought had been to run straight out, leap on the black horse, and make a dash for Bywater. But the soldiers were in the yard and before I could get the horse out of the stable they would have ringed me round. Besides such an act would be a confession of complicity. Then I thought of making an excuse to ride out openly—to say, for instance, that I was anxious about Thomasina Blackwood and must go to see how she was faring. But that—even if they accepted it—would accord ill with my having invited them to supper and most certainly Sir Walter would have insisted on accompanying me. No, I must think of something more crafty.

X

The meal lasted a thousand years. I sat there, noting the thickening darkness outside the windows. In May the nights are short, and Rawley, if he had not already set out, would be about to do so. Slowly, creakingly, he was moving towards the trap.

I was very gay. I gave, I think, a good impersonation of a woman with nothing on her mind save the entertainment of her guests; and that fitted in well with what I had to do.

When the meal was over I rose and moved to a side table where a silver dish held the last wizened apples of the autumn's crop.

"Now," I said, "I must ask you to excuse me for a few moments. Every night, without fail, I give my black horse his apples and he is more of a stickler for ritual than Archbishop Laud ever was!"

Laughter greeted that sally; but in the glass above the side table I saw them look at one another and make ready to move. Forestalling them, I said,

"You, Sir Walter, know my Barbary and his antics, but perhaps the captain might be entertained to see his performance."

They followed me out. In the yard the creak of leather and rattle of chains informed me that the troopers' horses were still ready.

"We should be fair," I said. "I expect your horses like apples, too."

"They're not accustomed to pampering, ma'am."

"Just this once," I said. I held apples to the questing velvet muzzles; I spoke into the long twitching ears. Then I opened the door of Barbary's loose box, called to him, and he came. He danced as I told him, rearing and pivoting on his back legs; he held up one hoof, then another; he whinnied to order. I handed the dish to Sir Walter at last and said,

"His best trick, for some reason, he will only do when I am on his back. Captain Allbright . . . please."

He helped me to mount.

"Kneel!" I said to the great black horse; and he buckled his knees and lowered himself. "Give him his reward," I cried, and as Sir Walter held out the apple I leaned over, saying, "Good boy, *good* boy!" Then I spoke into his ear. And at once he was up, a great mad thunderbolt of power, striking out back and front, gathering himself for the great leaping bounds which carried him out of the yard, not towards Bywater but in the other direction. I clung to his mane and screamed for help.

We thundered out of the yard and were halfway up the avenue before I spoke to him again and began to steer him cross the fields into the marshes—safe now, thank God, for the spring had been early and dry. Headed for Bywater by the shortest way, I got myself astride him and, lying low on his neck, said, "Run now; run as you never ran."

I reckoned that Rawley would still be on that part of the road where it ran alongside the river. It would be the action of a moment to back the team, unhitch and let the incriminating load roll of its own momentum into the water. Rawley could go back to his bed at The Ship, and the horse and I would finally come to a standstill somewhere quite incredibly far from Bywater. I might even stage a minor accident. . . .

Nobody, I thought, could blame me for overestimating my control over a horse which most people already regarded as a dangerous demon and certainly no one would believe that the refusal of the troop horses to budge an inch could be in any way due to me! Later I learned that they did stand fast, even when prodded with pikes; and I learned too that nobody had any difficulty in believing that I had bewitched them.

I found the wagon just where I had reckoned. It was blazing fiercely, and of the four or five dead men around it one was Rawley.

So now I do not care what they say about me, or what happens to me. My spirit is already dead in me. My flesh shrinks from the thought of death by burning. Yes, that appalls me and I can only hope that what Thomasina said on her visit to me is true—that the smoke chokes the victim before the flesh chars and the boiling blood bursts the veins.

There, I have set it all down, honestly. And what does it all amount to? Five times in my lifetime—is it five?—there was Robin's whistle, Rawley's letter, the petticoat, Charles' letter, and Cromwell's manifesto; yes, five times something which I have held in my hand has communicated something to my mind. Twice—once over the matter of Robin's innocence and once in the matter of Rawley's affection—I have imposed my will on my circumstances. And always I have been able to make animals obey me implicitly. Does this amount to witchcraft? Am I damned not only in this life but in the life to come? I cannot remember ever wishing, or working, ill to anyone. I cannot, even now, wish positive ill even to those who tell those twisted, lying stories about the transparent black dog in the harvest field.

No, if I could wish anything it would be that I might die, quickly, easily, before the faggots are lighted.

Interlude

Lady Alice Rowhedge was found guilty of witchcraft and condemned to be burned. In the brief interval between the delivery and carrying-out of her sentence, she was taken back to the cell in the old Bridewell in the Friargate at Baildon. She must have gone and stood by the narrow window, unglazed and rendered still more narrow by a rusty iron bar. What happened, happened so swiftly that people going home from the trial and arguing about her guilt, or her innocence, actually *saw* and stepped aside to avoid a small black dog which was proceeding along the Friargate in peculiar circular fashion, seeming to wish to bite his own tail and crying as he went.

Alice Rowhedge—with what was almost her last breath—said that she saw the dog and imagined that he had a thorn in his flank. She called him and he came and she put out her arm, not without difficulty. The dog bit her, sinking his teeth into her hand, not once or twice but many times, for on account of the narrowness of the window and the angle at which her arm was held she could not easily withdraw it. The dog ran on as far as the corner, where a blacksmith, recognising the nature of its ailment, clubbed it to death with his hammer.

Inside the cell Lady Alice told the gaoler what she had done and what had happened and added, in what he called a wondering voice, "No dog ever bit me before!" Then in almost no time at all she fell into frenzy, and from frenzy to coma, and died.

Only the most stubbornly rational people—and they were rare at the time—reminded themselves and their hearers that the dog was real enough to have been killed by a blow from the blacksmith's hammer and that its wretched little carcass had lain on his dunghill for days, plain for all to see. The vast majority believed that a dog of quite another kind, the dog of the harvest field, had come to save the witch from her just deserts.

An abbreviated version of the story which she had written while she was awaiting trial was printed under the title of "A Witch's Confession," and a copy of it found its way into every household where one literate person lived, and even the least superstitious people were forced to admit that she *had* after all, died before the faggots were piled. Her story, with many variations, many embellishments, was told by the winter fires and under the summer trees, told so often that it became part of the folklore of the region.

After the King had been executed—another thing to argue about; for even in Suffolk, where most men had been against him, there were those who thought that such an extreme action boded no good—Merravay was taken in hand by the Commissioners and divided into three portions. The two that consisted of land only found a ready market, but the third, consisting of the house and gardens and about thirty acres of land, was hard to dispose of. Merravay itself had become a place to avoid, for dark and sinister stories were creeping around. And the house staring there blank-eyed across the fields, deep in its grounds where the nettles and brambles encroached upon the pinks and lilies and roses of Lady Alice's garden, grew daily more like a place where ghosts would walk than a place where people should live. Only little boys, inspired by greed and bold in company, would venture there on sunny afternoons to snatch nuts from the shrubbery and pears from the sheltered walls; then, retreating with their loot, they would tell tales of strange things seen and heard and resolutely braved.

One such party, early in a new season of nuts and pears, did receive a genuine fright; for Phyl Whymark, the woman from the tavern, suddenly appeared from the house and ordered them to be off and not come back. Merravay was her property, she said.

From a safe distance the boys mocked her, mocked her claim to ownership. But it was valid enough. And the older people, with longer memories, said, "Ah, so she got it, after all!"

The Matriarch

THERE's no doubt about it, I ain't as spry as I was!

It's as much as I can do to stagger out here into the sun and drop down in this chair like a sack of meal.

But then, I reckon I must be close on ninety. Nobody can know for sure; they kept no count of birthdays when I was young. I got meself born, and I've kept meself alive, and when I come to take stock I can't help thinking that I ain't done so badly. A mite of luck, but in the main hard work and mother wit hev got me where I am today.

And where am I today? I'm sitting in the garden at Merravay, and I can look to right and left and straight ahead, and, for all I'm so long-sighted, as far as I can see belongs to me, my own, my very own.

Maybe I was meant to hev it; for there was a time long ago, though to me that fare like yesterday, when Sir Rawley Rowhedge was minded to marry me. He would hev done, too, but for the spells put on him by that whey-faced cousin of his—her that would hev burned for witchcraft if the Devil hadn't snatched her away. Nowadays folks make mock of witches and such-like, more fools they! I could tell 'em something; but I don't. What happened betwixt Rawley and me was our business then, and I've kept the secret all my life.

Till I took up with Rawley I'd kept meself to meself, and that weren't so easy. For one thing my mother was a byword for loose living; for another I went up to London every year, driving geese. We lived rough, sleeping in stacks and ditches along the road, and I was reckoned to be pretty. . . .

When Rawley took up with me and spoke serious about marriage I reckoned that was the reward of virtue—the virtue I'd often fought tooth and nail for; and when he fell under the spell and jilted me and give me fifty pounds, I reckoned that was the wages of sin. Between the two there was a bit of my life I never cared to think on. He was a right proper man, Rawley was; and I could never bear him much grudge; it wasn't his fault.

I was heartsick, but people like me don't brood over their feelings, leastways not their softish ones, and I plucked meself up and reckoned meself lucky to hev the money. And nobody was scornful to me. People reckoned he'd just hung about our place time he was drinking to drown his sorrow, and the one he was thought to hev jilted was Miss Headway.

I looked round for a way to put the money to good use. I did think about heving a pastry-cook's shop, for I was a fair hand at cooking; but there'd be no customers much in a village and I hated all towns. Moreover, by this time, my mother was dead and there was only one of my brothers—if you can call 'em that—living at home, and the way he was going on he didn't look like making owd bones. So I thought I'd wait a bit, and if he drunk hisself to death in good time, I'd spend my money making the tavern a better sort of place, the sort travellers would pull in at.

I found out a lawyer man that everybody spoke well of and went and arst him about putting money somewhere safe where it could breed a bit. I laugh to myself even now when I think about that first little business betwixt Mr. Turnbull and me and where it all led to in the end.

I'd no sooner laid the money away safe than I found I was in the family way. Christ in glory! I was so savage I could hev kilt myself. I'd allust set myself to be a cut above my mother, who'd had a bastard most years, and here I was, going the same road.

There was a chap or two would hev married me if I'd played my cards right, but I was still sore for Rawley and couldn't fancy any of 'em. So I told meself I'd get out of this fix same as I'd got into it, secret-wise.

First of all I tried every old-wives' cure I ever had heard of, mainly through hearing my mother say she wouldn't touch 'em. I jumped off ladders and heaved the heaviest things I could find, and one night went and stood in cold water up to my neck. But my John was a sight stubborner then than he ever was in later days. In the end I knew I'd either got to stand and brazen it out or get away. I towd my brother I was off to London to try to pick up a little money and threatened him well what I'd do if he burnt the place down or anything else silly time I was away, and off I went.

I knew where to make for—the Poultry Market, where hundreds of geese waddled in and were killed and dressed every day and where anybody that could see and had two hands could hev a job.

I wasn't exactly a stranger, and my home was nothing to be homesick for, but, God, I was miserable that time. I hated London, and the Poultry was a stinking place even for London, and the people I worked and lived with were low, scum of the earth. Still, it was good place to hide in.

I worked hard and laid by a shilling or two, and when my time came near I bargained with the woman at the house where I'd been sleeping to let me hev a room to meself for a bit. She towd me about a place started up by some kind ladies, a laying-in place for poor women, but I didn't want nothing like that. Nor I didn't want her messing about. I towd her so. The night I went back, feeling a bit queer, I give her two shillings.

"Thass rent till I get about again," I said, "and you keep outa my way."

She laughed. "You don't know whass coming," she said. "You may be hollering for me afore you've done."

"I may holler, but you keep out. I paid for this room and if you bust in, I'll claw you," I said.

I shoved a brukken chair under the knob of the door and settled to wait. I'd helped my mother more times than I could remember; I knew just what to do . . . and what not to do.

Next day, or the one after, I meant to go out of that room with my waist in the right place and nothing to show that any man'd made free with me.

I was my mother's second or third, and by the time I was of an age to help her she'd hev a baby as easy as she could wring out a cloth, so I'd no idea what heving a first baby meant. By noon next day, when the baby was born, I was that wore out with the pain and the struggle that what I had planned should happen damned nearly did happen, willy-nilly. But I roused myself enough just to take a look at the thing that had caused me such a lot of trouble . . . and with that one look I was undone. John and me hev been through a lot of things together, but I never loved him more than I did at that minute.

II

I could hev stayed in London, where one bastard more or less didn't matter; but I wanted my child to grow up in a healthier place; so regardless of shame and jibing, back to Nettleton I went as soon as I could face the trudge. And once there I cast round in my mind for some way of making a little money at the same time as I tended the baby and looked after what trade there was at the tavern.

I hit on pork pies.

I've worked hard all my days, but never harder than in the next few years. I reared, killed, and cleaned my own pigs, sold the choicest joints and made the rest—down to the shreds of meat that I could scrape from the toes and the jaws—into pies. There was the tavern, too; and a baby that I tried to bring up clean and healthy, and my brother well-nigh as helpless and a sight more nuisance. But I managed.

All this time the Witch, Alice Rowhedge, was living smooth and soft up at Merravay. She'd had a baby, too; a boy, a fine handsome little chap, but not a patch on mine, or so I thought. Hers was more like Rawley, with the same chestnut-coloured hair; my John took after me and that was lucky. I could see Rawley in him though.

I had kind of cherished the notion of getting him a bit of schooling and give him a push up in the world that way; but he never took kindly to learning. Any other sort of work he was a wonder at, very willing and very strong.

The years went by, my brother died, John grew, the war broke out, and the tavern trade dwindled, but the pie business flourished, and John and me had laid penny to penny till we'd got another fifty pounds to set aside with that that Rawley had give me; and we was looking about for a bit of land to rear more pigs and geese on, when Captain Samuel Fletcher came into our lives.

Him and half a dozen troopers arrived one afternoon and billeted theirselves on us. The men went into the bar-room, what was hardly ever used for its proper purpose; for, what with the rules and the scowlings, you could hardly sell a drink them days. Captain Fletcher follered me into the kitchen and after beating about the bush for a bit arst me if I could let him hev a sup of something. I was wary and said no at first, but then I see he wasn't trying to trap me, he was a proper drinker and he wanted something badly. So I went down the cellar and brung up some good owd October ale and a little brandy that I'd been howding on to. He was as happy as a yard dog let off the chain for a bit.

He got to telling me what he suffered in Colchester, where the taverns were shut down, and I towd him how I was planning to get out of the trade and get some land and he said, "Ma'am, take my advice and wait. There'll be land going begging when this is over."

"How so?" I asked.

"Once Cromwell is safe in the saddle," he said, "he'll take the land off all them that fought for the King. And once they get to breaking up the big estates, mark my words, land'll be mighty cheap."

"Not about these parts. Them with land about here are all for Parliament."

"I know one who isn't," he said, making a knowing sort of face. I arst who, but he was a man who could keep his own counsel even in his cups, which is a thing I respect.

Then he suggested that he should give me a regular order for pork pies.

"Delivered to me, at Colchester barracks. And to my mind, ma'am, all a good pork pie needs is a drop of something to wash it down."

"And to *my* mind," I said, "there's nothing easier to carry in and out than a nice bit of washing. You send me your dirty linen. . . . For send bare pies amongst a lot of soldiers," I said, "I just dare not."

We understood each other.

Thass funny to think that about this same time the Witch up at Merravay was setting about her bit of smuggling.

I've never been much of a thinking woman, I been too busy; but now and then thoughts'll go through your head time your hands are busy, and one thing I thought once is this. Loving a person and hating one are alike in this—you take note of what they do, where they go, and what happen to them. I *hated* Alice Rowhedge so much that if somebody'd stood at the crossroads and said her name in a whisper I'd hev heard it.

Well, things went wrong with her and she was carted off to gaol. At first we thought it was for helping to get arms to the King and, of course, there was nothing I could say; but when it come to witchcraft that was different. I knew she'd put a spell on Rawley; men don't suddenly, overnight, fall in love with their ugly cousins that hev been living under the same roof with them for years. Alice Rowhedge was there when Rawley's wife died, but he hadn't turned to her then, he'd turned to me. So though I wasn't going to say ought about the one spell I *knew* she'd worked, I could and did say about the time when I was stooking at Merravay. . . .

III

After a bit the thing what Captain Fletcher said would happen, did happen. They put Merravay up for sale; but I could hev cried with vexation because of the way they did it. No separate fields and pastures the same as I'd been counting on. Three big lots they cut it into; the New Holding land and the Merravay land next to it was one—and Sir Walter Fennel bought it; the Slipwell land and the other part of Merravay on that side was another—bought by Mr. Blackwood of Muchanger; the house and two fields and meadows made the third. It was as plain as the nose on your face that Sir Walter and Mr. Headway had had a say in the dividing; not that I minded their getting what they wanted; what raised my gall was the thought of the two fields and meadows near the house, any one of which would have suited my purpose, all going back to wild while the house went to rack and ruin. Nobody wanted that lot, for people who looked to live in a great house wanted more land, and people who wanted a little land didn't want a great house. So there it stood, shorn of its acres, useless as a ship gone aground.

I was still smarting when one day Captain Fletcher came grinning into my place and I rounded on him pretty sharp.

"That was rotten bad advice you give me," I said. "But for you and your land going begging I'd hev bought Croop's meadow time that was for sale. I went and let that go; and now I shan't never get the bit of land I hanker after."

He grinned and I went on: "And I should like to clout the head of the fool that divided that place."

"Clout away," he said, and stuck his close-cropped skull towards me. "You!"

"The same, ma'am. I'm one of the Commissioners. The army is in command now. Bless you, I thought I'd done you a good return for favours received. I knew that neither of the bespoke customers needed a house . . . so I tucked away a nice little thirty-acre bit *under* the house, so to speak . . . and then you go for me like a vixen!"

"If you did that you're more of a fool than I thought you! Thirty acres and a mansion; what use is that to a poor woman like me? All I've managed to scratch together in twenty years' hard grind is a hundred and fifteen pounds."

"Well, offer me that!"

"For Merravay and thirty acres. Man, you're mad."

"Maybe. Go on, make a firm offer and it's yours. Not today; not tomorrow . . . but before the year's out. 'In default of better offer,' see? We must do things orderly."

"But suppose you have a better offer," I said, very dry in the mouth.

"Well," he said, dragging out the word. "I'm only one of four, and there're strict eyes everywhere; but there are ways and means. For one thing it's a very bad-reputed house. They say the Witch walks there. Of course . . . that wouldn't bother a sensible woman like you; but, being an honest man, I should be bound to warn any prospective buyer. Shouldn't I?"

"You ain't mocking me?"

"I'm dealing with you, ma'am, as you dealt with me, fair and square and underhand. And now, have you anything to wet the bargain?"

I never said nothing to nobody, not even my John, in case things should go wrong. The best part of a year went by and sometimes the impatience in me was like a pain; another season wasted and me getting older and the land going back to wild. They say in our parts, "Fallow hath no fellow," but they only mean for a year.

However, the day came when Captain Fletcher visited me again, this time with another man, and all very strict and stiff. They had come to tell me, they said, that since no better offer had been made for Merravay, they would take mine, ridiculous as it was.

"I don't know about ridiculous," I said. "There ain't so many people want a house where queer things are to be seen and heard, nor land so weeded over that you can't tell ploughland from pasture. I made my offer afore the weeds had got such a howd!"

That changed his tune for him!

IV

Knowing what I knew about Alice Rowhedge's power, and hearing all the stories that were springing up and spreading about the house, it is a wonder that I didn't feel a bit funny about going to live there, especially as I'd been one to speak against her; but to tell the truth I never give the haunting a thought. I went up alone to look at the place for the first time as soon as I'd handed over my money and got the keys. There'd been a red climbing rose over the porch and part of it had come loose and grown right over the door, so I had to fight my way in, scratching myself something cruel. I'd expected it to be musty, and dampish and darkish inside, but it wasn't; it was warm and dry and sweet-smelling and there was nothing but the silence to show that nobody'd been there for a long time. I walked all through, thinking about the uses I could put some of the rooms to, and if I thought of anybody it was Rawley; which room had he slept in, where had he taken his food? And what would it have felt like, I wondered, to hev come in, married to him, with the place all furnished? I'd hev been shy and awkward, and scared of the old grandmother; now I was bold and certain of myself, and knew I'd got the best bargain in the world. Maybe that suited me better, after all.

I was in the kitchen then, looking round and planning how John and me'd live there and how he'd come in when the day's work was done and how I'd be getting the meal ready time he washed. It'd suit us fine, I thought. And then I heard the laughing. High and shrill and merry, as though somebody'd heard my thoughts and laughed with a—Ah, so you may think! Alice Rowhedge had always been a one for laughing when she was little, given half a chance. For just a minute I went cold, and caught my breath. . . . Then I realised that the laughing came from the garden, and out I went and found six or seven little urchins getting pears off the trees by the wall. I towd them to be off and not come back, and they ran a little way and then stood and mocked me, "Owd Phyl Whymark, t'ain't your place."

"Oh yes it is!" I said. And that was the first time I said it. And somehow after that it seemed true. And—So much for ghosts! I said to myself. Let that be a lesson to you.

I'd been to Mr. Turnbull, of course, to get back my money and the interest it had gathered, and I'd asked him, this time, to lend me fifty pounds to buy stock with. He said something about security.

"You write yourself a paper," I said, "to say that do I die or come to ruin, you're to hev fifty pound worth of stock."

"But if you were ruined, Mistress Whymark, there might be no stock."

"Well, the house and land can't get away. Write it so."

He coughed and fidgeted about with the things on his table; then he said,

"I think it would be bad to burden a property with a mortgage so soon. Tell me—you hold your tavern freehold, do you not?"

"I did; but I just fixed to swop it with Matt Bowyer for his owd mare and wagon."

"Has that transaction taken place?"

"We talked about it last night."

"The licence to brew and sell ale is in order, I take it?"

"Oh yes; but that ain't worth much these days."

"Slightly more than a mare and wagon, I think. I believe I could get you fifty pounds."

He did, and six months later they made a loop of good hard road that just reached the old tavern, and the coaches came. But I didn't grudge it; I'd been prepared to take an owd horse and wagon for the place, so I hadn't been wronged; and the new road made it easier for me to get my stuff to London. I began on that right away, heving no truck with the little towns what could get more stuff when they needed. My time in the Poultry Market had taught me what a hungry place London was. Whereas geese might open at two shilling apiece in Baildon or Colchester and drop to eightpence when folks'd sell at a loss rather than trail 'em home again, in London there was always a hundred daft people rushing about to find a goose after nightfall, even on Christmas Eve itself.

At first, heving set everybody plenty of work to do, I'd go up with John to show him where to go and how to do his deals, but he took to that the same as he always took to anything real and in the way of work; so then I could stay at home. I had broody hens sitting and fatting hens penned all over the ground floor of the house. I had geese in the orchard, and sheep under the trees in the avenue, pigs in the yard, and calves in the meadows. Sometimes it fared to me that I was feeding half London, I poured food out at such a rate; cheese and butter, bacon, meat and table fowls, eggs and cream. I used to work till I was past speech, well-nigh deaf and blind. I never did stop except to throw a bit of food into meself and John when he was home; and at night I used to drop onto my bed, in my clothes as though I'd been stunned. And I know that old Noah packing his Ark never got so many living creatures into a square yard as I did at Merravay. Every penny I made I put straight back into the place and in ten years I never bought myself nothing but footwear and a herring now and then. I couldn't grow herrings and I was inordinate fond of them.

V

One morning—a lovely June morning it was—I noticed my hands while I was milking; and they was the hands of an owd woman, all gnarled and twisted like tree roots. And I did a bit of reckoning and knew I must be fifty, maybe a bit more. Getting along; soon be going downhill . . .

That day I said to John, sudden-like,

"Did you ever think about getting married?"

He gaped at me. "I been thinking," I said. "I'm getting on. I should like to see my own grandchildren."

"You ain't sick, are you?"

"You know I'm never sick—ain't got time. But I reckon that if you're going to marry you should do it soon. You're thirty!"

He didn't say anything, or seem to think any more about it, and I reckoned that that'd be another thing for me to handle. So I looked around for a good strong girl, a farmer's daughter, likely to be a good help to us, but at the same time bright and lively. And I picked just the one, a girl named Hester Fulger that made beautiful lace in her spare time. I thought I'd ask her to dinner one Sunday, for though I'd never had no advantages I knew how things should be done. Any girl bidden to Sunday dinner to a house where there was an unmarried man knew which way the wind was blowing. But afore I got so far with my plans John went off to London on his next trip, was away two days more than I'd counted on, and got back just as the late summer dusk was coming down, bringing a girl with him. He walked into the kitchen, howding her by the hand, and before I could speak for the surprise at seeing her he said, "Mother, this is Alison, my wife."

I never see, in all my days, a poorer, more dwindling, more scared look-ing creature. She was clean, and had a sort of prettiness with her great tangle of curls and huge eyes, but she was about the size of a twelve-year child that has never had a square meal in all its life and expected every-body it met to give it a clout.

"Married?" I said; and the word went on ringing through the kitchen.

"Two days ago," said John.

"I'm afraid this has given you a shock," said the girl. Her voice surprised me; it was sweet and clear and very sure.

"I am a bit took aback," I admitted. "Hev you and my boy been long acquaint?"

"Two years," she said. I wanted to ask where he had found her. I tried to take comfort in the fact that she was too shabby to be a street whore. I turned back to the stove to hide my mortification.

John said, "Whass for supper?"

"A bit of gammon and peas."

"That'll do. Only Alison can't eat fat, so give her my lean and me her fat, will you."

It was only a little thing, but I do believe it was the first time in all his thirty years that he'd handed me an order. While I dished up he took her cotton bonnet and hung it on the peg over his working clothes and set her in a chair by the table, as if she was the Queen, and she turned her great eyes about, taking it all in, missing nowt and saying nowt. I took my place, feeling ill at ease, but trying not to let the upset put me off my food, trying to think of the next job waiting for me. It was no good, there across the table she set, my daughter-in-law . . . where I'd meant to make a bid for Hester Fulger. Oh, it was hard!

She ate very dainty, taking her time, and now and agin wiping her lips on a bit of a handkerchief. And for all her eyes looked so scared, she wasn't as nervous as I was; for though I couldn't find a word to say and could only look at her and then away agin, quick, she looked me full in the face as if she was taking my measure, and once she smiled, a right sweet, friendly smile, but not as if she was asking me to like her, more as though *she* was minded to like me. In one of my sharp glances I noticed her hands, thin and small they were, like a little bird's claws, but red and rough with hard work. Taking them into account and the smallness and the frightened look, I guessed that John had picked her up out of pity, same as he might a stray kitten. There was a very gentle streak in my boy. Nice for her, but what about me, counting on a good strong girl to take on when I got older; and what about the healthy great boys I'd pictured in my mind's eye?

Next morning when John took his place aside me at the early milking, I said to him sharp and sudden,

"What come over you, boy? And where did you find such a dolly?"

At The Shepherd and Dog, just behind the Poultry, where he lodged in London, he said. He'd had his eye on her for a long time, feeling sorry for her doing menial, ill-suited work. "She looked like a flower on a muck heap," he said.

I nearly said that we hadn't much use for flowers at Merravay; but I held my tongue. He was my boy; we'd stuck together through thick and thin; and if he wasn't as bright and sharp as I could hev wished at times, maybe he wasn't to blame for that. I wasn't going to quarrel with him on account of that little bit of thread!

Then presently we went in to our breakfast, and there she was, with it all ready and neatly set out. She'd found, somehow, the one tablecloth I owned, the one I'd washed and got ready against the day I arst Hester Fulger to Sunday dinner! And she'd put a few rosebuds in a mug in the middle of the table, and got water hot so we could wash our hands. Something new had come to Merravay . . . and I suppose you couldn't say that it wasn't wanted.

So in time we shook down together; though there were odd minutes when I was minded of the Bywater man what caught a mermaid in his net and brung her home and married her, minutes when I would think— What a tool for a busy woman to hev to put up with! She couldn't push, she couldn't pull, she couldn't lift. She wasn't unwilling, she just hadn't no strength. She'd wash—she was a great one to wash—but by the time she'd got the things soaked they was too heavy for her to lift and wring out; and though she took to the dairy work very kindly, when she churned I had to heave the cream in and then listen till she called, so I could tip the butter out; else she'd turn the churn over, trying. There was things she could do that I couldn't, read and write and reckon in her head, and she sewed beautiful; she mended us up very tidy; I never was much good with a needle and I never had time.

She quickened sooner than I'd thought for, but she carried the baby so ill that I often wondered whether it'd come to anything. I used to look at her and think of myself in like case and think maybe, in a rough and ready way, the burden is fashioned to the back. What she'd hev done wringing geese's necks and taking their insides out up to the very day, God alone knows. Then her time came and for a bit we reckoned we'd lose her, and it was then that I knew I had a fondness for her. My best Dutch cow calved the very same day . . . but I stayed by Alison, though John had fetched the doctor and I wasn't needed all that much.

The baby wasn't the poor pingling little thing I'd expected, and in a way braced myself to take and add to my load. A great lumping girl it was, and Alison said it must be named Phyllis for me.

Less than a year later Alison was in the family way again and this time we all had hopes of a boy. Young Phyllis was doing well; the place was prospering. Things looked fair and pleasant for us, and then the blow fell. And what a blow it was!

VI

Along come Mr. Turnbull one afternoon, when I was just laying the oak logs to my smoke oven to cure a couple of pigs, and say he's sorry to bring me such tidings but the fact is that Merravay, and all the land to it, do now by rights belong back to Sir Charles Rowhedge what fought for his lawful king.

We'd known, of course, that the King was back in London; good for trade that was, too. We knew owd Oliver—the tavern-shutter—had been dug up and hung in chains . . . just like the Witch in her writings said she had seen him. A rare stir in Nettleton that caused. But apart from the men what had signed the order for the owd King's killing they said nobody was to be punished . . . but I could see in the blink of an eye that Mr. Turnbull, what had been a good business friend to me, thought it right and fair that I should be cast out of Merravay . . . and if that wasn't punishing!

"But I paid for the place. All legal and above board."

"Ma'am," he said, "you made a token payment to them as had no right to sell. Count yourself fortunate," he said, "that so small a sum was involved. There are those in England today, thousands of them, especially in the West country, who are going to lose property for which they paid the full market price."

"Lose it? You mean just go away and leave it . . . have nothing?"

"Not perhaps so precipitately as that. Sir Charles, who has been engaged in the nutmeg trade in the Dutch East Indies, has arrived in Amsterdam, from whence he has written to me. I have written to inform him of the . . . er . . . position and he will probably come to see about things for himself. But I thought it only fair to warn you that Merravay is no longer yours."

I set the logs right and closed the door of the fireplace, opened the oven and saw the smoke flowing smoothly through. I took up one half carcass and hung it carefully on the hooks. Two pigs . . . four sides of bacon . . . mustn't waste or fumble . . . they at least were *mine*. But I felt sick.

"You have done well out of your venture, taking it all in all," said Mr. Turnbull, as though he was chiding a child for sulking when a treat was over.

It was true; I'd made profits; but they was all out there, walking about, eating their heads off, past profits carefully bred back to make future ones . . . it'd have been better if I'd bought meself diamond rings, or stuffed money into a mattress. Cut the ground from under me, and my stock was nothing but a liability—or so much dead meat!

I shut the door of the smoke oven very carefully so as not to check the flow.

"I sincerely hope," said Mr. Turnbull, "that you will be successful in finding alternative accommodation. You are lucky in having had a little warning. . . . I have heard of others less fortunate."

But what comfort was that to me?

There followed another bit of my life that I don't ever want to think about.

One thing that made me mad was that when those who'd sided with the King had held on and been fined and sold some land to pay the fines the people who bought that land weren't to be turned out. Not far from us the Hattons had been fined and sold a bit of the Mortiboys estate, and the man who bought that was reckoned legal owner still. I'd bought Merravay at bargain price, that I'd never deny . . . but it was the best price Fletcher and his friend could get. I'd bought it, bought it . . . worked and slaved over it, put my money back into it, and I had less rights than a squatter. It didn't seem fair. They talk about angels in disguise; Captain Fletcher was the Devil got up to look like an angel, so far as I was concerned.

Still . . . I plucked meself together again; it was no use setting down and crying. I took a sharp look at my stock and I knew there was two things I must, at all costs, save out of the wreck—my brood mares and my Dutches. The mares had a story of their own. Lady Alice Rowhedge had done her riding on a famous black stallion; and after she was tried there was talk about killing him, but Mrs. Blackwood, who was Rawley's daughter by his first wife, took the animal away to Muchanger. There she was the only one with a good word for him; he behaved like the Devil, savaging stable boys and always trying to break out and get back to Merravay. Maybe he started the stories of Lady Alice riding that bit of road.

When I first went to Merravay, I bought, cheap as I could, a work mare that was owd, had had a hard life, and was past all foolery you'd have said. My John, who was good to dumb beasts, fed her up and fussed her, and she got right frisky and one fine morning we found her and the Witch's stallion in the meadow together. In due time she dropped a foal— a mare—that was a rare freak; because put to a work horse, she'd give you one twice her own size, heavy and solid out of the ordinary, and put to a riding horse, she'd drop something lighter and swifter and more shapely than was ever seen in our parts. Whatever went into her came out *more;*

if you'd put her to a jackass she'd have handed you something with ears a yard long. I'd reared two of her mare foals, one heavy and one light, and they'd dropped some extraordinary young 'uns, the heavies heavier and the light 'uns lighter than any ever known. I meant to howd on to them two mares come what might.

Then there was my Dutches. They had a story too. While owd Oliver was still fighting the Dutch, one of their ships was brought into Bywater. The captain had had his wife and child on board, and he'd got a cow and her calf, too. They was for sale—by orders of the Mayor of Bywater— one day when I happened to be there; and lots of folks had gathered round the pen to see them, they being curiously marked, pied, black and white. I noticed that when the calf—a heifer—had suckled its fill the cow's bag wasn't half empty and I thought—Thass a good yielder. I made up my mind that if the bidding wasn't too sharp I'd try for the pair myself. And though folks had come to stare few made bids for animals they didn't reckon to be a canny colour, so I got them cheap; and then, keeping a sharp look out, I heard of a man called Stebbing, in the Yarmouth trade, that had brought a cow and a bull of the same kind back from one of his voyages; and I swopped his bull's service for my heifer calf and for a year or two we went hither and thither till I had a herd. He never got one because most of his animals died, eating yew. Dutches give more milk, and more cream to it, than any kind known and I could ask almost any price I fancied for a heifer calf.

So the first, the least, thing I must do, knowing I was to be chucked out of Merravay, was to find pasture and shelter for my Dutches. And till I began to try that I never knew how much people was against me. No! No! No! Nobody'd rent me house room.

In the end I was so desperate that I thought of Strawless Common. So I went out there and tried; but there wasn't a cottage to let and the grazing rights went with the cottages and the rough lot that lived there said if I put my beasts on it they'd stone 'em.

It was coming home from Strawless that I heard the Witch laughing.

I ain't a fanciful woman, as I'd proved; but I hadn't ate for days, nor slept for many nights, and I was ill with worry. For many a long year I hadn't given the Witch a thought, except that now and again, with my broody hens setting in her big hall, and my motherless calves sucking gruel in her withdrawing room I'd now and then thought—Ha! And it's me and my boy and my creatures that hev Merravay now!

And now she was laughing at me. Her boy was coming to drive me out and I couldn't find a corner for my mares and my Dutches. Them that laugh last laugh loudest . . . and she was laughing last. And I heard her, just like she used to laugh when she was little and could get away from her Granny and come out where I was getting the geese ready.

Hearing the laugh, it struck me I was going crazy, and small wonder. John was gone to London, all ignorant of what was toward; and Alison I couldn't bring myself to tell, her being in the state she was; there wasn't anybody that I could talk to.

I got back to Merravay and there was Phyllis tied into a chair, and Alison, wearing a pretty apron, with a meal that I had no taste for, waiting. And she said,

"There's a letter for you, Mother Whymark," and she took it from behind the salt jar on the dresser.

I took it and turned it about in my hands. I knew Mr. Turnbull's seal. The fool, I thought, writing to me, when he knew I couldn't read. I laid it on the table and made a show of eating, feeling sick and sicker . . . I knew what was in it . . . the date by which we must be gone.

Alison lugged Phyllis off to bed, and as soon as I was alone I broke the seal and looked at my letter. A date, I reckoned, might be set down in figures. But it was just a mass of words. I set there staring. Alison came back and began to gather the crocks.

"Leave them," I said. "Look, you'd best come and read this to me. But I don't want you to fret. I've known about this . . ." I tapped the letter ". . . for a week or so now, and I ain't yet worried my way out. But I shall, my dear, don't you fret. Just read out what it say and let's know the worst."

So she read it out. It was all a mass of long, learned words, but the gist of it was plain enough. Sir Charles Rowhedge had decided that he never wanted to see Merravay again, since he had heard from Mr. Turnbull the details about his father's and mother's deaths. So he'd given the lawyer the office to sell the estate, either in whole or in parts. For the house and thirty acres now in my "temporary possession" Mr. Turnbull thought a thousand pounds a fair price and was giving me the benefit of the first refusal.

"There you are, my girl," I said, when she'd done. "That's what I've been living with these last weeks. We're homeless. And whass worse I can't find a place for the Dutches!" Then I remembered the state she was in and that we was hoping for a lusty boy, so I pulled up short and patted her shoulder and told her again not to worry. I'd think of something, I'd manage.

And as I said that I heard the Witch laugh again; and suddenly something went snap in my head. I knew I was walking up and down, up and down the length of the kitchen, beating my hands together and talking, talking, telling her everything that I had tried, the rebuffs I'd met with, the hatred I'd uncovered. I knew I was doing wrong, for Alison started to cry, and I turned on her and said, "Cry. Go on. Be glad you *can* cry! I wish to God I could."

Then she was taking me by the arm and pushing me into a chair. "You must be calm, Mother Whymark," she said. "You'll wake the baby and drive yourself to distraction. We'll think of something. We're not ruined yet. . . . Look, I'll get you something to drink. Something to put heart into you." She walked towards the dresser and I thought she was going to get a mug and fill it with milk, and I said, "It's kind of you, Alison, but milk wouldn't settle in me now. I feel right sick. But I'm all right. I'll steady meself."

She stood by the dresser and laid her hand on the side of it and looked at me very odd.

"I couldn't help finding out," she said. "There was such a mass of cobwebs behind it that one day I got a man from the yard to shift it for me. You needn't have bothered to hide it from me. Working in an inn set me rather against it. . . ."

I didn't understand; and when I see her, what never could heave anything, take and try to shove the great dresser aside, I was afraid she'd took leave of her wits.

"What are you doing?" I asked, sharp-like, "and what are you talking about? You come and set and calm yourself."

She gave the thing another piteous little push and said, half crying, "I can't budge it. You ought to have had more foresight and kept at least a little brandy where one could get at it."

"What brandy?" I got up and went over to her quickly, calm and sensible again now that she'd gone distraught.

"The brandy that's in the cellar."

"What cellar?"

"Down behind here. . . ."

"I never knew," I said. I took and give the dresser a mighty heave and there, sure enough, was a door, matted with cobwebs again. "Christ in Glory!" I said.

"I thought you'd put it there on purpose. I'm sorry . . . I've wronged you in my mind."

"This dresser . . ." I gave it another bit of a shove ". . . was here when I come; I thought it was a fixture. Mrs. Blackwood took the movable stuff. You say you been down there, Alison?"

"I peeped. I wanted to know what you were hiding from me."

"Git a candle," I said. I pushed the door and it give way, it wasn't locked though there was a great keyhole. A short flight of steps, made of red brick like the house, led down into the dark. Alison come along with the candle, and, bidding her be careful, I led the way down.

It was a great cellar, and as far as the light of the candle reached we could see the casks alaying on the brick stillions and the bottles on the racks. I was dumb-struck. But I could see what had happened. Rawley had been fond of his liquor, and had had some connection with ships and foreign parts; when the war started he'd laid in stuff to last him a lifetime; and when the end come, somebody, some faithful servant maybe, failing to lay hand on the key had done the next best thing and shoved the great dresser in front of the door. And but for Alison's craze to root out spiders nobody'd ever hev known what was hid. So here it all was, French brandy enough to float a ship, in a manner of speaking, and other things as well; wines from France and Spain and Madeiry and the clear fiery stuff that the Dutch drink. It was like some poor toper's dream. In one little bin there was even a lot of homemade stuff, cherry and damson and sloe brandy in pretty little flasks sealed with pig's gut; they gleamed red and purple like jewels in the candlelight as I hauled them out.

Rawley's gift to me, made all unbeknownst. That was the thought that went through my head. And there was a picture, too; Rawley laying dead in his blood, the Witch gone on her last wild gallop, the soldiers prowling through the house, and some foresighted creature shoving that dresser in front of the door!

And then it come to me what all this stuff was worth. With the King back and everybody wishful to make merry there was a great dearth of real good liquor in the land. Put with the mite I'd saved, what I could raise selling off stock, the price I could get for this wondrous store might just save us. And with that thought I came over all weak and wobbly.

"Ally, we're saved," I said, and I leaned myself up against a cask and began to cry like a baby.

Alison turned and scuttled up the stairs, leaving me in the dark. And I thought of the Witch laughing at me, just a minute since, and Rawley saving me. I'd allust known it wasn't just a lustful passing fancy he'd had for me . . . he'd meant me to be mistress of Merravay, and spite of all, spite of the spells and everything, it had come about.

Alison come back with a couple of mugs. She took up a bottle at random and very expert knocked off its neck against the wall. She splashed some of the liquor into the mugs. It was Dutch snaps, and snap it did. It fair took my head off. "Oh Ally," I said, when I got my breath back, "if you hadn't been such a spider-chaser!" And I started to laugh.

VI

So the time come when we began to see the fruits of our labours. London kept growing and prices went up and we was all ready to make the best of 'em. I was still working from dawn till dark—and beyond—but in such good heart that the work came easy. In the year 1670—the year when Alison bore her son at last, her second child had been a girl, called for *her* mother, Maud—I had enough money and enough pluck to buy back the New Holding land from the Fennels. They'd put a lot of money into some wild-cat scheme for starting a company to trade against the big East India Company, and they'd come to grief and had to sell acres to get clear. And after that nothing went wrong for us; we was proper farmers at last, not just dealers and hucksters.

There was one more baby, another girl, named Agnes, who turned out just like me to look at but feather-brained. The owdest, young Phyllis, hadn't my looks but she was most like me inside. Right a dangerous little girl she was when young, for you had but to say, "No, my dear, you can't manage that yet!" and next thing you knew she'd managed it and stood there looking at you, a bit sneering. Long before she could reach the table she'd stand on a stool and make bread, grunting and clenching her little teeth and kneading away at the dough as if it was her enemy. Maud, the next one, I hadn't much use for, a whining child and very jealous of Phyllis, who was two years owder in age and twenty in all that mattered. The boy, called John like his father, came just right—when things was going well; he hadn't Phyllis' fighting spirit; very easy going he was, happy and idle. Just the stuff to make a gentleman of.

Alison often said I spoiled John, and maybe I did. *My* John took and died the year after Agnes was born. He wasn't much more than forty and there should hev been long years ahead of him; he'd never ailed to my knowledge, and the day he died he ate his dinner as usual. It got dusk and then dark and in the end I went to call him to supper and there he was, dead on the stable floor with a bucket of water overset beside him. That was a sore blow to me; and it changed something inside me. All the scraping and striving didn't seem much good when folks could take off and die young like that. He'd never had much out of life except hard work and hope for the future, and just as the good times was coming . . . So maybe I did pander to the boy, giving him what I'd hev liked to give his father.

And the money kept pouring into Merravay. There'd been two laws passed that did me a power of good. One kept out the cheap foreign corn and the other kept out the cheap Irish cattle. In Ireland, I was towd,

there's rain every day and the grass is knee-high; the Irish put a bull and
some cows in a field and then lay down on their beds and wait till 'tis
time to drive the young down to the cattle boats. Costing nowt to rear,
they sold very cheap and was a thorn in the flesh to such as us. Owd
Oliver was allust fighting the Irish, but he never had the sense to deal 'em
a blow that way. King Charles did, and I blessed him for it.

I was able to lay money by now, as well as set the house to rights and
send Johnny to a right good school that Alison knew about.

Alison came into her own at that time. Never in all my days had I
touched a curtain, nor trod on carpet, nor seen any eating tools except a
knife, a two-pronged metal fork, and a horn spoon; I was more ignorant
even than girls what had gone into service. But Alison knew all about
such things.

I liked everything she bought, it was all good solid handsome stuff and
I paid for it gladly. Johnny had to hev a proper home to come back to
and not be shamed; but feel at home in the rooms that Alison furnished
I just could *not*. I felt I must walk on tiptoe and speak in a whisper. All
them lovely shining things was mine, but they didn't know that, and there
was no way of letting 'em know. They just shone at me, scornful.

And then there was clothes. All my days I'd worn a short skirt, well
clear of the mud and dust, and a bodice with sleeves that'd roll up out
of the way; on my legs I had knitted hose and on my feet what was called
in our parts "high-lows"—higher than shoes to keep out the mud, and
lower than boots to be easy to get in and out of. A good pair, well nailed,
would last ten or twelve year and they shape to your feet; they get wet
and fold in the right place and though they seem as hard as wood they're
a lot more comfortable than any soft shoe. But, of course, in my rig I
looked what I was, an owd workwoman.

That didn't suit Alison; so she bought a roll of plum-coloured silk
and she made a dress. Lovely she made it, with lace ruffles and everything . . . Lord, if I could hev had that when I was a wench! But I was
too owd. The waist of it nipped me so I had to breathe careful, and the
skirt was so long and full that I tripped over it and nigh fell flat on my
face.

The girls laughed and Alison got cross with 'em, fearing I'd mind. I
just said, "Unhook me, then I can laugh too!" For there is something
good and comical in sparrers got up in pheasants' feathers. But I said,
"I'll wear it, Ally; I promise you. 'Tis a beautiful gown and I thank you
for sewing it. I'll lay it by and keep it for the weddings."

And then Ally said, in a bitter sort of voice that she didn't often use,
"Weddings! Where're they going to find husbands I'd like to know."

That was what we call a "lickser," meaning anything, a question, or a job, or a situation that hev you licked. There was Phyllis, on the plain side, mighty proud and masterful, handy and smart, she'd hev made any man a good wife. But what man? The poor was scared of us, the better sort scorned us. There we was, so far as marrying was concerned, neither fish, fowl, nor good red herring. No decent sort of farming man would hang round a plain girl, however good, for fear of being thought after her money. And I doubt whether Phyllis would hev taken a poor chap.

And there was Maud, a bit better looking, but a misery and given to good works. Cracked on the parson, she was . . . but he was married well and truly, with six little 'uns.

And there was that good-looking young scatterbrain Agnes, without a thought in her head except horses—but it was early days to worry about *her*.

But the days mounted up; same as the pence that turned into pounds. And it come to the time when Johnny was finished at Cambridge and was coming home for good. Alison said, "I just hope that he'll take an interest in the land and the stock. That is his only hope. . . ." She'd been ailing for a bit, so I was gentle with her and just said,

"Hope of what?"

"A happy full life," she said. "He'll have no friends here, will he? Nobody to talk to . . . to associate with. And I'm so afraid that he'll turn to London, where any young man with money to spend is welcome and fussed over. . . . It's such a pity . . . because, given half a chance, he could fit in here so well."

And I groaned to myself. I could send Johnny away and buy him an education and give him everything that was needed to make a gentleman of him. But there was no denying that once back at Merravay he'd be just the grandson of owd Phyl Whymark, who'd come from the tavern with her bastard, got Merravay for a song, and made a fortune.

I said, a bit harshly, "Ally, when I was his age I was hard put to it to keep myself and my child with food to eat. And I still reckon that two meals a day and roof overhead is the main thing to strive for. The rest is just trimmings! Either they come of their own accord or they ain't worth worrying about."

But for all that I was as glad as anybody when it turned out that Johnny wouldn't lack company, for a while at least; for when he come home that summer he brought his own with him. And what company, too! Young Lord Thrapston, no less, that was son to the Marquess of Whardale—lucky for him to be born in the purple for he was a nitwit if ever I see one. So far as I know he never did but one sensible thing in his life, and that was taking up with our Agnes.

Just at this minute he was in trouble. He'd got into debt and gone gambling, and his father, a very furious owd man by all accounts, had said he'd have his hide when next he set eyes on him, so he dussn't go home, and had to go what he called "to ground" till such time as his aunt, as was away drinking some special waters at a place called Bath, could get up to Leicestershire and talk the owd man round. So without a roof to his head or a penny in his pocket he was glad to accept Johnny's invitation to ride home with him and stay with us for a bit.

He wasn't like anybody we'd ever seen before. Since he'd gone to school and all that, Johnny had allust seemed sort of frisky and nonsensical to me, but set aside his friend Toby, Johnny looked as sober and solemn as a Baptist minister. Still, daft as he was, allust larking about and laughing, he had a way with him, though not much to look at, too much nose and not enough chin; and I reckon that Johnny had warned him to look out for *me*, for he did seem to go out of his way to be civil.

He'd been with us three weeks when he had a letter from his aunt that set him whooping and halloing as though he'd started a fox. She'd talked his father round, as he had said she would, and he was free to go home; and I was looking forward to the day when he did for Alison would keep me rigged out in the silk gown and in place of my comfortable high-lows a pair of thin shoes, no more than slippers, in which my feet seemed to hit the ground cruel at every step. But he didn't shift and he didn't shift and there was Agnes looking as mischievous as a monkey . . . and next thing I knew they was talking about being in love and going to get married.

Oh-ho, I said to myself, so the wind is blowing from that quarter again, is it? Well, it ain't going to blow Agnes what it blowed me! Maybe there's a body in Leicestershire clever with spells too! Though that weren't really what I feared, more the father and the argumentating and maybe auntie shedding a tear or two. So I took Agnes by the scruff of her neck and shut her in her bedroom and I took his lordship and I talked to him like he'd never been talked to before. But he held that he was serious; he'd never seen a girl like Agnes, he said, nor never would again and he was ready to marry her tomorrow.

"Then you'd best go down and fix things with Parson," I said, "for next time you see Agnes will be at the altar at church!"

He said so long as I was willing for him to see her there that was all he arst, and he grinned at me cheeky and went and got on his horse and rode off hell for leather.

But he didn't come back, and he didn't come back. And Alison cried and scolded me as if I was a babe, using all the long words she knew. She said that but for my interference all *might* have come right; I'd scared him off and ruined Agnes' chances. Johnny remembered hearing of somebody up in Norfolk that had a hunter to sell, and took hisself off to get free of the unpleasantness. Phyllis and Maud went about looking smug and self-righteous.

After a bit I let Agnes out, and she was no mite concerned.

"He'll come back," she said. "And if he don't, there's other fish in the sea!"

But he didn't come back and I was priding myself that at least, thanks to me, there was no harm done, and trying to make Alison see a bit of sense and make the other girls keep a civil tongue in their heads to Agnes, for the whole of that week and the best part of the next.

And then he did come, bringing the aunt he set such store by with him. She was a widow, a Lady Pernherrick, very rich and as odd as they're made. The main thing that I remember out of the confusion she chucked us all into is her looking Agnes over as if she was a horse she half meant to buy and saying,

"Hmmm, not bad, not bad at all. Time we had some new blood in our family. Getting very parrot-jawed."

Agnes bore the scrutiny just right, looking neither shy, nor saucy, nor put about; she'd been in the dairy when the owd dame arrived, and was wearing her print dress open at the neck and rolled at the sleeves and she did look pretty as a picture. Alison behaved very comely, too, though fussed inside I know. She got busy with refreshments and Agnes said,

"Now, if you'll excuse me, I'll go back to my butter; it was on the turn."

And his young lordship looked at me and said, "With your permission, Granny Whymark, I'll go with her."

VII

After that, little by little, I began to loosen my grip on the family, though I kept howd of Merravay. It was partly the company that made me fall into the background. There was no lack of company once the news of the wedding got noised abroad. I fitted out Agnes in the proper manner and I give her six hundred pounds for a dowry; and you could see people think, as if their heads was glass, that what was good enough for the Whardale family might just about do for *them*. If it'd heppened sooner I reckon Phyllis and Maud would hev got husbands too, but they was a mite owd and not much for looks, and there was allust a shortage of young men in our parts—among the gentry, I mean; and of course after Agnes' catch the others wouldn't look at nothing less. So the comings and the goings and the matchmakings all fixed upon Johnny. I'd hev been the last to grudge his company but 'twas no use pretending that I took to the Fennels and the Headways and the Blackwoods, neighbours though they were and try as they did to suck up to me late in life and say I was "a character." When I was trying to hire a bit of land for my mares and my Dutches, and willing to pay whatever might be asked, they'd had no doings with me. So I never mixed with 'em, and kept meself to meself when there was parties.

There was a time when it looked as though Johnny might marry Miss Caroline Blackwood, and that give me a bit of worry. For they were cousins of a sort. Mrs. Thomasina Blackwood was Rawley's daughter by his first, foreign wife; she'd had a lot of children and Miss Caroline was the last of 'em. With animals I'd bred cousin to cousin, and closer relations too, many a time; but now and again I'd wake in the night and picture to myself Johnny marrying Miss Blackwood and bringing forth something not quite as it should be, a kind of punishment for me keeping my secret all these years. But there was nowt I could do except hope for the best and things worked out all right. Johnny went off merrymaking with Agnes and Toby and came back engaged to marry a young cousin of theirs. Poor as a church mouse she was, for her father'd been one of the King's men that had stayed and been fined heavy and sold land that had to stay sold; but she was a lady in her own right, which was one in the eye for the neighbours. I was mighty well pleased.

And oddly enough it was over Johnny's getting engaged that me and Phyllis had the nighest thing to a set-to that we ever had.

"I suppose you're *pleased* about this," she said in a tight, sour voice.

"I ain't sorry," I said. "Somebody young and well bred is what I allust hoped for for Johnny."

"For Johnny!" she said in a wild way, "for Johnny! That's all you ever think of, you and Mother. Maud and me could work like black slaves and feed in the kitchen like labourers but the house must be set out for Johnny! Maud and me could work without wages and be grateful for a new pair of shoes so the money can pile up to make our brother a gentleman and he can marry a lady who'll despise us, and treat us like dirt!"

"Howd on, now," I said. "I look to live long enough to learn her her place if she come treating anybody like dirt. While there's breath in my body I'm mistress here, and master too, and don't you forget it!"

"But even you can't live forever. What's going to happen then? Johnny'll have Merravay, of course; he's the boy, he's the heir! No matter that he can't tell a bull from a bullock, and is wasteful and careless and brainless. Oh, I can see him, with his lady wife to help him, going through what we've sweated to store up, like a knife through butter . . ."

"Do we start measuring sweat, Phyl, I reckon I'm still a bit ahead of you. Naturally property go to the man that carry on the name and the family, so it allust was, so it allust will be. Granted you've worked, good and hard, and been careful and managing and saving, and I been pleased to see you so. But 'twould be no manner of use you having the place, for you're another that can't live forever and you're a bare branch. . . ."

With that she bruk out crying, a thing she hadn't done since she was a toddler, and then only with rage. Cried and carried on, saying how unfair everything was and that she'd give her whole life to Merravay and now was to be chucked out, and how I was taunting her with not being married. Finally I spoke to her right sharp.

"Here, that'll do, my girl!" I said. "D'you take me for a fool? Thass right bad luck to talk of death and willing, but I'll tell you this for your comfort. Nobody but yourself'll ever chuck you outa Merravay. D'you think I'm one to forget how when you was a little mawther you'd help me with anything you could set hand to? You should know me better. Moreover I ain't blind to what Johnny is, but he is as I made him, as I planned he should be. So I've made my will, all right and legal, and there 'tis, set down by Mr. Turnbull, that you and Maud are to hev a home here at Merravay and one quarter of the profits between you—and thass fair, for Johnny will hev a wife to keep and a family to rear, God willing."

I'd made that will after a lot of thought and turmoil. And Phyllis' share had been part justice and part craft. I knew my Johnny and I knew my Phyllis, too. She'd see her share didn't dwindle, and, looking after part, she'd be bound to look after the whole.

But was she grateful?

"I'd rather you left me something of my own, Gran. A bit I could make something of. Leave me New Holding; the house is half down, but it'd do and it's good land . . ."

"But I've been scraping and striving all my life, Phyl, to get the land *together*; I can't go mincing it up. The more acres together the cheaper to work and the bigger profits. Why, girl dear, I mean to buy back the Slipwell land if ever 'tis for sale; I might live to see that day."

"Buy back!" she spat at me. "As though it had once been yours! Land and money, land and money, that's all you ever think of. I'm trying to talk to you about *my life*. If Merravay had been mine I'd have given my life to it; but it isn't and never can be! And I'm not a brick of the wall or an acre of land that you should treat me as part of it." She stood and breathed hard. "Go on then," she said, "buy your land, get it together, keep it together! And in the end you'll lay under it. Under six foot of graveyard clay, like the rest of us."

The funny thing was I'd allust thought Phyllis was fond of me.

"Aye, so I shall. And I shall lie quiet and with nothing on my conscience about the way I've treated you, you young hussy!" I said.

But I wasn't really angry with her. She got her temper from me, and her land hunger. She was the most like me of the lot. But that was all the more reason for chaining her down.

However, as it happened, two things got together to make me think things over. One was that I couldn't take, try as I would, to Johnny's wife. She was pretty, with eyes the colour of bluebells and hair the colour of primroses, and she was small and sweet-mannered, but I distrusted her from the start. I could do with some gentry—Lady Pernherrick I'd truly liked and one or two more that came to the wedding. It was the woman in Lady Rosemary roused my gall; I'd have felt the same about her whoever she was, wherever she'd come from. Sly, a worker-round, and spiteful.

The other thing was that when Caroline Blackwood married somebody in the West Country her owd father and mother decided to sell Muchanger and go and live near her. An owd admiral wanted Muchanger but not all the land, so I seized my chance to buy Slipwell; and that brought me close to Mr. Turnbull again and one day I opened my heart to him.

"You know how I've left the main part of my property," I said. "But I don't feel right easy in my mind about Phyllis. I want her to stay here so long as is possible, but I can see trouble that might brew. If it so happened that her temper was too much tried . . . I'd like her to hev something to fall back on. But it mustn't be open . . . do she wouldn't try at all. And I want her to try."

So he set his wits to work and in the end I altered my will entirely. She was to stay at Merravay and hev her share as arranged so long as she wished. But if she married—I put that in for cover—or at any time decided to leave Merravay and break with Johnny she was to consult Mr. Turnbull. And I left the New Holding land not to Johnny, but to a trust until otherwise claimed, Johnny to pay a peppercorn rent which was to provide a harvest horkey for the workmen. It was all wrapped up in whereases and aforesaids and renewable tenures and conditional something elses, but he'd got it clear. If ever Phyllis and Johnny parted company New Holding would be hers. But she wouldn't know that till the break was made. So she'd stand till the end and howd her own . . . I hoped for all their sakes.

With that done, there wasn't much for me to bother about. So now I take things easy. When the sun shine I creep along to a sunny place, between the porch and the jut of the house and just sit there. The garden hev come on wonderful; the stone-pot things that once made handy feeding troughs for my beasts are set back on the wall and they're full of flowers, stiff tall things called tulips that come from Holland, like my Dutches. And over the wall there's a field of corn, doing well; thick and green with hardly a weed in it. And beyond that and to both sides 'tis all mine, gathered together with hard work and a bit of luck.

But I ain't as spry as I was . . . and often, time I've got meself out here and looked around and done a bit of thinking, I'm right glad to shut my eyes and hev a bit of a doze. . . .

Interlude

The death of old Mistress Whymark—as she had come to be called in her later years—caused hardly a ripple. She was immensely old and had been, for some time past, feeble of body and inclined to wander in her mind. Her last will and testament gave pretty proof of her senility.

She was not forgotten. Her achievement took its place in the folklore of the neighbourhood and was often mentioned as an example of what sheer hard work and tenacity of purpose could do. Her name was generally mentioned with respect; money was money, after all; and in that period of wild and often fatal investments, when so many fortunes vanished overnight, the possession of solid money and untrammelled acres attained an enhanced importance.

The old woman's shrewdness and driving energy appeared to have passed in greatest measure to her eldest granddaughter. Mr. John Whymark was careless, good-natured, open-handed, and convivial, and much—particularly in the early days of the marriage—under the thumb of his pretty wife. Miss Phyllis Whymark took up, was driven into, and finally unable to desist from, an attitude of permanent opposition.

In any dispute about management and husbandry she had one strong ally, her dead grandmother; and she could always say,

"But I can't allow that. That would jeopardize Maud's share and mine. I must guard our interests." Also it became increasingly plain that when Phyl's judgement was respected things prospered; when she was crossed they tended to go wrong.

Accepting her authority in most things, Mr. Whymark, nagged by his wife, sometimes defied her over matters of personal expenditure. "God knows what you do with your money, Phyl; surely I can do what I like with my own!" The most contrary thing he did was to plant an avenue of lime trees and turn two good fields into park land. Miss Whymark, having invoked Granny's name in vain with a monotonous mention of turning in graves, actually wept over the waste of good ploughland. She avoided the avenue and on the rare occasions when she went to the village, would plod on foot across the fields and emerge near a miserable little holding called Church Farm, from whose few acres a man named Fulger wrested a poor living for himself and his family.

There she would sometimes see a thin lanky boy and a thin small girl immensely busy at tasks only just within their capacity to tackle. The sight gave her peculiar pleasure. So young, so hard-working, they would get on in the only way which Miss Whymark valued—Granny's way.

Then one day, on skirting the yard of the small holding, she heard sounds of merriment. The erstwhile admirable Fulger children appeared to have acquired a very beautiful little pony with a fine saddle and harness.

More spoiling, thought Miss Whymark quite sadly; and she walked on, wondering, as she so often did these days, what the world was coming to.

The Governess

THE first actual money that Luke and I ever earned was sixpence a week for enjoying ourselves.

Luke was twelve then and I was ten, and we'd both been hard at work for as long as we could remember but we'd had no wages—nor looked for any—until the day when Father came home and said,

"Old Mrs. Maybrook called me across the road today as I came home from the smithy. That child is to have a pony and it is to be stabled here, there being no room for it at their place. She'll pay two shilling a week for its feed and grooming and you two'll tend it. You'll have sixpence a week—to save."

"How'll she buy a pony? Through the parlour window?" Mother asked.

Years and years of being married to Father hadn't quite got Mother out of the way of making little jokes. I could see the point of that one, and if Father hadn't been there I should have laughed and Mother and I would have gone on wringing the last bit of fun out of it. The point was that in the whole three years that the Maybrooks had lived in Nettleton nobody had ever seen Mrs. Maybrook out of doors. She'd moved into Ivy Cottage, a very gloomy little house near the church, and there she lived with a surly old maidservant and a little girl—about my age—who was reckoned to be her granddaughter. Anything to be done out of doors the servant did, but now and again when she was ill Mrs. Maybrook would rap on the parlour window and attract somebody's attention, then stand back in the shadow and give her orders and presently put the money on the window sill. The old man who sometimes did a day's work in their little back garden said she acted the same way when she gave him his directions; he said it was because she was so pocked she didn't look human.

Everybody was sorry for the child. Even Luke and I who worked hard and were often scolded and punished wouldn't have changed with her, cooped up in that dull house with two old women. It was nice to think she was to have a pony.

I don't know how Mrs. Maybrook managed to buy the pony, but it came within a week, and it was as pretty and dainty as a lady. Luke and I fell in love with it at first sight and gave its toilet far more attention than we gave our own, which was apt to be scanty, especially on cold mornings. We harnessed it up and tried it; we'd never ridden a proper saddled pony before. It was just my size, but when Luke, who was very big for his age, was on it, he looked like a duck's egg in an ordinary egg-cup. I told him so and we both laughed and Father put his head out of the barn and said, "Stop that foolery." He always feared that if you were laughing you were wasting time.

"And," I said softly, when Father had taken his head into the barn again, "you look a bit like Jesus on the ass's foal on Palm Sunday."

Luke said, "Shush," very shocked. But it was true. In those days he had a sweet, patient, long-suffering kind of look, and that, with his clear grey eyes and mass of light brown curly hair, gave him a saintly air, as if he didn't quite belong to this world. He was a proper Fulger; Father must have been very handsome before hard work and bad temper scored the lines on his face. I took after Mother, small and brown-coloured, and lively and merry—when we were let to be.

The afternoon came when the old maid from Ivy Cottage hobbled along to our place, holding Luella by the hand. I'd seen her before, of course, but never close to, and never dressed up as she was that day. She had proper riding clothes, made to her measure, dark green velvet they were, and a little hat with a feather. In her hand she carried a small crop with an ivory handle.

Luke and I always kept the pony fit to go into a parlour, and in a moment we had it saddled and led it out, very proud.

"There you are, love. There's your pony," said the maid.

Luella did not move forward; she stood there looking timid and reluctant.

The old woman turned to us and said, "Now don't you let her fall off, or the creature run away. And bring her back at four, up to the house. I can't come out again."

Luke looked at me; so, though I was a girl and the younger, I had to speak up.

"We were told to look after the pony. We can't take her out on it. We both have jobs to do."

"Your father about?"

"He's ploughing. If you want to ask him you must go to him and don't speak till he turns at the furrow's end."

"You're sharp!" she said with disfavour. "Mind you don't cut yourself!"

She stumped off and I looked at Luella.

"Most likely he'll say no, so you'd better let us help you on now."

She looked at me and at the pony and at Luke and then back at me again; then she said,

"To tell you the truth I'm rather scared of it. This wasn't my idea at all."

That was the first time I had heard her speak, and for a moment I could only stand and go on hearing her voice after it was silent; she spoke so clearly, with such sweetness, the words coming out so gently and yet so firmly. I could hardly bear to use my own voice after that. I said, as coaxingly as I could, but sounding gruff and rough all the same,

"There's nothing to be scared of. It's easy! Look, shall I show you?"

I scrambled onto the pony and rode round the yard.

"He's as gentle as a lamb," I said.

I brought him to a standstill near her and hopped off.

"Now you try."

"But I can't get on."

Luke spoke for the first time.

"I'll set you up," he said, and came forward.

I held the pony's head and Luke went to lift Luella. Immediately the pony pivoted sharply, so that Luella almost fell with Luke atop of her.

"Now no fooling about. That ain't what you're paid for!" said the old servant, hobbling back. "Yes, thass all right; your dad was sensible. So just be careful. There's no need for her to be venturesome; she ain't going to be a jockey."

With that she departed. Later on, when I knew the Maybrook household better, I realised that this incident was very typical. There was the care and the carelessness side by side; the pretty pony, the elegant clothes, the escort to our yard; but whether the pony were gentle or vicious, Luke and I fitted or unfitted for responsibility, nobody bothered to ask.

II

That was the beginning of happy times for us. Over the plough handle Father had bargained sixpence an hour for our time. ("I never reckoned Father rated us that high, boy," I said to Luke, "just think what we earn in a week!")

It was a mercy we weren't paid by results, for Luella never did master the riding; to the end it took both our efforts to get her on and less than nothing to topple her off. And the pony was no help. He was an angel with Luke and me, and a devil with her. But once she got over her first fright of him she didn't mind; she'd laugh and say, "You ride him," to whichever one of us was due for a turn, and then, with the other she'd play tag or Granny Grumble, or just saunter along and pick flowers. She'd never had any young company before and seemed to cling to us; when we parted she'd watch us out of sight and keep waving and calling.

Towards the end of September that year there came a day which we, being hardy, called "fresh," but Luella soon had a blue-white face and chattering teeth; so we took her off the pony and all had a good game of tag to warm her up; however she caught cold and didn't come out for several days. Then one day the old maid came stumping along to ask if I could go and keep her company. Highly elated, I put on my Sunday gown and shoes and went to Ivy Cottage and spent the afternoon in a paradise of dolls and draughts and dominos and musical boxes. That day I didn't see Mrs. Maybrook; the servant brought tea and cakes to the room we played in, and we drank the tea from the dolls' cups and cut the cakes into tiny pieces to fit the little plates. I'd never spent such an afternoon in all my days and went home dazzled.

Soon after that there was another message from Ivy Cottage. I saw the servant arrive and leave, looking utterly disgusted; and I waited, with my heart in my mouth, to know what she had come for. Nothing was said that day, but when Luke and I were in bed I could hear Father and Mother threshing something out in the kitchen below, Mother's voice quick and eager, Father's slow and grumbling.

In the morning Father said to me, "Tuesdays and Thursdays you get up early and do all your jobs and then go along to Ivy Cottage; and mind how you behave."

It was not to play, this time; it was to have lessons with Luella's governess, Miss Pelham. They thought Luella would learn better if she had company.

Luke, seeing me off, said, "Dog's nails! I wish I could come too!" (In the old days people used to say "God's nails" when they wished to be emphatic and "Damnation" when they were annoyed; now, because of chapel and the text "Swear not at all," they said "Dog's nails" and "Tarnation" instead.)

Although Luella had chattered freely while we were out together she'd never said anything about her home, and we'd never asked any questions; and it was quite a surprise to me to discover that Mrs. Maybrook was not her granny, but her mother. Mrs. Maybrook was very little older than my mother; it was the scarred face and widowed way she dressed that made her seem so elderly. But the mystery remained, even when one was close to, almost part of the family. It took me a long time to gather, bit by bit, that Luella's father and brother—a good deal older than she—had both died of the smallpox, which had ruined Mrs. Maybrook's looks; and that Luella had only escaped because she was put out to nurse. Even then I knew enough about things to know that only rich, fashionable people put their children out in that way, and the idea didn't go alongside the dull little house, the one servant, and Mrs. Maybrook's clothes, and other evidences of very modest means. At the same time, everything in the house was on the rich side, velvet curtains and silver things and such, and once when Luella and I were playing "dressing up" and she was a princess, Mrs. Maybrook let us have things out of her jewel box. I can believe now that they were neither so many nor so wonderful as they seemed to me at the time, but it did seem strange to me that she should have rings and brooches that she never wore, and only one cross old servant and a man odd times for the garden.

She had a voice exactly like Luella's, but with sad notes in it; she was a sad creature. There were times, though, when she was different. Now and then, on those winter afternoons when Miss Pelham was ready to go and catch the coach back to Baildon—it touched Nettleton on Tuesdays and Thursdays, that is why the lessons were on those days—Mrs. Maybrook would drift in, carrying a square bottle with a gold pattern on its sides and two little glasses that matched.

"You must have something to keep out the cold, Miss Pelham," she would say. Miss Pelham would say, "That is very kind of you," and take her glass and sip daintily. Then she would go . . . and times, if the road was slippery or there was anything to carry, she would take me with her, which Luella and I hated . . . other times I could stay for a little while; and then Mrs. Maybrook would fill her glass again, and again, and grow merry, telling us funny stories and making jokes and imitating everybody, even Miss Pelham, not unkindly but in the funniest way. Then her voice lost its dreary sound and was like music. She could say my name, Deborah, so that it didn't sound plain at all. I used to sit there, listening to her and thinking what a shame it was about her face, and how she was paying me to play and to learn, which I'd always wanted to do. (Father had asked a shilling an afternoon for me, though I still did my work at home!) And for Christmas that year she gave me a red woolsey dress.

Then the spring came and the outings started again. I was glad for Luke's sake, because although I always told him every single thing that had been done or said at Ivy Cottage he had felt cut off.

One morning, late in April and lovely weather, Luella said, as we heaved her onto the pony,

"Let's go to Merravay."

That suited me, because Merravay lay near to the woods which, I'd heard tell from children with more time for idling, was a famous place for flowers. I ran to get a basket and when I came back I found that Luke had turned the pony's head towards the fields.

"It'll still be a bit miry at Vinefields Bottom, Luke," I said. "Wouldn't it be best to go through the village and up at the front?"

"You couldn't get near. They've built a great wall round and put a gate with lodges. And two fields gone to waste planted with trees. Dint you know?"

"Oh, I want to go *near*. I want to see the house," Luella said.

"Why?" I asked.

"Oh . . . I've just heard a lot about it."

"So have we—and nothing in its favour, eh, Luke?"

We had heard enough about Merravay. Within the living memory of people like our old great-aunt Hester who lived with us, the Whymarks had made a fortune at Merravay, all out of sheer hard work; and the old woman who had done most of the work had lived to be ninety, so in holding her up as an example to the young the old people could very truthfully say, "Hard work never killed anybody!" Sometimes when Aunt Hester droned on about it I used to think to myself, Maybe not, but hearing about it is killing me! Of course I daren't say it, and of course nobody ever did die of boredom or great-aunt Hester would have been knee-deep in corpses.

From our little field the ground sloped down to the swampy bit where the kingcups grew and then up and up. We reached the top of the rise and were at the edge of a field of young corn. On its farther side was Layer Wood, and to our left, slightly downhill, stood the house. Luella turned the pony and sat there staring while Luke and I took a good look at the place about which we had heard so much.

It was a big house, with many windows and clumps of chimneys; the bricks of the walls and the tiles of the roof were a pretty colour, an orangy pink, like hawthorn berries when they first start to ripen. The colour showed up pleasantly against the dark green-black of two huge trees and the shining green of the lawns. But . . . it was just a big house.

"Oh," said Luella on an outgoing breath. "Oh. Yes it is beautiful. Better even than I expected."

She seemed quite overcome. So I looked again. The field at whose edge we stood was divided from the garden by a deep ditch that was like a long narrow horsepond drained dry in a drought. On the house side the dip was topped by a low wall, the same colour as the house, and along its edge there were some things like fir cones made of grey stone, and between each pair of cones there was a big grey vase full of yellow flowers—daffodils maybe. Back of the wall there were yew trees, like those in the church yard but cut into shapes. All very pretty, neat, well cared for, but it didn't rouse in me the kind of excitement that came on me when our lilac tree bloomed, or when I thought of that distant wood full of primroses.

"Isn't it beautiful? Luke . . ." Luella turned to him.

"Lookit the stacks!" he said, craning his head. "Eight, ten, and I can only see a corner of the stackyard. Dog's nails! And lookit the far side, out towards Slipwell. Beasts without number!"

"All got together with the sweat of the brow, lad," I said, imitating as best I could Aunt Hester's voice. "Do you work as hard, you may do as well. Hard work never killed anybody."

But the joke fell flat. They just went on staring. So I looked towards Layer Wood. Except for a few hawthorn trees that were freckled with green and some firs which stood here and there along the edge, the whole wood seemed to swim in a purple-pink haze as the swollen buds shone in the sunlight. I could just imagine how the pale tide of primroses shimmered under the trees.

"Oh, come on!" I said. "You've seen the house. Let's go to Layer."

Luella ignored me, but Luke shook himself free of his trance, and said, "Aye, come on. Our time'll be up!"

"You go," said Luella, "I'll stay here."

"And the pony'll run away with you as soon as we've gone," I said petulantly.

"Oh, take the pony!" She dismounted in a way which, but for her smallness and lightness, would have been comically clumsy.

With me on the pony and Luke loping alongside we soon reached the wood; and it was just as flowery as I had heard it was. The primroses were huge, the biggest I had ever seen, and the most fragrant. Every stem was four inches long, and I made up my mind to borrow one of Mother's precious glasses, so that the pink tips would show, blushing and beaded in the water. In those days flowers meant a great deal to me, and while I gathered the primroses greedily I saw with delight that the bluebells and foxgloves and windflowers were coming on. It was like Heaven, only there the flowers, they said, never died, so how, if the primroses lasted the year round, the later ones would find room was a mystery. But I remembered that once when I had voiced a similar perplexity about something I had heard in chapel, Father had sternly bid me to bear in mind that with God all things were possible.

As we went back—Luke riding this time—we could see Luella standing just where we had left her.

"Can *you* see anything to stare at like that about that house?" I asked.

"Only the stacks. Thass a rare pity, Deb, that we ain't got more corn-land. Still, I reckon I'll make my fortune out of beasts!"

As we pelted down towards Luella we called, but she only waved a hand and went on staring.

"She's daft," I said.

"Daft as a hen with its head off," Luke agreed; but his tone was tolerant rather than critical.

It took all our persuasions and finally mention of the scoldings and beatings that awaited us if we outstayed our time to get her to move, and when she did she looked back and said,

"I wish I lived there."

"Why? It's so lonely," I said. "I'd rather live in *any* house in Nettleton. What d'you say, Luke?"

"Not *any* house, Deb," he said cautiously. "Say Squirrels, or Curlew, or Monks." He named the three best farms in the parish.

"But that is a beautiful *house*," Luella said dreamily. "I shall come here again."

"So shall I," I said, thinking of the bluebells and foxgloves.

Yet, for one reason or another, we never did, though all through that spring and summer we had many pleasant outings, mainly without Luke, who, to his disgust, was kept at home to do "real" work, though, so far as I know, Mrs. Maybrook still paid for his time. Not that it mattered, except to Luke, for I was quite capable of managing the pony.

III

Then came the winter day when both Luke and I fell victims of the sweating sickness, which carried off more than a few that year.

Mother, who had great skill with herbs and simples, set about brewing one of her noxious remedies. It was market day and Father went off to Baildon, promising to bring back a lemon if he could find one not too dear. And then, through my whirling, throbbing head shot the remembrance that this was the day when I should go to Ivy Cottage for my lesson.

"You must let them know," I moaned.

Mother said that with all this illness about they would guess, but my muddled mind had fixed on that and I kept on till at last she said,

"Well, I daresay Aunt Hester could make her way there at a pinch. It's a straight road and everybody's gone to market now."

Aunt Hester took kindly to the idea.

"Aye, I'll go. And I shall take some of my lace to show the lady."

I was vaguely against that for no reason I could exactly name, but I was too grateful that she should go at all to say anything. In her youth she'd been a great maker of lace. I always thought that was what had ruined her eyesight. She'd made so much that she still had furlongs of it laid away in well-chalked linen to keep it from turning yellow. It was sixty pounds, saved from years of lacemaking and lent to my father, that ensured her a home with us. Even after her eyesight failed she had gone on peddling lace until some knave in Baildon paid her with a bad shilling. Now and again one of her regular old customers would come and buy a length out of the chest and that was always a great day, but such days came seldom.

Mother said, "Yes, do," and went on pounding away at the rosemary and nettle leaves with the rolling-pin.

Aunt Hester was so long on her errand that we had drunk the brew and were so muddled in our heads that I was never quite certain whether this happened or whether I dreamed it——

It seemed to me that she came back, blundering as usual over the threshold, clinking some money in her hand and saying that Mrs. Maybrook had bought a dozen yards of her best three point, and adding,

"I know something."

"Say it then, say it. Can't you hear my calves blaring?"

"I know who old Mrs. Maybrook is."

"Well, we all know that!"

"Ah, but thass just what you don't know! She's Miss Blackwood, my Miss Caroline that used to live at Muchanger."

It seemed to me that Mother began to pay attention.

"How d'you know? Did she make herself known to you?"

"No, but I heard her voice. And I've told you a dozen times that the strength of my eyes have gone elsewhere, nobody hear like I do, and I'd know her voice anywhere."

"You hear well, I will say. But if 'twas so, surely we'd know. The gentry, the Fennels, and the Headways would all be around her for the sake of old times."

"Ah, but they don't know. 'Tis only my ears know. She's come down in the world and lost her looks, but she crept home at the end, same as I should have done if I'd moved with the family that time. She never wanted to go, Miss Caroline didn't. . . ."

"Well," said Mother, "well, fancy . . . oh them calves! All right, all right, I'm coming."

It seemed to me that after she had gone Aunt Hester pottered about, muttering to herself about somebody who'd been treated badly, played fast and loose with, been homesick for years, and now come home to die. And it seemed to me that presently she turned to me and said that this was a secret, not to be mentioned.

I may have dreamed it all, for presently I was riding wildly on a see-saw, putting a wreath of buttercups round our sow's neck, quarrelling with Luke about who should lick the honey spoon and a thousand other things which I can't remember at all.

Then I was clearly myself again, and Luke and I both had quinsies in our throats. And one day when Luke could speak, he asked who was looking after the pony.

"The pony's gone," Mother said.

"Gone where?"

"How should I know, child? A man came and took it away. Now you know as much as I do, so don't ask any more questions."

It wasn't until we were almost well again that we learned that both Mrs. Maybrook and the old servant had caught the sickness and—as Mother said, not having anybody to make them a good brew—had died.

"Then who sent for the pony?"

"The man mentioned Mr. Turnbull. But it was your father he talked to, not me."

"And what happened to Luella?"

"Mr. Turnbull is looking after her."

So that was the end of being paid to be idle and to have lessons. And most likely we'd never see Luella again. What a hateful world we had struggled back to.

One day I said to Aunt Hester, "You were right about her coming back to die."

"Who?"

"Mrs. Maybrook." But she pretended not to know what I meant; and then I could not be sure what I had remembered and what I had dreamed.

IV

Father worked harder than anyone I ever knew, and had the worst luck. Nothing he ever did turned out right. When I was almost thirteen we were so poor that it was decided to put me to service, a fate which, being the only girl in the family and always with a job in my hand, I had hoped to escape. I'd heard some horrid tales about the way servants were treated, and Aunt Hester's admonitions to me—and she should know, she had been in service all her life till her eyes failed—did nothing to reassure me. They were so much concerned with humility, and truth to tell, I was, at that time, rather a proud little girl. I'd always been quick and handy and good at contriving, and sometimes even Father who was quicker with blame than praise would say, "Let Deb try," when there was anything particularly tricky to do. Also I'd done very well with the lessons at Ivy Cottage; Miss Pelham knew who paid her, of course, and so refrained from comparisons, but Mrs. Maybrook herself said my writing put Luella's to shame. I could sew neatly too, and I had once cherished hopes of being apprenticed to the dressmaker in Baildon; but for that one had to pay a premium and then earn nothing for four years at least. So it was service for me; and because Lady Rosemary Whymark happened to come— on Lady Fennel's recommendaton—to buy some of Aunt Hester's lace for edging handkerchiefs and Aunt Hester happened to mention that I was in need of a place, it was to Merravay that I went as a kind of maid-of-all-work when I was just one month short of thirteen years old.

I'd been there six years and worked my way up to be Miss Sophie's personal maid and even to do most of her ladyship's sewing, when I heard that the three young Whymarks were to have a new governess and that her name was Maybrook. I began at once to think about Luella.

In all that time we'd had but one bit of news of her. One day Luke had done a thing quite unlike himself, he'd gone to Mr. Turnbull's office and asked about her. Mr. Turnbull, Luke said, was very civil and kind and told him that she was at school in Epping, quite well and happy, and that he saw her regularly and would, on his next visit, say that someone who remembered her had inquired after her. "But for all that he never asked my name," Luke said. Sometimes, before I left home, he and I would occasionally say, "Do you remember?" and Luella would come to mind. But for six years I had only seen Luke on my free day, the last Saturday of each month except December, and he was always busy and growing up so swiftly that our childhood, our shared memories, had fallen into limbo.

Now, hearing the name Maybrook, I could only hope that Luella hadn't been reduced by circumstances to become a governess . . . or that if she had she was not the one doomed to come to Merravay. I'd lost count of the governesses who had been there in my time, but I could say for certain that they had all been miserable. It was, without any obvious reason, a most unhappy household, full of undercurrents, changing allegiances, conflicting loyalties.

At first sight, and afterwards, down on my knees scrubbing and polishing, I thought Merravay a large house, but the whole of Suffolk would hardly have been wide enough to contain its inmates peaceably.

The master, Mr. Whymark, was a very easy-going, good-natured man for nine tenths of the time. He would shut his eyes and ears to the perpetual squabbles about him and often let them develop when a word from him could have quelled them. Then he would suddenly lose his temper with everybody, just and unjust alike, and stamp and shout and either fling out of the house or shut himself in his library and get drunk. Every time he did that the disputants would drop the original quarrel and begin blaming one another for upsetting poor John.

Lady Rosemary was that sad thing—a pretty woman who was growing old and resenting it. She still had eyes like frozen forget-me-nots and a great sheaf of honey-coloured hair in which the white ones hardly showed at all, but the skin round her eyes and under her chin was crinkled like young beech leaves, and she was too stout. Provided that she believed you were devoted to her personally, she was pleasant to work for, though tyrannical in her demands. She seldom lost her temper, and could say the most waspish things in a cool, controlled voice. Once, they said, she had been extremely poor, but an uncle who had gone to Virginia at the end of the war had left her a good deal of money and a tobacco plantation, so she could afford to indulge her whims. Yet most of the rows in the house were concerned, directly or indirectly, with money. For, living at Merravay, were two Miss Whymarks, and the elder was parsimonious past all belief. Even my poor mother who never had a penny to spare, was not so mean, so watchful, so worried over candles, logs, wasted crusts. Most people think of ruin as something which might, if they are not careful, come upon them some day; Miss Whymark faced ruin, and spoke about it, every day of her life. She also made constant reference to her Granny—the old tavern-keeper whom Aunt Hester so much admired; Miss Whymark evidently admired her too and kept her memory green by acid remarks about "the old days" and "Granny's time" and the probability of Granny turning in her grave. For some reason which I never understood Miss Whymark wielded enormous power, both within doors and without, and everybody went in dread of her. But there was this to be said in her favour; she was the same every day, and if you worked yourself silly, never answered back, never wasted a grain of salt or a half inch of candle you did at least know where you were with her.

With Miss Maud it was entirely different. She was just as queer, not with meanness, for she could be extravagantly generous, but with imagining that she was being slighted and insulted. Even over food; whatever was carved she would cast sharp little glances at all the portions and unless hers was ostentatiously the best she'd push it away, burst into tears, and run off to her own room, where she kept great stores of sweets and cakes and a little outfit for making drinking chocolate. She was as susceptible to gross flattery as she was to imaginary insult, and was forever taking sides, having favourites, carrying tales. Nothing was real to her, and for that reason she was very dangerous. Still, she did a lot for the church and for the poor, of whom there were plenty, especially after Strawless Common was enclosed and the cottages were turned off.

Of the eight children born to Lady Rosemary five had survived; the deaths had occurred to the middle ones of the family, so now two were fully grown and three still in the schoolroom.

Mr. Roger was old enough to be soldiering abroad when I first went to Merravay. He came home during my third year there, invalided out of the army, looking very sickly and much older than his twenty-seven years. After staying at home for eight or nine months he went off to Virginia to see to some business in connection with the tobacco plantation, and he had stayed away. I had seen little of him; he was very quiet, though restless in the house, and well liked by those who came into contact with him.

Miss Sophie had grown to young womanhood during my time; she was two years older than I. When she was older and more settled she would probably be considered handsome, for she had inherited her father's brilliant colouring and height, but she was too thin and awkward to be a pretty girl. She was clever in a way which was no help to a young lady of her kind; she read everything she could lay hands on and could talk about what she had read. Lady Rosemary checked and chided and snubbed her at every turn, and did her best to prevent her from reading; consequently Miss Whymark encouraged her and frequently snatched up the London papers as soon as they arrived and carried them off to her room, where Miss Sophie could read them undisturbed. This action was purely perverse upon Miss Whymark's part, for the whole world might have sunk under the sea or gone up in flames without rousing in her one flicker of interest, provided Merravay remained untouched.

The three young children, Miss Julia, Miss Arabella, and Master Billy, were, despite their material comforts, more pitiable than enviable, for around their innocent heads unpredictable disputes of ancient origins were likely to break out at any moment. They were pampered, scolded, admonished, and cosseted by the four adult women according to mood or arbitrary situation. So they were growing up secretive and defensive, prepared to regard all grown-ups as potential enemies. Very often in the lapses between governesses it fell to my lot to take them for walks, while Miss Sophie took charge of their lessons, which she did very happily and efficiently. She had offered to take on the work permanently but her ladyship scoffed at the notion, "You don't need anything else to round your shoulders and screw up your eyes, my dear," she said. When they were without a governess they took their midday meal with the family and the sessions at table were very trying.

One of them might leave a little scrap of fat on the side of the plate.

"We were told to eat what we were given," Miss Whymark would say. "If we had wasted good food things would be very different here at this moment."

"Poor Julia is like me. I never could eat fat. Leave it, darling!" The indulgence in her ladyship's voice could not disguise its challenging quality.

"Well, let us hope these good times will continue, so that we can afford such fastidiousness. We should be ill prepared for a setback now, what with the waste of good food within and the waste of good land without."

The grass had grown smooth over the fields that had been turned into park land, and the young trees were branchy, but no resignation had grown over Miss Whymark's resentment at the loss of the arable land.

"Surely, Phyllis, the reason why most gentlemen's residences stand in parks and not in fields is to show that they can afford to spare a little ground. And for the same reason there is no need for the children to lick their plates as though they were starving dogs."

At this point the master would get up and go. Then Miss Maud, if she were at odds with Lady Rosemary, would make her contribution, "Every time I go into the village I see *many* poor little children who would be only too glad to eat that meat. Julia dear, clear your plate in gratitude to God who has provided so well for you." But if she had fallen out with her sister, Miss Maud would take a different tone, "Really, Phyl, what a fuss to make about a little bit of fat! All the scraps go into the swill pail!"

Her ladyship was then quite likely to say, with marked ingratitude, that the swill pail was not a subject to mention at table.

With slight variations of subject and side-taking this kind of scene would be repeated more frequently than anyone could believe possible.

The new governess—Luella or another Miss Maybrook—had the house by the ears some days before she arrived.

On a late January morning I was seated by the big window in Lady Rosemary's room, the one known as the Queen's Chamber. Her ladyship had attended a ball at Baildon on the previous evening, had risen late, and was sitting by the fire, drinking her morning chocolate. I was mending a lace flounce which had been trodden on and torn. At the moment Lady Rosemary and Miss Whymark were allied against Miss Maud, who was vehemently supporting the rector over the tithes; and as a sign of the brief, uneasy allegiance Miss Whymark came into her sister-in-law's room and accepted a cup of chocolate.

"Johnny has a new bee in his bonnet now," said her ladyship conversationally. "He thinks that governesses don't stay because we are so unpleasant to them. He read me a lecture on kindness to poor creatures. For what it is worth I pass it on . . ."

"If you have Miss Runackles in mind, Rose, I can only say that to me waste is waste and the hussy who wastes in this house gets short shrift whether she is governess or scullery slut."

"Johnny also thinks," the cool voice went on, "that the room we give the governess is dreary."

"Perhaps he would like her to have my room," said Miss Whymark very tartly.

"Well . . . of course, he is very muddle-minded," said her ladyship, not denying or confirming the possibility of such an audacious suggestion. "But, naturally, I should never entertain such an idea. No, actually I intend to give Miss Maybrook Sophie's room."

"But Sophie won't like that!" said Miss Whymark.

"No. But the move might serve to draw her attention to the fact that at Ockley there are eighteen bedrooms of which she could take her choice. I haven't told you about last evening! I was so infuriated. There we stood, having just arrived, and Sir Frederick came across to us, making it quite plain that he had been waiting for her. She said, 'Oh!' And what do you think Johnny did? Whisked her off into the dance, under the poor boy's nose. A father dancing the first dance with his daughter. There I stood, not knowing where to look or what to say. I was never more mortified!"

"Johnny isn't in favour of forced marriages," said Miss Whymark in a voice that indicated that she, too, thought them obnoxious.

"What a strange term! Forced! It just happens that that poor infatuated boy sees something in Sophie that eludes everyone else. That he is the most eligible young man within fifty miles has hardly any bearing on the matter, he is the only man not entirely senile who ever looks at her. But I could see how dashed he was. A few more incidents like that and she won't have a partner at all."

"She's still very young."

"She's twenty-one. That may seem young to you, Phyl. To me it seems dangerously old. I've seen too many girls go right through the wood, picking and choosing, and come out with a crooked stick at last—or no stick at all."

That was a direct challenge to Miss Whymark; for there was a legend in the house that both the old ladies had been very choosy in their youth.

"Well," said Miss Whymark, very slowly and clearly, "I should be sorry if you hoped, by putting Sophie in a poky room, to influence her attitude. For I have seen what happens when people marry for the sake of a comfortable home."

That was a frank production of the old well-gnawed bone. To my astonishment her ladyship ignored it.

"The one good thing about this idea of pampering governesses," she said in a ruminative voice, "is that it made Johnny see sense about the alterations. A house where the simple business of allotting everyone a habitable room causes such a commotion is obviously too small or badly planned. And when you think that one day Roger will bring a wife home, and that there are still two girls in the schoolroom . . . well, something must be done. Anyway Johnny at last sees the necessity and I am going to write to that man Kent this very day, before he has time to change his mind again."

That put spark to tinder and started a row of quite extraordinary violence. The idea of altering Merravay came into direct conflict not only with Miss Whymark's parsimony but with her sentiment as well. Merravay had been good enough for Granny, it should be good enough for anybody.

They wrangled, entirely forgetful of my presence, for several minutes.

"For two pins I'd persuade Johnny to build an entirely new house, fit for civilised people to live in, and leave this Merravay barn to you."

"Nothing would please me more," said Miss Whymark, stomping off to take counsel with Miss Maud.

I had finished my work, but was wise enough to stay with my head bent and my hands apparently busy for a moment. Suddenly her ladyship became aware of me,

"Deborah," she said, "I am planning some changes. Daisy can do what is needed for Miss Sophie, and I want you to take charge of the schoolroom. I seem to remember Miss Runackles complaining that the food there was always cold and the fire unsatisfactory. We want Miss Maybrook to be comfortable, so that will be your main duty in future. Of course, you will still have time to do things for me. Yes, that is a very neat piece of work, hardly detectable. Hang it away carefully."

Her ladyship was going to keep her bargain; the new governess was to be comfortable. And poor Miss Sophie was going to lose her bedroom and her maid . . . Daisy was a heavy-fisted, hard-breathing half-wit.

The quarrel about altering the house went on, making itself felt in many strange ways. With Miss Whymark more violently economical than ever; with Miss Maud rushing out the drawing-room one evening in tears, wailing, "Little did I think when I used to get up in the dark on winter mornings that I should live to see . . ." And finally with Mr. Whymark standing in the hall and shouting at the top of his voice,

"For God's sake, Phyl, stop dragging Granny in. Bless her heart, *she* spent money on Merravay as soon as she could afford it. Why shouldn't I? And let me tell you that if she is turning in her grave it's because you're trying to make her out as damned mean as you are. She wasn't, by God, she was a riotous old girl! Though why the hell she fixed up such a punishment for me I shall never know . . ."

VI

The day of Miss Maybrook's arrival came; it was a day when the coach did not run into Nettleton, so it was arranged that the cart from Merravay should go to fetch her from Baildon. But it turned out a pouring wet day and at midmorning Lady Rosemary decided to send the carriage instead. She had forgotten that this was one of the days when Miss Maud, carrying her own little locked tea caddy, was to go and favour the rector's wife with her company, her criticism, and advice, all washed down with the best Suchong.

At two o'clock, from the window of her room where she was changing her dress, Miss Maud saw Jack Lantern putting the horses to the carriage and screamed down that he was early, the fire wouldn't be lighted in the Rectory parlour. Lantern shouted back that he was off to Baildon and would drop her on the way.

"That you will not do," said Miss Maud, and still wearing her shabby dress, with her hair in disarray and the tea caddy clutched to her breast, she scampered downstairs, muttering that fifty years ago when she had sat up all night dressing fowls for market she'd imagined that she was laying up comfort for her old age. Was some chit of a governess to be considered before her now?

Her ladyship, appealed to by the coachman, said laconically that if she had said once she had said a hundred times that a place like Merravay should have three carriages and it was entirely Miss Whymark's fault that there was but one.

Miss Whymark said of course the two errands could be combined; Miss Maud got into the carriage and said she should scream if it moved an inch before three o'clock. In the end it was decided to send the slow cart to Baildon after all; and the governess was expected to arrive, no doubt soaked to the skin, some time between six and seven o'clock. So soon after five I made a handsome fire in the schoolroom and the children settled down by it to roast chestnuts, gloomily speculating upon the nature and appearance of their new governess.

I was drawing the curtains when I heard my name called and ran down. Her ladyship was standing in the doorway of the drawing-room, with Miss Whymark close beside her. Halfway across the hall Miss Maud, just back from the Rectory, was rubbing a few rain spots from the tea caddy. Briggs the footman was just behind the screen, slowly closing the door and lingering to see and hear as much as possible. And just inside the screen stood Miss Maybrook—Luella—explaining in the voice that took me straight back to childhood that having decided that she was not to be met, she had hired the post chaise!

I have seen a flock of sheep with young lambs, all at variance with one another, turn, as one animal, to face a strange dog, then draw together, heads outward, and present a united, defiant front. It was just like that. A governess . . . hiring a post chaise . . . seven shillings . . . What was the world coming to?

Having told me to take Miss Maybrook to her room and then show her the way to the schoolroom, her ladyship backed into the drawing-room, followed by the Miss Whymarks. Briggs stuck his nose in the air and stalked into the kitchen to make his report. Luella and I stood face to face.

She was much altered; but for the voice—and of course the name— I doubt if I should have recognised her. I had always thought of her as a pretty little girl. Even making allowances for the effect that her clothes and her cleanliness, her smooth hair and skin had had upon me I still think that as a child she was pretty. But all the prettiness had vanished. She looked at least thirty years old, pale and thin, hollow-cheeked and sharp-nosed. Her eyes were enormous, slightly prominent in their hollows, with thin, veined lids edged with long lashes and set under thin dark brows which ran from a little frown mark over the nose, upwards and outwards to her hair. Her mouth was enormous too, deeply curved, with the lower lip turned out in a wistful, discontented, yet very sweet way. I stood and stared at her, thinking that if I had met her in a street and she had asked the way I should have told her, unknowing, and then gone on wondering why I was suddenly thinking of Mrs. Maybrook and Ivy Cottage.

"But you're Deb . . . Deborah Fulger, surely. Do you remember me . . . Luella Maybrook?"

"Of course," I said.

"How lovely," she said, and stretched out the hand she had ungloved. I had taken care of my hands, making excuses to myself about the impossibility of doing fine needlework with rough fingers, but as I put mine out to meet Luella's it looked and felt, for all my care with the goose grease and witch-hazel, as big and coarse as a ploughboy's. Hers was nothing at all. There was just nothing of her except those great eyes, that mouth, and the voice.

"Oh, I am glad to see you again," she said as I lifted the shabby little valise. "I've thought of you and Luke so often. Those happy days we had. And then I didn't even say good-bye to you; you were so ill. I always meant to write to you; but I was so miserable . . . whenever I started to think about those days I just cried, so the letter never got written."

"Luke once asked Mr. Turnbull for news of you. He said you were well and happy."

"He may have thought so. He wanted to, I expect. Men can believe anything they want to. Well and happy . . ." she said with surpassing bitterness. "Still, I survived. And here I am. I owe that to Mr. Turnbull at least. Deborah, what are they like? The children?"

By that time we had reached the bedroom door, and I said apologetically, "I meant to light the fire, but I didn't think you could be here for at least an hour."

She told me about the taking of the post chaise.

"They all seemed *shocked*. Are they poor, Deb?"

"Heavens no! The old one who stood in the doorway is fanatically *mean*." I set the valise on a chair and went across to open the door of the clothes closet, which in this panelled room wasn't easy to see, and as I did so I told her a few things about the characters of Merravay's inmates and what to be careful of . . . "that is if you *want* to stay here," I ended.

"But I do. Of course I do. It did seem the greatest good fortune . . . when I heard from Mr. Turnbull I could hardly believe . . . I always so wanted to live here." She made a funny wry face, "In my innocent childish dreams, Deb, I used to plan that someone left me a fortune and I bought it; or I married a very rich man who bought it for me. I never saw myself coming here as a governess. . . . Still, here I am, and I must make the best of it. But that's enough about me. Tell about you. Have you been here long, and are you happy?"

"Six years; and I'm *settled*."

"And Luke?"

"He has the farm now. He's doing quite well. My father died, very suddenly two years ago." For some strange reason I heard myself saying aloud something that had been in my mind ever since Father died, something I never had said, or dreamed of saying to anyone. "We all thought he was vilely bad-tempered, but the truth was that he'd been ill for a long time and nobody knew."

Luella had been bent over the valise. She straightened and turned to me.

"Poor Deb. Does that worry you? You mustn't let it. How could you know? Perhaps he was proud of not complaining. And anyway, as far as I can remember he *was* a cross man, well or ill. I used to shake in my shoes if he looked at me. And think how he used to shout at Luke who was always trying so hard."

That speech soothed a sore place in my mind. Father had grown more and more cantankerous and had made Mother and Luke most miserable. He'd sent me to service and took my wages every quarter without saying so much as thank you. When Aunt Hester died and left her sixty-pounds share in the farm equally between Luke and me he never even told us, and there were times when I felt I positively hated him. Then one morning he'd walked into the kitchen and said, "I feel queer," and fell on the floor. Mother could see that he was past her help, so she sent Luke full pelt for the doctor. Father was dead when he arrived, but he was young and curious, and there had been two cases in our neighbourhood where women were suspected of poisoning their husbands; so he stripped the body. He found a lump the size of a bladder of lard in Father's groin and said it was a wonder he'd kept on his feet, leave alone done so much work, because he must have suffered agonies.

After that I had felt very badly about the way I had felt towards him. I'd wake sometimes in the night and think of him, mad with pain and taking it out on Luke and Mother; and working on and then dying, like a sick horse. And I'd think how he'd never known any success, and never had a drink or any fun, not even a really good meal. It seemed pitiable and heartbreaking.

"I know just how you feel," said Luella. "One of my pupils died suddenly after being peevish all day and I'd chided him. Oh dear . . . I think of it still sometimes; though Heaven knows I paid for that! My next place was quite unbearable. So bad that I left without giving notice or waiting for my wages. *That* was why I wrote to Mr. Turnbull; I knew he still had a little money left over, and I just asked him to send me some. When he sent it he said he'd heard about this job."

We had not closed the door behind us and now, far off along the gallery, I could hear Miss Whymark's stumping tread.

"I mustn't stand here talking," I said, "I'll show you the schoolroom. Then I'll light this fire and afterwards you can unpack in comfort." As I spoke I thought how delightful it was to have someone to talk to at last; and how very remarkable it was that Luella should be prepared to take up our friendship where it left off, not a bit conscious, apparently, of the difference in our positions.

We met Miss Whymark just where a lamp hung on the wall, and as she was carrying a candle, and I was too, we could see one another clearly. I stepped back, and she stood and regarded Luella with cold curiosity. I felt that she had come up to see what prodigal act this extravagant taker-of-post-chaises had committed within ten minutes of her arrival.

"You look very young for a responsible post," said Miss Whymark—surprising me. "How old are are you?"

"Twenty, ma'am; and I have had three years' experience."

"You look delicate, too."

"Apart from a cold I have ailed nothing since leaving school, where I had all the childish complaints—an advantage to a governess."

"That is a highly unsuitable dress you are wearing."

I had been a little surprised when Luella took off her shabby hooded cloak and revealed the dress. It was sombre in colour, a deep lavender grey banded with purple velvet; it was not over-extravagant in style, but it looked costly.

"I'm sorry you should think that, ma'am," said Luella in a voice which held interest, a trace of surprise, but no embarrassment. "Lady Hereford gave me this gown, since I had no mourning of my own."

"Mourning?"

"For little Lord Henry who had been my pupil, poor child."

Oh dear, I thought, this is a bad beginning; two titles mentioned so soon; and Miss Whymark had scant respect for the aristocracy. I waited for some scathing words. But when she spoke, after another long assessing look, Miss Whymark said civilly,

"Well, I have no doubt you are hungry after your journey. Schoolroom supper could be early this once. Deborah will see to it. Good evening."

Unperturbed by the encounter and quite unconscious of her luck, Luella followed me to the schoolroom, where the children, counting upon a later arrival, were in the middle of their chestnut-roasting. They looked up guiltily.

"Hullo," said Luella. "You do look cosy. And what a lovely smell. Oh, chestnuts! Now how could you guess that I should be hungry?"

She knelt down on the hearth, holding her hands to the fire and turning her gaze almost gravely from one flushed young face to another. Some kind of trust was established immediately, for before I had finished drawing the curtains and making the table clear for the untimely meal they were peeling nuts for her and saying, "Have this, it's bigger." "No, this, it's cooked all through," "No, this one, Miss Maybrook, I did it specially for you."

Downstairs in the kitchen I found that Briggs had reported that the new governess looked harmless enough.

VII

Her ladyship had lost no time in sending for Mr. Kent, and before my February Saturday was due (a day to which I looked forward most eagerly, because I could tell Mother and Luke about Luella) he arrived to look over Merravay and work out the best way to make it larger and more up-to-date. Such improvements had been in her ladyship's mind ever since she and Mr. Whymark had visited the house in Leicestershire where the Miss Whymark who had made the fashionable marriage lived. Moreover at Muchanger, a nearby house, a beam that was said to have smouldered for six months, which might be true for it was solid oak and measured two and a half feet each way, burst into flame in the middle of a windy night and half the house was burned down. Muchanger had been rebuilt in the new style, and after that her ladyship had nagged and cajoled and finally bargained to get Merravay altered.

I saw Mr. Kent arrive on a mild blue and white February morning. He was shabby; he looked awkward and surly; and he rode on what was plainly a hired hack. But I was interested in him, because, secretly practising my reading at every opportunity, I had saved old papers from the lighting of fires, and seen in one a brief account of a quarrel he had had with someone who employed him. And I thought him lucky to have been chosen by Lady Rosemary to work on Merravay, because she was a lady who was very much copied, and if he pleased her it was more than likely that he would be altering houses in Suffolk for years.

He alighted and then walked all round the house, staring, before he rang the bell. Then he went in and was closeted with her ladyship and plied with refreshments for almost an hour. The master, like Pilate washing his hands, had left the house early and gone to shoot at Mortiboys.

Presently her ladyship went out with the architect, and they paced up and down for a while and then crossed the dip and stood in the field. Mr. Kent waved his arms about and looked like a scarecrow in a high wind. And then he was back in the yard, wrenching the hired horse from the first good meal it had had in its whole life, poor thing, by the look of it, and off he rode, with his head sunk between his shoulders, and with a dour, defeated look on his face. I guessed that he had failed to satisfy her ladyship and I felt sorry for him.

But it wasn't that at all. From the conversation which Briggs overheard that night at table, the truth drifted down to us. Mr. Kent had refused to touch Merravay. He said that he had never before seen a house, particularly an old house, which his fingers hadn't itched to improve; but Merravay as it stood was perfect. He wouldn't touch it himself and he hoped God would strike dead anyone who attempted it.

Here Briggs had the exact words to report.

"So I said to him, 'Mr. Kent, houses are made to be lived in, not looked at!' and he said, 'Aye, and paper is made for wrapping things; and there are shops in London now where they'll slap a pennorth of brawn in paper for you. But if some lout went to wrap my pennorth in a page of Shakespeare's sonnets I'd cry shame on him . . . as I do on you.'

Then he asked me who designed this house and said whoever did it was an artist. And then he went off."

That was the first, I might say the only, time that I ever heard of a man sacrificing a chance of winning bread and butter, not to mention fame and fortune, for the sake of an idea. I still could not see exactly what was so special about Merravay, though I went to the top of the field and looked again, hard, earnestly. Nevertheless I could never think of Mr. Kent, obviously poor and in need of a job, riding away from a promising, sizable one because he didn't wish to spoil something he thought beautiful, without feeling respect and a kind of awe.

Soon after that came the last Saturday in February and according to my habit I left the house just before the midday meal. Since Father's death I had gone home more gladly, for Mother's merry spirit, never entirely subdued, had bobbed up again; and Luke regarded me as a shareholder in the farm. Mother thought, or pretended to think, that part of Father's trouble had been due to bad feeding, so nowadays she kept a good table; and curiously enough the extra outlay was not noticed, for in the very things where Father had failed, try as he might, Luke was succeeding.

I was hurrying home, thinking of the welcome and the toothsome dishes that awaited me, and of all the things I had to relate, when I met Luella and the children coming in from their morning walk. She asked me where I was going and said she would like to come with me.

"I'd like it, too . . . but . . ."

"Oh, they have plenty to do," said Luella. And they all three began saying what they should do: work on a sampler, mount and label a collection of winter berries, read. No other governess had succeeded in teaching Billy to read, but Luella had made him a book of his own, called "William Whymark's Book." It had pictures of familiar objects, with short sentences printed under them. The first picture was a little boy, lopsided of face; under it it said, "My name is William Whymark. I am a nice little boy and I will learn to read."

"Run along then. Don't make a noise, and have lots to show me when I come back," said Luella. Falling into step beside me, she said, "After all, teaching them to be self-reliant is part of the job."

"You're very clever with them," I said. "Their other governesses seemed to hate the sight of them and yet were afraid to take their eyes off them. And always complaining. Not entirely without cause. They once put a frog in Miss Runackles' bed!"

"How detestable. I should retaliate with three hedgehogs if I could find them!" She linked her arm in mine. "Will your mother mind my suddenly appearing like this? Oh, I do so want to see her, and Luke, and the place again. I always longed to be asked into your house. Oh, what a long time ago it all seems."

We walked along briskly, talking of this and that. She said what a good thing it was that Merravay wasn't to be altered.

"It would just have been too ironic if they'd started to tear it down the moment I came back."

"I confess," I said, "that I don't understand it all. What is it that attracts you so much?"

"Why do *you* love flowers so much?"

"I've never asked myself. I just love them. They're beautiful and . . ." I groped for a word which would express the inexpressible, handicapped by the fact that I was never called upon to converse about ideas . . . "well, silly as it sounds, they seem to *promise* me something. Don't ask what, Luella, I couldn't tell you to save my life . . . but it is true, just one flower can seem to promise something that hasn't to do with hard work, meals, making ends meet, being down to earth . . ."

"That is it, exactly. All things that are just beautiful carry that promise . . . in different languages to different people."

"Promise of what?" I asked, half fearful.

"I should think . . . Heaven. Tell me quickly, Deb, when you think of Heaven what is it?"

"Layer Wood in every season at once," I said without hesitation.

"Yes. And I think, 'In my Father's house are many mansions' . . . and all like Merravay. And the idea of many mansions in a *house* has precisely the same magic . . . other-worldly . . . preposterous touch as your every season at once. D'you see?"

We went on, walking and talking so fast that we made ourselves breathless. Presently Luella said,

"Do you still read a lot?"

Despite all effort at control the red colour flared into my face. My reading at Merravay was a guilty secret. I felt that the purloined key of the bookcase and the most lately "borrowed" book, both safe under my bolster, must be imaged in my eyes—I saw them so clearly—as I asked, uneasily,

"What makes you ask that?"

"The words you use, the way you put them together . . . that's all"; she was sharing my embarrassment. I realised that during this walk with its delightful resumption of good fellowship I had forgotten to keep my usual check on my tongue. Guilt and secretiveness had now such a hold on me that I was careful never to use, in ordinary circumstances, any word that Daisy might not.

"Well . . ." I said, deciding to tell a half-truth, "yes, I do. After you went away I was at home for a year and I didn't see a written word of any kind. When I went to Merravay I was surprised to find that I *could* still read. So for practice I read the papers when they are weeks old and used for lighting the fires. And I write too. I copy pieces out of the paper sometimes, and I write what the weather is like and what flowers are blooming. *But* nobody up there knows, Luella, and I don't want them to."

"Why ever not?"

"I might find myself in the schoolroom!" It was a stupid reason, but all I could think of at the moment. Fortunately at that moment we reached our yard gate and she had no chance to ask why I feared that fate.

Mother and Luke were astonished to the point of incredulity to see Luella, but delighted too, and when the exclamations ended we settled down to what, I think, must have been the merriest meal ever to be eaten in that house. Since Father's death Mother had resumed her making of homemade wines, elderberry, cowslip, and blackberry, and now, with many apologies for their lack of maturity, she produced samples of all kinds and we grew very lively. Luella seemed to slip into place with unbelievable ease; even the silk dress did not strike an incongruous note. Only her voice, her clear laugh, did that.

We lingered over the meal and then Mother and I went into the scullery to do the dishes. Luella offered to help but Mother would not allow that, so we left her with Luke by the fire. After a few minutes Luke put his head and one arm round the door and picked up the wooden pattens which Mother used when walking in the yard.

"I'm going to rack up now," he said, "and Miss Maybrook wants to come with me. I'll take these."

From the unglazed hole in the wall that served our scullery for a window, I watched them crossing the yard, Luella walking clumsily in the pattens, and laughing at her clumsiness. At the miry part by the pigs' pen she stumbled, and Luke took her elbow to steady her. Luke was laughing too, and I realised suddenly that I had never seen him really merry before. In Father's time he had been suppressed and subdued, and then at a stride he had passed to responsibility and the deadly seriousness that goes with ambition. But he was laughing now.

"She've turned out a lot better than I should've expected," said Mother, dropping a pinch of wood ash on a greasy plate and scrubbing vigorously. "To tell the truth I allust thought she was a mite dim-witted."

"Ah, that was because she couldn't manage the pony," I said, thinking that even then she had managed *us* and we had managed the pony for her. I looked back over the month she had been at Merravay—a whole month—and nobody, not even Miss Whymark, had yet found a word to say against her.

That evening Luke drove us back to Merravay in the cart. He and I were the best of friends; he had, at Father's death, told me that a third of the farm was mine. I had always returned to Merravay on foot, feeling very cherished and privileged if he strolled with me, in winter, until the lights of the house were visible across the fields. It had never occurred to him to drive me, and in justice to him I must say that the idea of being driven had never occurred to me either.

VIII

Quite early in March another architect, of whom her ladyship had heard a good report, came to make a visit of inspection. He was young and good-looking, well dressed, and full of confidence. He measured and tapped, walked about the house, and stared at it from various angles, and then retreated to the library to draw some preliminary sketches. When they were complete Miss Sophie borrowed them and brought them to the schoolroom to show Luella. I was there and she invited me to see them too; because she was well disposed to me just then since, though it was no longer part of my duty, I helped her with her hair and her clothes. I had, one evening, almost been caught doing her hair when her ladyship suddenly came in to tell her daughter which dress to wear; luckily I heard her voice and hopped into the clothes closet and hid myself. Afterwards Miss Sophie and I laughed almost hysterically together, and some sort of barrier fell and never went up again. Luella also helped with the constant titivation of the wardrobe—even her ladyship would ask her advice; for, with Lady Hereford, Luella had lived in London and had had opportunities to see the ladies of fashion.

So now we all three bent over the sketches as though they were dress patterns. I could see at a glance that Mr. Armitage's alterations were to be fundamental; the house's new face was to be flat, with many windows set in rows, and instead of the deep old porch the new door was to have a pillared portico.

"I tried not to like it," Miss Sophie said. "Poor Aunt Phyl is so upset because what she calls 'Granny's garden' will now be built upon; and the window tax will be calamitous. But now I have *seen* it. . . . Don't you think it is impressive—and so well designed?"

"It would be fine on any other house," said Luella. "I shall go on hoping to the very last minute that something occurs to baulk these plans."

"Well nothing will," said Miss Sophie in a pleased way. "Mamma is delighted with them, and with Mr. Armitage."

Two evenings later, after the architect had ridden away, Mr. Whymark came to a belated realisation of the extent of the alterations planned, and once again there was no need for us to wait for Briggs or Parker to bring news from the front of the house to us in the kitchen. The master, really angry and a little flown with wine, could make himself heard at Slipwell.

Where, he demanded to be told, was it proposed that they should live while the whole of the front of the house was pulled down? Yes, he knew he had promised, though how the devil he'd been such a fool he didn't know; but he'd only meant a couple of extra bedrooms and new doors and windows if she set such store by them. Live in a house with no front he would not!

There was then a babble of female voices, the words indistinguishable, and then the master's voice again.

"You keep out of this, Phyl," he roared. "All right; you agree with me; I don't want your blasted agreement. It's this everlasting pull devil pull baker that's been the ruin of this house. Am I never to have any peace? It's a bit late in the day to point this out to you all, but this is *my* house and you'd do well to remember it. All of you. Parker! Bring a fresh bottle to the library!"

And it was then, according to Parker, that the door opened and Mr. Roger walked in, saying,

"This sounds just like home!"

He had always looked old for his years and he had aged considerably in the two and a half years he had been away. A wig was now more to him than a sign of rank or mark of fashion; it was a necessity. The yellow sallowness of his skin had darkened and his face had fallen into grooves and lines—all melancholy; he looked rather like a hound. But he had a smile of singular sweetness; it was not merely a stretching of the lips and a brightening of the eyes, it was a lighting up, a rearrangement of his whole face. My work, of course, did not bring me near him; and Merravay, despite her ladyship's complaints, was big enough to allow two people under its roof to meet by accident very rarely, but on the few occasions when I did see him I found myself waiting for that smile, the sudden flash of sunshine in a sombre sky; it reminded me irresistibly of Mother's wryly merry looks behind Father's back in the old days.

Mr. Roger's arrival did a good deal to console her ladyship for the blow dealt her over the alterations. For four or five days everything was pleasant and lively and excited; parties to celebrate Mr. Roger's safe return, and reciprocal parties in other houses. And then everything changed.

For all this part of the story I had to rely upon what Luella, coming home with me in March and April, could report.

Mr. Roger had gone out to Virginia, it seemed, because the overseer of the plantation—sometimes called the agent, too—had died, and it was necessary to appoint another person, completely trustworthy and knowledgeable. That was soon done, but by the time it was arranged Mr. Roger had become deeply involved in the business of slaves and slavery. When he had learned all there was to learn about the slaves on the plantation, which would one day be his own, he had set out and visited dozens of others, places where rice was grown, and cane sugar and cotton.

What he had seen and heard appalled him. He had all the facts set down in a number of little black notebooks: the numbers of slaves on various plantations; how many died, were bought, sold, born each year; their weights, their rations, hours of work, diseases and punishments. He had come back to England with all this carefully gathered and meticulously recorded information, with the avowed intent to try to have the whole system abolished. He began by offering her ladyship a paper upon which she had only to write her signature and the two hundred slaves on her Virginian property would be free. That must be the first step, he said, because it would be a hopeless handicap to his campaign if people could turn round and say that his mother was a slaveowner.

Legally—as Luella pointed out to me—her ladyship, being a married woman, owned nothing; but in point of fact Mr. Whymark had always refused to have anything to do with the American property. I imagine that he resented it because it had made his wife independent, able to follow her whims. He now pursued his established course. To Mr. Roger, when appealed to, he said, "It is for your mother to decide"; and to his wife, "You must do as you think best. In your place I'd sign."

Two days later he said he didn't intend to have his life made miserable by the discussion of the woes of a lot of black fellows he'd never set eyes on, and forbade the mention of the subject in his presence.

The sense of conflict made itself felt throughout the house. We all, willy-nilly, began to take sides. I had no particular love for her ladyship; she had treated me fairly but had never done anything to endear herself to me, and I knew very well that if, one evening, lacing her into her gown I had dropped dead, she would have minded the resultant confusion and loss of time far more than my demise; but I could see her predicament. Mr. Roger was her eldest son, her best beloved child; he had been absent for overlong, she was delighted to see him home; she was mildly shocked by a few carefully selected incidents which he related to her and she wished to please him. But he admitted that by freeing her slaves she would, temporarily at least, reduce her income; and since she was now going pig-headedly towards a modified alteration of Merravay she needed the money because it bolstered her authority.

Miss Whymark, because anything likely to reduce her ladyship's power seemed most desirable, was an abolitionist; Miss Maud said that if the slaves could be sure of enough fat pork and meal to keep life in their bodies they were better off than many poor people in Nettleton. Miss Sophie, anxious to do anything, short of marrying Sir Frederick, to please her mother, said, not without truth, that a careful investigation of the ordinary farm labourer's conditions of life and labour would expose some shocking facts. Luella, partly because she was very tender-hearted, and also—I think—because loss of money would restrain her ladyship's rebuilding, was firmly on Mr. Roger's side; and when she found that he needed several copies of his charts and facts and abstracts written out, offered her services.

I was, I think I can say with truth, an entirely disinterested abolitionist. And it was not Mr. Roger who had converted me. It was somebody called Thomas Rowhedge who had been dead for almost a hundred years.

Soon after I first went to Merravay a brick in the breast of the chimney in the Ship Chamber became porous and a great dark patch came through the plaster. During the process of taking out the faulty brick it was discovered that the panelling on one side of the chimney was not solid; it was the front of a cupboard, and the cupboard was full of ancient books. When they had been cleaned and their leather bindings polished, they were housed in a special glass-fronted bookcase in the library, and during my time as maid-of-all-work it was one of my tasks to dust them occasionally. It was then that I discovered, to my delight, that I remembered how to read. For a week or two I contented myself by peeping into the books and reading a page at random while I was supposed to be dusting, and then one day I came across a thick, leather-bound book, written by hand, and noticed the name "Alice" recurring. A Lady Alice Rowhedge who had lived at Merravay many years before, and who had been—they said—a witch, had become a part and parcel of the folklore of our district, and many a winter night I had sat by the fire at home and listened to Aunt Hester's tales about her. A dark, shuddering curiosity seized me as I handled this book, and presently, when I left the library, it was hidden under my apron. Five minutes later it was under my pillow. I was fortunate in having been put to sleep in a little room directly under the rafters, reached by an almost perpendicular ladder which even Miss Whymark in her visits of inspection never climbed, a room cruelly cold in winter and roastingly hot in summer, a lonely, unenviable eyrie of which I remained in undisputed possession.

That book was, from my point of view, disappointing, but it had given me a taste for reading in bed, and for several weeks after that I "borrowed" books from that case. Then her ladyship caught Miss Sophie reading something which she said was most unsuitable and she locked that case and carried off the keys. The case left open contained books of surpassing dullness; most of them were ones which Mr. Whymark had had when he was a young man at Cambridge; some of them weren't even in English. But by that time the reading habit was strong in me; and when I had been reduced to carrying *A Mirror For Magistrates* to bed with me, I realised that I had only to ask her ladyship for the key under pretence that the locked books needed dusting. I never gave it back to her.

Amongst the books with which I was thus guiltily free to indulge was a slim, handwritten one containing a play called *The Middle Passage*. Under the title Thomas Rowhedge had written,

"This Drama is rooted in a True Story, told me many years since by my Father, who was himself the Sea Captain."

It was all about slaves and the things they endured on their journey from Africa to America. It made terrible reading, but there was poetry in it too. In the end the Captain, to the detriment of his pocket and the extreme fury of his partner, turned them all loose on a desert island, saying,

"It may be that you die here. Even so,
Die as free men whose hands, too late unbound,
Have failed to wring a sustenance from this soil,
That shall be my blame too, an added guilt
To that I bear already. But from hence
It shall not be my profit. Not for me
The Judas coin with blood upon its rim."

I didn't believe, of course, that a rough sea captain would talk that way to black men, or that they would understand him if he did; but it was good to read; and it set me against the slave trade and everything connected with it. So when Luella offered to make the copies for Mr. Roger, I volunteered to help her. We used to work in the schoolroom at night, after Miss Whymark had made her last round and the house was quiet. Despite the fact that Luella had had years of schooling and much more practice, I still wrote the better hand; but if Mr. Roger ever noticed the difference he never said anything. He himself sat in the library all through the lovely month of April, sorting the papers and scribbling away like a clerk. With every passing day her ladyship regarded him with more disfavour, and when he began sending letters to Sir George Fenstanton, who was our Member of Parliament, and trying to enlist his interest in the business, she went about with a tragic face, burst into angry tears frequently, and said, not caring who overheard her, that to have thankless, unloving children was the hardest fate a woman could have. She said that Mr. Roger was trying deliberately to ruin her, to take the roof from over her head, the bread from her mouth.

During this same month of April a rumour began to creep about the kitchen that Sir Frederick Fennel had proposed to Miss Sophie and been refused. This remained rumour until, during the Easter week when the balls began again after the Lenten lapse, I received first-hand proof of it.

Her ladyship's own maid—Kate, Luella, and I were helping to dress her and do her hair, and I was watching for an opportunity to slip away and see what sort of mess Daisy had made of Miss Sophie's hair, when the young lady herself, wearing a wrapper, came in.

"Mamma, do you wish me to wear the yellow or the blue?"

Without turning her head, upon which Luella was erecting one of the new high fashionable coiffures, her ladyship said quite sweetly,

"Neither, my dear. I do not intend that you should accompany us this evening. Since you have decided to emulate your aunts you may as well stay at home with them. Miss Maybrook! That last pin pierced my scalp!"

Not altogether by accident, I thought, catching sight of Luella's face. Even the fanatically devoted Kate looked troubled. The cold venom, the unkind timing of the announcement, had not been pleasant to see.

"As you wish, Mamma," said Miss Sophie.

"She'll learn," said her ladyship pleasantly. "I can see that I have been overindulgent with my children and the result is a headstrong wilfulness. Still . . . it may not be too late to rectify matters."

Rectifying the results of almost thirty years of what she called indulgence towards Mr. Roger took the form, a few days later, of refusing to entertain Sir George Fenstanton and the Bishop of Bywater. He asked her at table, in Briggs' presence, so we all had a first-hand account of it.

"If those two, lately at daggers drawn, propose to visit you together, Roger, we know why! All right, Johnny, I am not mentioning the subject! I may not be clever, but I have sense enough to see that when a politician and a churchman get together some third person is about to be robbed. I do not intend to receive them under the roof that they and you are trying to rip from over my head."

"Don't talk such nonsense, Rose," said Miss Whymark. "This house stood here years before any of those black men were born and will stand long after they're all set free or dead. I do resent the way you talk as though Merravay depended upon a few poor slaves."

"Did I or did I not say that I wouldn't have this thing discussed in my presence?" Mr. Whymark shouted.

"Roger brought it up. That's all he thinks about," put in Miss Maud. "I tried to make him interested in the poor Thackers, turned out in the road with eight children, but no, they ain't black enough to . . ."

Then, Briggs said, they all began to talk together. Mr. Roger accused his mother of trying to build a fine new house out of dead Negroes' bones; Miss Whymark accused Miss Maud of spoiling the Thackers, who should shift for themselves. "It was a regular bear garden," said Briggs.

That evening Luella said that we must work extra hard over the copies; she had seen Mr. Roger sometime during the day and he had told her he was off to London in the morning and wanted the papers to take with him.

We worked late, thinking the house asleep, and when Mr. Roger came in I was caught unawares. There was no time for me to lay down my quill and pretend to be busy with some much belated domestic task as I usually held myself ready to do.

He had been working too; there was ink on his fingers and a blob of it on the end of his nose. He had discarded his wig, and the few remaining strands of his rust-coloured hair were all on end. His neckcloth was loosened, and he looked more like an over-driven scrivener than the heir to a fine estate.

He took in the situation at a glance.

"Ah! So that's how it's done. I often wondered. Bless you, child. I thank you from my heart. As for you," he turned to Luella who was ruling a line to frame a column, "but for your help I should have been another month. I truly cannot express my gratitude . . ."

She laid down the ruler, stood up and stretched and yawned, as gracefully and unself-consciously as a cat. He stood smiling, the lines in his face softening out and changing as a dark furrowed field changes under the touch of the sunshine. And then, as he looked at Luella, the smile died out, and for a moment, or less, for a mere second, before his face resumed its everyday expression, there was something else. . . .

"You know, I take this as a symbol . . . that two young people should sit up o'nights, spoiling their pretty eyes to help the cause. It proves to me that, once the facts are known, all right-minded people . . ."

He broke off at a sound beyond the door.

"Miss Whymark," said Luella in a horrified voice.

"It's all right . . . she's with us . . . I'll explain."

The door opened after a knob-fumbling pause and there was Mr. Whymark.

"Thought I heard voices," he said in the staccato voice which came upon him when he was drunk. He stared at us all. "Wanted to see you before you go. Off tomorrow? That right? Wanted to say . . . all a great pity, very great pity. Mustn't mind your Mother, y'know, very excitable, always was, always will be. 'Nother thing too, wanted to say. Ah, yes. Mustn't get carried away. Take little chaps that climb chimneys. Know what? They all die before they're twelve. On paper, my boy, on paper. 'S'fact. Read about it 'tother day. Die before they're twelve. But you go 'long Goose Lane, old Sweeper Armstrong, claims to be ninety, put's son to the trade. Young Sweeper as old as I am, lot healthier; regiment of youngsters, all climbing chimneys and lively 'scrickets. See what I mean? Mustn't get carried away; make crass fool of y'self."

"I see exactly," said Mr. Roger. "I won't do that. Everything I say is soundly based on fact."

"So you reckon to set Thames on fire with all that paper, eh?"

"I hope to convince somebody who can. Sooner or later."

"Well," said Mr. Whymark, staring round aimlessly for a moment. "Well, wish you luck, m'boy. Ha . . . 'nother thing. Money. Can't do without it, y'know. More pull in a good dinner and a bottle of the right stuff 'nin all the talk in the world. And even if you do turn the black chaps loose, don't mean we shall go on the parish. Plenny money here, trust old Phyl for that."

"I have all I need at the moment, sir," Mr. Roger said, the smile lighting his face again. "But I thank you for the thought; and even more for your good wishes."

"'Snothing," said the master, waving his hand in the air. "Just heard voices and came along, say a friendly word. G'night."

He wheeled round with a lurch and then, arrested by something, turned again and peered at Luella.

"You . . ." he drew back, shaking his head. "Just f'r a moment, mistook you. Very peculiar thing. . . ." Muttering, he took himself off.

"If they were *his*, he'd free them tomorrow," said Mr. Roger, gathering his papers together.

"Because it would—for him—be the easiest thing," said Luella.

Mr. Roger looked up sharply. "All too true! Do you see through everybody as clearly as that, Miss Maybrook? Let's hope not, eh—er—Deborah? Still, that sort mustn't be discounted, you know; they have the will to good; in mass they form a power called public opinion. Well, thank you again, both of you, more than I can say. Good night."

"Well, that's over and done with, thank God," said Luella, yawning again as she dropped the lid on the ink bottle. "And tomorrow is your free day, Deb. Your mother did say . . . but would it be more change for you to go alone?"

"Of course not. And I'm sure they'd both be horribly horribly disappointed," I said.

IX

She came home with me in April, and we gathered primroses together again; and in May when the cowslips were in flower and the lilacs shyly showing their colour. My days at home had always been very cheerful since Father—poor man—had died, but Luella's coming contributed something else, something special. Both then and later, I gave hours of thought to the problem of Luella—and not without cause. I never put my finger exactly on what it was she did to people and for people, but I think I was near it when I concluded that she was a little like a flattering looking-glass. She was always herself and allowed you to be yourself, but in her presence, under her response to you, you were a little more how you would like to be. That, and her boundless capacity to enjoy herself . . . and, of course, the other thing which still eludes me, the thing there is no word for. It wasn't that I was charmed with her and therefore imagined her to be charming; there was the way in which the children had taken to her, the fact that in strife-ridden Merravay she had no enemy.

On our April day she asked again to be allowed to help with the dishes and my mother laughed and said, "All right then, love, come along," and taking one of her own print aprons she wrapped Luella in it, greatly amused because it was so much too wide. "The scullery is a hovel," said Mother. "My bowl is cracked and the dishcloth is the tail of one of Luke's owd shirts, but you'll hev to excuse all that," and plainly she knew that Luella would, otherwise she would never have let her cross the threshold.

In May that year the weather turned gloriously warm and on my free Saturday I decided to wear my summer "tidy" gown, but it had rotted while laid away and it split when I put it on. So I donned one of my clean working prints and rather morosely set out side by side with Luella, who was wearing a sprigged muslin, light and airy and very pretty. I grumbled a bit and she said,

"Ask Luke to buy some stuff for you next market day, and I'll make you a dress just like this. You need six yards, and three yards of ribbon. You should have a cherry colour. We could sew in the evenings and have it ready for the next outing."

"We shouldn't be able to collect the stuff till then," I said, still depressed over the split dress.

"Don't be so silly. Luke could bring it up, couldn't he? Or you could walk down to fetch it. It's light till nine."

The gulf between us, so often firmly bridged by her friendliness, by the memory of old days, by the hospitality of my home, suddenly yawned. Miss Whymark—I think because she was afraid that servants would *feed* their visitors—had made a rule forbidding relatives and friends to call upon them except in cases of emergency, in which she must first receive the caller and hear the business. As for running home to fetch a parcel . . .

Embarrassed, and more cross then ever, I explained this.

"She really is . . ." said Luella, as always instantly understanding. "Well, all right. I'll fetch it for you. After all in my last post I had a free day each week."

Luke, of course, willingly accepted the errand, but when we explained about Luella coming to fetch it, alone, on the evening of market day, I saw something happen to his face. And I thought to myself, Yes . . . like everybody else he has fallen in love with her, or maybe he has been all along. It was natural, perhaps inevitable. But I was filled with foreboding.

That deepened when, about ten days later, as we were putting the final stitches to the new dress in the last light of a lovely, lingering summer evening, Luella said,

"There, Deb, it's lovely and you'll look lovely in it. And I promised Luke that you'd ask for permission and we'd go to the Fair with him."

"The Midsummer Fair!" I said aghast. If there was one person in our district more averse, more opposed to the two fairs that took place, one at midsummer and one at the end of harvest, than Miss Whymark herself was, it was my brother Luke.

"Yes, the Midsummer Fair," said Luella, biting off her cotton.

"But Luke . . ." I began and stopped. No point in letting her know how completely off his head she had driven him. It must be that; nothing else would explain this sudden change of front. "Luke doesn't realise," I said. "Miss Whymark never allows anyone to go to the fairs."

"But I promised. I never have seen a real old country fair. But I've heard about them. Deborah, they still have *mummers,* simple little plays done in mime, just like the mediaeval days . . . now, in the eighteenth century. Did you know *that?* And climbing greasy poles to win a pig, and prizes for making the ugliest face through a horse collar. . . . All the old things that have amused people for hundreds of years; and all dying out except in remote places like this. Deborah, I would love to see it."

"Well *you* can. I can't. That is one of Miss Whymark's rules. No fairgoing. You see, there is another side to it. People go wild and get drunk and very mediaeval indeed. They reckon that two thirds of the bastards in the villages around . . ."

"Deborah, there are people who go blind because they read too much, people who die of over-eating and over-drinking. The world is full of fools."

"I am just trying to explain how Miss Whymark sees it."

"And I am trying to explain how *I* see it. Look, I'll ask her for us both. I did promise Luke."

"But it isn't a thing that decent people . . . Oh, Luella, how can I explain. It's all so outdated. Poor, rough people stick to the old things, they don't know any better . . . but the others move on." Was Luke, my dear brother, so serious, so ambitious, really one of the "poor rough people," or had Luella's desire to see the mummers persuaded him?

Suddenly it came to me that I was worrying myself unduly. Six years under Miss Whymark's inflexible rule now enabled me to say, quite light-heartedly,

"This isn't for us to decide, Luella. You ask Miss Whymark." Stupid old woman, she betrayed me! She couldn't, she said, permit me to go, because that would create a precedent of which the other servants would take advantage. But she was sympathetic . . . mark that . . . sympathetic with Luella's desire to see the mummers, and if she was *sure* of a reliable escort . . .

"I wouldn't have credited it," I said when Luella told me.

"She even asked me, since I *was* going, to take note of the prices of cheesecloth and knitting needles. She wrote the Baildon prices down and if the Fair ones . . . Deb, what is the matter? Why are you looking at me like that?"

"I've just thought of something else, Luella. You see . . ."

The thing I had to say seemed to choke me.

"Well?"

"You see . . . when a girl goes, by herself, to this particular fair, with a man, it's supposed to be a sign . . ."

I still couldn't say it. Luke so simple, unable to read or write, dear to me, oh, very dear to me, a good man, but for all that, with his muddy boots, sweaty shirt, hard hands, not to be thought of . . . a cat may *look* at a king but . . .

"A sign of what?" asked Luella crisply.

"Special favour," I gulped out. "You see . . . lots of country men are shy, they can't say things. So to make it easy for them there are these old customs. And the Midsummer Fair . . . it's easier for them to say, 'Come to the Fair' than 'Will you marry me?' But it means the same."

"Deborah, really. I never heard anything so entirely old-fashioned! It's just a spectacle, something to look at. And Luke didn't ask me alone . . . we were both supposed to go. Practically his last words to me when we parted were joking ones about minding to have this dress ready for you. And it is; and you shall go. I shall ask her ladyship . . ."

"Luella, please! If you did that Miss Whymark would make my life a misery for months. She'd take it as a direct insult and never rest till she'd . . . why, she might even give me the sack. Even if you did ask and got permission, I simply dare not go."

"This really is a very difficult household," said Luella. "I had set my heart on going, and I promised Luke."

"I'm not preventing you. I'm just pointing out what it means."

"Luke has more sense. Still . . ." She broke off and brooded for a moment, winding a strand of hair about her finger. "You may be right. But there's so little time now. If we could catch Lantern we could send Luke a note."

"Luella, you know he can't read!"

"Well, he said he would wait for us at the end of the avenue at ten o'clock. One of us must run down and explain. I don't trust Lantern to deliver a verbal message."

"There again," I said, "I can't go galloping off at ten . . ."

"Very well, then, I will."

She set off next morning just before ten, wearing her working dress and no hat. I lingered over my work in the schoolroom, wishful to hear how Luke had taken the disappointment. She didn't come back. Presently the children had finished the tasks she had set them and I took them out for a long walk, starting off along the avenue. There was no sign of her. It was a perfect day for the Fair, warm and sunny with a little brushing breeze.

She came back at dusk. Her peculiarly white skin was powdered with freckles across the nose and brow, her hair was a tangled froth of curls, and out of their hollows, deepened and darkened by fatigue, her green eyes shone like water. She was laden with fairings; a pair of fine white stockings for me to wear with my new dress, wooden dolls with painted faces for Miss Julia and Miss Arabella, a monkey on a stick for Master Billy. She had even remembered Miss Whymark's needles and a great roll of cheesecloth. And she had a wonderful time—a perfect day, she called it.

I had saved some oatcake and a glass of milk from the schoolroom supper and she settled down to it, talking all the time. "I really shouldn't need any food at all. Luke and I have been eating and drinking most of the day. But I am hungry. Oh, I must tell you about the plays. Deborah, you would have loved them; they were enchanting . . ." She rattled on while I lighted the candles. Then, as she tilted her head to drink her milk, the heavy tangled hair swung backwards and I saw something glitter in her ears.

"Did you get a fairing, too?" I asked.

"Oh, yes, these . . ." She loosened the earbobs and laid them in my hand; little daisies with petals made of silver and a scrap of yellow stone for centres. "Aren't they *pretty?* The prettiest on the booth. Luke gave me them. And I gave him a wonderful pocketknife. . . ."

So now, by all the traditions of our countryside, the wordless proposal had been made and accepted, and Luke had every right to regard her as his pledged sweetheart.

But that was too absurd even for me to say aloud.

X

Nevertheless, on our June free day, which came round soon after, I could detect a subtle change both in Mother and Luke. That was not really so surprising. To people of leisure and education it might seem strange to build any permanent plans upon the foundation of four or five visits and an outing; but for working folk that was the way. With free time so scanty and distances—on foot—so great, the business of court-ship must be reduced to the minimum, and rely largely on symbols. I'd known many girls get married on the strength of an invitation to Sun-day dinner and two or three subsequent walks.

It was not that Luke made any open display of feeling, he was not the kind to do that; but his eye dwelt upon Luella with a possessiveness that was new; and when, in the evening, I remembered that it was time to call for the new shoes which Farrow the cobbler was making for me, he was not slow to say, "Then if you start out a bit afore us and Luella and me walk the field way and take it easy, you'll just about get there together."

"We'll wait for you, Deb," said Luella. "At Vinefields Bottom, you know, where the pony once threw me off into the mud."

Such references to our childhood days were often on her tongue and, hearing this one, I wondered whether she realised that those days had gone, that we were not children any more, that walking with a young man through the fields, on a June evening, might have some significance. I pondered the matter all the way to Goose Lane. I told myself reasonably that there would be nothing so startlingly strange, so fundamentally in-congruous in her falling in love with Luke. He was very handsome then; the long-suffering, saintly look had disappeared, his face had hardened and now wore an expression of resolute intent which, if it were baulked, as Father's had been, might deteriorate into the same surliness. He was ambitious, too, and seemed, so far, to be lucky in all his dealings. He would make a good husband . . . for some girl. . . . But, perhaps because I had so chancily attained the state myself, and had been so hard put to it to maintain my hold, I did set a disproportionate value on being able to read and write, on the wider interests, the ability to take impersonal views, to converse as opposed to making flat statements. I knew that for myself I could never contemplate marriage with an ignorant man, and therefore it was highly unlikely that I should ever find a husband, and I knew that compared with Luella I was ignorant indeed.

But then I had never been in love. Was Luella?

July and August passed all too quickly, as they always did, as May and June had done. Soon winter, with the mud and the biting wind and the early dark, would be upon us again.

In July Mr. Roger came home, for the Parliament gentlemen had all gone to their country homes to overlook their harvests. He told Luella, who told me, that he had gained a hearing from one or two influential people and "planted a seed here and there." Her ladyship seemed pleased to see him again, and had evidently decided to treat his activities as a form of unimportant sickness from which he was almost recovered and which need not be mentioned any more.

The corn ripened and harvest began and soon everyone was thinking about the horkey, the high light of the Merravay year.

As was their custom her ladyship and Mr. Whymark went to stay with his sister, Lady Whardale, in Leicestershire, leaving home a week or ten days before the Feast. They had made a point of being absent just then ever since the two fields were turned into parkland, for at the horkey Miss Whymark always made a speech at the table and that year she had been tactlessly blunt in her remarks about how the founder of the feast would have felt about the innovation. Her ladyship, younger then, and more impetuous, had jumped up and protested and there had been a scene.

This particular horkey was entirely a Whymark festival, Miss Whymark's festival. Some money had been left by the old lady and just for once in the year Miss Whymark spent lavishly; she had even been known to contribute a little of her own money in a year when prices were high. In fact any careful observer—as I, in my necessarily limited way, was—might observe a change come over Miss Whymark the moment that the master and mistress drove away. During the fortnight of her undisputed reign she was less carping, more genial; partly it was excitement over the feast and partly, I think, a kind of endeavour to cast blame for the unpleasant atmosphere usual in the house upon the absent Lady Rosemary. And relief may have had something to do with it, too.

Two days before the event, when we were already beginning to bake and boil, and clear the centre of the great barn where the long table was set out, Mr. Armitage arrived.

Her ladyship had written to him earlier in the year, cancelling the ambitious plans for the new front in a mood of angry despair. Later her spirit had revived and suggestions for the extra rooms and some modification of the frontage had been made, and she had written again, asking the architect to pay another visit. Perhaps he was annoyed, or wished to assert his independence, for since then nothing more had been said or done. Now here he was and her ladyship was in Leicestershire.

Miss Whymark was not so busy with her plans as to forget that she was opposed to any alterations to the house But she did not make the obvious move of sending away the young man who had come to make plans for its alterations. On the contrary she set herself to woo him. She insisted that he stay, she lodged him and fed him well, and several times during the next day or two she dragged herself away from her delightful preparations to walk about and talk to him. Once when I went to find her and ask something I heard her telling him what Mr. Kent had said about the house. There was no doubt that she was a wily and forceful old woman . . . probably not above a little bribery; it was quite possible that her ladyship might return to find that Mr. Armitage had deserted the cause.

There came the day when the last load of corn, decorated with ribbons and boughs and flowers and topped by "The Maiden," was dragged into the stackyard; and another year's harvest was safely in. The first cask of ale was broached and then the labourers went to their homes, whence they would return, washed and reclad, accompanied by their womenfolk, to sit down at six o'clock to partake of the hospitality of a woman long dead.

The meal lasted for a long time, for these were guests who did not, every day eat their fill and Miss Whymark had provided nobly, with succulent cold roast sirloin, hams, pork pies, and pasties, with pickles and sauces, tarts and jellies, cakes, biscuits and sweetmeats, all washed down with ale in plenty, and tea and homemade lemonade. This year as usual she made her little speech, glorifying her grandmother's memory. She could say, "Those of you are old enough to remember with me . . ." in a very moving way which set the older people nodding their heads and thinking sentimentally of days which seemed golden in retrospect, not because of old Mistress Whymark's goodness and kindness but because they themselves were young then, and more vigorous, more hopeful. This year Miss Whymark struck what was, for those of us who understood the situation, a very topical note.

"We meet here, every year, to remember, to look back. It is a custom, an *old* custom, and none the worse for that. There are those in this world" —she looked directly at Mr. Armitage—"who do not fully realise the value of the old, the tried, the proved. There are those who cannot see that there are some things so old that they are nearly holy. . . ." She went on at some length, and a great gloom descended upon the company, who, hearing the trend of the speech and missing, perforce, its point, began to wonder what it boded. Later on I heard speculations voiced; was this the last horkey? Was everybody over fifty going to be sacked? Was Miss Whymark going to retire?

When she ended her speech and the applause had died down, Mr. Armitage, quite uninvited, rose to his feet.

"Madam," he said, "you have entertained me royally, and your speech has given me a great deal to think about. May I, in return, attempt to entertain you? I cannot, alas, sing for my supper like the boy in the nursery rhyme, but I can . . . Ah, I'll start with Master William Whymark. He looks a nice little boy, doesn't he; I believe his book says that he is a nice little boy; I am astonished to find him so greedy! What can he be doing with this and this and this."

Quick as light, from Master Billy's ear, from the back of his collar, from his curly topknot of hair, he produced an orange, a mince pie, and four sugar plums.

Before the laughter had died down, and while the children still stared, wide-eyed, he turned to Miss Whymark.

"I'm practically a stranger here, but I have seen, in a short time, that yours is a hard task, madam," he said dolefully. "You have all these rapacious, wasteful creatures to look after. Let me see if I can help you a little. Is that of use?" He took a candle out of her cap, another from her fichu, an egg from her elbow, two sausages from between her shoulder blades. The slight edge on his words delighted the company, everyone of whom had, at some time, suffered under Miss Whymark's parsimony. She was flustered, and astonished, but true to her character; as he juggled with the egg she called out, "Be careful; be careful." And then the mirth was unrestrained.

Through it, he said to Parker, "We know you are careful of the silver, but must you carry it on your person?" From Parker's pocket he drew four silver spoons.

When he had finished he sat down, not in his old place but next to Luella, near enough for me to hear him say,

"That went well didn't it? Was I word perfect?"

"You were *wonderful*," she said, "you remembered every tiny thing. And how you could, and do the juggling as well . . ." So she had pointed out the idiosyncrasies upon whose frank, but not unkindly, mention so much of the success had depended. Mr. Armitage looked at her approvingly, and settled down with a smoothed, pleased look; he evidently liked being told that he was wonderful. Luella had done it again.

Then there was the dancing, with old Mortlock and Young Lantern playing their fiddles and Miss Whymark stepping stiffly out, first with Parker, and then with the bailiff and two or three more in strict order of seniority. A few old people stood, or sat aside remembering with discomfort the implied threat of possible changes to come, and picking their teeth. The young ones romped through the ancient dances and the presence of Mr. Roger, Mr. Armitage, and Luella added to the extra merry mood which the juggling display had begun.

Luella romped like a child, completely unself-conscious, utterly given over to the process of enjoying herself. Once, and not so long ago, I should have done the same; now I derived more pleasure from watching. And amongst the things I saw that evening, and marked and remembered, was the expression on Miss Sophie's face as Luella, one arm linked in Mr. Armitage's, the other in the clean-smocked shepherd's, rollicked through the movements of "Three Meet." Envy, admiration, wistfulness, wonderment, they were all there.

A fortnight later, when Mr. Armitage had gone his way and the master and mistress were home again and the chestnuts—always the first to hope or despair—were showing some lemon-yellow leaves, everyone was surprised that Miss Sophie, returning from one of her solitary rides, announced that she was going to marry Sir Frederick Fennel "very soon." I was not surprised. I knew the exact moment when she had made that decision. For I also, in moments when my lack of certain things has been borne in me, have thought—Ah, but this, and this, I have and may be sure of!

The engagement—Miss Sophie's grasping at the one thing she could be sure of—pleased everyone; and several people, recovering from their surprise, claimed credit for bringing it about. Her ladyship held that it had been her stern treatment which had resulted in the change of mind— the thought of the dull home-keeping winter had brought the silly child to her senses. Mr. Whymark said that he had always been of the opinion that so long as the girl wasn't pressed or bullied nature would take its course. Miss Maud said frankly,

"Well, I gave her some advice, based on my own experience. I said, 'Roger will bring a wife home one of these days, and you'll find that living in your brother's house isn't all honey, however kind *he* may be!' That made her think."

The wedding had been arranged for the second week in October. How many people, I wondered, saw the significance of that? Miss Sophie's birthday fell in the following week; she would be twenty-two. She would be married before she was twenty-two. In her present mood that mattered.

It mattered to me, too; for I lost my September Saturday because there was so much to do, cleaning the house and making ready for the Whardales, who must, of course, come to the wedding and must stay at Merravay. And if I had ever yearned and longed to go home for any reason but sheer homesickness, it was just then.

For when I went home with Luella on the August Saturday, Mother had said, "You girls must fend for yourselves today. Mr. Loveridge, across at Squirrels, stuck a fork through his foot day afore yesterday, and I'm seeing to the brews and plasters." She was very busy and important, and sure of her skill in cures; she said he would mend.

But in little more than a week Jack Lantern, who brought us the village news, told us that Mr. Loveridge was dead. I felt, on the verge of my mind, sorry for his wife, a town-bred woman and helpless, and his six-year-old son; but they would be all right, in a way; for Squirrels was their freehold and known as a splendid farm. It would sell easily. Another week passed and Jack Lantern, not without a trace of awe in his voice, said to me one morning, "So that brother of yours has took over Squirrels! Well, to be sure, some people get on in this world!"

My curiosity swelled like a boil, and one day when Luella told me that she was going into Baildon with Miss Sophie to buy materials and engage the services of the best local sempstress to help with the dresses, I said, "Luella, please make some excuse and stop at the farm and ask what this is all about."

She came home with quite a story. Mrs. Loveridge hadn't had complete faith in Mother's remedies and had called in the doctor, who had made mock, in a pleasant way, of the plaster of dock leaves and iris roots which she had applied, and he had taken it off and put on his own. According to Mother, Mr. Loveridge's foot had started to rot from that moment and he died. The widow immediately veered round and was full of remorse and kept saying that if only she had trusted Mother. . . . Then Luke had looked after the business of getting her harvest in, as he would have done, as a matter of course, for any neighbour in similar plight and so she felt kindly towards him. And she didn't want to stay on the farm herself; nor did she want to sell it, because there had been Loveridges at Squirrels since the beginning of time. And the upshot of it all was that she had agreed to let the farm to Luke on a ten-year lease, on condition that when her boy was fourteen Luke would take and teach him to run it, and that he would not cut down the rose that sprawled over the house front, or the lilacs which Mr. Loveridge had planted to screen the privy.

Squirrels had always been well handled and the land was in good heart; such a farm was very rarely for hire, and in getting a lease on it Luke had had a piece of luck that fell to no more than one in a thousand.

Luella had had no time to gather details, and I did not know then that Mrs. Loveridge, despite her distress and her sentiment, had fixed a rent which, if Luke worked twenty-four hours a day, kept his health, and met with nothing but good fortune, might still leave him a small margin of profit.

During the next week—the one before the wedding—I heard from Jack Lantern that Luke had already found a tenant for our old house, but was going to keep the land. The tenant was a cousin of Farrow the boot-maker, a Kersey weaver whose lungs had weakened; he wanted the house, the orchard, and a shed or two where he could keep a goat and a few chickens to eke out what he could earn by field labour in good weather when he felt able.

To hear all this in bits and pieces was very irksome, and as soon as the wedding was over and the house guests gone I asked Miss Whymark if I might run home for an hour one evening.

Luke was out and Mother was alone in the middle of her packing and sorting, muddled, distracted, but happier than I'd ever seen her in my life. Despite the fact that the light was failing and I had but a short time to stay, she loaded me with bundles and baskets and hurried me off, across our orchard, through a gap in the hedge, and over the meadow that divided the two houses. A well-defined track showed me how often she had come and gone that way during the last few weeks. She talked in-cessantly, breathlessly, as we scampered along.

Squirrels was a good big solid old house, with one or two panelled rooms and a multitude of cupboards.

"Now this is what I call a farmhouse!" said Mother with deep satis-faction. "It's like the one I was born in. Ah, I give up a bit when I mar-ried your poor father! But then I thought and hoped he'd get on; and why he never did is a mystery; he worked hard enough. Still . . . And to think that I can get out my bits of brass and copper that my granny give me that've been in a box under my bed all these years and never had room to set out. Oh, I'll hev a nice kitchen again! Now come and see what'll be the parlour."

We stood in the thickening twilight in the big square room. It had two windows and the red rose, which must not be cut, grew all about them, with a belated bud or two close to the panes.

"You know, Deb," said Mother in a less excited voice, "I never said a word, but I hev worrited myself of late. I could remember how I felt once the first glow had wore off and there I was, with that place in the passage where you knock your head twenty times a day, and nothing but pegs on the doors for your clothes. Well, that just show, no sense in worriting. Things kind of work round, if you wait. And Luella'll hardly know she ain't at Merravay, once this is set out. . . ."

The chilly little wind of the autumn night moved in the rosebush and set the buds tapping against the window.

"You seem . . ." I began, and stopped. "Isn't a bit soon to take for granted that Luella——? Or do you know something that I don't?"

"Well, bless my soul! Nought's been *said*, at least to me, but surely we all know. Why, she went with him to the Midsummer and everything. And look how they carry on, laughing and skylarking about. What could be plainer? And him talking about buying a *carpet!*"

What could be plainer?

The wind was in the big chimney now, making a plaintive sound; and the buds, the last, too-late buds tapped at the glass, as though asking for shelter.

"I don't know," I said. "Sometimes . . ." But what could I say?

Mother suddenly laughed with just a hint of mischief.

"I know what ails you, my girl. You're just a thought jealous. You marnt be that, now. Your turn'll come."

I was spared having to answer that because she suddenly clapped her hand to her mouth.

"Dog's nails! I left a beef pudding in the copper. It'll hev boiled dry and that boy ain't had a proper meal since the day afore yesterday. We must get back. You can see the bedrooms another time."

Luke was swilling himself under the pump when we trotted into the yard. He seemed surprised to see me.

"I been wanting to hev a word with you, Deb."

"I mustn't stop now. I'll see you on my day," I said.

"No, I'll come a step with you."

"But you're hungry and the pudding's spoiling."

"That can wait." He picked up his jacket and shrugged himself into it and then called to Mother that he'd be back in ten minutes. I was terrified that he was going to talk about Luella; but he began with a half-shamefaced apology.

"I ought to hev talked it over with you, Deb; but time was short and I knew I'd never get a chance like that again. Now I've got to spend what is yours by rights, as well as my own, stocking the new place; and if you should want to get married I couldn't give you your portion straight out like I allust meant to, see? But you'll be better off in the end. In two or three years' time, if my beasts go ahead like they are doing now, and corn keeps its price, we'll be well-to-do, Deb. Only just now we must sow before we reap, see?"

"That's all right, Luke. I'm not thinking of getting married. You're welcome to use my share for as long as you like. I'm glad you've had the chance. I hope everything goes well with you."

And now don't say anything else; let me go back with my doubts; let me not have to say anything about what is too formless, too uncertain, to be put into words.

I mentioned the meal waiting.

"Just a minute," he said. "That ain't all. I been wanting to talk to you about . . . Luella and me."

Exactly what I had dreaded.

"You see, like I said just now, putting money in afore we can take it out I'm going to be short of *spending* money. It was in my mind to ask her at Christmas. Back in the old place I could've spared a guinea or two to hev things nice. Now that look to me as though we've got the parlour and nothing to put in it. But I don't want her to think I'm shilly-shallying. What d'you think I oughta do, eh, Deb?"

Despite his quietness he was usually so sure, of himself, his plans, his rightness, that this clumsy, hesitating bid for help and direction struck me as horribly pitiful.

"You should talk to her," I said at last.

"Well, I hev tried. But you know, I ain't handy with words and she sort of head me off and go rattling on about something else. She on't be serious."

Deadly serious himself, of course, he was attracted by her apparent lack of seriousness—just as, no doubt, long ago that dour man our father had been attracted by Mother's lightness of heart. Strange how things fell into pattern.

But I knew that Luella could be serious enough when she chose to, and my foreboding deepened with the thought that when she headed him off she did it deliberately.

"I ain't asking she should scrub floors and feed calves. Time we're married I mean to hev hired labour, and if I can't, damn-all-to-Hell, I'll sit up o'nights and do things with these hands. You tell her that, Deb, and tell her thass up to her to say whether we do it Christmas, or wait a bit."

"Damn-all-to-Hell, Luke, d'you know what you're asking? I can't go telling her things like that before we even know whether she wants to marry you or not. Have you ever even made it plain to her that *you* want to marry her?"

"I been more or less courting her since the first day she come back, ain't I? You never see me so much as look at any other female, did you? I took her to the Fair . . ."

"That's just it," I said angrily. "All these silly old customs. A man has a tongue in his head, hasn't he, and could ask a plain question without making such a morris dance."

"Well, a word in season wouldn't cost you nothing, Deb; and it'd clear the way for me a bit," he said, unruffled by my sharpness. "Thass all right for folks that are handy with words; I ain't. I start and get all tied up and then off she go on another tack and I'm lost. You just edge a word in for me, sometime when you're heving a chat. Eh, Deb?"

"I'll see. I think the best thing for you to do is show her the house and everything next time we come, and then ask her. Then you'll know where you are. And Luke . . ."

"Yes, Deb."

"You mustn't . . . I mean, don't count too much, or be too much disappointed. You see . . . nowadays everybody doesn't attach such importance to things like going to a fair."

He laid a heavy hand on my shoulder.

"Hev you got any reason to say that? Any reason to think . . ."

"No. Truthfully, Luke, none at all."

No reason for anything I said, or thought; no reason for feeling cold and empty and sad and sorry for everybody. . . .

Let him ask her and have done; the thing had been on my mind, a vague disquietude ever since the February evening when he had driven us home.

XI

That last Saturday of October was one of those rare lovely autumn days; it began with a mist like a bloom on a grape and opened out to a noon of marigold yellow and closed with an evening of hyacinth blue, full of the scent of apples and burning leaves. Luke wasn't home when we arrived; he had gone to one of the farm sales, of which there were always plenty round about at that time of year. Mother, Luella, and I spent the afternoon moving the last few things across from our little old house into the new one. I was glad to be so busy, for I was as nervous as though I were the one who was to make the proposal, or to receive it. For one thing I was terrified lest Mother should say something tactless and premature to Luella; but I wronged her there. Luella of course, threw herself into the moving, the rearranging, the admiration of the rooms, with exactly the enthusiasm which she would have shown over a dolls' house which two children had just acquired.

At dusk Luke came home, pleased with his purchases. He was wearing his market clothes, buff breeches and a bright blue coat with brass buttons. He looked extremely handsome, solid, reliable, and genial.

We sat down and ate the first meal that Mother had cooked in that kitchen. When it was over I saw Luke look at me and tighten his mouth.

"I reckon you've seen the house, Luella. I want you to see the barn. Mrs. Loveridge said 'twas a thousand years owd and used to be the main house. 'Sbig as a church." He lighted two lanterns and led Luella away.

Mother and I washed the dishes. Then we polished and set out the cherished pieces of brass and copper ware.

"And there's another thing," said Mother suddenly. "There's room for *me* here. I allust wondered whether the time'd come when Luella might feel about me the way I did about your great-aunt Hester. Not that I *grutched* her houseroom, poor soul, but she did fare to be allust underfoot. That on't be so here. So long as I'm useful I can busy myself, and when I'm useless there's room for me to be out of sight and out of mind."

"I hope that time is a long way ahead," I said. I wondered what was happening in the barn.

After what seemed a long time they came in. My first thought was that Luke had baulked his fence, for he did not look like a man whose suit had been accepted, or rejected; and Luella, very white and small-faced, looked even less like a girl who had been proposed to. For one demented moment I thought that she had expected Luke to speak and been disappointed when he didn't.

They admired our handiwork, and we all ate plum cake and drank a glass of elderberry wine. Then Luella said,

"It's a nice night, Luke, and the horse has been out today, so we'll walk home."

"Right you are," he said. "I'll walk with you to the avenue at least."

"But you're tired, too."

"A bit of a walk on't hurt me," he said. Voice, manner, everything, just as usual. Just as usual his leave-taking with his mention of seeing us next month "or maybe afore."

We began to walk through the deeper darkness of the avenue, through the light brittle fallen leaves, which gave off a dry autumnal scent. Luella walked in silence and I was just about to say some trivial thing when she said,

"Luke just asked me to marry him."

"I'm not exactly surprised," I said; though I was surprised to know that he had done it after all. "Well?"

"I didn't know what to say." Her voice sounded far away, lost. "It's very difficult, Deborah. Marriage is such a *final* thing . . ."

"That, I should imagine, is what people in love like about it."

"In love . . . when you're all dazed and dazzled, when you're not yourself at all. In that state you have to make a decision that affects your whole life, everything you do, and have, and are, from that moment on. It's a frightening thought, Deb."

"Yes; I suppose it must be." But what did you say to him? Tell me, without my having to ask.

"You look round," she went on in that remote voice, "and what do you see? Most people would say they married for love . . . and they end like the Whymarks. I'm inclined to think that the more you follow your heart the worse you feel when you wake up one morning and find that it misled you."

"I think you're unduly cynical, Luella. Is that bound to happen?"

"I think that love—not the kind part, the friendliness and the working together; they last—but this thinking that the sun rises and sets with the one person, and the . . . the physical part, that *is* bound to wear off. Time alone would . . ."

"What did you say to Luke?"

"Almost exactly what any well-reared young woman is told to say in the circumstances." She gave a sudden laugh, harsh, almost hysterical. "That I wasn't sure—and that, God knows, is true—that I must have time to think. Straight out of the book, Deb, word for word."

Well, that suited Luke exactly; no wonder he'd looked so calm. My spirits rose a little. This seemed an apt moment to say my few words. And since he had come into the open himself it would do no harm to mention my certainty that he would make her a good husband, and was utterly devoted to her.

"I know. I know. Anyway, if I do marry him, I shouldn't mind the work. I should delight in it. And I could help in other ways—read the papers for him, and do accounts, for he'll end with a bigger business than he can keep in his head, smart as he is in his quiet way . . ."

"Luella, you *are* in love with him!"

"Yes. Oh yes, I am. At least I have this. . . . Oh, Deb, you'd never understand. In some ways you're still such a child; you have never . . . I mean all your ideas are out of a storybook. Fall in love and live happily ever after. Dear Deb, I hope *you* will. You might. You *are* single-minded!"

"You're not." It was half question, half statement. "Luke is," I added, as she did not answer.

"I know. And they're the ones who get their way in the end."

"In this case, I truly hope so."

"Thank you, Deb. That was a pretty speech!" She laughed in the old light-hearted fashion, thrust her arm through mine, and, saying that it was turning cold, hurried me towards the house at such a pace that further speech was impossible.

I felt quite gay too. I believed that she was being a little coy and shy and girlish.

Early in November somebody got up and made a speech in Parliament about the slave trade and its iniquities; and then the papers took up the subject and printed some articles and dozens of letters. Mr. Roger's name was mentioned several times. My turn to study the papers would not arrive for two or three weeks, but I heard all about it from Luella. Her ladyship, faced with the fact that what she had determined to regard as a foible, a bit of child's play, was being seriously discussed in London, reverted to her earlier attitude, and tears and angry recriminations became an everyday occurrence. At the end of the week Mr. Roger went to stay at Ockley with Miss Sophie, who, as soon as the wedding ring was on her finger, had proceeded to take a subtle revenge on her mother. It was a simple one, too; it consisted of charming, affectionate behaviour to everyone else and cold, flat, formal behaviour to her ladyship. A typical example was one morning when she arrived, carrying an enormous bunch of lilies, the like of which I—or indeed many people in England—had never seen before. They were shaped like the white ones which fill cottage gardens in June, but they were pale rose-pink in colour and splashed with purple at the heart. And this was November. At Ockley they had hothouses.

"Sophie, how beautiful!" said her ladyship.

"They are pretty," said Lady Fennel coolly. "They're for Aunt Maud, for the church."

"I'm afraid the cold will kill them," said her ladyship after just a second's recoil.

"If they can survive here. . . ." Lady Fennel shivered inside her furs. "This room is like an icehouse. How poor Deborah can sew at all! No wonder she has chilblains. Have they started this year yet, Deborah?"

"Ockley is too warm," said her ladyship. "And that is why, in my opinion, Freddie takes cold so easily. Such a pity! I always think a man with a heavy cold . . ." she made a grimace of disgust.

With things on such a footing between them it was natural enough that Lady Fennel should now take sympathetic interest in her brother's cause.

On the last Saturday of November I had to go home alone. Luella and the children had gone to Ockley for four days. The rector at Ockley was a very old man and fond of old customs; he had revived a winter merrymaking known as a "church ale," a thing which few villages had had since Cromwell's time. There were mummers there, too; and if her ladyship resented the fact that now every member of the family except herself had been invited to Ockley for some special occasion, she gave no sign, merely saying that it was instructive for the children to see things which would be done away with by the time they grew up.

From that visit Luella returned in rather low spirits which I attributed to the cold which she had caught. Ockley was splendid, she said, and Lady Fennel had been more than kind, and the church ale had been most entertaining. But all this I gathered by questioning; the usual rippling enthusiasm was absent.

I passed on to her the invitation which Mother had sent, for her to go home for Christmas, any day, all days, when she was free. I, of course, did not go home at all in December.

"I don't like to go to your home to be merry, Deb, while you have to stay and work," she said. "Anyway I can't begin to think about Christmas yet. This cold and everything . . ."

"Poor Luella," I said. "I believe you should be in bed. You look feverish." I put out my hand to touch her forehead and see. She shrugged away from me.

"You shouldn't hang about me. You'll catch it. I'm all right. I'm better. It's just . . ."

The days moved on and it was the seventeenth of December. The day of the Christmas Market, when they judged the fat bullocks and gave the prizes. After the judging the beast was sold, with butchers competing heartily for it; then it was paraded round the town with the crier going ahead, ringing his bell, calling out the weight of the bullock, the name of the man who had reared it and of the butcher who had bought it. Everybody then ran hotfoot to the butcher's to bespeak a joint of that beef for Christmas, and it was a standing joke that whatever the bullock weighed alive, it weighed two tons dead, since no one was ever disappointed of his order. Joke or no joke, it was a fact that the winner of the first prize put ten pounds into his pocket, sold his animal in a competitive market, and gained himself a reputation as a breeder.

It was one of those days with a hard dry wind when fires burn fiercely, consuming solid logs as though they were paper. Midway through the morning I carried a fresh basket of logs to the schoolroom and just as I reached the door it opened and Mr. Roger, whom I thought to be at Ockley, stepped out.

"Ha . . ." he said, in a manner quite unlike his own. "I hoped I'd see you—er—Deborah. Wanted to wish you a happy Christmas and . . ." he pressed a guinea into my hand and laughed. "To buy a new pen with, bless you!" He patted me on the shoulder and went running downstairs.

The children were not in the schoolroom; Luella was alone, looking so small-faced, so pale and shaken, that I dropped the log basket and ran to her, asking,

"What's the matter? What happened?"

"Nothing. Nothing, Deb." She linked those little white birds' claws hands and moved them up and down in a distracted gesture. "I must get the children in. He told them to run away for a minute and they did so without their coats, in this wind. They'll catch their . . ."

She moved towards the door. I reached out and grabbed a handful of her skirt. I heard my voice, thin and strangling, say,

"What did he want? What did he say to you?"

"Deb . . . I can't. I've hardly . . . later on . . . Deb, please." She put out one hand and pushed mine away with them, then lifted it to her cheek, driving her knuckles against the flesh. Then she was suddenly calm. There was a rustle of silk, a waft of perfume from behind me.

"So you came too," Luella said. I turned.

"I thought it best. Nobody knows better than I how nasty Mamma can be," said Lady Fennel. "Good morning, Deborah."

It was both greeting and dismissal, delivered in the way that gentry are born with. But I didn't move.

"Look, Lu, I think this may be very unpleasant. You'd better come back with me, now."

"I must get the children in."

"Deborah can do that. You come and get some things together. I know, my dear, I saw every sign of storm. Let Roger face it. . . . There, what did I tell you?"

From downstairs there came a wailing scream, and then the sound of commotion; voices, doors slamming.

"I've had enough scenes to last me the rest of my life," said Lady Fennel coldly. "I'm having no part in this one. I came to spare you. Come along." She took Luella quite roughly by the elbow and begun to hustle her out of the schoolroom. I caught her by the other arm,

"He asked you . . . and you . . . ?" I knew, of course, but I wanted her to tell me. To my surprise she gripped my hand and used it to steady herself against the impetus of Lady Fennel's pull.

"Wait a moment, Sophie. I can't just run away like this. I haven't committed a crime! Yes, Deb. Mr. Roger Whymark has asked me to marry him and I have said I will do so."

"That is all I wanted to know," I said. "I hope you'll be as happy as you deserve."

"And Mamma," said Lady Fennel, "is going to call you ugly names and derive great pleasure in ordering you from the house. You're a fool, Lu."

"I know."

"And you're shaking with fright. Mamma will come screaming at you and you'll fall in a fit, that's what you'll do."

"I am not frightened. Why should I be? I am worried about those children. If you, Deborah, would be so good as to go and look for them, I could stay here in case her ladyship should wish to speak to me; otherwise I must go myself."

"I'll go," I said, and went to push past them as they stood in the doorway.

"I still think . . ." Lady Fennel began again.

The children when I found them were wearing their coats and hoods, and because I wanted a little time to think, and thought that they would be as well out of the house for a while, I took them for a long walk along the edge of Layer Wood where we were sheltered from the wind. So I missed what was, by all accounts, the most spectacular and noisy scene ever to take place in Merravay.

When we got back the house had the air of having been battered into silence. Her ladyship had taken to her bed; Miss Whymark had taken refuge in her accounts; Miss Maud had gone to the Rectory with her story, and since Luella was nowhere about and her brush and comb and a few other things were gone from her room I gathered that she had, after all, gone to Ockley. Mr. Roger was still in the house, waiting for Mr. Whymark's return from the Fat Stock judging. And of course rumour and counter-rumour had the house by the ears. They even said that her ladyship at one point had thrown a vase at Miss Whymark, who was taking Luella's part . . .

I should have found it all very interesting and very amusing—if it hadn't been for Luke.

I should have thought it very right and proper, highly suitable—if it hadn't been for Luke.

I should have regarded it as highly romantic, especially as Luella had such strong feelings about Merravay—if it hadn't been for Luke.

But there it was. My dear, serious-minded, single-minded Luke had been jilted—there was no other word for it—and I honestly felt worse than if I had been jilted myself.

At intervals all through the afternoon I had thought about how he would take the news and every time I felt as though someone had kicked me in the stomach.

And there was Jack Lantern, about to go home, carrying the news; and Miss Maud even now telling the story at the Rectory. I couldn't leave Luke to hear it from the lips of a casual gossip.

At seven o'clock I put the puzzled children to bed and then I did what I had never done before, walked away on a working day without asking leave. Whom could I ask, anyway—go to Mr. Roger, reading in the library, and say, "I must go and tell my brother that you're going to marry the woman who for the last seven weeks has been making up her mind to marry him?" Look him in the eye and say, "You be careful! She's in love with Luke Fulger; she's marrying you for another reason; she doesn't believe in love because it wears out." All so true, so reasonable . . . and too fantastic to consider for more than a moment.

I battled against the wind all the way home; and there was Mother alone.

"Luke meant to go to Baildon, but he heard of a sale—a man died over at Minsham and he thought he might pick up a few things cheap. And what brought you, my dear?"

As she asked the question she opened the door of the oven and took out a loaf of currant bread, whose readiness for withdrawal from the oven she tested by turning it over and rapping its bottom with her knuckles and then holding it to her ear to listen to its response.

"It's done," she said, and busied herself. The scent of hot bread was for once not appetising to me.

Presently we heard the creak and rumble of wheels.

"Ah, so he got a wagon. He took just the horse, in case."

He'd got the wagon. He was pleased. He came in. He ate great helpings of the mutton and apple pie—ordinarily almost my favourite dish. Tonight I couldn't look at it, though I had had nothing to eat since breakfast. I felt like a hangman watching a condemned man take his last meal. And then I felt I was exaggerating; and I wished I'd been in love myself and had some other standard than books to judge by; and I wished that Mr. Roger had died in Virginia, or on the high seas; and I wished that Luella had never come back. And I wished, almost most of all, that it hadn't fallen to me to break this bit of news.

Most of the time we were talking about Christmas and finally, when Luke had eaten his fill, he got to his feet, took a candle in hand, and said to me,

"You come here a minnit, Deb."

He led the way into the cold, almost unfurnished parlour. On the old table that used to be Aunt Hester's there were two parcels.

"Thass for you, with my best wishes," he said, pointing to one of them. It was a cloak, grey and smooth and fine, a lovely cloak, lined with red. Choking, sick, I thanked him and did what he was obviously yearning for me to do, looked at the other, smaller parcel.

A little fur tippet. Small, but so smooth and light and silky that I could see that it was the best of its kind . . . even her ladyship, though she had bigger and more, had no better.

He took it up in his great brown work-scarred hands.

"She'll like that. I did what you said, Deb, and asked her straight out like and she ain't in no hurry; so, seeing's I got time to get carpets and such like, I reckoned I could get her a pretty present. . . . And that is pretty, ain't it?"

And if I cry now, just cry and run away without saying a word as I long to do . . . he'll be like Mother and think I'm jealous! Oh God, what did I ever do that You should bring me to such a pass?

"It's lovely, Luke. Lovely. Fit for a queen. You have the best of taste. But my cloak is even better. It'll last me a lifetime. Oh Luke . . ." I leaned against him. "I am grateful . . . and I do love you. . . ."

"Why, Deb," he said, "there ain't no need to carry on that way about a little owd Christmas present. Tell you what, you put it on now. I'd'a kept the horse hitched if I'd known you was here. S'nasty owd night."

"The wind was against me coming. It'll blow me home. I will wear the cloak, Luke, and I'll be proof against anything. Will you come a step or two with me?"

We stepped out into the tearing wind, turned the corner of the house into a sudden calm, and stopped to gather our breath. And then, like a surgeon who must inflict agony and can best show mercy by being swift, I laid hold of his arm and said,

"Luke, I came to tell you. Luella is going to marry Mr. Roger."

He said nothing. His arm went stiff under my hand and I heard the breath go out of him. Presently I heard my own desperate voice explaining, consoling; and then we were at our yard gate, across the road in the teeth of the wind again, under the lighted window of The Evening Star, in by the way that the coach passengers used, into a warm, blazingly bright room; still with my hand stiff on his stiff arm; and still he said no word.

In the bright room, loud with voices, confusingly full of men, I turned and looked at Luke. The wind-whipped red was still in his cheeks, but all round his mouth and the root of his nose there was a white shadow as though a chalky finger had brushed him. And his eyes were blank, stunned.

A man . . . landlord? . . . wearing an apron, bald, holding a ladle, came bustling about.

"Well, if it isn't Mr. Fulger himself. Just talking about you. Congratulations, I'm sure. Mr. Everton, sir . . ."

Another man, red-faced, beefy, thumping Luke's wooden shoulder, shaking his wooden hand. Congratulations indeed. Thirty years in the cattle trade, never seen, never hoped to see, a better beast than the one which had just won Luke the Fat Stock Christmas Prize.

"And what shall it be, sir? On the house, I insist. This is a great day for Nettleton. We're pleased and proud indeed."

Ha, I thought . . . Luke is an up and coming man who has just taken over a big farm and never set foot in this place before. But it was possible that they were pleased . . .

"Brandy," Luke said, breaking the silence at last.

"And the young lady. Will she partake on this great occasion?"

"Brandy," Luke said again.

I put on a false, gay, rallying voice. "Luke, you forget. The news must have stunned you. I will take a small glass of Madeira, if you please."

I might have been thrust into a place where no lady should be, but I would show them I knew what a lady might drink. And though to mention being stunned by news was so cruel that I flinched as I said it, it was sensible, too. It offered some excuse for the way he was behaving.

"But you must have known there wasn't a beast to touch it," said Mr. Everton. "Why, alongside yours the rest all looked like Pharaoh's lean kine. . . ." Somebody asked facetiously what breed that was; somebody else said well, be fair, the second-prize winner had beef on him too; somebody took Luke's glass away and gave another, full. When he had drunk that he drew a long deep breath.

"I clean forgot the bullock, Deb. Little owd Weaver took it in for me and I got thinking about the sale; then my supper and then . . . Clean forgot."

"You've got that sort of a mind, Luke. And if you'll think steady about the next thing and never look back, you'll be all right."

Then they were surging about him again, asking him questions, refilling his glass. Every minute took us one pace away from the dreadful thing; so I waited, patiently, though I would not let anyone fill my glass again.

The wag-on-the-wall clock over the fire jerked along to nine.

"I must go," I said. "I shall be locked out."

"It isn't every day you have a thing like this to celebrate," said the land-lord.

"She's right though. Must be getting along."

"We'll hope to see you again, Mr. Fulger."

"Aye, and afore long," Luke said.

The moon had risen and rose high, with wind-driven clouds scudding across her face, so that moments of pitch darkness were followed by moments of brilliant, unreal light. Once the lights of The Evening Star were behind us we might have been in the middle of the desert; it was not a night to tempt anyone abroad and in winter the village people went to bed early to save fuel.

Luke and I walked in silence; that and the rushing wind, the fact that the one glass of wine in my empty stomach had seemed to affect my weight, and the confusing alternations of light and dark made everything seem unreal and dreamlike. Wake up and think—What a hateful dream, thank God it isn't true!

Then all at once I heard the sound of a horse's hoofbeats. We were then on the stretch of road which led only to Merravay and then on to the Lower Road, which nobody used in winter because of the mud.

The wind made it difficult to be sure of direction and for a moment I thought the sound came from behind us; that would be Mr. Whymark coming home, very late from the Fat Stock Show. But next time I caught the sound I was sure that it came from the road ahead of us, and it was coming towards us, fast.

And suddenly I thought of Lady Alice. It was on just such nights as this that she was said to ride abroad. Ordinarily I regarded the legend with some scepticism, but tonight I was in a state to believe everything. I grabbed Luke's arm and said,

"Can you hear a horse?"

He listened. "No."

That increased my cold panic; for it confirmed the stories of how two people could be walking, arm-linked through the night, and one would see and hear the phantom while the other declared that nothing but the wind went by.

"I can. And it's coming from Merravay and the Lower Road. *Her* ride. Oh Luke. It's Lady Alice!"

"Don't be so sawney," he said and listened again. "I hear it now. 'Tain't galloping."

I too had heard the pace slow down; but then, sometimes, passing people, she did slow down and lean from the saddle the better to cast the evil eye on them. Every story I had ever heard came back into my mind.

I cast about for somewhere to hide, but the hawthorn hedges on either side the road were as high and solid as walls.

"At least stand back," I whispered; and I pulled him close to the hedge.

The horse, moving at a steady trit-trot, was close to us when the cloud moved and the whole road sprang into light. Luke and I, in the shadow of the high hedge, were partly hidden. I cringed and closed my eyes. But at the last moment some strange compulsion came upon me. I *had* to look. And there was Mr. Roger on his brown horse with the white blaze.

Fright had driven every bit of sense out of me. With relief as sharp as pain, I said, "It's Mr. Roger."

In the next half second I was alone under the hedge. Tattered by the wind there was borne back to me the sound of hooves, of pounding feet, of Luke's voice calling.

The moon went in again. In the sudden blinding darkness I dragged myself from the hedge in which I had been half embedded and set out towards them on legs that seemed to be made of flannel. Two dozen yards of road stretched on and on, an endless journey.

Then it was light again and I had reached them. The horse stood broadside on, and Luke and Mr. Roger were grappling together. Urgent in my mind was the thought of Mr. Roger, so light and thin and brittle-seeming, Luke so heavy, thick-muscled, and strong; two such ill-matched men mustn't fight. I shouted to them through a mouth stuffed with chaff, and put out my flannel hands and seized Luke by the coattails. Something, elbow or fist, came up and hit me under the chin. Sparks of light burst out from the top of my head. My teeth had gone into my tongue and my mouth was filled with blood. I tried to scream again but nothing came but a blubbing sound. I spat, and just managed to call Luke's name.

Another cloud moved. There was a thump, a grunt and the slither of feet in the mud. Then quietness. The next burst of light showed Luke on his feet, Mr. Roger spread-eagled on the ground. His wig and hat, still wedged together, lay between him and the horse.

I wavered forward and knelt down and set my hands on him. I'd handled enough dead fowls and rabbits in my time to know the "dead" feel. It wasn't there. Immediately my mind began to work again, smoothly and sensibly.

"He's only stunned," I said. "Take his hat, ditch that side, get some water."

Running home as I had done, I had gone in my apron. I took it off and used it to dribble the cold water over his face. Then I remembered that most gentlemen carried flasks when they rode abroad. Luke found it and handed it to me, but Mr. Roger's flask had not been unstoppered lately; I had to hand it to Luke to unscrew. There was no more than a teaspoonful of brandy in it, and, careful as I was, it seemed to run out from his mouth uselessly.

"I never meant to kill him," Luke said. I went on dripping the cold water.

"Perhaps . . . the doctor . . ." I said at last, thinking sickly of all the miles between us and Baildon.

Luke turned towards the horse. Stopped and stripped off his coat and the fisherman's jersey which Mother had knitted.

"Keep him warm," he said, handing the garments to me. As I was wrapping them I saw Mr. Roger's face begin to twitch. His eyelids flickered, opened, closed again.

"It's all right . . . he's come round," I said.

His eyes opened again, looked at me, recognised me.

"Deb," he said, in a puzzled way.

"Yes. It's all right. We'll look after you."

"Shouldn't speak with your mouth full," he said in an inconsequent way, giving me that singularly sweet smile. After a moment he said, "I'm all right. Was I thrown? Belle'd never . . ." He began to struggle up. Luke leaned down and lifted him as though he'd been a child who had tumbled.

"Fulger," said Mr. Roger. "No coat. Cold night, too."

"We're quite near the Lodge, sir," I said. "Could you sit on the horse if Luke lifted you? Or shall he carry you?"

"I can walk. I haven't broken anything. My wig . . . where is it? Feel the cold, you know." I set his wig, muddy as it was, on his head.

"All this is very odd," he said in the same bewildered way.

"I hit you," Luke said in a humble, broken voice. "I'm main sorry now. I was out of my . . ."

"Don't bother him now," I said. "Let's get to the Lodge."

"Ockley," said Mr. Roger clearly. As he said it he sagged, bowed forward with a stream of blood and vomit gushing from his mouth. And once more my hands knew; live weight and dead weight are not mere butcher's terms.

It was Luke who broke the immeasurable silence.

"I'll carry him to the Lodge. You get back to Mother and warn Tad Thatcher on the way."

Tad was constable that year.

"I can't do that. They'll hang you." My bitten tongue had swollen, every word cost me agony, but I must talk now if I never did again.

"I kilt him."

"You did not. You hit him. It was an accident. You had cause; and drink in you too. But they wouldn't . . . no, Luke, if I can manage . . . this must be between us two forever."

"A man should take his punishment."

"You'll be punished . . . your conscience . . . all your life," I said cruelly. "But there's Mother . . . worked so hard, helped you, d'you want her to end in the poorhouse and me be branded murderer's sister all my days? Don't ruin us all for one unlucky blow. Let me look at you!"

I inspected his face.

"He hit me more about the body like," he said simply, and I found that heartbreaking—summing up as it did in so few words the dead man's lack of viciousness even when attacked.

"Hands," I said sternly. One knuckle was barked a bit.

"Suck it." I ran my eye over his clothes. If he'd gone to the Fat Stock Show he would have worn his best, and the mud on his breeches' knees where he had knelt would have shown. On his stained workaday ones it was unnoticeable.

"Put on your other things. Now listen. You must do exactly what I say. Back to The Evening Star. You set me on my way . . . went back to celebrate. Buy drinks for everybody. Go home. Don't say a word . . . ever. Do that and I can save you."

"But Deb . . . I'd as lief hang as live now . . ."

"So you think now. You wouldn't when you found yourself in the lockup. For Mother's sake, Luke. Hurry. Be too late soon." Oh, if I could only get him moving. What could I say?

"Most likely they'd hang me too, Luke, for helping you. I can't hide my mouth."

That did it.

"But what'll you do, Deb? Alone here with *that*. Murder can't be hid."

"Never you mind . . . less you know . . . better. For God's sake, move!"

The moment he turned and began to walk woodenly away I set the horse's head towards Merravay and dealt it a blow which set it galloping off. With any luck it might go rushing past its own gate, and even if it failed to do so the people in the Lodge would have heard galloping and be unlikely to be able to say positively whether they had heard one horse or two.

Then I waited for a little while. I was not frightened. I stood there in the dark, alone with a man just murdered, and worked everything out as though I were doing a sum. Afterwards, as long as I lived, I was to go through the whole thing in my dreams, starkly terrified, and wake screaming; but then, when it mattered, I was calm.

I ran to the Lodge and shouted and threw things at the window until Bert Baxter put his head out. Presently I was mumbling out my story—so exact in many details; how I had just left Luke, and turning the bend in the road had seen Mr. Roger struggling with a man. How I had been hit myself. The man—a stranger—I said, had thrown himself on his horse and galloped away. The Baxters had heard a horse . . .

At some point of my story somebody whipped round and asked what I was doing out that night, and even for that I had an answer. I had so wanted to know whether Luke had won the Fat Stock Prize.

Interlude

Deborah Fulger's story was accepted without question. People found it easy to believe that the assailant was a highwayman lying in wait for some market-merry farmer jogging home from the Fat Stock Show. Only a stranger to the district would have gone into ambush on a road that in winter led nowhere except to Merravay.

Sir George Fenstanton, who had been extremely fond of Roger Why-mark as well as interested in his schemes, had another theory. He believed that the anti-slavery campaign had alarmed someone with vested interests, someone powerful and unscrupulous enough to hire an assassin. Occasionally in his cups he was heard to say that he could make a shrewd guess and that if only he had a shadow of proof . . . but that was never forthcoming.

In the early days of his grief Sir George swore that he would continue Roger's work; but he was not the stuff of which reformers are made, and in the end his contribution to the cause was accidental and posthumous.

During his lifetime he had gathered together, and had had printed and bound in fine Morocco leather, every word which Roger Whymark had ever written on the subject of slavery. Decades after his death a friend of his grandson's, a man named Clarkson, rode over from Bury St. Edmund's and was shown into the library to wait because Sir Philip was down at the stables to overlook the dosing of a favourite hunter. The monograph lay, as it had lain for years, on the writing table, side by side with a silver inkstand, arid as the Sahara—Sir Philip was no scholar. Mr. Clarkson, a hopeless print addict, picked it up and began to read and never noticed that the ten minutes he had been asked to wait had stretched to fifty. When his friend, soiled, sweating, and apologetic, did arrive, Mr. Clarkson raised a face upon which horror and excitement conflicted.

"This," he said, holding out the monograph, "is the best prepared and correlated mass of evidence on any subject that I have ever seen. Years old, of course, but nothing's ever been done. Conditions are worse now, if anything. Would you mind if I borrowed it? I'd like Wilberforce to see it."

Sir Philip, who could read if he had to, just as he could bear toothache, said that Clarky could have the whole damn library for all he cared.

"Who exactly was this Roger Whymark?"

Sir Philip knew all about that. He described the tragedy and went on to say how after it the family had split up; they'd built a fine new house at New Holding and only an old aunt and the family governess had gone on living at Merravay. They'd sealed themselves in by planting a shrubbery across the top of the avenue.

"Like in the story 'Sleeping Beauty.' Only they weren't. At least, I never saw the old aunt, the other I did, once. Enough to frighten the French. She's dead now and she left the house back to the Whymarks. I hear old Bill's trying to sell it."

Sir Philip naturally knew about the Whymarks whose eccentricities and bargains and quarrels had been the subject of dinner-table chat. He was not familiar with the story of Luke Fulger, who at the opposite end of the social scale had become a legendary figure. Humble people still spoke of him as proof of what could happen when a man let success go to his head. Sober, hard-working, sensible chap that he seemed, he'd won the Fat Stock Prize and that had ruined him, for he went on drinking to his victory till the day he died. There never was, there never would be again, such a drunkard as Luke Fulger was. From the night of the Show onwards nobody ever saw him sober.

And when he died his sister Deborah, the best sister ever a man had—she'd stuck to him through thick and thin and even found him a wife, hoping to reform him—had put a stone over the grave. A plain stone with just his name, the dates of his birth and death, and the words, "He will be long remembered." And those words were truer than most such cut in stone over graves; for people were still saying—as naturally as they said, "Hard as iron"—"Drunk as Luke Fulger." Not that anybody ever was, of course.

The Nabob

THIS evening, entering the house, I had for the first time a sense of owner-ship; that inner confidence of possession which says, "Mine! My house! My hearth!" Why that feeling should strike with such poignancy at this late hour I cannot imagine. It has always been fairly plain that I had only to outlive Father to inherit Merravay; and he has been dead for almost a month. Moreover for six years, ever since his stroke, I have been master here; but it wasn't until today when I made my will, naming as my heir a young man for whom I care very little, that I felt the place to be really mine.

In the room which I invariably use when alone, a comparatively small and cosy apartment with a little ship forever sailing across the chimney-breast, all the papers relative to Merravay were still lying about. I say "papers," though this is so old a house that some of the deeds are written upon leathery parchment in script that is, to me, almost illegible. A name, a date here and there, stand out.

Unlike Ockley, where the Fennels have lived, father and son, for three hundred years, or Mortiboys, which the Hattons claim to have been in the family from Saxon times to within living memory—when Chris Hatton staked it on a gambling game—Merravay has changed hands several times; good business for the lawyers, for even when, as happened in 1729, it passed from Whymark to Whymark, it was the subject of formal and com-plicated transfer. One Whymark received it in exchange for some land at New Holding, where their present family house stands. Earlier, in the middle of the previous century a Phyllis Whymark appears to have bought Merravay twice! She could not sign her name; instead there is, in each case a large, firmly inscribed cross, and written below it, "Phyllis Whymark, her mark."

I sat for an hour looking through the deeds and thinking. In these dry and dusty documents with their formal phrases one aspect of Merravay's history is told. What of the human stories behind? For wherever living people meet there is a story. I, for instance, have inherited Merravay in the most normal way; I take my place in the company of its owners as "George Frederick Sandell, my beloved son." Neat, dull, ordinary. But behind that there is a story too. The story of what I paid for my heritage. But the paying has been so protracted and so subtle that I am at a loss to say exactly what I gave. The self-dramatising devil that lurks in us all, prompts me to say, "My soul"; but that would surely be an exaggeration. A scrap of integrity here, a bit of self-esteem there, a little cowardice, a little cynicism, a larger amount of what sometimes seems to be a ridiculous obsession.

It began in the November following my sixteenth birthday, when Father came home from India, unexpected, unannounced, and took me away from my school at Withernsea. I had spent ten years all but a term there, and been dully miserable all the time. There are, I believe, worse schools, places where boys are starved, savagely beaten, and taught nothing. Ecclestone House was not like that. Mr. Ogilvy loved to teach and was, on the whole, sparing with punishment, though he could lay on at times; and nobody *starved*, though a constant diet of bread, potatoes, and porridge induced in us a perpetual, nagging residue of hunger for something else, so that we nibbled hips and haws out of the hedges, chewed leaves of wild mint, and avidly devoured apples no larger than marbles. Our way of life, our surroundings, were of unrelieved dreariness, all cold and grey and dull. Most of the boys had begun life, as I had, in warm sunny places overseas, pampered, perhaps spoiled, by native servants; Ecclestone House specialised in caring for boys whose parents were abroad. Only a few of us could look forward to a holiday or to a visit from a relative. In ten years I had only left Withernsea once. Time, thus unbroken by things to look forward to or back upon, stretched endlessly. As a forcing place for scholars Ecclestone House was unsurpassed. With every other outlet for interest closed, all but the most congenitally stupid boys sought what relief mental effort could offer, and Mr. Ogilvy could point proudly to many old boys who had done very well in after life.

I was just a dull, average kind of boy; without, I think, much imagination; and to this day I believe that if Father had removed me one year earlier we should have got on well together. That I should have been much happier, I know for certain.

But during my last year, a new parson came to Withernsea, and very soon evinced interest in the school. Ecclestone House being run on what was known as "sound Church of England principles," the clergyman was naturally persona grata within its walls. He liked boys; he saw that our lives were dreary and pitied us; he also, I suspect, saw us as potential raw recruits to the cause he served. He used to ask us, two or three at a time, to his house, where, having regaled us with strong, sweet tea, inch-thick slices of sparsely buttered toast and very solid seedcake—all of which, unluxurious as it was, seemed to us like heavenly manna—he drummed into us, bluntly and openly, the principles of his Methodist-flavoured faith. His religion had little to do with dogma or ritual; it was not highly coloured and perhaps not very spiritual; it was vigorous, earthy, and militant; and it boiled down, really, to the simple order, "Put yourself in his place." He told us that it was good for us to be cold and hungry because when we got out into the world we could then sympathise, in the real sense of the word, with those countless people who were doomed *always* to be cold and hungry. By example as well as precept he bore home to us that "Put yourself in his place" did not mean just another man's place; it applied equally to women, and to animals. Christ's words, "These my little ones," he said, meant every living thing on earth except one's self.

To this day I can never think of the Reverend James Carter without thinking of the parable of the Sower and the Seed. So much that he said must have fallen on the stony ground, or in the weed-choked place; but there may be many men in the world who stop for a moment now and again, and think, and measure, as I have done, their conduct against the standard that he set. And I hope that to bolder, more positive characters than mine, he has been an inspiration. To me he has been little more than a hair shirt, worn secretly.

The first person to whom I began applying the principle of justice to all, was Mrs. Ogilvy. In school she was known as "the old hag," and was credited with every meanness, every furtive shift, known to woman. Our parents—those who were abroad—were charged five pounds a year for our clothing; yet everybody knew that only when a boy was about to leave, or go home for the holidays, was he given a new garment. Mended, patched, let out, taken in, clothes were passed from boy to boy in endless line. We held that against her; as we held the dull food, the thin blankets. It was easy to think of her as a harpy, battening upon our privations. Then one day I looked at her and saw her with Mr. Carter's eyes, and I saw her as a fellow victim—either of Mr. Ogilvy's greed and mismanagement, or of a system which compelled them both to make the lowest possible charges in a competitive market. Anyway I saw Mrs. Ogilvy as a woman, past her first youth, continually harassed, running Ecclestone House with such poor help as could be obtained, since nobody with any choice would work there. She always wore a kind of linen cap in the house and her face sagged heavily, like a hound's, but one day a strand of hair broke loose and fell along her cheek, and mingled with the grey of it there was a glint of yellow, and I found myself thinking that once upon a time she had been young and her face hadn't sagged and her hair must have been pretty. And perhaps Mr. Ogilvy—young then, too, though that was unimaginable, even to me—had loved her and told her how pretty she was!

And, oh dear! I thought to myself, how sad everything seems when you start putting yourself into another person's place; and now I can't bring myself to say that my Sunday jacket is inches too small.

So I was wearing it, and the breeches that must be hitched dangerously low if they were to meet my hose, and the shoes with the patches-upon-patches, on the day when Father arrived and Mrs. Ogilvy came and told me to make myself tidy and go to the parlour because he had come.

The man in the parlour, standing by the too-recently lighted fire and sipping, with an air of distaste, a glass of that Marsala known to the school as "parent-juice," was a stranger to me despite the fact that I had prided myself on my exceptional memory. They say that white children who start their lives in tropical countries mature early; that may be true. Or it might be that for ten years I had been in the same dull place, with very little to overlay the vivid memories of childhood. I believed that I remembered my father, my mother, my ayah. I am certain that I remembered my ayah's earrings; three strands of copper wire threaded through a blue bead, and the left-hand bead chipped in two places. But the man in the parlour bore no resemblance to the parent I had remembered, who was red-faced, fleshy, blue-eyed, and cheerful-looking. This man was tall, stooping, and very yellow; even the whites of his eyes were yellow. His face was heavily lined and his mouth was a thin, greyish-purple gash. Nothing familiar and nothing pleasant.

I recovered myself quickly, bringing Mr. Carter's principle into play and I thought—Well, he saw me last, a fat, curly-headed six-year-old, all in white, fresh from the ayah's hands; and what does he find! A lanky scarecrow, overdue for the barber, with legs and arms sticking out in all directions. I mustered a sheepish grin. Father came over to meet me, set his hands on my shoulders, and kissed me.

"I'd have known you, anywhere," he said. "The hair alone! Not to mention the nose. . . ." He stood back, looking at me with, for a moment, undisguised satisfaction. Mr. Ogilvy, not much interested, for he had grown used to men coming from the ends of the earth to claim boys they had not seen since infancy, muttered something about there being a remarkable resemblance, and went on to say that I had been a good, untroublesome pupil. As he spoke Father's look of satisfaction changed to one of deep disgust.

"They aren't your best clothes, are they?" he snapped.

With a nervous, side-sliding glance at Mr. Ogilvy, I nodded.

Father said, "Well, I'm damned. . . ."

He swung round and began to rate Mr. Ogilvy who said,

"I'm afraid that is not my business, Mr. Sandell. All what I call the domestic side . . ." At that moment Mrs. Ogilvy, who had hastily changed her gown and put on a clean cap, came sidling in. "Ah, my dear, how timely," Mr. Ogilvy said. "Sandell's father was asking about his clothes. They do look a trifle small. Perhaps you should explain that Sandell has grown, rather phenomenally, in the last week or two."

There followed a thoroughly nasty little scene. Mrs. Ogilvy said—which was not true—that the tailor was making me some clothes. Father pointed to a mend, a patch, a place where the jacket I was wearing had been let out, and expressed his doubt that this had been made for me, had fitted me, so lately as last year. He did not lose his temper; he did not raise his voice; coldly, relentlessly he stated his grievance. Mr. Ogilvy glared at his wife and her face, after going dark red with angry confusion, began to quiver. Seeing that, I said, "It is, Father, entirely my fault. Two Sundays ago, when I put on these clothes I realised that I had grown out of them. But I knew Mrs. Ogilvy was planning for the tailor to come . . . and I didn't expect to grow quite so much in just a fortnight. . . ."

"Quiet a minute, my boy. Let me speak," said Father. And speak he did, to such point and purpose that Mrs. Ogilvy began to cry and Mr. Ogilvy offered, with injured dignity, to return Father five pounds if he wasn't satisfied.

"Never mind that, now," Father said, a little mollified by the offer nonetheless. "The boy is alive and looks well, that's all I care about. D'you own a topcoat, George? Get it then, and we'll go."

"You mean now? Am I leaving today?"

He nodded, and I went bounding away, so full of joyful excitement that I thought I might burst.

At Hull, where we stayed for a few nights in an inn which seemed unbelievably luxurious to me, though Father had many faults to find with it, I was fitted out with clothes and had my hair dressed; then we drove, by post chaise, to Peterborough, where my sister Olivia was at school. I asked Father whether he intended to remove her as precipitately as he had done me, and he replied that he wasn't sure, a great deal depended upon Olivia and upon the school. Olivia was almost two years older than I, but we had come to England together in charge of a woman friend of my mother's who was bringing her own children home. Once during our ten years of exile that same woman, kind soul that she was, had invited us both to spend Christmas with her family. I had not seen

Olivia since then though we wrote to one another two or three times a year. I tried to tell Father what she was like, but apart from the fact that she was amiable and pretty I could find little to say. I could inform him that she liked her school, for during that brief holiday I had listened with astonishment, incredulity, and envy to her account of it. And when we arrived the homelike, easy-going atmosphere of the place made itself felt in a moment.

Olivia had quite grown up, though she was not now as tall as I; she was dressed in a way becoming to a young lady and bore far more resemblance to the mother I just remembered than to the sister I had seen five years before. She was very pretty, with a face like a kitten's and extremely black hair which grew off her forehead in a point.

She came into the room where we were waiting, a little shy, but demure and with a smile ready. I thought that Father would be delighted with her. But his manner was strange, stiff, and quite unaffectionate. I put that down to shyness, and to her looking so like Mother, which probably waked sad memories in him. Having shaken her by the hand and asked her abruptly how she did, he stood back and stared while Olivia turned to me and put her arms about my neck and kissed me and rubbed her cheek against mine and said how lovely it was to see me. Then she said,

"And dear Papa! After all these years. Oh, isn't it exciting? Oh, I could cry for joy!" And she did begin to cry.

"Now, now, there's no need to be silly," Father said.

At that moment one of the Miss Rossiters, followed by a maid with a tea tray, came bustling in. She was a very animated and garrulous old lady and passed over the awkward moment by asking Father a series of questions that needed no answers. Then she said, "Come now, Olivia dear, dry those happy tears and pour tea. Exhibit to your Papa those pretty manners which we have tried to inculcate."

Olivia's dimples peeped, her cheeks went pinker as she sat down behind the tray. She asked in the prettiest possible manner,

"How do you like your tea, Papa. With cream? Sugar?"

"I never drink it," he said.

"Well," said Miss Rossiter gaily, "we know what to say in that case, don't we, Olivia?"

Olivia was obviously disconcerted; but she said,

"I say, perhaps you prefer sherry or Madeira. Many gentlemen do."

"But not to *me*, dear. To your guest."

More confused than ever, Olivia repeated her words to Father.

"That is right, child," said Miss Rossiter. "And *then* you ring the bell."

Father said later that it was at that moment that he decided to remove Olivia from school. "Damn play-acting. Time she learned sense!"

II

We spent the next few weeks moving about, looking at properties that were for sale in the east of England, the part which Father preferred because it was driest; and so, in early February, we came to Merravay.

A handsome old man, mounted on a large grey horse, met us at the lodge gates.

"The house is rather difficult of access, I fear," he said when he had greeted us. "So I came to show the way." He led us along an avenue of limes to a point where the trees went on but the road was blocked by a mass of shrubs, dark laurels and lilacs just pricked with green buds. On our left several trees of the avenue had been removed to make a gap, and beyond this another avenue of younger trees led away and ended in a great white-pillared house in the Palladian style.

"Of all the stupid things they ever did," said the old gentleman in a confidential, conversational voice, "blocking this avenue was the silliest. That is my house," he pointed to the big white one. "Merravay lies there." We could see, at the end of the closed avenue, a cluster of tall, rose-coloured chimneys. "And now we must take the cart track," he said, and led the way between two trees on the right-hand side to a beaten path only just wide enough to allow passage for the carriage. It skirted the closed avenue for a while and then curved to end in the stable yard at the back of the house.

It struck me that Father was well disposed towards Merravay from the first. In other places which we had inspected his first words had usually been of a critical nature. Here, as soon as he alighted, he stared round and said, "I like that. I've seen several places where what they called the 'home farm' was a mile or more away. Difficult to keep an eye on."

"We could go in at the back, I found both keys," said Mr. Whymark with almost childish pride. "But I think you should see the front first."

He opened with some little difficulty an elegantly patterned gate of wrought iron, set in a length of red wall, and ushered us into a moderately well kept garden. But he sighed as he looked round.

"Dear me! What an air of neglect. I send over fairly regularly and have it tidied, but it's painfully obvious that nobody has *loved* it lately. Do you like gardening, Miss Sandell?"

"I've never tried. I think I should," said Olivia.

"Now we'll take this little path and come out at the end of the garden. Of course the best view is from the top of the field. Still, this gives some idea . . ."

We emerged by a low red wall, set with grey urns filled with daffodil spears, and there we turned to face the house. I thought it very beautiful; and evidently Mr. Whymark had some feeling for it too. He looked at it for a long moment and then gave another gentle sigh.

"Isn't it *grim?*" Olivia whispered to me, catching my arm as we followed Father and Mr. Whymark up to the house.

"I rather like it," I said. And a moment later, when the great door was opened and we stepped into the hall, I suffered that emotion which, in other circumstances, is known as love at first sight.

I was so fascinated by the place, so anxious to look in every nook and cranny, literally feasting my eyes, that I could not wait for Father and Mr. Whymark to make their more systematic and leisurely progress. Dragging Olivia by the hand, I went from room to room, upstairs and downstairs, delighting in all I saw. The two men were still upstairs when Olivia and I came back into the great hall, and there I knew the full measure of my enchantment when Olivia said,

"Oh I do hope and trust Father doesn't buy *this* house! It's *much* the worst we've seen."

In the past weeks Father had so often checked and snubbed and chided her and told her not to be silly that she had developed a meek, almost mute manner in his company, and when she was alone with me, indulged in a compensating exuberance. So I ignored a good deal of the emphasis in her words.

"Why don't you like it? I think it's beautiful!" I looked round as I spoke. The hall was as long and wide and high as a small church. Just inside the door was a fixed oaken screen, most delicately and exquisitely carved. At the farther end a magnificent staircase led up to an open gallery. At the foot of the stairs the banister rails ended in a great solid post carved into the figure of a man, so lifelike that one could see the ripples in the hair of his head and beard. He leaned on a staff, and the set of his shoulder, the bracing of his hands on the staff, gave one the impression that he was holding up the staircase.

"Look at *him!*" cried Olivia, following the direction of my stare. "Imagine taking a candle and going up to bed past him! Oh, I should be terrified. Dear George, George darling, I do beseech you, try to persuade Father not to live here."

"But he's a benevolent old fellow," I said, going nearer to the figure. "He'd wish you pleasant dreams as you passed." But that wasn't true! There was a sternness about the carved face.

"Oh, but look," I said, "it's Moses with his stick turning into a snake. Why, Olivia if this were in a church or anywhere except a private house people would go to see it. It's a wonderful piece of carving—it's a work of art!"

I put my hand over the knotted, gnarled wooden ones that clenched the stick, and felt what I can only call a satisfaction. At the same time, through the great window I saw a view of the garden, the green of the grass, the warm rose of the wall, the dark field, the wood beyond.

"And what a view!" I said.

"What of? A ploughed field and a wet wood. Oh George, no! Truly it frightens me; there's something terribly unfriendly about it. Hateful."

"Now that is silly," I said. "Considering that it's empty, and has been for five years I believe, it seems to me extremely welcoming. Think of that one we saw at Kelvedon. This doesn't seem like an empty house at all."

"No; it doesn't. It's haunted, George; that's what it is. And the ghosts hate us for disturbing them."

I knew enough by this time to realise that her opinion would not influence Father in the slightest; I had no fear of that; what I minded was that she should say such things about the house I liked so much. So I said peevishly,

"Oh, for Heaven's sake, Olivia. Don't talk such absolute nonsense."

She saw that I had lost patience and began in her pathetic, eager-to-please, frivolous little way to try to make me laugh.

"It was nonsense. I was joking. But, George dear, can't you just imagine . . ." and she started to rattle off an account of just what ghosts Merravay might harbour, headless ladies and men dragging chains.

Charm, particularly charm of speech, is difficult to define and impossible to describe. Odd little turns of phrase, the timing, the glance that accompanies the words, all mean so much. But whatever it is, Olivia had it in full measure, and soon I was laughing and protesting that now she was frightening me.

In the midst of this a sound on the stairs made me look up and there was Father, followed by Mr. Whymark, coming down. Father was looking at Olivia with such cold distaste that the laughter died on my lips. It was a look of physical revulsion, such as a man might turn upon a dish which had once badly disagreed with him.

Mr. Whymark said genially,

"I can't tell you how it delights me to hear young voices in Merravay again. I spent my early childhood here, you know. I had two sisters, not much older, and after Miss Maybrook became our governess we had very merry times. She was so kind to us . . . and so gay. Poor girl." And again there came that gentle little sigh.

Father said briskly that he had still to see the buildings and wanted to get back to Baildon before dark.

On the way home he said that if the question of access could be settled to his satisfaction—meaning that if Mr. Whymark knocked the cost of making a new avenue off the purchase price—he was prepared to buy Merravay.

"Did he happen to tell you why the old one was blocked?" I asked. I was in that state of mind towards the place, which, in the case of people, leads one to ask where they were born, what games they played as children, what is their favourite book.

"Oh, some long-winded story about a row between his mamma and an aunt. So far as I could make out, the aunt liked the house and his mamma loathed it—his elder brother came to a tragic end, or something. The aunt owned the land were the New House stands, so they swopped. And they couldn't share the avenue—which by the way I don't wish to do either —so she had it blocked. And then some jumble about the aunt leaving it to, why yes, that governess he mentioned, who lived there all alone apparently, like a hermit, until five years ago, when she died and left it to him. He's been trying to sell it ever since. I should say he's hard-pressed for money. Small wonder! He told me he'd been married three times and had eleven children in all. Talkative old fool; but if we mean to settle here it'll pay us to humour him . . . up to a point."

I was so delighted that Father liked Merravay that I could overlook his attitude towards a charming old gentleman.

III

One of the things I had said to Olivia in an endeavour to cheer her, once we knew that Merravay was to be our home, was that no house should be judged in its empty state. Imagine, I said, the difference which carpets and curtains and pictures and furniture would make. That remark was both prescient and an understatement. I had no idea then of what Father intended to do. Lodged in a warehouse at Hull were five or six enormous crates containing things he had brought from India. Their freightage must have cost a fortune, for each of them displaced its own bulk in tea, or pepper or cloves or nutmegs—all very valuable commodities. Father had brought rugs and carpets, so silkily smooth, so brightly coloured, that it seemed wrong to lay them on the floor and walk over them; he had brought yards and yards of the thin embroidered silk which at that time, I learned was being hung upon walls in rich houses and imitated in paper for the decoration of homes less wealthy; he had brought cabinets and chests in red or black lacquer heavily gilded; and there were dozens of ornaments too, some beautiful, some grotesque, made of ivory and ebony, of silver and mother-of-pearl, of jade and soapstone.

Even the ordinary household furniture which we bought during visits to London—visits which included my introduction to theatres and tea gardens and coffeehouses—was all beautiful and all costly; elegant rib-band-back chairs, sideboards and tables and chests of drawers in satin-smooth walnut wood.

Father paid me the intoxicating compliment of inviting my opinion about everything he bought. My taste, like any other hobbledehoy's, was unformed and dubious, but I knew what was elegant and pleasing even then. Sometimes the expense worried me, especially as Father often grumbled about it and tried to haggle with the shopkeepers. Once I mentioned the matter and he laughed,

"Bless you, boy, I could buy the shop and the man who owns it and never notice. But it doesn't do to let them know; they'd fleece you!"

Sometimes, when the burden of choice between two things weighed heavily on me, I would say, "But which do *you* prefer, sir? After all you have to live with it."

"You have which you like. It'll all be yours one day."

Perhaps I dwell unduly on those days, when everything seemed wonderful and exciting, rich, pleasant, colourful and comfortable. But even then . . . there were moments. One I particularly remember. On a miry day, on a bit of bad road, going uphill, the horse in our hired carriage, a poor thin old beast, made heavy going. I said I would get out and walk to the top.

"Damn silly idea, get yourself muddy," said Father. He leaned and called to the driver.

"Get along! Use your whip, man! What's a whip for?"

Settling back, he went on to talk pleasantly on the subject which I had interrupted.

I should, of course, have known then.

We moved into Merravay around midsummer, and with the sunshine without and the splendour within there was little to remind us of the day of our first visit. The drawing-room walls had been hung with the silk, a deep maize-yellow embroidered with flowery boughs and bright birds. In other rooms where the surface of the panelling did not lend itself to hangings the oak had been painted, white and gold, or pale bluish-green. The great open hearths in most of the rooms had been enclosed with slabs and pillars of marble, and provided with basket grates, graceful as Grecian urns. But the hall—the place which at that time I liked best—was almost untouched. Father had decided that the stair posts and the fine screen would be ruined by being painted, so he had left them and the walls in their natural state, and he had retained the open hearth there, too. But to compensate for the lack of colour he had gathered against the

dark background all the brightest of his Eastern treasures; the most glowing rugs, the red laquered cabinet and chest, great bowls and vases of
painted porcelain. Just to look at the colour, so lavishly spread, was to
know a lifting of the spirit.

It may be because I had left a place of bright sun and gaudy colours
and lived so long in grey Withernsea, where the schoolroom floor, the sea
outside, and the sky above were all the same dull neutral hue, that I was,
and shall always be, susceptible to brightness, even to the extent of loving
a dirty gypsy woman because of her scarlet neckcloth, even to the extent
of liking to see poppies in a cornfield, indicative of bad husbandry as
they be.

I know that when I entered Merravay for the first time after everything was in place I thought—I shall feel pleasure every time I come in
here, no matter what happens.

I should, in fact, have been perfectly happy during our first months at
Merravay if only Father would have been nicer to Olivia.

Nothing she did, nothing she said, could please him, that was the truth
of it. I'd been long enough with him now to realise that he didn't care
for women at all; he always spoke contemptuously of them, but he could
be, and often was, perfectly civil when face to face with a woman of his
own class. To Olivia he seemed unable to be civil; and at the same time
he seemed unable to let her alone and allow her to avoid him, as she tried
to do. Like a man with a sore thumb, he must keep picking.

"Where's your sister? What's she up to?" he would say. He would
enter the house, "Olivia! Olivia! Oh, there you are . . ." and launch into
some complaint, nothing too trivial, nothing too absurd. He had a curious
theory that women must be kept busy, otherwise they got into mischief,
grew fanciful, took to tea-drinking and gossip. In this belief he assiduously
invented little jobs for Olivia. His linen was badly laundered, Olivia
must do it; yet to judge from the resultant, never-failing complaints she
was worse than any laundress could be and keep a job. The maid who
cleaned the silver dropped and dented one of the branching candelabra,
Olivia must polish it in future; and it is a fact that from the moment she
took on the task he never touched or saw a piece of silver without giving
it the closest scrutiny, and nine times out of ten he would find something
to rebuke. It was like a sickness. He had bought, in London, one of the
new pianos, and Olivia, who had learned to play a little and had a good
ear and clever fingers, liked to play. The music she made was always
wrong, too loud, not loud enough, miserable belly-aching stuff, a silly
tinkle. But when in despair she ceased to play, except when he was out
of the house, that wasn't right either. Why had he given all that good
money for a silly toy if it were never to be used?

It all sounds petty and trivial, almost laughable, and sometimes indeed Olivia and I did laugh together—a little hysterically—about it, but it was hateful to watch, a continual jarring of the nerves. In the beginning I had occasionally put in a politely worded, mild, reasonable protest: "That's hardly Olivia's fault, sir," I would say. He would retort, "It's none of your concern, my boy!" or, "I know what I'm about, George," and I soon learned that by speaking I did more harm than good, for always later on he would be more actively disagreeable to her. I should, of course, have hated it had he taken a similar attitude to me, but at the same time I did not enjoy the pointed contrast. Sometimes Olivia would say, half laughing and half crying, "Oh you're all right; you're *George, my dear boy*, the fortunate fellow who can do no wrong!" And to that I could only reply, "I believe he's a woman-hater."

"Then why did he ever bring me here? He could have left me at Peterborough. I was much happier there, George, truly. If this goes on I shall write to Miss Rossiter and ask if I can go back and teach the small girls. I shouldn't want any wages."

"You'd do better to stay here and get married," I said.

And indeed as time went on the idea of Olivia's finding a husband and having a home of her own became to me as delectable an idea as ever it could have appeared to any girl herself or to the most scheming match-making mamma. I grew more and more inclined to shuffle off a feeling of guilt and responsibility where she was concerned by thinking that this state of affairs couldn't last forever; Olivia would soon find a husband and be out of Father's clutches.

Nor was it by any means a far-fetched idea; for one of the fears which Olivia had voiced, the fear that life would be very lonely at Merravay, proved to be entirely unfounded. We had no sooner settled than Mr. Why-mark invited us all to dinner "to meet a few neighbours," and soon we were entertaining and being entertained at least once a week and some-times more often. Perhaps it is the ever-present danger of life becoming dull in the country which makes country people really cultivate and bother about their social activities; I know that all around us were people who seemed to enjoy the company of their fellows and to be extremely tolerant of one another's little peculiarities, and to be willing, though with a certain understandable caution, to welcome newcomers into their circle. Very soon Father gave a special Indian dinner, with curries and strange pickles and fruits and sweetmeats, and with Candy our Negro servant in his finest clothes moving round like a shadow; and that was a great suc-cess. It was plain that the new state of Merravay's interior impressed every-one very much. And Father, without making any particular effort to be agreeable or ingratiating, seemed to strike just the right note, particularly when he confessed that he knew absolutely nothing about English agri-culture and expected that for a year or two he would lose money. At that the English countryman's desire to be helpful with dictatorial-flavoured advice came uppermost. Almost every man at the table immediately of-fered to ride over and just cast an eye on this and that. Then Sir Evelyn Fennel, who lived at Ockley Manor and was related to the Whymarks in some degree, said,

"You'd do better, Sandell, to get a good steward. Otherwise you'll have civil war. Great-uncle William here on my left will tell you to plant seeds in the dark of the moon, he is so old-fashioned, while Hodge here on my right is so much day-after-tomorrow that he's taken to marling his land." Everyone laughed.

Father said, "As a matter of fact I have engaged a foreman who seems to know his job; a fellow called Tom Fulger."

There was a tiny silence.

"He's knowledgeable enough," said Mr. Hodge at last, a little grudg-ingly. "Worked one time for Coke at Holkham. Yes . . . he knows his job."

"Well . . . what don't you like about him?" asked Father, going in his direct way to the heart of the matter.

"Damned revolutionary," said Sir Evelyn. "You keep your eye on him. He had the nerve to say—and in a public place—that any labourer that was worth his salt was worth ten shillings a week! That's where the rot starts. *They* don't want it; they haven't got wit enough to think up such nonsense; but you get one or two big-mouthed malcontents like Tom Fulger rip-ranting about and then there's trouble."

I came to know Tom Fulger very well during the next year or so. Dur-ing the September after our move to Merravay I had my seventeenth birthday, and shortly afterwards Father asked me in a kindly casual way whether I had any ideas about my future. I had none; I was enjoying my present way of life and asked nothing but that it could continue. I hesitated to confess this lack of ambition and enterprise to a man who so often spoke about "making opportunities" and "taking time by the fore-lock" and so on; therefore I said,

"I haven't given the matter much thought, sir. Have you anything par-ticular in mind?"

"I'm asking you."

"Well . . ." I said.

"Surely to God, boy, you know what you *want*; or what you *don't* want. The world's open to you. Would you like to go to the University, travel a bit . . . ?"

"If it were merely a question of what I should *like*, I should say that I should like to go on living as I am at the moment but to have more to do with the land, the farming side. That does interest me and if I learned about it, properly, one day I could run it for you."

"Nothing would please me more. But why be so timid about it? It's the thing I should have suggested myself, but I wanted you to choose."

"Well, I thought perhaps you might think that it was . . . unenterprising. That perhaps you thought I ought to go out and tackle the world, like you did, Father."

"I had to, my boy; if I hadn't it'd have damned soon tackled me. But you're different; you can have what you want, do what you like. And you don't have to thank me," he said with a note in his voice that I had never heard before. "You're part of the prize I wrung out of the struggle. When I was your age I was sweating over ledgers in an airless hole in a dirty stinking place called Kumalpore; and God help me if I made a blot. Yes sir, no sir, let me kiss your arse sir, to clods and clowns that hadn't half my brains or my breeding if it comes to that. And when I see you at the same age, George . . . I'd see you off on the Grand Tour, or to Cambridge, or if you wanted to go and make a young ass of yourself in London, it'd all be one to me, because it would be like having it myself."

I heard those words then and I felt warmly, gratefully, towards him for saying them, for lifting the burden of gratitude from my heart, for making so free with all that he had. But later on I saw what lay behind them. I was nothing really, just a peg upon which he could hang another self. That was why I could have a fine new saddle horse in the same week as he had grudgingly handed Olivia the price of the cheapest possible muslin dress, and told her to buy the stuff and sew it herself. But that, as I say, came later. At the moment I was delighted because he was pleased with my choice of occupation, and delighted that I was to stay at Merravay, to know it better, to serve it.

IV

In that way I became, to an extent, Tom Fulger's pupil. He was a tall lean fellow with a face like a saint in a stained-glass window and a remarkable repertoire of swearwords. His family had lived in Nettleton since the beginning of time, and his grandfather had been, by all accounts, a substantial farmer. One day when we were driving into Baildon market he pointed out to me the house in which his grandfather had lived and where his own father had been born. It looked a big, solid, prosperous place.

"That's why I never touch a —— drop of the —— stuff, not even home-brewed," Tom said, leaving me to guess the connection. "I had an old great-aunt, my granfer's sister, wonderful old woman too she was and kept things together longer than they'd have held otherwise, and I've heard her say that he was all right, doing wonderful well, taking prizes with his beasts, and God knows what, and then one day something upset the old sod and he went and downed a glass of —— brandy. And never stopped. Drunk hisself out of Squirrels, drunk hisself out of Church Farm, drunk hisself out of two or three jobs old Deborah got him. They still say around these parts, 'drunk as Luke Fulger.' And all on account of once being upset in his belly, or maybe it was toothache. Soaking old sod, I hate even to think about him!"

I thought, but I did not say, that probably it was a Fulger trait never to do anything by halves. Tom was the most thorough man I ever knew. And just a little demented. He thought every man, irrespective of whether he owned property or not, should have a vote; he thought every labourer should have ten shillings a week; he thought every child should go to school; he thought all foxes should be shot, all race-horses put to work, and only big, healthy bulls allowed to run with the cows. There was hardly a thing which had come under his notice about which he had not had some thought, and most generally his thought was in direct opposition to everyone else's. He afforded me a great deal of entertainment and presently, when I had come to realise how sound and right all his ideas about agriculture were, I sometimes asked myself whether a man could be so sensible in one direction and wrong in all others. And that, of course, was a dangerous line of thought.

When I look back on that year and the next one I feel like a very old man. I suppose that if one is ever to have boundless enthusiasm and endless energy one has them at seventeen, eighteen. And perhaps the change of diet had an effect on me. I could rise at first light and be out with Tom, who had no nonsensical ideas about "gentleman farmers" or lily-white hands. Later in the day I could shoot or hunt or ride with Father, spend another couple of hours with Tom, play cards or dance all evening. I've ridden home from a ball at the Baildon Assembly Rooms, changed my clothes, and spent the rest of the night in the lambing pen and not felt a penny the worse.

Olivia and I had no lack of friends of our own age. Of Mr. Whymark's third family two girls and one boy were still under twenty, a gay, high-spirited trio; the girls particularly were allowed more freedom, both of speech and movement, than was common. It was young Phyllis Whymark's hoydenish ways which precipitated a scene in our family.

Father, although thinking little of Mr. Whymark's capacity for business, was well aware of his social value and did nothing to discourage friendship between the two houses. Olivia was always at liberty to accept the frequent invitations to the New House, to ride, to picnic, to go shopping with Phyllis, who had developed for her one of those doting friendships in which girls delight. One bright April morning Phyllis came galloping over to know whether Olivia would ride to Ockley with her. Olivia came out to find me in the yard. "Do you think I might go? Father isn't here so I can't ask *him!*"

I said that naturally she could go. I had not noticed that before each previous outing she had had to seek permission.

"Oh yes," she said, when I commented on this. "Always. Cap in hand, 'Please, Papa, may I go?' Just like school. Well, have I your permission then, George?"

"Oh, don't be silly," I said, a little embarrassed; and then to cover the brusqueness, added, "Enjoy yourself."

She came in just before dinner; I had spent the day on the farm and come in and cleaned myself early; Father, who had been to Muchanger, was still upstairs, changing. Finding me alone, Olivia lingered for a moment, abandoning the quiet, repressed manner which she now as a matter of habit assumed upon entering the house. There was a new baby at Ockley and Phyllis was to be its godmother; there were hothouses at Ockley and in them the strawberries were already almost ripe. The simple, innocent excitements of the day were held out for my sharing.

"Well, miss, and where have you been all day?" asked Father from midway down the stairs. He looked quite savage.

"At Ockley, with Phyllis, Papa," said Olivia, instantly deflated. She moved to the stairs and stood aside to let him pass her and then began, quickly, to mount them. Father walked to the centre of the hall and said, "Come here!" He raved at her for several minutes, going on after he had reduced her to tears.

Once I said, "Look here, sir, she did consult me and I . . ."

"Keep out of this, George," he said and raved on. Olivia, crying, said, "But you weren't at home, Papa; so I asked George . . ."

"Will you leave George out of this?" he said furiously, and raved on. Finally he dismissed her to her room, saying that he did not wish to see her at dinner.

I made a cub's move.

"If Olivia has no dinner I don't want any either," I said.

"Now for God's sake don't you start!" he said; and taking me by the arm, hustled me without ado into the dining room just as Candy padded in with the soup tureen.

I sat down in my place, realising that I had put myself into a ridiculous position. Whatever I did now, whether I ate or refused to eat, I should look silly. And at the same time—so lacking in dignity is crude nature—I realised that I was extremely hungry. The plate of soup which Candy placed before me both looked and smelt painfully appetising. But I did not take up my spoon. I folded my arms and sat there, feeling a fool and looking like one.

After a moment Father cocked an eyebrow at me and said,

"George, you look exactly like a dog 'On Trust!' Eat your dinner, boy, and don't be so ridiculous."

"I know it's ridiculous," I said, "because it makes no difference to the situation whether I eat or not! All the same I think you were very unjust and unkind to Olivia just now and it isn't the first time either."

"Well, suppose we discuss that afterwards. Argument at table leads to indigestion. Richard Whymark was at Muchanger today and gave me a message for you. The pups are ready to leave their mother and he'd like you to have first choice. Young Stephen Fennel is going over there on Thursday, so if you want the really first choice you'd better try to get there tomorrow."

"Thank you for telling me," I said in a voice I tried to make cold.

He was too wily to repeat the friendly overture. The rest of the mealtime passed in silence, giving me ample opportunity to think "I am right. I am right," and then to wonder whether the need to think so repeatedly wasn't in itself a sign of weakness.

We went back to the hall, where a fire was burning. Father took his usual chair and stretched his thin yellow hands to the blaze, then, rubbing them together, leaned back and said in a conversational tone,

"So you think I'm unjust and unkind, eh?"

"To Olivia, sir; not to me. And that makes it rather hard for me to say . . ."

"Go on. State your case."

"Well, just before dinner, for instance. You shouted at her that you would not have her careering about the countryside, her whereabouts unknown, her company unapproved, and her behaviour uncontrolled. But if you had been here and asked for your permission you would have given it, I think. Well then, I fail to see how an exchange of words between you could make all that difference to her whereabouts, or her company, or her behaviour."

"Very lucid, George. Very true, too. Up to a point. The point being that in leaving the house without my permission she was flagrantly disobedient. It was no crime to go, with Phyllis Whymark, to Ockley, to see a new baby, I agree with you there. But the trouble with females is that given an inch they immediately take a mile and if, on this occasion, she escaped without reprimand, next week she would be off without leave on some less innocent errand."

I almost said, "That is silly!" but checked the words just in time.

"Well, are you satisfied?"

"I don't want to offend you," I said, "but it isn't just today's occurrence. You are, to my mind, very hard on Olivia always. She does her best to please you, but you never are pleased. She's young and inexperienced in housekeeping, but in that matter you behave to her as though she were forty and judge her harshly; and then in other matters you treat her as though she were a child; so she is never right. And it makes me unhappy to watch."

Remembered, that speech sounds mild and reasonable; but then it seemed bold and challenging, and I waited with lively apprehension for the wrath that must surely follow. But Father said nothing. He got up and went to the red lacquer cabinet and took out the brandy. He poured some into a glass and drank it in a manner contrary to his habit. He was—at least by Suffolk standards which were all I knew—fairly abstemi-ous, and would sit for a whole evening with a similar measure of liquor, sipping and toying with his glass.

Filling the glass again, he closed the cabinet and returned to his chair.

"It's a pretty good rule, you know, George, not to bother about what can't be helped."

It was difficult to find an answer to such a pontifical statement, so I sat still and waited.

"And if a . . . well," he looked up and smiled, "let's say a yellow dog with very floppy ears bites you, it's understandable that in future you don't care for yellow dogs with very floppy ears. You agree?"

Father's speech, though often pungent and succinct, seldom tended to-wards the metaphorical. That it did so now showed, like that gulping of brandy, that this was a critical moment.

"Well, sir . . . that would rather depend. Quite a different yellow dog . . ."

"Bitch, bred of the bitch that bit you?" he asked, raising his heavy eyebrows. "Have I said enough, George?"

I could have left it there, I suppose. But I said,

"Either too much or too little. You seem to be implying . . ."

"Telling you, my boy, telling. I can't like her, George. That's some-thing you'll have to accept if you and I are to remain on friendly terms. Every single thing about her, her size and shape and colouring, the sound of her voice, the very way her hair grows . . . and that laugh! You may not believe it, but I have *tried!* And it's useless. Simply by existing she sets my teeth on edge."

"Because she is so like Mother?"

"That stumps you. Well, there you are, you forced it on me, George. You started it. So you'd better know. Your mother isn't dead. So far as I know she's still living in a dirty little bungalow at Kumalpore with a down-at-heel scrivener with the lung rot. And, by God, I hope she's hungry!"

I'd remembered her, pretty, kind, and gay; and dead, preserved from change and age, static, enshrined.

"I was busy," Father said in a flat harsh voice, "busy trying to make money. I'd always given her everything I could; I wanted to give her everything that there *was*. But women are like that, George. You might as well know it now. Offer them a daisy and they want the moon; climb the sky and drag down the moon by sheer force and nothing will please but the daisy. While I was sweating my guts out *he* was playing his damned little tinkles; putting Hindu songs into English and setting them to music. Hindu love songs . . . out of a country where women are less valued than cows. My God! The top of my skull still lifts when I think of it."

I said the only thing I could think of. "I'm terribly sorry."

"Why should you be? Sorry for yourself, perhaps. I offered . . . when you and Olivia came home—I could have afforded it then—I offered that she should come with you. But the rot had set in; she couldn't leave then. So tuck this away in your mind, George; never let a woman get the upper hand of you; they're all as false as Hell. And now let's forget it. We've survived, and that is the main thing. Have some brandy . . . you look a bit white about the gills. Mustn't take it to heart, you know."

It was only later on that I realised that my protest, the revelation it had provoked, and the understanding of Father's attitude which the facts had engendered in me had done nothing to help Olivia or to soften her lot.

And whenever I think of Olivia I think of Candy too, because all my memories and all my remorses are inextricably tangled.

Candy was an African Negro whom Father had bought in Zanzibar; he was often referred to as "my man, Candy," and it would have been as true to have said, "my slave, Candy." He had been bought for money; he received no wages; Father regarded him, and Candy regarded himself, as a chattel.

Coming through the Bay on the voyage home Candy had met with an accident and had broken a leg, so Father had left him in Hull in a hospital for the sick poor, and I only learned of his existence after Father

had decided to buy Merravay and was, one evening, discussing the staff
we should need in the house.

"A cook and three maids will be plenty," he said. "Your sister will make
herself useful and my man Candy will be both footman and butler."

"Who is Candy?" I asked. Father explained, and I with some muddled
recollection of Mr. Ogilvy's dissertations about socmen and serfs said,
"But I thought one couldn't have slaves or be a slave in England."

"That's as may be," said Father. "When you go to London you'll see
every other fashionable lady attended by a little black boy. They buy
them young, give them plenty of gin, and make them sleep in cupboards
to keep 'em small. They put collars on 'em, too, like dogs. I once saw one
with a collar studded with garnets and turquoises; very pretty." He smiled,
"I shan't put a collar on Candy, he's an ugly old devil, but you'll like
him; I never saw his equal for getting a shine on boots. You look in-
credulous, George! See here." He reached for the paper, turned it about,
and held it to me pointing to a column. And there, sure enough, were
several advertisements for black boys, wanted, for sale, or lost. The lost
ones, I noticed, were all pock-marked and bow-legged; the ones for sale
all handsome and very accomplished.

"Well," I said, "I never knew that!"

"If you will forgive my mentioning it, George, there were one or two
things omitted from Mr. Ogilvy's curriculum!" He smiled as he said it
and I smiled back.

"Can he speak—and understand—English?" I asked.

"Well enough. His last master was Portuguese, but I've had him nearly
two years. I'd made up my mind to retire and that was my last visit to
Zanzibar and I'd heard such accounts of English servants from people
fresh out from home, I thought I must make sure of one good servant.
And Africans are much stronger than Indians. . . ."

Candy came down from Hull in the wagon with the crates of furnish-
ings, and my first thought about him was that he was very ill clad for
the English climate. It was a day of bitter March wind and he was
wearing a pair of thin cotton trousers and a short jacket of the same
stuff. His huge feet were thrust, hoseless, into a pair of shabby shoes. He
was a good deal older than I had expected him to be; his close-curled
black hair looked as though it had been lightly powdered; and he was
less black than I had imagined, for at that moment he was the curious
pinky-grey colour which Negroes go when they are ill, or cold, or
frightened.

"Poor thing," I said, "he's frozen. He must have some warmer clothes."

"He's all right; he'll warm up when he starts moving about. What he certainly is, is damned filthy." Father turned to Candy and said, as one says to a child, "Dirty! dirty!"

Candy's eyes rolled like loose marbles in their sockets.

"Four days, no water, no wash. All ize, ize. No water."

"Plenty of water here," Father said. "Help with this stuff and then wash!"

That was a day when we were only at Merravay in order to see the furniture safely in, and just before dusk we drove back to Baildon to the inn where we were staying. When we went towards the carriage and Candy climbed up beside the driver I was horrified to see that he had taken literally Father's orders to wash. His coat and trousers were now clean, but quite wet and already plastered to him by the wind.

"He's wet, the fool," I said, "he'll catch his death. Shall I give him my coat."

"George, please," said Father, putting one hand on my arm and pulling me into place beside him, while with the other hand he drew up the rug. "He's all right. He'll take no more harm than a dog would. You must get that into your head. You might just as well go and give your coat to one of the horses."

If Candy had sneezed or snuffled next day I could have said, "There, I told you!", but he did not. He took no apparent harm at all.

The next time—or at least the next time I remember—that I spoke up on Candy's behalf was, oddly enough, the time when I thought he would be too hot. It was when we finally moved into Merravay and I discovered that Candy was to sleep in the chimney room, which was just a space partitioned off around the main chimney stack of the house. The whole of one side of it was made of the red brick chimney; there was floor space about six feet long and four wide, and it had no window. Three little round holes bored in the top of the door which divided it from the passage admitted the only air.

"He'll stifle," I said.

"You'll see," said Father.

But, just as Candy had not frozen, so he did not stifle. I used to remind myself of that, trying to believe that Negroes were different, less sensitive. I had to take comfort in that thought if I could, for Father was hard on Candy; just as he was hard on dogs and horses, hard on Olivia, hard on everybody except me. I really must have been the world's worst simpleton, always to think myself exempt; never to guess that he knew all about the hair shirt Mr. Carter had slipped over my head; never to guess that I was as much his slave as Candy.

I didn't. I went on my gay, happy way, thinking how lovely everything was and how much I should enjoy myself if only . . . if only . . .

if only . . . thinking that Olivia would one day marry and get away . . . thinking that Candy after all must be made differently . . . thinking all the coward's thoughts.

V

Time slipped away. I found myself devoting more and more attention to the farm. Father took singularly little interest in it though he would walk around the yard every now and then and make a great fuss if a bucket or a wisp of hay were out of place; he liked it all spic and span and he liked to show visitors round. But the ordinary routine bored him, and I came, almost unconsciously, to look upon my work as my refuge.

Olivia had her twenty-first birthday. Father gave her a pear-shaped ruby on a gold chain and then cut into her timid expressions of gratitude and pleasure with the remark that she was now an established old maid. Long before this, towards the end of our first year at Merravay, Olivia had put into action her threat of writing to Miss Rossiter to ask if she could go back to Peterborough as an unsalaried teacher. Miss Rossiter had written her a long letter, rich, I suppose, in sorry wisdom. Any girl, she said, who had a home and a father who was willing and able to provide for her, should thank God every morning and evening for such blessed security in a world where so many unfortunate females had none. Dozens of women, some as young as fifteen, some as old as fifty, had applied for the last post they had advertised and almost had said that they were willing to work for no salary; some had even offered small sums of money as well as their services in return for bed and board. So would dear Olivia—the letter ended—please cultivate a meek and cheerful spirit even when things were a little difficult, and remember always to count her blessings. . . .

When I read the letter, I said,

"Well, I never did think it a very good idea. You stay here and get married."

And steadily, over the next three years, whenever I thought of Olivia I assured myself that she would get married; she was so pretty. But though at parties and picnics men paid her plenty of attention and she never lacked partners at the balls we attended, somehow no young man, to my knowledge, ever sought for Father's permission to marry her; and all too soon she was twenty-one and Father, when at a loss for other taunt or gibe, could always remark that she was becoming an old maid.

Just before my birthday, my nineteenth, Father surprised me by announcing that he had invited an old acquaintance, a Mr. Douglas Booth,

to come and stay. My surprise arose from the fact that Father seemed to
have severed all connection with his past; and although he spoke freely
and authoritatively about India and Indian affairs—then much to the
fore on account of the trial of Warren Hastings—I do not remember hearing him mention any one of his former associates by name. I evinced
some interest in Mr. Booth, but Father had nothing much to say about
him, save that he had known him years ago but had not seen him since
his return to England. I was left to judge for myself that he was a man
for whom Father had some regard. It was arranged that he should oc-
cupy the master bedroom, the one which local legend, confirmed by Mr.
Whymark, said had once been slept in by Queen Elizabeth. And Olivia,
whose wardrobe was, for a girl in her position, very modest, was given
permission to buy two new dresses.

Mr. Booth arrived on the afternoon before my birthday. He was considerably Father's senior, small, very dried and brittle looking. To begin
with he seemed painfully nervous and shy, but later on his manner
showed traces of aggressiveness and self-importance. His carriage, his
horseflesh, his clothes, and appurtenances were evidence of his wealth,
and he irritated me on the first day because when he was looking over
Merravay he followed each favourable comment by another which
showed that, compared with his own place in Berkshire, Merravay was
very small beer indeed. I remarked upon this to Father who said,

"Well, I believe Gore Park is quite palatial. He inherited it from his
grandfather, who made a great fortune before the public conscience became quite so tender about such things."

"Oh," I said. "I thought he'd been in India with you."

"So he was. He held an official post. But he's regarded as the only man
who ever went to India and came away with nothing but his pay in his
pocket. A phoenix!"

"Is he married?"

"Not that I know of," Father said carelessly.

That evening Mr. Booth regained the ground he had lost in my opinion
over Merravay by being very pleasant in a nervous, unobtrusive way to
Olivia. He asked her if she played the piano and she said she did but
had not practised lately.

"If it wouldn't trouble you, I wish you would play a little for me. I
am exceptionally fond of music and used to play myself . . . before . . .
well, my handicap . . . you know." We had all noticed that the first
and second fingers of his right hand were missing; he referred to the
loss as though it were something to be ashamed of.

Olivia glanced at Father, he nodded. She went to the piano and
played with nervous clumsiness at first and then with more assurance. Mr.

Booth named several of his favourite tunes, some of which she knew and some of which she had never heard, and he listened with unassumed interest and pleasure. When she had finished he thanked her and said she had a very pleasing touch. Father stayed silent; Olivia blushed.

Next morning, learning that it was my birthday, Mr. Booth apologised, too effusively, for not having known and come provided. He insisted that I should accept a very fine seal from his own fob. In the evening, when several neighbours came in to dine, and to dance later on in the hall, he apologised again for his inability to dance—perfectly understandable on account of his age—and instead of retiring to play cards with the other old gentlemen, he hovered about, looking like a little grasshopper, on the verge of the gay crowd. I thought him pathetic and once stayed out from the dance to talk to him; but he said he was enjoying himself, the music gave him pleasure, and he liked to see people making merry. At Gore Park, he added, there was an enormous ballroom with mirrored walls. "But seldom used; all too seldom used."

Next day we went to Ockley to shoot partridges, returning for late supper in the evening. The principal dish was a large game pie which Mr. Booth praised quite fulsomely.

"Yes," said Father, "Olivia has turned out to be quite a skilful little housekeeper."

Even then no breath of suspicion stirred in my mind. I was simply glad that someone for whom Father seemed to have regard should say the things which I often wished to say about Olivia but knew would be ineffectual coming from me. Old, ugly, fidgety, and annoying as he was, I felt my heart warming to Mr. Booth for pointing Father the way to a better appreciation of Olivia.

A very pleasant week followed. Mr. Booth had arranged to leave on market day, so, knowing that I should be up early and breakfast alone, I said good-bye to him overnight. When I shook, with an inward shudder, his cold, scaly, mutilated hand, and uttered the conventional hope that we should soon meet again, he said shyly,

"Indeed I hope so. I hope to see you all at Gore Park. I particularly want to show you my home farm. And the whole estate, of course; eighteen thousand acres in all."

"I shall look forward to that, sir," I said; and took my leave.

Next day, coming back from market, about to enter the house from the rear, I heard a little tapping sound from over my head, and I looked up and saw Olivia signing to me from her window. As soon as I had divested myself of my boots I went along to her room. Pressed against the glass her face had looked very white and distorted, but that, I told myself, might have been a trick of the light.

She must have been crying for hours; her eyes and her nose were puffed out of shape, and at sight of me she began to cry again so violently that it was some time before I could understand the reason for her distress. Then it came out.

"Oh, George. Father says I am to marry Mr. Booth!"

I said—I shall always remember the words—"I wouldn't let you."

At that she flung herself into my arms. "I thought you'd be on my side."

"Of course I am. I never heard anything so ridiculous. Why, he's older than Father! Father must be stark staring mad."

"With rage, now he is. I said I'd rather die."

I could understand that. This bit of news had scraped from my mind all pretence that I liked the man because he had been pleasant to Olivia and civil to me. I knew that all along I had seized on the small bearable things about him because I hated the sight of him and felt guilty for taking such a dislike to any human creature. Now I could admit to myself that I loathed him, everything about him; the dark, reptilian, leathery skin, the pale, bright, reptilian eyes, the scanty, scurfy hair and the bad teeth. And that sly, creepy manner. And his age! How could he dare to think of marrying any pretty, fresh young girl, leave alone my sister?

"I'll go and talk to Father now," I said.

Father was dressed for the evening; Candy on his knees was easing on the light, buckled shoes.

"Ah, George. I was coming along to talk to you while you changed. I've something to tell you. You're late, aren't you? Run along, I'll be with you in a minute." Candy rose and went to the chest, sprinkled a fine linen handkerchief with lavender essence, and presented it humbly to Father, who accepted it without a glance and tucked it into his cuff. "Come along," he said, "I'm damned hungry, but you must change; you smell, George. What is it, pigs or yokels?"

"I'd better say what I have to say now."

"Oh. I see. Five minutes, Candy. Well, George, I take it you've been treated to a display of hysteria. I was coming to warn you. I expect Olivia cried on your shoulder and said that she would rather die, eh? Women use these expressions so lightly, you know; many would rather die—by their own evidence—than pass a spider in the open road. You mustn't take that to heart, George."

He said all this in a light, flippant way which was somehow more deadly than anger would have been.

"I'm not going to stand by and see Olivia married to that little toad," I said hotly. "He's old enough to be her father and as ugly as sin. The whole idea is so revolting I wonder you entertained it long enough to tell her about it."

"Well, I agree that it is rather a striking example of Beauty and the Beast, so far as appearances go; but it's the right way about, you know. Now if you contemplated marrying an ugly old woman, George, I should take a very different view. As it is, I am delighted."

I could see that. My fury mounted.

"Yes; but then you've never had any natural feeling for Olivia, have you? I happen to be very fond of her and I won't stand by . . ."

"Don't repeat yourself, George. Time's short. As for that accusation . . . if I were as doting a father as old Whymark I could hardly hope to arrange a better match for my daughter. Mr. Booth admires her very much; he is in a position to give her every comfort; I'm sure he will be kind to her, and once she has forgotten about the handsome young man that every girl expects to find round the next corner, she'll be very h——"

At that moment the great gold-and-silver inlaid, pearl-and-coral encrusted elephant bell which Father had brought from India, and which served as a gong, rang out.

"I shall begin," said Father, moving away from me.

I tried to hold on to my bold, angry mood, while I hastily washed and threw off my market-day clothes; but when I rushed down to the dining room, ready to take up the cudgels again, Father, with a sidelong glance at Candy, began at once to talk upon some trivial subject. He put himself out to be pleasant, and since I knew that to anger him would be of no help, I contrived to be pleasant, too. Imperceptibly the atmosphere warmed.

Candy put the port wine, the fruit dishes, and a bowl of walnuts—the first of the year—on the table and withdrew.

"Now," said Father, "we can continue. Bawling her head off and talking about dying, she upset you, I know. She was just being girlish; they always behave that way when they're first proposed to."

"Olivia was genuinely distressed. And so should I be. God! In her place I should be thoroughly sick at the thought."

"That is one of the troubles with you, you know. I've often noticed it. You will always go putting yourself into somebody else's shoes— Candy's, Olivia's, even a horse's. That is such a waste. You can't understand how they feel, you only judge by how *you* would feel in their place. Naturally the idea of yourself in bed with old Douglas hugging and kissing you makes *you* feel sick. If it didn't there'd be something seriously wrong with you! Where it's a matter between man and woman it's entirely different. Damn it, George, have you never seen a fine lady give a hearty kiss to a filthy sweep who had crossed her path and brought

her, she thought, luck? Make a little allowance for sex, boy. And for God's
sake don't go and encourage her whimsies. It is a pity she got her word in
first."

"That makes no difference. Even is she wanted to marry him, Father,
I should hate the idea. He's too old, and ugly, and creepy. I want Olivia
to marry somebody nice; somebody she *could* be fond of."

His thick eyebrows arched quizzically.

"Have you a candidate in mind, George? Take your time," he said, as
I hesitated. "All these avid suitors take some counting, don't they?"

"Well," I said, "I know that just at the moment . . ."

"Come, come," he said with testy good humour, "face facts, George.
She's twenty-one and there's a dearth of young men. Of old Whymark's
eleven, only three were boys and it's the same wherever you look. Also,
much as this will shock your tender susceptibilities, there's this to remember. Love fizzles out and the lucky people are those who have something
left when the kissing is done. Can't you see that she's damned lucky to
get such an offer? And believe me, once the first coyness wears off she'll
realise it. Poor old Douglas, he was too shy to speak; he asked me to
prepare the way and then he'd write her a nice little letter. By the time
that arrives she'll have come round and be as pleased as a dog with two
tails. You'll see. So don't you worry, George; and don't encourage her to
keep up this play-acting. And now, since we're alone for once, how about
a game of chess?"

In the next few days he ignored the subject.

Olivia and I talked of the matter when we were alone and she certainly
didn't seem to be affecting the deep revulsion she professed; and whenever I was with her I shared her feeling and repeated that of course the
idea was absurd, untenable, that of course I was on her side and would
support her in her refusal.

Then one afternoon two letters arrived, one for Father, which I didn't
see, and one for Olivia. It was a stilted, pompous little letter, and it
said that the proposal it conveyed was made with Father's full knowledge
and approval.

"You see, they settled it between them," said Olivia.

Father was out that evening. Next morning, having been out for a
couple of hours, I came in to breakfast to find him literally forcing Olivia
into a seat at the table.

"You will sit there and eat your breakfast properly. Pretty, eh? You
look like an old woman who's lived through a famine! You'll eat your
breakfast and then you'll write that letter."

Olivia dared not refuse the food he kept thrusting at her, but she cried
all the time, and there is something about a person who is eating and

weeping that is, well, unendearing to say the least of it. I was shocked
to find that my pity was giving way to irritation, as pity so often does
in the end. After the nasty meal was over, Father tried to force her
into the library to write and she refused and he started to shake her and
I said,

"Stop that," in a high shrill voice quite unlike mine.

"Yes. That was a mistake," said Father as Olivia wriggled out of his
hands and ran loudly crying upstairs. For the first time since the affair
had been mooted he seemed to lose a little of his composure.

"Look here, George. That letter must be answered. More hangs on this
than you know. She's carrying coy reluctance just a little too far. Go and
see if you can talk sense into her."

I went up. Olivia turned and said, "Oh, poor dear George, I've made
you fall out with Father."

I remembered all the things he had said about women being different,
and being coy and being hysterical and being silly about spiders and
kissing sweeps.

"Now for God's sake, Olivia dear," I said, "be quite honest with me. Is
it just . . ." She looked at me and I was ashamed. But as though she had
sensed my Father-instilled doubt, she jumped from the bed upon which
she had flung herself and went to her dressing table.

"He thinks I'm pretty, does he?" she said. She took up the scissors and
with three sharp snaps of the blades cut off all the little curls which clus-
tered about her forehead Then she dragged the points of the scissors
down her face from just below the eye to the jaw. The parallel furrows
leaped up, beaded with little drops of blood.

"All right," I said, answering something that hadn't been put into
words. "I'll tell him. Don't worry any more."

Father was waiting.

"It's useless," I said. "She just can't do it; and I don't want her to."

"Let's go for a ride," he said.

It was one of those mellow autumn mornings when the thin mist shreds
away and the sky is harebell blue, and everything wears a gentle, wistful
look. Father led the way along the narrow headland that divided the front
field from Layer Wood, which was blazing with copper and gold and
sharp yellow. Single damp bright leaves fell slowly down, spinning.

Speech was impossible while we rode one behind the other; but at
the top of the field Father halted and I drew up beside him. From this
point one had the best view of Merravay, for the field ran down towards it and the trees rose behind it so that it seemed to be cupped in
the loving hand of the earth. This morning the worn old walls, the

slightly uneven roof, were drinking in the sunshine and giving it back again in a glow of apricot and rose and tawny. A thin column of smoke from one of the chimneys went spiralling up, blue against blue. In the garden the flowerbeds were fragile patchwork against the solidity of the lawns, the carved yews.

I had meant to speak as soon as we halted, but, having looked at Merravay, I was compelled to sit and stare for a moment, thinking that I had never seen it so lovely.

It was Father who spoke first, breaking the silence by saying in a rapid, staccato, strangely distinct voice, as though addressing someone slightly deaf or stupid,

"Look here, George; this has gone far enough. I gave you several perfectly good reasons for my approval of this match; there is another which I wasn't particularly anxious to talk about. But since you are so stubborn and will insist on encouraging her, I must tell you. You've read all this ridiculous nonsense about Hastings, I suppose. All right! Now when they drop the net for big fish they take small ones, too. An inquiry of that nature turns up a lot of things one believed to be done with and forgotten. And I've realised in the last month or so that at one point I am vulnerable. It would be very useful for me to have Douglas Booth on my side."

"You mean that you did something . . . and now he's blackmailing you!"

Father laughed.

"Really, George, you do so tend to melodrama. If there is blackmail in it, the boot surely is on the other leg. I'm the blackmailer. I've got what poor old Douglas wants; and whether he would ever be called upon to repay me is very much a matter of chance. I just want to make sure that, in the event, he would stand by me. You're not the only one who likes Merravay, you know. I'm fond of the place, too."

"What has Merravay to do with it?"

"I should not, if it came to the point, sit there waiting for Messrs. Fox and Burke to slap *me*, George. My gains, ill gotten as they may seem to such sentimentalists, cost me dear, and I shall hang on to them. At the first breath of trouble, unless I can be sure of Douglas, I shall sell out and go abroad again."

He paused to let that sink in.

"And I still think," he continued, "that Olivia would be better off in her own home, with a rich and doting husband and a pack of children—she's the sort who would breed once a year—than she will be as governess or companion to a lady! For I tell you frankly, George, and you can tell her, that if she doesn't go to Gore Park she doesn't stay at Merravay. As it is, the effort to be fair and just to her is just a little too much for me and after *this* . . . if she defeats my neat little scheme for self-preservation by sheer pig-headedness . . . I doubt if I could keep my hands off her. You saw what happened this morning. If she won't go my way, she must go her own, and discover just how much fairness and justice there is in this world."

I said the only thing possible for me.

"The day Olivia goes out to earn her living, sir, I shall go with her."

What effect I expected that speech to produce I find difficult to say. I knew, or thought I knew, that his affection for me, though rooted in his self-love, was firm and strong. But he was evidently one of the "if thy eye offend thee, cast it out" manner of men. He turned and gave me a long assessing look and then said in a reasonable way, far more chilling than any sneer,

"Well, if that is the way you feel, George, there's no more to be said. You're a nice-looking boy, you write a clear hand and have pleasing manners when you choose. You'd be worth every penny of eight shillings a week as a clerk; I started with less. In that case Mr. Booth can hang himself for all I care. I always had a nagging desire to be a country gentleman and I thought you liked Merravay. I was prepared to settle and found a family. But without you it would be pointless to stay. So if you've had your fill of it we'll say good-bye to Merravay as soon as possible."

With that he swung his horse round, set it to the low fence between field and meadow and went galloping off, leaving me with his last words ringing in my ears.

I often wondered whether he used the phrase "Good-bye to Merravay" deliberately or not.

The next four or five days were as wretched as any I remember. Olivia kept to her room. Father and I met at table after the first evening when I absented myself and he sent Candy to fetch me. "I see no reason why we should avoid one another, George," he said. "You're young and romantic, I'm old and practical, and we take different views, as men are entitled to do; but let us behave in civilised fashion."

My interviews with Olivia were just as trying in another way; she cried and cried and kept begging me to make it up with Father. I had told her, so far, only that Father had threatened to turn her out and I had said that I should go, too; I hadn't mentioned Merravay. She had written another letter to Miss Rossiter, explaining that now she was about to be homeless, and begging her to employ her or find her employment of any kind.

"She'll help me now that my circumstances have changed, George; I am positive of that; and truly I should be happy, glad, pleased to go from here if only you hadn't said that you'd come too. It's so much worse for a man to be poor. Nobody expects a woman to have anything, anyway. And I shall have a place to go. It was a kind, noble gesture, George dear, and I do appreciate it, but you're making everything so much more difficult for me."

Constant crying and misery had marred what looks the scissors had left; and, looking at the bristly hair and deeply scratched face, I kept thinking—Yes, that was a gesture too; and whom did it hurt?

"Do please say that you'll stay with Father."

My jangled nerves gave way,

"God damn it all, Olivia, why should I? He's kind enough to me, but the way he treats Tom Fulger and Candy and you sets my teeth on edge. There are times when I hate him, and I won't go trailing about the face of the earth in his company just for the sake of his filthy money!"

"What d'you mean by trailing about, George?" she asked, suddenly quiet and intent.

"Well," I said, confused, "nothing really. But there is some sort of threat; he may have to leave Merravay. It's some sort of inquiry or something which Mr. Booth could ward off if he was so minded. That's one reason why Father is so . . . oh for God's sake, Olivia, don't *cry!* I didn't mean to tell you that. I was just trying to show you that I might as well go with you of my own free will as wait and be chucked out."

"And now I've lost Merravay for you," she cried, and threw herself face downwards on her bed.

"Well, if you can't discuss the thing reasonably . . ." I said, and went away.

On the fourth or fifth morning, at breakfast, Father said to me, "Has Olivia written at all?"

"Not to my knowledge."

"Well, tell her to do it today. A civil, decent proposal demands some answer and there's no point in being more offensive than necessary. Tell her, too, that she'd better start looking about for a post. *I* meant what I said, George."

The slightest possible emphasis on the first pronoun fired my temper.

"So did I," I said.

"Then you'd both better start looking!"

He ate some food rather more quickly than usual; then, emptying his mouth, said,

"This is all your doing. If you hadn't backed her up she'd have given in within twenty-four hours and written Dear-Mr.-Booth-you-do-me-too-much-honour-and-what-kind-of-ring-can-I-have? As it is, she thinks you'll bring me round. If George is for me, who can be against me? They're all as crafty as foxes, and she thinks she's on a safe bet because I'm fond of you. I *am* fond of you, when you're amenable, but I'm damned if I'll be blackmailed, even by you. You've turned against me and I'm one of those who do not love their enemies."

"A few days ago," I retorted, "we were civilised people taking a different view—or so you said. Now you call me your enemy."

"A few days ago I was counting on your fondness—not for me—for Merravay, George. So we're all wrong. And why God Almighty ever took into his head to make women I shall never understand. Surely his infinite wisdom could have devised some less troublesome way of propagating the human race. Everything ruined by one cock-snitched little bitch's whim . . . encouraged by *you*. You'll remember that to your sorrow!"

He was going to spend the day at Muchanger, and shortly after breakfast rode off.

I had arranged to work with Tom that day, but suddenly I had no heart for it. My future at Merravay, learning about and then managing the land, the crops, and the flocks, was like a path seeming to lead on and then stopping suddenly. I had no future here.

I wandered idly into the garden. There was a slight autumnal chill in the air that morning, but the sun was shining on the dew that lay like silver on the lawns and sparkled on the thousands of cobwebs which stretched from leaf to leaf. A brilliant cock pheasant rose from a bed of marigolds and flew to the red wall, where he rested for a moment between two of the grey urns and then flew on to the field. The furrows lay striped in dark chocolate and faint purple. The wood blazed with a last desperate fire.

"I saw Father leave," said Olivia, coming up softly behind me.

"Yes, he's gone to Muchanger."

"Did he say anything?"

"Yes; he said you must write to Mr. Booth today. And he said we must both begin to look about for jobs. And he said everything was my fault." I tried to speak lightly but failed to keep the inward dreariness from sounding in my voice.

Olivia plucked a marigold and stood staring at it as though counting its petals.

"George dear, do please give in. I'll tell you something . . . I didn't think either of you would hold out so long."

I laughed. "That's exactly what Father said. We must be a very stubborn family."

"I'm being stubborn for my own benefit, George. You're doing no good at all. I do with my whole heart beg you to make it up with Father."

"I tell you I don't care about Father."

"But you do about this place."

"I shall survive."

She turned and stared at the house.

"Isn't it strange," she said musingly, "I hated it from the first; you loved it; but it was inimical to me from the beginning. Like a person. Quite apart from any other reason I shall be glad to leave the house. If it belonged to me absolutely I shouldn't want it, shouldn't want to live in it."

"If it belonged to me absolutely . . . Look, Olivia, we're wasting time again. We must make plans, think what we're going to do."

"I think I should write that letter first."

"It would be as well," I said. She turned and went into the house.

In less time than I expected she came to the door, the letter folded and sealed in her hand. "I've done it," she called brightly.

We walked towards one another, and when we met she held out the letter, address uppermost, very clearly written.

"Doesn't that do Miss Rossiter credit?" she asked.

Something cold and gall-bitter rose from the pit of my stomach to choke my throat. Oh yes, I thought, you may well be gay, now. You're leaving a critical parent and a home you hate . . . anything to you will seem an improvement.

Just at that moment Phyllis Whymark arrived; she wanted Olivia to go with her to Baildon to match some ribbon.

"Of course," said Olivia, "I was going to take this to post anyway."

"What on earth have you been doing to yourself?" Phyllis asked.

"A series of accidents. I burned my hair with the curling iron and scratched my face on a rosebush."

"I've been in the wars, too. Look, young Billy hit me in the mouth with a ball; took one tooth out, clean as a whistle. I shall never get married now!"

"Married!" said Olivia. They went off laughing.

A day at Muchanger seemed to have restored Father's good humour too. Olivia had not returned when we sat down to dinner, but since she was no longer expected at table her absence was not remarked upon, and he seemed to go out of his way to be entertaining, giving me a lively account of his day's doings. It was impossible to avoid the thought that with Olivia out of sight and mind, with Olivia safely away, we two got along pretty well. A self-pitying consciousness that I had made a fool of myself to no purpose came inevitably upon that thought's heels.

We were halfway through the meal when the door slammed, and before I could do more than hope that Father would not connect the sound with Olivia, she had reached the dining-room door and stood there, look-ing pretty and in some way different. Her riding clothes were worn and shabby, but they had been made for her and fitted better than some of the clothes she had made for herself, and the little cocked hat hid her spoiled hair; the flush of a day in the open did something to conceal the marks on her cheek; but the difference lay deeper than mere appearance. She moved and looked like a free woman at last; as though the shy, de-mure schoolgirl had spent three happy, successful years somewhere and now looked in to visit us.

Father looked at her, his ordinary expression of cold distaste shot through with positive venom. For the first time in years she met his look without flinching and stared back, her eyes as hard as his own. My heart began to beat with a nervous flutter.

"This is an unexpected honour," said Father with heavy irony. "But I trust that you do not expect to dine here. You are both late and un-welcome."

"I dined at the New House," said Olivia. I caught her glance and signed to her to go away, but she stood her ground and it occurred to me that she might be a little flown with wine. The females at New House were very free in such matters and often stayed at the table with the menfolk, sharing the port wine.

"It's all right, George," she said, answering my sign, "I have some-thing to say to Father."

"Nothing that you have to say would interest me, now, miss. Get out!"

"All the same, you should know," said Olivia hardily. "I wrote to Mr. Booth this morning and accepted his proposal."

Astonishment held us both speechless for a moment. Then Father said, "Well, I'm damned!" and began to laugh.

I said, "Olivia, you didn't!"

"I hope that pleases you both," she said, and her glance flicked, like the very tip of a whiplash, from Father's face to mine; then she turned and walked, very straight-backed, to the door.

"There you are. What did I tell you? That's women for you, George. Unpredictable as the wind. All that fuss, and she meant to have him from the start."

"She did not! She changed her mind this morning. And I know when . . . and why . . ." I was almost crying, so sharp and terrible was my remorse, my knowledge of my secret disloyalty, my recognition of a flash-ing relief.

"You must have been remarkably eloquent, George," said Father.

"It's nothing to laugh at," I said savagely, jumping up from my chair. "And she shan't do it. I shan't let her. I'd sooner see the place burned. . . ."

I went blundering towards the door, but Father, from his end of the table, was quicker, and he stood there with his back against it.

"Don't be in such a hurry," he said quietly. "Such militant chivalry will keep for a minute. Sit down and hear what I have to say."

"You won't talk me round," I said. But I let him push me back into my chair.

At that moment Candy returned and I realised that all this shattering little incident had happened in the time it took to change plates between courses.

"Oh, take it away, and yourself with it," snapped Father, motioning the dish away. "Put the decanter on the table and get out."

As soon as we were alone again he poured wine for us both and then, for just a second, sat silent, twirling the stem of his glass between his fingers.

"It would be most unkind of you, George, to withdraw now whatever it was that you said, or did, this morning! I mean that. You see, you'd be taking away her excuse for doing what she wants to do, what she has wanted all along to do."

"I don't believe that."

"You can test the truth of it presently; but I won't have you for the second time go blundering in blindfold. On that first evening, if I'd caught you before she did, I could have explained, warned you, and none of this fantastic muddle would ever have arisen. You see, George, he is ugly, and he is rich, a most damning combination where women are concerned. A woman could marry an ugly poor man and still feel noble, or a rich handsome one and feel romantic. D'you follow? What Olivia was waiting for was some reason that would be acceptable to that vanity which women carry about with them like a set of scales—and you gave it to her. Her warped female sense of values would seize with delight on the notion that she was saving you from exiling yourself. I'll bet that she was writing that letter before whatever it was you so fortunately said was out of your mouth."

To myself I admitted the truth of that—the apparent truth; but his whole premise I could not accept.

"I will take back what I said if she will take back what she wrote." I tried to remember exactly what I had said; so little; so vague; it must have been my manner rather than my words which had provoked that impulse of self-sacrifice.

"Well, you can try," said Father calmly. "It would, as I say, be unkind; and I think it would be useless too. She knows that such offers don't come every day. Also, if she hasn't whispered it as the most deadly secret to

Miss Whymark, who by this time has told everyone within reach, I'm a Dutchman." He paused while I thought about that.

"I'd rather have her silly then, than sell herself in a loveless marriage to that little toad on my account."

"You know, George, you are most devastatingly like a woman in some ways—the way you talk. Sell herself! Loveless marriage! Old maid's twaddling stock phrases! And the way you shift ground. This morning apparently you conveyed in some way your wish for a match to take place; the moment it's settled you're all against it. It's time you grew up, you know. Men know what they want and take it by hook or by crook if they can, and are glad. If you feel impelled to pity *some*body," he said, a malicious grin beginning to slide over his face, "pity poor old Douglas. He'll have to line up with me now; and then start at his inflexible age to accommodate himself to Olivia's whims and fancies."

"Not if I can prevent it," I said.

"Run along and try," said Father settling back and lifting his glass.

Olivia listened politely to all I had to say, but she would not budge an inch. At one point, made cruel by exasperation, I cried,

"I believe Father is right. I believe you want to marry the man after all. And you're the girl who would rather die!"

"I'm not," said Olivia, giving me a strange look. "That girl did die, writing the letter. I'm a different girl, George."

"Oh, don't talk rot," I said, and my voice sounded like Father's.

"It's true. I am different. Why, I actually heard myself boasting to Phyllis about the glories of Gore Park!"

I gaped at her. So Father had been right about the whispered confidences. Probably right about the secret wish to marry. . . . Despite that creeping doubt, however, I continued to argue and plead until at last Olivia said, "Really, George, I did think that now I should be left in peace."

V

I suppose that the final, the fatal, defeats never come to a man from the outside; they are inflicted from within. And I suppose that those inner defeats are never the result of one great battle; ground is lost inch by inch. What Father stood for as opposed to what I tried to stand for was not triumphant until I began to believe that he was right; but the struggle had begun long ago. Perhaps as long ago as the day when we met in the Ogilvys' parlour. I could look back and think, if I hadn't been so easily silenced when I tried to speak up for Mrs. Ogilvy . . . if I had got out on that hill and walked in the mud . . . if I had stood up more resolutely for Candy . . . I should have altered not Father's nature or behaviour but my own; I should be a stronger character. It was the dreadful weakness of my own character that distressed me most when I thought about Olivia; the weak hysterical support, the weak self-pitying withdrawal of it; the weak tardy effort to replace it.

Outwardly all went very well. The wedding, by Olivia's express wish, took place before Christmas. Father, pleased with her at last, did everything in fine style and gave her a generous marriage settlement. Two of his casual prophecies were fulfilled; she bore her first son within a year and within six years had five, all healthy and surprisingly handsome. And, given her inch she took her mile; Mr. Booth certainly had to accommodate himself to her whims and fancies. It would be difficult to find a more masterful and exacting wife, a milder, more tolerant husband. Sometimes it is easy for me to believe that Olivia Sandell did die that sunny autumn morning, and went, a wistful little crop-haired ghost, to join the ones she always said haunted Merravay.

I lived on, most enviable young man; but something in me had been damaged. For one thing I could never marry, never again feel at ease with any woman; Father's cynicisms and Olivia's transformation combined to put that out of the question. And with men I became conscious of a feeling of inadequacy. I could still work and do business with them but I could not share their pleasures. With the passage of time I became misanthropic as well as misogynous, quite against my will.

I never opposed or openly criticised Father again. The impulse would arise sometimes, especially when, during the troubled time six years ago, wages became a matter of hot dispute, but as soon as I had convinced myself that he was wrong I would remember the number of times when he had been proved right. I never even argued with him again. And he seemed to lose interest in me. Our relationship settled down to a placid coolness to which his illness and long immobility hardly made any difference at all. Six years ago Tom Fulger—long since gone from Merravay, which I was capable of running on my own—came as the representative of the farm labourers to see Father about raising the winter rate of wages to match the rising price of goods. Father, who had never liked Tom, lost his temper and had a stroke. A few days later, without telling him about it, I raised all the wages. After six years, during which I visited his room every morning and evening and saw to it that everything was done to alleviate him, he died. And after the funeral I moved into the great bedroom, where I had always wanted to sleep.

Romantic, defeated, impulsive warm heart turned cold, unfriended—for that raising of the wages set every neighbour against me—a self-hater, a weak, poor-spirited fellow, I sit here tonight and know that I am happier and more fortunate in the final issue than anyone else I know. For I love, with an unchanging love, something that cannot change. And today, with the willing of Merravay to Olivia's third and favourite son I have shaken off an old nagging sense of indebtedness. If I liked the boy better my sense of repayment would be that much less complete; willing it to him, as Olivia asked me to do, hurt so much that now I feel I owe her nothing. Tonight Merravay really belongs to me.

Interlude

George Frederick Sandell Esq., of Merravay, died as he had lived, an eccentric.

Even before his father died he had gained himself a reputation for sloppy sentimentality, and during his term of office as a Justice of the Peace he caused scandals and made many bad neighbours by his lenient sentences to poachers. In the end sentiment killed the miserable, puling fellow.

A hot-headed agitator called Tom Fulger, who had once been manager at Merravay, sided with the labourers during the riots and stack-burnings which broke out during the demand for higher wages or cheaper food which followed the end of the Bonaparte wars. In Suffolk the Yeomanry was called out one November and Fulger was shot through the head.

What must Mr. Sandell do but order a stone to be put over his grave?

Several people thought that the rector of Nettleton failed in his duty in allowing the erection of the stone at all. The rector, however, perceived a golden opportunity. Mr. Sandell was far less regular at church than a gentleman in his position—for the sake of setting a good example—should be. The rector said that when the stone was set up there must be a proper dedication service. He planned to speak very frankly at that ceremony.

Mr. Sandell protested that there was no need for a commotion; he only wanted Tom's grave marked so that in years to come, when the workers had got a fair bargain, there'd be something to show whom they had to thank for it.

The day of the dedication dawned clear and bright, a typically English April day. The rector, warned by his wife who was weatherwise, put on his hunting boots and wore a number of warm garments under his cassock. When the driving sleet came down he stood his ground without marked discomfort. Most of those who had come to watch and listen had understood from the rector's opening sentences that the rector's views were as sound as their own; they retreated to the shelter of the church. Mr. Sandell, bareheaded, stood as though in a dream, staring at the ornate stone, over which the sleet was sliding, blurring the words:

TO THE MEMORY OF THOMAS FULGER

WHO IN HIS DEVOTED ENDEAVOUR

TO ATTAIN

BETTER CONDITIONS

FOR

HIS FELLOW MEN

LAID DOWN HIS LIFE.

Even when the rector's sonorous phrases had come to an end Mr. Sandell stood there. He was seen to shiver as he at last walked to his carriage; and ten days later he was dead of inflammation of the lungs.

His heir was a nephew, who upon taking up his heritage, added the name of Sandell to his own of Booth, and, largely on that account, he was regarded with considerable suspicion for a time. But he, thank God, had no nonsense about him; he took after his grandfather, the old Nabob. He was entirely sound over matters like poachers, wages, and trespassers.

He became extremely popular. He married one of the Fennels of Ockley and slipped into place in the county like a hand into a glove. Once again the great hall at Merravay became the scene of gay gatherings. All was well.

The Poacher

WHEN I was seventeen I was sent to Merravay in disgrace. I had committed the heinous crime of falling in love with the wrong young man; then, forbidden to see or speak to him ever again, I had proceeded to fall—in conventional fashion—into a decline.

My papa, who was very angry with me, approved of Merravay as a place of exile because it was one hundred and fifty miles away from Archie; my mamma, in whom rage had given way to exasperated concern for my health, thought that the good country air and a change of scene would be beneficial. So a letter explaining the circumstances was sent to Uncle Alan, and back came an invitation rendered lukewarm by the accompanying apologies. He was afraid, he said, that I should be lonely in his womanless household; and he was afraid that I should find life at Merravay dull in this season; and he was afraid that if they were hoping for some young man in Suffolk to prove a counter-attraction they would be disappointed—there was a great dearth of young men.

The fact that winter was approaching was one reason for Mamma's desire to get me away; for in the garrison town where my papa was stationed at that time the winter was the gay, social season; and since I could not be left at home without arousing comment, or be taken out without the risk of seeing Archie, it would have been a very awkward situation indeed. And nobody cared, I least of all, how dull life at Merravay would be. I felt that every place where Archie was not, was hateful; and besides, was I not going to die very soon?

Of course I can look back on it now and laugh, and feel a little sorry for my parents, and put all the blame on *The Posy*, that apparently innocuous little magazine. Until I was fourteen and my mamma for reasons of economy dismissed my governess, I had nothing but contempt for *The Posy*, for at that time I was interested in everything under the sun except clothes and love stories; but once Miss Tibbenham had gone I seemed to be stranded in a mental desert, and *The Posy*, which Mamma took regularly because it had fashion pages, was the only oasis in that desert. It seemed harmless enough and was highly thought of by all parents. Its fashion pages told us what was being worn just then, and how to reconstruct an old garment to look like new; it had a "Household Management" page, mainly hints on how to be mean with food and strict with servants; it had a "Pretty" page telling us how to deal with freckles and such things; and it had a serial which invariably lasted just six months. Twice a year for three years we were regaled by a new version of the same story; there was always a girl, crossed in love, who fell into a decline and died. She lay, pale, "beautiful in death," with her long hair streaming, and covered with roses in each one of the six stories.

So, of course, when I was seventeen I fell in love, was crossed, and fell into a decline. I had mistimed things somewhat, for unless I lasted out until the summer, which seemed unlikely, there would be no roses for me.

However, I went to Merravay, as to death, and made no protest.

It was a place often mentioned in family circles, generally with an accompanying comment about Uncle Alan's luck and Grandmamma's unashamed favouritism for him. My grandmamma, whom I could just remember as a strict, intimidating old lady, had spent her girlhood at Merravay. Her brother, who never married, had made Uncle Alan, her third son, his heir, and everyone believed that Grandmamma had ordered him to do so. They said also that my oldest uncle, who inherited Gore Park, had greatly hoped that when Alan went to Merravay Grandmamma would go to end her days there; but she did not. She stayed at Gore Park and retained her martinet sway until the end.

A young male cousin of mine had once stayed with Uncle Alan and reported that the shooting in East Anglia was superb but that Merravay itself was a dull hole: and an elderly female cousin, who had for a short time kept house for Uncle Alan after the death of his wife many years ago, still spoke of Merravay as the most beautiful place in the world; but she was given to easy enthusiasms, as spinsters so often are.

II

Complicated arrangements for my safe escort across country were made, and I arrived safely one fine September afternoon and went straight to bed. Self-inflicted as my woes were—or as, looking back, I see them to be—they were real enough then and I was genuinely ill. Uncle Alan's first comment, when he met me at the coach stop, was that I looked more ill than he had expected and that he hadn't realised that I was "a doctor's case."

He was a tall, stout, handsome, self-indulgent and, up to a point, genial man; his wife, of whom he was reputed to have been very fond, and his six-year-old daughter had both died during an outbreak of cholera which had swept through the country like a plague. His son was, according to family parlance, "damn odd"; he was scholarly and spent most of his time abroad, brooding over the ruins of old cities, Jericho, Babylon, Thebes. Papa and my two uncles whose inheritance had been small professed to pity Uncle Alan for having so odd a son, just as they professed to pity Uncle Frederick, who had inherited Gore Park, for his gout. It consoled them for their envy.

Uncle Alan was obviously ill at ease with a strange young female, and an ailing one at that; but he had made meticulous arrangements for my comfort. I was installed in a vast, beautifully furnished bedroom and given a maid, Susan, to attend me. One of the symptoms of decline, as laid down by the stories in *The Posy*, was that the subject should eat nothing, or almost nothing; and I hadn't been in Merravay for twenty-four hours before I realised that Uncle Alan's food was far more difficult to resist than Mamma's "invalid diet" had been. Mamma's idea had been to offer gruel, steamed fish, and blancmange; Uncle Alan appeared to think that if one couldn't eat a roast partridge one might be tempted by oysters, a smoky-hot puffy omelette, breast of chicken in cream sauce, or peaches in brandy.

But it was not, I must contend, the food which brought me round. I was still miserable enough to be resistant to that. It was Uncle Alan's embarrassed, clumsy, almost boyish concern which brought me downstairs on the evening of my third day in his house. And after that I had something new to think about.

I went down, making what I thought of then as a valiant effort, thinking that if I were going to die, I might as well die on my feet. We dined together and afterwards sat in the drawing-room, an immense apartment, beautifully furnished. He asked me if I played chess—I didn't—or the piano, which I did a little. I played for quite a long time, sometimes with tears in my eyes because music is of all things the most conducive to emotion. At nine o'clock Clayton, the manservant, brought in the tea tray, ordered specially for me; and when the tea was drunk Uncle Alan said, "Maybe you should get back to bed now."

I rose obediently and bade him good night and he uttered some of his awkward, kindly intentioned words, so that I almost cried again. Then I walked to the door, opened it, closed it behind me, and was immediately seized by what was perhaps the first genuine emotion I had known since Miss Tibbenham had read me some of Macaulay's poems.

It was a highly unpleasant emotion too. Sheer stark terror. And utterly reasonless.

The hall at Merravay is very large, not like the hall of a house at all, more like a church or a barn. But everything that could be done to soften its austere appearance had been done. The stone floor was almost completely hidden by lovely rugs; the furniture was beautiful. On a bed of ash in the huge hearth three enormous logs were blazing, lending their light to supplement that of the two lamps and many candles. There was no reason at all why I should be frightened, should stand there by the closed door of the drawing-room, paralysed by terror, with cold sweat breaking out all over me. Nothing to see, save the big gracious apartment; nothing to hear.

To be frightened was an entirely new experience for me; I was far from being a nervous creature. My sheltered life had prevented me from ever being very greatly tested, but the common everyday accidents of life had never found me wanting. An unruly hired horse had run away with me and finally thrown me, but I rode again next day; and once when Miss Tibbenham and I had been left alone, with only a daily woman, she had gone out to the chemist's one evening, slipped on an icy path, broken her ankle, and been taken in by some kind people near by; I'd slept alone in the house for ten days then—which every girl of twelve wouldn't do! The daily woman had made quite a fuss about it, making me go round and lock every door and shutter the windows before she left at dusk, and predicting the most shocking possibilities.

Now here I was, utterly unable to cross a room because I was frightened. Of nothing!

I stood there, shivering and sweating and waiting for whatever it was to pass over. But it didn't. The terrible fear—fear of nothing—mounted and mounted. I wanted to scream, but though I opened my mouth and tried to, no sound emerged. How long I stood there I don't know; or how long I should have stood there. I knew that Uncle Alan was in the drawing-room, I had only to take a step backward and turn the handle and I should be with him. I longed to take that step, but I couldn't move.

It was he who moved. He was a pipe-smoker; but he was too polite— just then—to smoke a pipe in his own drawing-room in the presence of a female. After I had gone—and how avidly he must have been waiting for that moment—he came to fetch his pipe from the library, where, I discovered, he usually sat when alone. He opened the drawing-room door and walked straight into me.

The terror, whatever it was, receded at once with the opening of the door, with his first step into the hall.

"Good God!" he said, as his stout warm body hit my cold shaking one. "I thought you'd gone to bed."

My first impulse was to gasp out that I had been frightened. But something that was half common sense and half good manners rose up in me and took charge. Poor Uncle Alan . . . a sick girl thrust on him was surely bad enough . . . spare him the mad fancies.

I said in what struck my own ears as an amazingly ordinary voice, "I just wanted your arm . . . on the stairs."

"Poor girl, poor girl," he said, "I didn't think of it. Very remiss of me. Well, here we go. Lean on me."

He scooped me across the hall and up the stairs and into the warm lighted room where Susan was busy with the bed-warmer and the hot milk of the bedtime ritual.

I was too near the edge of sleep to come back and start worrying when I realised that from the moment when I had said good night to Uncle Alan I hadn't thought about Archie at all. For the first time in months I slept without crying myself to sleep.

III

I have heard old ladies say tartly that a sharp smack of the face is the best remedy for hysterics; it may be that a sharp shock of fear is the best remedy for decline; certainly I woke next morning with something other than my love-sickness on my mind.

The memory of the terror was still vivid, and as soon as I was fully awake I began to dread a similar experience. Unless I stayed in my room—a thing I felt less inclined to do now than at any time since my arrival—sooner or later I should be obliged to face that walk across the hall alone.

Yet, now that I was capable of thinking about it, and of taking courage in the bright morning sunshine, the place drew me. I felt I must look at it, investigate, search for some explanation. I was up and dressed by eleven o'clock.

The hall faced south and had two enormous windows through which the sun spilled slantingly; on the bed of grey ash two logs burned; the place felt warm and looked gay. I stood at the bottom of the stairs and stared for a long time; nothing sinister met my eyes. With a feeling of daring mingled with scepticism, rather like that with which children play Old Man, I went and stood by the drawing-room door, exactly where I had stood last evening. Then I walked slowly round, looking at everything and touching some things and finding nothing frightening at all. I didn't know what I was looking for, but if I had come upon a suit of old armour, or a skull made into an inkstand, or a hideous foreign idol such as I had seen at Gore Park and other places, I should have regarded that as the focus of evil, probably made up some story about it, attributed my suscepti- bility to my low state of health, and been, if not comforted, satisfied. But there was nothing; and finally, having walked all round the hall, I sat down on the window seat farthest from the stairs, full in the sunshine.

I was on my feet again in a minute. Absurd and ridiculous and im- possible as it seemed, even to me who was on the search for the absurd, the ridiculous, the impossible, to sit down there in the full sunshine was like lowering oneself into a well of icy water. It wasn't just the deathly cold; it was the awful feeling of misery and despair.

I had bounded away from the window seat and now stood two feet away from it in a place where the sun lay on the floor. Warm sun.

After a while I walked to the other window, touched the smooth, age- polished wood of the seat there; it was almost hot. I went back and timidly, but with dogged curiosity, felt about the other window. There was no detectable draught but there was the chill, a chill which not only af- fected one's flesh but seemed to pierce one's very soul, so that the light went out of the day and there was nothing but utter desolation.

I was familiar, of course, as who is not, with a ghost story or two, "The Flying Skull at Francoy Abbots"; "Maria Marten"; "The Nun at Borley"; but in all of them something was seen or heard. No story that I knew had ever mentioned cold as a sign of haunting; yet as I stood there I was perfectly certain, as—with very little else to go upon—I am sure to this day that the far window seat in the hall at Merravay is a haunted place.

IV

Apart from exercising craft and guile to ascertain that I never had to cross the hall alone after dark, there was nothing that I could do. I daren't mention the subject to anyone; I daren't ask a question. Now that I had been jerked back into life and found myself capable of taking an interest —however morbid—in something outside my own affairs I realised how idiotic my recent behaviour had been. Doubtless to other people it had seemed so all along, and if I now started to talk about a haunted window seat they would be justified in thinking me quite demented. And I must admit that now and again the thought that I might be going out of my mind did occur to me! Obviously I was not a very steady-minded girl. I could now go for increasingly long periods without thinking of Archie at all, and when I did think it was with hardly a pang—yet the past week I was prepared to die for love of him. Had I merely fallen into a fresh state of delusion; changed an imaginary grief for an imaginary terror?

All this went on below the surface. Poor Uncle Alan was delighted by the outward change in me; and attributed it to the air and the food. He began to take trouble over my social life. He had several friendly neighbours; the Fennels, to whom he was related by marriage, were within easy visiting distance, and the Whymarks, though their house was hidden by the trees, were practically next door.

I particularly remember a visit which Uncle Alan and I made to the Whymarks early in October. For one thing it was the first time that I had been on horseback since early summer when the storm broke over me and Archie. For another there was at New Holding a very old lady, Miss Phyllis Whymark, who said that she remembered my grandmother and that I was very like her to look at. That pleased me, because my grandmother had been accounted very handsome in her day. Miss Whymark opened her mouth and pointed to a gap in a set of otherwise remarkably sound if yellowed teeth.

"I do so well remember," she croaked, "the day after I lost this tooth I went over to Merravay and there was your grandmother, my dear, in worse case. She'd burnt her hair off curling it, and torn her face on a bush. We laughed and said that now we'd never get married. And believe it or not, as soon as we were alone she told me that she was going to be married before Christmas. I was so jealous I could have clawed her eyes out! Ah, but that's a long time ago."

We had lunch at New Holding, and after the meal some of the young ones led me off to see their puppies. As a consequence my boots were caked with mud, and being town-bred and used to my mamma's house-proud ways, I didn't enter Merravy on my return. I went to the back door, sent Susan up to fetch my house shoes, and called to a boy in the yard to come and pull off my boots as I leaned against the wall.

The main back door at Merravay had a porch, one side of which, at that hour of the afternoon, caught the westering sun. I moved into the sunny place, braced my back against the wall and lifted my foot, and stood there trapped within another circle of the same icy cold, the same deadly misery, as lay about that window seat. It struck with the same impact as a pailful of cold water, strongly thrown. I gasped and gave a violent shudder. The girl Susan, standing by with my shoes in her hand, said,

"You didn't ought to stand there, miss. Thass the one sunny place in the yard and thass allust cold."

I put my hand on the red, warm-looking wall.

"Yes," I said carefully. "It looks warm but it strikes cold."

The boy tested it and said shyly,

"That fare warm to me like, miss."

"You got so much muck on your hands, Sam, you couldn't feel nothing," said the girl sharply. "You didn't ought to handle miss's boots even with them hands."

He went very red about the ears and as soon as he had dragged off the second boot, went hastily away. Susan was still stooped over my shoe, and I said in as casual a way as I could manage,

"There's the same cold current of air, or whatever it is, in another place, I've noticed. I wonder if you have ever . . ."

"Ah," she said, with a wealth of meaning in her voice, "that winder in the great hall."

I could have kissed her.

"Set to clean it, I was soon arter I come here, miss. Never again. No, not if I was sacked for refusing."

"Because of the cold?" I asked lightly.

"No, miss. Because of the badness. It's there, too," she said, looking towards the side of the porch which we had instinctively left as soon as my shoe was on. "Thass all very well for folks to mock, but this was the Witch's house when all is said and done."

"What witch?"

"Oh, thass a long way back, miss; hundreds of years ago. But there's them that hev seen her tearing past like the wind on a great black horse; honest, steady folks, miss." Susan's face had gone very white and stiff-looking. I shivered, this time from a cold that came from within me. I told myself that this was all nonsense, ignorant country superstition; but after all I had used the word "haunted" in my thoughts about the cold place in the hall; and if one were credulous enough to think of a window seat as being haunted, why boggle at talk of witches? And why also, with a most practical view of the nonsensical, proceed to point out to oneself that the ghost of the witch, riding a ghostly horse, would surely confine its activities to the out-of-doors?

I had no sooner thought of that than Susan said,

"I allust reckon, myself, miss, that Lady Alice used to sit by that winder and make her spells and such; and there by the porch I reckon she used to keep her nasty beasts."

Thinking it over, I came to the conclusion that Susan's explanation was as likely a one as any I should ever think of. And though it left me far from satisfied, it was the only one that I was ever likely to get. I had to adjust myself to it. But, perhaps because I had never taken witches very seriously, the atmosphere which lay about that window seat had seemed to me much more dreadful than any one would have expected to be left there by a maker of spells.

Lady Alice Rowhedge, I discovered, however, had left a mark on more than the atmosphere of her old home. I never mentioned her—both from caution and delicacy—to my uncle; but a chance word, intentionally dropped here and there, brought me a good deal of information. In the country memories are long, and so are lives. One day, over at New Holding, I dragged the conversation round to the subject and learned to my astonishment that there before my eyes was someone who had known someone who had known someone who had actually seen the witch. This old Miss Phyllis Whymark had had the story from her father, who had it from his aunt, another Phyllis Whymark, who had it from her grandmother, another of the same name, who had been present at the trial when Lady Alice was found guilty and condemned to be burned. It had happened in the days of the Civil War . . . but it seemed suddenly as near as yesterday as I sat and listened to the old woman's croaking voice. And yet even then I was not content. This something, this palpable evil, which haunted the hall at Merravay and haunted me, so that I was driven to the most shameful devices to avoid going into the place alone after dark, never *really* in my mind, seemed to be linked with the Witch; and when old Miss Whymark ended her story with the ritual words "All nonsense of course," and popped a strong peppermint in her mouth I said,

"That is really very interesting! Are there any other phantoms at Merravay?"

She laughed and choked on the peppermint. "You're just like your grandmother, my dear! Ah, she was a one for ghosts! She once told me something she daren't even tell to her brother George that she was so fond of. She once *saw* something."

"What? Where?"

"A boy, just about to be taken with a fit. In the hall. She said he looked so real that she went to help him and found that he wasn't there at all. Very upset she was at the time, I recall, and I had difficulty in persuading her that it was all imagination."

"Do you believe that?"

"Dear child, what else could it be? Bodies are shovelled into the ground and spirits go off to God or Satan according to their deserts."

"I wonder," I said. "I wonder whether a very strong feeling mightn't leave a mark, stay there and go on and on . . . still being felt . . . like weather. I mean . . . if you woke up just after a thunderstorm, you'd know . . . by the atmosphere . . ."

"Heaven save us," said the old lady. "If people's feelings lasted like that the world would be so full of them we should all go about with no room for our own. Isn't that so?"

And that so exactly, though unwittingly, described what had happened to me in the hall at Merravay that I could only say:
"Yes, of course, that is quite true."

V

Well, now I come to the really incredible part of this story.

My Uncle Alan's bugbear was poachers. Quite a large portion of the Merravay estate was taken up by a wood, called Layer Wood. Up to the time when he inherited the property there had been what was called a "right of way" through it; it was the shortest path between the villages of Nettleton and Clevely. Little girls went there for flowers, little boys for nuts, and all too often, according to my uncle, men went there and "knocked off one for the pot." For poor people the times I look back upon were hungry times.

Uncle Alan, who set great store by his pheasants, closed the path at both ends and put up notices. Then he engaged a number of keepers. And finally he set mantraps. By his account—and I must confess that I never heard the other side—he was within his rights, but he met with a good deal of opposition, especially over the closing of the path, which was a right of way by ancient custom that even the rector recognised and supported. However, Uncle Alan had won in the end; Layer Wood was "preserved," and anyone who trespassed there risked falling into a mantrap, while anyone who poached risked the utmost rigour of the law.

Midway through November, on a very foggy evening, Uncle Alan and I were playing chess, the rudiments of which he had managed to teach me, when there came a noise and a stamping and the sound of men's voices approaching the front of the house from the garden.

Uncle Alan cocked his head and said, "That's Palmer, by God!" and jumped up and was across the hall and had the front door open before I could catch the table and steady the chessmen which his precipitate departure had disturbed. He had left the door open and I could look through it, across the hall, and see, as though in a theatre, the scene that was taking place there. Palmer, my uncle's head keeper, whom I knew by sight, and one of his underlings held between them a wretched-looking boy of about my own age. I couldn't see much of his face, for he sagged between the two men, but his very black shaggy hair and something about him made me think of gypsies. Presently, after a good deal of talking in the thick, slurred Suffolk voice, which at that distance I could not understand, Palmer pushed the boy forward. Then I was almost certain that he was a gypsy. He had one of those big-nosed, high-cheekboned faces which

at the best of times have a hungry, haggard look, and for the boy this was
not one of the best of times.

It may be weak in me, but I never like to see dogs with their ribs showing, or horses with thin drooping necks, or people who look miserable.
This, I know, is no virtue in me; I just hate the feeling of discomfort that
they rouse in me. Once when I was quite small I was so affected by the
blue fingers of a flower-girl that I wanted to give her my little muff.
Mamma explained that the girl didn't mind cold hands, she was used to
them, and would instantly have sold the muff and bought gin with the
money, and that I must try not to be a silly little girl.

I was no longer little and had—I thought—become rather less silly lately,
but my heart went out to this boy who looked so cold, and hungry and
thin and captured. The other three looked very well pleased with themselves, and presently Uncle Alan rang the bell and Clayton came, and
went, and returned with two big mugs on a tray. I thought—Oh dear,
nothing for *him*; and he looks as though he could do with it.

Then they all four went out by the door that led to the kitchen quarters
and for a few minutes I had something else to think about. The door
between the drawing-room and the hall was open and I was alone: was
that the same as being alone in the hall? Would the terror come stalking
in? The obvious thing to do was to get up and shut the door; but that I
could not do. I could only sit there and wait.

I was pathetically pleased to see Uncle Alan when he came back, and
he was pleased to have someone to whom he could tell his tale. At last
the expense of the mantraps had been justified. In the fog last night
that little devil of a poacher would have got away if he hadn't stepped
on one of them and been nipped by the ankle.

"*Last* night?"

"So Bowyer says. Anyway he was there at six this morning, but Bowyer
knew he was snug enough; and Palmer was having his day off, so he
left him there till they made their night's rounds."

"In a trap. Is he much hurt?"

"Of course not. Just nipped."

"He must have been very cold . . . and hungry."

My nice kind uncle, who had pressed all those tasty dishes on me and
taken such pleasure in my better appetite, laughed jovially and said,

"He'll be hungrier by the time he gets to Baildon gaol!"

"Is he on his way there now?"

"Dear child! In this fog? It's worse than last night's. He's in the old
buttery. When I first became a J.P. they would insist on hauling offend-
ers up here at unearthly hours—so much nearer, in many cases, than the
lockup in Nettleton—I just had to find somewhere to put them. Now let

me see . . . my dear, I'm quite sure you've been cheating. Never in a thousand years would I allow my queen to be. . . ."

"You got up so hurriedly that you knocked the table. I just gathered them up anyhow."

"Then there's no point in going on, is there? And I apologise, my dear, for the suggestion that you cheated. Your Aunt Mary," he broke off, horrified. I realised that never before had he mentioned his dead wife by name. In a flatter voice, but with obvious, calm resolution, he continued, "She would cheat me, but so prettily. Draw my attention to something, you know. And then move a piece. And I never let her know I knew!"

That was somehow so pathetic, so revealing, that the distaste I had been feeling for him because he had laughed about the poacher being hungry melted away, or was overlaid. As soon as I had dismantled the board and was ready he lent me, as was his habit now, his arm to the top of the stairs.

In my room Susan was busy with the warming pan; the hot milk which I was supposed to drink last thing at night stood in the hearth, and a plate of cheesecakes, a comestible which I had once been edged into admitting to liking, stood on my bed table.

Conversation, as Susan helped me to undress, turned inevitably upon the poacher. Susan, from whom, because she had been sensitive to the cold spots, I hoped for something else, was full of glee because he had been caught. She was Nettleton born and bred and all against gypsies.

"Thass been them all along, miss. Mr. George was real soft about them, I've heard my father say again and again. Said they was colourful! Thass on their account Layer was closed and set with traps. But for them and their thieving ways honest folks could still go there for primroses. They come, they take what they fancy, and off they go, leaving us to bear the blame. Now they've got one. And I'm glad!"

She said much the same thing in several different ways; then she said good night and left me.

For what I did next I take no credit for kindness, but for boldness . . . yes. It was not kind of me to wish to feed the boy; it was simple self-defence. I couldn't lay my head on the pillow and sleep, knowing that he was hungry; the jug of milk, the dish of cheesecakes, kept yelping at me reproachfully. But it was—considering the circumstances—very brave of me to step outside my bedroom door. Brave because, from the first night of the terror, my own room had possessed a compensating quality of sanctuary. All terrors bring their own cures. If you are frightened of the dark the first dawn glimmer can scatter them; if you fear spiders the mere removal of one can bring peace . . . and from that, so small a thing, up and up to the very fear of death with its mitigation through the hope of life everlasting, every dread is balanced in the human mind by the compensating factor of dread removed. To me, once night had fallen, there was the terror in the hall . . . and, had I ever been called upon to face it, the similar terror of the back porch. I could take temporary refuge in the drawing-room, the dining room, or the library; my bedroom was my absolute sanctuary. To leave it once I had gained it called for an effort more violent and more sustained than any I had ever made. To any rational person my dilemma must seem incomprehensible; but to me it was real and painful; either I must get into my bed and lie all night worrying about the hungry young poacher in the old buttery, or I must open the door and go down—not through the hall, for I could take the backstairs—but through the open dark, where the terror, apparently confined to one place, might possibly be at large.

Oddly enough what the poacher might do to me never once entered my mind.

I had a little blue silk bag with a pattern worked on it in beads. I set the jug of milk in the centre of it and wedged the cheesecakes all round. I could hang that on my arm, carry a candle in the same hand, and still have one free for opening doors.

The first one I opened timidly. I was out on the gallery which ran along above the hall, which was the haunted place; and before I took a step out I waited. If I felt the cold, if I sensed the terror, back I meant to bolt like a rabbit. But there was nothing. I took the few necessary steps along the gallery and then turned sharply to the right, into the passage that led to the top of the backstairs. Halfway along it was the room which one of the Whymarks, who knew Merravay well, had said was the schoolroom when their family lived there; and at its far end was a ladder which led to the space under the rafters. Compared with the front part of the house this was all ugly and grim and outwardly far more frightening . . . but I felt no fear there. It's all right, I thought to myself. Truly if, just in the passage, I had been joined by two or three friendly and quite unfrightened people I could not have felt more reassured. The knowledge that the terror was limited, that so long as I did not go to meet it in the hall it could not come to me, did a great deal to restore me to my natural confidence.

Except for the setting in of a great iron stove at one of its open hearths, the kitchen at Merravay has been unaltered for generations. I found what they called the old buttery by sheer accident, recognising its new purpose from the heavy padlock on the door and the opening in its upper panel. The aperture was no bigger than an ordinary book and was divided into halves by an iron bar. Having found what I had set out to find, I hesitated. The boy might be sleeping the sleep of exhaustion, and if so it would be small kindness to wake him back to his woes. I stood and listened, and I heard the straw rustle as he moved. Stepping up to the door, I held my candle high so that he could see me, though I could not see him, and I said,

"It's all right. I've brought you something to eat."

For a moment there was no answer; then the straw rustled more noisily and there was a dragging, shuffling sound; and into the faint radiance of the candlelight, just behind the bar his face emerged. A hoarse, choking voice said,

"'Sthat true? You ain't making game of me?"

"Oh no." I set the candle down and began to fumble in my little bag. I handed him a cheesecake. I expected him to snatch it and start eating, but he held it in his hand, looking at it as though he doubted whether it were really food. Then he said,

"God bless yer! But if yer could . . . miss, I'm perishing for a drink of water . . ."

"I have some milk. . . ." But the milk was in the jug and the aperture was too small to allow of its passing. The boy had his face close to the bar now, and I could see the avidity in his eyes, the cracked dryness of his mouth. "Just a minute," I said, "I'll have to get a little mug." I hurried back to the kitchen and snatched a pewter pipkin from a hook. I filled it and passed it in carefully. The boy drank, passed it back to me to be refilled, and emptied it again. And again, until the last drop had gone.

"God bless yer," he said again, more clearly. "You saved me life, I reckon." He ate a cheesecake then, cramming it into his mouth so fiercely that the good crisp pastry broke and he lost some crumbs.

"Take your time," I said. "There are three more." I handed them in one by one. He licked the last crumb from the palm of his hand and asked,

"What made yer do it?"

"I thought you looked hungry."

"For a minnit I thought you wus a angel." I saw his face change. Its open pathos gave way to craftiness.

"Miss, lemme out," he said, and as he spoke he put his face to the opening and stared at me with such urgency, such pleading, and such wiliness that I stepped back a pace.

"I couldn't. Even if I wanted to. You're padlocked in."

"I know that. But this here winder is on'y boarded over. I on'y want a bit of a tool. Knife'd do. They took me knife. Hand us in a knife, miss."

I just stood and stared at him, and, encouraged by my silence, he began to talk so quickly and so brokenly that I only caught a phrase here and there. He spoke about being transported for seven years at least, being loaded with irons, starved, and beaten; he said he hadn't touched a pheasant, that there was enough gypsy in him to prevent his having a fair trial.

One had, of course, heard stories about convict ships and settlements which, even if exaggerated. . . . And he was young, and so thin.

Also, just at that moment I was feeling a strong dislike for my kind uncle, by whose orders a boy who had lain for a night and a day in a trap had been locked up without being given so much as a cup of cold water. And, not being country-bred, I was insufficiently convinced of the sacredness of pheasants.

At that moment my candle flickered; looking at it, I realised that very shortly I should be in the dark. The effort to think clearly and quickly, the excitement of making a sudden and unconventional decision, fluttered my heart and dried my throat. I turned without speaking and hurried to the kitchen, where I first found a new candle and then looked round for a tool. I looked with a certain wistfulness at a heavy, sharp-edged wedge rather like a big chisel, which was used for jointing carcasses; but I was cautious. If the boy failed to get out . . . So I chose an anonymous-looking knife with a short stout blade.

When I got back to the door the boy had retreated to his straw and was crying in harsh gasping sobs which stopped when he saw the light. He came to the opening with tears making little runnels of cleanliness on his dirty face.

"If you don't succeed in getting out you must account for the knife," I said, and handed it in. He put his mouth to my fingers and slobbered at them like an affectionate dog. "I hope you do get out and then keep out of trouble," I said. I was backing away while he blessed and thanked me, and then he said with another abrupt change of manner, "Wait, lady. Look I got sumpin for yer." He fumbled about in his clothes. "They dint find this when they went over me. Got it in me mouth, see! Hold yer hand, miss. I mean it. Buy yerself sumpin pretty. Thass all right, I never stole it. I come by it honest, give yer me word."

His thin dirty hand had come up to the lower edge of the opening, and between its fingers and thumb was what looked like a golden guinea.

I gasped. Not with the surprise which the boy evidently expected—for he said slyly, "There now! Go on, take it. S'real!"—but with some other feeling for which I have no name. To say that I knew makes at once too great and too small a claim, but there is no other word. I *knew,* instantly and surely, that the gold coin between the gypsy's finger and thumb was connected in some way with the hatred and misery and despair which lay over the cold spot in Merravay hall and by the back porch.

"Where . . . did . . . you . . . get . . . that?" I asked.

"Up in the wood," he said without a second's hesitation. "Time I was in the trap, scratching about. Under a lotta leaves that was."

"Is it a guinea?"

"Course it is. Here, see for yerself." He stretched his hand past the bar. "I ain't never handled one afore, but I know a guinea when I see one. Take it. It's yours."

"I don't want it . . . I mean . . . thank you very much for wanting to give it to me. I couldn't take it. I would just like to know . . ."

"Look at it; see for yerself. All right then, hold the candle and I'll tell you. This side there's a old woman on a stool, and some words writ. This side there's a flower, rose outa the hedge. That got the right edge, too, ridgy. Thass a guinea all right. And I come by it honest, like I told yer. And I'd like you to have it . . . Whass the matter? D'you hear sumpin?"

The more he thrust the coin towards me the worse I felt, for the little shining coin seemed to hold the very essence of whatever it was that affected me with such terror. I knew, just as people know the first onset of a familiar pain, that unless I went quickly I should be too frightened to move.

"Good-bye," I gasped out. "Good luck."

"Just a minnit, lady," he said. "I wanta get on but I gotta say this first. I ain't Gyptian proper, I don't know the words, but I give yer the blessing. May yer marry a rich man that'll be good to yer and have plenty of strong healthy children and live to be old with yer own teeth and when yer . . ." But I had started to walk away, to scuttle like a scared rabbit making for its burrow.

In the morning when it was found that the boy had gone there was a considerable fuss, which would doubtless have lasted longer and caused me more secret embarrassment had not my cousin Rupert arrived home suddenly. At first I was a little frightened of him; he had an odd, abrupt manner and a way of saying things which would suddenly make you see them in a new way. He had no trace of Uncle Alan's geniality of manner, but now and then when they argued about things like wages, corn laws and pheasant preserves he would say, in his offhand, dry way, a word or two which led me to think that he might be, at heart, the kinder person of the two. We didn't get to know one another very well until he had been home for about a fortnight. Then there came an evening when Uncle Alan was out and we were alone together. It drew on towards bedtime and I began making my wretched little plans. When my uncle was at home the matter of going upstairs presented no problem. Once he had got the idea of helping me upstairs at night it had become a habit with him, and though I was now quite able-bodied he helped me and would have gone on doing so, I suspect, if I had lived with him for twenty years.

Suddenly Rupert looked up from his book and said,

"What is it that you're so scared of?"

Questions rapped out like that often receive a truthful answer, and this one did.

"There's something in the hall that I don't *like* by day and just can't face at night."

"Show me," he said, and stood up and reached out his hand to me.

"It's nothing you can see. It's just a feeling . . . it's . . ."

"A miasma?"

"I don't know." I didn't like to say that I didn't know what the word meant.

"Show me where."

I went out into the hall with him and pointed.

"Do you feel it now?"

"Oh no. Only when I am alone. And it isn't just my fancy . . . one of the maids . . ."

"Now who started this? You or the maid? You see, I've often noticed about maids; they come from crowded little hovels and the mere *space* frightens them."

"Oh, I felt it before I ever spoke to her about it."

"It's strange," he said, musingly, and—I was glad to see—quite seriously, "how eclectic these things are. Hit and miss. I only once knew a case when everybody was affected. We were digging just south of El Khasan and a workman turned up a bit of a bowl—he was about to pick it up, but didn't; instead he turned and ran, and so did we all, fifteen of us, including a stout old German professor who hadn't run for thirty years. Sheer, reasonless terror. Now, tell me more about this."

I told him from the beginning; and at the end I said, "And there was the coin too . . ."

"What coin?"

"I can't tell you. It is a secret."

"Describe the coin." I did so as well as I could. "That would be Elizabethan or Marian . . . about the same period as the house, you know."

"I wish I could tell you about the coin. All about it. You could go and look. There might be something that would explain . . ."

"Then why not tell me?"

"I'm not sure about . . . well, at least I know that you aren't quite as strict and fierce as Uncle Alan is about it . . . but I don't quite know how you feel about pheasants."

"I like to eat them roasted." He smiled at me, suddenly young and friendly. "Tell you a secret, I always come back to Merravay when my appetite gets the upper hand. Like a bird migrating. I sit down one day, wherever I am, to the usual makeshift meal and think—They're roasting pheasants at Merravay! And home I come. There now, your coin-secret could hardly be more self-revealing and shameful than *that*. Tell me. Did you find it in a pheasant's gizzard?"

When he smiled like that I felt that I could tell him anything. I said, "Promise not to tell Uncle Alan. He has been so very kind to me. And he'd be so upset and angry."

"So he would if you went and told him that I came home for the sake of the food! All right, I promise."

So I told him. And he laughed and said, "You did absolutely right. And this is all very interesting. I'll ask Palmer in the morning where that trap lay, and I'll go and pry about. Like to come with me?"

"I would! I longed to go by myself, but I didn't dare. I did find out exactly where the trap was. You needn't ask Palmer. But I might get scared."

"With me to hold your hand—or to run with you as the case might be?"

"No," I said, after I had thought for a little. "I think that, with you, it would be all right."

And it was. The trap was still in the same place and Rupert looked at it and said, "Most likely he'd scratch about, as he called it, in this direction, trying to pull himself up by these hazel twigs. And it slopes a little. One should always allow for the force of gravity. We'll try in this direction first."

The trap had been set with cruel cunning on the old path, so that anybody who blindly persisted in using the right of way would fall into it. On the inner side of the path there was a little clump of hazels standing in the piled-up drift of the leaves of many autumns.

As soon as I arrived at this spot I began to wish that I had not come. It was a crisp, bright morning, and I had company, but I felt uneasy, depressed in my spirits, and afflicted with a curious physical feeling, as though my clothes or my skin did not fit. I looked at the trap and thought of the boy lying there all night and all day, and that was a bad thought too; but below and beyond that there was more. At the same time my morbid curiosity was lively; I knew that we were on the right track; this place, the back porch, and the hall at Merravay had some dark connection.

Rupert pushed in amongst the hazels. I started to follow and then drew back.

"I think I shall stay here," I said.

"Wise," he said, "these leaves are soaking wet."

I looked up and down the path. It had been closed for only a few years and was still used by the keepers, but it was rapidly being grown over; the blackberry brambles particularly had thrust out aggressively so that in places they almost met. I thought again what a pity it was about the pheasants. This must have been a very pretty, pleasant path between two villages. I pictured people on it, very trite pictures: little girls in spring, gathering primroses, little boys in autumn, gathering nuts, and in the long warm summer evenings, young lovers wandering with their arms about one another.

Presently I heard Rupert say, "Ah."

"Have you found something?"

"I think so. Oh yes!"

"To do with it?"

"I should say so. Stay where you are."

"What is it?" I called sharply, because now I was all curiosity.

"I'm coming," he called back, and in a moment he pushed through the bushes. He looked a little queer, half-excited and half-concerned. He had pushed back his sleeves, and his hands to the wrists were covered with soil and bits of crushed wet leaf. Holding the left one out stiffly so that he did not touch me with it, he laid his left arm over and round my shoulders while the other hand held out for my inspection what looked like a little heap of dirt with several gold coins bedded in it.

"They look like . . ." I pried one loose and rubbed it on my hand-kerchief. "It is the very same!" I said. What the gypsy boy had called an old woman on a stool was a queen on a throne, and his hedge rose was the Tudor emblem, exactly like the ones that were the motive of so much of the carving at Merravay.

"You were right. Elizabethan, Rupert, it says so . . ." So far curiosity and what one might call the heat of the chase had sustained me, but now I knew that I felt towards this coin as I had done towards the one in the gypsy boy's hand. "It feels the same, too," I said, and dropped it back into Rupert's palm. "Oh, was that all you found? Nothing to tell us any more, nothing to explain? That place in the hall, and by the porch, and now here . . . all connected. And all awful." The arm about my shoulders tightened.

"Darling," said Rupert, "to find so much in so short a time proves my extraordinary prospecting ability, don't you think?"

"I know. Of course. But we're no farther. I wanted something that would explain, that I could settle down with and know that it made me feel this way because of. . . . You know I went all round Merravay for days, looking for a nasty idol, or one of those horrible inkstands made out of a skull . . ."

Rupert gave me an odd swift look and I thought—Yes, now you'll think I'm morbid and hysterical.

"We'll come back when it isn't so damned wet in there. And with a spade. I'm not used to doing my own digging, you know."

"Of course not," I said penitently. I stood looking at the clump of hazels which held—I felt—the clue to the mystery.

"Let's go back," said Rupert, dropping his arm and offering me the crook of it. "I do want to wash!"

On the way back I thrust away all thought of what he had not found and we talked animatedly about what he had. He said that the coins must have belonged to a rich person, or to a very miserly one who saved small amounts and then converted them into a few pieces, for coins of such value were rare in Elizabeth's day, being worth thirty shillings apiece then, which was five or six pounds by our reckoning. He said too that he believed the little lump of stuff in which the coins were embedded were the rotted and altered remains of a leather bag and that the one piece of gold which the gypsy had found had probably been pushed out by the growth of a root, or picked up and dropped by a magpie. And that was all very interesting to me; I liked to hear Rupert talk.

VI

We did not make our second visit to Layer Wood; the weather turned cold, with a bitter wind from the east and sharp sleet storms. My papa, who within his sphere was a man of influence, succeeded in getting Archie posted to the West Indies; my mamma suffered a recurrence of migraine. So they decided that I had imposed upon Uncle Alan's hospitality for long enough, and wrote to suggest that I should go home for Christmas. This suggestion raised very mixed feelings in me. Apart from the terror I'd been happier at Merravay than in any place where I had ever been, especially since Rupert's return; the prospect of returning to take my place as a dutiful daughter in the strictly regulated treadmill of social life in a garrison town had very little appeal for me. I told myself, pretty sternly, that I had fallen victim to the comfort, the indulgences, that I had received at Merravay. And every evening, when either Uncle Alan or Rupert walked with me across the hall and up the stairs, I told myself with another kind of sternness that it would be pleasant to return to a place where I *could* go upstairs alone.

I was running all these thoughts through my mind one evening, three days before I was due to go home, when once again Rupert and I were alone, this time in the library. Because of my imminent departure the last week had been a round of gaiety with dinner parties at home, at

Ockley, New Holding, and Muchanger. Rupert and I—who had reached a point where we could sit together by the fire and each read a book and look up now and then and make, or answer, a remark, and read again—had of late had no chance to spend such an evening together.

On this evening, though I was holding a book I was not reading; I was thinking my thoughts. I wished that he would put aside his book and look up and talk to me on this—this which might well be the last time we ever . . . Something swelled in my throat at the thought and tears came pushing up and under my lids. I stared hard at my book until I had controlled myself.

Just then Rupert closed his book with a snap.

"Charlotte," he said, "I want to ask you something and I don't want to be clumsy. You see, from something Father said I gathered that . . ." He halted, choosing his words, and I said boldly:

"Oh, that is all ended. It wasn't *real*. It sounds a strange thing to say, but that . . . whatever it is out there"—I nodded towards the hall—"put it out of my head completely!"

"How?"

I heard myself saying, in carefully chosen, scrupulously measured words, exactly how I had known that my lovesickness was a matter of imagination. I ended with the words:

"I'm probably giving you the impression that I am utterly shallow-minded, but that I can't help. Honesty compels me to admit that your Merravay ghost, whatever it is, drove Archie clean out of my mind."

"I've been wondering," Rupert said, "whether it would make any difference if that end of the hall were walled off. You see, Charlotte, I love you. . . ." His face, the lamplight began to whirl before my eyes in a crazy fashion; his voice, saying things about being diffident in case I was still in love with Archie, about being willing to live elsewhere if I found Merravay frightening, seemed to come from a long way off. The voice, the words sounded as cool and reasonable and dispassionate as I knew Rupert to be at heart; but somehow, there we were, midway between the two chairs, locked in an embrace which wasn't cool or dispassionate at all.

"I've been in love with you, Rupert, ever since the evening when I knew I could tell you *anything*," I said. Then I thought about the haunted place and how it had shown me the truth about myself and Archie. Even at this moment when my cup of happiness was full to overbrimming, that mattered somehow. I dragged myself out of Rupert's arms.

"Wait here," I said.

I went out of the library. I closed the door behind me. The hall was lighted by a single lamp; the "bad place" lay in the gloom. I walked towards it. There was the terror; there was the despair; there was the deathly cold. I walked into it and I knew the day must come when Rupert and I must grow old, and impotent, and then die. I stood there knowing in one concentrated moment all the despair which poor human mortality brought face to face with eternity can know . . . but I wasn't frightened any more. I thought: That is how it is, how it always has been and always will be. All we can do is to snatch at this moment, the time which is ours, and make the best of it.

I went back to Rupert and said:

"It is all right. Whatever was there is gone. I'm not frightened any more."

Then he told me that on the morning when he found the coins he had also found a skeleton. He, of course, was used to ancient bones and was not much shaken, but he had feared the effect of his find on me and hurried me away. His work had led to an understanding of the importance of burial rites, and therefore he had arranged that these bones should be given Christian burial. Dear Rupert, he believes that that may have brought rest to the uneasy spirit.

He says the bones lay in peaceful, sleeping fashion with one hand under the skull and the other laid upon something which, though rotted past recognition, might have been a book; and I know that he believes that someone, when this house was young, used to sit in that window seat and read and one day went into Layer Wood to read, fell asleep, and never woke. That person set great store by Christian burial and could not rest without it.

I think otherwise. It wasn't a bookworm, it wasn't a witch who made that emotional mark on Merravay; it was a lover. I know because my false love couldn't face whatever there was there; my true love could. And those coins were somehow deeply concerned. But it is all a mystery which I accept, just as I accept the fact that I have never lost a tooth and have been blessed with six handsome, healthy children, all boys. . . .

Interlude

Strangers to Nettleton still stop to stare at and remark upon a number of cottages which, though too old and individual to be Council houses, bear evidence of having been planned and built with more taste and care than is common, and of having been erected, all twenty-four of them, at the same time.

Though their style is ornate and old-fashioned they are pretty enough and they have worn well. They stand, two by two, each with its strip of garden in front and a larger patch to the rear; each with its own wash-house, shed, and outdoor convenience; and with two wells to serve the two dozen.

In the centre of each frontage is a lozenge-shaped piece of stone bearing the letters RBS and the date 1875. That was the year when the railway went through to Bywater and Mr. Rupert Booth-Sandell sold some land profitably.

In the same year he invested money in the Great Eastern Railway Company and that was a profitable investment. In 1880 he built what is known as the Institute—used as a village hall to this day. During the following year the Tudor almshouses at Baildon, reared and endowed by the terms of the will of one Thomasin Griggs, widow, were found to be finally past repair. Mr. Booth-Sandell built new ones, single-storied versions of his Nettleton cottages because he felt that old people should be spared the effort of climbing stairs. The lozenge on the almshouses displays the initials of Mrs. Booth-Sandell.

Those were the settled, spacious days, and Rupert and Charlotte Booth-Sandell were typical of their class and generation. Until quite recently it was possible to find ancient men and women who would speak nostalgically of the "old master and mistress," of their generosity, their dignity, their family of lively handsome boys, the glory of Merravay during their régime, the way the carriage lights shone on the trees of the avenue when the Booth-Sandells gave a dinner party, the ox-roasting to which the whole village was invited when Mr. Booth, the heir, came of age. Ah, they were the days, and gone forever.

And if the wages of the farm labourers were never more than twelve shillings a week, and sometimes as little as ten, nobody was ever stood off in the winter; and the moment there was trouble in the house there was the old mistress on the doorstep, ready with an offer of help. And food was cheap, and the new houses, let for one and sixpence a week, had enough garden to grow vegetables for any family, however large.

In 1890, in the glowing mellow sunset of the century, Mr. Booth Booth-Sandell succeeded his father. Gradually the twilight descended.

Things were never the same at Merravay. For one thing Mr. Booth, for all he was so handsome, never married. Too gay and frisky in his young days, and later on too crusty. But although he was never the man his father was, and of course not nearly so rich, he was popular enough with the village people, for he could be unthinkingly generous, and he was always one for a joke.

The Heiress

Of all the self-imposed burdens under which mankind struggles, family loyalty is, I think, one of the heaviest. I notice that modern people tend to be very casual about their obligations in this respect, but those of us who are now called, somewhat scornfully, "the Victorians," were so schooled to a sense of duty towards those of our own blood that we must either perform it or suffer pangs of conscience. So I must sit down and pen the invitation which, if it is accepted, will spoil what remains of my life. I have no choice.

The exasperating part of it all is that I never liked Merravay; I never liked my Uncle Booth; I never liked my cousin Maude.

Maude and I and another cousin, a boy who died in his early teens, were the only children in our generation; of my grandmother's six sons one, the eldest, my Uncle Booth, remained unmarried, and two others were childless. Maude and I were almost of an age, she was about six months older than I, and in those far-away days visits were often arranged and long journeys undertaken because our parents thought it would be nice for us to meet. I remember her as a thin, leggy child with a mane of very curly pale auburn hair and the freckled skin which often goes with it. She had a high-bridged, arrogant nose and curiously narrow, very bright blue eyes. Her parents, who adored her, had spoiled her shamelessly and she had no fear of anything or anybody. I was rather a timid child myself, and most of our meetings seemed to end in some kind of trouble which she instigated, mocked me into, and then sailed out of, unrebuked, while I was taken aside and punished. I thought this decidedly unfair; my parents seemed to believe that they were omniscient; surely they should have seen how things were, I used to think.

One of the places where we used to meet was the family house in Suffolk, then the property of my Uncle Booth. It lay in a very remote place amongst fields and woods but it could hardly be called inaccessible, for the railway ran to within two miles of it. The shooting there was reckoned to be above average, and every year my father and Maude's and my other uncles endeavoured to get to Merravay at some time during the autumn and to arrange their visits to overlap as far as possible. So far as one could judge, this desire to get together at least once a year was not due to any deep-rooted affection; they quarrelled, they criticised one another, they took sides, but they all seemed to enjoy the reunion, and when increasing age, infirmity, and finally death broke up the family circle it was easy to look back and be rather sentimental about it all.

Merravay was a Tudor house and considered very beautiful; remarkable, they said, for having stood for three hundred years without being added to or altered. Of that fact the kitchen quarters bore witness. Uncle Booth had made one innovation; he had installed a bath. Apart from that the house remained, even to the rugs on the floor, exactly as Uncle Booth's great-great-grandfather had had it when he came from India and settled down at Merravay. The garden was delightful, but I always thought that the place as a whole was gloomy and when—as time went on—it became my duty to make occasional visits there alone, doing my duty to Uncle Booth, I always went reluctantly and left with joy.

I was never at ease, for one thing, with my uncle. He was odd and arbitrary and even in his more genial moments inclined to poke fun at one, to make outrageous statements and watch for one's reaction. His father, my grandfather, was still remembered in the neighbourhood as a liberal-minded, open-handed man. Cottages which in their day were models, and almshouses and public buildings all bear his stamp, RBS, and the date. There are boys now at Baildon school and at the universities profiting from the scholarships he founded. Uncle Booth had been known to say that his father had been extravagant in *his* way and thus curtailed extravagance in his heir.

My father died suddenly, and at a comparatively early age, when I was sixteen. We were left badly off, and I think Mother would gladly have gone to live at Merravay; but she was not asked to do so, and if she made any overtures they were disregarded. She was very anxious, however, that I should ingratiate myself with Uncle Booth. The death of my boy cousin had removed the obvious heir. Mother always knew when Maude had been to Merravay and would tell me, rather reproachfully; and I would say, "But Maude *likes* Merravay." Maude had told me so herself, times without number. She always said it was the most beautiful house in the world. I think she was sincere, too. Often when we'd stayed there together I'd seen her, before breakfast, go running to the end of the garden, scramble up onto the wall between the urns, and sit there swinging her long thin legs and just staring, and staring, as though she were in a trance. It would be no hardship for her to spend part of her holidays there, for though she got on with Uncle Booth little better than I did, she wasn't afraid of or embarrassed by him and always had an answer.

Her parents were wealthier than mine and more worldly. At sixteen she was sent to a Paris finishing school, and a year and a half later she was presented and launched upon a London season. Everybody said that she was a raving beauty. Certainly she had got rid of her freckles and gained control of her limbs; and with that blaze of hair and those ice-blue eyes she could not help but be noticeable; but I personally thought that she was still too thin, and too tall, and too high-nosed to be beautiful.

"She'll make a wonderful match, I expect," said my mother with a little sigh.

Actually I was married first, and if getting a man as near perfection as a human being can be counts for anything, mine was a wonderful match, though it cost my poor mother many a sigh, not small ones either. I married the local doctor. That was considered little short of disgraceful, especially as he had no private money, no connections, and was only a junior partner. But I knew my mind, and for once I dug in my heels and stood up for what I wanted. Uncle Booth could not come to the wedding —he had just suffered his first slight stroke. He sent me a cheque for twenty pounds and a grumbling letter because I had not taken Ian to be looked over.

"I'm afraid you've done for yourself there," said my mother.

She said it again when, almost a year later, Maude was married and from Merravay! She said she had always hoped to be married from that house. And of course the enormous hall, which takes up such a disproportionate part of the ground floor in that house, lent itself to such an occasion. I did not go to the wedding, it was only a few weeks before I had my baby; but I heard vivid accounts of how wonderful Maude looked coming down the great staircase in her wedding dress and veil. Uncle Booth's present to her was an enormous ruby on a thin gold chain to wear as a pendant; and we were told that some old lady, a remote relative, one of the Gore Park Booths who was at the wedding, said that it was an heirloom which should never have been in our part of the family at all.

My son, my dear Angus, was born while Maude was on her honeymoon in Venice. I was perfectly content. I was very busy, too busy to bother much about anything outside my own household. In the next five years I went to Merravay only once, just for a day, to take to Uncle Booth a few things of my father's which my mother, on her deathbed, said she wished him to have. Poor mother, she was hopeful to the last;

she tried to make me promise to take Angus, too; but I travelled third-class and it was hot weather; I left Angus at home in his cool clean nursery. The stroke had affected Uncle Booth's speech and made him even more difficult to talk to; otherwise he was unchanged. So was Merravay.

When Angus was five and we were in process of changing his nurse for a governess, something happened to me. To my mind. For one thing I realised that though Maude had now been married five years she had had no child; and I also realised that Ian would never make money. He was too kind, and too careless. I wanted nothing for myself . . . but for Angus, I suddenly knew, I wanted everything. We could, we would, afford a governess . . . but away ahead in the years I could see many other needful, desirable, or merely pleasant things which would be, unless circumstances changed, unattainable. And there was Uncle Booth, a man of property; and here was Angus, as handsome, well-set-up, delightful little boy as there was on the face of the earth. All suddenly I realised how *my* mother had felt about Merravay and why she had cried when she compared the twenty-pound cheque with the great ruby.

I wrote to Uncle Booth suggesting that Angus, whom he had not yet seen, and I should spend a few days at Merravay. The letter which came back was kindly enough and when we arrived our welcome left nothing to be desired. It was obvious that Uncle Booth had taken pains to ensure our comfort—even to the extent of having two steps made so that Angus could get into the high bath. But almost immediately he started making the gibing remarks which I always resented, even when they were aimed at me alone.

Angus had the grave, speculative stare which all children of that age adopt towards strangers. Uncle Booth stared back at him and then said, "Boo!" so sharply that the child jumped and backed away. I had told *him* how he was to behave, and he was trying to obey orders; he wasn't prepared for foolery on the part of a poor sick old man. To me Uncle Booth said, "Take him away, Catherine. He's a nice little boy, I'm sure, but he's got such a bedside manner I expect him, every minute, to ask have the bowels worked today."

I thought that was unforgivable; a backhanded slap at Ian, an insult to Angus. And it was rude to mention bowels thus gratuitously to me!

That was not a successful visit. On the last day of it Uncle Booth received a letter from Maude. He laughed over it.

"What a gel that is! Listen to this. 'Edward is going to divorce me. May the black sheep come and graze at Merravay before being sheared in public?' Joking about it. That damn fool of a husband of hers doesn't know what he's losing. There aren't many with Maude's spirit. Now you can make yourself handy, Catherine. You can write for me." He sat down and dictated the letter straightway. A hateful letter. I know it began,

"My dear Maude,

I was shocked and horrified by your news. So far as I know we have never had a divorce in the family. God knows what things are coming to when a decently bred, decently reared young woman like you can be accused, openly, of adultery . . ."

It went on like that, bitter, vituperative. And it ended by saying,

"Of course you may come and hide your head at Merravay; blood is thicker than water they say; besides the thing might as well end where it began. So come and wear your penitent's sackcloth where you wore your bridal satin."

Was it all meant as a joke? He'd told me, often enough, that I had no sense of humour. I could understand and laugh at Ian's jokes; that was one bond between us, we laughed at the same things. For the life of me I couldn't see anything funny in this. In Maude's place I wouldn't have accepted such an invitation even if refusing it had meant that I had to go into cheap lodgings in London.

I went home next day. Maude went to Merravay and stayed there for several months. It was a particularly nasty divorce. Her husband was as vindictive as he had been doting; and a young, titled girl who had had what was called an understanding with the co-respondent committed suicide in a fit of disgust, so there was a great deal of publicity. Everybody expected that in the end her fellow sinner would feel compelled to marry her. Whether he ever offered to or not the family system of communication—what Ian always called "the jungle drums"—never informed me; they did tell me that Maude said the young man was a handsome ass and that his asininity was responsible for the whole catastrophe and she did not intend to marry a fool.

She had no need to. She married Sir Theodore Audley; thus gaining at one stroke another rich, doting husband, a title, a great Palladian mansion in Wiltshire, an imposing house in St. James' Square and a shooting lodge in Scotland. She also gained, and filled as though born to it, a place in that half-raffish, half-royal circle which was such a feature of Edwardian society. She remained childless.

Early in the summer of 1912 the jungle drums informed me that Uncle Booth considered himself neglected by me and mine; and that he was in failing health. In mid-July I received a letter, a formal invitation to Merravay for a month. One sentence in it roused my resentment.

"Bring your husband," it said, "I have reached the state where a private physician seems to be called for." That didn't seem to me to be the right way to ask a busy man to give up his holiday.

"He's old and crotchety. Take no notice," Ian said. "You and Angus go for a month. I'll come down with you and stay a week, and then again for a week at the end."

"You probably won't," I said. "He'll insult you funnily or be funny insultingly and you'll leave and never come back. I wouldn't go near him again if I didn't feel it my duty to Angus."

"You visit your Uncle Warren . . ." Ian said.

"Because I'm sorry for him. His son died, and then his wife, and he's poor . . ."

"And dipsomaniac and dirty! Dear Cathy; at the bottom of your heart, you know, you're afraid that you might seem to be a fortune hunter. So you feel *bound* to take offence at Uncle Booth."

"Is it that? Do *you* want me to be nicer to him, about him?" I asked, a little bewildered.

"Makes no difference to me," Ian said. "I can give Angus every advantage that I ever had, and more. But it does seem to me that you're a bit mixed about your Uncle Booth. He *can't* be worse than Warren."

"All right. I'll try again. We'll all go and be nice to this poor old rich uncle of mine. . . ."

Whether age and illness had improved Uncle Booth's manners or whether Ian and Angus being there made things easier I cannot say. I only know that that was the best visit I ever had at Merravay. For one thing the weather was lovely. It is a little strange how those two or three summers immediately preceding the fatal summer of 1914 seem to glow with more than sunlight. Even Merravay seemed to lose its gloom.

Ian and Angus established surprisingly friendly relationships with Uncle Booth, and Angus was praised for the way he took to riding; he had never had much chance to acquire horsemanship, but he proved to be fearless and to have what they call "good hands." "As good as Maude at the same age," said Uncle Booth. We understood that praise could go no further.

During our last week Uncle Booth's lawyer came and was closeted with him for the best part of a morning; and after that I did permit myself a hope or two on Angus' account. There was no doubt that Maude would inherit Merravay—Uncle Booth had several times mentioned her devotion to it, as a place; "She doesn't come to see me, you know. She comes to count those houseleeks on the roof!" But Angus, I thought, had made his mark and would be remembered.

We had been home three days when I heard that Uncle Booth had

had another stroke, likely to prove fatal. I went back at once, but he was dead when I got there. Maude had arrived a few hours earlier but had had, she said, no speech with him.

We were alone together there for that evening. Now and then it struck me as rather sad that we should both be so calm. Maude's manner was brittle, but no more so when she said, "I shall miss him; he was always *there*," than when she said, "This soup is almost stone-cold." I hadn't seen her since her second marriage, and to me she looked surprisngly young and almost intimidatingly sophisticated. I was almost sure that there was rouge on her cheeks and lips; she wore diamonds in her ears and on her fingers; and she smoked—absolutely naturally and with no air of bravado—cigarette after cigarette, using a long holder that looked to me as though it were made of jade.

I noticed at once that out of the confusion which inevitably follows a death, had emerged the idea of Maude being the centre and head of the house. That was hardly to be wondered at. Despite her busy social life and her travels, she had spent much more time at Merravay—though I had stayed there more recently. She was older than I; she was—if Uncle Booth could be credited with such a conventional preference—his favorite niece; and all servants being snobs to the bone, they enjoyed saying "Her ladyship this" and "Her ladyship that."

It was a lovely late summer evening, and after dinner Maude and I, by common impulse, escaped from the hushed house and went into the garden. Dusk was creeping in from the fields and the wood. Merravay had always struck me as being an unnaturally quiet place, even when allowance was made for its remoteness. Tonight the quiet seemed almost unearthly, although when one listened one could hear the soft mourning of doves, the twitter of smaller birds settling for the night, the clatter of the last train running through to Bywater.

In the rose garden the second-crop roses, which had been buds when I left three days before, were full out, wide-hearted after the day's warmth; and from the herbaceous border waves of heavier perfume from lilies, late stocks, and tobacco flowers came to meet us as we strolled. At the very end of the garden, where the urn-topped wall divided it from the field, we stopped and turned, leaning back against the still-warm bricks.

"It is," said Maude, looking to left and right and then straight ahead to the house, "the most beautiful, perfect place in the world."

Ordinarily she had a crisp, light way of speaking, just flicking her words and dropping the emphasis in unexpected places. Ordinarily she would have said, "the *most* beautiful place." But tonight her voice was deep, caressing, and she gave "beautiful" its full, brooding value.

Ordinarily I should have questioned her verdict; Merravay was solid, spacious, and had certain historically interesting features, but it was too grim and gloomy to be beautiful in my eyes—very much as Maude was too angular and high-nosed; yet the thought of Uncle Booth lying there in his vast high-windowed bedroom, dead and really unmourned, depressed me so that I didn't feel like arguing. I felt empty and forlorn; I longed for my husband, my child, my own neat, snug house and garden. All the sadness about this place, the age-old, ingrained gloom which I had always felt, seemed to rise like a tide and engulf me. On a sudden impulse I moved nearer to Maude and took her arm. Inside the billowing chiffon sleeve her arm felt hot, almost feverishly hot, and surprisingly frail.

"It's sad," I said, without choosing my words, "to die and have nobody to mourn you."

Maude jerked her arm away. "We can't all be founders of families," she said. "Who d'you expect to cry over a selfish old bachelor? And he's oblivious to whether we cry or gloat."

That struck me as exactly the thing which Uncle Booth would have said in the same circumstances.

"You and he were very much alike in some ways," I said.

"That's why we got on so badly. We saw through one another. He knew why I came here; he knew what this place means to me."

That was true. I'd heard him say so.

"That mystifies me, Maude. You have three, is it three? houses. You see and stay in all kinds of magnificent places. What is it about this place? To me it seems a gloomy old barn, it does really . . . but Ian, my husband you know, seemed terribly taken with it too."

Maude stared straight ahead towards the house, which loomed dark and menacing against the fading green of the evening sky.

"I don't know," she said at last. "It's just something . . . The first time I ever came here I wanted to stay; I asked my father to buy it. I've always come back and when I'm away I dream of it. It's my place. It is *so* beautiful. It's one of those things which nobody can explain." She fitted a cigarette into the holder, struck a match, and narrowed her eyes against the flame. "Talking of crying," she said abruptly, "I did cry, for pure happiness then, the night Uncle Booth promised to leave it to me. So if I cried now it would be hypocrisy."

So he had promised Merravay to her. That was no surprise to me; it had been understood more or less all along. Just a thousand pounds for Angus, I thought; just enough to see him comfortably through school and started in life. And there was this to be said for Merravay going to Maude; if Uncle Booth had left it to either of his brothers, Ernest or Warren, the only two left, he would have felt bound to leave money for its upkeep.

With Maude that would never arise. So perhaps . . . with luck, just a thousand pounds for Angus.

Uncle Ernest arrived early next morning. He had spent most of his life in the colonial service and had retired with a knighthood and a pension. He lived in a not-very-luxurious club in London and seemed glad to get to the fleshpots of Merravay. But he grumbled, almost automatically, at everything. A damp patch and a crack on his bedroom ceiling caused him great concern.

"Well," he said, looking from Maude to me, "whichever one of you gets *this* handsome property gets a white elephant, let me tell you. Roof's in shocking condition. Ceiling over my bed! Sword of Damocles nothing to it. Have you seen it?"

"I've seen the one in my own," said Maude. "But I've been up in the roof. There's no worm or dry rot. The tiles just need relaying and replacing in parts."

"That'll cost a pretty penny."

"Five or six hundred pounds," said Maude as though it were nothing.

"Not that *we* need worry, yet," Uncle Ernest proceeded. "Tricky chap, Booth; always was. Probably left the place to Dr. Barnardo's Homes. Short of his leaving me my father's gold watch, which I always coveted, nothing would surprise me!"

Well, Uncle Ernest had his surprise. Uncle Booth had bequeathed him not only the coveted watch but all his personal belongings, studs, cuff links, cigar cases, guns, everything in his cellar, and the sum of a thousand pounds.

That was one of the first of what seemed an interminable list of bequests. One would have thought that this was the will of an unusually sentimental man who was either fantastically generous or prodigally rich. Dozens of servants, past and present, people for whom Uncle Booth had never had a good word to say, all remembered; the Almshouse Trust, at which he had jeered; the Scholarship Fund, which he had pretended to deplore. A veritable shower of gold fell upon all; and still there was no mention of Angus. How rich had he been? What would be left?

At last Mr. Turnbull paused, cleared his throat slightly, and read out the final phrases. All the contents of the house he left to Maude; Merravay and the garden to me.

I swallowed something sour and choking that came up from the pit of my stomach into my throat. I felt Merravay with its mediaeval kitchens and sagging roof fall like a dead weight on my shoulders. I knew a moment of bitter disappointment. Then I braced myself. All right—I thought

—you wanted to surprise everybody, but I am not surprised; I always thought you were a horrid old man, and now I know it. I could see that the will had been the last of his verbal quips. What perverse pleasure he must have derived in sitting down on that fine August morning and planning a surprise for everybody. Surprise a kitchen slut with a legacy of fifty pounds; surprise Angus, the obvious heir to everything, by not even mentioning him; surprise Maude, who had three houses full of furniture . . . surprise Catherine, who didn't care for Merravay. I am not surprised, Uncle Booth . . . but Maude . . . oh dear. For the first time in my life I could think, "Poor Maude."

I took a careful glance at her; she was sitting as though someone had taken a sharp sword and run her through. There was now no doubt about whether she rouged her face; the harsh colour stood out like clown's paint, her nose looked like a bleached bone. As I watched she stood up, straightened herself, and without a word to anyone stalked out of the room.

I thought to myself that I would be ashamed to make such an exhibition of feeling. After all I was equally, or more, cruelly disappointed, mocked. I was a woman who had to look pretty sharply to the butcher's bill, who had to live in a town two hundred miles away, who had a child to provide for. And all I'd got was a liability. She could have Merravay; I'd sell it to her; thank God there was one person on earth mad enough to want it and rich enough to indulge the whim.

I muttered a word of excuse and ran after Maude. She was in her room, hurriedly throwing her clothes and toilet articles into a dressing case. I was breathless from my run up the stairs and along the gallery, but I managed to gasp out,

"Maude, you can have it. I don't want it. I never did. And I couldn't afford . . ."

"Get out of my sight," said Maude. She cast at me one look in which all the hatred and accusation in the world seemed concentrated; a mad look.

"Don't take it so hard," I gasped. "I'm terribly disappointed too. But we can come to some arrangement . . ."

"I'm not going to *buy* what is mine by right. I never want to see the place again!" She snapped the dressing case and went to the bell, jerking the pull crazily.

"I'll give it to you . . ." She gave me another mad look. "Maude, you must see that it isn't any use to me. I couldn't live in it; I couldn't have the roof mended."

"Insure it and burn it down," Maude said. "Oh, Beales . . . I'm leaving immediately."

Even the rule about behaving oneself before servants was no rule to her. I said, "Good-bye, Maude," in as normal a voice as I could manage. She swept past me without a word.

Then began the terrible time during which, were I a fanciful woman, I would say that I was justified in all my feelings about Merravay, back and back to my earliest recollection when I was frightened of the place. It had seemed to threaten me, and Heaven knew it now carried out its threat in terms of near ruin. We couldn't leave it empty and uncared for and allow obvious decay to add itself to the hidden flaws; we had to find wages for a caretaker and a gardener. Upon our limited means the great house fastened like a bloodsucker.

I wrote three letters to Maude, each more beseeching than the last; she answered none. A formal letter from a firm of furniture removers, asking for access to the house for four days, informed me that she was about to remove the furniture. I shut myself in my room then and cried a little in secret. There were things of great value at Merravay; if only Uncle Booth had. . . . I know the Bible explicitly states that to him who hath shall be given and from him who hath not shall be taken that which he hath . . . but I had never expected to be obliged to interpret that so literally.

Once I knew that Maude was adamant I did everything possible to sell the place. Advertisements which stressed its historic value, the scenery, the shooting, photographs over which even Ian would brood and say, "It really *is* beautiful," appeared in all the papers. Numbers of house agents had it "on their books." But the stark fact which I had recognised before Mr. Turnbull had finished speaking just would not be gainsaid. Nobody wanted a great crumbling house in the depths of the country with nothing but a kitchen garden attached to it.

One day, when I was obliged to go there, I tried to cheer myself by playing a game. I arrived at Nettleton station and drove to Merravay in a ramshackle cab, pretending that I had never seen the place before, had been attracted by the advertisement, and had come to inspect it.

It was an experience to frighten the hardiest. Stripped of the furniture, the house was simply not habitable even in imagination. I stood in the drawing-room and looked at the walls, realising for the first time that the silk which covered them had once been deep yellow. Wherever a picture had hung or a piece of furniture stood against the wall, it was bright yellow still, with birds and sprays of flowers embroidered on it in delightful colours; elsewhere everything had faded to a dim greyish buff, marked with brown stains where the damp had crept in. In places it was frayed, in others torn. Imagine any woman standing there and thinking, "my drawing-room." That alone . . . and then there were the kitchens, grim vaults.

No, it was hopeless. I realised it then. What should I do; what could I do? I thought of Maude's remark, another one of those that old Booth himself might have made, about insuring it and burning it. Really, if I could have hoped to do so without exposure I should have been tempted. And certainly if I could have wished the place out of existence it would have vanished there and then. But it stood there fundamentally solid enough. The roof might leak, but the timber was sound. I looked at what seemed like acres of flooring, smooth and shining, honey-coloured; at what seemed like miles of panelling, much of it beautifully carved; at the staircase, as good as the day it was completed; at the roses and ships and other things which decorated the chimney breasts. Had they no value?

Then I went out into the kitchen garden. It was a wildly prolific place; Uncle Booth had employed two men and a boy, and the garden produce at Merravay had always been one of the joys of a visit. I had kept on one man, the eldest of the three, paying him a small wage and allowing him to make it up by selling what he could. I had also arranged to have boxes of stuff sent to me by rail, but that was highly unsatisfactory. Now, carefully tended, basking in the sun, the wealth of it, great plump shining strawberries, thick tender asparagus, early peas, tended to exasperate me almost past bearing.

On my way home in the train I made up my mind. Next day I wrote a letter to the Baildon agent, who, being at hand, could better deal with it. I asked him to try to find a buyer for the kitchen garden, and to sell the house if he could to a "housebreaker." Ian was very much distressed. I said, "What else can I do? Almost two years, and it's costing us money all the time. If I can just get a thousand pounds . . ."

"For almost the first time in my life," he said, "I wish I'd devoted a little more attention to money."

But it worked out in the end. A builder named Hoggett offered a thousand pounds for Merravay as it stood. The agent, shrewd and energetic fellow, took him over and persuaded him, on the strength of the staircase alone, to raise his offer to fifteen hundred pounds.

On the last Saturday of July 1914 I received a cheque for the whole, minus the agent's fees, and when I subtracted the sums I had paid out in wages and the cost of my journeys to and fro and the other expenses, I reckoned that I had almost exactly the thousand pounds for which I had hoped. I'd finished with Merravay.

Nine days later war was declared. Ian joined the Army Medical Corps and after that I had something else to worry about. I don't think I gave

Merravay another thought until the other day when I heard that Maude was hard up and homeless. All her husband's houses passed to a nephew when he died, and Maude had squandered the money he left her, as well as her own, in unwise speculations and endless house-movings. They say that between 1919 and 1938 she moved house, buying and selling and losing money on every deal, no fewer than fifteen times. That must be an exaggeration.

What could I do but write and invite her to share my tiny flat, even though I am told that she once described it as "one cell in an egg box"? I suppose the whole thing would strike Uncle Booth as a most delectable joke.

Interlude

When Joe Hoggett wrote the cheque for fifteen hundred pounds and so became owner of Merravay, he was putting his name to nothing so mundane as a money order. He was signing a declaration of faith.

Several times during the past weeks he had said, "Don't you believe it. There ain't gorn to be no war. Stands to reason . . ."

He knew all the reasons and could reel them off, pat.

On the last Sunday of July he drove out from his neat villa, Jesmondene, on the outskirts of Baildon, to inspect again, this time with a possessive eye, his latest purchase. He took with him his wife and his daughter-in-law, who were always pleased to have an outing on a fine Sunday afternoon, and were today excited by the prospect of seeing Merravay, of which they had heard a great deal. It irked Joe that his son, Joe Willie, was unable to accompany them; his absence quite spoilt the day.

Joe Willie did not share his father's confidence in Germany's awe of the British Navy, in the Kaiser's blood relationship to the British Royal Family, or in any of the other things which Joe thought of when he said, "Stands to reason . . ."

Joe Willie had been, for the last two years, a member of the Suffolk Yeomanry, the Loyal Suffolk Hussars. Old Joe had nothing against that; he was proud that Joe Willie, son of a working builder, should take his place amongst the sons of farmers and gentry—and be the best mounted of the lot. Joe had taken that showy, spirited black horse as part payment of a bad debt when the Whymarks "went up the spout" as he termed it. Joe Willie, looking very smart and handsome, had gone off to what he called "exercises" on this fine Sunday.

Mrs. Hoggett and Rosie, after a glance at the outside of the house and a more prolonged stare at the hall, both of which Mrs. Hoggett pronounced "gloomy" and Rosie "romantic," went off, woman-like, to the kitchen quarters, leaving Mr. Hoggett to take—a little shamefacedly, for it was Sunday, after all—a folding rule from his pocket and just run it over, just to make sure, just to confirm . . . He *knew* that he had made a good bargain, really; but his original offer had been for a thousand . . . and though he knew and was sure, he just wanted to *make* sure.

Once, while he was running rule and eye over the panelling, the thought struck him, cold, stomach-shaking—Do that come to a war and Joe Willie go, it'll be like this a long time, me alone. . . . But then, thass daft. There ain't gorn to be a war. Stands to reason . . .

In the kitchens and pantries and storerooms the two women were having a wonderful time. Mrs. Hoggett's father had been a butcher and had enjoyed Mr. Booth-Sandell's esteemed custom; she had always regarded the family with genuine awe. Seeing the kitchen in which that meat had been prepared for table was a shock to her.

"Well, if I wasn't seeing it with my own eyes I *never* would have believed it. Swanking about like that, ever so lordly, and living so shabby. Look at that old sink. All hollowed out with wear. You couldn't clean it, not if you wanted to ever so. Well, I never did."

"I don't suppose the old man ever saw his sink," said Rosie. It was a reasonable statement, but there was just that something in her voice which made Mrs. Hoggett suspect that once again she and Rosie weren't seeing quite eye to eye. That often happened; though they were the best of friends, really. Still it was with a certain asperity in her voice that she said in the bathroom, "He did see the bath I s'pose!" They stared at the mahogany-surrounded sarcophagus that stood high and lonely in the centre of a moderately large room.

Rosie agreed, for a moment, that the new bathroom at Jesmondene was preferable to this; then she looked out of the window and wasn't so sure.

Again Mrs. Hoggett sensed the lack of response; Rosie wasn't quite the homey, companionable daughter-in-law she'd hoped for, but she suited Joe Willie; and though she seldom said the absolutely right, cosy thing, she never said the downright wrong one.

The three met in the hall. Joe Hoggett was jubilant. He'd been right as usual. The staircase and the fireplace alone were worth the money; then there was the panelling and the flooring, all solid oak as good as new and better; and the tiles—it was curious how, these days, lots of people building a new house didn't want it to *look* new, liked the old tiles.

"Well, my dears," he said, closing and locking the great door, "Joe Hoggett weren't far off the mark there. Thass a bargain all right!"

"When I think," said Mrs. Hoggett, "how in the old days he'd come to the shop and sit there in his gig and give the window a clip with his whip to draw attention, ever so lordly and all the time . . . Well, if I hadn't seen with my own eyes . . . !"

Joe Hoggett helped the women into the high dogcart, gathered the reins, clicked his tongue to the horse, and then turned to take one last look at the house which he meant to carve up as a butcher carves up a carcass. The doomed and threatened house stared back at him.

"I call it a shame to pull it down," said Rosie in a strained, desperate voice. "It's such a beautiful house."

"Thass better; thass a beautiful bargain," said Joe easily. "You wait till Joe Willie see what his old dad've pulled off this time!"

But Joe Willie never saw the wonderful bargain; he rode away on his handsome horse, came home for one leave that was reckoned in hours, and went to meet death in the Dardanelles. Joe Hoggett's zest for money-making was quenched; there was no point in it now, for Joe Willie had left no child. There was some slight satisfaction in lending Merravay to be used as a military hospital where men less desperately wounded than Joe Willie might be mended; and when, its purpose served, the place came back into his hands he was spiritlessly relieved to sell it to the first bidder.

During the next thirty years the house changed hands seven times. A new law protecting ancient and historic buildings prevented anyone doing with it what Joe Hoggett had planned to do; a brief period in the ownership of a capricious millionaire saved it from falling into complete decay. In 1940, for a fortnight it sheltered a number of evacuees who would have stayed longer if there had been a cinema and a fried-fish shop within easy reach. Later in the war contingents of soldiers stayed long enough to write rude words on the plaster and carve their initials on the panelling.

Peace came; the old house stood and awaited the next turn of fortune. One thing only seemed certain—the time had come when Merravay must work for its keep.

The Breadwinner

In 1946, when David was what they called "rehabilitated," we set out to look for a little place in the country where we could cultivate a market garden and bring up a family. We had about three thousand pounds between us and when we had discovered that people were asking five or six thousand for two acres of chicken-sickened ground and an asbestos-board bungalow so small that David's claustrophobia became rampant at the sight, the miracle happened and we found Merravay.

It was an old Tudor house in Suffolk; quite genuine, spacious, and beautiful. It had been modernised after a fashion some years before; it had a banqueting hall and a musicians' gallery and—what mattered more to us—a big kitchen garden and some substantial outbuildings. During the war it had suffered; as David said, looking round, "The legions have camped here," and perhaps that was one reason why it was for sale so cheaply. They were asking three thousand pounds for it. When I brooded over the possible folly of buying an historic mansion to house two adults and one child I could find three points in favour of the project; first was that even on our first visit of inspection David had stayed indoors for a full hour without making one of his pitiable little excuses to go outside; secondly I could see that—should the market-garden idea fail—there was room here for me to take paying guests; and thirdly I was a fool. "Knaves and fools all pay in the end but the fools pay first!" I was fool enough to fall for the charm of the house. Its air of having seen such better days, of falling into decay so graciously, of wanting to be loved and used gently again . . . oh, I don't know! I was just a fool!

We put down our ready money and I sold the best of the things my grandmother had left me and we bought fifty handsome Rhode Island Red pullets scheduled to begin to lay in November, when eggs, scarce and dear, command good prices. That sounded promising, and we were also encouraged by the fact that the old man who had had charge of the garden on a "sharecropper" basis while the house was empty decided to stay and work for us. He was the recipient of a pension of some kind which made it inadvisable for him to *earn* more than thirty shillings a week. His method of recompensing himself more adequately had worked well in the past and probably he saw no reason to alter it. But it broke down in September, when I went into a fruit shop at Baildon to try to sell some green figs and was informed that they always bought figs from Merravay which were better than mine. That was indisputable! The wretched old man had risen earlier and picked more discriminately. Attempts—almost pathetically well meaning on our part, at least—to reach some less cutthroat arrangement met with marked non-collaboration from him and finally, with the remark that he was used to working for gentlefolk, he left us.

However that was just at the beginning of the long spell of severe weather for which the winter of 1946–47 is memorable, and as there was nothing to do except feed the hens and wait—and pray—for eggs and look for the places where snow had penetrated the roof, we bore up bravely, saying that there was no better place to be housebound. The hall made an excellent playground for a young child, and the fireplace took kindly to a diet of wood cut from the overgrown shrubbery.

In the following spring I made my first tentative suggestion about taking in guests. David wriggled away from it. He didn't actually *say* that an Englishman's home was his castle or that it was a man's duty to provide for his family . . . that was all implied.

And there were, of course, several stones unturned, many avenues unexplored—to hell with clichés! We tried goats and bees and mushrooms, we tried dog-breeding; we grew pyrethrum and scabious and lavender and potted plants. We tried everything!

And then, one day, driving in from Baildon, David overtook Ginger Whymark, whose car had broken down. Once upon a time the Whymarks had been the big noise in these parts; they'd owned Merravay and sold it and built a great new white house near by and lately sold that to an agricultural college and moved into their own lodge cottage—a bit added to. The old man had managed to retain the shooting rights and every autumn he had a big party; very favoured old friends screwed themselves into the limited accommodations at the Lodge, the others went to The Evening Star in Nettleton, and soon after David had become—and I had forced myself to be—friends with Ginger Whymark, the woman at The Evening Star fell ill on the very eve of one of the old man's parties and Ginger came across to ask a favour . . . would I, could I, put up four decent old chaps? Just bed and breakfast, she could manage everything else.

I'll be honest. I didn't much care for Miss Whymark with her marmalade-coloured hair and her hearty voice and her abounding energy —they said she did all the housework at the Lodge single-handed, bred her dachshunds, looked after an old aunt across the way as well, and still had time to hunt or go beagling when chance offered, a reputation which made me respect and admire and . . . is there a word for it? Resent doesn't quite do, nor does fear. . . . Anyway, that doesn't matter. What does is that I seized on her suggestions and took in the old men, who were perfect pets, and when David saw that the sun did not fall out of the sky at the sight of Captain and Mrs. Stamford taking base coinage in return for hospitality the way was opened for me to do what I had been longing to do for months—start Merravay as a guest house. I sold a few of my remaining treasures, a Bow clock, some bits of Chelsea china, and a lidded wassail bowl—the only complete one, I believe, outside a museum, in all England—and with the proceeds I bought the necessary furniture and paid for the necessary advertisement, and before long my guest house was on its feet and staggering along.

II

It would be ridiculous to pretend that the guest house made much profit; what it did do was to work in very well with David's various activities. Vegetables and fruit, eggs, rabbits and fowls I could have at cost price, and since I could now order with comparative lavishness at the Baildon shops their owners were more inclined to buy what we had to sell. By May of 1950, when the lilacs and mock orange in the overgrown shrubberies at Merravay were scenting the air for miles around and every day ended in a kind of cuckoo-haunted dream, I could look round, not with complacency but with some satisfaction. We were solvent; people who had stayed once had come again and recommended us to their friends, and Ginger Whymark had heard of someone who had two old horses in need of a good home and we had offered to take them, "meat for manners," so now we could offer riding as one of the amenities at Merravay; and my main worry was that David was overworking. Since the guest house had got going he had suffered a decline of spirits, had more than once said something about being a failure and having made a mistake in coming to Merravay. This I attributed to the fact that he was working too hard as well as resenting the establishment of the guest house.

The overwork, at least, was remedied. Early one morning, driving back from Baildon, he saw a man sitting by the roadside, endeavouring to hammer back—with a stone—the loose sole of his shoe. David's all-embracing sympathy came uppermost; he stopped the car, spoke to the man, brought him to Merravay, gave him a meal and a rather better pair of shoes. The man was a Pole; whence he came, whither he was bound, we never knew. When he had eaten and was reshod he looked at the garden and said, "I dig. I am not beggar men." And he dug until the next mealtime; after which apparently his pride demanded that he should dig again. At nightfall he slept in the loft and was then so deeply in debt that he must dig all next day.

He looked harmless enough; a thin, clean-looking little man with closely cropped hair and very bright blue eyes, but, as I said to David, he might be a thief, a murderer, for all we knew.

"Damned good worker though," said David. "We could use him."

At the next feeding time David asked casually,

"Know anything about horses?"

Something happened to his tight, bony little face.

"Me. To know about horses." He dived into an inner pocket and brought out a wallet, grey-edged from wear, held together by a rubber band. He selected and held out to us a photograph of himself in the high boots and trim uniform of the Polish cavalry, seated upon a much too tall, lively-looking horse. I could think of no comment which would not—by implication at least—be hurtful, but David said, in just the right tone,

"Ha. Cavalry! Yes, I'd say you knew about horses."

"Against tanks they were no good," said the little man, replacing the photograph and busying himself with the rubber band. "Much later I have Spitfire. Was good."

"The operative words there are 'much later,'" said David with one of his brief, sudden accesses of bitterness.

"Please," he said, not understanding. But after that he was, all at once, one of us, and we were privileged to call him by his name, which was Stanislav.

Largely thanks to his efforts, Merravay was looking its best when Miss Julia Spenwood came to stay with us for a fortnight of recuperation after an operation. Somebody had recommended her; and she looked so frail, so faintly distraught, that at sight of her some Little Mother of All The World instinct rose up in me. I plied her with Bovril, Ovaltine, eggs beaten in milk, and in return she ruined me.

She arrived on a Saturday and on the following Thursday went to town to keep a pressing engagement, she said. David drove her to the station to catch the one good "up" train and arranged to meet the good "down" one in the evening. She wasn't on it; and in the morning I had a letter thanking me for my care of her and saying that urgent business had compelled her to remain in London; would I send on her belongings. She enclosed a cheque for the full fortnight.

Nobody in Nettleton was sufficiently hard up or enterprising enough to deliver Sunday papers, but they were obtainable at the station between the hours of twelve and one, and on the Sunday after Miss Spenwood's departure one of the people staying in the house who was fond of riding rode in to fetch them. I was busy getting the lunch but I did notice that all my guests had congregated in a little bunch about the papers as though something interesting was afoot. Some particularly gory murder, I thought, knowing the Sunday papers. But while I was clearing the tables the old dear who had fetched the papers lingered, hovered, hesitated, and then handed me one paper folded small and said, "I think, Mrs. Stamford, you should see this." He hurried away and I looked at the headline, which asked, in bold thick print, "Another Haunted House Near Borley?" Underneath was a small but beautifully clear photograph of Merravay. Below that was a spiel about poor Julia Spenwood, the fashion editor of the paper, who had been ill and gone to Merravay for her convalescence and who, after four days, had been forced to flee the place because it was so dreadfully haunted. There was no mention of what she saw, felt, or heard, apart from a "feeling" on the stairs, a "cold place" in the big hall, but it was a clever piece of sensational journalism. I could see exactly what it meant. It was Miss Spenwood's "comeback." Poor old dog Tray, sick and blunt of tooth, had nearly been shut out but he'd managed by chance to grab a hare and had carried it home and was now reinstated in the very middle of the hearthrug.

A cry of "Fire" could hardly have emptied the house more quickly. By Monday midday everybody—with some fatuous excuse or another—had departed. The week's post brought me several cancellations, a letter from a medium who wished to hold a séance in our haunted house, a letter from a woman whose own house had been dreadfully haunted and successfully exorcised, and an anonymous communication furiously denouncing me for trying such a cheap advertising stunt. In the next fortnight I received no requests for accommodations, and the only people who came to the house were a few sensation-seekers, hoping, half frightenedly, to find another Borley. It seemed to me that I had been ruined by an irresponsible journalist and should have some redress; so one day I put the article and the letters of cancellation into my bag and drove into Baildon to consult young Mr. Turnbull, the solicitor who had dealt with the transfer of Merravay.

At home, to David, I had always managed somehow to make light of the disaster, but as soon as I began to describe it to someone who would not be inwardly *hurt* by the implication that I needed to make a living out of paying guests, my control wavered. My voice and my hands shook, my head jerked, my eyes filled with tears.

Mr. Turnbull listened gravely and—I thought—sympathetically; then he studied the newspaper cutting and the letters.

"Most unfortunate, and, I realise, infuriating for you. But in law, I'm afraid, you have no redress. You see it would be difficult to prove conclusively that Merravay is not haunted and even more difficult to prove that Miss . . . er . . . Spenwood was not genuinely of the opinion that it was. And she could certainly produce—not evidence of haunting, but evidence that she was not alone in her opinion."

"You mean that other people have said so?"

He nodded. "As a matter of fact my attention was drawn to the subject some years ago—before the war. There was some trouble about leasebreaking. The house was rented at the time. The tenant tried to plead that it was haunted as an excuse . . . that didn't work, of course. But I looked up the story. Very interesting!"

"Tell me."

"Well, I shouldn't wish . . . though there's nothing actually frightening . . ."

"That kind of thing never frightens me," I said. I could have added that I had enough real terrors to contend with, getting into debt, finding a new and really serious leak in the roof . . .

So he told me the story of Lady Alice Rowhedge, the witch of Merravay whom some remote ancestor of his had attempted, unsuccessfully, to protect when she was tried for witchcraft in the middle of the seventeenth century. She was supposed to ride a great black horse, on windy nights at certain seasons, along a certain stretch of road; at other times she walked about in the house, brewing potions, making spells. "Three hundred years is a long time, Mrs. Stamford, but the story seems to crop up fairly consistently. Miss Spenwood wasn't being very original." He smiled and went on, "This story, you know, will either die down and all will be as before; or else you may find that your ghost is established and becomes an attraction. Then you could charge half a crown for admittance, and sell wildly expensive cups of tea."

"To a lot of stupid neurotics!"

"Oh, don't be harsh on us! I visited Borley several times; and the fact that the ghost story interested me took me to Merravay in the first place, and as a result, when somebody wanted to demolish it *I* put a stop to that scheme. You owe your ghost a little, Mrs. Stamford."

"Maybe," I said, getting to my feet, "it would have been better for me if it had been pulled down."

His manner grew more serious.

"The guest house really mattered?"

"Why else should I bother?"

"Well . . . of course, it's not for me to make suggestions. But if you find that people like to visit, but are averse to sleeping in, the house, you could try making it into a club. A relative of mine did that with her white elephant of a house and says it pays and she hasn't to make beds, a job she happened to abhor."

"That would mean getting a club licence."

"Which wouldn't be difficult. I could do that for you."

I thanked him for his kindness. Halfway home I stopped the car and, bowed over the wheel, gave way, for the first and last time, to a bout of lachrymose self-pity. Everything we had tried so far had come to no good and had cost money; even the bee-keeping scheme! And I had just invested in a store of sheets and towels. Now I must go marketing for glasses, liquors, and a club licence. It seemed a little too much! But by the time that I had repaired my face, stiffened my courage, and got ready a cheerful, optimistic mood in which to meet David, my mind was made up. I'd try another thing; Merravay should become a club.

The way one thing links up with and leads to another is very strange. Spite and rancour had taken me to Chris Turnbull and much resulted from that visit. Not only did he get me the licence, he made the club.

There is another strange thing—the way wars work out for different people.

My war had been dull; and because I was bored by it I had taken a course in cookery, found an unsuspected talent, and gone on and on.

David's had been disastrous. He'd just reached captain's rank when he was taken prisoner and pushed into a camp where he was senior officer. In those days, before it was proved that the Japanese intended to disregard all conventions, David, who knew the rules, often ventured upon his pitiful, futile protests. One of these concerned overcrowding and lack of exercise, and he used the unfortunate expression, "boxed up." The Japanese to whom he made his complaint said, "Bad exaggerations. I will show you boxed up. I will demonstrate to you categorically boxed up." David being six feet tall, the box they made for him was exactly five feet six inches each way, and he spent nearly two years in it. He emerged wildly claustrophobic.

Chris Turnbull's war, beginning with a wound at Dunkirk, had put him into a hospital bed next door to Jimmy Rorke the film actor, and there had started one of those apparently incongruous friendships which astonish everyone except the participants.

So now Chris could say to me, "It is nice to have somewhere to bring Jimmy and Mavis when they come for weekends!" And local people could say, "Let's run out and have a meal at Merravay. We might see Jimmy Rorke and Mavis Mallinson!"

And I could cook, especially the kind of exotic meal for which people are willing to pay a disproportionately high price. I still think that I could have made a great success of Merravay as a club and dining place had nature seen fit to endow me with cast-iron feet, a solid timber backbone, and a dozen hands. As it was I had to have help; and to need help in England nowadays is to rank with the piteous drug addict who must pay blackmailing price or perish.

Of course I could always advertise "bus passes gate." It did just that, at forty miles an hour, twice a day, making for the Nettleton post office, where it stopped. But "help" didn't like that; and after some harassed and distracted months, some comic, heartbreaking experiences, I settled down to run the place with the assistance of one good, steady daily woman and a fugitive succession of girls who thought they'd rather like to do a little waitressing, and, of course, the invaluable Stanislav, who took on voluntarily the work of bar-man. Each afternoon he would stop work, take a bath, put what looked like Dorofix on his hair, and with an expression which would have become his sainted namesake—dogged resignation—get behind the bar, and proceed to act with his usual dexterity and care for our interests. Out of the tips that came his way he hoarded enough to buy what I hope is the noisiest motor cycle ever made, and often, when we had made everything tidy for the night and I had tottered to bed to lie beside David, who had been asleep for hours, I would hear that motor cycle go roaring away, lonely and raucous through the dark. Stanislav seemed to need so little sleep, lucky man. My own need was chronic and cumulative. I could have lain down at any moment and slept for a week, a month, a year, forever. Shopping, catering, cooking, making out the menus, totting up the bills, being pleasant to people; being a wife to David; being a mother to young John, who was now, thanks to the club, a weekly boarder at a decent little school and whose week ends must somehow be made to seem happy, normal interludes . . . it all took toll and sometimes I would catch a horrifying glimpse of myself in a glass; light-brown hair dusted with silver; face thin and lined, rouged and powdered too hastily into a caricature of itself; eyes too wary, too watchful. But one day—I told myself after each such glimpse—things would alter; I'd have time; one day I'd go to the hairdresser's; take forty-eight hours off and sleep . . . one day something would happen.

And one day something did. I went to answer the telephone's shrill summonses and instead of the table reservation I expected it was a personal call from London for Mr. David Stamford. A friend of his, one Eddie Blenco, much blessed by me because he had once sent me a hundredweight of sugar—he had a plantation in Jamaica—was in London and wanted David to go up to see him. I remember saying, "You go. The trip will do you good. Stanislav and I can manage." Somebody, somewhere, filed that remark away!

David went and came back to tell me that Eddie Blenco had had to have an operation which might alleviate, but could not cure, his complaint. He knew that his active days were over and he needed somebody entirely trustworthy to go and manage his plantation.

"But you don't know anything about sugar cane," I said tactlessly, and saw David's face darken.

"I am prepared to learn. Besides the place is crawling with people who know everything. What Eddie wants is somebody he can trust to go and look after *them*. And look, Jill!"

He whisked out and showed me a photograph of a long white single-storied house with a deep verandah. In the foreground was a garden, neat but luxuriant, and behind it a mass of palms.

"Ours," said David in a voice of intense gloating. "No rent, free service . . . and a thousand a year!"

It was his great moment! Man the provider had gone out and brought home the carcass and I spoiled it all. I said,

"But what about Merravay?"

He looked at me and said, "I never gave it a single thought. It was a gaff. Just a place to get away from."

That reminded me of the old David; of the dashing headlong way in which we had got married, decided to have a child, bought Merravay. And though I was glad to see this resurrection of the spirit I felt compelled to say,

"But we gave three thousand for it." And then the devil made me add, "I'm not budging from here till I see that money again."

III

Just before he left—which was three months and about thirty disappointments later—David said, "You must be the most pig-headed woman God ever made. So we paid three thousand for the damned place! Can't you see that we've lived here, three of us, for five years? It owes us nothing! For the last time, will you shut the door on it and come with me?"

"I daren't," I said. I thought of the chance of his not liking the job, not being able to stand the climate, of the plantation failing, of his falling out with Eddie. Three thousand pounds was three thousand pounds; a nest egg, education for John, food, a roof, a bridge to the next venture.

"All right," David said. "I shall go. I won't smoke or drink; I'll live on sugar cane; I'll take odd jobs and cheat and swindle everybody, and *I'll* give you three thousand for the bloody house. Nobody else will . . ."

"For the house perhaps not; but for the club as a going concern somebody might. And I just feel I must stay here until somebody does. . . ."

Stanislav promised to stay and look after everything. David promised to find him a place on the plantation. Chris Turnbull promised to keep an eye on us. I promised to take the first reasonable offer for Merravay. Even young John promised to be a good boy.

So David left and I was appalled by the sense of loss which his going inflicted. Of late we had spent little time together, rising up half asleep, utterly uncommunicative, to go about our separate chores, to meet over hasty meals, and eventually to go, at differing hours, back to our work-induced slumber, side by side. There were days when we had hardly exchanged a dozen words; but he was *there!* I could save up things to tell him when the opportunity occurred, could amuse myself by collecting, polishing up, making more amusing or significant the trivial things that happened in the course of the day's work. Now I missed him terribly; far more than I had during the war, for then our brief times together had not led me to rely upon his mere physical presence. I decided that in the past I had never been sufficiently sympathetic towards widows, especially those who had enjoyed a longish married life. . . .

The year crept up to its summer peak and then began to go down the slope which, beginning gently with August and September, would lead precipitously to the winter depths, when it would be dark in the morning when I rose and there would be no one to speak to, and dark again in the afternoon long before the most avid-for-drink member came into the bar. David wrote regularly; and every letter mentioned the warmth, the sunshine, the beauty of the country, the plentitude of things like domestic labour; every letter said, "Put on your hat and come!" And each time the temptation to do so became a little more insidious, to be balanced by the determination not to do so becoming a little more stubborn.

On the last Saturday in August my dear daily woman, Mrs. Baxter, told me that she was leaving; she was going to marry the village constable who lived next door to her. I was not surprised; she was so pink and placid and comfortable that she was sure to marry again—I would have married her myself had I been qualified to do so! But the news dismayed me.

"I'd have done it over Bank Holiday," she said, "but I wasn't sure of Annie Coote till this last week."

"A bridesmaid?" I asked, forcing myself to take interest.

"Bless you, bridesmaids! And Ager my third! No, Annie's for you. She's niece to my first, and a rare good worker. And she'll live in. She'll wait, too, trained she is. You'll be set up with Annie!"

Touched by this solicitude for my well-being I gave Mrs. Baxter the only thing I owned which had ever evoked her admiration—Granny's bow-fronted china cabinet, which still emptily mourned the treasures I had been obliged to sell. One of her husbands had been a champion winner of fairground ornaments and the cabinet would show off the prizes "a treat."

And for some time after Annie's installation I would have given her aunt-by-marriage the same thing daily, I was so grateful. Annie was about thirty-six, past the silly age, tireless, willing, quiet. A real treasure until she fell out with Stanislav.

In the beginning she seemed to like him, did little things for his comfort, spoke him very fair; and to say that he rebuffed her would be untrue; he met her overtures with the same monosyllabic courtesy which he used towards me and the club members. Annie, not understanding, felt herself snubbed and rebounded into frank hostility. I noticed the rasping little speeches which he seemed to ignore, but it was difficult for me to interfere until one morning when, carrying in some pot plants, he dropped some soil and fetched a brush and dustpan and swept it up.

"While you're about it you might as well make a job of it," said Annie. She pointed to some cigarette ash.

"When madam wish me to sweep she tell me and then I sweep," said Stanislav. His voice and the glance he shot at me were both imbued with challenge. I said—truly—that he had enough to do without sweeping. Annie, with a mutter about dirty foreigners and cheeky Poles, turned away. Best to ignore it all, I thought; but later in the day when Stanislav and I were checking supplies behind the bar he suddenly said,

"To be called dirty by that peasant! Pole I am and proud to be. Yes, despite all, proud! And never will I carry that cow on my motor bicycle. There is trouble! She wait every time and wish I should carry her. Should I take her on my motor bicycle and rape her in ditches she like me well. Otherwise I am dirty Pole. I do not forgive her. Never!"

"Well," I said, "I'm not suggesting that you should take her as passenger or anything like that, but I wish you'd forgive her and bear with her. She helps me so much. And it's for such a short time. Things are going so well. We've made twenty new members. Very soon I shall sell the club and you and I will be on our way to the Captain." (Stanislav having learned David's rank always used it punctiliously.)

"It is in my mind," he said, "that raping in ditches is not such thing as should be said to ladies. Please forgive me, madam. I was too angry!"

I forgave him. I realised that what he had said was true enough.

Our waitress at that time was a rather pretty, cheerful, bumbling little girl named Nancy Peake. I'd never been able to teach her much, but she'd taken a liking for Annie and begun to model herself on her, and very often Annie spent the afternoon in the Peake house. One morning—it was late in October but more like November weather, a day of dark drizzle— I was coming back from shopping and overtook, halfway up the avenue, a little thread of a woman who was stumping along through the wet leaves. I stopped and said, "Are you going up to the house?"

"I am," she said.

"Get in then, I'll run you up."

"But I'm Mrs. Peake. And you're Mrs. Stamford. I know you, though you don't know me. And I've something to say that on't be to your liking, so you don't want to go giving me no lifts! You go along. I'll be there presently."

I grinned. Unsuspecting, simple fool that I was, I grinned and said, "Now what could you have to say, Mrs. Peake, that would make me unwilling to give you a lift? What is it? Does Nancy want to leave?"

"She don't want to, but she's gorn to. Ah, that she is. We're poor, but we've allust been respectable, Mrs. Stamford. Nancy ain't staying in a place where there's carrying on! Oh no! There's right and wrong and how you and your husband, poor man, fix things between you is your affair and I ain't interfering; but where my Nancy is concerned, thass different. We're poor but we've allust been respectable and respectable we stay. Thass all. Thass what I come to say and I said it, to your face!"

She whisked around and stamped off in the direction of the village. I sat for a moment, feeling stunned and a little sick, and then I realised that it was Saturday; that every table was booked. Without Nancy I should be in a muddle. I turned the car and drove back to Nettleton, hoping that Mrs. Baxter . . . Mrs. Ager . . . might be free to "oblige" as she had occasionally done at a pinch.

Mrs. Baxter was pleased to see me, but it was clear that Mrs. Ager was faintly alarmed and no little embarrassed. She asked me into the parlour, where the cabinet was now a cage for a menagerie of pottery animals of unlikely proportions, and avoided my eyes as she said that Ager didn't really like her to take odd jobs. "You see, with Ager there's this, ma'am. He really do hev his position to think of; and to tell you the truth he ain't quite so easy handled as my others, so you see . . . I'm sorry. And I wouldn't like you to think that I paid any attention to that Annie and her wicked tongue. Told her straight I did, only last week, that the worst thing up at Merravay was her evil mind. But thass the Cootes all over; speak evil of somebody they must, and now they're done with me they start on you! And I'm right sorry I ever recommended her to you!" Then suddenly her wavering gaze came to rest on my face; her blue eyes were troubled, oddly innocent and yet corrupt with wisdom. "You know how it is, ma'am. For one that'll give you the benefit of the doubt there's ten that on't."

It was too late to retire into dignity and pretend that I didn't know what she was talking about; besides, it would have been utterly untrue. I knew. I simply said that I was sorry that she couldn't come and help out that evening and retreated.

IV

I suppose that anyone with a grain of sense would have gone back, sacked Annie and closed the club, admitting defeat. But at the mere thought of so doing, something—mainly panic, I suppose—rose in me and made it absolutely imperative to stay in Merravay until I sold it or died. So I said nothing; I worked side by side with my enemy and I held out until the first week of December.

There had been a long spell of fog, the worst weather for me for it made catering almost maddeningly difficult. At six o'clock I'd look out into a white blanket and resign myself to an unprofitable evening; at eight o'clock a dozen hungry people would arrive, clamouring for food. Either the fog had cleared for a bit or else some bold spirit had suggested risking it. Or again there would come an evening when the fog seemed to have lifted, and I'd cook, and nobody came; and Annie, Stanislav, and I would eat, all next day, lavishly, heartbreakingly, things like wienerschnitzel, warmed up. And David's last letter had said, "Do give it best, darling! If only you would we could still be together for Christmas." And I thought, if only I could! And I saw three thousand pounds, made visible in the shape of very black pound signs, leggitty little beasts, tearing away from me, never to be recaptured!

However, that morning, the first Saturday in December, dawned bright and clear and the weather forecast said that the fog had finally lifted. The telephone rang and rang; by eleven o'clock every table was booked. My spirits rose as I set about making the pastry.

It was Stanislav's day for having his fortnightly haircut, so with the car piled high with greenstuff and some pot plants, he had gone into Baildon early. John was paying his weekly visit of devotion to Ginger

Whymark's latest litter of dachshund puppies—a fact for which I was later to be supremely grateful.

For suddenly the kitchen door burst open, and there was Stanislav, one half of his head ruthlessly clippered, the other still bristling with its fortnight's growth; his face was blue-white, his ears blazing red. Without a word he walked over to where Annie sat cleaning silver, and smacked her face twice; his palm hit her right cheek, his backhand her left, with a sound like a pistol shot.

Before he could hit her again I had him by the elbow, clutching with both hands and throwing all my weight against him. Annie saw her chance, got up, overturning her chair, and made for the door, screaming like a banshee. Stanislav jerked himself free and would have followed, but I was between him and the door and just managed to rush across, slam it, and set my back to it.

"Have you gone mad?" I gasped at him. For a moment he glared at me so savagely that I expected him to charge the door and fling me aside. In that moment I could hear Annie's screams, evenly spaced, diminishing in volume as she fled down the avenue. And I saw the madness—not the fury—go out of Stanislav's eyes.

"She is vile, wicked woman! Such things she is saying of me. I wish very much to kill her!"

"I could see that."

"If you should know what she is saying . . ."

"But I do. I've known ever since Nancy left. But she was *help!* Now look what you've done, you silly hot-head!"

"This English phlegm! This nation of shopkeeper! Never shall I understand. She is help, and so to be free to be saying untrue vile things so that barber men are winking and making filthy jokes to me. Two times he makes the joke. The first time I am not believing the ears; then I understand. I do not think he makes any further joke today!"

Apprehension seized me.

"Oh, what did you do? You didn't . . . ?"

"I am meaning to knock his teeth down the throat. But they are false teeth he is having and fall on the floor instead. Is funny!"

He gave a short, sharp bark of laughter in which I had a hysterical impulse to join. "Is funny" indeed. . . .

"Now we shall have real trouble . . . police . . ."

I could see the headline in the paper, "Pole Strikes Barber"; I could imagine the exposure of motive, all the hints and rumours which I had tried to ignore, creeping to the surface like worms after a rain.

"Can be fined," said Stanislav. "Can be in prison. Better than sit in barber chair and hear . . ." his hot little blue eyes glanced away from me, ". . . dirty jokes about me and that filthy bitch!"

The lie—and all that it implied—touched me. Suddenly something absolutely female and atavistic stirred in me. Angry, bristling, ridiculous little man, he had struck blows and would doubtless perjure himself in defence of my "honour." The clash of pennant-fluttering lance on blazoned shield, the "pistols for two" in the dawn, had narrowed down to "Pole Strikes Barber; Fined Thirty Shillings," but it was chivalrous still.

"Well," I said weakly, "all that must wait. The first thing is for you to find another barber and have your hair finished. You can't go about looking like that!"

"Will finish him presently, myself, with horse clippers. Meanwhile . . ." He snatched up the rag which Annie had dropped, plunged it into the plate polish and began to work on the silver with all the vigour of unexpended rage.

I stood for a moment, looking at all those forks and spoons which must be set out in order, collected, and washed. I looked at my unfinished pastry; at the slate upon which I had written the names of those members who had booked tables; I thought of the gallons of soup; of the mounds of vegetables. Weakness washed over me like a wave. I had tried, I had done my best, and I was beaten; why not admit it? I couldn't cook for and wait upon thirty people single-handed; nobody could. Moreover, by this time the rumour of Stanislav's assault upon the barber would be all over Baildon, lending point and substance to the scandal. Could I face the furtive, curious eyes?

I had only to lift the telephone; cable first to David, and then make a series of calls saying that, having no help, I was obliged to close the club. Let people think what they liked—they'd think the worst anyway. And I wanted, oh, how badly, to share with David the exquisite humour of "but they are false teeth he is having." After all, I thought, there are other values in the world beside material ones; why ruin your happiness trying to salvage three thousand pounds?

To this day I don't know why I didn't lift that telephone. . . .

But I didn't. And by six o'clock the tables were set and the fires made up; Stanislav with his skull shaven was behind the bar and I was in the kitchen. John, I might add, was in the Heaven of Heavens because Ginger had given him one of the puppies; its nose was a fraction of an inch too short, or its tail a fraction of an inch too long, so in this world of curious values it wasn't marketable. He'd taken it to bed with him and retired early, and willingly, because he thought it might be tired. They were asleep, curled up together when I looked in before going down to make my last stand.

Good evening! Good evening! Yes, isn't it lovely to have it clear again. Oh yes, of course you can have dinner. So difficult to make arrangements beforehand in this weather. David? Oh, he's very well, thank you. I heard from him this week. Plenty of sun there! Oh, hullo . . . if only I'd known you were coming I'd have made you one of your special dishes. An omelette will do? Of course. Cheese or mushroom? (Nothing to me, dearie, dash it off in no time.) David? Oh, very well, thank you. Yes, I hear every week; sometimes twice. A drink? That's kind and I could do with it, but I just must get back to the kitchen. Single-handed tonight. Yes, isn't it awful? Stan's hair? He does look a bit odd, doesn't he? Rather *too* short; maybe somebody "got in his hair" as they say. (Oh yes, I'm a wit, I am!)

I was back in the kitchen, having "shown" myself and faced them, or at least those who had come early, when the telephone rang. It was Chris Turnbull.

"Jill? Look, I know it's a bit late, but I've had a young American wished on me. Nice. Mad on old houses . . . so I thought. . . . But if it's awkward we'd eat at The Evening Star and then, if we survive, come on later."

"If you really had my good at heart, Chris, you'd drive out here full speed and take on the bar for an hour while Stan helped me to dish up. I'm entirely on my own tonight. If you would . . . and then eat later, I'd do you proud. . . ."

After that, what with the steam, the heat, the haste, everything melted into a kind of nightmare. I drowned in a sea of soup, potted shrimps, smoked salmon; I fought my way through a jungle of roast pheasant, filet steaks, with or without garlic, dear member? I climbed great mountains; potatoes, peas, braised celery, and what-sweet-would-you-like? I ran marathons; cheese, black or white coffee, and can-I-have-my-bill-please? There was Stanislav, useful as another pair of hands to me, never hesitating, never needing direction, never forgetful; breasting the wave, thrusting through the jungle, climbing the steeps, running the race by my side. And we did it. At about ten o'clock somebody looked out and said, "Fog coming up again," and fifty thousand people said at once, "But the forecast said . . . my bill please . . . swallow that down and let's get going . . . good night."

After that there was a great quiet.

There is something about complete exhaustion which is akin to one stage of drunkenness; time seems to skid about. I heard the last car start. I was conscious of nothing but a grinding agony in the small of my back and a peculiar feeling of being hobbled. I looked down and thought, Good Heavens! Elephantiasis! Huge bags of jelly were bulging and shaking where my ankles should have been. Another day like this and I'd have to have one of—no, two of those little carts they tie on to fat-tailed sheep.

Then, without the slightest idea of how I came to be there I was sitting by the fire in the hall. A cup of coffee and a brandy glass stood on the table beside me. Stanislav was clearing the last things from the deserted tables and Chris Turnbull and a craggy-faced young man with dark red hair were helping him.

I called to Chris and—just as in drunkenness—my voice came out peculiarly high-pitched and clear.

"Leave it, Chris; leave everything. There'll be plenty of time to clear up in. I can't go on like this. I'll just have to shut down and go to David."

"I think that would be wise," Chris said.

There, I've said it, I thought; that makes it real.

Then I lost another moment, during which somebody must have brought a stool and propped my feet on it. The place was tidy and Stanislav had gone. Chris was sitting opposite me and his friend stood by the foot of the stairs, running his hand caressingly over the almost life-size figure of Moses which stood there. The sight called to my mind the number of things about Merravay which were unique and lovely. Now that I had, by a single decision, severed my connection with the house I could afford a moment of admiration for its beauty and regret at its fate. I looked ahead and saw it deserted again, given over to the bats, the owls, the ghosts.

"It isn't my fault," I said aloud. "I've done my best. I could truly say that everything we ever tried here was doomed from the start. Chris, I believe you were right about Alice Rowhedge. She didn't want us here, so she put spells on us. Well, now she can have it, all to herself."

"Now isn't that curious," said the young American, who had been crossing the hall as I spoke. "Alice Rowhedge did you say? That was my mother's maiden name!"

Finale 1953

Between a young Cavalier named Charles Rowhedge who disappeared into the East Indies in 1662 and a Thomas Rowhedge first heard of as one of the few survivors of an ill-fated party making the overland route to California in 1841, there was a gap which nothing but imagination could ever bridge satisfactorily.

In course of time Mr. Christopher Turnbull, eager as ever for any activity more to his romantic taste than the routine duties of a country solicitor, managed to unearth the fact that a Thomas Rowhedge, in the island of Banda, in the year 1749, had added his shaky signature to a protest sent by the nutmeg growers there to the Dutch East India Company's Office in Amsterdam. That was the end of the trail in the East.

In the West the name Thomas Rowhedge occurred in a list of five people, all that remained of a party of twenty-three who had been snowbound on Trucksee Lake for five months during the winter of 1840–41. Their trials and escape had been lent some notoriety by the suspicion—and rather more than that, since one man, almost demented by his experience, confessed to it—of cannibalism. Another survivor, in his deposition, was recorded to have said, "I went by Tom Rowhedge and he never so I never." There were a few other small indications that this Thomas Rowhedge had been a person of influence and integrity, and the family which he had founded in the sunny valley of the Sacramento had always cherished his memory.

It would have been nice to think . . . but there was the gap.

There were clues. The tendency to choose Thomas and Alice as names for first-born sons and daughters; the fact that, although the first Californian Rowhedge married a woman with some Indian blood, many Rowhedges were red-haired; and there was a mention of that somewhere in the original Alice Rowhedge's confession. Very little to go on, as Thomas Rowhedge Anderton was the first to admit. And even within his own mind he regarded his feelings with a degree of cautious scepticism. He knew that he had always been extremely, almost excessively, Anglophile; he had come to England early in the war as a member of the Eagle Squadron and he had never felt wholly at home anywhere else since then. And he had fallen in love with Merravay at first sight. Long before Mrs. Stamford had let fall the name which started his imagination leaping he'd thought that of all the houses he had seen that was the one he liked best, would most like to own.

Properly approached—Chris Turnbull had said casually—Mrs. Stamford would take five thousand pounds for it, he thought. Her husband was in Jamaica and she was very anxious to join him there.

That certainly was cheap for a house with a room still called the Queen's Chamber where the first Elizabeth had slept; for a house with a rose garden that had been laid out by a convicted witch . . . and cedars said to be brought from Lebanon seven hundred years ago.*

* Possibly exaggerated, but one held to be 600 years old was felled at Assington, Suffolk, in 1952.

And Amanda, so homesick, so terribly out of place in America, would surely love it.

Also, he wanted it himself. And his experience in wanting things was extraordinarily scanty. His mother, once widowed and twice divorced, and the resultant circle of suitors, stepfathers, relatives, and friends had seen to it that his wishes were not only met but often forestalled. By the terms of his father's will he had attained an independent income when he was eighteen, and at twenty-one he had inherited the bulk of his grandfather Rowhedge's solid if unspectacular fortune. He was a very enviable young man, and one who might have been sadly spoilt. But his tastes had remained curiously simple. He had once quite shocked a young newspaperwoman who was gathering material for a restaurant-sponsored column of nonsense about what and where people liked to eat, by saying that his favourite food was radishes and bread and butter. The young woman, privately thinking this a facetious snub, saved her face by giving the dish the name by which she had recognised but not deigned to order it during her one holiday in France—*radis au beurre*. But it was an honest answer, and revealing. Revealing too was his certainty that Amanda, when she heard that he had bought, on the impulse of a moment, an old historic house in England, would be not merely approving but transported with delight. For he and Amanda saw eye to eye in everything.

Amanda was half-English by birth and entirely English by education, that was what had attracted him to her in the first place. Her mother, after years of unhappy marriage to a Wiltshire landowner who liked to go to sleep in a chair after dinner and finally allowed himself to be divorced so that he could do so in peace, had gone back to America and her family. She had taken Amanda, aged seventeen and just released from school. Amanda was coltish and shy, years younger, by every sophisticated standard, than her cousins and their contemporaries. Even when she had been coiffured and dressed and equipped to pattern she had failed dismally to fit in, and the chance introduction to Tom Anderton came as a godsend, just in time to save her from developing an inferiority complex.

Soon after her eighteenth birthday they became engaged; gratitude on her part, Anglophilism on his, masquerading as love. Their mothers opened the debate as to whether an Easter wedding with lilies, or a June one with roses, would be preferable. The debate continued.

One of Amanda's American uncles, who suffered from asthma, always wintered in Florida, and being fond of youthful company, and rich enough to command it, he always set out with an attendant bevy of nephews and nieces. This year Amanda was invited, and since Tom had pledged himself long ago to act as best man to a friend who was about to marry in London, it all fitted in well.

Just before he left America Tom looked in at a party where he talked for a while with a quietly spoken, shy-seeming Englishman who turned out to be Jimmy Rorke. In the course of the conversation Rorke said that he thought the really loveliest part of England was a bit one never heard about, not the famous Constable country, but the region just north of it, over the border, South Suffolk. Tom confessed that that was a part which he had never heard of.

"I go there pretty often. I have a friend there, Chris Turnbull; he's a solicitor in a place called Baildon." He went on to say that Chris was brilliant, could have done anything, but had chosen to bury his talents, in a way, because there had been Turnbulls practising law in that town for four hundred years and he hadn't the heart to break the line. If Tom should happen to go that way and cared to look Chris up and say . . .

"Maybe I will," Tom said.

And there had come a time when the wedding was over, and he was feeling lonely and yet unwilling to go home . . .

That was how it had happened.

With one thing and another he was only just back in time to keep Christmas with his mother, and immediately after he set out for Florida to see Amanda. He took with him two dozen photographs of the house. The ones of the interior, taken in powerful artificial light, were clear and dramatic; the outdoor ones, for which the photographer had been obliged to depend upon the vagrant, pale sunshine of a winter's day, were less successful; they suggested a sombreness, a look of brooding age, that was only just short of sinister. But Amanda would understand; when he said that the house was built of old brick Amanda could imagine . . .

She had no need to.

"It's the spitting image of Daddy's house. I knew it! The moment I read your letter I thought—Heavens! It sounds just like Hadwyke! Darling, what can have come over you?"

"But it's beautiful! Here, just look at this. That shows the screen in the hall. Silvery grey and so finely carved. And then this room where Queen Elizabeth . . ."

"Darling, it's always her, or Anne Boleyn! I can't believe they spent their time rushing about sleeping in different places just to give people something to talk about later on. Can you?"

Outside a voice called urgently, "Mandy! Mandy!"

"Well, we don't have to live in it, do we?" said Amanda, shuffling the photographs into a heap and standing up. "Get your bathing things, darling. The others are waiting."

He knew he hadn't even reached first base. She wasn't in the right mood. Now he came to think about it she hadn't been in the right mood ever since his arrival. There'd been a slight undercurrent . . . as though he'd offended her in some way and she was bearing a grudge. It couldn't be because he'd bought the place without asking her . . . or could it?

He probed the point at the first opportunity, which was not very soon. For something had happened to Amanda during his absence. She seemed to have become very popular. She'd always been rather out of things; now she was the centre . . . it was "Mandy" here and "Mandy" there all the time and she appeared to like it. But at last he did get her to himself and he asked his question.

She said, "Yes, I do think it was pretty highhanded."

"But, honey, there wasn't much time. This Mrs. Stamford wanted to make the sale right away and I knew that you wanted to get back there and it was the loveliest old place we'd be likely . . ."

"I can't think what made you imagine that I wanted to go back. I don't, Tom. And if I did it'd be Mother and Hadwyke all over again. It was the house that finally got her down, you know. Besides . . . I like it here. And you should have consulted me. . . ."

Fortunately the full irony of the situation escaped him. Being engaged to him had given Amanda just the confidence that she needed to make the grade in her new circumstances. Having made it, she need no more be bothered with this dull young man. And he had liked her because she was English and homesick and different.

If he had come straight home without visiting Jimmy Rorke's friend they would probably have had the June wedding with the smother of roses upon which her mother had set her heart, and a little later on some other catalystic circumstance would have revealed, more disturbingly, how little in love they were. As it was, the broken engagement hardly mattered at all. An old house, thousands of miles away, staunchly facing the blizzard-laden east wind of its four hundred and seventy-fifth winter, had merely forestalled one more divorce.

By the third week in January Tom was back in Nettleton, with the full approval of his mother, who was absolutely certain that Merravay was the Rowhedge ancestral home and that the blood of baronets ran in her veins. When the weather was warmer and he had the place comfortable she was coming, with a number of her cronies, to use the house as a headquarters for her Coronation visit.

He was camping in one room while workmen swarmed through the house, installing bathrooms and central heating. A plump, cheerful woman whom some people called Mrs. Coote, others Mrs. Baxter, others again, Mrs. Ager, and who didn't seem absolutely sure herself, came up each morning and made his breakfast and tidied his bed. He was completely happy, though at times he would have liked someone with whom he could have shared his happiness and his enthusiasms. And even that he found. . . .

One morning, after a fortnight of loneliness, he went into Baildon and was driving back when he overtook a tall girl who was plunging along through the rain. She was ill clad for such a day. A scruffed old leather jacket shed the water from her shoulders, but below it her tweed skirt hung soggily and a pair of thin, high-heeled shoes sucked at the mud; her head was bare and her bright yellow hair, misted with raindrops, shone like a halo. She carried a parcel which looked heavy and from which the soaked newspaper in which it was wrapped was peeling away.

Tom passed, slowed down, stopped. Despite the unsuitable shoes and the parcel she was loping along at a good pace and soon drew level.

"Could I give you a lift?" he asked.

"That depends where you're going," she said crisply. "If it's only into the village it's hardly worth while mucking up your beautiful car. Thanks all the same."

"I'm going through, to Merravay."

Grey-green eyes, narrowed against the rain, widened and regarded him with frank interest for a moment.

"Oh . . ." she said; and the single word implied that she had heard a good deal about him. "Well, in that case, I should take it kindly." Before Tom could reach out and open the door she had done it for herself, had heaved the parcel into the rear seat and lowered herself into place beside him. She brought with her a faint feminine scent of cosmetics mingled with that of wet leather, wet hair, and something else dangerously near to being downright nasty.

"This is the second time this week that the car has broken down and this time they don't hold out much hope. I shall have to get a bicycle." She pushed that thought aside. "So you're Mr. Anderton. I'm Ginger Whymark—we're the nearest thing to a neighbour you have; we live in the Lodge at the end of the other avenue. Tell me . . . is it true that your folks only bought Merravay in order to rip out the stairs and fireplaces and take them off to the States?"

"Why no! My folks as you call them haven't had anything to do with it. My father's been dead nearly twenty years and my mother's quite crazy about the place, so far. She's coming over in May—if I can get it clear by then. I don't expect she'll want to stay long. But I'm staying."

"It's you then, you own it?"

"That's right. I own it."

"It was just that you look a bit young to go owning houses," she said. "Nowadays, around here anyway, you have to save hard till you're forty in order to buy a caravan. Still, I'm glad, by God, that *that* tale isn't true. I've a very soft spot for that house. I was so *relieved* when the Stamfords took it but anybody could see with half an eye that they'd never hold out. They were the nicest people, but like children, always trying out something new and never giving anything time to get going. I did try to point that out. It was just the same with my dachshunds. I mean if at the end of the first year I'd decided—as well I might—that they weren't a paying proposition and gone rushing off into great Danes or Pekes or something the way the Stamfords would, well, I shouldn't be where I am today!"

"And where is that?" he asked, matching her frankness.

"I'm recognised as one of the best breeders of dachshunds in England. Not wishing to boast—but Monarch of Merravay simply swept the board. . . . Oh!" She put a long, thin, hard-worked-looking hand to her mouth and shot him a glance. "The place was empty then, when I started, and didn't look like ever being occupied again and Merravay went so well with Maid, Matriarch, Monarch, Mischief, and Midget. Lodge wouldn't go with anything except Lousy!" She laughed, with just that touch of wryness which David Stamford had found so engaging, especially when he was having a bad day. "And," she said meditatively, "it was meant to be a bit of homeopathic magic, like African witch doctors pouring a libation to bring down the rain."

"I don't follow."

"Of course not. Well . . . there was a time when I did just hope that the Stamfords would just hold on until my great-aunt . . ." she laughed again. "Damn it, she is ninety-four! It had gone though my mind in demented moments that if the dogs did well, and if she really left me what she says she will because I mend her fuses and chase the burglars from under the bed and bully her butcher, I just might have . . . But of course that was a pipe dream. And I couldn't have left my parents. And I couldn't have kept the place up. I should just have moved from room to room, one jump ahead of the rain; and in the end the roof would have caved in on me. But how could man die better? Oh blast! I was afraid of that!"

Heaving and shrugging, she freed herself of the leather coat, then, rearing on one knee, leaned over to wrap the parcel. As she did so the unpleasant odour of which Tom had become increasingly conscious, and which had somewhat inhibited his full response to her chatter, became more noticeable. Was there, he wondered, proper bathing accommodation at the Lodge?

"Gah!" said Miss Whymark, "it's high this week! That is the one thing I don't like about my job. Even when it's fresh I have an absolute horror of horse meat."

"I once heard a professor say that all true Anglo-Saxons have," said Tom. "He said it was on account of the horse once being a sacred animal and subject to a tabu."

"That's interesting; feasible, too, I should say. Look, I wonder would you mind dropping me here. I've just remembered I must go along Goose Lane and pick up my heavy shoes. Old Farrow promised them for this morning."

"Down here?"

"Yes. But don't come. It's a vile bit of road and you couldn't turn . . ."

"I could back, I guess."

It was all too apparent that Miss Whymark was not accustomed to much consideration.

She re-entered the car, carrying, unwrapped, exactly the pair of shoes one would have expected her to be wearing on such a morning. She inspected the clumping new soles with considerable satisfaction.

"Nice neat job," she said. "How he does it I can't imagine; he's as blind as a bat!"

Was it possible that the poor girl had but the one pair of heavy shoes?

"Oh!" said Miss Whymark as they passed the mouth of the chestnut avenue which Nabob Sandell had planted. "I meant to get out here. Now you'll have to turn in *our* avenue and the College traffic has churned it into bog—tractors, you know." The avenue of limes, the cause once of so much dissension, came into view. "When my family lived at Merravay, this was the avenue up to it. There's quite a fascinating story about the family quarrel which resulted in the shrubbery being planted across its upper end."

"I didn't know you ever lived at Merravay."

"Not me; the Whymarks. Oh yes, we lived there, years before New Holding was built. Now, keep well over to this side . . . aah! Just missed it! That's grand." Once more she forestalled his effort at courtesy and was out of the car in the rain and the mud, whipping out the parcel before he had pulled on the hand brake. "Now come in and have a drink. Father has two or three friends staying; they should be shooting, but it's too wet. I bet they've been drinking for hours!"

On the inward side of the little Lodge cottage a considerable extension had been made in modern style. Tom could see a wide bay window with a bank of exotic hothouse flowers just behind it; and behind the flowers, drawn by curiosity to the window, were a number of elderly male faces, all of them, Tom thought, bearing a marked resemblance to the late Sir Aubrey Smith. The owner of one face came nearer the window, beamed at Miss Whymark, and pointed to the flowers with a gesture of exaggerated complacency and triumph.

"Lovely! Lovely!" she shouted. "That is Sir Stephen Fennel," she said, turning to Tom. "He's brought Mother some flowers. Poor old dear, it was touch and go this year but he managed to keep his hothouse going by not having a fire himself. He sits at night with his feet in a muff. . . ."

A curious, inexplicable shyness descended upon Tom.

"I mustn't come in now, thanks just the same," he said. "I've got some stuff aboard that the men are waiting for."

"Some other time then. Any time," Miss Whymark said equably. "And I've no doubt that when Mother hears you are really going to *live* at Merravay, she'll rout out a hat and pay you a formal call. That is," she added gloomily, "if they ever get the car going again. She can't walk far these days."

"Well, I'd be glad . . ." he began; but probably that wasn't quite the thing to say. "I would like very much to show you what is being done up at the house."

"And I'm all agog to see." She pondered. "I tell you what I could do. I walk the dogs most evenings. I could walk that way. I often did when the Stamfords were there. Then seeing it empty again and the rumour of the staircase being ripped out depressed me so much, lately I've avoided it."

"This evening?"

"There again, it depends. If Sir Stephen stays on, I *might*. If not they'll need me to make a fourth—at bridge."

"You might even give me a word or two of advice about furnishing. I took over a few things from the Stamfords; but for the rest, well it's all kind of new to me."

"My experience of furnishing has been confined to fitting nine-footer sideboards into rooms twelve feet square *and* leaving room for the door to open. But of course, if you really . . ."

"I do," Tom started to assure her; then he realized that she was standing, without hat, without jacket, in the rain. And he thought—I'm as bad as the rest, using her rough.

"Come up as soon as you can. I'll be looking for you," he said quickly, and drove away, followed by her voice thanking him heartily for the lift.

It was raining more heavily now, a silver-bead curtain suspended from a slate-grey sky. The men who should have been crawling about the roof had taken shelter in the kitchen and were busy with yet another brew of tea. One of them, a Nettleton man, was holding the floor.

"Mind you, I wunt want a word of this to git to *his* ears. Let him spend every duzzy dollar he got afore he wake up to the fact that this ain't a house to be *lived* in! 'Tis well known, in these parts, to be haunted. Ah, I see you grinning into yer mug, young Saunders! That don't alter fax. Why, only a year or two back there was a whole crowd of right smart people staying here and they all upped and went, saying they couldn't sleep for the moaning and groaning. Bit in the paper about it there was. Then you go back to afore the war. Lord Clumberly took it and what he warn't going to do with it . . . coo! Lady Clumberly come down once, just the once and never no more. Work stopped and up for sale again. 'Twill be the same agin now, you'll see!" He drank deeply, and looked with pleasure on his audience.

"I can remember further back than that even. A sensible owd working chap called Joe Hoggett bought it; he come up here one Sunday arternoon, and never set foot in the place no more; and if you so much as mentioned it to him he'd blench and look at yer as if you was talking about Owd Nick. And now I bin in it I know why. You couldn't call me chicken-hearted," he said modestly (he had gone, very reluctantly, to the "old" war, and at Vimy Ridge, chiefly because no other course had seemed open to him, had held a machine-gun post single-handed and had been awarded a Military Medal) "but you wouldn't catch me spending a night here; no, not if you was to offer me a thousand quid."

"Little Mrs. Stamford slepp her all by herself," somebody contributed.

"Ah. So they say!"

"What about that there Pole?"

The conversation showed signs of drifting.

"But what is it all about? What does the haunting?" asked an electrician from Colchester.

He genuinely wanted to know, but to conceal his serious purpose he winked right and left as he spoke, pretending to be leading on this credulous Nettleton fellow.

"Ah, wink away," said the Nettleton man, who was sharper than he looked. "There's them that hev laughed for years about the walls of Jericho tumbling down when Joshua's trumpets blew and now they've dug the place up and found that they did fall down. Thass the same with this. There's the story they tell in the village, and if that ain't good enough for you go and look in Baildon museum and see the thing writ out. There was a Lady Alice Rowhedge, hundreds of years ago, and she was a witch and she made spells and bargained with the Devil to get this house for her own. And the Devil did her! So now she can't rest nor cease from tormenting till the Rowhedges hev it agin."

"Reglar Boris Karloff you are!" somebody said. "Make my flesh creep. Still, so long as I'm out afore dark."

"And not a word, mind. Don't forget the dollar gap!"

"Time he've finished here the balance'll be on the other side I should reckon!"

Tom entered—as he always did, for the sake of the joy the first sight of the hall invariably gave him—by the big front door. The lacy screen, the massive, gently mounting staircase, the figure of the old man leaning on the staff, the eighteen-inch-wide, honey-buff planks of the floor, the long taut stretch of the gallery, the Tudor roses over the cavernous hearth —he looked at them, one after another, and knew that his pleasure in them, sharp as it had been, was today increased. A little dragging sense of loneliness had vanished. It would be ridiculous and naive to bank too much on the strength of a single meeting . . . but he had been definitely attracted to her, even when he was wondering about that odd smell. And of course the setup . . . shooting parties and patched-up shoes, hothouse flowers and foot-muffs, formal calls if a broken-down car could grind out two more miles . . . that all savoured of the Deep South. But anything less like a southern belle . . .

Obviously she had the heck of a life, a very bad deal; but it hadn't got her down.

She'd wanted Merravay herself, but she didn't grudge his possession of it. She was glad. She didn't like to see it empty. When she came . . .

Yes, he'd have a fire in the big hearth of the hall—he hadn't tried that yet. He'd put his two chairs and the rug close to the fire. Drinks? He had plenty, and it might be that after the walk she'd be ready to eat, too.

And she'd come along, glad to see the lights in the windows, and he'd open the door and say, "Welcome to my home!" No, that sounded a bit pompous. He'd say, "Hi there. Come in."

But the fact remained that after the way Amanda had behaved about it, and the way that his mother had snatched at the whole thing, not because it was what it was, but because of what she chose to make of it, the idea of the arrival of someone who felt—and with more reason— about Merravay as he felt was extremely exciting and satisfactory. Probably, when she'd rested and had something to eat and drink, they'd go over the place together. She could tell him details of that family quarrel which had resulted in the closed avenue; and he could ask her—because it was quite clear that one could ask her anything—what was behind this hint of haunting. Gosh, there were so many things. . . .

Making his preparations, mental and material, for his first visitor, Tom felt he had come home.

THE TOWN HOUSE

The Town House

All of the characters in this book are fictitious,
and any resemblance to actual persons,
living or dead, is purely coincidental.

Part One

MARTIN REED'S TALE

I

Few born serfs, like me, could tell you their birthdate, but I was born in that memorable year of 1381 when the peasants, armed only with the tools of their trade, supported by a few soldiers, back from the wars, and a few priests with hearts of compassion, rose up against their masters, against the laws and the customs that made a serf the property of his lord. They gave—according to the stories—a good account of themselves: the men of Kent reached London and forced the King himself to lend ear to their grievances. In the end, though, they were disbanded by trickery, sent away soothed by false promises, and the freedom they dreamed of did not come in their generation, nor the next. So, when I was born in the autumn of that year, 1381, I was born a serf as much the property of my Lord Bowdegrave as the horse he rode, and—at least until I reached working age—of less value; for his horse had an Arab strain, far more rare and precious than my Saxon peasant blood.

My mother died at, or soon after, my birth, and although some woman must have suckled me, or fed me with pap, I have no memory of it. For me life began in the forge, where my father worked and where I learned not to touch hot things because they burned, not to get in his way because his hand was heavy, and not to go too near the horses' heels. I was working the bellows—and doing it properly—when I was still so small that I had to stand on a great stone in order to hold them level with the fire.

For his work on my lord's horses and harness and field tools and armour on occasion, my father, being a villein, received no wage. He had his hut, a strip of land in each of the three open fields, and the right to eat his dinner at the lowest table in the hall. When he worked for other people he could make his charge in coin or in kind, and he was not unprosperous. Some years before the rising of 1381 there had been a great sickness in which many people had died; skilled smiths were not as common as they had been. On some manors my father could have hoped and tried, by industry and thrift, to have saved enough money to buy his freedom, but my Lord Bowdegrave was a lord after the ancient fashion and boasted that never, on any of his three manors, had he manumitted a serf for money. My father knew this and therefore, given the choice of a coin or payment in meat or drink, he would choose the latter, so in our hut we ate well and I grew taller and stronger than most of my kind.

Maybe my wits profited from the good food, too, for when the time came for me to learn the Catechism and Responses our parish priest praised me often, and in the end was taken with the notion of making a clerk of me. He was himself the son of a serf, baseborn like me and set free by Holy Church, and he hoped to push me through the same door.

To my surprise my father was in favour of the plan. He was already showing signs of the dreaded smiths' palsy, that ungovernable shaking of the hands which results from the strain of lifting the heavy hammer and from the jar and thud of its fall. It was, as yet, slight, just a tremor which increased towards the end of the day, so that sometimes in the evening he would slop a little ale from his mug, but he knew what it heralded. He knew, too, that, on the manor of Rede, the old and the infirm had little to hope for. He would, of course, be entitled to a place by my fire, a share of the food of my table, but it would be a place and a share measured by the size of my family and the generosity or otherwise of the woman I married. He rightly reckoned that as the father of a celibate parish priest he would fare better, so, looking ahead, he allowed me time to take my lessons.

Learning came easy to me. I was, naturally, idle as all boys are, and earned myself many a buffet, but the priest said I had the makings of a scholar and would do him great credit in later years. As time went on I would relieve the tedium of the lessons by concocting questions which I hoped he would not be able to answer; the hope was justified more and more frequently. He had forgotten much of what he had learned. At last, in the summer before I was ten years old, he went to Norwich and bespoke for me a place in the monks' school there, where he had got his own learning. After that there was only one thing needed to set me on my way to clerkdom, and that was the permission of my Lord Bowdegrave to leave the manor and his service. The priest never doubted that permission would be given.

"My lord boasts that he has never sold a serf his freedom, but he will not hesitate to make a gift of you to Holy Church," he said.

My Lord Bowdegrave was seldom at his manor of Rede; he had two others, one in Lincoln, one in Kent. This last was his favourite, being within easier reach of London, but the others were visited each year immediately after harvest, at which time even the most trusty steward might go a little awry in his reckonings. Also, after harvest, when the great field was all a-stubble, was the best time of the year for hawking.

It was in the first week of October in the year 1391 that I first came face to face with the man who owned me. My face and hands had been scoured, my hair was newly shorn, and I was wearing a clean smock. I was very much frightened. The priest, who must have been—I now realise—a very simple and unworldly man, had warned me that my lord would surely wish to test my abilities. I must be prepared for questions; I must not answer hastily and without thought, nor must I answer slowly and thus appear stupid. Above all I must speak up so that I could be heard, and with the very greatest respect.

The steward had plainly prepared my lord for our appearance, for as we entered the great hall, he said, "Ah! The smith's son. I remember."

Fright boiled in my throat. I knew I could never answer a question, no matter how simple. Fright laid a heavy hand on my neck, so that my head was bowed, my eyes fixed on the rushes, fresh spread for my lord's visit.

Above me the voice asked one question.

"How many sons has the man?"

The steward said, "This one, my lord."

"Then he cannot be spared. Bad clerks are plentiful; good smiths are few." Thus briefly was my future, the priest's hopes, my father's old-age comfort disposed of. From my lord's verdict there was no appeal.

I was able then, for some reason, to raise my eyes and look into the face of the man whose lightest word was to us, his villeins, weightier than the King's law or the edicts of our Holy Father, the Pope in Rome. It was a handsome, well-fleshed face, highly coloured; stern too, as befitted a man of consequence, but not ill-natured. From the height of his chair on the dais he looked down at me, and his light hazel eyes took my measure.

"You're a stout, likely-looking lad," he said, "far more fitted to handle a hammer than a quill." Having thus dismissed me, he lifted and crooked a finger and said, "A word in your ear, Sir Priest."

What the word was was not for me to know, but I noticed that from that day onward the priest favoured me no more but seemed rather to avoid me.

The priest may have suffered some disappointment. Now that I am older and know more, I can see that, having made the one great stride from serfdom to clerkdom, he had shot his bolt; he had ended as a priest in a small, poor parish. Had I become the scholar that he thought I had it in me to be, then he would have been more, for great scholars remember their teachers and many a man of small learning is immortal because he taught the rudiments to one who has become famous. But this, of course, I only guess at.

My father and I, on the other hand, suffered nothing so positive as disappointment. I had been dreading the discipline of the convent school and the break with everything I knew, the harder lessons, the competition with boys born free. And my father was consoled for the loss of a more secure old age by the thought that in the immediate future he would have my assistance at the forge. Also—and this I have seen proved many times in later years—it is seldom those who are oppressed who resent their oppression; they wear it as they wear their clothes. Serfs, when they rise against their serfdom, are always led by free-born men. There was nothing of resentment in us. My lord had spoken, and as he said, so it would be. I went back to the forge and the anvil; I began to take great pride in my strength, and later in my skill. Smith's work is a man's work, and it was quite as much to my taste as the question-and-answer work with the priest, who would drub my head if I erred.

So, year followed year; life went on in the old pattern. I grew, and I learned, toiling on the working days and making merry on holy days. I might well have lived and died at Rede, one of my Lord Bowdegrave's possessions, had I not fallen in love.

II

LOVE is not, it is rightly not, a thing for every day, for ordinary people. Love is for the minstrels and the singing men to make tales of. That way it is safe.

How often have I heard a singing man strum his lute and raise his voice:

> "A gracious fate to me, to me is sent;
> Methinks it is by Heaven lent.
> From women all my heart is bent
> To joy in Alyson."

There is a pleasant thought, set to a tunable air, and suitable for a singing man who means nothing by it. Pity the poor fool of a man who, in this our life, suffers such a fate; who goes mad and sets one woman above all others, above all else. I know whereof I speak, for such a poor fool was I.

Men of property choose women who will bring them good dowers;

acres to link with their acres, coin to rattle with their own, or a good name to boast of, or some other advantage: poor men, when the itch comes upon them, take the wench who is handiest, or, if they are uncommonly prudent, have a care to pick one with sound limbs, sweet breath, and—so far as such things can be judged aforehand—an amiable temper. And they all do very well, since any woman can bear a child or boil a dumpling.

But I . . . I must needs fall in love!

There was, at first sight, no reason why my love for my sweet Kate should cause any upset. She belonged to our manor of Rede, and her father was, like mine, a villein. He was a shepherd and lived on the sheep run, over by the river in a remote and lonely place; and since Ancaster Church was nearer his hut than ours of Rede, he and his family went to Mass there; so I was twenty and Kate was seventeen before I noticed her, and then it was only by chance.

I was by this time a skilled smith and more active than my father, so when there was a job to be done at a distance I was the one to go; and on an April afternoon I was coming home from Ancaster, walking downhill towards the river where the steppingstones were, when I saw, on the Rede side of the stream, a child—as I thought—washing some linen in the stream. That was an ordinary sight enough on an April day when the body-clothes worn through the winter could be sloughed off and cleansed, and I took no notice until a woman came out of the shepherd's hut, walked towards the child, berating her as she walked, and then, snatching up a broken branch that lay nearby, began to lay on heavily.

That again was no extraordinary sight, and it was not for me to interfere between parent and child; only the priest, or perhaps the steward, had the right to do that. The little girl took the punishment without outcry and, for all I knew, deserved it. But after a moment, I, who all my life had seen women beating their children, was struck by the ferocity with which this woman went about the job. I splashed over the stones, and on the other side slowed my pace and at last stood still. The woman seemed to be in a killing rage, and the prevention of murder is every man's Christian duty. So I said:

"Have a care, good wife. Such heavy stripes might kill the little wench."

From what Kate told me later I have no doubt the woman would, sooner or later, have done that, but not out in the open under the eye of a witness. She gave me a savage look and laid on three more blows, as though to prove her right, but they were lighter ones, and then she threw down the branch and went stamping and grumbling away back into the hut.

My fate then made me go to comfort the child, and as soon as I was within arm's reach of her I saw that her smallness belied her years; inside the torn dress was the white curve and the pink bud of a girl's breast. I looked on it and was lost.

I am not a poet or a singing man to tell of love. When I think of what made her dearer to me than any other, I can only say that she was so small, so light and thin and small, like a little bird, a little rabbit. To the end of our days together I never grew used to the smallness of her, and my hands—sometimes against my will—always went gentle when they neared her. For the rest, her hair was the colour of new-run honey and her eyes as blue as a speedwell.

I held her close to me for comfort, and, dragging down the end of my sleeve, I dipped it in the water and wiped away the blood where the skin was broken. She cried then. That was ever her way; to bear the blow, no matter how heavy, with fortitude, and then melt at a word or touch of kindness. When she was quiet again I asked for what reason her mother dealt so ill with her.

"She is not my mother. She is my father's new wife and she wishes me out of the house."

"To go would be better than to be treated thus roughly," I said.

"I cannot. The steward orders me to stay. I help my father with the sheep."

"Then he must stand between you and the woman."

"Ah, but she lays about him with her tongue," Kate said. "I should think shame to tell you what she says of us if ever he even looks at me kindly."

I held her in the crook of my arm and thought more rapidly than I had done for years, since I had done the last time the priest questioned me. Up to that moment the business of bedding and breeding had troubled me less than it does most men. One day, I had said to myself, I should marry and get a son to work in the forge when I, in my turn, began to shake and shudder, but it had never seemed an urgent or even a desirable business. There had never been a woman in our hut, and Father and I had managed very well; we were peaceful and better fed than most. But now I knew. . . .

"Be of good heart," I said, "and keep out of the woman's way as far as you can. I shall be back tomorrow, to see how you fare." I dared not say more lest I should raise a hope which it would be cruel to cast down. Rede, though in many ways a manor far behind the times, was well run, and the priest kept the Kin Book in order to make sure that no marriage was within the forbidden degree. There were the laws of the Church to be minded, and other, unwritten laws which ruled against the wedding of double cousins, that is, cousins related upon both sides. Experience had proved such unions to be bad alike for mind and body, harelips, fits, deafness, dumbness, and blindness had been the penalties of such near-incest in the past. So, on all properly managed estates, even the lowest hind had his "pedigree," and it must be consulted before leave to marry was given.

When I left Kate I went straight to the priest's house. I told him that I wished to marry Kate, daughter to the shepherd, and he said something which I always remembered.

"I have watched you, Walter, my son, and it has vexed me lest, all unwitting, I made a monk out of you when you were young, yet failed to bestow the benefit of clergy upon you. I was not to blame."

"I know that, Father. You had no cause to be vexed for me."

"You are twenty years old. Half your life is sped."

A cold thought for a man in love. I shuffled it off, looking at him; he had been in his middle years when he taught me.

"Ah," he said, "clerks live longer That is the rule. Measure your years not by mine but by your father's. He lacks a year of his two score and he is an old man."

That was all too true. Oh, hurry, I said in my mind; open that Kin Book, give me leave to marry Kate, for twenty years is all too short a time. And yet, if we cannot marry, twenty years without her will last forever, they will last so long that I cannot live them out.

He used his finger on the page of parchment which, with other pages, all of slightly different size and tied by thongs onto a stave of wood, made up the book. Sweat broke out on my forehead and around my mouth. Weeks, months, years went by; and at last he lifted his head and said:

"You are no kin to her."

I thanked him as though he, and he alone, had arranged it.

It was too late, that evening, to disturb the steward; but early next morning, before he went out on his rounds, I went to him.

"Ha!" he said. "And about time too. By the Rood, I don't know what is happening to you young rascals. Too idle to breed! With labour so scarce, too." That reminded him of something else. "The wench must stay at her work," he said. "So she does that, nobody minds in which hut she sleeps. Except you, of course." He gave me a nudge and a leer. "You can tell shepherd that the bride fee will be two geese, rightly fattened. That being settled, I am sure you will have my lord's permission to marry. It is a pity that you must wait until his harvest visit."

That day I whistled as I worked, and as soon as I could down tools went, without waiting for my supper, over to the shepherd's hut and said to that weak-minded man, "I have, from priest and steward, permission to marry your daughter, Kate."

The woman looked pleased, but he grunted, and said something about talk coming cheap; he was a poor man with a wife and two children younger than Kate; where was the merchet coming from. He supposed I had never even thought of that; young men in their heat never remembered that every time a girl married the lord exacted his due.

"But I have remembered. Steward said two fat geese, and them I will provide."

"Three," he said, "can be fattened as easy as two. One for me, two for my lord, and the bargain is made."

"It is made," I said, and struck hands on it. "And now," I said, stepping back and including the woman in my stare, "any blow on Kate's body will be a blow on mine, and I will repay it fourfold." As I spoke I knotted my great fist and the muscle on my forearm leaped up and quivered. Shepherd bleated, like his own bellwether:

"The children have run overlong unmothered. Their new mother did no more than mend their manners."

His other children were boys, aged about seven and nine, and hardy looking. They bore no marks of ill-usage that I could see, whereas my poor Kate was all swollen and marked from yesterday's beating.

"Any correction that Kate needs from this day forward *I* will tend to," I said, smiling at her and feeling my heart go soft. "As for you boys, if the woman bears on you too hard, kick her back. You're two against one, or, if you, shepherd, had the courage of a louse, three. What did she bring as her marriage portion? A gelding iron?"

"Take your foot from my floor," the woman cried furiously.

"Gladly," I said, and, taking Kate by the arm, I drew her out and we went to a place where a bent hawthorn, just coming into flower, leaned over the stream. And there I held her close and we talked. I said:

"My pretty one, you shall be safe with me."

Safe with me. Yes, I said that. I looked down the years and saw her in our hut, eating fatly of food I had provided, growing smooth and sleek. She was so small and I was so strong; I would never even let her carry a bucket of water from the well. Her work as sheep-girl I could not order, but I would put fear into the shepherd, so that the hard tasks did not fall to her. She should be safe with me.

III

Now here is something which men born in free towns, or on the manors of more enlightened lords, may find hard to believe: or they will believe that it was true in times long past, not in my living memory. But I swear, by all that I hold holy, it was true at Rede. It was the custom which our Norman masters brought with them. Having a little learning, I can give it its proper name, *jus primae noctis*, but we called it First Nights; and it meant simply that the lord of the manor had the right, if he so wished, to take any serf-born girl's maidenhead. Whether he exercised the right depended upon many things, the man's own lustfulness, age, or disposition, the way the girl looked, the fashion in the district. On many manors it was regarded as outmoded, like the Twelve Days of the Lord of Misrule at the Christmas season: but in this, as in other matters, my Lord Bowdegrave was old-fashioned, and here and there about Rede manor, and about his others I have no doubt, the long straight Norman nose, the cleft chin, the bright hazel eyes which were the visible sign of the Bowdegrave breed could be seen, incongruous in a peasant face, bearing witness that he had not only exercised his right, but done it potently. Of late years, however, age and an increasing heaviness—it took two stout men to heave him into his saddle by this time—had cooled his ardours, and for several seasons past he had contented himself with kissing the prospective bride if she were comely, or giving her a smack on the rump if she were otherwise.

Occasionally, during the weeks that followed my bespeaking of Kate, I thought upon this matter. It seemed to me impossible that any man, however old, however much he weighed, could look upon my Kate and not desire her. Yet, strange as it may sound to any not serfborn, I was not unduly disturbed. This matter of acceptance of circumstance cuts very deep. Think of those born humpbacked, deaf, blind. They accept their fate and bear it. I was born a serf. If my services were required even in the next village, Ancaster, to shoe a horse or mend a plough, I must ask the steward's permission before I could step across the boundary between Rede and Ancaster. Think how irksome that rule would be on any free man. To me it was nothing. In the same way it was . . . well, almost nothing, that the unlikely might happen and my Lord Bowdegrave should claim his First Nights right upon Kate. She would be mine for the rest of our lives. He could not be prevented. There lies the whole crux of the matter; what cannot be prevented must be borne, like unseasonal weather, mildew on wheat, murrain in cattle. Through May and June and the months that must drag until our lord's harvest visit, every time I thought upon the matter I told myself: There is nothing I can do; it is unlikely that he will claim his right, but if he does what is one night?

That was a year of most remarkable fine weather. With the new moon of June the heat set in, and by mid-July the corn was ready for reaping. Without hitch or hindrance, without so much as a summer shower to halt it, the harvest went on, and before the end of August, a full month early, the stubbles were cleared. My Lord Bowdegrave, informed of this, put forward his visit, and my time of waiting was cut from October to September.

I had ruled myself well. To a degree the season had been in my favour; hay-time and harvest are busy times for smiths, and this year, since they followed so hard on one another's heels, I was doubly busy. Also Kate's father, resenting, perhaps, my words about the gelding iron, had sent Kate farther and farther afield as pasture became scarce. So I saw her but rarely. However, late in August, the grass having grown again on the lowland by the river, the flock came home, and one night, under a lopsided moon, she and I lay together.

It was sin; but she was guiltless. God and all the saints are witness to that. I did it deliberately, courting all blame. I had heard that day, somewhere in the yard, that my lord was on his way to Rede, and I thought: He is old and clumsy, and he does not love her. She is very small. There may be hurt and it is better that I, who love her . . . That was part of my thought, but not all. There was the reined-in desire of the last five months, and there was the wish to forestall, to be first, despite all custom.

Afterwards I took her face between my hands with their calloused palms and blackened nails and I said, "Now you belong to me."

So then my Lord Bowdegrave came to Rede and there was much commotion, with the paying of the rents and the taking of tallies of all his stacks and beasts and flitches and honeycombs. Then, one fine morning, Kate and I were called into the hall, just as, long ago, my father and I had been called when it was to ask consent for me to go to the monks' school. Walking over the fresh rushes, hand in hand with Kate, I was grateful that that consent had been refused.

I had warned Kate not to make herself look pretty. I still, in my serf's heart, admitted the old lord's right, but by the mere action of forestalling him I had taken a step out of bondage. I had risen up, under the moon, and said, "You belong to me"; later I saw the falseness of that. If you lay claim to a piece of land, you should be able to prove your right in the face of all men; if you cannot do so, any man who trespasses there does you more wrong than if he walked on common land. I was anxious, therefore, that she should not appear in the hall with her hair newly washed and streaming over her shoulders, wearing the wreath of flowers which marked the bride-to-be. Kate had laughed and asked, "Shall I smear wood ash on my face?"

Even had she done so it would not have hidden the fine shapeliness of her bones, the thickness of her honey-coloured hair, or the blue of her eyes. I saw the old man look at her; first with that pitiable, old-man lustful look, wishing he were ten, twenty years younger; than in another fashion. Even as the steward hastily named us, Walter, the smith's son, Kate, the shepherd's daughter, no relation according to the Kin Book, I saw the old man straighten himself and shift a little in his seat.

"Both of this manor, which will neither gain nor lose labour thereby," chanted the steward.

"Have done," said my lord. He dragged his eyes away from Kate, and, shifting a little more, turned to me.

"You're my smith, eh?"

"Yes, my lord."

"Then this is an ill choice, surely. You need a wench capable of working the bellows for you at a pinch, and breeding good strong boys. This little maid is altogether too fine and delicate for your purpose." His face had grown fat and purple since I last looked at him; in it his eyes shone, his lips were wet, with lechery. He leaned forward a little and reached out his great mottled hand to take Kate by the wrist.

"I can find you better employment; in the still room of my house at Abhurst. You'd like that, eh?"

Without giving her time to answer—for what did it matter whether she said yes or no?—he said to the steward, "Have her ready to ride, pillion to Jack or Will, when I go."

To describe a moment of boundless rage, folks often speak of "seeing red." A true word. I saw red then. My Lord Bowdegrave, the chair upon which he sat, the tapestry on the wall behind him, the steward standing by, were all gulped up before my eyes in a great red wave, into which I plunged my fist with all my weight behind it. I felt, but did not see, the smash of my knuckles upon the great leering face. The next instant something hit me across the back of my skull, and the redness gave way to a burst of sparks and then to blackness.

The utter black pricked out with stars, and there I was, lying flat on my back with my face to the sky. There was not an inch of me that was not in pain. My hide had been broken in a score of places, and the whole of my body was set stiff in a case of dried blood. Somebody had given me a monstrous fine thrashing. I moved myself carefully and found that none of my main bones were broken; then I rolled over on my face and was sick and felt better for it. Bit by bit I came to myself. I was stark, stripped of my hose and shirt, and I lay on the dung-heap. Left for dead, I thought to myself. Remembering what I had done, and why, it struck me that maybe I should have been better dead, which thought, naturally, brought me fully back to life. I gathered myself together, piece by piece, and reeled into the forge which was handy, and where we always kept a bucket of clean water to slake our thirst. Feeling my way to it, I dipped the horn mug and drank again and again, taking in, with the cool blessed water, the full sense of the plight I was in. I must get away, and I could not go naked. I staggered away to our hut.

There was a strong smell of onions, and the fire upon which my father had cooked his supper was still a small pink glimmer on the hearthstone. He lay in his bed. I threw a handful of dry sticks on the embers, and as the flames leaped he moved, lifted his head, saw me, and crossed himself hurriedly, saying, "God betwixt me and harm."

"It's only me, Father."

"A ghost," he whispered.

"My living self." The flames gained power, and he could see me, horrid as any ghost, stripped and all bloody.

"I gave you up for dead," he said.

I was his son; we had lived together in fair amity for twenty years, and of late I had carried the weight of the work. I did not blame him for leaving me where I lay; I had done an unforgivable thing and he had his own safety to look to. But he had come home, cooked his onions, laid down to sleep. At the back of my mind something stirred, a whole thought in a breathing space. That was to be a serf. A serf had no right even to human feelings; it was only by throwing away all claim to human feelings that a serf could support his way of life. I had, this very morning, acted like a man, not a serf; and with what result!

"Small thanks to those who beat me that I am not dead. And if I am here by morning, dead I shall be." I forced my bruised, stiff limbs to move more briskly. I had dressed in my best to wait upon my lord, so now I must don my stinking working clothes. Then, because our hoard was hidden in the earth under his bed, I had to ask my father:

"Give me my share of the money we have saved."

He got up, grumbling.

"Less the price of the three geese your share is," he said.

"But I am leaving the geese with you. Father, I must go far away. Who knows what may befall me? A penny may mean life or death to me."

"And who is to blame for that?" Recovering from his fear of being visited by a dead man's ghost, he began to rate me. Mad, reckless, ingrate. That ever son of his should lift violent hand against his lord. Shame, shame, undying shame; and worse. Punishment for him for breeding and raising such a rogue.

"You showed your colours plain enough when you left me for dead on the dung-heap and came home and roasted your onions. You have nothing to fear. Who else, when I am gone, can shoe a horse within ten miles?"

"That is true," he said, comforted again.

Yet, when he had unearthed our little hoard, he divided the coins into two heaps, then took from mine the sum I had paid for the three geese and added it to his own. I protested at that.

"The sixpence for the geese should be laid aside first, then the sum should be divided. The way you have it now, you are twelvepence to the good."

"You talk like the fool you are. You took out sixpence in April to buy the three geese. Now we divide into fair shares, and I take sixpence from your share and put to my own since I did not buy geese."

Nothing would make him see differently, and I dared not stay to beat it out with him. I took the twenty-one pence which was my share, put them, a half loaf, a piece of cheese, my knife, and a length of good cord into the little bag in which, when I worked away from home, I carried my noon piece, and then I was ready.

"You never saw me," I told him. "For all you know the crows picked out my eyes and the dogs ran off with my bones. If any speak to you of me, rail against me as you have just done."

I was on my way out, ducking at the low doorway, when he said in an uncertain voice, "God go with you, Walter." I remembered then that he was my father, growing old and tremulous, his working days almost numbered, and with no one now to depend upon. And he had taught me my trade without too much clouting. So I forgave him his supper, and the unfair division and made him a fair answer.

"God be with you," I said; and went out into the night.

IV

THE river bank, near to the place where Kate had been washing that day, was dotted with clumps of gorse bushes. I chose one close to the path worn between the shepherd's hut and the steppingstones where the family dipped their water, and there I hid myself. The gorse made an uncomfortable hiding place, but I was so sore all over that a few scratches mattered little. It was in my mind that I was most ill at ease. I had no certainty at all that Kate had been sent back home; it seemed far more likely that she had spent the night at the hall, in my lord's bed most like. But there was a faint, faint chance that she had come home, and I could not leave Rede forever without snatching at that chance.

Day dawned. A thin blue thread of smoke rose from the hole in the hut roof; the shepherd came out, eased himself by the wall, and went in again. Presently Kate herself came out, carrying a bucket. She must have cried all through the night; her face was swollen with tears. She looked stupid with misery and moved listlessly. When she was as near my bush as the path to the water would bring her I said, softly:

"Don't look round." I had debated with myself whether to say that first, or, "Don't be frightened." It seemed to me that a fright she would get over, whereas for me to be observed would be fatal. I quickly added, "Don't be frightened; and don't speak."

I cannot understand why all the mummers in the world—even when it is the Blessed Virgin to be represented—should be men. Women are natural mummers. Apart from a slight start when she first heard my voice, Kate gave no sign at all. She walked down to the river, dipped the bucket, and came back, leaning sideways against the weight. Level with me, she set it down and stood rubbing her arm and shoulder, at the same time yawning heartily.

I jerked out a few words, telling her that I meant to slip away to the woods.

"I'm not asking you to come. Every man's hand will be against me. And you could live soft at Abhurst. But if you *want* to come, I shall wait in Tuck's Oak till dusk."

I was not being unselfish. At that moment, much as I loved her, I was not sure that I wanted her with me. I felt weak and sick and sore, and I was about to do something new and dangerous, something I had never heard of anyone else doing successfully. A man about to jump from a great height, or swim a wide stream in the dark, is better off without a woman clinging about his neck, however well beloved she may be. Yet in my heart, if not in my head, I must have wanted her to come, else why had I not made straight for the woods and got away under cover of darkness; why was I prepared to risk waiting all day?

Kate took up the bucket and moved away, and in a moment I heard the voice of her stepmother, intent now upon currying favour with one who shortly might have benefits to bestow.

"Give me that bucket," she said, her scolding voice overlaid with forced good humour. "You don't want blisters on your hands tomorrow."

They went indoors; the thread of smoke thickened. Soon, I judged, they would be breaking their fast. I began to move. I went on my belly like a snake, from gorse bush to gorse bush, keeping alongside the river until I was out of sight of the hut. Then I went to the water's edge and laid down my leather apron and the little round cap, which all careful smiths wear to save their hair from rubbing against the horses' hides and picking up the running itch. I walked into the water, careful to make clear footmarks in the mud. I waded downstream in the water until my legs were so benumbed that they failed me; then I climbed out and made for the woods. I hoped that I had broken the scent which the hounds and my lord's huntsman would soon be following. I hoped that my off-cast apron and cap would look as though I had drowned myself.

Once safe in the great forest, I regretted having made tryst with Kate. "All for love," sing the singing men, and in their songs love risks all, conquers all, never doubts and never falters. But the Bible says, "All that a man has will he give for his life," and, for ordinary, frightened men like me, that is a true saying. I was in the forest by midday and could have made good progress during the hours of daylight, had I not promised to wait. I climbed Tuck's Oak and lay along a stout branch, sweating with fear at the thought of the hounds casting up and down the river bank. Would any see through my trick? Would the search be long enough and patient enough to pick up my trail again? I remembered the way my fist had smashed into my lord's face; he would feel the damage this morning; he would be after me for vengeance as well as for my value. The longest day's labour had never seemed so long as the few hours I waited; and they were few, for Kate came while it was still broad day. She brought a basket into which she had packed four goose eggs, some cold mutton, a loaf of bread, and some apples. She had thought to bring her winter's cloak.

At the sight of her, the realisation that she had chosen to be hunted with me, rather than to live at ease with our master, love leaped up in me again. I was glad that I had lain in the gorse and waited in the tree, and glad beyond all measure that she had come. I dropped from the bough, took the basket from her, and, holding her by the hand, set off in a southerly direction. She told me that the huntsman and two brace of hounds had found my hiding place in the gorse, followed it until it ended, and then, after casting about for an hour, returned. The man was carrying my cap and apron.

"And how did you get away so soon?"

"I said I must carry my father's dinner—for the last time. And for once she did not stand over me, weighing with her eye all that I put into the basket." She laughed. "Father said good-bye and he hoped that when I was in the still room at Abhurst I should remember that he was a poor man with several mouths to feed. I said I would. Then, when I left him, I came here."

"The hounds. If they are brought out on *your* trail?"

She laughed again. "The sheep always loved me. I had but to call and they would follow. They came after me almost to the wood's edge—Father was too busy with his dinner to mind them. When I was ready I turned and scattered them. It would be a rare hound that could scent me on ground sheep had been over twice."

"So it would. And you, my Kate, are rarer among women than that hound among hounds." I slackened pace long enough to kiss her heartily and then pressed on.

"Where are we going?" she asked.

"The only answer I can give you is away from Norwich. That is where they will seek us. So we must walk in the other direction until we reach a walled town."

That was another thing which every serf knew, it was part of his serf's heritage, the knowledge that if by some miracle he could ever escape from his manor and reach a walled town and there spend one year and one day, without being reclaimed or committing any offence against the town laws, then he would be a free man. Alongside this knowledge—which one might think any serf would try to use to his advantage almost as soon as he could walk—lay other knowledge all concerned with the risks and the difficulties and the ferocious punishments which awaited any who made an unsuccessful attempt. Once off his manor without leave, a serf was a marked man; for miles around a rider on a swift horse would raise the hue-and-cry, and while that was on any stranger would be challenged and asked to explain himself; when the runaway was overtaken he would be brought back, whipped, and branded. Such a fate few serfs were prepared to face in order to gain "freedom," which was just a word to them. The dues and the duties of villeinage might be heavy or light—it depended upon the lord of the manor, upon his steward or bailiff, upon old custom, but whether heavy or light they had worn calloused places upon the bodies and minds of the bondsmen, and, unless something out of the ordinary disagreeable happened, as it had happened in my case, no man in his senses would throw himself out into the unknown world. At least, so it was at Rede, which, as I have said before, was much behind the times in every way. I had never known a man to run away, and should never have done so myself had I not been driven. Having run, I intended, if possible, to make good my attempt.

I did not know then, though I know it now, that the great forest stretched, with but few large clearings, from the Wash to the Thames River, but I knew it was large and I hoped that Kate and I could stay in its shelter for a long time, and then perhaps emerge at Colchester, which was the only town besides Norwich which I knew by name. I knew it because of its oyster beds; every year, when my lord made his after-harvest visit, great creels of them were hurried up on horseback to lay upon his table. Where this town lay I did not know, except that it was southward, and my hope of reaching it was only a hope. For the woods, while offering shelter from the hue-and-cry along the roads, had dangers of their own. In the densest thickets there were wolves and the even more dangerous wild boars, and everywhere there were the game wardens. Merely by entering the forest, Kate and I were committing a felony and making ourselves liable to savage punishment, if caught.

All this we knew, yet, having found one another, we walked along in good spirits. On this first day of our journey the wood was mainly of beech trees, which do not encourage undergrowth. The great grey tree trunks rose straight and smooth as the pillars of a church, and under our feet was a carpet of leaves dropped in the autumns of bygone years. We travelled until a grey dusk was thick amongst the trees. Then I remembered stories of men who had been lost in fogs, or in forests, or in great open spaces like sheep runs and gone round and round, retreading the same path. Lest we do the same and find ourselves, in the morning, back at Rede, I called a halt. We threw ourselves down under a tree so old that its roots in places grew clear of the soil, making little low caves. We crouched in one, ate bread and mutton and apples, the first food we had ever taken together. I thought of that, blasphemously perhaps, thinking that it was a kind of communion; and as I did so Kate put up her hand and touched the twisted arch of root under which we sat.

"This is our very first house," she said.

Something began in my belly and swelled and swelled until it reached my head, I forgot all my fears, forgot our present plight and the future's uncertainties. I felt brave and powerful, tireless, undefeatable.

"You shall have better, sweetheart. I will build it myself, a snug, trig house, as sound as this tree." I reached out my longer arm and laid a finger on the tree trunk.

Kate laughed and said, "I'm glad you were touching wood!"

I laughed too. Rede seemed far away; here in the wood's quiet, with night gathering about us, we might have been alone in the world, another Adam, another Eve in a new Garden of Eden. We finished our meal and afterwards slept in each other's arms.

V

THE next four or five days—that is so long as the food lasted—were the happiest in my whole life. I can look back and see them, set apart, glowing with something more than sunshine. Since then I have never pitied idiots; for during that time Kate and I were touched by idiocy, not set free from the dangers and cares of ordinary living, but somehow not properly concerned. It was as though we had ceased to be Kate, daughter of the shepherd, Walter, son of the smith, and become people in some minstrel's song, walking through the greenwood, loving one another. "All for love."

The nature of the woods changed; the clear-floored beech trees ended, and we came to the thick forest, with undergrowth of hazels, brambles, and bracken, all closely woven. Sometimes we could turn aside to seek easier passage, sometimes I had to go ahead, hacking a way through with my knife. Still we moved on, careful to keep the sun upon our left hand until it was high, walking into its eye for an hour and then keeping it upon our right until it sank. We were sparing of our poor provisions, eking them out with blackberries and unripe hazelnuts, with sloes and crab apples that soured our mouths, but even so we came to an end and were face to face with the eternal problem of the poor, brought back to earth by the question which is for all but the rich the first and the last question: How shall we eat today? We learned, soon enough, that love is a business for those with full bellies. No, maybe there I wrong Kate and, through her, all women; I think they care more for love and less for their bellies than men do. She stayed cheerful long after I had begun to fret; she spoke gently and lovingly while my words grew few and sharp from hunger.

We say, lightly enough, the words "starve to death." Put like that, it sounds easy and brief enough, a man ceases to eat and he dies. The truth is that he does not immediately die. Death by starvation has many unpleasant stages. There is the belly pain, as though, within you, some strange animal hungered and, lacking other sustenance, gnawed at your vitals with sharp fangs. There is, following the pain, a constant desire to vomit, as though you would turn your empty belly inside out, like a beggar proving his pocket to be coinless. There is a shakiness in the bones, your hands fumble and grow clumsy, your knees give way. There is a ringing in your ears, as though bees hived there.

As our need to get out of the forest grew greater, we made less progress. We were weaker and we were forced to hunt. From the cord I made a rabbit snare, and we wasted hours sitting somewhere near, but out of sight, fretting over the loss of time and yet glad enough to have reason for inaction. I caught nothing.

Kate bore up bravely until we ate the hawthorn berries. They were plump and red and ripe and looked to us, in our hunger, as good as cherries. "Birds eat them," we told one another; and we ate them, in quantities. They did me no harm at all, but they turned Kate's bowels to water. Soon she was stumbling along, doubled over with pain and looking so wan that I was frightened. Up to that point we had been careful to make as little of ourselves as possible, but now I began calling as we went forward, cupping my hands to my mouth and uttering loud cries. Woodcutters, charcoal-burners, and game wardens lived in the forest, and now that we were starving the hope of falling in with some man with a heart of Christian charity loomed larger than our fear. Nothing answered me but my own voice, bouncing back from the trees. In all that time we saw nothing but one red deer, which flickered away like something seen in a dream.

We found no more hawthorn berries, but Kate's infirmity persisted; the time came when she could no longer walk at all, so I carried her; and I did not go straight forward, I took the easiest way. She never weighed much, but now she was variable. I'd pick her up and it was like lifting a kitten, so light she was; but as I went on she grew heavy and heavier. Sweat broke out all over my body, my heart hammered, my sight clouded. In the end I would set her down and fall prone, and she would creep away a little distance, behind the nearest tree or bush and then emerge, more deathly pale than ever. Through the ringing and buzzing in my ears a stern voice would say clearly, "Kate is going to die and you are to blame." Presently I would brace myself and try again. Again. Again. Making no progress, and the forest going on and on, and nobody in it but us.

From hunger sleep is no refuge; the starving do not sleep; they slip from one kind of misery to another; the gnawing pain goes on and so does the worry. I would lie down and think, imagine, dream, that a fine fat rabbit was kicking in my snare, then I would struggle up, shouting, to find that the piece of cord was still twisted about my wrist because I had lain where I had fallen and never set the snare at all.

It was a nightmare time.

Once I lifted Kate, turned dizzy, and only just set her down before I dropped her. She said, in a weak voice, gasping, "You can't . . . carry me . . . any more. Leave me. No need . . . for both . . . to die."

If I had had a known destination or any real hope of finding help, I might have been more tempted. But mere walking was not going to save me. Only a miracle could do that. I told her so.

"Only a miracle can save us now. And a miracle could happen here as well as at any other place." So I lay beside her for a little, gathering my strength, and then staggered a little distance and set my silly snare. That was the miracle I expected, a rabbit in my snare. As I set it I prayed, not in the manner I had been taught, but as though God were the steward and I were begging some small favour of him. "God, send a rabbit, please, God. A rabbit, God, please." The light was just beginning to fail; it was a time when rabbits were abroad.

When I got back to Kate she said, "I can smell . . . herrings roasting."

I almost wept then. I knew that delusion. It had been my companion for hours, days. As I walked I had smelt more food cooking than had ever been set on my lord's table; fat pork boiling with peas; roasting fowl; dried herring; new bread; seethed beef; dredged hare; onions.

"Poor Kate," I said. "My poor, poor Kate. Your hungry nose deceives you."

"But I can . . . can't you?"

I sniffed. I could smell it. A mouth-watering smell at any time. After the harvest of the earth came the harvest of the sea, and the dried herring would come in barrels to Rede. When the day's work was done Father and I would toast them, on long sticks, by the fire. We could have been doing it now, while Kate ate venison and syllabub at Abhurst.

Call me heartless knave if you will. But first go hungry for uncounted days; then make your own choice, love or a roasted herring. Lie weak with hunger on the ground and stare death by starvation in the face, and choose. If you say love, then I will call you saint and you may call me what you will. I am honest with myself. I wished myself back at Rede with a herring spluttering at the end of a stick, and Kate safe and full-fed in Abhurst.

I lay, wishing that, and the good smell continued. Presently I realised that never before in my delusions had the one kind of smell continued. Moreover, it grew more powerful. This, I thought, was because I was growing weaker, slipping farther and farther from reality. Perhaps, I thought, before we died we should taste food as well as smell it, God's final mercy. And from that I turned to thinking about dying, as Kate and I must do, unshriven, with all our sins upon us. Even the joys of our few happy days had been stolen. Unconfessed and unabsolved, they would weigh heavy in the scales. I was beginning, desperately, to try to recall the proper prayers for those on the point of departure when Kate nudged me.

"Go and . . . look. It can't . . . be . . . far away."

Even in that extremity my good strong body served me; lying prone, even in despair, had restored me. Standing up, without having to lift Kate, I found myself steadier than I could have hoped. Turning my head from side to side like a hound, and drooling water at the mouth, I set off in the direction from which the scent seemed strongest. A few paces brought me to a place where, in some time past, the forest trees had been felled. Where they had stood a coppice of bushes, elder and wild rose and hawthorn, had grown up. Close pressed and fighting with one another, they had woven themselves into a living wall. The strong scent of herrings roasting came from its farther side. I walked along the thicket, seeking an entrance, but there was none, and the scent grew fainter. I turned back and walked the other way. The fence continued, and the smell again faded. I was vastly puzzled. No house could be completely enclosed.

I staggered to the spot where the smell was strongest and threw myself at the bushes, thrusting my way into them bodily, hacking at them with my knife in a frenzy. The last line of them gave way before my onslaught, and I found myself standing at the top of a little bank, looking down upon a sight as astonishing as it was welcome. To left and right, as far as eye could see in either direction, ran a straight flat road, bordered on each side by thicket like that through which I had just forced my way. The road was thickly grassed, and at the point immediately below me stood a jenny ass with her foal. Nearby was a fire and over it, slung on a crossbar, the herrings. Standing guard over the whole was a little old woman with a donkey stick in her hand and an expression on her face that was at once terrified and defiant.

"Keep your distance!" she said. "I've nowt worth stealing, and if you come near I shall fetch you a clout."

I must have been a fearsome sight, bursting through the bushes, knife in hand, the bruises of my beating turning greenish yellow, the broken places now well scabbed, all in addition to my desperate, hungry look.

My wits were still with me, however. I did not move, but dropped the knife so that it fell down the bank almost at her feet.

"Good mother," I said, "I am no robber. We have gone astray in the forest and are like to die of hunger. Of your charity, let us eat." Then I remembered that I had money. "I am no beggar, either." I took out a penny and threw it after the knife.

"'We,'" she repeated on a questioning note. "How many are you?"

"Myself and my wife. She is in worse case."

"All right then." She stooped and picked up my knife and the penny. "No tricks, though. I'm old, but I'm lively."

I turned and pushed my way back through the gap, widening it as best I could, and walked to where I had left Kate.

"Was . . . it true?"

For answer I bent and lifted her. Hope had given me strength, and I was able to carry her to the gap and pull her through it. The old woman was still on guard, but at the sight of Kate her manner changed.

"Poor creature," she said, and coming forward helped me to bring Kate down the little bank and place her by the fire. Then she quickly slid the herrings from the stick, cut great slabs from a round brown loaf, and said, "Lay to. And God send Grace on the food."

I ate as I had never eaten before, but Kate, after a bite or two, sickened again.

"Poor mawther. She has clemmed overlong. Her belly is shrunk. If only . . ." In her face, brown and wrinkled as a walnut, her faded eyes snapped and sparkled. "God be thanked," she said. "We have it!"

She routed about amongst her belongings and found a little wooden bowl.

"You must hold the donkey steady," she said to me. "She's not been milked this way afore."

If ever there should come a time when dancing bears are so common that they no longer draw a crowd, an old woman, a young man, and a jenny ass in milk should go the rounds. I was too anxious about Kate to be other than vexed by the performance and the time it took, but even then I could see its comical side, especially when the little foal, shrewd enough to see that it was being robbed, came butting in. However, at last we had a cupful of milk in the bowl. Kate drank it and it stayed down. The old woman slipped some more herrings on the stick.

"Maybe St. Christopher knew what he was about when he let my basket break," she said. I then looked at the two osier baskets which stood by the fire and saw that the bottom of one of them had given way.

"I'd have been a mile or two farther along the road if that hadn't happened," the old woman said. "Couldn't go scattering the good fish, so I thought I'd stop and mend it up while I could see; then I felt hungry and reckoned I'd eat first."

"And we smelt your supper and were saved," I said, looking at Kate, who was holding the bowl in both hands and sipping slowly, but steadily.

"Slip a bit of bread down with it, afore your belly shuts again," the old woman said, handing her a slice. Kate ate, obediently, and when that stayed with her too I knew the worst was over.

When I was full to bursting, I licked my fingers and offered to try my hand at mending the basket. I used a piece of the cord and some young hazel wands. Kate curled up under cover of her cloak and slept; the old woman and I sat by the fire. She had lost all fear of me by that time, and when I needed my knife for the work, handed it back with a grin.

"I was flummoxed to see you," she confessed. "Mostly I'm on the lookout for trouble, but on this bit of road I never seen another living soul, not in all the years I've travelled it. None else know of it, and I ain't likely to tell them."

It was a strange road, like none I ever saw before or since. Under the grass, which was shallow-rooted, were large flat slabs of stone, set edge to edge. I scraped away the grass to have a better look at it.

"It's a wonderful good road for a loaded donkey," said the old woman. "Pity there ain't more like it. I blundered on it by accident."

She told me how, years before, with another donkey, she had camped for the night on a common and waked to find that, despite his hobble, the donkey had strayed. She thought she could hear him moving behind some breast-high bracken, and, looking for him, had found the road.

"That was the end, all grown over and known to none. But it looked to me to run the same way as the other, so I reckoned I'd try it. And I'm glad I did. It's ten miles of easy going for the beast, and nice for a lone woman to have a spell with her mind at rest without fearing to be set upon. The ghosts I don't mind. They don't heed me, nor me them."

"Ghosts?"

"Aye. The like of no mortal men they are. Marching men, with short skirts, like a woman's but up to the knee, and shining helmets with brushes atop. There's great silver eagles on poles going ahead of them. I've seen them many's the time. The first time I was too scared to breathe, but I crossed myself and they went by without so much as a glance."

"You have a stout heart," I said.

"For some things. I'm feared of robbers. And of the time when I cannot get around to sell my herrings." She watched me work for a while. "By your hands," she said, "you're a smith. I've an idea that you broke your time and ran off to get married."

An apprentice who left his master before his time was up was in fault, but he was not the marked, hunted man that a serf was who had run from his manor, so I nodded.

"Ah well, there's good masters and bad. Was yours a beater?"

I nodded again, thinking to myself that in the morning I must warn Kate to tell the same tale.

"There's a smith in Baildon who *might* take you—if you was well spoke of by somebody he knew, like me."

"Would you so speak?"

"I might. You seem to me a decent sort of chap. And it'd cost me nowt."

"I should be grateful to you all my life," I said. "Is Baildon where you go to sell your herrings?"

"One of the places. It's a fine large town with the best market in these parts. And it's a long way from Norfolk," she added slyly.

"How do you know that I am from Norfolk?"

"By your tongue. Hereabouts we talk different. We sing our words. Silly Suffolk, some call us, but in the old days it was Singing Suffolk. Still don't worry about that, we'll fash up a tale to explain. There, you've done a good job on that basket; good as new."

We were on the move early in the grey and rosy dawn, for the old woman was anxious to get on. She and I breakfasted on herrings, from which Kate still turned sickened away, but she ate heartily of the bread.

"The little mawther can ride the ass for a bit, you and I'll hump the baskets. We'll go faster that way."

Old and shrunken as she was, she set a fast pace, one which I, carrying one basket, could only just manage, and to which the donkey held unwillingly, urged on by a light blow now and again. The foal frisked along, light as a leaf, unaware that his unburdened days were numbered.

Three miles along the road we came to a wide-open space, which had also been cleared in some past time and was now all grass and self-sown bushes. Above the tangle some white columns rose, one complete, twice my height, and beautifully carved at the top. Others were broken.

"There's a good well here," the old woman said briskly. "This is where I aim to spend the night when I'm this way."

There was a well in Rede manor yard, but nothing like this one, all buried in bushes and weeds. This was a basin of that same white stone as made the pillars and shaped something like a church font, but one side was higher than the others and had a horse's head carved upon it, the water ran in a clear steady trickle out of the horse's mouth, into the basin. We all drank from it.

"Now we'll load the donkey and go in proper fashion," our guide said. That done, she took the animal's bridle and dragged it forward, through some bushes and a belt of trees, and in a few minutes we stood on a piece of common ground, beyond which was a sight that to me was new and most marvellous. When I say new, I mean to my *eyes*. Inside my head a picture something like it had formed when I had heard anything about Jerusalem. But my imagination had been small and mean compared with this reality. This town was walled, though in places the wall had been neglected and allowed to crumble; inside the walls were the crowded roofs of a multitude of houses, and rising above them were some great towers, taller than the highest tree I had ever seen. One in particular seemed to soar into the sky, with buttresses and pinnacles of extreme grace and beauty.

"That is Baildon Abbey," said the old woman, seeing me staring. "Don't stand goggling now. If Armstrong takes you, you'll have plenty of chance to look at it." She urged on the donkey and we left the common for the highroad, which was crowded with marketgoers. There were men driving cattle and sheep and pigs, women carrying fowls and eggs and baskets of fruit and vegetables, other laden donkeys, people on horseback, even a litter or two.

"I didn't know," said Kate in an awed voice, "that there were so many people in the world."

"Any others with herrings; thass what I want to know," said the old woman. She looked sharply about her. "Not that I worry much," she went on contradictorily, "bringing fish this far is more of a trudge than most folks'd face. We go this way."

Directly ahead of us was one of the town's gateways; some people entered it, others swerved aside and followed a track worn close to the wall.

"A new order last year. Market dues used to be collected on the market place, but the poor fellows wore themselves out, walking round. So now us with stuff to sell walk round, to the north gate and pay as we go in. They chose that gate because it's nearest the Abbey—not so far to carry the bag!"

A monk—the first of his kind that I had ever seen—stood in the archway, accompanied by two ordinary men. As each marketgoer drew level with the monk he looked over the produce he carried and without a moment's hesitation decided whether the dues should be paid in cash or kind. He touched nothing: if cash were demanded, one of the laymen received it, if the due were to be paid in kind, the other took charge. It was all done swiftly and in order and in a singular silence. There was no haggling; the dues were paid in sullen silence and no one said much until out of earshot of the monk. At a safe distance grumbling began. I later learned that there was a kind of justice about the dues, ruled by the law of supply and demand. The monk might take, for example, a fowl from one woman and a pound of apples from another, unfair on the face of it; but inside the market that day fowls were plentiful and cheap, apples scarce and dear. From the basket that I had mended he demanded a score of herrings. Once out of earshot, our friend said sourly:

"There's robbers in all shapes, but them in cowls is the worst. They say that some of their takings come back again as alms and such, but I never took charity yet and never want to."

The market place was a great open square immediately in front of the Abbey's main gateway. Here on the cobbles some people took up a stand and began to cry their wares as a means of drawing attention; others moved to and fro amongst the townswomen who had come out to do their marketing. I saw several females of a kind new to me, well dressed, with rings on their fingers and elegant headgear, followed by maid- or menservants, carrying baskets. In my simple way I took them for great ladies, never having seen one, for if my Lord Bowdegrave had a wife he never brought her to Rede. It was a surprise to me to learn that all this grandeur appertained to the wives of burghers who had been successful in their various businesses, and an even greater surprise to know that these grave-faced, sedate women were in many cases breaking the law by dressing themselves so fine. In the towns ordinary folk had become so rich that they could afford to ape the nobility, and laws were passed saying at what rank one might wear velvet, satin, or the better kinds of fur. The laws were not heeded. In fact that was one of the first things I noticed about life in the town, the ordinary people were far less humble and conscious of their state than even the freemen on the country manors.

There was no other herring-seller in Baildon that morning so Old Betsy—as I heard her called—soon emptied her baskets. One man even made an offer for the donkey foal, to which she replied shortly that she'd think about selling it when the creature was weaned. Then she said to me:

"Come along, and I'll take you to Armstrong, and be on my way."

Leaving the Abbey behind us, we climbed a short steep street called Cooks Lane, in which almost every shop was a food shop, out of which came odours that set my mouth watering anew, and from there we turned left into a narrower lane that smelt of hot iron and scorched hoof-horn. The smithy was set back from the street and its wide thatch stuck out, supported by roughly trimmed tree trunks, so that the animals awaiting attention and the men with them were sheltered from rain or sun. The space was crowded, and the smith with three apprentices were working at full pelt. Old Betsy pushed her way in, leaving Kate to hold the donkey and beckoning to me to follow. When the smith, between jobs, straightened himself, he saw her and said:

"Thass no good, dame. You must wait your turn today. I'm too busy to draw breath."

"Then I'm doing you a favour. I've brought you my young kinsman, a good smith, in his sixth year. His master died, poor man, and his forge was took over by a man with four sons, so he wouldn't take over the 'prentices."

"You want I should take him, eh?" asked Armstrong, looking me over with a calculating eye.

"You'd be doing yourself a good turn."

"In his sixth year. I don't like other men's 'prentices, they ain't trained to my ways. Besides, though I got work, I'm short of room. These three lay all in one bed as it is."

"He'd find his own bed. He's married."

"What! In his sixth year! Scandalous."

"Thass different in Norfolk where he come from. They ain't so hard-hearted; they make allowances for human nature."

"Let's see your work," Armstrong said, speaking to me for the first time. "Clap a shoe on this nag."

My hands were less steady, my movements less sure than usual, because so much depended upon how I showed, but I did the best job I could.

"Passable," Armstrong said, without enthusiasm, when I had done.

"Well, do you take him, or don't you?" Old Betsy asked shrilly. "We can't stand about all day, waiting on you."

"Tell you what I'll do," the smith said, narrowing his eyes. "I'll take him, but not as a six-year man. He go back to five; that'll give me a chance to undo the bad ways he've learned in Norfolk where everything is so different. He find his own bed, I give him his dinner and his dole at Christmas and Whitsun. Are you agreed?"

"Thass for him to say," Betsy said. She looked at me and managed to convey, without a word, that in her opinion I should be wise to accept the offer, since one in my position was not likely to get a better.

"I agree," I said, "and I thank you."

"Well you may," Armstrong said. "And all here will witness the agreement."

All the men within hearing nodded and said, "Aye. Aye."

"Start right in, then. How're you called?"

Mindful that I might even yet, even at this distance, be hunted, I renamed myself there and then.

"Martin, sir," I said.

I know now that amongst sailors there is a superstition that it is unlucky to change the name of a ship. Perhaps it does a man no good either.

VI

So I was established and had a footing, however humble, in the town, and could not be driven out as a vagrant, and Kate found work the next day in a bakehouse in Cooks Lane. The work was hard and heavy, the wages very small, but—and this meant much to us—she was allowed to bring away, at the end of her day's toil, a good quantity of unsalable stale bread.

We started off our life in Baildon in a lodging about which one of my fellow-apprentices told me, saying it was a cheap place. It was in a loft over a stable and contained six straw-stuffed pallets laid close together on the floor and a cooking stone under a hole in the roof. There was a trough of water in the yard below. The beds, at that time of the year, when people were on the move, were always occupied by travellers of the poorer sort, tinkers, drovers, tumblers, and bear-leaders, and by the humble pilgrims to St. Egbert's shrine in the Abbey. The loft had a stench of its own, a mingling of the stable smell from below, of years of careless cooking on the greasy hearth, of sweat and foul breath and human excrement; Kate and I found this irksome, for, though neither of us had been bred to be fastidious, we were used to fresh country air, and to stinks so accustomed as to be unnoticed. In this lodging place the stink changed from night to night and always, it seemed, for the worse. Still, it was a shelter, the cheapest one available, and, had I been earning only a little, we should have stayed there. As it was, what Kate earned just sufficed to feed us, and week by week I had to pay the rent out of my small store of money. I was ignorant of town life and had imagined that I might earn a coin or two by doing odd smith jobs for people, as Father and I had done in and around Rede: two things defeated that hope. For one thing Armstrong was a hard master, and we apprentices often worked far into the night; after the horses had all been shod and taken home we worked, by fire and candlelight on ploughshares and harrows, and chains, and spits and iron sconces. The other thing was that in towns all labour was organised into Guilds, which were communities of craftsmen, governed by strict laws, all of them aimed at upholding a monopoly. An apprentice to the smith's craft, for instance, was forbidden to work for hire outside the place where he was apprenticed. If he did so, he would be punished, and, worse yet, it would count against him when, his apprenticeship completed, he applied for journeyman status and admission to the Guild. The person who employed him would also be in trouble, since every Guildsman in the district would be against him, refuse perhaps to do the most urgent job for him for a period varying from a month to six, and, if the man himself were a Guildsman of another craft, his own members would regard him as a traitor. There were some forms of work which I would have been allowed to do. I might, for instance, have helped to drive cattle to market, or dig somebody's garden, but such jobs must be done in daylight, and I never had a daylight hour to spare. The smithy closed early on Saturdays, and then another rule came into force; every apprentice was bound to go and practise shooting at the Butts on Saturday afternoon; so I had only Sunday, when nobody wanted cattle driven or gardens dug.

I had not been in Baildon long before I saw that I had exchanged one servitude for another; in place of my Lord Bowdegrave I had a trinity of masters, Master Armstrong, the Guild, and money.

One wet October evening a man known as Tom the Juggler came to sleep in the loft. It was Saturday, one of the two market days, and he was grumbling that the weather had ruined his trade; people were not going to stand in the rain to watch his tricks.

"Another day like this," he said, "and I shall be sleeping in Squatters Row."

"Is that cheaper?" I asked, wondering whether all my inquiries had missed some useful piece of information. He laughed.

"It's free, you fool."

"Where is it?"

"Down by the Town Ditch. Grant you it stinks, but not worse than this. Only trouble is, the roof leaks."

"Maybe I could mend it. I'm handy," I said. He laughed again, as though at some wonderful jest.

Next day, when he took me along to the place he called Squatters Row, I understood his merriment.

It was at the rear of the Abbey, on the side farthest from the market place. It was a street, a good deal wider than any other in Baildon; one side of it was bounded by the Abbey's eastern wall, the other by the backs of houses, some of them slaughterhouses. The street sloped towards the centre and there ran the Town Ditch, the drainings of all the gutters and privies in the town, the blood from the slaughterhouses, the overflow from pigsties. It had, at some time long past, been decently covered in by an arched hood of stone, stretches of the cover still existed, but in the main it had given way. The stench was loathsome, but, as Tom the Juggler had said, not much worse than the loft when it was fully occupied.

"But I see no place to live hereabouts," I said.

"Use your eyes," he said; and pointed across the Ditch to the Abbey wall. It was heavily buttressed, and the buttresses stuck out to within a few feet of the Ditch, making, as it were, compartments with three walls. I looked along and saw that several of these compartments were occupied; most were open to the sky and to the Ditch, some were roofed over by pieces of sacking or sailcloth, supported at the front on poles.

A sick feeling of defeat squirmed in my belly, and when Tom the Juggler laughed I could have hit him.

"The north wind's the sharpest," he said. "You want to get the wall between you and it." I noticed then that he had brought along his pack. He crossed the Ditch at a place where the arch still held and chose his buttress, throwing the pack down.

"There're worse places. If you want to come back, say so, and I'll keep you the stall next door."

It was still raining, but the rain was coming on a wind from the west; I noticed that the tall wall of the Abbey sheltered the ground immediately below it to a distance of some feet. The buttress would keep off the north wind which brought the snow. I could do better than rig a flimsy bit of sailcloth on four posts; I could fix timbers to the wall and the buttress and lay a thatch over. I could make a fourth wall. With what little money I had left I could buy the materials for that work, and enough timber to make a table and two stools, straw and sacking for a mattress. All at once I could see the little hut completed, weatherproof, even snug. And ours alone. After the lack of privacy in the loft, that in itself seemed a blessing.

"I shall stay. And I'm very thankful to you."

"Then your wife can cook my supper," said Tom the Juggler.

I hurried back to our lodging, where Kate was doing some washing, and told her I had found a place. I warned her that it was in a foul place and in the open, but that I had plans for it.

"Just so long as we can be alone at night," she said. So, when the washing was done, I led her to the spot and tried to make her see the little hut as I had seen it in my mind.

In our lodging we had been among the poor, now we had joined the destitute. Our permanent neighbours were a one-legged sailor who lived alone, a man who was deaf and dumb, his wife and four children who had not inherited his infirmity, an aged crone, who, when anyone would employ her, acted as midwife and layer out of the dead, and an evil-living young woman who twice a year was whipped through the streets for harlotry. As well as these, Squatters Row had a drifting population of people who had failed to find, or could not afford to pay for, a bed for the night. As the weather grew worse these grew fewer in number.

Before winter set in I had made a hut, just as I had planned; we had a table and two stools and a mattress stuffed with sweet fresh straw, much better than our louse-ridden bed in the loft, and, rough, humble, and cold as it was, it was, as Kate said, "our second house" and it became home to us. That we should be happy in such circumstances and that the meals we ate there—often no more than hunks of four-day-old bread thinly smeared with fat—should seem like feasts to us may sound strange, but is nonetheless true. We were young, we had our health, love was still lively and so was hope. If we were lucky, in a year and a day we should be free. In two years I should have served my time and be a journeyman, working for a daily wage. Then things would change. We had a great deal to look forward to. We had another advantage, too, and one which is, I think, sometimes overlooked when people think of living in great poverty; the smallest thing extra, or nicer than usual, was a wonderful treat. I remember Kate coming home with a skip in her step because, there being a shortage of stale bread, her mistress had told her to take a fresh loaf.

"Feel it," she said, thrusting it into my hand, "smell it." To the full-fed it would be a rare dainty indeed which could bring such pleasure.

The year and the day, so important to us, passed. On a September Sunday evening we could look at one another and say: We are free. On the Monday, Lord Bowdegrave could ride up to the forge where I worked, recognise me for his smith's son, and no more lay claim to me than he could to Master Armstrong. Only the serfborn can know or guess or even dimly imagine what that moment meant to us.

We were spending the evening as we, and many of our kind, spent all our free time in fair weather—gathering firewood on the fringe of the common ground. The forest there belonged, like most of the things around Baildon, to the Abbey of St. Egbert, and the Abbot granted the townspeople that privilege; any dead wood which could be found within thirty paces of the boundary might be collected and taken away. Kate and I were indefatigable woodgatherers; often through the past winter our less active or less provident neighbours had come to warm themselves, sometimes to cook, by our fire. On this evening we were making two faggots of what we had collected, a large one for my back, a smaller one for Kate's, when she said:

"Thanks to the Virgin, our child will be free-born."

God forgive me for the way my heart went plummeting down. A first child, indeed any child, should be a wished-for, a welcome thing. But I was earning no wage, nor should be for another year. It was Kate's meagre money and the bread she brought home that stood between us and hunger. And I had known all along that the work in the bakehouse was heavy, too heavy for her frail body; how long, with another burden within her, could she stay at work? And what would happen when that time was outrun?

There was that side to it; and there was another. It went hard with me to think that our child would be born, and live its first year, in a makeshift hovel by the brim of the Town Ditch. As month had followed month since our arrival in Baildon, I had hoped that God in His mercy was seeing fit to withhold parenthood from us until we had a home ready for a child.

Now all the cheer that the day had brought me failed and faded. Walking home, bowed under my faggot, I knew the first faltering of hope. I looked into the future and saw, not the neat little house in some more habitable part of the town, but Kate and I and our family condemned to live our lives out in that stinking place of outcasts.

Kate said, "Don't be angry." And that made me ashamed, remembering how, on a like occasion, the deaf-and-dumb man had beaten his wife until she was black-and-blue.

"I'm not angry," I said. "How could I be? It takes two to make a baby. But, Kate, I am worried."

"God and St. Katherine will take care of us—and the baby," she said. "They always have done. We've done very well so far."

"That is true. But I was looking ahead. You can't stay in the bakehouse when . . ."

"Then something else will turn up," she said, with the utmost faith. "You'll see."

Hating to drag her down into my own state of discouragement, I said no more. I only hitched my load a little more firmly onto my shoulders so that I could spare a hand to ease hers a little, thinking, as I did so, of the flour sacks, the loaves, the firing of the oven which she must manage, with none to help.

VII

KATE must have known about her state for some time before she told me in September, for the baby was born in February. The baker's wife had kept her on until Christmas and then told her not to come back, because it worried her, she said, to see Kate straining herself to do the work.

"Once your belly is out beyond the point of your nose when you stand upright, you should be careful," the woman said. "If you don't, the child'll come feet first."

Kate had argued that in the country women worked in the field sometimes until the very day the birth took place.

"Maybe, but I don't have to watch them," said the baker's wife.

All this Kate told me, making light of it and still saying that when one door shut God opened another. I could see, however, that she was a little dashed that another door had not opened already. And none did, just as I had feared. After Christmas was the worst time of the year to go looking for chance employment; even the markets grew small; there were few travellers and no pilgrims in the inns; housewives were saving their work for the spring. Everything was at a standstill.

Since September we had saved what we could, but it was pitiably little and we were once again on the very verge of starvation when that other door did open.

Ordinarily both Kate and I were out of our hut and away early in the morning, and did not return until late in the evening, so of the ordinary comings and goings of our neighbours we saw very little. Now, doomed to stay at home, Kate noticed that every morning the sailor with the wooden leg and one of the children of the deaf-and-dumb man left Squatters Row together just before midday and came back carrying food. She asked where they had been and was told, "To the Alms Gate."

"And the monks give you food? Would they give me some?"

"Brother Stephen would. Brother Justinius would not," Peg-Leg said. He knew all the rules. He explained the situation to Kate in his own simple words. The monks had plenty to give away. Baildon was a very rich Abbey and had in time past been heavily endowed by wealthy men who had sought favour in the sight of Heaven by remembering the poor in their wills. There had been a time when anyone, needy or not, deserving or not, could present himself at the Alms Gate and be fed; but after the great upheaval of the rebellion in the year when I was born, people in high places had become alarmed at this "indiscriminate charity," as they called it. They said it encouraged indolence and the habit of drifting from place to place. So a law was passed saying that alms were to be given only to those who were not able-bodied.

This was a law which admitted of varying interpretations. Some monks said that they had no time to waste on making a close physical inspection before handing out a bowl of peaseporridge or a hunk of bread, or who would split a hair of logic by arguing that a man in the throes of hunger could not rightly be said to be able-bodied. There were others who accepted the law as it read and made it an excuse for reducing the scope of their charity.

In Baildon, in the main, the law was accepted. Dummy, our deaf-and-dumb neighbour, for instance, could hope for nothing at the Alms Gate; he was able-bodied, that is, sound of wind and limb. Peg-Leg, on the other hand, was accepted as a responsibility, and so was Dummy's child, because she had been knocked down by a bullock running wild from the shambles and she had grown crooked.

A woman like Kate was a debatable case, and as, Peg-Leg said, it all depended upon which of the two almsgiving monks threw up the hatch in the Alms Gate which lay just beyond the Bell Tower. Brother Justinius argued that pregnancy was a natural state and that a woman heavy with child was in no sense disabled; Brother Stephen, on the other hand, counted heaviness of body and shortness of breath as a disability.

"There you are," Kate said to me, after learning all this from Peg-Leg. "I told you we should be cared for."

She joined the miserable little crowd at the Alms Gate and came away, empty-handed or happy, according to which monk was on duty that day. Brother Stephen even carried matters so far as to now and then dole her out a double portion, saying, "You must eat for two."

I invented a tale that Master Armstrong had taken pity on me and offered me a breakfast piece in addition to my dinner. This meant that I went to work every day with an empty belly. In fact the dinners which our master provided were as scanty as he dared make them, and the weather being very cold and wet, I grew thin and low-spirited. Those who have never hungered think little of food, those who are hungry think of little else. I confess that there were many times between Christmas and the birth of my first son when I would have exchanged even my freedom to be back in the hut behind the smithy at Rede, with the fat pork cooking in the pot. I had to find another, a longer way home. Cooks Lane, the shorter way, was so full of mouth-watering smells; and then I would be home and Kate would have something left from her dole if it had been a good day with Brother Stephen at the hatch, and she would offer it to me and I could feel the wolf look come into my eyes.

However, the child was born, whole and sound. The old woman who was our neighbour—her name was Agnes—came and gave her assistance. And hardly was the baby born—it was a boy—before the old woman said:

"There, my dear, you've a fine lad and now you can claim your Trimble."

It was so early in the morning that I was still there, and I asked, "Her *what?*"

"Her Trimble," said Agnes. "God bless my soul. Where were you reared never to have heard of that saint among women, Dame Trimble?"

"Let me hear now," I said.

So, what time she bound the belly-band firmly about my son's raw navel, she told me about Dame Trimble as the story had been handed down a hundred years or more. A young girl, one of a large family reared in dire poverty, had gone to work for an old wool chandler, who married her and soon afterwards had died, leaving her well-to-do. She had no children of her own, but was all too well aware of the hardship which childbirth means to poor women. She was shrewd, too, and dealt wisely with the fortune she had been left, so that she died rich. She had founded a charity, now known familiarly as "The Trimble," by which any poor woman in Baildon—poor meaning any woman whose husband was not a full journeyman or its equivalent—could claim upon the birth of any child, meat, bread, and ale for forty days following, a woollen gown, a hood, and a pair of shoes.

"Dummy's wife is still wearing the one she got with her first," Old Agnes said. "She sold the others. There's a good market for such. And the food and drink are good too, very generous. Enough for the woman, and her man, and a bit over for the midwife if the family ain't too large, as in this case."

"Who hands it out?"

"The monks. At the Alms Gate. One of the parents has to take the child and show it. It's the father's job, though I've known mothers to crawl out on the second day, them with no men to rely on. Dame Trimble made no difference, she didn't even say *respectable* women."

So, on the next day, I had to forgo my dinner and run home and take the child to the Alms Gate. I felt silly and sheepish, expecting to be the butt for jeers, standing there with a baby in my arms; instead I found myself an object of envy. And well I might be. Brother Justinius was doling out the usual peaseporridge and bread, but at the sight of me he called out to someone behind him and bade me wait a little. Kate's Trimble, when it came, was food for a family, more food and better than I had seen at one time since I left Rede.

"The gown," Brother Justinius said, "according to the rules, must be of the woman's own choosing, and the shoes made to her measure. So they must wait. By what name is the child to be baptised?"

"Stephen," I said clearly. Kate had chosen the name, long ago, because Brother Stephen had been kind to her.

"These Norman names, how fashionable they grow," said Brother Justinius, with something sour in his voice.

I put on my most stupid, dull-witted look and said, "Norman is it? We thought it came from the Bible."

He gave me a sharp look. "It is to be hoped that you are not tainted with Lollardry, to be forever referring to Master Wycliffe's Bible."

"Master Wycliffe? I do not know him. Is he a Baildon man?"

"Oh, get along with you," Brother Justinius said crossly, and slammed down the hatch.

I hurried home to Kate with all the good food, and a little tale to make her laugh.

Dame Trimble's sweet charity carried us bravely through the next weeks; there was enough for Kate and me, and most often Old Agnes as well. Kate got back her strength and I gained some flesh. The baby throve surprisingly, and although he had been born a full year before my plans made me ready to welcome him, now that he was here I loved him very dearly.

April brought in the softer weather, with its one disadvantage to us who dwelt in Squatters Row; when the gutters of the upper town ran freely, the Town Ditch often brimmed over until its stinking waters lapped our doors. Still, summer was coming in, and by the first week in September I should have served my overlong apprenticeship and be earning. Hope stirred once more.

The town itself was growing; every market day brought more people. A shipowner from Bywater came inland and began to build a fine new house which employed a number of masons and carpenters. Master Webster, the chief wool merchant in the town, bought a new string of pack ponies. At the forge we were very busy. But when, at the end of six weeks, Kate began looking for work, she found it hard to come by. One reason was that she refused to leave Stephen in the charge of Dummy's wife, who had offered to look after him with her own, for twopence a week.

"I know her looking after," Kate said. "One of hers has been run down by a bullock, and one drowned in the Ditch. Stephen goes with me."

By that time I as beginning to be anxious again.

"If she had twopence a week for minding him, it would be to her own interest to keep him out of the Ditch. In any case it might be as well to leave him while you hunt for work, even if later, having proved your value, you took him with you."

Nothing, however, would persuade Kate from her course; she was sure the right job would turn up. And in mid-May she found work as a picker in Master Webster's woolsheds.

The fleeces were cut off the sheep in the spring and bundled up, just as they were, and brought into Baildon. Master Webster paid a price which took into account a certain amount of rubbish, burrs, caked dung, leaves, bits of stick and mud. The bigger merchants—many of them overseas in Flanders—paid so much a pound for clean wool, so the fleeces had to be picked over carefully. The picker knelt or squatted as she worked her way through the wool, and the unchanging position became tiring; the oil and odour of the fleeces saturated her clothes, her hair, her flesh even. Kate bore it cheerfully, saying that she was used to the smell of sheep, and that Master Webster had been kind about letting her take Stephen. When he could crawl, she pointed out, the woolshed would be a far safer place for him than the bakehouse would have been.

Alas, before Stephen could crawl, Kate was with child again. This time she was dismayed.

"There'll be only eleven months between them. If Stephen isn't walking, I shall have to carry them both to work."

"But I shall be earning," I told her.

She smiled as though it hurt her.

"I know. But there will be four to feed then."

She had carried Stephen cheerfully and willingly and never ailed much. This was different. She was sick and miserable. I was little comfort. To me there was something wrong, almost obscene about this begetting without being able to support. I was ashamed, and that made me peevish. It was at this time that something went out of our hut, something which had made it, despite its squalor, a happy home. Kate and I now seemed to take an unholy pleasure in making sharp remarks to one another. One day, when she was complaining, I said:

"I warned you, didn't I? You would have been better off at Abhurst."

She swung round on me like a swordsman.

"You mean you'd have been better off as an unmarried apprentice, with your feet under somebody else's table."

The weapon to wound was there, at my hand, and I seized it.

"If it comes to that, I *am* an unmarried apprentice," I said.

Kate shot me a glance of hatred and then began to cry.

"That's right. Throw that in my face!"

We had never been married. We had arrived in Baildon as man and wife and never dared risk drawing attention to ourselves by offering ourselves to be wed. There was that question, ordinarily so harmless, to us so dangerous, "Of what parish?" It would have been easy to lie, but Holy Church has a long arm. It might have occurred to the priest to make inquiries whether these unknown people were free to marry, and that would have been disastrous. Sailing under false colours, we had come into Baildon, voiced for by Old Betsy, and under those same false colours we must go on.

Now, sobbing bitterly, Kate poured out all her hidden shame and doubts. No wonder, she said, everything went wrong with us, living in mortal sin, as we were. And if she died in childbed, as well she might, she would go straight to Hell as a wanton. She went so far as to ask whether being born free could make up to Stephen and the child that was coming for their bastardy.

Her distress distressed me. I said I was sorry for having spoken as I had, and we kissed and made up. But every quarrel—of which this was but a sample—took something from us which no reconciliation could fully restore. I understood, during the next few months, what makes men go and drink themselves silly in the alehouse. I should have done so, many a night, had I had any money.

VIII

THE day dawned that brought the end of my apprenticeship. Nothing had been said overnight, but I had not expected any sign, for during my two years at Armstrong's I had seen an apprentice become a journeyman. (Journeyman does not mean a man who journeys to his work; it means a man who works by the day, *jour* being the Norman for day.)

It was one of those enchanted days of late summer touched by the first breath of autumn, golden and blue and heavily dewed, as I set out for work, carrying Stephen, as I had done for some weeks, and walking round by Master Webster's woolsheds. Even Kate was more cheerful this morning.

I went, as soon as I reached the smithy, to the nail where my apron usually hung. It was not there. I pretended great surprise and anxiety. Then the others gathered round me, chanting:

"He's grown too big for his *apron*
He'll have to get another one."

The reply to this sally varied with the nature and wit of the new journeyman. I said, "How can I get another. I've earned nothing yet!" and that was well received, with more laughter.

I then went to take up my tools. They too were gone, and again I pretended concern. They gathered round me.

"He worked so hard for a dinner a day
He wore his hammer clean away!"

The next remark was prescribed. I must turn round and cry in mock dismay, "What shall I do?"

Then they all bellowed, "Become a journeyman!"

After that there was a moment or two of jollity, with good wishes and drinking, turn and turn about, from a jar of ale, which, according to rule, should be provided by the senior workman present. It was an understood thing that, on such a morning, the master should allow ten minutes for the little ritual. On this morning my apron and tools were returned to me, and I was, at last, I thought, a journeyman of the Smith Guild in Baildon town.

Presently Master Armstrong arrived, stood by my shoulder while I finished a job, and then said, "Step across the road with me. I've something to say to you."

The Smith's Arms stood directly across the road from the forge; we took a seat on the bench and Master Armstrong called for ale. This, I thought, was another stage in the process of being recognised as a journeyman. When the ale came I expected him to speak some words of salutation, but instead he took a deep draught and then wiped his mouth on the back of his hand.

"You ain't going to like this, Martin," he said. "But thass no good blaming me, nor nobody. Rules is rules and they hev to be kept. Last Guild meeting I brung up your name and said you'd done your time and was a handy skilled worker; but they ain't taking you."

The cobbled lane, the forge opposite with its smoky red fire, and the haunches of the waiting horses and donkeys began to rock and swing before my eyes, slowly at first and then faster, until all I could see was a blur. I realised that my eyes had filled with tears; I was about to cry, like a child.

My throat ached and felt wooden. I lifted my mug and took a tiny sip and swallowing it eased me so that I was able to say:

"In God's name, why, master?"

"You worn't born here. And do you go back where you come from, you'll fare no better. There they'll hold agin you that you didn't do your full time there. See?"

At that moment it seemed like a cruel blow aimed at me personally by malignant fate. Later on I understood better and knew that I was but one of many men of all crafts who were, in the towns, superfluous to requirements. All through my lifetime, ever since the great rising of 1381, on all but the most old-fashioned manors the serfs had been buying themselves free and had thus been at liberty to apprentice their sons how they would. So every year more apprentices qualified to become craftsmen than old craftsmen died or retired, and those safely inside a Guild were casting around for excuses to keep the young men out. Often the excuse was flimsy, invented. In my case there was no need. I was a "foreigner"; my exclusion needed no cunning twist and would cause no searching of conscience on anyone's part.

"What's to become of me then?" I asked.

"Ah," Armstrong said. "Thass the question. But I got the answer. I'm sorry for you, Martin, and I'm making you this offer outa goodness of heart. You mind that. I brung this up at the Guild meeting, too, and they was all agreed. You can't be a full journeyman, nor claim the rate laid down for such. But you can go on as a *paid* apprentice, see? They looked up the rules, laid down in past years when there was a shortage of apprentices. They was paid then, anything between quarter and half the standard rate; and you being a handy sort of chap, I'd give you half."

I looked at him, and quickly away, lest he should see the loathing in my eyes. I'd had, from eating at his table and a hundred other little things, evidence of his meanness and cunning. Pretending to do me a favour, he had prolonged my apprenticeship for a year. Now, pretending to do me another, he was getting a skilled, finished workman at half rate.

But I had no choice. Half pay was better than no wage at all. I said humbly, "Thank you very much."

He jumped up quickly and said, "Let's to work then."

All that day, added to my own bitter disappointment, was the dread of the moment when I must tell Kate. She did not, however, weep or rail against Armstrong and the Guild; only the deepening of the lines in her face, the increased droop of her mouth, betrayed how shrewd the blow had been. I had dreaded her tears, and yet now, perversely enough, I wished she had cried. I might then have been moved to take her in my arms and comfort her. Once in a hard winter I saw a tree entirely encased in a coating of ice. Our poverty and our worries, and our defeated hopes, were putting a similar casing around our souls. Soon we should have lost even the memory of love, and be dull, plodding work animals, no more.

Kate had said miserably that there would be but eleven months' difference in the age of our children, in fact there was less than that, for Robin came into the world a little before time, a small, ailing baby, unlike Stephen. When I carried my second son to the Alms Gate I was the subject of coarse jests about being such a quick worker. "Do you get any faster," one man said, "you can knock off work and live on your Trimble."

This time Kate sold her woollen gown and the hood. Since her place in the woolshed had not been filled, she dragged herself back to work at the end of a week, frail as she was.

"That way we shall get something in hand," she said fiercely. "We can save my wage so long as the Trimble lasts. With two to feed—and God knows how many more on the way. . . ."

"There'll be no more, Kate." That was a promise which would cost me nothing to keep. I was not like my neighbour Dummy, who could go through the performance which ended with a baby while feeling nothing for the woman he bedded with. Yet, though our joy in one another had been lost, somewhere between Stephen's birth and Robin's, we were still a unit, we two against the world, as helpful to one another as we could be, a good wife, a good husband, good parents so far as our means allowed. Kate still washed and mended and cooked. I mended the roof and hunted for firewood, and every morning and evening I went to the woolshed so that I could carry the heavier child.

On one cold March evening, miserable with falling sleet, I found Kate awaiting me at the gate, with something of liveliness back in her face again. When I went to lift Stephen she stopped me, laying a hand on my arm.

"The ponies from Bywater have just come in," she said, "and without Old John. He dropped dead on the road. If you went to Master Webster now you might get the job."

It was a sensible suggestion; and Kate knew that ever since September I had longed for a chance to leave Armstrong; for I held in my mind the certainty that if he had stood up for me strongly enough, saying that he *needed* me as a journeyman, his word would have carried weight, even against the rules. Yet pride is a curious thing and will pop up in the unlikeliest places.

"But I'm a skilled smith," I said, without thinking. Those few words said it all. I'd strained and sweated, and waited and almost starved in order to be a smith, not a pack-whacker to a pony train.

"On half pay," Kate said.

I knew the need to defend myself. "Should I earn much more, if anything? Pack-whacking is an unskilled job; anybody can do it and that sort of job comes cheap."

"They get about. They pick up things. They do errands for people along the road and get gifts that way. I've seen Old John come in with food for a week." She tightened her arms about Robin and braced herself to move.

"If it's beneath you to care whether we eat or not . . ." she began sourly.

"I'll do it. Where shall I find him?"

"In his office. Through the yard, there, to the right, where the light is."

"You take the baby home," I said. "I'll bring Stephen." He could by this time walk a little, and holding his hand I went into the wool yard and knocked on the door.

The room inside served as office and living room, was well lighted and warm. Tally sticks stood in every corner. Master Webster stood by an open cupboard on whose shelves lay samples of wool.

"Well?" he said.

"I'm told that one of your pack-whackers is dead. I wondered if you would give me his job."

He pinched his upper lip between his finger and thumb, pulled it out and let it go again.

"You're a foreigner. I'd sooner hev a man that knew the roads."

"I could learn my way about, master," I said humbly.

"Wasting *my* time, meanwhile. You're the smith they wouldn't let into the Guild, ain't you?"

I nodded, gritting my teeth together, for I saw in this the beginning of a hard bargain. The man nobody wanted.

"Pack ponies are hard on their shoes," he said. "Now *suppose* I rigged up a forge, right here in the yard. Could you shoe the ponies as well as drive 'em?"

"Of course I could."

"It'd hev to be done on the quiet. Now and agin I'd hev to send a beast to Armstrong or Smithson, and if they queried why my trade dropped off, thass easy explained, ain't it? Pony's likely to cast a shoe anywhere."

"That is so," I said.

"Mark you," he said, "I'm doing you a favour. Making a job for you, you might say."

"I'm truly grateful."

"So you should be. Now, as to wages . . ."

I saw his fingers working as he reckoned. They tapped out a sum which was fourpence more than I was earning at Armstrong's. With a gallon loaf costing a penny, it was an increase worth considering; and I bore in mind Kate's words about a pack-whacker's chances to earn a little extra here and there. So I sold myself into another bondage for an extra fourpence a week.

IX

WITHIN a week I was well aware of the advantages in my new job. For a trained craftsman, who had mastered his trade and passed his apprenticeship, to become a mere driver of pack ponies *was* a comedown, but it had its compensations. As Kate had said, we got into the country, and it was in the country that food was plentiful and cheap.

When I joined Master Webster's teamsters it was winter and we were not collecting the dirty fleeces from farms and sheep runs, we were carrying the picked-over wool down to Bywater.

Bywater was a small port, much smaller, we understood, than Dunwich or Yarmouth; but it had obtained, during the reign of the great King Edward III, one priceless privilege. It was allowed to export a certain amount of wool, in defiance of all the rules governing the staple. This was because at some critical moment during the King's wars with France, this small town's fishing fleet had chanced to be in harbour, and had been able to offer the King eighteen vessels for the transport of troops to France, shortly before the great Battle of Crécy. The privilege of being able to export wool freely was its reward.

The Bywater people often laughed and joked about the privilege, saying that, when King Edward granted them the favour, the limit he had set on their export had been far in excess of all the wool shorn in East Anglia, for Norfolk and Suffolk and Essex were not then reckoned to be sheep-rearing districts. The favour was, they said, "like giving a one-legged man permission to dance a jig." But things had changed since then; sheep runs had been established on many a ploughland, and in my time Bywater exported every bale of wool the license allowed.

Ships that set sail laden with wool returned with other commodities, and there were goods to be found in Bywater that could be obtained nowhere nearer than London. On the very first journey I made to Bywater we were stopped by an innkeeper at Nettleton. His little daughter was ill and he wanted an orange for her. She had once eaten an orange and all through her fever had craved another. I was lucky and found four, and when I delivered them into his hands on the return he almost wept with gratitude. He took me and my fellow-driver, a lively little hunchback called Crooky,

into his house and gave us each a mug of his best October ale. Then he
asked which would we rather have, sixpence apiece or our pick out of
his storeroom. Crooky, who had no family and was a drinking man, chose
the sixpence. I went to the storeroom and stared about at more stacked-up
food than I had ever seen in my life.

"You mean I can have anything?"

"Anything you can carry. Could you have seen the little wench's face
when I put the thing into her hands! Take what you like and call me still
your debtor."

I chose a great ham, which, sliced into pieces by any of the keen
knives in Cooks Lane and sold piecemeal, would have been worth four
shillings.

"And I'd sooner give you that," said the innkeeper, when I had made
my choice, "than the sixpence yon fellow took. The pig it came off fed on
the scrapings of the plates, and drunk the wash-up water, and the smok-
ing was done by the fire that we cook on. So it cost me nowt."

That was my first experience as a doer of errands. Others followed. Not
all the people we obliged were so deeply grateful and wildly generous,
but I always remembered a farmer's wife who had broken her needle. She
lived a long way from the road we travelled and had twice walked the
five miles and stood a whole morning in the biting wind to catch us on
our way down to Bywater. She gave us the errand, and the money for
two needles and asked us when we should be returning. We told her, and
when we came clattering along, the unladen ponies trotting and thinking
of their own stable, there she was, with two grey geese on long leads of
plaited rushes.

She said, in a shamefaced way, "Would you take these in payment?
The needles had to be paid for in coin, and I have no more, nor shall till
the calves are sold. But they're good geese, right fat."

"A goose, for carrying a needle!" I said in astonishment. "Payment
enough and over."

"But I can't walk to Bywater—the calves would starve; nor I can't sew
with a goose, and my poor man's hose all agape. I'm much obliged to you
both. Besides," she said, grinning, gap-toothed, "the geese cost nowt. Gan-
der do his work for pleasure, goose lay the eggs. All summer they keep the
grass down so I can walk dry-foot to tend the calves. Whass to a goose?"

I could have told her. To a goose there were some feathers to add to
the collection in order, one day, to have a feather pillow. Then there was
a fine hot savoury meal, and fat to spread on our bread on many a cold
morning; and bones to boil, with an onion or two, into a heartening
broth.

Oh, and there was more to it than that. There was me saying to Kate,

"You were right. Snatching at Old John's job was the best thing I've done so far."

And there was Kate, with some of the worry eased out of her face, smiling at me with some of the old sweetness.

To the poor so little means so much.

When the sheep-shearing time began and we started making journeys to outlying farms and sheep runs to bring in the fleeces, there were more errands and more rewards. Now, with both of us in employment and a good deal of our food costing nothing, we began to lay aside a penny here and there, in the renewed hope of being able to hire a house somewhere far from Squatters Row.

There seemed no real reason why the secret of the work I was doing for Master Webster in addition to my pack-whacking should ever have been discovered. He was a very cunning man. He knew that the other drivers would soon notice if, bringing in a horse with a loose shoe, or an unshod hoof overnight, they found it wearing a bright new shoe in the morning. So he made a new rule, the teams were to be driven in rotation. In this way, in the course of a few days, I went out with each team, and, on our return to the stable, would take careful note of the state of the hoofs of the ponies with which I had made that journey. Crooky was well known to be unobservant and unheeding; he would leave a pony with a strained fetlock, or a sore back, and walk straight away to his drinking. I always walked away, just as lightheartedly, but, when there was a job to be done, I went back, late at night, was admitted by Master Webster, and went to work in the forge which he had set up in a little shed to which only I had the key. Every now and then, just to avert suspicion, a pony would be sent for shoeing to Armstrong or Smithson.

So, for six months Master Webster saved himself money and all was well.

One night, late in September, I had been working and was on my way when I turned a corner and ran into a man who was lolling there by the wall. He reeled and had so much difficulty in recovering himself that I judged him to be drunk and clutched at him, steadying him with my hands. His hands clutched at mine, and at the same time he fell against me, his face buried in the shoulder of my jerkin.

I said, "Hold up, man," or some such words, and he pulled himself straight, let go of my hands, and lurched off.

I thought no more about him until, four or five days later when I came in with a load of fleeces from Clevely and reached home, I found Master Armstrong sitting on one of our stools.

"I wanted to see you, Martin," he said. "Your wife said you might be back today, so I thought I'd wait a bit."

Kate turned from the hearth where she was cooking supper and over his shoulder made a face at me.

"Master Armstrong came yesterday and waited a long time," she said.

I had a wild hope that perhaps in the last six months he had missed me, had persuaded the Guild to admit me, or, next best thing, was now willing to re-engage me at a full journeyman's wage and be hanged to the Guild.

"What is it, master?" I asked.

"Thass this," he said. "You're doing Webster's smith work; and thass agin all the rules."

"Why should you say that?" I put on an astonished face.

"Now don't play no fool's game with me. We know. Smithson's first man, Nobby, ran into you the other night. Your hands was black; he'd washed his, but he gripped yours and blacked his, see? And you reeked of the forge."

"I did indeed, after he'd reeled against me, and so would any man. As for my hands—I'd just helped to unload twelve ponies, three hundred pounds of filthy fleeces apiece, marked with tar some of them."

Armstrong grinned. "You're a sharp one. Then how do you explain *this*? Ever since March, when you took up with Webster, that look like his ponies don't wear out their shoes. I noticed, Smithson noticed, but it worn't till we put our heads together we knew we'd *both* been done. I reckoned he was doing the jobs, he reckoned I was."

"Ponies don't mind where they cast a shoe," I said. "And you can't run a pack pony on three legs. We have to get work done at the nearest forge."

"That seem a rare rum thing that only this summer them ponies cast shoes so far afield so often. Me and Smithson, we still got our memories, mark you. 'Twasn't this way last summer, nor the one afore. Where's the difference? The difference is that Webster hev now got working for him the rascal I took and trained out of goodness of heart, and is now plying the trade I taught him to do honest men out of work."

That, in a way, I could deny. I wasn't doing it to spite honest men. I was doing it to keep myself alive. So I said, "That is not true, master."

"Thass true. And you know it. And now I'm giving you fair warning. There's ways of dealing with fellows who run agin the rules. Either you stop doing Webster's smith work, or we'll find a way to make you." He stood up and stamped out of our hut.

Kate pulled the pot to the side of the hearth and came and gripped my arm.

"Oh, Martin, what will they do?"

"Tackle Webster. He's a Guildsman too. He'll be savage at having to give up his fine penny-saving scheme and sack me. He never wanted to employ me anyway. He called me a foreigner."

"We never make any headway," Kate said drearily. "Every time we do a bit better and begin to hope, something happens."

Next morning, as soon as Master Webster appeared in the yard, I told him of Armstrong's visit and threat.

"Did you admit doing the work?"

"I denied it, but he is sure nonetheless."

"Then his case stands on the word of a drunken apprentice who ran into someone in the dark. And that against mine, mark you. We'll take no notice. The next pony to need a shoe shall go to Smithson, and that will keep him from siding too hearty with Armstrong. For the rest we'll go on as we were. It suits me well."

"It suits me. But Master Armstrong said there were ways of dealing with those who went against the rules."

"He said truly. But they must first prove that I'm breaking a rule. And of that I'm not so sure. I never seen any rule saying a man may not employ his private smith if he wants. I ain't flaunting the business, as you well know, there's nowt to be gained by falling out with your fellows. But first they must prove that you are doing smith work for me, and next they must prove thass agin the rules. And all that will take time. We'll go as we were."

By mid-October all that year's fleeces were in and our journeys to outlying places ceased. From then on, until winter weather closed the road, we carried the picked-over wool to Bywater, Lavenham, and Melford.

On our outward journeys, when the ponies were loaded, we never travelled after dusk. Wool was valuable and there was always the risk that the pony train might be set upon by rogues who could easily find, in any port, some ship's captain who was not too nice in his inquiries as to where the wool came from and whose it was. Our summer journeys were different, the raw dirty fleeces were not so immediately marketable, and to pick them over demanded some settled headquarters, which robbers lacked. In summer we often moved loads at night, but in the winter we only travelled after dark when the ponies were unladen and we were making for home.

Crooky and I were doing that, rattling along at a good pace, coming back from Bywater one November night. He rode the first pony, I the last, and we were urging the string along because there was fog about. We rode easily; having nothing of value to care for, our one concern was to get back home as soon as possible.

We reached a place where a narrow bridge spanned the river, some five miles out of Baildon. It was the same river which ran through Baildon and turned the Abbey Mill at Flaxham St. Giles. Once we were over the bridge, the river ran alongside the road on our left hand, and for us the bridge had become a landmark. Many a time Crooky and I, crossing it, had shouted to one another, "Nearly home."

This evening, Crooky, riding ahead of me, shouted back, "Nearly home!"

"God be thanked," I shouted back. I heard his pony's hoofs sound hollow over the bridge, and the next and the next. . . . I was almost on the bridge myself when something dropped in front of my face; it fell to my waist and there pulled tight and jerked me off the back of the pony, which kept up its trot. I shouted, "Crooky! Crooky!" but he didn't hear, or took no notice. And as I fell over the pony's tail and hit the road, blows began to shower down on me. The rope which had lassoed me held my arms fast, I was utterly defenceless. I remember thinking that this was how they dealt with those who went against the rules. Then somebody hit me on the leg, causing such sharp agony that I cried aloud. Another blow fell on my head, and the pain ceased.

When it began again I thought I was back at Rede. It was like waking from a dream, all about running away and trying to make a life in a place called Baildon, and having two children and a makeshift hut in Squatters Row. I was Walter, the smith's son, who had hit his lord in the face and must get away sharply if he wished to live. I tried to raise myself and a quiet voice said:

"You must lie still or you will undo my work."

I opened my eyes then and saw, not the dung-heap in Rede yard but a smooth whitewashed wall. Yet there was a connection with Rede—that same thirst which had sent me staggering to the bucket in our forge.

"I'm thirsty," I moaned.

"A good sign," said the quiet voice. And in a moment my head was lifted a little and the cool hard rim of a mug touched my lips. Beyond it, hanging in space it seemed above me, was an old man's face, pink-fleshed, deeply wrinkled, with faded blue eyes, the whole enclosed in a monk's cowl.

"Brother . . . Brother . . ." I said in a fumbling way.

"Sebastian," he said. "I am the Infirmarian. You are safe and not much hurt except that your leg is broken."

He lowered my head and I lay still, thinking: My leg is broken. Broken bones will knit themselves together, but like a thread which has been tied they are shortened. I thought that. Then I remembered that what I had just lately thought to be a dream was real enough. I lived in Baildon, had a wife and two children, and had found it hard to make a living when I was whole and well. Henceforth I should be a cripple, a beggar.

"It had better been my neck," I said.

"And who are you to be giving orders to God?" asked Brother Sebastian, in a humourously rebuking voice. "You should lie there and be thankful. You could have lain in the road until you died, but for a mule's cast shoe. Brother Bartholomew was collecting the Nettleton rents and should have been home before Vespers, but he was delayed. So he found you. And here you are in experienced hands. I mended the leg of a lay brother who fell from a ladder two years since, and a bad job I made of it. But I know where I went wrong, and with you I have made good my error. Poor Edgar's set like a dog's back leg, but on yours I have tried a new trick. A broomstick, tied firmly in three places. Aha, that wayward leg may think to set all crooked, but governed by that broomstick it shall be."

"I am thankful," I said. Then I thought for a moment and asked, "Is it Thursday still?"

"No. The bell for Matins sounded half an hour ago. It is Friday."

"I have a wife. She expected me back for supper on Thursday. She will be worried."

"She knows. Brother Stephen recognised you and a message was sent. So calm yourself; lie still and be thankful and let your wounds heal."

Lie still, perforce, I must, but I was neither calm nor thankful. Brother Sebastian, along with his tender, careful ministrations to my body, tried to minister to my soul. He spoke often of faith in God, of the will of God, of the beauty and virtue of unquestioning acceptance. I listened with my ears, while my mind went its own way; it was all very well for him, who had never had to grapple with the world, who if he hungered did it voluntarily and would be rewarded for his abstinence in Heaven. He could look down along the years—those few that remained to him—and see his life, peaceful, neatly ordered by the ringing of bells, pottering along until he died. I lay there, a young man yet, a man with a wife and two children, and saw myself limping and starving through the years.

Brother Sebastian and every other monk who came in contact with me showed me kindness. Brother Stephen sent frequent messages, and alms sometimes, to Kate, and every time she sent back word that all was well. My most urgent question—Is Master Webster holding my job open for me?—was either never asked, or never answered, or the answer suppressed.

"Time enough to fret about work when you are fitted to do it," Brother Sebastian would say.

Despite my fretting my flesh wounds healed and my broken bone knitted. The day came when Brother Sebastian removed the broomstick and, having allowed two more days for the limb to strengthen, helped me to stand up and test the virtue of his new experiment. Up to a point it was good. My leg was straight enough, but it had set quite stiff and about two inches shorter than the other. I walked, if anything, more clumsily and painfully than Peg-Leg.

The straightness was all Brother Sebastian cared about. Fingering my shin gloatingly, he said, "Thanks be to God who brought the broomstick to my mind. The stiffness will wear off with use, you will find. And I will myself make the shortness of that leg the subject of a Novena."

"Do you hope for a miracle?"

"Why not? I shall pray, and so must you, and you must have *faith*. Many much lamer than you have been restored at St. Egbert's shrine."

That, I knew, was true. The wealth and fame of Baildon Abbey was rooted in the miraculous reputation of the Saint. I knew his story by this time. In life he had been king of a tiny kingdom, part in Suffolk and part in Essex. This was in time long past, before one king ruled all England, in the dim ages, before the Normans came. Egbert's enemies had been the Danes, wild heathen men who had come to rob and burn and rape in that part of England that lay along the sea. In one of his battles Egbert had been captured; but he had been so doughty and valiant a foe that the Danes' leader had offered to make an ally of him, give him high rank in their order, provided he would abandon the Christian faith and worship the heathen gods. He had refused and been killed. The monks of Baildon —then a small, poor wooden convent—had sought for his body and buried it in their tiny church; and then the miracles had begun. Then had come the pilgrims in search of further miracles, and the gifts had poured in. The miracles could hardly be disputed. During my three years in Baildon there had been several; a young girl had been led to the shrine, jerking and twitching in the throes of St. Vitus's dance, and walked away in full control of her limbs; a man set fast in all his joints, just able to put one foot before the other, leaning on two sticks, had hobbled into the Abbey church and walked out, firm and upright, leaving his sticks laid across one another in the form of a cross at the spot where he had prayed and been healed. There were others, all well vouched for. But—and this is what stuck in my mind—both my afflicted neighbours, the deaf-and-dumb man and the man with one leg, had, in their time, asked a miracle and come empty away. And it seemed to me that Peg-Leg, at least, had asked the impossible. Had he really expected a brand-new leg to grow out of his stump, and how—all at once, or inch by inch? And had their failure been due to lack of faith in themselves?

I was not pondering these questions for the first time. I had often thought about them while I was working. I had come to the conclusion— which may be a blasphemous one—that St. Egbert's miracles acted, not on the affliction, but upon the person who was afflicted. The jumping, jerking victim of St. Vitus's dance, for instance, might have stood by the shrine and prayed and believed that St. Egbert was helping her to hold herself still, and in that belief held herself still and then known that if she could control herself for one minute she could do it forever. The same with the man who had stiffened. Maybe he had waked one morning a little stiff, and coddled himself and grown stiffer; maybe he liked to be pitied, maybe he welcomed and traded upon his affliction. Then a time came when he wished, for some reason, to be like other men, so he made his pilgrimage and, standing there, leaning on his sticks, thought that he could stand upright and unaided if he *tried*.

In such miracles I could believe. But in a miracle that would add two inches to my short leg, no.

However, all that day Brother Sebastian kept me on the move; two other beds in the Infirmary were occupied, and he made me help to wait upon the invalids. After each clumsy walk he would say, "Rest now," and then, when I was rested, set me in motion again.

That evening he gave me an enormous supper.

"Eat heartily," he said. "Tomorrow I shall dismiss you and you will need all your strength." When I had eaten he said, "And now we will go and see what St. Egbert has to say."

I had noticed before that they always spoke of their Saint as though he were alive and aware.

For me it was a tiring and worrying walk. The Infirmary lay in a remote part of the Abbey, rightly, for often it housed sufferers from diseases which could be caught by others. We went along passages, up and down stairs, once across a piece of garden; and as I walked, my hand on Brother Sebastian's shoulder, I thought miserably that if this were the best I could do with aid, it did not matter whether Master Webster had held my place for me or not. I could never work as a pack-whacker again. And though I could perhaps at a pinch have stood on my toes on the short side, and plied my smith's trade, nobody would employ me now, even at half rate.

I was panting hard when we reached a great doorway with torches in sconces on either side, and with a small door set in the one half of the large ones.

"Get your breath," Brother Sebastian said. "And *pray!*"

We went up the steps and in at the small door. The vast church was but dimly lighted, just enough for us to see our way. The tall columns of the nave soared up into darkness, but at its end there was a light and a sparkle.

We walked towards it, side by side, Brother Sebastian silently in his soft cloth shoes, I going stamp and shuffle as I put down my good leg and then swung the stiff one round.

The light and the glitter came from two sources. There was the altar which lay beyond the reredos screen, and the shrine itself which was on this side, slightly to the left. There were candles innumerable, and their lights were taken up and thrown back at us, many times magnified by a thousand shining surfaces. The shrine, and this is true, was invisible under a thick pelt of gold and silver ornaments and jewels of every colour. Hundreds of people every year through hundreds of years had lain their offerings there. It was like looking at the sun at midday in the summer; my eyes blinked and squinted, unable to take in any one thing because the whole was so dazzling.

I was speechless with awe, but Brother Sebastian might have been in his own Infirmary.

"The Saint's real tributes lie there," he said, after giving me a moment to stare and wonder. He pointed to a space beyond the shrine, where sticks and crutches, leather neck braces, slings, and bandages lay all in a jumble.

"There, you have seen what he can do. Kneel down and ask him to act for you."

I tried. I tried to force out the prayer for the cure for the shortness of my leg, but it would not be. I found myself praying, with the utmost urgency: Let me find some work that I can do. Let me not be a burden on Kate. No other thought would come into my head, and I went on praying the same thing over and over, until at last Brother Sebastian touched me on the shoulder.

"We must not tire him," he said. And something impatient and evil moved in me. I wanted to cry: How can you tire someone who has been dead and at rest for hundreds of years? And I knew that there would be no miracle for me.

Brother Sebastian, after he had spoken to me, had moved away and was now on his knees on the step which led up from the nave to the choir stalls. I stood up and went, stamp, swing, shuffle, until I stood behind him.

The altar was a gold table, bearing a jewelled crucifix and two seven-branched golden candlesticks. It was backed by a screen, also of gold, divided into a number of oblongs, each one a picture, done in glowing colours and worked in some way I did not understand into the gold. There were three rows of them, twenty-six to a row. From where I stood it was impossible to see them clearly.

Brother Sebastian stood up. He knew he had failed, or I had failed, or St. Egbert had failed, and his manner took on a curious resemblance to that of a workman, say a smith, who has done a bad job and knows it and uneasily tries to divert attention by mentioning the weather or inquiring after the health of the customer or his family.

"You are looking at the screen. It is interesting. Come and regard it closely. It is one of our treasures." We went forward.

"Two hundred years old," he said. "You see, the pictures in the centre row represent scenes from the New Testament, those above and below, scenes from the Old. But each three have a common theme. How many do you recognise?"

I looked at the three pictures in the centre.

"In the middle," I said, "is the Crucifixion. Above it Abraham is prepared to sacrifice Isaac, but sees the ram caught in the thicket, and below is Jephthah keeping his vow by sacrificing his daughter. These three pictures have sacrifice as their common theme. Is that right?"

"Go on," he said.

I looked about. In many of the sections the light just shone back at me, off the surface of the gold and the inlaid colours, carrying no meaning. I was, after all, an ignorant fellow. Here and there a picture had meaning.

"On the left there. In the middle is Our Lord Jesus Christ feeding the five thousand. Above is the prophet Elijah and the widow woman of Zarephath with the unfailing barrel of meal and cruse of oil. Below, that same Elijah is being fed by the ravens."

"You are right. And what is the theme?"

"That God, if He wills, can provide."

"Right again. That is what I wished to point out to you, but you pointed it out to me. Bear it in mind. In a few minutes the bell will ring for Compline. Come, I will help you back to bed."

On the way back we neither of us spoke about the miracle which had not happened. Brother Sebastian talked about the altar screen, saying that, beautiful and valuable as it was, it was in the wrong place. It should be in some parish church where the priest could teach those who could not read the Bible truths by its means. Then he said suddenly:

"You have more learning than most. Where did you come by it?"

"I always heeded what our priest had to say."

"You should thank God for a good memory."

The good memory which so often reminded me how I had said to Kate, "You shall be safe with me." Something to be grateful for indeed.

That was my last night in the Abbey Infirmary, and it was a poor one. I slept in snatches, each full of strange and sometimes sinister dreams. Once I dreamed that my leg, like Peg-Leg's, was cut off at the knee and that St. Egbert answered my prayer for a miracle by causing me to grow a golden leg, very marvellous to look at, but too heavy for me to drag; I lay on Rede dunghill, unable to walk and lamenting the miracle. Then I dreamed that Kate and I and Stephen were *really* starving, sitting before our hut, bowed over with the pain in our bellies. A great bird came sweeping down, carrying Robin's dead body in his bloody beak. Kate said, "It will be all right to eat this meat. It is a gift from God."

From these and similar wild dreams I woke sweating, to lie and face the old gnawing anxiety again until once more I fell into uneasy slumber. I was glad when the bell rang for Prime.

I rose and began to dress and found that my right shoe was missing. I hunted for it until the Infirmary servant brought the breakfast and then sat down to eat my porridge while it was still warm. I had almost finished when Brother Sebastian came hurrying in, carrying my shoe.

"The miracle!" he exclaimed. "The miracle, Martin. It happened. In my old head! Look." He held out my shoe onto which had been tacked, very neatly, another sole, two inches thick.

"Try it. Try it." He was as eager and impatient as a child. "The thought came to me at Matins, and I asked Brother Anthony, our shoemaker, if he could do the work. He stayed up and worked instead of going back to his bed. How is it now?"

I stood up and stood level.

"Most wonderfully easy." I began to thank him, but he cut me short.

"Thank St. Egbert, who put the thought into my head. Now, when the stiffness has worn off, you will hardly be the worse for your mishap."

Once more I tried to thank him. He stopped me again, tapping my hand with his finger.

"Wait. There was something else I had to tell you before you go. Now what could it be? Nothing to do with your leg or my work . . . that is why I have forgotten it. But I shall . . . Oh yes! Martin, you live in Squatters Row as they call it."

"Yes."

"Well, be warned by me. Begin to look for other accommodation. There is talk of clearing that wall and covering in the Ditch and making all tidy there. The Prior and the Cellarer were talking only yesterday. The Bishop of Dunwich came to visit and entered by the east gate and made some unfavourable comment. They're bound to take some action."

I'd had less than a moment to savour the joy of the shoe that mitigated my lameness.

"I don't suppose it will happen tomorrow or even next week," Brother Sebastian said kindly. "Our present Cellarer is too old to move quickly, but . . . well, I thought I would warn you."

I suppose I should have thanked him for that, too. As it was I took leave of him sullenly.

X

KATE's greeting of me was proof that our sharp words towards one another, the way we now lived, hardly touching one another, and all the worry and all the woe had not really set us apart. When I hobbled home she cried, partly at grief to see me so lame, but mainly with joy at seeing me again. She said how much she had missed me, how greatly she had longed to come and nurse me herself, and I in turn said that I had missed her very sorely, thought of her by day and dreamed of her by night. I could hardly tell her what form those thoughts, those dreams had taken.

Soon, however, I had to ask the question.

"And has Master Webster held my place for me?"

All the joy, the young-Kate look went out of her face, leaving the harassed, irritable one which was her everyday one nowadays.

"No. He put a new man on the very next Monday. I went to him, Martin, I spoke for you. I went on my knees, and I cried. He took no notice. Then I lost my temper and told him flatly he was ungrateful when you'd been hurt beating off robbers on his behalf."

"They weren't robbers," I said. "There was nothing to steal that night—except the ponies, and they made no attempt upon them. They let Crooky go by, and the ponies, until the last that I was riding. I think even Crooky knew."

"Knew what?"

"That I was to be set on. You were here, Kate, when Armstrong said they had ways of dealing with those who went against their rules."

"But they might have killed you."

"They probably meant to. In any case, lying out all night I should have died. It was only lucky chance that I was found."

"Then they're murderers. And they should be punished."

"Who by?"

"The law. The constable."

"I have no evidence against anyone. Whom could I accuse? It was dark and foggy. I never saw a face, or heard a voice."

"Then if it was Armstrong's men, it was because you were doing Webster's smith work and he should have stood by you."

"Maybe in a way he has; maybe he put on the new man just until I was better."

Kate shook her head.

"No, I made sure of that. And he seemed so against you, somehow. I think he would have sacked me, simply for being your wife, but Margit got married and left us shorthanded on the floor."

"Why should he be against me? I always served him well. I shall come along in the morning and see him."

"I don't think it will do a ha'porth of good," Kate said.

In the morning I dropped Kate and the children at the door of the wool-shed and went to look for Master Webster. He was in the stables and the moment he saw me his face darkened.

"What d'you want?"

I forced myself to be meek.

"I've come back to work, master."

"Not here. I've no use for blabbermouth jugheads."

"Me?" I was never more astounded. I was of sheer necessity the soberest man who ever wore shoe leather, and I never talked to anyone. Even Kate hadn't known why I worked so late so often, until Armstrong had come and let it out.

"Yes. You. You got yourself tipsy in the Smith's Arms and bragged about what you were doing here after dark."

"I haven't been in the Smith's Arms since the day Armstrong broke it to me I couldn't join the Guild. Who's the liar who said he saw me there? I'll break his neck!"

"Shouting at me won't mend matters. This was all gone into at a full meeting of Guild aldermen."

"What was? You know yourself, I told you at the time, that I was spied on and reported to Armstrong and that he came and saw me and threatened me. You said take no notice and go on as we were."

"Nobody spied on you. You made that up when you realised, sober, what you'd said in your cups. And it was a poor reward for my pandering to you."

"Pandering to me?"

He fixed his eyes on some point behind me, over my shoulder, and said in a wooden way which told that he was repeating something said before, "You wanted to keep your hand in—on the smith work—and I was silly enough to let you shoe a pony now and then. For practice, against the time you hoped to get back into the craft. Ain't that right? Out of charity I did it."

I saw his plump red face, the eyes avoiding mine, the lips moving, spilling out the lies; and then the red mist came down and blotted it out. I could feel, beforehand, the supreme pleasure of smashing my knuckles through the mist and onto that well-padded jaw. But this time I held my hand. Hit him and, shorthanded or not, he would give Kate her quittance, and what she earned was, at this moment, all there was between us and starvation.

Whirling about, at the back of my mind was the thought that free men can suffer humiliations deeper and more hurtful than any serf can ever know. In order that Kate and Stephen and Robin should eat tomorrow— for myself I did not care, I never wanted to eat again—I must accept this lie. I could see exactly what had happened; the Guild aldermen had held a solemn conclave; Webster, a member of the Woolman's Guild, had offended the Smiths by using me, a non-member, to do smith work; and the Smith's Guild had committed, not a fault, but a breach in manners, by spying upon Webster. So there had been a meeting of all the aldermen, intent only upon smoothing the whole thing over. Webster had lied about employing me, and Armstrong had denied the spying. No matter what it took of lies and falsity to do it, the firm, unbroken face which the Guilds as a whole presented to the world outside must remain uncracked. Throw lies, throw a living man's body into the breach, and then seal it over with cakes and ale and renewed vows of brotherhood and fair dealing.

And I, for the sake of a loaf of bread, dared not speak.

Jesus Christ! I said to myself. If only a miracle could happen and I could deal with them all as they have dealt with me, with joy would I rub their faces in the dirt!

I knew I was like a child, beaten by his father, thinking, *When I grow up!* But there was this difference. The child will surely grow.

I went out on the hunt for work. The town was growing in size and business was flourishing, but work was hard to find. Out in the country more and more acres of arable land were being turned into sheep runs, and one man could tend the sheep where twenty had been needed to plough and sow and reap. Those put out of work came flooding into the towns, so that there were three men for every job. A good deal of the work going forward was building, and with my stiff leg and built-up shoe I did not look a likely digger, or climber of ladders. I was passed over again and again.

Soon, alongside Dummy and Peg-Leg, I was waiting at the town gates every morning, ready to fight for any despicable little job that might be going, to hold horses or walk hounds while their owners went into the Abbey to visit the shrine, to carry baggage, to lead the way to inns. Sometimes, standing there amongst the riffraff, I would think how far I had fallen, a smith, a craftsman who had served his time. By comparison my father's life, bound as he was, had had dignity and purpose. I'd run a long way and borne a great deal and got nowhere.

Now and again, having done a job and taken the meagre pay, I would go into the country and buy apples or plums or eggs on some day that was not market day, and come back and hawk them through the streets. The walking tired me and I grew lopsided, since the easiest way was to hitch the whole right-hand side of my body when I swung that leg forward. Dummy's brood, on the rare occasions when they were sufficiently full-fed to feel sportive, took to imitating me behind my back, as they did Peg-Leg.

I never passed on to Kate the word that our very hut was threatened, but some time during that summer the old midwife and layer-out, Agnes, came back from making a baker named Barnaby ready for his grave with news which seemed to excite her. She said that Barnaby had left all his money for the building of some almshouses and that as soon as they were standing everybody in Squatters Row was to move into them. It was strange to hear how that drunken old slattern, who lived under a piece of torn sailcloth, spoke of having a house again as though that was the one thing she wanted. But nothing came of it. The Barnaby houses were for eight widows whose husbands had been Guild members.

"And there goes my last hope," Agnes said, and went out and got herself most enviably drunk.

Dummy's wife said, "They are only one up and one down, they'd be no good to my lot. Laying heel to head, we go from here to there." She indicated the space between two buttresses.

So Squatters Row went on just as before, and that summer we had a new kind of visitor. The pilgrims brought their own parasites, bear-leaders, tumblers, dancers, and singers, but this was something different, a travelling friar, poorly dressed in a grey hood and gown of the coarsest stuff, and with his feet bare in the dust. At night he slept with the rest of us outcasts, between the buttresses, by day he went about preaching. He'd follow a performing bear or some other entertainer and wait until a crowd had gathered, and then he would call, in a very powerful voice, "Brothers! I bring you good news." His news was the Fatherhood of God, the brotherhood of man. The more frivolous, or the rough in the crowd, would jeer and pelt him, but he would stand his ground and sooner or later he would speak against the Abbey and the monks. He would say that it was wrong for professional religious to be great landlords; he decried all pomp and ceremony; he said that Christ only once in His life rode, and that on the back of a humble ass, how then could abbots and bishops, Christ's representatives on earth, go mounted and robed like temporal princes?

I do not doubt that he was honest and sincere. I suspect that his decrying of rank and power, his praise of humility and poverty were, in a manner, like the clapper, or the whistle by which other people gained the crowd's attention. For afterwards would come the real sermon, urging the

virtues of charity and mercy, chastity and honesty, with many a text and
story from the Bible to illustrate his point.

Moving around as I did, working or searching for work, I heard him
often. Kate, shut away in the woolshed, had no such chance, so over supper
I would tell her something of what he had said, or how he had been
pelted.

One evening she fell thoughtful and after a time said, "He is a stranger
and sounds good of heart. Could he *marry* us?"

"I don't know. If he has taken priest's orders, yes. But all monks are not
priests, maybe all friars are not."

"You could ask him. Go now."

"Oh, not out there, with so many listening who think us married
already."

"No. Get him out of earshot if you can. I know, bring him here, ask him
to sup with us."

"But we've eaten," I said, looking at the bare platter.

"I should think my breakfast tomorrow, aye and every morning I have
left to live, a small price for such a favour."

"So should I, of course. Of course," I said, and ran out into the night.

Squatters Row was fully occupied, and the friar had taken one of
the least favourable places, midway between two buttresses, with no corner to huddle into. He was eating a slice of rye bread and when I proffered my invitation to supper he said:

"That is kind of you. I have enough here. Perhaps tomorrow . . . if
you can afford it."

"Oh yes," I said. "Truth to tell my . . . my wife and I," I had to say that,
for there were ears all about, "my wife and I wanted to ask you something
. . . a favour. Would you come indoors with me? It is very near."

"Of course," he said, and heaved himself to his feet.

Inside the hut I closed the door, which hung awry from two hinges
of leather which I had made, and wedged it close. In the faint light of the
dying fire we all looked into one another's faces for a moment, none of
us speaking. The friar broke silence, looking at the children in their bed by
the inner wall.

"They are sick?" he asked gently.

"No, Father, asleep, I hope," Kate said. "My . . . this man and I have a
confession to make and a favour to ask. We have lived as man and wife
for four years now, but we were never married. . . ."

"And now you wish to be?"

"Yes," I said, "but not openly." I told him—not everything, but all he
needed to know—of our circumstances; how we had intended to marry

and been prevented through no fault of our own, and had come to the town as man and wife and then dared not betray our state.

"You have been living in sin; you know that?"

"We know. And we have suffered for it."

"And during this time you have performed your religious duties, always with this sin unconfessed and unabsolved?"

"Yes." He looked so grave that the consciousness of sin did come upon me. I must confess that in the rough and tumble of daily living the matter had troubled me very little; I had only thought of it occasionally as having been a mistake, the cause and reason for some of our misfortune.

"But you are free to marry? And during this time you have been faithful to one another?"

Kate said, "Always, Father." And I said, "Unswervingly." And that was true. I had never even looked with desire upon any woman save Kate and not for lack of temptation. During my pack-whacking days the chances had been plentiful.

"This can be mended then," the friar said. "Tomorrow you will both fast all day. At about this time in the evening I will come to you and you may make your confessions, and in that state of Grace you shall be wed. We will then break fast together."

We thanked him heartily and he went quietly away.

Next evening we fed the children and put them to bed early. Kate scrubbed the rough board which was our table top, and set out upon it the meat pie she had bought in Cooks Row, a fresh loaf, and a dish of red-cheeked apples. She was in high good spirits, calling this our wedding feast, and regretting that we had no wedding garments.

"Like the man in the Bible story," I said.

"But he was sent away. That can't happen to us."

We had left the door open and made up the fire with dry sticks which gave light but little heat; and in the light I looked at her with new, searching eyes, making compare with the girl who had entered the hall with me at Rede and roused an old man's lust. Hard work and poverty and misery had aged her by five times the four years that had gone by since then; her face was thin and lined, her hair rough and lustreless as hay. I thought how lightly the years would have touched her had she gone to Abhurst, and I remembered again those silly words, "My pretty one, you shall be safe with me."

"It's the Guilds that have ruined us," I burst out suddenly. "They threw me out to rot and when I refused to rot they broke my leg. Kate, I never meant it to be this way, I meant to take care of you and cherish you."

"And so you have," she said, and came over and put her arm about my neck and kissed me. "Few men are so careful about fetching water and carrying the heavy loads. Who else would have walked with me to work every day, to spare me? You say what *you* meant. *I* meant never to say a sharp word to you, and Heaven knows I've said many. But from tonight I start afresh."

I pulled her close. I felt tenderly towards her, though there was no desire in me.

"Few women," I said, "would have been so patient and worked so hard. Who else would have kept food on the table and washed and mended and made a home as you have?"

These were not romantic speeches, but they were sincere and more suited to our state than any flowery words could be. And I was angry that immediately afterwards my empty belly gave a loud rumble.

"I'm hungry too," Kate said. "All day I've been too much excited to notice, but now I am hungry and he is late."

Presently we were asking one another whether the friar could have forgotten us and reminding ourselves that he had spoken of breaking fast together; if he intended to fast with us, surely his own emptiness would make him think of us.

Kate began to fidget, going to the door to peer out and complaining that it was too dark to see.

"Go and see if you can find him," she said. I walked the length of the wall. I could not see the friar anywhere.

I went home again, and we waited.

It was after Curfew, so we dared not replenish the fire, and sitting in the dark the time stretched out endlessly, but at last it was eleven o'clock; we heard the bell tolling the hour.

"He isn't coming," Kate said.

"Something must have happened to him." I remembered how some of the rough people had jeered and pelted him. I remembered, too, that many of the things he had said about monasteries and the conduct of the monks were offensive enough to make the Abbot take action against him.

"Have you seen him at all today?" Kate asked.

"No, I've been off the streets all day today. I offered to guide some pilgrims to the Angel Inn, and while I was there I got a job sawing wood. I'm going there again tomorrow."

"He promised to come," Kate said, and the old complaining note was there in her voice again. "I really thought that at last we . . ."

I realised that marriage meant much more to her than it did to me; a woman who lives out of wedlock with a man is called a whore; there is no such damaging term for the man. I made a great effort to comfort her. First I said, fumbling about in the gloom for the knife and the meat pie:

"Let's have our supper. Everything looks worse when your belly is empty." And then, between the mouthfuls, I said what were perhaps the first fanciful words I had ever said.

"Kate," I began, "when Brother Sebastian took the broomstick off my leg and found that the bone had healed up short, he said he would pray for a miracle. We went together to St. Egbert's shrine and prayed there. Nothing happened to the bone in my leg, I didn't expect anything, so I wasn't disappointed; he was. But a few hours afterwards he thought about thickening the sole on my shoe, and when he told me about it he called that the miracle. You see . . . the thing you ask for comes, but not in the shape that you think. We thought that tonight the friar would come and marry us, but he didn't. Kate, really, if we could only understand it, we *were* married, that night by the river under the hawthorn tree . . . and tonight we were, in a fashion, married again when you said I'd been good about fetching water and I said you'd been good about mending and making a home. Try not to fret about the words that haven't been said over us. We are, in very truth, married."

"The friar himself said that we had lived in sin."

"Dummy and his wife were properly married, I've heard her boast of it to Loose Liz. Look how they live! Worse than animals. They make the beast with two backs, and as soon as a child comes of it he beats her black and blue. Their crooked child takes dole at the Alms Gate, and Dummy meets her on the way home and eats his fill without a thought for his wife's hunger. Kate, in all the time that I was a pack-whacker I never ate a mouthful of what I was given until I was back here and sharing with you. When the friar asked us had we been faithful to one another, we could both say yes, and truly. How could any ceremony make us more married than we are?"

She did not answer immediately; but after a moment she said, "All that is true; but there is another side to it. The friar said we were living in sin and that every time we went to Mass with that sin unconfessed and unabsolved we were sinning anew. And our being faithful to one another can't help them being bastards." Even in the dark I could see her arm fling out towards the bed where the children lay. "Nothing but ill-luck ever since we've been here, and now nothing but ill-luck to look forward to."

I pitied the misery that sounded in her voice, but it made me impatient, too. It may be true that misery loves company, but it finds its comfort in a different misery, not in a reflection of its own.

"I did my best and there's nothing more to do. Let's sleep and forget it," I said.

THAT summer had been unusually wet and wet it continued over harvest, so that some of the poor thin crop was lost in the gathering, the sheaves standing mouldering in the fields. It was clear that bread would be scarce throughout the coming winter. Part of the blame for what happened next can be laid on the fear and ill-temper which this prospect roused in the hearts of all but the very rich. But something must also be blamed upon the friar, who had appeared in our midst, sown his seed of discord, and vanished; and a great deal of blame must be laid upon the Abbey, in particular the Cellarer, who dealt with many things affecting the good or ill-will between the monks and the townsfolk.

There were two rights which the Abbey held and which I had never, during my years in Baildon, seen exercised. One was the right to *all* the dung dropped within the town boundaries; that is not merely in the streets and market, but in stables and smithies and cowsheds and pigsties. This did not mean that all the dung went onto the Abbey lands, but it did mean that anyone who wanted to use his own manure on his own land or garden must buy it back, *in situ*, from the Abbey Cellarer. That this right had fallen into abeyance I knew from my years in the smithy. Master Armstrong had derived a small but steady income from the sale of dung dropped by horses waiting to be shod.

The other right was to demand that all corn within an area of ten miles should be ground at the Abbey Mill, which stood a little way out of town on the south side, at Flaxham St. Giles. That this right had not been exercised for many years was proved by the existence of another mill, on the north of the town, which was now being worked by the son of the man who had started it. Two easygoing Cellarers had followed one another in office.

Now, in this year of poor harvest, a new one was appointed, a young man, energetic and avaricious. One of his first acts was to have cried through the town the announcement that in future the Abbey Mill must be used for all corn grinding, and that the rights to the town's dung would be strictly enforced. Next day the Abbey servants, with a flat cart, went about the town, assessing every dungheap and what was not paid for there and then was loaded onto the cart and taken away. The Cellarer himself, riding a grey mule, went out to the North Mill and curtly informed the young miller that he was welcome to grind any corn brought to him from any place more than ten miles distant from Baildon market place, but no other. That meant ruin to the miller, and two days later he drowned him-

self in his own millstream. The Church refused him burial and he went
to a suicide's grave at the crossroads.

This story rang through the town, adding to the ill-feeling which the
enforcement of the old rules had brought about.

Worse followed; for as soon as the monopoly of milling was assured, the
charge for milling was raised. It had been one fourteenth, that is a pound
of flour for every stone of corn ground, henceforth it would be two
pounds—one seventh. This was bad for everybody, since it put up the price
of bread.

Everywhere now people were speaking against the Abbey and the
monks, and it was curious to hear, mixed with the straightforward grumbling voiced in their own simple words, the echo of the friar's accusations.
Even those who had listened to him least had picked up from those who
had given him their attention some phrases which sounded foreign on
their tongues, "appearance of sanctity," "abuse of privilege," "temporal
power," "private lechery." Many of them hardly knew what the words
meant, but they did know that they were speaking against the Abbey and
the monks, and whipping up the ill-feeling.

Nothing might have come of it, but in early November the Abbey of-
ficers arrested a man known as John Noggs, who kept a little alehouse
just inside the west gate of the town. He had set up and been working a
small hand mill, and his customers had been seen to arrive with sacks of
corn and to depart carrying sacks of flour. The power to turn the stone
was supplied by two simple-minded boys, and if it ground one hundredweight of corn in a full day's work that was its limit. Still the new Cellarer was a man rather to take account of the breaking of a rule than of
the damage done by the breaking. He was also a man to judge the customers of the illicit mill equally guilty with the miller. Within the next
few days several more arrests were made. One of those accused of cheating the Abbey of its rightful dues was a respectable, solid townsman who
owned a cook shop, and one was a poor old woman who had gleaned diligently all through the harvest and taken her gleanings to be ground where
the charge was lighter; the others I knew nothing of.

Immediately all the ill-feeling came, like a festering boil, to a head. The
whole town was now united against the Abbey. Over most matters it was
difficult to get the comfortably off to join with the poor, or the merely poor
to join with the destitute, and there was a severance, always, between those
within and those without the Guilds. Now the arrest of the pastry-cook,
who was a Guildsman, was an affront to them all, the fate of the innkeeper-
turned-miller was of concern to the middle sort, and the very poor were
all agog in sympathising with the old woman. The sullen grumbling

changed to a more active, though still vague feeling that "something should
be done."

At this moment there popped up a very ancient fellow, half blind and
more than half rambling in his wits, who could remember back to when he
was a little boy, when on a somewhat similar occasion the townsfolk had
all joined together and shown "them" that even "they" couldn't have everything their own way. The squabble then had concerned the taking of eels
from the river—another Abbey right—and when the townspeople had
done considerable damage to the Bell Tower and the main gate, the rules
had been modified. The old grandfather, after years of obscurity, suddenly found himself the centre of attention. The little house of his granddaughter with whom he lived was always thronged with people anxious
to hear his tale of what had happened seventy years ago. He conveniently
forgot, or left out of his tale, anything which the townsfolk would not find
agreeable, and the effect was to make them feel that they were a pack of
powerful wolves who, for many years, had allowed themselves to be bullied by a few bleating old sheep and who had only to show their teeth to
turn the tables. Very soon, before the arrested people could be brought
before the Abbey Court, an attack on the Abbey was being planned.

I heard all about it. I was always moving about the town, here and there,
in search of work. I was hungry and poor, one of the oppressed whose
bread would be dear, whose feelings would veer towards the old gleaning
woman. By the simple process of listening and saying nothing I learned a
great deal. Sometime in November, at the dark of the moon, the Abbey
was to be attacked. The monks would then be in bed and sound asleep;
they retired soon after Compline, which was at seven in the winter, and
slept until midnight when they were roused for Matins. It was not badly
planned. The postern gate in the great main gateway was to be forced by
means of a battering ram, and then a body of apprentices, armed with the
bows and arrows with which they practised on Saturday afternoons, was
to march in and demand the release of the prisoners. The aldermen of the
Guilds, dressed in their livery, and unarmed, but under guard of another
group of apprentices and journeymen, were then to go and negotiate with
the Abbot, or the Prior, and get the charge for milling reduced again to
one fourteenth and the claim on the dung waived. All this under threat of
real violence, letting the riffraff run wild through the Abbey, and firing
timbers and thatch. This, according to the old grandfather, was how the
townspeople had conducted their business seventy years ago, and they had
won what they asked for. Why shouldn't it happen again?

Now it is true that an ordinary poor man like me can go through a lifetime without once testing his loyalty to anything save his own belly and
his own family. In the main he cannot even be said to be loyal to his own

kind, since at any moment he is prepared to snatch a job, or a crust, from another man exactly like himself; I had done it many a time by the town gateway. But it is equally true that some extraordinary circumstance may arise and the most simple man must ask himself the question: Where do I stand in this matter? and the answer is there, clear and certain as soon as the question is asked.

Such a testing point I had now reached, and there was no doubt at all in my mind that I was with the monks. I had lived in the town for over four years, and the only kindness that I had received from anybody had come from within those Abbey walls. Brother Justinius was mean; the increase in the milling charge made my bread dear, but those facts looked small when placed beside the alms Kate had received in both her pregnancies, the fair, just way in which the Trimble charity had been administered, the careful attention I had been given in the Infirmary, and the way Brother Sebastian had devised and Brother Anthony had carried out the scheme to make me less crippled.

I owed the Abbey a good deal. And I hated the Guilds, their aldermen, their journeymen, and their rules.

At the same time I will not pretend I was ruled either by gratitude or hatred. Expediency played its part. The old grandfather might remember only that the townspeople had gained their point about the eels; the fact remained that after seventy years the Abbey still governed the town; and even if the townsfolk had won back their right to go eel-fishing, the Abbey had retained every right that mattered. It seemed to me that I should do myself no harm by trying to get into favour with those who would surely get the better of the dispute in the long run. I might even contrive to put in a word for my little threatened house. If I warned the monks in time, they would be grateful and then I could say, "Please don't demolish my neat thatched hut with the rest of Squatters Row."

I was obliged to settle all these things in my mind rather quickly when it came to the point. After all the weeks of grumbling and plotting the decision to make the attack on the twelfth of November was only settled on the evening of the eleventh. On the morning of the twelfth I was helping a man to slaughter a pig; we had its throat cut and its guts out when the man's neighbour looked over the wall and passed the news. I stood for a moment with my filthy hands hanging idle and the scent of blood in my nostrils and ran through all the arguments again. The townsfolk who had never shown me any kindness at all, or the Abbey which had given me alms and mended my leg? The townsfolk who would never do me any good, or the Abbey which might grant me the right to go on living in my hut?

I made up my mind, and, striking my leg in a gesture of sudden comprehension, I exclaimed, "Holy Mother, my shoe! The monk Anthony is the only one who knows how to mend it. If trouble is brewing, I should get it done today."

The man I was helping gave a loud yelp of laughter and smote me on the back.

"Thass the way," he exclaimed. "Take the honey before you smoke out the hive. Get what you can out of the rogues. They'll hev more than shoes to mend tomorrow, I'll warrant."

I limped along to the Alms Gate and stood at the end of the little crowd who were drawing their dole. Brother Justinius was on duty, for which I was a little sorry; but when my turn came at last, I took off my shoe and, leaning against the hatch, said, "Brother Justinius, I have some information which is of importance to the Abbey."

I spoke softly, for there were some who, having snatched their dole, were eating it then and there.

The monk had his wits about him. Taking the shoe, he said in a loud, scolding voice, "What again! I declare you wear out more shoes than a tinker's ass! You'd think Brother Anthony had nothing else to do. Wait there."

He slammed down the hatch.

I curled my barefoot round the shin of my other leg and leaned against the wall. One by one those who were wolfing down their food finished it and wandered away; all but one, a stranger to me, his hand wrapped in a filthy, bloodied clout.

"Keep you waiting," he said, coming close to me. "Keep you waiting like you was a dog, for the bits they scrape off their plates." He cleared his throat and spat out his rancour.

"I must wait," I said. "Only the monk can mend my shoe."

"That may be. But if they was the kind brothers to everybody like they make out to be, wouldn't they say, 'Come in. Sit you down,' not, 'Wait there.' Same with the food. Why, once I heard a friar preach, telling about Our Lord Jesus Christ. . . ." He crossed himself piously. "*He* fed five thousand once, and He said, 'Sit down on the grass,' He said, 'and be comfortable.' And He didn't hev no hatches and waiting about till the hour struck. Fish He give them, too, and when their bellies wouldn't hold another bite He filled baskets for them to take away. Maybe you never heard that tale."

"I've heard all the tales," I said shortly, wishing he would take himself off.

"I'm a stranger here. I s'pose you don't know a place where I could lay, cheap, for the night."

"As it happens, I do." I directed him to the loft where Kate and I had lived during our first weeks in the town. I praised it, saying it was so good, so cheap that if he wanted to get a bed he should hurry. As I talked he began to unwind the rag from his hand. Under it flesh and bone were whole and sound.

"The monk will return in a minute. If you want to eat here tomorrow . . ." I said warningly.

He winked at me and hurried off. All poor men took it for granted that they were in league together, I thought. I was the one exception.

As soon as he had gone Brother Justinius opened, not the hatch but the whole door.

"Come in," he said.

The room was small and square with wide wooden shelves on the walls to left and right of the door. There were the remains of the loaves, and the big bowls of peaseporridge, cooked and allowed to set firm and then cut into sections. Someone in the crowd must have claimed Trimble too, for there was a joint of beef, glazed and brown without, pink and juicy within, which even at that nervous moment brought the water gushing into my mouth. I was meat-hungry. The thought struck me that had I stayed until that pig was dismembered, I should have been given a couple of trotters, or even maybe a hock.

"Now," Brother Justinius said briskly, "what is it that you have to tell?"

Tell him, I thought, and he would push me out, go to his immediate superior and say, "A man at the Alms Gate just told me . . ." How much would that profit me?

"It is for the ear of my Lord Abbot alone."

He looked at me. Kate went round my head and those of the boys every month with a pair of borrowed shears, and my time to be shorn was about due. Where I was not patched I was ragged, filthy from my last dirty job, and wearing but one shoe. A likely visitor for the Abbot!

"Who sent you?"

"Nobody. My own conscience compelled me."

He gave me a cold cynical look and said, "Oh, come along. What is it you have to say?"

"It is of importance. I can only speak of it to my Lord Abbot."

He said to me with great seriousness, "Do you know what you ask?"

And I said to him, with equal seriousness, "I know what I have to tell."

I could see him debating with himself whether or not to open the door and push me out. Finally he snapped out the one word, "Come."

He opened a door in the wall opposite the hatch and set off, at a great pace, along a stone passage, so cold with the stored-up chill of many sunless years that my teeth began to chatter. After what seemed to my bare limping foot a long walk, he stopped and threw open a door, saying in exactly the voice he had used before:

"Wait here."

The room was warm, with a good fire on the hearth and settles on either side. I went and warmed myself, slowly turning round like a roast on a spit, then I sat down. Something about the way I had been received, and this long waiting, started a doubt in my mind. Might it not have been wiser to stay with my own kind, outside these walls, thrown myself wholeheartedly into their plot, perhaps distinguished myself by boldness in the assault, so that they would say: This man must be admitted to the Guild forthwith; he is worthy to be a journeyman?

Well, it was too late now.

The door opened and another monk entered. I jumped up, forgetting my bare foot, lurched, and had to catch at the settle to save myself.

"I trust you are not drunk."

The voice was no more friendly than Brother Justinius', but it was different, cool, distant, very faintly amused. The face, narrow within the cowl's shadow, matched it, thin, sharply curved nose, arched brows above bright, intelligent eyes. There was nothing about his garb to mark him from any other monk, but I knew at once that I was in the presence of someone important.

"I am sober," I said. "I am lame without my shoe."

"And you have some tale to tell. What is it?"

"Are you my Lord Abbot?"

"No. But you must make do with me. I am the Prior."

It took all my courage to say again, "It is a matter of importance. It should be for my lord's ear alone."

"I *am* his ear. Come now, I am waiting."

I gave in and told him all that I knew. Except that his eyes narrowed a little as he listened, I might have been telling him that the weather was cold. When I had done, he asked one question.

"Why have you turned traitor to your fellows?" His tone was curious rather than accusing or malicious, yet it shamed me.

"I bear them a grudge for several wrongs they have done me. I was well treated in the Abbey Infirmary when my leg was broken. And I hope for a reward."

His glance brightened.

"I see. Well, rest assured that if your tale is true, you will be *well* rewarded."

"It *is* true. Why should I come and tell . . ."

"I have no time for that now. Wait here."

He went away, swiftly and silently. Soon the door opened again and Brother Justinius entered. Behind him were two men, servants, one of whom carried my shoe.

"Brother Anthony says that the upper hardly justifies a new sole, but it will last a little time. Put it on. Then these will show you the way."

He left us, and when my shoe was on one of the men said, "This way," and went ahead, the other fell in behind me. I suspected nothing. The two men might be on their way to town on some business, they might even have homes there and be about to return to them. I did notice that we were not going along the long cold passage that led to the Alms Gate, but there was nothing strange about that either. The Abbey had many entrances, and the Alms Gate, so far as I knew, was only used for its special purpose. Once we emerged into the daylight and crossed a paved courtyard, and I noticed that even out-of-doors the short winter light was waning. The next passage into which we plunged was almost dark. The man ahead of me stopped suddenly and threw open a door, and, instead of going through the opening himself, stepped aside and waited. The man behind me gave me a slight push and I went through the doorway, not into the twilit street as I expected, but into the pitch dark, full of a stench which even I, accustomed to the Town Ditch, found sickening. Before I could turn the door behind me slammed to with a horrid, final sound.

XII

STUPID bewilderment was, for a long time, the only thing I could feel. Why do this to me?

Afterwards came terror. I had heard—as who had not?—of the deep dungeons under great castles where men were thrown and forgotten, left to starve to death or be eaten by rats or go mad and beat their brains out against the walls. Those dungeons had a Norman name, "oubliettes," sinister indeed. Somehow I had never dreamed that an Abbey would have such a place. Even when Jack Nobbs and the others had been dragged off and imprisoned, I had imagined them in a less comfortable Infirmary. Now I knew. I was in even worse case than they were, for they were accused of an offence, they would be brought to trial. I might very well just disappear and never be heard of again. Nobody outside these walls knew where I was.

Sweat of fear streamed over my body and dried cold as I thought about Kate and the children. I had never supported them, but there had never been a day when I had not somehow managed to contribute something to the household, even if it were only a bundle of firewood; and I had kept the hut standing and moderately weatherproof. Apart from that most material consideration, there was Kate's anxiety to worry over. Our first fond love had worn away, like the nap from a woollen garment, but below, the fabric of unity was still strong; if she had failed to come home one evening I should have been distraught; I credited her with full as much concern for me.

I should have said that it was impossible to find any spot in Baildon out of the sound of the Abbey bells, but here the silence was as complete as the darkness. The cold had driven me to burrow into the heap of stinking straw, and I lay there for hours wishing with all my heart I had kept clear of this business, imagining Kate going home and waiting and wondering, waiting and worrying. For a long time misery kept me from feeling hungry, but as the slow hours dragged by the gnawing began in my vitals. I was schooled to the feeling of not having had enough to eat, it was almost a constant state with me since my accident, but this was the painful urgent need to eat *something*, anything, the need that will drive a man to beg or steal. Presently, useless as I knew it to be, I was beating with my hands on the door and shouting.

Nobody noticed, probably nobody heard me. I remained alone with my fears and my hunger and the deadly cold which bit deeper as my hunger increased. In the end I was driven back to the straw again, and, comforted by the warmth, fell into a state which was neither sleeping nor waking. Sometimes I was almost asleep, my miseries of mind and body became a little blurred, and behind my shut lids scenes from my past drifted by, small and very clear. Then I would be jerked back to the straw and the hunger and the terror.

Once, thus jerked back, I had a new thought. I was going to die, and I was afraid to die. Keeping alive had been such a struggle that I had spared little thought for the state of my immortal soul; even the friar's words about attending Mass while in a state of sin had soon been, if not forgotten, pushed aside. Kate and I could not suddenly absent ourselves, and we could not be married openly without putting the brand of bastardy on the children, so we had gone on as before and I had not worried about it until now. Now not only that great sin but dozens of small ones must be remembered in torment. The lies I had told, one way and another! All out of necessity, one might say, but each one a handing over of my soul to the Devil, the Father of Lies. I had more than once stolen things in the market—and never given the matter another thought. It hadn't seemed sinful then, merely common sense, two eggs slipped from a basketful while the owner turned her back meant a meal for Stephen and Robin; I'd taken the nails that held my hut together from Armstrong's stock—we made nails in slack hours at the forge, and I had taken a few from a chest containing hundreds. Such petty pilfering I had not even confessed when I might have done, they had weighed so lightly on my conscience. Now they loomed enormous, and presently, thinking of death and the Judgement, I reached the point where even my running from Rede assumed the character of a sin. I was Lord Bowdegrave's property and I had removed myself. . . .

Some remaining crumb of sanity became active then and I thought: How ridiculous! How can a man steal himself? And I laughed. The sound frightened me. I clapped my hand over my mouth. Mad, mad! Locked up in the dark, starving to death, and going mad. The next step was to beat my head against the wall and add self-destruction to my other sins.

I was at the door again, beating on it and screaming, not this time saying I was hungry, starving to death, this time begging for a priest, beseeching them not to let me die with all my sins unconfessed and unabsolved.

As before nobody came.

Beating on the door and shouting had been too much for me in my weak state; sweat poured off me again, my heart thudded so hard that it struck sparks from my eyeballs. Without knowing that I had fallen, I found myself on the floor. Then the cold struck again and I crawled back into the straw, turned weakly warm, almost drifted into sleep again, and then was jerked back.

This time it was hope which tugged me. God was merciful. Jesus Christ, in His earthly life, had been poor. Mary the Mother knew how one felt about one's children and their hunger. I could pray for pity and understanding and forgiveness.

So I knelt on the damp stone floor and prayed, passionately. I mentioned every sin I could remember, even my running away from Rede, which I could see now *was* a sin, in that it was evidence of my discontent with the condition to which it had pleased God to let me be born.

I prayed for hours. I prayed until the sweat ran down my face and dropped on to the floor and as it ran I began again.

"Sweet Jesus Christ, who in Gethsemane . . ." For He, too, knew the sweat of agony.

Then I swooned, or slept. From kneeling on the floor I was lying in the straw, which had, all at once, lost its stench. I was waiting for something, something of which I had been given warning, a pleasant and comforting thing.

What did I expect? Some voice in the silence, something luminous in the dark?

When it came it was merely a thought in my head. I *had* no soul. Serfs had no souls. They were treated like animals and they were animals. The pretence that we were immortal, with Hell to fear and Heaven to hope for, was simply a trick to make us well behaved.

How simple and how sensible, I thought. No master, no steward, however watchful, could keep an eye on us all the time, it is therefore greatly to their advantage to teach us, "Thou shalt not steal," and make us believe that thieves go to Hell.

Priests pretend too; it keeps the churches full and Peter's Pence rolling in. That must be true, because monks are religious men and if they believed that I had a soul they would never dare leave me to die here with my sins unshriven.

Strange as it sounds, the thought that I had no soul was the most comfortable notion that I had ever had. It removed the fear of Hell; it lifted all responsibility. I had lived as an animal and I should die like one. Like an old horse or a dog, past all use and a waste to feed any more. All this fuss about marriage, I thought. We coupled like dogs who don't expect to be chanted over; and as for those eggs . . . who calls it *sin* when a starving cat sneaks off with a fishhead?

Freed from the fear of Hell, I curled up in the straw and made ready to die.

Everything rocked a little, the darkness lifted, the walls melted away, and I was lying on the grass under the little crooked hawthorn tree, freshly green and white, just breaking into blossom. I could smell it, cool and scentless.

"You," I cried. And all at once I understood everything. Nothing to do with priests or sins or being forgiven, nothing to do with anything there are any words for. Just the beauty of the tree and my acceptance of it, promise and fulfilment all in one. And what there are no words for.

Now I could die.

All nonsense, of course.

The voices reached me first.

"Complete misunderstanding. 'Hold him safe,' I said. The order was perfectly clear."

"A gross mistake indeed; but that can wait. Brother Sebastian . . ."

"Hold the light a little closer."

Hot tallow dripped on my cheek; I opened my eyes and closed them again, the light struck so painfully.

"Why, this is the man Martin whose leg I mended. Give me the cup."

Something wet on my lips turned to fire in my mouth.

"Come, rouse yourself, man!"

". . . to reach such a state in little over twenty-four hours."

"Probably he was fasting when he was thrown in. Come, drink properly, wake up and drink. You waste more than you take."

The cool voice, which I recognised as the Prior's, said, "This noxious air, as much as the fast, is responsible for his state. Unless we move soon we shall all be insensible."

I made a great effort and mustered my voice.

"Why?" I cried. "Why did you leave me to die? I came to bring you warning."

"Drink," said Brother Sebastian, pressing the cup to my mouth again.

"Everything shall be explained presently," said the Prior. "Get him out of here, give him food. Then clean him and dress him anew. When he is ready, bring him to the Abbot's parlour."

Whatever it was they had given me to drink had gone to my head, so that my ears rang, and when at last they heaved me to my feet the floor seemed soft and yielding and a long way away. Brother Sebastian, carrying the candle, moved ahead, murmuring gentle encouragements. One of the men who ordinarily collected the market dues helped me along.

In a small warm room they sat me down and brought a basin and towel so that I could clean my hands before I ate. They served me barley broth, a roast capon, dried figs. Gradually my head cleared and my spirits rose. They seemed, after all, well disposed towards me. I had done them a service, been ill-used. . . . I began to think about reward, began framing in my mind the plea for my little hut. Surely now that would not seem much to ask.

"Now, Martin," said Brother Sebastian, "having restored the inner man, let us attend to the outer. That dungeon reek clings hard."

He led me to the laundry, where stone slabs, hollowed into basins, ran the length of one wall, and a great fire burned, with huge iron cauldrons swinging above. Hot water, tempered with cold, was poured into one of the basins. Brother Sebastian handed me a square of strong lye soap.

"I should get right in and wash all over, hair as well, if I were you. Our Abbot has a fastidious nose. Clothes will be brought you. I must get back to my duties. Fare you well."

The clothes, brought by a servant as I towelled myself, were such as I had never dreamed to wear, a rich man's clothes. Soft woollen shift, clinging close and warm from neck to knee and down the arms to the elbows, a fine linen shirt, hose and tunic of smooth grey cloth. The touch of them against my freshly scoured skin gave me a sense of well-being, of bodily ease that I had never known before. I had known its shadow once or twice, back at Rede when I was very young and a few of us boys had stripped and plunged into the river on a very warm sunny day, but we had come out and donned our creased, dirty clothes.

I remember thinking that the clothes themselves were a kind of reward, and that the shift was big enough for Kate to cut up and shape into warm garments for Stephen and Robin.

I was stooping to put on my old worn shoes when the door opened and there was a young monk, with a pink, girlish face and his sleeves rolled over his elbows. He had a pair of shoes in his hand.

"Made hurriedly and from memory. We trust they will fit."

They fitted much better than the old ones.

"Then . . . if you will come with me. . . ."

We went along passages, up and down steps, and at last came out into the open, where immediately I smelled the sour harsh scent of slow-burning wood, like that which fills a room where a log has rolled off the hearth. I stopped and sniffed and said:

"Did they get in then, after all?" If so, all my effort had been wasted and there would be no reward.

"Nobody got *in*," he said gently. "We were prepared and the main gate was reinforced. They tried to batter it down, and failed, so they set it afire. We welcomed its destruction, it was never worthy of its place. The new one is to be made from cedarwood from the groves of Lebanon." His voice took on a dreamy, ecstatic note. "Cedars are long-lived trees. It may even be that St. Egbert's new gate may be made from a tree which cast its shade over Our Lord."

"But you said you were prepared."

"Oh yes. Our Abbot has fifty knights to call upon; there was time to reach two of them, and their meinies. But our rule forbids us to strike the first blow. Once the gate was burned and the attackers were inside . . . then the archers and pikemen went into action."

"And drove them off?"

"Very easily, I believe."

Most cheerful news. "We were prepared," he said. "Time to reach two of them and their meinies." All thanks to me!

We were walking along a path, grey-paved, between two green lawns which ended in a laurel hedge through which the path went on. Behind the fence was a low stone building, made of dressed flint and owning a high, arched doorway, flanked by several windows in each side. The windows were glassed and just caught the last rays of the sinking sun.

At the doorway the monk halted.

"The Prior awaits you in the anteroom," he said.

I went in, blinking in the sudden light of a huge leaping fire and three or four candlestands. There was a long table in the centre of the room and at it a monk sat writing. The Prior stood at his elbow, reading every word he wrote. He gave me a brief glance of recognition, looked down again, and said:

"That will do well. Seal it."

The scribing monk took a bar of sealing wax, held it to a candle, dropped a great blob on the bottom of the parchment, and the Prior took up a gold seal and stamped it down. Then he rolled the parchment into a tube and said to me:

"There you are. Smelling sweeter, I trust. Follow me."

He opened a door at the back of the room and I followed him.

It was like walking into an oven, but the little figure seated in a chair close to the fire was all shrouded in fur, a great shawl of it lay across his shoulders, and another covered his legs. A woollen hood such as peasants wear in the fields in winter was pulled low over his ears and brow. His face was as brown and wrinkled as a walnut, and his lips a thin blue line. He looked a hundred years old. Only his eyes were lively.

The Prior went close to him and said in a high, penetrating voice, "My Lord Abbot, here is the man Martin, whom you wished to see."

Turning back to me, he said, "The Abbot is very deaf. Speak loudly or not at all."

In a high, thin monotone the Abbot said, "Ah yes, yes indeed. We owe you a great deal. I wished to thank you. Also I wished to hear why it was that you sided with us rather than with your fellows."

I said, in my loudest voice, "They refused me admission to the Guild."

He gave me an odd little smile and looked over my shoulder.

"What does he say?"

"He says that the townsfolk refused to admit him to the Guild."

"Ah, those Guilds. Most regrettable! Becoming so arbitrary. I'm not quite sure how far the Guilds were involved in last night's affair." He looked inquiringly at the Prior. "However. The Guild refused to admit you, so you turned against the Guild. And very fortunate for us that you did. Quite right of course in *any* circumstances." He nodded and smiled at me approvingly, and I thought that now was my chance.

"I had another reason, my lord," I said loudly.

Once again the Prior was obliged to repeat what I had said.

"Indeed. And what was that?"

I turned helplessly to the Prior, who said, with a sly smile, "Now you see the truth of what I said. I *am* my lord's ear. Very well, tell me and I will speak for you."

"They speak of clearing Squatters Row. I built a little hut there. I know I had no right to build, but I didn't know that at the time. It is the only home I have and it is not unsightly. I wondered . . . I mean I thought that if the information I brought you served your purpose, you might perhaps overlook . . . might allow my little hut to remain."

This stumbling speech the Prior compressed into two clear sentences. I watched the old man's face and saw with dismay that the request found no favour with him.

"The Cellarer tells me that the spot is a disgrace, a mere rubbish heap thrown up against our walls. It does not offend my eyes or nose, I never go abroad now. But we have visitors. What do *they* think when they see human beings living like pigs within arm's reach of the most splendid shrine in Christendom? The Cellarer tells me that nobody entering by the east gate can fail to see the place—and smell it."

It was, once again, a verdict against which there was no appeal. Forbidden to be a priest, I thought; forbidden to be married; forbidden to be a journeyman; and now, forbidden to remain in my hut.

"You have the parchment?" the old man asked the Prior.

"Signed and sealed, my lord."

"You see, we had thought of rewarding you by giving you what all poor men seem most to desire—a piece of land. Perhaps you know it—just outside the town on the south—the Old Vineyard they call it. The blight persists there, and I understand that we already have as much acreage under plough as we can handle. So it is yours, in perpetuity, in return for a red rose on the last day of June each year—a formality which shouldn't cause you any inconvenience. Give him his copyhold."

The Prior pushed the rolled-up parchment into my hand.

I tried to shout my thanks. Whether he heard or not, I could not know, but the Abbot nodded and smiled again. Then he said, "On the other hand it is poor gratitude which gives with one hand and takes away with the other. Also they tell me that the land is full of stumps, which must be cleared before it can yield any crop. What will you eat while you labour, and where will you live? I think," he said, looking past me at the Prior, "we should give him some money, too."

"As you wish."

"Give him fifty marks."

"My lord! Fifty marks is the scotage for the three Flaxhams in one year."

"Sir Alain and Sir Robert reached us, with their men, did they not? If that rabble had made an entry, it would have cost us fifty marks many times over. Fifty marks is no more than his due. Give it to him."

The Prior pulled aside a piece of tapestry hanging on the wall and opened the door behind it, went through, and closed the door carefully behind him.

I said, "My lord, I know not in what words to thank you."

The Abbot said, "It is useless to speak to me. For some reason, known only to God, I am deaf to all voices but *his*." He looked towards the door. "Very occasionally he thinks that gives him the right to dictate to me." He smiled and nodded his head.

I thought that if I could not speak I could act my gratitude, so I dropped to my knees, took the old man's thin cold hand, and kissed it. He withdrew it hastily and patted my shoulder.

"Don't let the aspect lead you to think that you can grow vines on that field. Six years ago the blight struck there and, though we rooted out every stump and ploughed it over and laid it fallow for a year and then planted strong new stock, still the blight remained. I went out to see for myself, I remember—one of my last rides. It was a sad sight—a very sad sight. Ah . . ."

The Prior returned, carefully closing the door again and drawing the tapestry over it. He carried a linen bag tied at the neck. He said to me, in the cool, amused voice which showed that he had recovered his composure, "My Lord Abbot must set high store on the people of Baildon. Our Lord Himself was betrayed for only thirty pieces. You have all this—and the Potter's Field as well!"

He could have said sharper things and caused me no twinge.

"Please," I said, "tell him how very grateful I am. All my life I have been so very poor . . . and lately lame as well. All that I have tried has been of no avail. Now I can begin again. I am so very thank . . ." I choked and tears came into my eyes.

The Abbot gave me one of his bright, shrewd glances.

"You would be wise—for your own sake—to conceal the source of your money."

I nodded to show that I understood, and the movement brought two tears spilling over.

"We are grateful to you," he said. "Go in peace."

The Prior came to the door with me.

"The east gate is nearest for you. Besides the great gate is closed."

The clerk, without being bidden, rose from the table and led the way. On this journey I saw several groups of pikemen and archers as well as a few men in armour, but they, like everything else, were just the background of a dream to me.

It was almost dusk. I intended to go to Webster's and fetch Kate and the children home, for the last time. I would put my arms about her and say, "Don't ask questions now, I will tell you everything when we are home, but, sweetheart, we are *rich!*" We would walk slowly down Cooks Row, that street which we so often avoided because of the sight and scent of food so far out of our reach, and we would buy everything we fancied. When we were home I would make a fire, not sparing the wood because in future we could have as much wood as we wanted. Over supper I would tell her the story and speak of what I planned. Dear Kate, she should never lift a finger outside her own house again.

Something sloughed off my soul, like the scab from an old sore, and all at once I was able to look beyond that happy supper table. Kate and I could go to bed together properly again. Another child would be welcome now. In every way we would start anew.

I reached Webster's gate just as one of the wool-pickers, a bent old woman with screwed-up, half-blind eyes, was coming out. She stopped by me and said, "Kate ain't bin to work today. Master's rare and vexed."

I turned and began to run, as quickly as I could in my new shoes, towards Squatters Row.

Interval

I

THE man with the bear came into Baildon just before dusk. November days are short. They are cold, too, and the man, heavily muffled, thickset, and clumsy, might, in outline, almost have been another bear, forced to stay upright. As though to prove his claim to be human, he talked to himself as he walked. Very often children, keeping at a safe distance, would call after him, "Talk to yourself, talk to the Devil."

He was telling himself that leading a dancing bear was all right in the summer, but misery in winter. He said there ought to be a place where bears could be left at the end of September and collected at the beginning of April, well fed and kept in training. There was no such place. He reminded himself that even when a bear-leader had money for a lodging for himself and could find a place that had a stable where the bear could sleep, nine times out of ten they wouldn't have you in—horses didn't like the bear smell.

Every time he reminded himself of this, and felt the bitter wind, he looked at the bear with hatred and dragged viciously at the chain. Every time he did so, the bear looked at him with a curiously similar expression. In their imposed physical likeness to one another, in the flashes of hatred, and in their dependence each upon the other for the basic necessities of living, they were like an old married couple.

The man's name was Tom, and he was known on the roads as Pert Tom; the bear, neutered at the beginning of his training, was called Owd Muscovy.

As Tom had suspected, there was no lodging for man *and* bear; he took the rebuffs philosophically. It was some years since he had been in Baildon, but he remembered it well and knew of a fairly snug place in which to spend the night, a place where several people lived between the buttresses of the Abbey wall, and made their little fires and were willing—for a small consideration—to allow a stranger to warm himself and cook a bite of food. On his last visit there had been a woman, living behind a screen of tarred canvas, who—again for a consideration—had been willing to grant other favours. That, he remembered, must have been all of five years ago; probably she'd moved on, and in any case she would have aged. Still, in November a man couldn't be too particular.

When he reached the place it was very much as he remembered it, except that in one corner, between the wall and the buttress, someone had built a tidy little hut, with a thatch to its roof and a hole for a chimney, the hole carefully plastered round with clay to keep the straw from catching alight. Pert Tom looked at the place speculatively. If the owner of the place was good-hearted, he might find shelter for the night after all. At the moment the place was deserted and he wandered on, found some campers whom he remembered from his last visit—a very old woman and a deaf-and-dumb man and his wife, whose family had increased considerably—but the woman who had slept behind a piece of canvas and been willing to share her bed with him was not—to his disappointment—there.

"They laid onto her so hard last time she went to be whipped," the dumb man's wife explained, "that she mended her ways. She went off into the country to work in a dairy."

"What a cruel waste," Pert Tom said.

He began his preparations for the night, settling down in the corner opposite the little hut. He hobbled the bear by fixing the chain around one foreleg and one back, removed its iron muzzle, and gave it its supper. Always, wherever he was, he fed the bear first and when, as sometimes happened, there was only food for one it was the bear which supped and he who hungered. There was no sentiment concerned, he was capable of using the bear brutally, but to keep it in good fettle was simply common sense. When the beast had devoured its bread and honey, he slipped back its muzzle and went to sit by the dumb man's fire. But he kept his eye on the hut, and in the very last of the light saw a small woman, a girl almost, with two young children, enter it and close the door. He waited a little while, then, muttering that he was going to turn in, he went to the corner where the bear was asleep, lay down beside it, and waited again. He could see by the light that came through the ill-joined timbers of the hut that the young woman had got the fire going. At what he thought the right time he rose, went softly across the space, and knocked on the door. Kate opened it. Against the smoky red fire glow he saw the halo of her pale

hair and missed the lines of worry and disappointment on her face. In
his smoothest, most wheedling tone he said:

"I wondered if you could oblige me with a drop of hot water. I got a
pinch o' ginger in my pack. With hot water and honey that make a rare
warming drink. Ever tried it?"

"No," she said flatly. "I can let you have some water if you've got a
crock."

He was trained to take in as much as possible at a glance. One sweep
of his eyes informed him that, although, having a roof over her head,
Kate might be said to be better off than he was himself, she was yet pit-
ifully poor. The two children were eating bowls of water gruel, the very
cheapest form of food, and they were eating it hungrily. But he noticed,
too, that a mattress, made of sacking through which the straw was bursting, lay against the back wall, taking up indeed more than a half of the
floor space. Better than lying on the bare ground in the open.

"I've got a bowl." In a moment he was back with it; he brought also his
pinch of ginger and his pot of honey.

"I thought maybe the lil dears'd fancy a spoonful of the honey in their
gruel," he said.

She was ashamed that even a stranger, begging at her door, should have
seen how poor the children's supper was.

"You are kind; but they've finished now."

"Honey," Stephen said.

"Be quiet. Now, if you'll give me your bowl . . ." She took it, poured
into it the small amount of hot water left over from the making of the
gruel, and handed it back to him. Outlined against the hearth, her figure
looked slim and shapely—too thin, but he wasn't fussy.

"I brung the ginger," Pert Tom said coaxingly. "If you never tasted it,
you should. Go down right warm, like a fire in your belly."

"I believe you. I've no time to try. I have a lot to do and my husband
will be home any minute."

She spoke the last words in a very clear, significant way.

"Well," he said in a deflated tone. "Thanks for the water."

He returned to his corner, drank his warming brew, choking a little,
put his pack under his head and, cuddling close to Owd Muscovy for
warmth, began to drift towards sleep as easily as an animal. Once, just
before sleep took him, he was not unhappily aware of his woman-hunger,
a mistake to drink the ginger, he thought, it was well known to heat the
blood; if he'd known the woman was waiting for her husband and would
refuse her share of the precious stuff, he'd have saved it for a more promising occasion. Then he was asleep.

The bear, stirring restlessly and grunting, roused him. He doubled his fist, thumped the heaving bulk beside him, and growled, "Lay down!"

The bear, ordinarily—and with good cause—extremely obedient, continued to stir and grumble, and presently Pert Tom was wide awake and aware that something was, if not wrong exactly, out of the ordinary. There was a distant noise which roused a confused memory of his soldiering days; and overhead the sky, without star or moon, was curiously light with a pinkish-yellow pulsing glow.

"You're right. Something's afoot," Tom said to the bear, and got to his feet, shivering in the brittle cold of the night. The confused noise sorted itself out into the sound of men shouting, some heavy thumping, and—was it possible?—the twang of bowstrings. Nearer, and quite distinct, came the sound of movement from the hut in the other corner. The pulsing light leaped again in the sky, and he could see the woman in the doorway.

There was something intimate about the two of them being wakeful at this hour of the night, and he forgave her for her earlier unfriendliness. He ambled over and said, "Whass going on?"

"They're fighting." He could hear that she had been crying. "And Martin must have gone and got mixed in it. He isn't home." She gave a sharp sob. "I never thought they'd do it," she said, a wild note creeping into her voice. "And I never thought he'd have so little sense. . . . If he's hurt . . . Oh, if only I knew!"

The sky lightened and darkened and the distant noise increased.

"'Sno use me going to look. I don't know your Martin."

"I know that. I want to go myself."

"Then why don't you?"

"The children. If I take them and he's hurt, then I've got both hands full and couldn't help. And if I leave them and they woke . . . with all this noise and nobody . . . The others have all gone to watch. They ran past minutes ago." She leaned forward and put a hand on his arm. "Would you watch them for me, just five minutes while I go and look or ask . . . ? Somebody must have seen him."

"I don't mind," he said, without enthusiasm.

"Oh, thank you! If the little one wakes, put his thumb in his mouth, but the big one, say Mother won't be a minute."

She was gone, running like a deer.

"So, after all, I'm *in*," Pert Tom said to himself, ducking his head and entering the low dark hut. He remembered, from his single searching glance, the position of the hearthstone and the fact that at one side of it lay a heap of dried twigs, and on the other some more solid pieces of wood. He took out his flint and tinder and soon had the fire alight. He squatted on his heels, warming his hands and the inner sides of his thighs. As the light strengthened he looked about him again. The two children

lay against the wall, foot to foot, wrapped in a piece of woollen cloth.
The unoccupied portion of the mattress, with another cloth crumpled
across it, looked comfortable and inviting. He threw two pieces of wood
onto the fire and went and lay down. He teased himself pleasantly with
the idea of the woman lying here beside him, and dozed a little, losing all
consciousness of time.

He roused when Kate came back.

She was no longer crying. The scene outside the Abbey gate had
shocked her into calmness; she had been obliged to stare into the face of
dead man after dead man in her search for Martin, fourteen in all, some
horribly mutilated by arrows. She had not found him, nor anyone who
had seen him lately, but a woman had told her that some of the men of
the town had been inside the Abbey when the archers took them by
surprise. She felt certain that Martin was there, dead; and mingled with
her grief was a deep resentment that he should not only have joined the
rabble in their stupid quarrel, but been in the forefront of the attack.
When she thought of him lying dead she was ashamed of that feeling,
but it was there just the same. Torn by two such conflicting emotions
and denied the relief of tears, she had fallen into a stunned, somnambu-
listic state in which she was conscious of a single purpose—she must get
home to the children. The sight of Pert Tom sprawled on the bed did not
surprise her, although she had forgotten him, and when she had thought
of the children had visualised them as being alone. She was past feeling
anything so trivial as surprise; in a world where Martin was dead anything might happen.

Tom propped himself on one elbow and waited for her to speak. After
a minute he said, "You didn't find him?"

Such a stupid question merited no answer. She sat down on one of the
two stools and stared at the fire and presently said, "*Why* did he have to
join them? They'd treated him as badly as they could. He was a good
smith. . . ." As she spoke those words the tears almost came, for she saw
Martin as he had been on that evening at Rede, striding back, full of
youth and power, from his work at Ancaster and coming to her rescue.
A hard bitterness dried the tears. "A *good* smith," she repeated, "but they
wouldn't let him into their Guild. And then they broke his leg and lost
him his job. He didn't have to side with *them*."

"How d'you know that he did?"

"If he didn't where *is* he? Never once since he lost his job has he been
away for the night. And I know what he was doing today. Helping
with a pig-killing, just over the Ditch. And I know what happened. . . ."
She lifted her head so that the firelight shone in her eyes and on her

lips. "He thought he'd get back in with them, show them what he was made of. The fool!" Grief and fury came together in the last word.

So far as Pert Tom was concerned, she might have been speaking in a foreign tongue. Lust was lively now and he saw every hope of gratification. He got to his feet and laid a heavy hand on Kate's clenched in her lap.

"Like ice," he said. "I'm gonna get my ginger and we'll put the pot on and hev a nice hot drink. Pull you together better'n anything."

She said nothing; when he returned she was sitting as he left her, staring into the fire. He was putting water into the pot and the pot in the heart of the flames when she said, as though continuing a conversation, "We never even said good-by." Then there was another long pause before she spoke again.

"It was all on account of me that he came here and was so wretched. He'd have been better off at Rede. He said so. No, I said that. I used to say a lot of things I didn't mean."

The water boiled and Tom made his brew, using the last of the ginger and stirring in the honey with a liberal hand.

"Here. You get that down. You'll feel better in no time."

"As though I could," she said, speaking directly to him for the first time. "Nothing could make me feel better except the sight of Martin coming in that door."

"Drink it and try."

She thought that in his dull un-understanding way he was trying to be kind, so she lifted the bowl and sipped and coughed.

"Go down so nice and warm, don't it?" He swilled his own with gusto.

Spices were so expensive that only the rich could afford to buy them for their flavour; to develop a market among the poorer people, the merchants had craftily spread the rumour of their aphrodisiac virtues. Pert Tom, because he was ready for Kate and warmed by his ginger, all too easily believed that the sip or two she had taken would render her complacent.

"Don't let it get cold," he urged her. She lifted the bowl and drank its contents in that same sleep-walking fashion. He waited another minute, then he said, "Don't fret. There's as good fish in the sea as ever came out."

"What do you mean?"

"This," he said; and took hold of her, his purpose quite plain.

She woke then and remembered that her first feeling towards him had been one of distrust. He was big and hot and heavy; he reeked of bear; it was like being mauled by a bear. He had his face at her breast—in dreadful parody of a nursing child—and she could feel the heat of his breath through her clothes. She pushed, but he only pulled her closer. She wanted to scream but knew it would be useless, there was no one to hear except the children. She went limp in his hold and let him pull her down on to the bed. Then she said:

"Wait," and made the first motion of unfastening her dress. Just as he'd expected, Pert Tom told himself. Then her hand moved, quick as a slithering snake, and she had snatched a piece of burning wood from the fire and was on her feet, standing over him, threatening him with it.

"Get out," she said.

He jumped up and stood hesitant, face to face with her in the tiny room. He had only to get hold of her arm and twist it. . . . But she jabbed at him with the flaming branch; the heat scorched his face and singed his beard. He backed to the door which opened outwards and was unlatched. With the opening of the door under the pressure of his body a draught of cold air came swooping in; the flaming tip of the branch flared more fiercely and a piece of it dropped off and onto the edge of the straw-stuffed mattress which broke eagerly into flame.

Kate did scream then and tried to stamp on the new flame, but in a second her skirt was blazing. She threw the branch towards the hearth and stooped, smacking ineffectually at her skirt. Then she grabbed at the children, calling them by name, shaking Stephen awake and trying to lift Robin. They woke and shrank, screaming, nearer to the wall, away from the blazing edge of the mattress, the blazing of Kate's skirt.

"Help!" she screamed to Tom. "Help!"

It had all happened so quickly that he was still pressing his hands to his smouldering beard. But he had his wits about him. Save her, help her out, and what would be the result? Trouble. People were always ready to believe the worst of any stranger. She'd tell how the fire started and the least that would happen would be that he'd go to the lock-up; and nobody would care for Owd Muscovy. You could lose a good bear that way. Better let the bitch burn.

He put out his hand and pushed the door shut. It took another movement of air with it so that the flames leaped up with a hollow roar. Before he could have counted ten, before he dared withdraw his hand from the door, the inner side of the low thatch was alight.

He stepped back then to a safe distance. There was a moment when the woman and both the children were screaming together, then the thatch fell in on them, throwing out showers of sparks and little clots of burning straw. The screams stopped. There was a smell of burning flesh and then, after a minute, mingling with it, the stink of smouldering fur.

"Owd Muscovy!" cried Tom, and ran to the corner where the hobbled bear was plunging about, alight in a dozen places.

"Lay still. Lay! Down! Down! Down!" said Tom, beating at the thick greasy fur, tearing off bits of burning straw. He was not even conscious of the pain in his hands, he was so intent. The first lesson a bear-leader learned was that it did not pay to have too shabby or openly intimidated a bear; people liked to think that the bear was much stronger than any man and that but for the muzzle and the chain would tear its leader to pieces.

"Holy St. Ursula," Tom moaned. "You'll look like the moths hev been at you."

Even when his pelt was out of danger the bear, in whose early training fire had played a part, was nervous and shivering. Tom would have calmed him with an untimely offering of bread and honey, then remembered that he had taken the honey into the hut. All wasted and the ginger, too!

"And all over what?" he asked himself. "Slice off a cut cake that'd never been missed. Silly bitch! What got into her?"

He looked back at the hut then. The poor flimsy timbers of its front and side wall had fallen inwards over the whole, and had almost burned themselves out.

"Need never hev happened," he said. "Could hev been as nice as nice."

In a mood of self-pity, and with no twinge of conscience, he again settled down beside the bear and slept so soundly that he did not hear the other residents of Squatters Row return from their sight-seeing.

With morning light shining on the ruin, the dumb man's wife and Old Agnes found the destruction of one small hut of far more interest and moment than the burning of the great Abbey gate which they had seen during the night. They asked the inevitable question, "How did it happen?" and Tom had his tale ready. He had waked to find the hut blazing and had done his best to save whoever was inside. He had his blistered hands, his scorched face, and raggedly singed beard to show. Nobody for a second doubted the truth of his story. Dummy's wife managed, without exactly saying it in so many words, to imply that such an accident could have been expected, if you couldn't have a proper house the only thing to do was to make your fire in the open, as she had done all these years. The accident, in fact, was the result of trying to set yourself up above your neighbours. Old Agnes, remembering that Kate and Martin had dealt more fairly with her over the Trimble than her clients ordinarily did, said that perhaps it was a mercy in disguise—if Martin were really dead; it was a hard world for widows and orphans.

Pert Tom was praised for his attempted rescue and sympathised with for having wandered into Baildon just at this time. Nobody would be in the mood to be amused by a bear's tricks today. The town was in mourning, some said nineteen men dead and many more injured. And all for nothing.

Tom believed that trade would be bad, and soon after breakfast was on his way towards the north gate of the town when he saw a new detachment of soldiers marching in. They moved with the dogged, flat motion of men who have marched through the night, so it was likely that they had come from a distance. The fighting seemed to be over, and they wouldn't be marched back without a rest. Soldiers were good customers, easily amused and very open-handed. He turned himself about and followed them back into the centre of the town.

The Market Square was scattered with the litter—some of it curiously irrelevant—that was left by street fighting. There were the spent arrows, the burned-out torches, the thrown-down clubs, and sticks which might be expected, but there were also bits of clothing, part of a wheel, a cooking pot, some grey wool on a spindle. Patches of blood showed where men had fallen dead or injured, but all the bodies save one had been removed. An old woman and a boy of about ten were struggling with the corpse of a heavy man, the old woman crying and hysterically admonishing the boy.

"Hold his legs higher. Higher. You're letting his bum drag on the ground."

Pert Tom remembered how, after the Battle of Radscot Bridge, he had come across a dead man with a ring on his finger. It was that ring which had enabled him to buy Owd Muscovy, a two-year-old, fully trained. He went carefully over this battleground and saw nothing worth salvaging except the spindle, which he put in his pack.

Inside the great stone archway the burned edges of the gate hung jaggedly. Two monks, their faces expressionless, as though every morning they measured up burned gateways, were using a yardstick. Soldiers stood on guard all along the front of the Abbey, and inside Tom caught a glimpse of archers, pikemen, a man or two in armour. The soldiers he had followed had disappeared through the gateway, but soon others came out in groups of three or four and made off up Cooks Row towards the alehouses. He followed and was soon giving thanks to St. Ursula that he had decided to stay in the town. The bear's tricks were well received, especially his imitation of a pikeman's drill with a little cane for a pike, and by two o'clock in the afternoon Pert Tom had collected as much as was needed to live luxuriously by his standards for the next four days, which was as far as he ever looked ahead. He found an inn not yet discovered by the soldiers and therefore spared the sudden inflation of prices, and took a leisurely dinner of boiled beef and dumplings, apple pie and ale. Before he left he had his wooden bottle filled with ale, and on his way back down Cooks Row he did some pleasant shopping; a meat pie and five pickled onions for himself, a pot of honey, apples, bread for Owd Muscovy, half a pig's head for the wife of the deaf-and-dumb man whose fire he hoped to share again.

For the town this might be a day of mourning, but for Squatters Row, never in any real sense part of the town, it was a jubilant occasion. Old Agnes had laid out six that day and had four more to do tomorrow. "Of course I could've done the lot today, but it don't do to hurry. If you make it look easy, they grudge your pay." She had bought bacon and ale for her supper, and was sharing Dummy's fire because she was too busy to make her own. Dummy had spent the day grave-digging and brought home a pig's trotter for each member of his family and ale for himself.

Just at dusk Peg-Leg arrived, begging to be told what had happened. He had been out of town for three days visiting a niece who lived in the country and had a tender conscience. Every now and then when he grew tired of the food doled out at the Alms Gate he would pay her a visit; she would feed him, mend his rags, call him "Uncle Jacob," and restore his self-esteem. Sometimes her patience and his good behaviour would last four, five days, a week; but sooner or later he would offend her and she would reprimand him, and he would return to Baildon, laden with the provisions which it eased her sense of responsibility to provide. On this evening, after an unusually brief visit, he was carrying a piece of pork, a dozen eggs, some flat oat-cakes sticky with honey, and a little sack of walnuts. He was easily drawn into the group and the tit-for-tat bargaining, promising a share of his pork when it was cooked in return for a piece of pig's head this evening, swopping some eggs for a mug of Old Agnes' ale and sharing out the walnuts amongst the children.

The air of festivity mounted until one child was bold enough to ask Pert Tom to put the bear through his tricks. Tom was not going to break an infallible rule for dwellers in Squatters Row.

"Owd Muscovy, he've earned his rest today. Tell you what I will do, though. I'll play you a tune on my whistle."

He played a merry tune, and the children began to hop and skip in time to it. Peg-Leg said, with a trace of wistfulness, "Nice to be young, and sound of wind and limb. I was a rare one at a hornpipe once on a time."

"Young!" cried Old Agnes scornfully. "I can shake a leg with the best. Aye, and after a full day's work, too."

Gathering up her skirts and exposing skinny legs like knotted twigs and huge flat feet, she began to caper, calling to Tom to play faster, to play louder. Dummy's wife sprang up to join her, and their antics made even the deaf-and-dumb man laugh; he rocked from side to side, making a hoarse wheezy sound, like a pair of bellows whose leather sides had cracked.

It was into this merry scene that Martin walked.

He saw first the black ruin of what had been his home. Breath and heartbeat stopped; then reason took control. A few yards away was the leaping fire, a crowd about it, laughing and dancing to music. They wouldn't be doing that if Kate and the children had been . . . No. The neighbours were celebrating a near-escape, Kate and the children were there . . . beyond the fire.

He walked towards it, and Old Agnes, spinning round, saw him, stopped dead, let her skirt fall, and stared. In a second they were all staring and silent; on the defensive, like cattle in a field when a strange dog enters. And he could now see beyond the fire. No Kate, no child of his.

"Holy Mother of God," Old Agnes said, "we thought you was dead, too."

"Dead." He repeated the word. "Too? D'you mean . . ." The rest of the question could not be spoken; his jaw jerked convulsively.

Old Agnes moved towards him and took him by the arm. She was suddenly sober and aware of how callous their behaviour must seem to him.

"Flared up in the night, your place did. But we thought you was dead too . . . she . . . Kate was running round, hunting for you and crying. And with all gone together there didn't seem much to grieve about."

He said, "Burned," but the shaking of his jaw mangled the word so that it emerged in a moan of anguish.

Agnes tightened her hold on his arm.

"Come and sit down, lad. Come to the fire and take a sup of ale. It'll ease you."

He pushed her off and took a few staggering steps back to the buttress which had been one wall of his home, and was now blackened by the flames which had destroyed it. He leaned his head against the cold stone and so stood.

He might have known. It was all part of his life's pattern; every small mitigation of misery had been immediately followed by some new misfortune. An hour ago he had been given the means to make his family safe and comfortable forever, so by some Devil's logic it was inevitable that now he should have no family.

He thought: She never had anything! And the tears came scalding into his throat and stayed there.

Back by the fire, where the silence continued, though the eating had been resumed, Old Agnes eyed Martin uneasily, and presently made her second imaginative leap in the day.

"Go and tell him you *tried*," she said to Pert Tom. "Tell him you did your best to save them. Show him your hands. It'll make him feel better to think somebody tried. Coming on us all playing the fool and making merry . . . Go on!"

Pert Tom rose and ambled over and stood beside Martin and said, "I did me best. Tried to save 'em. Burnt meself. Look."

Martin neither looked nor answered, but he put out his hand and laid it on Tom's shoulder. The bear-man could feel the ague-like shudder that ran through the other man's body, and, although he felt no guilt in the matter, something of Martin's deep misery was communicated to him.

"Once," he said, "a man that knew a lot about things towd me burning to death worn't as bad as it sound. Talking about holy martyrs, he was. He said the smoke sorta choked you and deadened your senses afore the fire took howd. Reckon thass true, too. They on'y screamed once."

Through the knot of pain in his throat, Martin said, "Pray God that's true." He used the expression from habit, out of earnestness. There *was* no God, or such things could never happen. How *had* it happened?

He forced out the question, adding, "She was always . . . so careful. I'd put in a good hearthstone, and clay round the smoke hole."

"I dunno. I woke up to find it all ablaze. Like I said, I tried, but that was too far gone, then. Burnt meself. Look." Once again he held out his hands. Some of the blisters had broken through hauling the bear's chain all day. All Martin could see was Kate, young and pretty, just as she was when she had come to join him under Tuck's Oak. But he managed to say:

"I'm deep in your debt for that much. Leave me alone now."

Tom went back to the fire.

"He hev took it to heart," he said to Old Agnes. "Pity. I know more'n one man'd think hisself well rid of his wife."

"They was different from most," said the old woman, thinking again of the Trimble.

The fire burned low, presently everyone save Agnes had left it. She took a good drink of her ale to give her heart and then filled the mug again and went to where Martin stood.

"Here," she said, "you drink this. I've had my losses, too, and I know what I'm saying. Ale'll ease you."

He made no move to take the mug, and she went on, "I been with death all my life, Martin, and folks in sorrow. Them that come out of it best take what comfort they can get and turn their minds to other things, even if thass only squabbling over the pickings. You can't bring Kate back, nor go to her till your time come. So you must bear up and comfort yourself."

"She never had anything; nothing but worry and misery and toil. And all my fault."

"Don't talk so daft," the old woman said sharply. "You couldn't help being poor. I never saw a man more ready to turn his hand to anything. I never saw a better husband neither. I've said that a dozen times, seeing you so careful about fetching the water and the firewood and all. Come on now, lad, don't add to your own load." She held the mug to him again. He took it, gulped down the contents, and handed it back.

"Now leave me," he said.

"You come and lay down," she insisted. "You can lay under my rug."

He said, "No," and flung himself down by the black ruin, the grave of all his love. The old woman sat down beside him, took his head in her skinny dirty claws, and eased it into her lap. Her kindness, or the ale—it was a long time since he had drunk anything but water—loosened something in him. Tears came, and with them words, such a flow of words as he was never to loose again. Everything he said was self-reproachful, all concerned with the ruin he had made of Kate's life, how he had promised that she should be safe with him and then robbed her of the only safety possible in this unjust world. Old Agnes hardly listened. She stroked his head and at intervals muttered a soothing word or two. "You couldn't help that, lad." "Aye, I know, I've been through it myself, long ago." "Ah, that's the way it is when you're poor." And once she said, "Dying young's no real hardship. Plucked off the bough, clean and sound. If you hang on, you rot. I've seen 'em, Martin, riddled with rot, stinking like corpses, but still alive. Kate and your little ones are safe from that, they're safe from everything now. We're the ones anything could happen to. We're in worse case."

II

PERT Tom had been born into an age and a community as devoutly mystical, as thoroughly religious, as any in the history of mankind. As a baby he had been baptised, as a child put through his Catechism. As an apprentice the only holidays he had known, the only landmarks in the year's toil, had been the festivals of the Church and the Saints' days. As a soldier even his oaths had been religious, since without belief there can be no blasphemy; and as a bear-leader he had never spent a whole day without passing through a town where a new church was building, or mingling with a group of pilgrims on their way to or from some shrine, or hearing a friar preach, some convent bell ringing.

Of it all he had absorbed and retained only one thing, as primitive and as personal as a savage's devotion to his household idol. Pert Tom believed in St. Ursula. That same fellow-soldier who had given him the information about the painlessness of death by burning had told him that St. Ursula was the patron saint of bears and bear-leaders—an excusable piece of misinformation based upon the likeness of the Saint's name to the generic *ursus,* meaning bear. When a dead man's ring provided Tom with the price of Owd Muscovy, he had thanked St. Ursula and adopted her as his personal deity. The Holy Trinity and the rest of the Saints seemed, like most respectable people, to be against him and his fellow-vagrants, but St. Ursula, whom he visualised as a stout, comfortable, vulgar, tolerant old woman, was firmly on his side. When a cunning idea slid into his head, it came direct from her; any trick he played had her nudging connivance; any luck that came his way was her work. She did not, like the rest of them, set a poor man any impossible standard of virtue. She made no demands. She entirely understood that he had meant Kate no harm and that it had been necessary to lie about the burns on his hands and face. Proof of her understanding and partisanship was there, concrete, indisputable. Look how he had been rewarded!

By April of the next year Pert Tom had some vague conception of just how full and rich his reward was to be, and it occurred to him, for the first time, that he should make a gesture of recognition towards this Saint who had been so overwhelmingly generous to him. So when, with the spring, the fresh tide of pilgrims and tumblers and minstrels and vagrants came pouring into Baildon, he began to look out for an imageseller, and before long found one.

The image-seller was of grave, almost priestly mien. He carried a tray of meticulously fashioned, beautifully coloured little images and a box of holy relics. He wore a hat with cockleshells which indicated—in his case falsely—that he had made the pilgrimage to the Holy Land, and his box contained, amongst other things, a sliver of wood, purporting to be a piece of the true Cross, two thorns from Christ's crown of mockery, and a two-inch square of St. Veronica's handkerchief. Most of the figures on the tray were of the Virgin, the rest were of female Saints after whom girl children were named. What parent, having named a daughter Agnes, could resist buying for her an image of the Saint, with the lamb at her feet?

All the figures were made and fired and coloured at a pottery in Wattisfield, where clay had been dug and worked in Roman times, and they were all made by one old man, who, though he worked quickly enough to keep four salesmen on the road from April to September, as well as supplying two settled dealers, one in Norwich and one in Walsingham, never turned out anything shoddy or slapdash. True, the colours of the Saints' garments were a little gaudy, customers liked them that way, but the tiny faces were virginal and saintly, pearly-pale, and wearing one of two expressions, gently smiling or gently sorrowful.

On this bright April morning, Pert Tom, now a gentleman of leisure, with money in his pocket, halted and looked over the image-seller's stock. He would know his Saint when he saw her, buxom, red-faced, her interest identified by a bear, or perhaps a goad, spiked collar, or muzzle. There was no St. Ursula; the old man at Wattisfield knew his business; little girls in that district were named Catherine, Ethelreda, Winifred, Edith, Agnes, Elizabeth.

"You ain't got what I want," Tom said reproachfully.

"And who was you wanting?"

"St. Ursula."

"Here y'are." He proffered a St. Ethelreda with her daisy emblem.

"That ain't my St. Ursula. She'd hev a bear."

"A what?"

"A bear. Growler. Got a bit of flesh on her bones too."

"Oh. That one! Sold the last a day or two back. Great demand. Bring you good health, good luck. Tell you what, I'll bring one on my next round. I'll be back here for the Lammas Fair. You live here?"

He must ask that, for an unpopular outlandish Saint, with a *bear*, would be quite unsalable, and Pert Tom, though he had now been settled for five months and looked like being settled for the rest of his life, still had a vagrant look, something of the roadster about him.

"I live here. All right. I'll look out for you Lammas time."

There must be some special interest, something extra behind such choosiness, and it might be open to exploitation.

"Of course, if you *liked* and was prepared to pay for it, I could hev her made with a bit of genuine relic to it—strand of her own real hair or something. Only that'd cost you, naturally."

"How much?"

"Two shillings," said the image-seller tentatively, ready to abate the price should this odd customer flinch.

"I could manage that. But I want her *proper*, bear and all. Not one of them poor peaked-looking things."

"You should mind your tongue, remembering who these are. And if you want the hair, then you'll have to pay half down."

Tom paid, calling upon St. Ursula as he did so to witness how heartfelt was his gratitude that he should take such a risk.

Weeks after, on the morning of the Lammas Fair, he took delivery of his order with loud complaints.

The old man in Wattisfield, who was a dedicated artist, had disliked being given definite orders; he had protested that though he knew more about the Saints than any bishop alive he had never heard of a St. Ursula who had dealings with bears. There was only one St. Ursula, a virgin, who with eleven hundred other virgins had been martyred at a place called Cologne by some people called Huns. A virgin Saint, and virgin Saints were all slender, pearly-pale, yellow-haired, gently smiling or gently grave. He'd been making them for years and he *knew*. "Flesh on her bones," the very thought was a heresy.

"But, master, I told him two shillings and he paid one down. I promised him real hair."

Even the artist agreed that such a customer merited some consideration. But when it came to the point he could not bring himself to sacrifice his artistic integrity to the extent of making a Saint as buxom as a washerwoman. He made a solid-looking brown bear to crouch at the hem of the blue robe, and the inclusion of a flaxen curl cut from the head of his youngest granddaughter cost him no twinge of conscience at all. If people were such fools as to believe that their silver could buy hair from the head of a woman dead and buried for hundreds of years, they deserved to be cheated. What could not be cheated, or ever would be, was his own standard of workmanship.

"Poor starved-looking thing! But for the bear I shouldn't've known her," said Tom, handing over his money grudgingly.

Still, there it was, he had bought the best that money could buy, and St. Ursula, who had understood so much, would understand that the false representation was not his fault.

He carried the little image home and set it on a shelf in the room that was his, the first room that he had ever been able to call his own.

"Set you there," he said, "and enjoy all you was so kind as to give me."

He thought of how, in the next dark winter, when the snow fell and the mud lay thick in the roads, the flames would leap on the hearthstone and the howling wind would drop back, baffled by the thick walls and the stout shutters, by the heavy door and deep thatch of the house that was already known as the Old Vine.

No member of any Guild had laid a finger on the house. Martin had planned it and done much of the work, the rest had been done by unemployables like Peg-Leg and Dummy. The monks' Old Vineyard lay outside the town walls where the Guild rules did not hold.

It was a small house, two tiny rooms and a kitchen, but there was as much sound timber in it as in many three times the size. The walls were made of oaken posts, planted at eighteen-inch intervals. Smaller beams were set aslant, joining the bottom of the one post to the top of the next, and the triangles thus formed were divided again, horizontally. The spaces were filled in with laths and the whole plastered over, once on the inside and twice on the outside. A brick chimney in the centre carried the smoke from both rooms and from the kitchen hearth.

"We'll have our own fire," Martin had said, already aware that although he had bonded himself for life to the bear-leader his enforced constant company would be intolerable. All that he had, all that he intended to have in the future, he was prepared to share with Tom, who had tried to save Kate, and with Old Agnes who had tried to ease his hour of misery, but his fire and his bed he must have to himself.

The little house stood at the lowest edge of the vineyard, close to the road, and adjoining it, sharing a wall with Martin's own room, was the new smithy, into which during the next summer season much of Armstrong's and Smithson's trade was to be diverted. Once the house and smithy were up, Martin's gang of cripples and misfits, who would work for any pittance and the certainty of one good meal a day, set to work upon a stable block, built of clod and wattle.

Pert Tom could see the reason for the house and for the forge where Martin was going to earn a living for them both, but the stables puzzled him.

"What d'you want them for?"

"I shall offer stabling, like smith work, at a price those in town can't match. To begin with, that is. Later I shall have horses of my own."

"And what d'you aim to do with them?"

"You'll see."

It was not a satisfactory answer, but one with which Tom must be content. To press a question was useless, although on that November morning when Martin had talked in stony-faced calm with Tom, one of his reasons for offering to take him into partnership was that he needed his company.

"There's not a man in this town that I can ever bring myself to talk to, except in the way of business, and that the least I can; and living that fashion a man could be struck with the dumb madness."

The other reason he had given was that he needed Tom's partnership as a screen for his own sudden possession of money.

"I've got it and I didn't steal it. More than that I can't tell you. Nobody could know what you've earned or saved over the years. It'd look natural enough for you to settle down, build a house and a smithy for me to work in, so that your old age would be taken care of. You could have come into Baildon with some such scheme in mind."

His real, his secret reason, the wish to share with Tom all that he should
have shared with Kate, he never mentioned to anyone. Nor did he ever
put into words his grudge against the town. When, at the beginning of
the second summer season, a deputation of the Smith's Guild waited upon
him and offered him full membership, even some seniority, admission at
once as a master man, if he would cease undercutting prices, he gave
no sign of the bitter, ironic amusement the proposal roused.

"I cannot see how that would work to my advantage," he said.

And this time, though the damage he was doing them was far more
serious than that he had done by shoeing Master Webster's pack ponies,
they hesitated about taking revenge by violence. For this there were two
reasons, he had his gang of riffraff, the poor without a craft, the disabled,
reinforced by tougher elements, an old soldier or two, one of Peg-Leg's
shipmates, a half-crazy priest who had been unfrocked. They owed an almost feudal allegiance to Martin, who allowed them to build another, more
solid Squatters Row at the back of his stables, who paid them when there
was work to be done and fed them between times. And there was also
a strong feeling throughout the town that Pert Tom and Martin, in becoming—as it seemed—tenants of a piece of Abbey land, had moved into
the shadow of the protection of that august authority. It was an authority
with which, at the moment, the townspeople had no wish to try another
throw. After their failure in the previous November the Abbey seemed to
delight in grinding their faces; even the rule concerning the eel-fishing
had now been revived and was strictly enforced. The town as a whole
had been laid under an obligation to pay a large part of the cost of the
new gate and was groaning under the imposition. Not until many
years had passed, and a King set an example, would the people of Baildon
defy their Abbot again.

The suspicion that the Abbey looked with favour upon Pert Tom and
Martin, who had taken a piece of unprofitable land off its hands, was
confirmed by the story of an amazingly out-of-character behaviour upon
the part of the new Cellarer. It concerned a horse, a young, strong horse,
newly broken, and brought to Martin's forge to be shod for the first time.
Its owner, an oldish peasant, was sitting on a bench waiting, when he
clapped his hand to his chest, gave a loud groan, and collapsed. He was
dead when he was picked up. It was evening when his eldest son came
to remove the body, and before he left he said to Martin, slyly:

"Now they'll come round to pick the heriot, and they allust take the
best beast. The horse is the best my father had. Would you let it bide—
just till the dues are paid."

Martin looked the young man in the face.

"Ask me to stable your horse and I agree. I make part of my living by stabling horses."

He had no intention of involving himself, though he would have agreed that the heriot was a peculiarly heartless exaction, for it meant that when a villein's family lost its breadwinner it also lost—to its manorial lord—the most valuable of its possessions.

"Then will you stable my horse until I fetch it and pay what I owe. They'll take the cow for heriot—and she's dry in two teats."

Nine or ten days later the Cellarer rode up on his mule and beckoned Martin from the forge.

"We understand," he said, "that you have in your stable a horse which is, by heriot right, Abbey property."

So the peasant was an Abbey tenant and had underestimated the thoroughness of the system.

"There are several horses in the stable," Martin said.

"This one is young, freshly broken. Its owner died here, suddenly."

"I know the one. I'll fetch it."

"No." The Cellarer held up a plump hand. "In this case, because there was some dispute about the heriot—they offered a cow, fit only for beef—the Abbot himself took an interest. He said that if the horse was with you, it should remain. He has asked from time to time about the Old Vineyard and was interested to hear that you had laid the rest of the field down to barley. He thought the animal would be useful to you."

Every word of this singular conversation was audible to the men waiting on the bench outside the forge and was duly reported in the town. What, men asked themselves, was so virtuous about growing barley? And why had such a valuable present been made to Martin, with no mention of Pert Tom who was understood to be the tenant of the land? When all the questions had been asked, and all the speculations made, and the gossip finished, one thing remained in the memory—the Abbot took an interest in the Old Vineyard. Martin in his upward spiral towards success met, therefore, much less opposition than he might have done.

Part Two

OLD
AGNES'
TALE

I

I NEVER knew my age by yearly reckoning, but a woman's life has mile-stones of its own, and by their measure I was an old woman, and had been for years, when Martin took me to live with him in the house at Old Vine and made me free with all that he had.

Before that, for more years than I can number, I'd lived in Squatters Row, amongst—save for a very few—the scum of the earth. For that I had only myself to blame, in the main. I'd had one knock as a young woman and never pulled myself up again. My family were decent country people, and my mother taught me her midwife's trade. When I married I got a good steady man, one of Sir Stephen Fennel's game wardens out at Ockley, where we had a tidy snug house on the edge of Layer Wood. We'd been married two years, and I'd just started a baby, when he died of a fever and the house was wanted for the man that took over his job.

What with the grief and the baby coming and all, I didn't act sensible; I went running round like a hen with its head off trying to find—not a job, as I should have done—but some little place to put my bits and pieces. That took some doing, and before I'd managed it, along came the bailiff and two men and put my furniture out. I never forgot that day; it was October and pouring wet, and there was my goose-feather bed that my mother had made, the chest my granny had left me, the chair my own father had sat down to die in, and all my other things, set out in the rain and the wind. I was like somebody crazy and stood there crying and howling.

After a bit one of the men came back and said he'd give a shilling for the lot. I took his shilling, got a ride in a wagon to Baildon, and went straight to an alehouse and got drunk. Whether it was that or the jolting in the wagon, I lost the baby the next day; and after that there didn't seem anything to bother for, except to earn enough to keep me in ale. I never tried for a steady job, or to try to get myself a house again.

Whenever I even thought about houses I thought of the one I'd had, and how I'd kept it clean and aired the bed in the sun and polished the chest and the chairs with beeswax. And yet I was a home-keeping body. All those years I never heard of a pig-killing without my fingers itching to do the salting and make the brawn and the sausages; I never smelt bread baking without wishing I'd had a hand in it. I hated the way I lived and the riffraff all round me; but all I ever did was get drunk and forget it. When Martin took his knock, which was so much like mine, the first thing I did was to offer him some ale and a chance to forget.

One knock didn't down him though, and the day came when he looked for me and said Pert Tom the bear-man and he were setting up in business together and had a house nearly built, and they wanted me to go and look after it for them.

I said, "I don't know. I reckon it's too late by many a year. I've lost all my housekeeping skills. And you've lived alongside me long enough to know my weakness for ale."

"I don't ask for skill. All we want is food on the table and a stitch put in now and again. And you're welcome to all the ale you can drink, and to anything else you want."

"You want somebody younger."

"I want you," he said. So I said I'd try.

I hardly knew myself. I found there wasn't a thing I'd forgotten. After all those years, living hand to mouth, I could still do things just as I'd seen my mother do them, and been taught by her to do them. Even her wonderful lardy cake I could make as though I'd been doing it all my days. I made a little garden and grew herbs and peas and beans and bushes of lavender and rosemary. As for the ale, now that I was happy I could take a pot and be content with that, just like anybody else.

It was like being born again, and it was all due to Martin who'd taken me out of the gutter. I'd always liked him; he'd been very generous over the Trimble; and now, what with the liking, and feeling sorry for him and admiring the way he worked and schemed, I came to love him. He seemed like my own, the son I never had.

I had three happy, busy years. Then one morning I noticed that my ankles were swelling. That was how Death first put his finger on my mother. Later would come the blue lips, the shortness of breath. Then I'd be useless. And what would happen to Martin?

There were, I knew, dozens of women who would come and keep house for him and Tom; but there is a difference between keeping house and looking after. I kept house for Tom, I looked after Martin.

If Pert Tom came home soaking wet—as rarely happened, for he could pick his time for going abroad—I'd say to him, "Look at the mess you've brought in!" and let him sit down wet or dry as he chose. If Martin came in wet and would have gone to his room to get busy with his tally sticks or some such, I would say, "Oh no, you don't. You put off your wet things and on with these dry ones, and drink this hot broth before you so much as sit down."

Once—the winter he started his wool-buying, and should have gone to Kersey and had a heavy cold—I took away every stitch of clothing he had, so he had to stay in bed.

I looked ahead and I could even see the new woman making more fuss of Pert Tom than of Martin. For one thing Pert Tom was supposed to be the one with the money, and he was cheerful and joking, while Martin was glum, on the sour side, all wrapped up in whatever it was he was doing, no matter what it was. Martin worked as some men drink or gamble.

To me and to Tom he was civil enough, so long as we didn't take liberties; even Tom held him in some awe. To speak to him on such a private business was taking a liberty, perhaps, still I did it.

I asked him, "Did you ever give a thought to marrying again?"

He gave me one of those black looks of his. They'd come over him since Kate's death. Before that I'd seen him look miserable, or hungry, dog-tired, or angry, but this was something different; there was a sort of power to that look, so that it was as bad as having another man curse you.

"It'd put some purpose to all this work and getting gear together," I went on. "You'll end a rich man, with no one to take after you."

"I'll leave a fund to pay nosy old women to mind their own business."

"I know I'm old, and maybe I'm nosy, but I would like to see you settled. The past is over and done with. A new wife in your bed and a new boy in a cradle and . . ."

He gave me another, even blacker look, one that cut clean through me, turned on his heel, and went out. I never mustered the courage to speak of it again.

Still, there are more ways of catching a cony than running after it shouting. I put my wits to work.

I didn't know any respectable young women, and none ever came to the house. There had been a time, when Martin first looked like being successful, when the townsfolk would have been friendly—they even invited him to join a Guild, after all; but he would have none of that. He never went into anybody's house, and no one visited us. So where to start my matchmaking?

There was Peg-Leg. He was the black sheep of a very respectable family and had a niece, out at Clevely, married to a yeoman farmer that owned his fifty acres; she must have been a very decent sort of woman too, for, riffraff as Peg-Leg had become, she never cut him off. I talked to him frankly, telling him what I was looking out for.

He laughed at first.

"Do the man want a wife he'd find one hisself. He get about, don't he, he must see dozens. He've lived alone three year now, and I reckon he must like it."

"He's never given the matter a thought, being too busy, first with the forge and the stabling and now with all this wool. There's a difference between going out to find yourself a wife and seeing a neat pretty girl doing the jobs about the house, waiting on you and listening when you talk. If we could find the right girl, it'd come over him bit by bit, without any thinking."

"Well, maybe. I'll hev a talk to Winnie about it, next time I go over."

But I hadn't got endless time; I couldn't wait.

"I tell you what I'll do, Peg-Leg; I'll give you the money to buy yourself a ride, and to take your niece a present."

"Where'd you get it from?"

"The housekeeping. I handle all." I was proud of that.

"All right then. Only don't set your heart on it too much. You know the saying about the horse and water."

A day or two later he set off for Clevely and he must have been on his very best behaviour, for he stayed ten days, and when he came back he was as pleased as if he'd thought of the whole idea himself.

His niece's husband had a sister named Jennie, eighteen years old, and, said Peg-Leg, as pretty as a hedge rose as well as being skilled in the house. Peg-Leg had explained the situation, and the girl and her family were willing. So I said to Martin that the work was getting a bit much for me and that Peg-Leg had a niece who would come and help me.

"Where'd she sleep?"

"With me. There's room." My bed was in a kind of alcove in the kitchen, the chimney stuck out and there was just room for a bed between it and the wall.

"Not much room. If that was shored up stronger," he said, pointing up to a kind of wide shelf that ran across one end of the kitchen, and was used to store cheese and bacon and onions—all of which we used a lot of, feeding so many men their dinners.

"All right. Maybe that would be best. Thank you," I said.

So presently Jennie came; and she was as pretty as a hedge rose, and almost as quiet. Asked a flat question, she'd say yes or no as the case might be; and passed the salt she'd say, "Thank you." For a sensible young man with the itch in his blood that would have been enough; but being so quiet and shy made her seem younger than she was, while Martin was years older than his age. Across the gap he only gave her the kind of attention he'd have given a child.

There was a fair while she was with us and I made an effort and went into town and bought her a headdress, the prettiest I ever saw, made of stuff so thin it was like cobwebs on a frosty morning, all draped over two pointed horns. It'd make her look older, I thought, and it couldn't help but be noticed. It would have made any girl prink and toss her head and flutter her eyelashes and *be* noticed; but Jennie wore it as though it were a woollen hood to keep out the cold.

After six weeks I knew it was hopeless and sent her home. Then Peg-Leg said there *was* another girl he knew, a cousin of Jennie's, not so pretty, rather older, but lively. He'd seen her at his niece's too, and she was enough to make a cat laugh at times.

Her name was Kate. I said we must change that, and she was agreeable, she liked being called Kitty. Her skin was sallow and her hair the colour of mud, but she was cheerful and amusing, and every bit as good in the house as Jennie. Even Martin smiled at her sometimes, with the smile which came rarely nowadays and always looked as though it hurt him somewhere deep inside. However, after a bit he began to make excuses not to sit down at table with us; he'd say he was busy and would have a piece in his hand. I got tired of having Peg-Leg sidle up to the door and ask how things were going, when nothing was going at all; and also I didn't trust Pert Tom; all the little airs and graces, the jokes and the glances that were wasted on Martin, found a ready mark with the bear-man, so in the end I thought it'd save trouble if Kitty went home too.

Tom, who was sharp enough in his way, had seen what I was up to. "You daft owd besom," he said. "Don't you know when you're well off? If Martin got married, his wife'd look round your greasy pans and show you the door."

"That wouldn't matter to me," I said, thinking of my legs and the way the swelling was creeping up. "I want to leave him *with* somebody before I die."

"I'm here, ain't I?"

"Fine help you are. You'd watch him work himself to death and never do a hand's turn."

"You can't say that. Didn't I take Owd Muscovy and my whistle, and go round gathering the crowd and yelling my lungs out about the cheap smith work and stabling to be found at the Owd Vine?"

"So you did. Three summers back. Just to get him more work than three men should've tackled!"

There was no love lost between Pert Tom and me. For one thing, after that first night I never believed that he burnt himself trying to save Martin's wife and children. I noticed next morning that the bear was burnt too; and it certainly hadn't tried to save anybody. Tom said it to boast and be admired, and it had paid him well. It seems that he'd saved a bit of money, not a lot, but enough to start a business with, and he wanted somebody to start up with that was capable of earning him a comfortable living for the rest of his life. Martin was just the man. It amused me, though, to see that, despite it being Pert Tom's money, Martin all along had stayed top dog, mainly on account of those black looks of his. Even while Martin was working from dawn to dusk in the forge and Tom was just idling about, Tom was never master. And later, when Martin went into the wool trade and had smiths working for him in the forge, and began to call himself with two names, Martin Reed, and was being called Master, the bear-man stayed plain Pert Tom.

Well, all I could do, having tried my hand at matchmaking and being acquainted with no other respectable young women, was to pray; and since by that time I couldn't get to church, the best I could do was to steal into Pert Tom's room now and again and painfully go down on my knees before the Virgin that he had there, calling her St. Ursula. I knew better; her cloak was true Mary blue, and she had the face of the Holy Mother. The bear was just there to show that even a savage beast could be tame in Her presence. At least, that is how I thought and believed while I was doing my praying that somehow or other Martin should find him a good steady wife that he could be fond of. Later on, when I saw what we got, I changed my mind, and I reckon Tom was right, that *was* St. Ursula and I'd annoyed her by calling her out of her name.

We got to June again and Martin was riding about, buying up fleeces. He'd been away two days and nights and was coming home for supper. I'd got a fowl on the spit, peas in the pot, fresh-baked bread, and a dish of little strawberries I'd bought from a hawker. Pert Tom was fidgeting about, wanting to begin, saying Martin had changed his mind and wouldn't be back that night; and I said I wouldn't cut the fowl and let the good juice run, just for him. It was well on into dusk and I'd lighted the candles when we heard the horse come in at the back and trot to the stable. Then we heard Martin, walking slowly.

"He's met with a mishap, or he's ill," I said; and I shuffled over to the door and opened it just as he got there. He'd got his arm round what I thought was a child and was helping her along. They were both smeared with mud and dripping with water.

"Oh, what is it? What happened?" I asked, the foolish way you do when surprised.

"Let's get in," he said. I pushed a stool close to the fire and he set her down. Her long black hair reached to the edge of the stool and water dripped from it to the hearthstone.

"I'll see to her," I said. "You go and put on some dry things. Tom, brighten the fire and mull some ale." It wasn't a cold night, fortunately, but the girl's teeth were chattering and Martin was all goose pimples.

I threw a blanket from my bed over the girl and stripped her, no hard task, she had on only a bodice and a skirt, such stuff and colours as no decent woman would wear. The bodice was made of red silk, frayed and worn web-thin in places; the skirt was all striped with different colours and had holes in it you could put your hand through. My work as midwife and layer-out made me knowledgeable about bodies, but I never, in all my time, saw a woman quite like this one. She was so thin, but not wasted thin, sinewy rather, square in the shoulder and narrow in the flank, more like a boy, and yet very dainty. And her legs, in proportion to her body, were the longest I ever saw.

I had a queer fancy, when I'd got her stripped and was rubbing her down, that this was the kind of body angels had perhaps, under the long robes, a body not tied down to any one sex.

At the same time I had a great dislike for touching her. I couldn't think why—for except for the river mud she was clean, cleaner than most folks I've had to handle. But she had the effect on me that mice have on some people, or cats, or harmless frogs. In the first instant, faced with a drenched woman, I'd snatched the blanket from my bed, but once it had been over her, touching her here and there, I knew I couldn't sleep with it again until it had been washed and hung in the air several times. I put my second shift on her—I was so well provided for these days I had three, just like a bride, and my best dress I gave her, too, knowing that I should never like them again. Shoes I couldn't lend her, mine were too big, and there was no need. I doubt if she'd ever worn shoes in her life; her feet were as hard as horn and so high-arched she could have stood on a good-sized pullet's egg without crushing it.

Martin came back into the kitchen, dressed dry and with his hair standing on end where he had rubbed it.

"All right now?"

"I am—thanks to you—very well."

Her voice wasn't like a woman's either; it was deep, like a low note on a fiddle and she certainly wasn't from our part of the country.

Pert Tom poured out the hot, spicy-smelling ale, and the girl took her cup without saying "Thank you," and sat hugging it to her chest and staring into the fire. Martin took his and sat at his own place at the table.

"Well, what happened?" Tom asked. "Why was you both so wet?"

They seemed each to wait to let the other answer, and both spoke together when they did speak.

"I fell . . ." the girl began, just as Martin said, "I fished . . ." He stopped and allowed her to finish.

She lifted one long thin hand and laid it to her flat wet hair.

"I am doing my hair, making the water my looking glass, and I fall in."

"And you fished her out?" Tom said to Martin.

"That's so. Is supper ready?"

"And waiting," I said. "Pull that stool in."

"You are inviting me?"

"You're welcome to your supper and a bed," Martin said.

"Is very kind."

"Where did you fall in the water?" Tom asked.

"Some place," the girl said.

"Flaxham St. Giles, by the mill," Martin put in.

"Where's your home?"

She hunched her small square shoulders. "Anywhere. Everywhere. I am on the roads and I make my living . . . Oh!" She dropped her knife and turned to Martin and said in the most heartbroken way, "My tambourine. I have lost my tambourine."

"Don't fret about that. We'll see about it in the morning. And if the worst comes to the worst, we'll get you a new one."

"Is very kind."

Pert Tom, who had travelled the roads himself, began to ask her questions about this person and that—a stilt-walker, a tumbler called Boneless, a man who swallowed knives. Sometimes she would say, "Yes, I know him," or, "He was at York last summer," but when he pressed for details her answers were vague and unsatisfactory.

"Mostly I am alone. It is better so," she said.

"And if you'd just escaped drowning by a hairsbreadth, Tom, probably some things would slip your memory," Martin said.

"Now somebody once towd me that when you drowned you see your whole life spread out like a picture. I allust wondered if that was true. Is it?" Tom asked.

"I do not know. I saw only a hawthorn tree. So pretty, green and white in the sun. I think to myself: Is Heaven, after all. Then here I am, being slapped in the face, very wet and cold. Sir," she turned to Martin, "I do not wish you to think me ungrateful, but I was . . . Oh well, it is over now."

When she said that Martin looked at her with a sudden, sharp interest, such a look as I'd never seen him turn on anyone, not even his Kate.

You'd look that way, maybe, if you were in foreign parts across the sea and suddenly heard somebody speak in your own tongue.

He stopped eating and seemed as though he was going to say something, but he didn't; the habit of easy talk had gone from him in these last years.

I thought over the words again, and couldn't find anything in them. This was June, the hawthorns would be in flower, and most likely the last thing she saw when she fell in the water was just such a green and white tree. And if it wasn't the words she said, it must had been her looks that suddenly made him come to life that way. So then I took another look at her.

I know that men and women see things differently, and I know that I was already against her, but even so she had no beauty, no prettiness. Her face was too thin, all mouth and eyes, and the eyes not set in right. Or at least it looked so. It looked as though her cheeks had been pushed up, leaving hollows where flesh should have been and a heap of flesh up under the eyes, shoving them out of shape. Her skin was all over alike, the colour of porridge. Her mouth, I grant, was as red as a berry. I looked at this face and I remembered what I'd seen of the almost breastless, unfemale body, and I shuddered as I sat there.

Pert Tom, as soon as he had supped, got up and went off for what he called his "last breath of air." That meant Dummy's daughter, not the crooked one, the younger, with the red hair, a very forward little wench, bound for a bad end.

Martin sat on at the table, and again looked as though he was going to say something, and finally did.

"Agnes will look after you. Good night," was what he got out. Then he went to his room and we two were left.

I didn't want her to help me clear the table. I knew that if she lifted the loaf and put it in the crock, I should not want to eat another slice of it. I didn't want her to touch anything; and that puzzled me, life had long ago knocked any fancifulness out of me. But there it was.

I said, "The bed's up there," and I pointed. "And the privy is outside, sharp to the left."

She went out and came in again and climbed the little ladder. I noticed that her toes curled round the staves, like fingers, and that seemed so unnatural that it gave me a shuddering grue once more. Her wet clothes lay on the floor, she'd never thought to hang them out to dry. I did that, because I didn't want her to have the excuse for waiting for them in the morning. For a little while they smelt of wet stuff drying, and then they smelt of wild thyme. The scent reminded me of the sheep run at Horringer, where I had lived as a girl.

In the morning she came down and picked up her clothes and in a minute was down again, wearing them.

"A comb," she said. "Could you lend me? That I lost too."

I had a comb, a good one, not a snaggy-toothed wooden one, a fine bone comb that Martin had bought for me one day when a pedlar came to the door. I handed it to her unwillingly, thinking: Another thing spoilt, I shall never really like it again. She ran it through her hair, which had dried out, black and glossy as a blackbird's wing, but almost as flat as when it was wet. She didn't plait it or knot it, just left it hanging, and that, for some reason, annoyed me, as well as seeing her with my comb, so I said:

"That skirt of yours isn't decent. Why don't you mend it?"

"I cannot sew."

"Rubbish. Any woman with hands and eyes can sew. What can you do?"

"I can play my tambourine. And I can cook a hedgehog."

"A hedgehog! That's no meat for Christians."

She made no answer, but went and stood by the door, looking out at the morning. I stirred the porridge, set out the bread, and drew the breakfast ale. Martin came in from the yard and stood by her in the doorway.

"Did you sleep well?" he asked her.

"Oh yes. Is so long since I sleep in a bed."

He came in and stood by the board, and I put the porridge bowl before him. He always took his breakfast standing. She stayed by the door. After a spoonful or two he said, "Have you had your breakfast?"

She turned around and leaning against the doorpost laughed.

"Once a day is for eating—with people like me." She smacked her flat stomach with her hand. "Get into bad habits and expect to be fed all the time. No!"

Martin, whose very smile had grown into something painful, actually laughed.

"One indulgence couldn't hurt. Still, please yourself. Now, where do I look for this tambourine? Where exactly did you . . . fall into the water?"

She squinted up her eyes so that they looked more misshapen than ever. "The name of the place? I do not know. There is a bridge."

"Stone or wood?"

"Stone. Two arches."

"Upriver from Flaxham. That'd be Marly?"

"Perhaps. After the bridge is a place for dipping water and there is my tambourine."

I knew that on this day Martin had planned to go to Hedingham, and that was nowhere near Flaxham or Marly way. Wasting his time, I thought.

"Most like it has been picked up by now," I said.

"I do not think anybody will do that," she said.

"I'll go and have a look. And if I can't find it, you shall have a new one."

"It belonged to my mother and I have just bought it new ribbons."

When he had gone I said to her, "Would it have hurt you to say thank you? Here's a busy man going out of his way, promising you new if he can't find your old—and that is most unlikely. And you can't even thank him!"

The bulges under her eyes lifted, squeezing her eyes as she smiled.

"You should know. You are a woman. If you thank a man, he thinks you are in debt to him and so he looks for payment."

"Not him," I said. "He's the kindest and best-hearted . . . This whole place is built up on his good heart, lame folks and daft ones and people in trouble or disgrace, people nobody else wanted." I thought of Dummy and Peg-Leg and Peter Priest, and a dozen more. Me too.

She said, "People nobody else will want, they are very cheap."

Something in my head went "snap" like an overblown bladder. The shocking part of it was that just for a second I thought: That is *true!* Just as he made that tidy little hut in Squatters Row, out of nothing, out of stuff other people would chuck away or overlook, so he's made all this out of human rubbish. Even Pert Tom's savings had been *used*, and Pert Tom so handled that he daren't bring his baggage into the house.

But that only lasted a second; it was like some of the things you see when you're very drunk; they seem very real and you're scared. Then they're gone. And that was gone.

I said, "I suppose you will have to wait to see if he finds your tambourine; and if you want to eat midday there'll be food here, but I'd thank you to get out of my kitchen."

She went off, and I began on my day's work, which was preserving gooseberries. Our young bushes were in full fruit that year, and some of Dummy's children had gathered them and picked off the tops and tails. I scalded the jars and packed them in close, got the cloths soaking in the mutton fat for the covers, and more mutton fat melted to pour over. Then Pert Tom, who was a slugabed in the mornings, came ambling in for his breakfast.

"Where's Martin's drowned cat?" he asked.

"Out. I'm busy. I didn't want her hanging round me."

"I reckon you'd better get used to it. I've missed my mark if he don't take up and marry her."

"Marry her. Rubbish!" But another overblown bladder had gone "snap" in my head.

"You ask yerself. Take the way he looked at her, promised her a new tambourine if hers was lost—and him so mean he didn't even hev a pair of gloves till you give him a pair for Christmas. You couldn't've missed *that*. If you ask me, she's cut to his measure, all skin and bone and grief, somebody to feel sorry for, just like his other one."

I dished him out the heat-up porridge.

"You knew Kate, then?"

"Kate?"

"His wife."

"This porridge is burnt, tastes awful. Kate, was that her name? I saw her, yes. I saw her go into the hut—like I say, all skin and bone and grief. And now he've got hisself just such another, after waiting so long." He laughed and pushed his porringer away. "Still, maybe she can cook."

"She can," I said tartly. "She can cook a hedgehog."

"A hedgehog? That ain't Christian food," he said, exactly as I had done. "Thass real Romany."

"And what's that?"

"Oh, foreign. Out of Pharaoh's Egypt, some say. There's one or two on the roads, but decent people don't hev nowt to do with them. They're heathen. They don't even lay together like other people, they do it cutting their thumbs and letting the blood mix."

"The tales you tell!"

"I only pass on what I hear tell myself. And of course if she is Romany I shall miss my mark, 'cause she couldn't marry him. They ain't allowed to stay in one place more'n a moon month; if they do they die."

He finished his breakfast and went off, it being Wednesday, to idle away his time looking round the market and sitting in one alehouse after another, listening to and spreading gossip. He didn't come in for dinner, nor did the girl, so I fed those men who were on wages-and-dinner terms, finished my gooseberries, and sat down to rest myself before starting supper. I'd hardly set down before Pert Tom came in, full of ale and something else. I could see before he opened his mouth that he had a fine tidbit to tell me.

He looked round the kitchen and up in the loft.

"Is she about?"

"No. You can see for yourself."

He pulled a stool near me.

"Now you listen to this. Know what we've got in the house now? A witch, no less!"

"Rubbish," I said, partly because his tales were so farfetched and partly because, like almost every other old woman who was poor and looked a bit wild, I'd had the word "witch" flung at me in my time. Nevertheless, when he brought out the word I thought: That's it! That accounts for the way I feel about her, not wanting her to handle my things, not wanting to touch her.

"Rubbish away. Only tell me this, where'd Martin say he found her?"

"Flaxham. By the mill."

"Right. And what lay upriver from Flaxham. Maybe you don't know."

"As it happens I do. A place called Marly."

"Right again. Well, Tuesday morning, yestiddy that is, a Marly man heard his dog barking early in the morning; he look out and what do he see but a young woman with long black hair raiding his hens' nest. He see her take two eggs, one she stuck in the front of her dress, the other she kept in her hand. Jest as he was he run out and ask for his eggs back. She say, 'Take it,' and give him the one in her hand. He say she've got another, she say she h'ain't, and he say all the time he can see it bulging out inside her bodice. So he go to take it, as who wouldn't? And she say to him, 'Don't you put your hand on me,' she say, 'if you do you'll be very sorry.' But he don't take no notice, he take the egg instead. And then what happen?"

"His arm dropped off at the shoulder."

"You're a funny owd crone, ain't you? No, what happen is that he go out to the hayfield and afore he've been there a quarter hour somebody unhandy with a sickle cut off two fingers for him. Now thass no good saying 'Rubbish,' the man that towd me had jest brought the poor man to the Abbey Infirmary; they'd stopped the bleeding with hot tar, but he was swelling up cruel. Only, here's the point to this tale. Everybody in Marly turned out to chase the witch, and by the bridge they found her. They tied her skirt round her knees and chucked her in to see do she sink or swim. And she swum! Straight downriver towards Flaxham, this chap say, sailing like a swan. Now do you believe me?"

I did. It all fitted in, even to her saying that nobody would have picked up her tambourine from the river bank. Of course not. Nobody would want to touch her gear. Just as, in my unknowing way, I hadn't wanted to touch anything she'd handled.

"Yes. For once I do," I said. "We must tell Martin."

"I can't wait to see his face. Fancy him swallowing that yarn about using the water for a looking . . ."

He broke off and turned his head sharply and looked towards the door. I saw his colour change and he crossed himself openly. I turned, too, and there she was, leaning against the doorpost and holding something in her hands. I slipped one thumb over the other in the shape of the Cross, under cover of the table.

She said, "To wagging tongues things sometimes happen, too." As she spoke she walked in and laid what she held on the table. It looked like a ball of clay, about the size of your head, loosely covered with dock leaves.

I've seen some frightened people, but seldom anybody worse scared than Pert Tom. He jumped up and blurted out, stammering and blinking, "I shan't say anything. I shan't mention it," and he hurried into his room, where, I knew, he would ask his St. Ursula to protect him.

The girl said to me, "You cross your thumbs, but you will tell Martin what you hear?"

"If my tongue still wags, yes. I'm so old that what happens to me doesn't matter any more."

She sat down by the table and folded her arms.

"Is all nonsense, of course. Alone, on the road, as I am most times, a woman must take care. The tale is a lie. Partly. Was Monday evening, not Tuesday morning; and there was no egg. You understand me. No egg. Me, looking for sleeping place, and the man, like all men. You should know, once a man has his hand *here*, who is safe? So his fingers are chopped. Every day, some place, fingers are chopped." She leaned sideways, still with her arms folded, and laughed. "If I could say a thing and make it *be*, I am not wasting my time chopping fingers. No. I would say: Let me dance like my mother! Oh, if that could be!" She sat up straight again and threw back her head, and for a moment in the stuffy kitchen it seemed as though the wind blew on her face.

I was old, and since I had come to live at the Old Vine I'd had a quiet life, nothing much to think about except whether to serve beef or mutton. So now, with so much, all at once, all strange and different, I was confused. Later, I thought, later, in the quiet of my bed, I'll think it all over. Just for the moment I wanted something real and firm to seize upon. And there was this bundle on the table.

"What is that?"

"Is a hedgehog. Is not food for Christians you say, so I will show you."

"Oh no. You're cooking no hedgehogs here. Not in my pots."

"He is needing no pot. He has his own. See." She picked up the bundle and stripped off the dock leaves. "We bury him, so, in the hot ash, and he makes his own pot. When he is ready we crack him and his prickles all come away with the pot."

She buried the thing at the fire's edge, pushed it inwards a little, and pulled a log over it. As she straightened up, Martin, back much earlier than usual, walked in, holding the tambourine.

"Here you are," he said.

She swooped forward and took it from him, the bells jingled and jangled, the ribbons, red and yellow and blue, green and purple and pink, just like the stripes of her ragged skirt, fluttered and shook.

"Oh," she said, "is so *so* kind! My tambourine." She drummed on it lightly with the fingers. "Not spoilt. I was afraid, out on the grass . . . Is good. Now, after supper, I will dance for you."

Pert Tom had to be called to supper, and came out like a dog with a bad conscience. Ordinarily after market day he would chatter on, and Martin would grunt and show little interest until Tom told of some mishap that had befallen some Baildon man, and then he would look up and grunt in another tone. But tonight Tom was silent, every now and again looking at the girl and, if he happened to catch her eye, shake his head a little and make a secret face, trying to reassure her that his tongue would never wag.

Presently Martin said, "What's the matter, Tom? No gossip going round today?"

"Not a thing. Not a thing," Tom said and bent over his food. He was eating what I had cooked, but Martin was eating the hedgehog.

She'd cracked off the clay, and I admit that the meat left inside looked clean enough and smelt very tasty; but I couldn't bring myself to try it, and Tom was too scared.

Martin said, "I will. Come to think of it, if nobody had ever tried anything new there'd be precious little to eat."

As he ate he praised it, and I tried not to mind or be jealous. After all, I longed and prayed that something would happen to make him shake off the dead past and come alive again, and if it took a wild thing out of the woods with a tambourine and a hedgehog to do it, who was I to complain? I could only hope that she would rouse him, make him feel that there was something left in life besides hard work and making money, and then go off and leave him to take up with a decent woman.

All through supper she sat, looking at the tambourine and now and again touching it. As soon as the meal was over she jumped up and asked Tom and Martin to move the table. They began to push it towards the hearth, but she said:

"No, no. The other way. Is better the light behind me."

When the space was cleared and we were gathered at the other end, she walked down towards the fire, keeping close to the wall and sidling along. Then she stood still, like a cat about to make a spring. And then, with a shake of the tambourine and a little hoarse cry, she leaped out into the centre of the space and began to dance.

I've seen many dancing girls in my day. In the old times, in Squatters Row, in a good summer I've known as many as four be there all at once, and late at night they'd dance, not for pay, but to outdo each other. Some were good and some were bad, but the best of them *was* only a girl dancing when all was said and done. This was something different. Dancing she really could cast a spell. What but magic could make that ragged gaudy old skirt shake out into blurred soft colours like a rainbow or the sunlight on the spray over a weir? How else could she move so that it was all movement, a bird in flight, a deer leaping, a tree swaying in the wind? The music was magic too, for a tambourine has but two sounds, the thrum on the skin and the jingle of the bells; in her hands it made real music in which there was a rush of the wind, the birds' calling, even the solemn chant of the Church.

As long as it lasted you could only sit and stare and wonder. Even I, an old woman, with all my fires quenched, could feel again the stir and the ache, not in the flesh, or for it, but for something more, that something which, when you are young, you think lies round the next corner, and when you are old you know you missed because it never could be there. Here, just for once, in the homely kitchen, against the light of the dying fire, it all was held out for us.

When she stopped it was like waking from a dream in which you are warm and full-fed, to find yourself cold and hungry again. We all three let out our breath in a great sigh.

She went and stood by the wall, breathing quickly and lightly. Then I could move my eyes. And just for once I saw Martin's stern thin face and Pert Tom's fat stupid one wearing the same look of naked lust.

The girl spoke first.

"You like?" She lowered the hand which held the tambourine and it gave a little tinkle, like the echo of the question. She dropped against the wall, hunching her shoulders.

"By my mother I dance like a pig. When my mother danced, when she ceased, men wept with the pain of it."

Pert Tom got up and blundered out of the house, leaving the door open; the cool air, faintly scented with hay, flowed in.

All very well for him, I thought; he can go and find his red haired baggage; Martin has his empty room, with tally sticks for company.

But Martin stood up and said, "You know, you've never told us your name."

"Is Magda."

"Magda." He repeated the name which was as strange as everything else about her, as though it pleased him. He said, "We could do with a breath of air, too." He went towards the door, and it seemed to me that he moved more lightly, more freely, leaning less to his limp than usual. She followed him, I thought unwillingly.

THAT evening they weren't out an hour, all told. I was just in bed when they came in quietly, said good night, and went to their separate beds. I thought to myself: Well, that's over; he's had his will of her and proved to himself that he can so far forget Kate as to go with another woman, and now if she'll just take herself off, everything will be all right.

In the morning, quite early she did go off, with her tambourine; but she was back, just before supper.

"So you've come back," I said.

"You think I will not?" She squinted her eyes at me. "Martin, he is the master here, is it not? He says I am welcome. Tonight I shall dance again."

"Dancing! That's all you think about."

"Yes and yes and yes. I have danced today. Look." She held out her long hand and showed me some coins in its palm. "I am not needing it, no supper to pay for. You can have it." She walked up to me and tried to put the money in my hand. I backed as though she had offered me something red-hot.

"I don't want your money. Save it and buy yourself a shift!"

She surprised me by giving one of the deepest, heaviest sighs I ever heard a human being give, though I'd heard the like from donkeys, already overladen when something else was added to their load.

"A shift, a petticoat, and shoes. And every night the certain supper and the bed. It is much."

"What are you talking about?"

"Things to *have*. Me, I have wanted only to *be*."

"Be what?"

"Such good dancer as my mother."

I said, almost against my will, "I fail to see how she could have been better than you were last night. I've seen a lot of dancers in my time, but I never saw anybody dance like you."

Something lit up in her face; she flung herself at me and would have hugged me, but again I backed away, this time almost into the fire.

"Don't," I said.

"You are not liking to be touched. Me, too, but with men only."

"Then you go the wrong way about," I said. "Any man, watching you dance, is bound to want to get his hands on you."

"But I am not dancing for men to desire me. I am not dancing to be

paid. Enough for supper and new ribbons for my tambourine sometimes. And now a new comb."

"Then why do you do it?"

"Because . . ." She paused, smiled, shook her head. "There is no because. To dance I am born, so I dance."

"To me that sounds daft."

"Must everything be because? There is a poppy, very red, beside the
road for just one day. Because? Is a red poppy. No good for eating. You
pluck him, he falls to pieces. Is enough for a poppy just to *be* a red poppy.
And so with me."

I couldn't find an answer except—poppies aren't people and people
aren't poppies—and that, because it sounded quite as daft as anything
she had said, I wouldn't say.

That evening I didn't stay to see her dance. I went and had a little
gossip with Peg-Leg. We spoke of this and that, and of the girl who'd
come into the house, and I mentioned what Pert Tom had said about
Martin being likely to marry her.

"He might at that," Peg-Leg said. "Once I sailed with a man that
had a monkey; he was more set on that monkey than most men are on
their wives. Then it died and his heart broke. A month or two after we
sailed into Tangier where there was plenty monkeys, cheap. I said to
him, 'Whyn't you get yourself a new monkey?' He turned white as a
sheet and he said, 'I'll never have another monkey as long as I live.' But
. . ." Peg-Leg paused and wagged a finger at me. "We went into Naples
and there on the quay was a cat, terrible looking, bones sticking out
and mangy all over. He took to that, and within a week was as fond
of it as he had been of his monkey. See? We did no good with Jennie and
Kitty, they was decent, home-keeping little bodies, they just called his
Kate to mind. This, by all accounts, is quite another pair of shoes."

"What do you know of her, barring what I've told you?"

"I seen her," he said simply. "And I was told she was dancing and
prancing and shaking a tambourine in the market place today. Can you
see Kate doing that?"

"I wouldn't mind," I said, "if I thought she'd make him happy."

"I don't reckon," Peg-Leg said slowly, "that men look to women to make
them *happy*. Martin had Kate and they got on better than most, but when
they wouldn't have him in the Guild, and then, later on, you remember
when he broke his leg and Webster sacked him—you couldn't say he was
happy, could you? Holy Mother, he was miserable as sin." He broke off
and rapped his wooden leg with his knuckles. "Meaning no offence, Agnes, you having been a woman once, women set theirselves a bit too high.
Could somebody come along to me and ask which would I rather, the

Queen of Sheba in my bed, or my leg back and be at sea again, I know which I'd say."

"Ah, that is because you're old."

"Old! God's blood, how old do you think I am? I'm forty. I'd just turned twenty-four when I was beached."

I'd always thought of him as being an old man.

"Don't you go fretting yourself over Martin," he said. "He's got his business. All he needs now is a boy to bring up in the trade, and he can as easy get that out of a slut as out of a mim little wench that couldn't say boo to a goose."

That at least was true, and I felt my heart lighten a bit.

"Maybe I'd better start fretting about myself for a change," I said. "Peg-Leg, if Martin should marry her, I couldn't stay in the house. The other night she brought in a hedgehog, and I said she wasn't cooking it in *my* pots. They'll be *her* pots. Everything will be hers, to use and handle. I couldn't bear it. Could I come and turn in with you for a bit?"

"I reckon so." He looked round the snug little hut. "Since I took up work again, I've let my mending go." Like all sailors he'd been handy with a needle. "You could stitch me up. And it'd be nice to find the fire going when I got home. You'd have to bring your own bed."

So I'd found myself a hole to run to if the moment of need should come.

It came, three or four days later, when Martin said to me, in his abrupt way, "I'm going to marry Magda."

"I hope you'll be happy," I said; and I meant it. "There's one thing you should know, Martin—or maybe she told you. . . ."

"What?"

"They say she's a witch, and was being swum that day you found her."

"I knew that. As soon as I'd choked the water out of her I cut the cord. I'd seen one swum before."

"And you don't mind?"

"I don't care what she is. She's the only woman . . . Who told you it was being said?"

"Pert Tom."

"You can tell him to keep his mouth shut."

"Oh, she did that, threatened to make his tongue drop out or something."

Martin laughed. I thought to myself: Peg-Leg can say what he likes, a woman can make a man happy or miserable; already Martin is a different man.

"There's one other thing. I told you some time back this was all getting

too much for me. You remember? I think now would be the time for me
to go. When's the wedding to be?"

"This day three weeks."

"Well, now, there's Dummy's Mary. She's crooked, but she's as strong
as a donkey for all that, and she often hangs around watching me work
and helping a bit. If I got her in and showed her how things should be,
then there'd be a new mistress and a new maid, and that is the best way."

"Maybe. Where'd you go?"

"I should go and look after Peg-Leg."

"I always meant you to end your days by my fire, with your feet under
my table, Agnes. But then I never thought . . ."

"But for you Peg-Leg wouldn't have a roof or a fire, so it comes to
much the same thing."

"In a way, I suppose. And we'd send your food across."

Stuff she'd have clawed over.

"I'd sooner manage on my own."

"Please yourself. You can have what money you want."

"That's kind. And any day I feel up to it, I'll go in the shed and pick
wool for a spell to help earn . . ."

He gave me a very black look and said, "If you think that's easy!"
He swung on his heel and limped away. I thought for a moment that
he had seen through my excuse for leaving and was annoyed, yet he
hadn't been earlier when I said I was going. It took me a moment or two
to realise that Kate had picked wool at Webster's, and this was no moment to remind him of her.

Pert Tom had his excuse for getting out all ready to his hand. All
these years he'd held onto his bear and been fairly regular about feeding
it and putting it through its tricks. Once, when he was grumbling about
what the animal cost to keep, I asked him why he didn't sell it.

"Easy come, easy go," he said, "and maybe one of these days Martin'll
bite off more than he can chew. First he hev a forge, then hev a row
of stables, then he hev a wool business. Grant he've been lucky, but build
a thing too high and it'll topple over. If it do, then out on the road we
go, Owd Muscovy and me, and no worse off than we was."

"Except that you'd have lost your savings." We'd been given to understand that it was Pert Tom's money that had started the business in the
first place.

Pert Tom laughed. "Ah yes, them savings! Well, they wasn't all that
much, and I've had years of soft living. And shall do, till Martin overreach
hisself."

"If you think he's overreaching himself, you should warn him. You're supposed to be his partner."

"I hate wasting me breath," he said. But he had held onto the bear; and when he heard about the marriage being so near he said to Martin, "I allust promised meself one more summer on the road, and if I don't go soon I shall be too owd. And you'll like the place to yourselves to start off with."

To me he said, "I give it a month, but a month alongside her is more'n I can manage. Half the time I'm frit of her and the other half I'm itching arter her, and I don't know which is worst."

"What'll you do if it lasts more than a month?"

"It can't. I towd you, they can't stay in one place more'n a month without sickening. I shall be back in five-six weeks, according to the weather, and you'll see, she'll be gone."

"Daft talk," I said. "In five-six weeks she may be three weeks gone in another fashion. I surely hope so."

He didn't even stay for the wedding, so he missed the feast Martin gave to everybody on the place. He had an ox roasted in the yard, and there was all the ale we could drink and plenty over. Even Martin, who'd never, in all the time I'd known him, taken a drop too much, was tipsy as soon as anyone.

Magda, for the wedding, had a dress, very costly, of crimson silk so dark it was almost black, she had shoes on her feet and her hair knotted up and fastened with a pair of silver pins. That way, she looked ordinary and decent, her skin very sallow between the dark of the dress and the dark of her hair; and she had none of a bride's happiness. She looked so downcast that I wondered if the shoes were causing her pain.

We put them to bed in proper style, and I myself put the salt and the handful of barley at the four corners, to make sure that they would be fruitful.

Peg-Leg was easygoing and I was comfortable enough with him, but for me everything seemed out of joint. I missed seeing Martin and seeing to him, feeling as mothers do when their sons marry and move away. I got into the habit of waiting about the yard just to catch a glimpse of him, judging from the way he looked and the way he walked whether things were going well. One morning, not long after they were married, he came out of the house and went towards the stables whistling, and I could have cried with joy. Immediately after I could have cried with rage at myself for letting such a daft fancy put me out of the house and out of his life. One day there'd be a baby there, his baby, and I should have no part in it. I was like a woman who, hungry as she may be, can't go to her own bread crock because a spider is sitting beside it.

Dummy's Mary was so grateful to me for getting her the job, and training her to it, that she was like a dog; she often used to come round to have a bit of gossip and ask my advice on this and that. She told me that the mistress did nothing in the house at all, still ate only once a day, and spent hours in Tom's empty room, playing the tambourine and dancing, all by herself. Martin had put his foot down about her dancing in the town and threatened, if she disobeyed him, to take away her tambourine.

"He should stop her dancing altogether," I said, when Mary told me this, "rattling her insides about that fashion, how can she hope to breed?"

Another time, a little later, Mary reported that the mistress had a cough, which she said was because she was indoors so much.

"She's not hobbled or chained," I said. "She could do a bit in the garden. The lavender isn't even cut this year yet, and the pea haulms yellowing where they stand. And couldn't she walk into market, like any other housewife?"

The year moved on and it was Michaelmas. Pert Tom had been away longer than he'd planned, because, I suppose, the good weather had lasted. I looked forward to his coming home, partly because I wondered what he would do, and partly because I wanted to tease him about being so know-all about Romanys and their not being able to stay anywhere more than a month.

October was two days old when, one afternoon, coming out of the woolshed, where I'd been picking (which is hard work and made me think of Kate, who used to do it all day long and with two children to mind), I saw Tom just shoving his bear into its shed.

"So you're back," I said.

"So I am, fancy you noticing," he said sourly, and kicked the bear to move it over.

"And she's still there. Using your room to dance in, so I hear."

"If I want me room back, I shall hev it. Remember how I got this?" He turned his face so that the scar the burn had left on his cheek showed up in the light.

"You'd not speak of that and remind him, just when he's begun to be happy again!"

"Why not? He was the one said we was to live together the rest of our lives. He was the one said no women in the house when I wanted to bed Joan in comfort. I'll remind him all right. I'll remind him of a lot of things."

I drew a bow in the dark.

"While you're about it, remind him how your old bear was burnt, too, helping with the brave rescue."

"What d'you know about that?"

"More than you think. A lot more than you think."

Where exactly I'd hit him I couldn't see, but somewhere, for, though he scowled he said, "I don't want to go dragging up owd things. Nor I don't want to go back on the roads. I've got soft and I'm too owd to lay out arter Michaelmas. Where're you living?"

"With Peg-Leg—and a right tight fit it is."

"Well, I shall see what Martin hev to say. Not that I hanker to be under the same roof with her, but this is my home, arter all."

So off he went, and that very evening when Peg-Leg came home he told me that he and several other men had been taken off their different jobs and set to build again.

"Starting tomorrow, digging holes for the posts. A rare fine big room this is to be, too; twenty feet by twenty and ten high. He talk of putting in a window, glassed."

"Just for Pert Tom?"

"No. For Mistress Reed. He had a special word for it. Ah, I got it, a solar he called it."

I tried to imagine such a large room and couldn't see where it could be on such a little house, not without blocking up a door or a window of what was there already. Unless he built it on the forge side.

"Is he aiming to move the forge then?"

"No. The other side."

"That'd block the way the ponies come in from the road to the yard."

"They're leaving that just as it is and building across the other side of it."

"Then there'll be two separate houses."

"No. Martin reckoned to roof over the way the ponies go in and leave that as a passageway. Then folks can get from the kitchen door to the . . . the solar, just stepping across the passage."

For the next six or seven weeks I used to go along every day and watch the work going forward. Apart from the big houses at Horringer where my father was shepherd, and Ockley where my husband was game warden, so of course I never was in them, only saw them from outside, I never had seen such a building. Even the floor was solid oak, every plank about eighteen inches wide and laid as level as a table. And they put in a window, like Peg-Leg said, not flat in the wall, but bowed out, right over the garden I'd made, so it only just missed my lavender bush. It was all made up of little panes of glass, greenish, about as big as the palm of my hand. All that, just for a woman to dance in!

I now had another spy inside the house, as it were. Pert Tom, who had often enough grumbled about my cooking, more to annoy me than because he had any cause, would come slouching round once or twice a week, and, without actually asking, would say something smelt tasty, and complain of Mary's cooking, and I'd give him a piece of whatever was going and he'd sit down and talk. He seemed to have lost most of his fear of Magda and to get along with her very well, "what little I see of her," he said. "I never hang around when she take that tambourine in hand, because thass the only time she's anyway tempting." He spoke as though, apart from her dancing and her lack of interest in the kitchen, Magda was ordinary enough and life in the house pretty smooth-running.

Once, a little before Christmas, he spoke of her having a cough and brewing up a cure for it; it smelt terrible, he said.

Then, even nearer Christmas, Mary came along one evening and begged me to go in and make the plum pudding.

"All them costly things," she said. "If owt went wrong and they was wasted, that would be a pity. 'Tain't like spoiling a pot of porridge, is it?"

I said craftily, "I'll come and help you, if we can do it some time when the mistress isn't about—then you can take the credit for it, you see. You wouldn't want her to know, would you?"

"She's in the solar every afternoon now."

"All right then. Now mind this . . ." I told her that she was to scrub the table, wash the bowl, the spoon, and the big iron pot, and scald the pudding cloth. "Never mind if they are all clean; it's a kind of magic rule, for making plum pudding everything must be washed afresh."

Even if I hadn't had this hatred of handling anything after those long thin hands had been on it, that would have been a wise order. Nothing in the kitchen was as I left it, everything was greasy and smeared and in the wrong place. I scolded Mary—not too much, for she had been brought up like a pig and only had three weeks' training—but I scolded myself most harshly for running away on account of a fancy. I should have stayed, I told myself. I'd come back, I told myself all the time I was chopping the suet; I'd humble myself to Martin, tell him I wasn't comfortable with Peg-Leg and beg him to take me back. I'd force myself to get over this stupid feeling; if Pert Tom could live in the house with her, so could I.

We had the flour and the suet and the eggs and the fine fat raisins all ready.

"We want a pinch of spice," I said to Mary. "Where do *you* keep the spice box? I always had it on the shelf here."

"I think it's in the cupboard."

"God bless you, girl, don't you *know?*" I exclaimed, and glared at her as she went to the cupboard.

Inside it was all of a jumble, in which she ferreted about like a blind woman, while I clucked my tongue, making the most of my impatience. She reached up to the top shelf and as she did so a little bunch of dried-up herbage fell out, she grabbed at it and missed it and it dropped near me. I picked it up, smelt it, and said sharply:

"Mary! Leave hunting that spice box and come here. What is this?"

And I thought: Jesus have mercy, if a poor ugly crooked girl like that can get into trouble! I kept my eye hard on her, but she neither blushed nor blenched.

"That? Oh, thass Mistress's stuff for her cough."

"Her cough! But this . . . How often does she take it?"

"I don't rightly know. From time to time she'll pour water on and drink it when it's soaked."

"I see. Best put it back. Then if you look behind that crock of mouldy dripping, you'll find your spice box."

She brought it to me, saying with a false little smile, like a dog in disgrace wagging its tail too fast, "You do hev good eyes, Agnes."

"Too good," I said.

We went on making the pudding, but my mind was on other things; the feeling that I must come back here and set things right for Martin's sake; the memory of that bunch of dried stuff with the faded flowers that had been pink and the pale rounded leaves with their pointed ends.

I was on my feet, the better to give the mixture the good sturdy whack that it needed, and saying, "Like this, see. Smack it about as though you were beating a bed," and just about to hand the spoon to Mary when the kitchen door opened and Magda walked in. First I was thankful that I was on my feet so I didn't have to stand up to acknowledge she was mistress, and second all my determination to come back and see Martin comfortable just ran away like water down a gutter.

She said, "Hullo, Agnes," as carelessly as though she'd seen me the day before. No surprise, no interest that I should be there, in her greasy, untidy kitchen, making her plum pudding for Christmas. I just gave her a nod of my head and turned to Mary.

"Now to do the thing properly," I said, "we have to have a chunk of wood, borrowed from a friend, to lay on the fire to start up the boiling. Go along to Peg-Leg's—there's nobody there but you must knock on the door and say, 'Can I borrow a log to cook my plum pudding?' You'll find some logs there, choose the biggest and bring it back."

Mary went off. I'd made the thing up on the spur of the moment, but it fitted, I thought, Christmas being the friendly season.

Magda was going towards Martin's room, now their bedroom, but I stopped her.

"I want to ask you something."

She turned back and said, "Yes." And at that moment the fright came on me. All those months ago, when Pert Tom had said she was a witch and I'd crossed my thumbs and thought that was why I didn't want any doing with her, I hadn't been really frightened. That is true. She'd threatened the tongue that wagged about how she got in the river, yet I had told Martin. I'd never been really scared. Now, all of a sudden I was. My breath seemed to catch. Still I said it.

"That stuff you take for your cough, every now and then. Do you know what that is?"

"Is a wildflower. Good for the cough."

She'd turned back and now stood so that the table was between us, and we faced each other as though we were fighting a duel or playing some gambling game.

"I never heard it was good for coughs. It has another virtue. . . ." Then I thought: That slipped out because you get used to speaking of the virtues of herbs, in this case it has no virtue. It'd be a virtue if she was a maid betrayed, or the down-burdened mother of a huge family. . . . I shouldn't have said "virtue." And of course I shouldn't, because she just said:

"So? Is nice to know!" and went sauntering into the bedroom.

I was so angry that I couldn't breathe. My heart came jumping up into my throat, beating like a hammer, bells rang in my ears, and for a moment I couldn't see except for sparks all shimmering against blackness.

I sat down and wrestled with my breath. I would breathe, pull it in, hold it, let it out. I could hear myself making a noise like a blacksmith's bellows.

Then there was Mary, so quick for all she was lopsided, back, lugging a great log.

"What do we do next, Agnes?"

And I managed to tell her, calmly, how to put the pudding into the cloth, leaving plenty of room for it to swell. And she did it. All the time there was no sound from the inner room.

It was growing dark.

"One more thing, Mary," I said. "Take the scissors and cut about an inch off the lavender bush. That has to boil in the water."

As soon as she had gone, I took the bunch of pennyroyal from the cupboard and dropped it into the heart of the fire.

III

I THOUGHT the matter over, by night as well as by day, for what remained of the time till Christmas. I felt it was my duty to tell Martin what his wife was up to, and yet I dreaded to upset him. I didn't want to make *too* much of it. There again, I thought, if I'd had any pluck at all, I should have been in the house, and seeing him often, able to drop a hint. However, my chance came, for this Christmas was to be a real merry one of the old-fashioned sort. Martin had a pig killed and roasted whole, and we all had our Christmas dinner on the big wool floor which had been three-quarters cleared. As at the wedding there was ale for everybody, and we sang all the old Christmas songs about the Three Wise Men and the Star of Bethlehem, and about the Holly and the Ivy.

Peg-Leg, like all sailors, was handy with his knife and could whittle any shape you asked; and I'd asked him to do a Baby, and a donkey and a cow about the size so that a small saltbox could be a manger for them. I put a wisp of straw in the box, laid the Baby on it, put the donkey on one side and the cow on the other, and set them all on a board to decorate the table at the end where Martin sat. I'd praised Peg-Leg's whittling and left it at that, and then, on the Christmas morning, when we stood together watching the pig turning on the spit over the fire in the forge, I did another bit of flattering.

"Peg-Leg," I said, "somebody ought to thank Martin for all this, and you're the one. If it's left to Peter Priest, it'll be all long words and no heart to it, and Pert Tom'll be stuttering drunk before the time comes. You're the one."

"Aye," he said, "I reckon I could stand up and say thanks for us all."

"And best wishes. I tell you what, Peg-Leg, say that while you're about it you'll wish that next year there'll be another baby at the table. That'll draw everybody's attention to yours."

"And thass a good wish, too," he said.

So all I had to do was to wait till Peg-Leg stood up and clapped his hands for silence and started to speak. Then I went and got as near Martin as I could, a little behind, so my mouth was close to his ear, and when Peg-Leg said about the baby, I muttered to myself, as any old woman of my age is entitled to do:

"And so there would be if she didn't keep swilling down that cough mixture!"

He heard, I saw him jump. He said, "What was that?" pretty sharp.

"What was what?"

"What did you say?"

"Did I speak? I reckon I was talking to myself," I said and wandered off.

I really did think to myself that that hint was dropped as well as ever a hint was. And it was noticed. It wasn't long after Christmas, the real cold weather was just beginning, when Dummy's Mary came along with some tale about the Master coming into the kitchen just as the Mistress was brewing her medicine and taking it and pouring it out at the back door.

"Thass all froze now, as hard and smooth as glass," she ended.

"Take a shovelful of ashes and put over it then, for Holy Mary's sake," I said. "We don't want anybody breaking a leg."

After that I just sat back and waited. The cold weather ended, the days pulled out, morning and evening, a few birds began to sing and even fly about with bits of straw in their bills, and it was spring again.

I stood one morning, where I usually did, and watched Martin mount and ride off somewhere. I remembered thinking that, badly as Mary managed in one way, she kept him fed and tidy looking. He did look just as usual. I stood there for a bit, enjoying the air, and along came Pert Tom to give Owd Muscovy his breakfast.

"Well," he said, "if you left on account of her, you can move back. Reckon I was right after all. She's up and quit!"

I had another of those turns when I couldn't breathe or see; I had to lean against the wall to keep myself from falling. He was saying something, but the ringing in my ears was so loud I couldn't hear what it was. I did my careful breathing, in, hold it, out, for a time or two and at last I could speak.

"What do you mean, up and quit? When, why?"

"I was telling you. You gone deaf? She took off yesterday morning and ain't been seen since. I reckon I miscalculated. That must be a *year*, not a month they can't stay in one place."

"Oh, stop that jabber! What about Martin? How's he taking it? Was he off just now, looking for her?"

"Not him. He's off to Lavenham. Know what he said, last night, when he come in and found her gone? He said, 'Well, you can't keep a lark in a cage, leave alone make a broody hen of it.' Then he set down and et his supper. If you ask me he've had a bellyful of her and is as glad to see her gone as I am. You'll come back now, eh, Agnes, and cook us some decent grub?"

My mind was elsewhere but my tongue answered him.

"You always used to grumble about my cooking."

"That was afore I tried Mary's!"

"I'll see. Most like she'll come back. She's like you, born to the road; this first spell of fine weather set her foot itching."

Maybe that was the way Martin looked at it. Maybe that was why he had eaten his supper and been so unconcerned.

But that wasn't true. He must have known she had gone for good, for that evening Mary came along, her eyes popping, to tell me that the Master, the minute he was home from Lavenham, had told her to take everything that belonged to the Mistress and put it on the fire in the forge.

"There was that lovely dress she had for the wedding, and the tawny woollen she had for the cold weather, and her shoes and everything, even the pins for her hair. And there was Tim, standing by with the bellows and the flames shooting up, you never see such flames, Agnes."

Oddly enough, I didn't picture the flames; I just saw her, going off in the old red bodice and striped skirt, carrying her tambourine, and her hair hanging. "There is no because. To dance I am born, so I dance." I thought of that. And I thought of Martin's remark about the lark and the cage. That showed understanding, and was a comfort to me, because a blow that you can understand never hurts so much as one which puzzles you. I also thought of Peg-Leg's words about women overrating themselves; this very morning Martin had gone off about his business in Lavenham. He'd survived a worse knock, he'd survive this. Some decent food and a clean bright kitchen, if they didn't help, wouldn't hurt.

I said, "So now there's no mistress in the house. It was bad enough when there was. I shall come along tomorrow morning, Mary, my girl, and put you through your paces."

She looked pleased.

So there we were, in well under a year, back just where we were. My only regret was that there was no baby. Nor would be now. Martin, grown even more silent, never thought about anything but work and business.

The big fine room across the passage was never used. I went in now and again to let in the air and watch Mary wipe away the dust. It was a sad room. I'd go in and think what a waste, his building this just for her to dance in; and I'd end by thinking I could see her dancing.

Amongst us her name was never mentioned, and for all the mark she had left on the place she might never have come at all.

THAT was the summer when Martin began to speak of buying a ship of his own to carry his wool overseas. It wasn't until well on into November, however, that he heard of a likely vessel for sale and rode off down to Bywater to view it. It was bad travelling weather, and hardly light all day long, so the trip would take four days at least, and his last words to me were not to worry if he was away longer.

I took the opportunity to make brawn, and on the third night turned one out of its mould to see what it was like. We had it for supper, and very good it was. When Mary went to set what was left away for next day, I said:

"Look, you were a good girl and worked hard on that brawn, you can take that piece along to your mother and show her what a clever girl you are."

Pert Tom and I drew up to the fire. He was a bit mopish just then, because Dummy's Joan had taken up with one of the young smiths in the forge and he hadn't yet found himself another hussy. Looking at him, across the hearth, I thought he wouldn't find it so easy this time, and the next harder still, until in the end he'd just be that figure of fun—an old lecher.

We spoke about this and that, and mentioned Martin and the ship, wondering if he'd struck the deal.

"If he don't this time, he will the next. He'll get whatever he's set his mind on. And arter the ship he'll be hankering for a sheep run, so that from hoof to loom ain't nobody making a penny 'cept him."

"Well, what's wrong with that?"

"Did I *say* owt was wrong? You take me up so sharp. I shall go to my bed."

He went off, peevishly, and I shut my eyes and dropped into a little cat-nap, the way old folks do. It was the door opening and a rush of cold air coming in that woke me. Waking that way, neither your eyes nor your wits work well for a minute, and when I looked towards the door and saw a bent-over woman's figure with a bit of grey woollen over the head and upper part of it, I *saw* Mary, and I spoke to her, pretty gruff.

"Don't stand there, letting in the cold." I was glad to see that, though she'd run off just as she was, she'd had the sense to borrow a bit of wrapping to come home with.

Then, before my eyes, the hunched-over figure straightened out and it wasn't Mary, it was Magda. It was Martin's wife, come back. She straightened herself and at the same moment reached out her arm and pulled the door shut. The bit of grey stuff fell back off her head and showed the short stiff spikes of her clipped hair, and the thin face, always hollowed, now like a skull covered with skin, and the queer-shaped eyes sunk back in dark circles.

She stood there, leaning back against the doorpost, just as she had leaned that sunny morning and laughed and slapped her flat belly and said that to eat more than once a day was to get into a bad habit. She looked, now, as though she hadn't eaten once a week.

I had no scrap of pity. Only anger that she should have gone off on a spring morning and dared to come back, with the belly-cramp of hunger on her, as soon as winter set in. I was so glad that he wasn't there, with that soft heart of his, under the hard shell, and I was thinking of things to say, harsh enough, scornful enough, to drive her away, when she said:

"Martin. He is not here?"

That brought the words into my mouth.

"No, he isn't. But if he was he'd say what I do. Be off. You went away of your own accord and hurt him sore. He's done with you. You aren't wanted here. Be off. Back where you came from."

She laughed; at least her lips curled back from the teeth that now seemed to be too many in her mouth, and a sound, like laughter, but with pain in it, came out of her.

"You mistake. I am not come to beg. I come to bring something."

"Your love and loyalty in return for a full belly! He saved you from drowning and what thanks did he get? He's away. He'll be away for a week. Nobody here cares about you. Go on. Get out."

It was November, and in November nobody has food to give away. I knew the signs. In twenty-four hours, without food and shelter, she would be dead. It was cold outside and she was starving. I wondered whether, breathless and clumsy as I was, I had the strength to throw her out. As I was wondering she bent over again, put her hand on her knees and braced herself, with a shudder, and the grey woollen, very slowly, slid down, down to the floor.

Then I saw; then I knew.

There is something almost uncanny about having plied a craft for many years; there can come a time when the plying of that craft can become all that matters. You are nothing, you cease to be, except as the tool with which the job is done. You don't even *think*. I didn't think then: This is Martin's child, that he wanted and I wanted. I didn't think: This is the woman whose touch, for me, would have made a bit of bread uneatable. There was no thinking. There was a woman, in labour, pretty far gone in labour, two good strong pains in four minutes, and there was Agnes, the midwife, who could ply her craft drunk or sober.

I wasn't even the swollen-legged old shuffler that lately I had been. I was across the kitchen and I had her by the arm and onto my own bed in the blink of an eye.

"When did you start?" I asked, as I'd asked a hundred times before.

"This morning. Early. In Sudbury. I think this baby will be born in a ditch. Like me."

"Twenty miles. You walked twenty miles? Like this."

"Is good to walk, I understand. Good, eh? How bad then is bad? Aagh!"

I remembered, without the least distaste, that lean sinewy body. And I said, with far more truth that I had ever said the words before, "You'll have no bother."

Then I remembered that hollow, starving look. I turned aside and pulled the pot of broth into the heat. It was part of the liquid in which the trotters and cheekbones for the brawn had boiled, good and strengthening. It was warm already and it began to bubble. I poured some into a cup and gave it to her.

As she sipped, I, Agnes the midwife, did what she always did, talked, tried to keep their minds off, tried to make out that this that was happening wasn't the end of the world.

"What happened to your hair?"

"Is sold. My tambourine also. Like this I cannot dance."

Another pain gripped her and the cup wobbled in her hand. I steadied it.

"Why did you leave it so late?"

"To come? Oh, many reasons. Is all a disaster. I go from here to find the wise woman. She is in York, and when I am come to York she is in Chester. And so it goes on. Then too late, or she is not wise enough."

I swear that it was Agnes the midwife, not Agnes, Martin's friend, who asked the next question.

"You tried to get rid of the baby?" It mattered, it meant upside down, feet first, sideways on.

"But of course. To a dancer a baby is ruin. Always I am hearing from my mother how good she is, until I come to ruin her. Aagh!"

She writhed and bit her lip. I took the cup from her; turned away, laid out my scissors and twine. You never made any show of them, but they had to be handy.

"So you've come from Chester?"

"From Chester. And not easy. My hair is sold, and my tambourine. I am to beg and to beg is slow. Too many people will say, 'You wish to eat you shall work.' So here I wash clothes and here I beat flax and here I cut nettles and so goes the time. But I am coming. Then, one day I steal. Bread. And I am not quick." Something that started out to be a smile turned into a grimace. She waited, drew breath, and went on. "Are most kind, these people. For stealing bread is a whipping or to stand in the pillory, but these are not suited to my condition. So I am locked in prison forty days. But still they are kind and they say poor baby to be born in such place and I am let to go." She turned her head from side to side on my pillow, and I saw the sweat spring out on lip and brow. Not long now. I took a cloth and wiped her face, as gently as I ever wiped any woman's. At the next twinge she muttered some words in a language I did not know.

"We're nearly there," I said, "it'll all be over in a minute or two."

At that moment Mary came in and stood goggling. I told her to get out fresh candles, "and the pepperpot," I added in a lower voice. I didn't expect any trouble, but it was as well to be prepared. I then sent her to her bed. I'd always hated to be watched at work.

A little time—more than I'd expected—went by. Magda was plucky; she bit her lip; she muttered the strange words; she moaned. Once she screamed.

"That's right," I said, "don't bottle it up. Scream all you want to."

I had forgotten Pert Tom, who, the next minute, opened his door a cautious crack and asked, "What's going on?"

He held his door ready to slam it to at once. (In the morning he said he thought maybe thieves had broken in and were clouting me; and I said, "If so you were ready with another brave rescue, weren't you?")

"Nothing for you to worry with," I told him. "Go back in and shut the door."

The next pang was weaker, and the next weaker still. She was young and sinewy, but she hadn't been looked after well and had come to the job exhausted and weak with hunger. Dallying at this point could be fatal. So I took the pepperpot, shook some into my palm, and held it under her nose. She gave a mighty sneeze and it was done.

The moment I had Martin's son by the heels, Agnes the midwife, spry, knowledgeable, intent only on the job, cleared off and left me.

First I had a good look at the baby. If Magda's own brew or the wise woman's muck had marked or marred him, I knew what to do; I wasn't having Martin saddled with something crippled or wrong in the head. So far as I could see, though, he was perfect, thin but healthy, and his first cry was real lusty. Then I paid particular attention to his face. There is a moment—and any midwife will bear me out on this—just one moment, when all the newly born bear the stamp of the man who made them. They may lose it and never have it again, but they all, boy and girl alike, come into the world looking like their father will look when he is an old man. Magda's baby was Martin at sixty, bald and wrinkled. Happiness flowed into my heart. Here it was, the boy he wanted, the boy I had wanted for him.

I knew that what I should do was to call Mary down, hand the child to her, and busy myself with the mother. I thought about it, knowing exactly what Agnes the midwife would do. I knew *I* couldn't do it. That old, shuddering loathing was back on me now: her precious load delivered, she had become once more the woman from whose lightest touch I had shrunk. But that was not all. I had no need to touch her. I could have called Mary and told her what to do.

The truth was, I wanted her to die. I thought how happy we could be now. What life was left to me I could devote to bringing up the baby. But not if she stayed. And she would. She spoke of a baby being ruin to a dancer. Besides, any woman, however wild, is settled by motherhood. Martin would be so pleased with the child that there'd be no question of forgiving her wandering off, it would just be forgotten; she'd be reinstated, more than ever mistress of the house, and I should be back with Peg-Leg.

Oh, I know that women do die in childbed, every day, every night, but not without a fight, not until every measure has been tried. Agnes the midwife had had many a hand-to-hand fight with death, and knew all the tricks.

I, I did nothing. I sat down with the child in my lap and saw to him, while behind me on the bed the Romany blood, the witch's blood, the woman's lifeblood soaked away.

Interval

Of Martin's ventures the Baildon people had said, "Ah, the bigger you blow a bladder, the louder the bang," and, "The higher a kite flies the farther it has to come down." As year followed year they waited for him to overreach himself, for the bladder to burst, the kite to fall. Nobody but Martin himself knew how often their ghoulish hopes had come near to being fulfilled. And he himself could not have said what it was that drove him, time and again, to take another risk, exchanging a certain, comfortable security for a touch-and-go chance. He just knew that he must go on and on.

Most of his ventures had an element of makeshift about them.

He went into the yard one morning, beckoned to Peg-Leg who was in the stables, and asked brusquely, "What sort of sailor *are* you? Could you take a ship from Bywater to Calais, or Amsterdam?"

"If she was sound, I could sail a ship to Constantinople and back."

"The one I have my eye on is old, but she's sound. How d'you know that you could?"

"It weren't my head that clumsy barber-surgeon cut off, you know," Peg-Leg said in an offended voice. "I'd done eleven years with the best sailing man ever breathed, devil in sea-boots though he was. And what you've learned at the rope's end you tend to remember."

"If I buy this ship, with all I've got tied up there," he nodded towards the woolshed, "I couldn't, straight-away, offer a hired captain enough to keep him honest. I've been over, I've seen all their tricks. Good wool marketed at half price, cash in their pockets and written off washed overboard or some such. One deal like that just now could be ruin. But a couple of honest trips, Peg-Leg, would see me clear, and after that you should have a share, a good share, one in forty of the whole cargo."

"You mean *me* be captain?"

"What d'you think I'm talking about?"

"Mother of God, I'd do it for nothing. I'd pay you to let me—if I had the wherewithal. I trudged, soon's I got this wooden leg fixed, I trudged from Bywater to Hull . . . Dunwich, Lowestoft, Yarmouth, Lynn, all the way to Hull. I begged for any job, just to be at sea again. Always the same answer: We can get plenty chaps with two sound legs."

If Martin remembered the time when he had been in a similar case, he gave no sign.

"It'd mean staying sober."

"I'm sober afloat. Sailors ashore . . . well, they make up for lost time. And beached like I was, in my prime. What other comfort was there? Look at Owd Agnes."

"Agnes?"

"Yes. Rolling drunk every time she had the money. Can't you remember? She steadied up as soon as she had a kitchen. I could steady up if I had a ship. You say you got your eye on one. How's she named?"

"*Mermaid.*"

Peg-Leg rubbed his nose. "I knew one by that name once, but that's a common name. Where do she lay?"

"Down at Bywater."

"Then s'pose we went down there . . . Is she manned?"

"More or less. The man that owned her was master; he's sick, he wants to sell, but the crew is ready to sign on with whoever buys her."

"They would be, ready and anxious. Then s'pose we go and go aboard, and you tell me where you want to steer for and I'll land you there."

"Yes," Martin said, "I think you will, Peg-Leg."

"I got a name," Peg-Leg said. "And it's Bowyer. Jacob Bowyer." He turned away to prop the pitchfork he had been holding against the stable wall. "Captain Bowyer," he said softly to himself, "Captain Bowyer of the *Mermaid.*"

The next sudden promotion from common yard hand to a post of responsibility was made when Richard was six years old, and concerned the unfrocked priest who had joined Martin's gang of workmen when the house was being built and the land cleared, and who had stayed on and had lately been working as a pack-whacker. He had a hut in the new Squatters Row behind the stables; it was set a little apart from the others, and he lived alone, aloof of manner, surly of temper.

One evening Martin surprised him by inviting him into the house and taking him into his own room, where upon the table a piece of virgin parchment, two newly cut quills, and an inkhorn were laid out.

"I take it you can write, Peter," Martin said.

"It's not a thing one forgets entirely."

"Sit down then." Peter did so and picked up one quill, rejected it, took the other, and said, "Who cut this? He was no scribe!"

"Cut it to suit yourself," said Martin, handing him a knife. Although he had cut the quills himself the criticism pleased him.

"What do you want me to write?"

"This. This is a deed of grant, made to one Martin and the heirs of his body, in perpetuity, of all the property and messuage known as . . ." He paused and the pen caught up with him.

Peter Priest looked up and asked, "What is this? A forgery?"

Still unoffended, Martin said, "No. A test."

He rose and went to the heavy chest that stood beside his bed and took out another parchment, one with a dangling seal. He took Peter's writing, and, scowling heavily, compared the two.

"There is a fault," he said at last. "You have spelt my name with an *e.*"

"*E* or *i*, both are correct. It is a matter of opinion, not a fault," Peter Priest remarked coldly.

"Otherwise it is well done. How is your reckoning?"

"By tally or mentally?"

"In your head, the answer then written down."

"In Roman figuring or Arabic?"

"Both."

"Try me."

Martin went to his bed and from there dictated four problems in arithmetic, laying out, behind the priest's back, the answers as he made them by tally.

"Read me your makings."

All but one of the answers fitted, and in that one, when they reworked it, the error was Martin's.

By this time the possible purpose of the test had occurred to Peter Priest; the accounts and records of the business had outrun Martin's ability to deal with them; so he, Peter Priest, was to be taken off the road and installed as clerk. The prospect was pleasing; how infinitely preferable to sit indoors, plying his real craft once more, instead of being on the roads in all weathers, handling greasy bales of wools, urging— sometimes having to pull for sheer force—pack ponies through the mire.

"You see," Martin said, "my way is slow and cumbersome, and can be wrong. That is why . . ."

He came round the table and sat down, facing Peter.

Why, Peter wondered, is he so cursed slow stating his business.

Martin was slow, partly because any but the briefest speech now came hard to him, partly because speaking of Richard brought the child to mind, and roused, as his actual presence did, many conflicting emotions. He delighted in the boy and loved him dearly, but he was an ever-present reminder, not of Magda, but of the two other little boys, especially Stephen. To be troubled by this, not to enjoy his fatherhood to the full, was he knew absurd, but he had felt from the beginning, from the day when he had come home and found the baby there, that in some way Richard was a usurper. For a long time even to watch the child being fed, and then later feeding himself, had been both a pleasure and a pain. Stephen, his first-born, had lived on water gruel, on stale bread thinly smeared with fat, and had spent his days on the stinking wool floor, and finally died because his father was trying to save the miserable hut which was all the home he had. Richard fed on the fat of the land, enjoyed Old Agnes' whole doting attention. Stephen had been a very good, quiet little boy; Richard was naughty and wilful. The whole thing was in such sharp contrast that comparisons forced themselves upon Martin many times every day.

At the same time, simply because he felt this way, he also felt guilty. It wasn't Richard's fault that he had been born after the tide of luck had turned. So, each time that the affection which should have streamed out, full and free, towards the new child suffered the inevitable check and recession, Martin would, by some act of indulgence, endeavour to make up to the boy. He could deny him nothing; he could never punish him

lest, into the punishment, should go some of this unjust resentment because Richard was Richard, not Stephen.

It had all mattered less, been more easily smoothed over, while Old
Agnes lived. Doubtless, in her time, Richard had been naughty, ungovernable, wild, but she had never complained; she had acted as a buffer, explaining, excusing, saying, "He is very young. He will learn," saying, "For
myself I like a lad to show a bit of spirit." Once, jerked out of silence by
her ridiculous attempt to defend some particularly prankish behaviour,
Martin had snapped out:

"Stephen was never like that."

And Agnes had made—for Martin—the most terrible answer possible.

"Ah, there's the difference between the colt fed corn and the colt fed
grass. You can't expect them to act the same."

Agnes had died when Richard was four, and within a week Dummy's
Mary was crying and saying she couldn't manage the housework and
Richard; he didn't come when she called him and when she picked him
up he kicked her. The answer to that had been a strong, active young
woman named Nancy, whose sole duty was to see to the child. She had
had one of her own, illegitimate, which had died at the age of two.
Martin, engaging her, had cherished the secret hope that her heart might
share, with his, the defence of memory, that she might be a little less
doting and lenient than Old Agnes who had never had a child of her own.
If Nancy arrived thus armed, she was disarmed almost immediately.
Richard was a remarkably handsome little boy, so charming when allowed
his way, so disagreeable when crossed, that anyone crossing him was almost bound to feel that the change of mood was in some way his or her
fault, not the child's. In a very short time Nancy, too, was enslaved. And
so had happened the stupid, inexcusable incident with the bear.

Richard was almost six, and ever since he could toddle he had seen
Uncle Tom go to the shed where Owd Muscovy lived, open the door,
and place food within the bear's reach. The muzzle, no longer needed,
hung on a peg in the wall, and the chain, attached to the bear's collar
at one end, was hooked at the other over a strong nail driven slantwise
into the wall of the shed.

Pert Tom, after that one summer on the road during Magda's brief
rule as mistress of the Old Vine, had grown slack and old. Dummy's
Joan's leaving him had, as Agnes expected, been a turning point in
his life. It, or rather the difficulty he had found in replacing the young
hussy, had loosened his mainspring. But he had kept his bear. And
when Richard was five, at Christmastime, he had actually brought Owd
Muscovy out on to the wool floor and put him through his tricks.

Richard watched, entranced.

"Uncle Tom, let me blow the whistle and make the bear dance."

"He wouldn't do it for you," said Pert Tom, who was the only person who ever treated Richard as an ordinary human being, an equal.

"Why not?"

"You ain't his master."

"Let me try."

"Get outa the way," said Tom.

Shortly after that Christmas, Richard began asking Martin for a whistle, and Martin remembered another little boy who had never asked for anything, had his pang of guilt, and provided the whistle.

The thing in itself was enough for Richard for a long time. He blew and a shrill level noise emerged. By accident he put a finger over one of the holes and a different noise resulted. Bit by bit, untaught, by a process of trial and error he learned to play a tune, one of those sung in the woolshed at Christmas, "The Holly and the Ivy." Once he could do that, he plagued Uncle Tom to teach him *his* tunes. Tom said, "One day" and "Sometime" and "Don't bother me now," but in the end he succumbed and after an hour or two with the child, said to Martin:

"He've got a true ear, and come to the point he's teachable. He'd got 'Gathering Pescods' and 'Granny's Bonnet' in nearly no time at all. If I'd had him on the road, with Owd Muscovy, I'd hev made a fortune."

The two tunes were all Richard wanted to learn. He played them over and over until he was sure, and when he was he set out to test them on Owd Muscovy.

The shed was never locked for the simple reason that no one except Pert Tom was ever likely to open it. Except for that one Christmas outing, the door had never opened except when the bear was fed or the shed cleaned, and when Richard opened it the bear ambled forward, expecting to be fed. Richard pushed past and went to where the extreme end of the chain was hooked over the slanting nail. Even on tiptoe he could not reach it, so he turned back, and, exerting all his strength, pressed the hook which held the other end of the chain to a ring in the bear's collar. The chain fell free, into the soiled straw on the floor, and Richard realised that now he had no means of leading the animal up to the kitchen door as he intended, to cry, "Come and watch, Uncle Tom," and demonstrate his disproof of the old man's statement, "He wouldn't do it for you." But he was undismayed; so long as the bear stayed on all fours—which he would do until the whistle sounded—his collar was within reach of Richard's hand; he could be hauled along by the collar.

Owd Muscovy had never before, since his remote forgotten cub days, been free of both chain and muzzle at the same time. Without them he felt, not liberated, but strangely vulnerable. Children he knew and hated, they tweaked and pinched and poked. Against them Pert Tom was his defence, and now here he was, stripped of his appurtenances, at close quarters with a child, and no Pert Tom in sight. When Richard attempted to take his collar, he backed away nervously but with a warning growl, and when Richard hung on, tugging determinedly, it was nervousness rather than vice that made him bite. His teeth closed on the child's forearm and, through the sound woollen stuff of his sleeve, inflicted only two incised wounds. But the blood sprang and the yell which Richard let out was a yell of pain as well as wrath. He loosed his hold on the bear's collar and ran to find Nancy. Owd Muscovy made no move to pursue him, nor, though the door stood open, did he immediately leave the shed; he emerged a little later, just as one of the pack teams was coming into the yard. The ponies, though weary, were capable of being thrown into a stampede, one of the pack-whackers was caught between a frightened pony and a wall and had his ribs crushed, and added his cries to the general pandemonium. Dummy's eldest boy was in the loft, pushing hay over the edge of it into the mangers, ready for the incoming team; he heard the shouts and the cries. "The Bear," "The Bear's on the rampage," and, with a heroism never given its rightful due, jumped into the manger, fork in hand, jumped from the manger to the stable floor, and ran out into the yard, where Owd Muscovy, by this time in a state of panic, had risen on to his hind legs and was doing his dance in an attempt to placate. Dummy's Jack charged and drove the pitchfork home into the hairy chest thus exposed; one prong must have penetrated to the heart, for within a few minutes Owd Muscovy was dead.

If Richard could have controlled his temper and his tongue, he would have emerged blameless, a victim of the escaped bear, like the clawed pack pony and the man with the crushed ribs; but, his wound smeared with tar and his pain deadened by a dose of laudanum, he was furious to hear that Owd Muscovy was dead.

"Now he'll never dance for me. And me going to all the trouble to learn the right tunes."

Pert Tom, inconsolable at the loss of his bear, which he had hated, exploited, cherished, and loved, all at once, said, "You! Thass it. You let him out, you little hellion!"

Martin said, "Tom. Mind your tongue!"

"Bugger my tongue! You let him out, didn't you? You opened the shed door."

"Bugger my tongue," said Richard, enjoying the sound of a new, attractive phrase. "I wanted him to dance for me, but he bit me instead."

"There you are," said Pert Tom. "Straight from his own mouth. He opened that door. So Owd Muscovy, the one thing I ever owned, is dead, just a lump of stinking carrion. Go on, sit there making your goddamn faces at me. Look what you've got, a great flourishing business, ships on the sea, and who knows what. Where'd it all come from? Something so dark and dishonest you never could say where. Had to pretend it was my savings. My bitch had to be bedded here and there, out on the hard ground mostly, yours gets a wedding and is called Mistress, and finely she served you. But you get this . . ." he flung his hand in Richard's direction, "and he go and let out my bear. So he's dead, my Owd Muscovy."

"Nancy, take Richard to bed," Martin said.

"I don't want to go to bed."

"You see," said Pert Tom. "Thass like the Bible say: 'If these things be done in the green leaf, what shall be done in the dry?' You see how he hev the upper hand of everybody here. You mind what his mother was. You're making a fine rod for your own back, and I only hope I live to see it beat you."

And so, in the end, Martin had realised that Richard must be tamed. And so, here he was, having put Peter Priest through his paces, saying, "What I want is for you to teach my boy."

Peter Priest's vision of a quiet, clerkly life vanished, leaving behind it a sense of loss so sharp that it hurt.

He said sourly, "I couldn't teach him. Nobody could. To teach a child you must be his master."

"That," said Martin, "is what you would be."

"And the first time I punished, or even chided him, he would run to you, wailing, and you would turn yourself inside out to make things right for him." He rose from his seat. "Thank you, no! Three hundred days a year in this part of the country the wind blows from the east, but I would rather walk into the teeth of it, running the ponies who can be beaten if needs be."

"Richard can be beaten—if needs be, but not over the head."

"Beaten. The young Master of the Old Vine?"

"How else could he learn?"

"How else indeed? Well, well. Even you, at last, come to the end of your indulgence and hand over! What do you wish him to learn?"

"To read what is written and write what can be read. To reckon, as you now did, in his head, and write down his reckonings in figures Roman or Arabic." Without intending it, his voice, as he said those words, took on a sardonic note.

"You see," said Peter Priest, "already you are against me. And what the parent is against how shall the child learn? The figuring, Roman or Arabic, are not terms of mockery, as you in your ignorance make them sound. I can slave out my guts teaching him, and you, with a few mocking words over the supper dish, can undo all I have taught him. I will stick to the ponies. You send him to school. From school he can't come running to cry and show his stripes."

Martin said, with a black look, "Sit down. Stick to the ponies, you say. Whose? Not mine. I can go to the town gates tomorrow morning and find a dozen pack-whackers. And, maybe not tomorrow morning, but some morning not so far away, I can find Richard a teacher. You have your choice, teach him, or take your foot in your hand and leave the Old Vine. If you teach him, I promise that, so long as you do not hit him over the head, what you do will be right with me."

"Why so shrewd about hitting over the head?"

"Once, long ago, when I was young, I had some lessons. And to be hit on the head made me more stupid."

"What would you pay me?"

"Twice your present wage. And you would live in the house, in comfort. I planned to build two rooms above the solar." He remembered the way in which Peter had asked about the figuring and added solemnly, "Meanwhile, you would have time to renew your learning and get the dirt out of your hands. Also you should have some garment more suited to your new position."

Peter Priest gave him a look of unadulterated hatred and said, "That could be seen to."

From that day onwards Peter Priest did no manual work at all; he would not even help with the building of the new rooms above the solar or the stairway that led up to them. He told Martin, arrogantly, that he would need books, and to buy books cost money. Martin asked how much he required, and Peter named a sum which made Martin gasp.

"By that reckoning a book costs as much as a pack pony."

"Why not? Ponies breed their young. A new book may mean a year's hard work for a scribe."

"The priest who once taught me carried his learning in his head," Martin protested, less from meanness than from his dislike of Peter Priest's tone.

"And he taught you so well that, when it comes to passing on what you learned, you hire another man to do it for you."

"Buy what you need," Martin said.

On the day when lessons were to start he was careful to be absent; he would be away four days, he said. Nancy had her instructions, and at the given time called Richard in from the yard, smoothed his hair with her hand, gave him a handful of currants, and told him to go up the new stairs to Peter Priest's room.

"What for?"

"You'll see when you get there, my poor lamb."

Munching the currants and licking his fingers, Richard marched up the stairs. The door of Peter's room stood open and just by the window was a table spread with unfamiliar objects. Peter had sent for him to show him something, just as the men about the yard would call and say, "Master Richard, look, I've found a young owl," or, "Master Richard, Peg's dropped her foal, like to see it?"

Richard walked over to the table without noticing that behind him Peter closed the door and shot the top bolt.

"What's this?" he demanded.

"Don't touch anything. Come here and wash your hands. And in future always come to me with clean hands."

Richard looked at the bowl of water.

"Nancy washed me this morning."

"Nancy washed me this morning," repeated Peter in a cruel mockery of the childish treble voice. "A great boy almost seven years old. Wash your hands and dry them thoroughly."

"I shan't. I didn't come here to wash!" He swung round and made for the door.

"You come here to take lessons. And the very first lesson is unquestioning obedience."

"Open this door," yelled Richard, having found the door bolted and the bolt just out of reach. "Peter, do you hear me? *Open this door!*"

Peter Priest walked up behind him, encircled him with his left arm, hoisted him from his feet, and brought his right hand down on the little backside thus exposed, once, twice, thrice, with a will.

"That," he said calmly, "is for saying 'shan't' to me."

Richard roared from pain and insult.

"Stop that. Stop it at once," said Peter Priest and shook him, until from sheer breathlessness he hushed the noise.

"Now come here and sit down." He pushed the boy towards the table and down into a chair. Richard jumped up at once.

"I don't want to. I'm going to Nancy. She's making me some gingerbread men and I . . ."

"You will have no gingerbread men, nor any other goody, until you know your letters, so you'd better listen carefully."

When he could repeat all the letters of the alphabet without prompting and recognise ten of them without hesitation, Peter Priest said, "That will do for today," and opened the door and let him go.

For today! There would never be another day like this! Never again would he enter old Peter Priest's horrible room.

Next morning, well before lesson time, he went towards the stables, intending to take his pony and be miles away before Nancy could even wonder where he was.

Peter was waiting for him in the dim stable.

"I anticipated some such trick," he said, and took Richard, not by the hand, or the arm, but by the ear. It really hurt, and, pulling away, jumping about, and trying to kick at Peter's shins only made it hurt worse.

Upstairs in the hated room, Peter Priest said, "I am now going to beat you for putting me to so much bother. You will have six stripes today. To-morrow, if you repeat this idiotic performance, it will be eight and the next day ten."

He laid on the stripes dispassionately, enough to hurt, not hard enough to cause injury, and then, putting aside the little cane, asked in a conversational tone, "I wonder how much you remember of yesterday's lesson. Let us see."

Richard, snuffling, said, "You just *wait* till my father comes home!"

"We will wait. Meanwhile, let us see how much you remember."

When Martin rode into the yard Richard was waiting for him, and he was hardly out of the saddle before the tale of woe began. The child had already witnessed the collapse of one small world. Mary and Nancy, though they petted him and spoke pityingly, had put up no real defence against Peter, and Peter had managed at every turn to outwit him. Even when he had rushed straight out the house before breakfast and hidden himself at the very back of the woolshed, Peter had found him—and that was ten strokes with the cane. The one thing that had sustained him was the certainty that when his father came home and heard of all this mistreatment, he would take full vengeance.

His father actually asked only one question, "Were you beaten over the head?"

"Why, no. He beat me here," said Richard, rubbing his sore seat.

"Then," said Martin, "he was only doing what I told him."

Quite slowly—because this could not be taken in all at once—the rest of the world began to quiver and crumble.

"You mean you *told* old Peter Priest to beat me, and lock me in and not let me have any gingerbread?"

Martin looked at the angry, handsome little face. Going on for seven years old; and if Stephen had lived to that age no doubt he'd have been picking wool alongside Kate and never have known what gingerbread tasted of.

Stiffened by that thought, he said, "Yes. He only did those things because you were naughty and disobedient, and would not learn."

So, there lay the world in ruin.

Slowly Richard said, "But I did learn. I know my alphabet, backwards and forwards, and when Peter draws the letters I can name them. Tomorrow I am going to draw them, too."

Martin's mind had done its familiar *volte face*, remember Stephen, feel guilty, pet Richard.

"There's my good boy," he said heartily. "And now come and see what I've brought you."

Never again, as long as he was in the schoolroom, did Richard give Peter Priest cause for anything but the mildest verbal rebuke. This fact Peter attributed—not without reason—to his own first firm handling. Richard became a good scholar, a little too studious indeed for Martin's liking.

Youthful resilience survived the shock of those four horrible days, but deep down the damage remained. The spoilt, arrogant little boy grew into a youth more than averagely handsome, talented, charming, a little too eager to please, more than a little lacking in self-confidence. The lack was not obvious and did not show itself in any physical way of slouch or stutter. Transmitting Martin's orders, his voice had the almost genuine ring of authority. He knew the business thoroughly and before he was twenty had made several visits to the wool-buying centres of the Low Countries. Yet even Martin could never deceive himself into thinking that the boy's heart was in the business. It was difficult to say where it did lie, with his books and his lute, perhaps.

The solar was furnished and in use now, Richard spent his evenings there and Martin tried to, but somehow he could never settle there for long, he'd get up and make some excuse for going into the yard or to the office, or even to bed. And as he retreated he would sometimes think that Richard's lute-playing in the big room sounded lonely. What the boy needed, of course, was a wife.

Not—and this thought always followed hard on the other—not a Baildon girl, Martin hoped; there were, after all, plenty of other places to choose from; and he would devise a trip for Richard, to Colchester, to Kelvedon, overseas again. And when the boy came home Martin's "Well, how did things go?" held an interest not entirely concerned with the business that had been the reason for the journey. Richard never had anything except business to report upon.

Presently he was twenty-four, and sometime during the following spring Martin spoke the words outright.

"Don't you think it's time you thought about getting married?"

Then, though neither of them saw it, the flaw in his confidence showed itself. Richard smiled his charming, rather secret smile and said, "I think I shall never marry. You see, I know the girl I want, and her parents would never allow her to marry me."

Everything tough and aggressive in the elder man rose to that challenge.

"We'll see about that," he said. "Who is she?"

Part Three

ANNE BLANCHFLEUR'S TALE

I

ON the morning when the whole course of my life changed, Mother and I were in our hall, busily contriving to make a new dress for me out of one of her old ones. In its day it had been a fine garment, but its day was long past. There were many threadbare places and the colours had faded. Our task was made the more difficult by the fact that, at sixteen, I already topped Mother by half a head.

"But there is a hem," Mother said, with her eternal optimism. "We'll let it down and hang it in the sun and it'll fade all over alike, I have no doubt."

The hem came down, showing the stuff in its original colours, green and crimson, in a sprawling, all-over pattern. Elsewhere the green had rusted, the crimson had faded until they were almost alike.

Mother saw me look glumly at it and said, "So long as you are tidy the *shabbier* you are the better. Your Aunt Astallon will take pity on you, I trust, and buy you a new gown."

Only by biting my lip hard could I hold back the sharp retort, words no girl should speak to her mother, especially one so kind and indulgent as mine. My Aunt Astallon was as likely to give me a new gown as she was to jump in the river, or walk out barefoot in the snow. But my mother had lived on hope—and hope alone—for so long that she could no longer distinguish between the likely and the unlikely. My father, though less resolutely cheerful, was well-nigh as feckless, and the wonder was, not that we should have fallen so low, as that we should, somehow, have managed as well as we did.

While I bit my lip and scowled we heard a horseman ride into the yard. Minsham Old Hall, as our place was called, was very old, built for defence, not for living in, and the only windows were set high in the walls and narrow. Mother had to hop on a stool to look out.

"I declare," she said, "it's Martin Reed again! What can he be wanting now?"

"The same as last time—his money," I said; and I intended no joke. Mother laughed, however.

"Poor silly man," she said; and hopped down and picked up the dress and gave it a shake.

Master Reed was the man who owned the sheep run near us. Once all the acres had gone with the Old Hall, but they had been sold away, years before we went to live in the house. Our few acres and Master Reed's sheep run were quite separate, and to reach his part and his shepherd's hut he had no need to come into our yard. For a long time after we moved into the house he was just a name to us, and then one day he had come, walking quickly for all that he limped, and asked Mother if she would, as a favour, heat a tar bucket for him. The shepherd he had then was ill or idle or runaway—I never bothered to hear the whole of it— and he'd come out to find several of his sheep flyblown. He'd found the tar bucket in the fence which was nearer our house than to the shepherd's hut and had run to ask Mother to lend him her fire for ten minutes.

Mother, of course, had been obliging, and while the tar warmed and he stirred it, she had stood by him talking about sheep. Mother could talk about almost everything, she'd had such a crowded life, moving about from place to place and always taking interest. She'd learned quite a lot about sheep when she was staying with her Uncle Bowdegrave at Abhurst in Kent, where the sheep were quite different from those in Suffolk, she said.

Stirring away at his tar, Master Reed shot her a look and said, "That's right, ma'am; shorter legs and blunter heads."

Then, his tar melted, he picked up his bucket and hurried away with the briefest of thanks.

But about three days later, when I was alone in the house, my father and mother having been asked to dine with the Fennels at Ockley, Master Reed came to our door and handed in a bundle of cloth, very fine, blue in colour. He said, and I remembered the exact words to tell Mother: "I don't like to be in debt. I borrowed your fire the other day. I hope this will be accepted as payment."

There was someone with him, sitting astride one horse and holding the other. I gave him no heed. To Master Reed I said, "But I am sure my mother would not wish for payment for so small a thing."

But he pushed the blue cloth towards me, and I remembered that my brother Godfrey—at that moment milking the cow—was being fitted out to go to our cousin Fortescue. So I made my curtsey and said:

"I thank you kindly, and so will my mother, though there was no need." But, handling the good cloth, I thought it would make a fine cloak for Godfrey. I had already started my round of visits to great houses and rich relatives and knew how important clothes could be.

The blue cloth made Godfrey a cloak, but three years later, when he must cease to be a page and become a squire, he needed another and more expensive outfit. And it was then that it occurred to my parents to ask Master Reed for a loan.

In fairness to my father I must say that when he borrowed he did have expectations. (Expectations have been our downfall.) Father's Uncle Dawnay was, at that moment, on his deathbed, and so far as we knew Father was his only kin. However, Uncle Dawnay, who had been a jovial sinner all his life, became frightened on his deathbed and willed everything he had to a Chantry, where Masses are being said for his soul to this day. (Mother, when she heard the sad news, said, "But I'd have prayed for him, night and day without ceasing if he'd left the money to us!" Then she'd laughed and added, "Of course I shouldn't, I should have been too busy spending it!")

Our debt to Master Reed was never paid, and on the May morning when he rode into our yard it was over three years old.

Our windows were not glazed—and never would be—so presently we could hear my father's hearty booming voice greeting the woolmaster, and Master Reed's gruff tones. We could hear the two voices, but not the words. Mother listened for a moment, her head on one side, then she said happily:

"They don't *sound* cross. We'd better try this on. An empty dress hangs longer than a full one."

I put on the dress and she walked all round me, looking at it critically.

"Oh dear, you need every inch of the hem down. We shall have to face up the inside. What with, I wonder? Something the same weight or it won't hang right." Then, to cheer herself, "We could *dag* the sleeves, Anne. Dagging is very fashionable, and it would cut away some of that worn edge."

You would have thought that the remaking of that old gown was the only thing in the world that mattered. With the wool-man in the yard, demanding his just due.

Presently we heard the horse trot away, and after a minute Father came in. He had his favourite hawk, Jess, on his wrist and he stroked her as he went towards her perch, transferred her onto it, and fastened the chain. Then he pulled off his glove and stood slapping it against his leg and looking at me as though he had never seen me before. I imagined it was the effect of the dress and hoped that perhaps it was not as ill-becoming as I had feared. Then he said:

"I want a word with your mother." I gathered up the long dress and went to the stairs. They ran up alongside the wall and were made of stone and had no handrail. At the top was a gallery, with the floor so rotted that you had to mind where you trod, and behind the gallery one big room had been partitioned into three. I couldn't hurry, and before I reached the room which I shared with my sister Isabel I heard Father say:

"That fellow Reed has just made me an amazing proposition." I was curious to know what it was, so I just stepped out of sight, leaving the door wide, and listened. ". . . wants Anne for his son, Richard. He's prepared to make a substantial settlement and cancel the debt."

Mother gave a sort of yelp; there is no other word for it. She sounded just like a dog that has had its paw trodden on.

"The saucy upstart! I trust you sent him off with a flea in his ear."

"Why, no. I said I'd think it over. Talk it over with you." She must have scowled, for he asked, in a surprised way, "You mislike the idea?"

"Mislike? Mislike? He must be mad to have thought of it. And you must be mad to have carried it to me. We've come low, Mary pity us! But not so low as that." Her words began to come out jerkily, and I knew she was throwing her arms about as she did when excited. "Look where you will, through the length and breadth of the land, and you won't find a girl with better blood in her veins. On both sides. Blanchfleur, Bowdegrave, Astallon, Dawnay, Fortescue. *And,* don't forget my grandmother of Ramsey, Royal Saxon. And you'd put my daughter to bed with the woolmaster's son. You should be ashamed."

"I didn't bed them. I only said I'd think it over."

"These jumped-up merchants with their new money, they think they can buy anything. If you wish to please me, Blanchfleur, get on your horse and ride after him and tell him my daughter is not for sale."

"I should never catch him," Father said truthfully. "Besides, perhaps Anne . . ."

"You are crazed," Mother said. "Since when have wenches ordered their affairs or been asked for an opinion. Up and after him. Tell him to buy his great silly son a wife where he buys his fleeces. My daughter is not for sale."

She had fallen in love with that phrase.

"The man spoke modestly and not in huckstering fashion. He said he knew the difference in their estates. I don't think he was in full favour . . . but the boy saw Anne once and fell in love."

"Fell in love," Mother repeated with great scorn. "The wool merchants

now must fall in love—aping their betters. What next? They'll be riding in tourneys, I suppose."

"Wool merchants have been knighted. . . ."

"That's enough," Mother said. "Will you ride after him and give him
his answer or must I?"

"You never even heard his offer," Father said. But the words were a
requiem for something dead and done with, not a renewal of live argument. In a minute he would be on his old horse, and, though it might be
suppertime before he reached Baildon, when he got there he would give
the answer that Mother sent.

I rushed out on to the gallery and cried, "Wait."

They stared up at me. I went halfway down the stairs and stopped.
Standing high made me feel bolder.

"He sets some value on me, which is more than anyone else does," I
said.

"I should box your ears," Mother said. "Listening in corners! And what
do you know about values? You have never had a chance. You're only
just sixteen. . . ."

"And I've been on offer for *years*. Who is her father? Good! Who was
her mother? Good again! *What is her dower?* How many times have I
been passed over for some snippet with teeth like a rabbit's and two good
manors? I'm sick of it. And another aunt saying I spoke when I should
have been silent, or looked up when I should have looked down. Blaming
me for what I can't help."

Every one of the shames and humiliations that I had suffered in four
years came back, as burning and hurtful as in the moment when they
happened. Rage made me feel as though I were drunken.

"It is the same with Godfrey," I declared. "Why wasn't he knighted
when he'd served his three years? For one reason only. A knight needs
equipment, and you couldn't and Uncle Fortescue wouldn't lay out the
cost. He'll spend his life polishing other men's mail and waiting, just as
you would have me wait for something that never comes. And I will wait
no more, I will marry the wool-man's son."

"I will box your ears. You are out of your mind. That a daughter of
mine . . ."

"Yes," I said. I could feel the sneer curl my mouth as I thrust out one
foot and held it clear of the stair. "Saxon royal blood in my veins! And
what on my feet?"

It was a little unjust. For my last visit—to my Aunt Bowdegrave—I had
been provided with shoes, but I had outgrown them and passed them on
to Isabel. For my forthcoming visit to Aunt Astallon I have no doubt
Mother would have procured me some shoes, somehow, from somewhere,

but at the moment I had a peasant's footwear, a roughly shaped wooden sole, with cloth nailed around it and tied in a bundle round the ankle.

"They are only makeshift," Mother said.

"Our whole lives are makeshift, and pretence, and believing what isn't true."

As soon as I said that I was smitten with compunction. With their faces tilted up towards me and wearing such shocked helpless expressions, my parents looked like two children, who had been playing happily that they kept house, and a grownup had come along and kicked over their make-believe furniture and said that the game was silly and unreal.

Father shifted his eyes and looked at Mother, waiting for her to strike, as it were, the next note in the tune. Every time I came back home—my eye made sharp by absence—I noticed that her ascendancy had increased; his movements, speech, and impulses were all slowing down, she was just as quick and positive and vehement as ever. This morning though, for once, she was at a loss, and looked as though she might cry. Upset by that, Father lashed himself into a rage and shouted at me.

"You're overripe, my girl; that's what ails you. You're ready for a roll in the hay with the pig-man." Whether he intended to or not he had forestalled Mother's tears. She rounded on him.

"Pig-man indeed. What a thing to say to your own daughter. Didn't her Aunt Bowdegrave complain of her prudery? And quite right too. A maid should be modest."

I said, "I shall marry the wool-man's son, who has made me an honest offer, or I shall go to the one aunt I have not yet visited—my aunt at Ramsey, and be a nun."

I then turned on the stair and made to go up, but I had forgotten the long gown, caught my foot in it, and fell to my knees.

From the hall below Mother wailed, "Saints have mercy. Nothing is more unlucky than to fall upstairs."

Where, I wonder, did that superstition have its origin? I can see that to spill salt, or to break a looking glass is in itself a misfortune, since both are valuable, and the glass at least hard to replace. But to fall upstairs . . .

Anyway, I had more important matters to think about. I had held over my parents the only threat that a girl could hold; from any other decision they could beat me off, by argument or force if needs be, but once a girl had declared her intention of taking the veil they would be hardy parents indeed who tried to stop her. My great fear, when I came to think things over, was that my parents might take me at my word, steadfastly refuse to let me get married, and so force me into the convent. Little as I liked my present way of life, I should like that of a religious less, especially at Ramsey, where my aunt, the Abbess, was very strict in keeping to the rules of the order. I had seen her once, at a wedding, and even on such an occasion when most nuns disregarded all the rules, she held to her habit, wore no jewels, ate sparingly. To be a nun at Ramsey was to be a nun indeed.

I began to wish I had never spoken those rash words; yet, when, some hours later, Mother climbed the stairs and came and sat on my bed and asked did I really mean what I had said, I replied with a firmness that astonished myself.

"Yes. The wool-man's son is the only one who has ever made me a serious offer of marriage; I suspect he is the only one who ever will. Unless I take it, I shall go to Ramsey."

"In which case," she said, pulling a sorry face, "we should see you seldom or never. Baildon is within reach, even with such poor horses as we can afford."

I said nothing.

"Anne, to please me, try once more. Go to your Aunt Astallon—it will be different this time; her own girls are married and gone. She could give you more mind. And you're prettier, you grow prettier every day. You have everything, except a dower. You'll make a good match, yet."

I stayed silent. And at last she said, "Oh, if only things had been different. . . ."

Upon that I almost broke down, thinking what her life had been. My father was the youngest son of a youngest son of a great family; he had, therefore, connections, ambitions, and military obligations without anything to support or forward them. His one hope was to have married an heiress, instead he married my mother who was, if anything, even more highly connected, but one of several daughters and but modestly dowered. For years, however, the insecurity of his position had not been evident; he was a good man in the lists in time of peace, a good soldier in time of war. Trailing his family after him, as a kite drags its tail, he had moved from castle to castle, from great manor to great manor, riding in tourneys, supporting this lord and that in their petty squabbles, making war on the Scots, and on the Welsh, cheerful good company always, Sir Godfrey Blanchfleur, most admirable knight-errant. Mother had borne seven children and four had died before she had a bed to call her own. We had all been born in different places, grand, high-sounding places, Beauclaire, Abhurst, Rivington, even Windsor, but Godfrey was thirteen, I was nine, and Isabel was three before we had a settled home, and that came about by accident.

Father was unhorsed in a tournament at Winchester, and fell on his head, denting his helmet so that it could not be removed in the usual way. They say that he was unhurt, rose unaided, and walked from the tourney ground to a forge where an unhandy smith, in hammering off the helm, damaged his skull. He lay like the dead for four days and when he finally rose from his bed his days as a fighting man were done. His left arm and leg, though whole and uninjured, had lost power, were weak and heavy; and he was slow, even in his speech.

He was no whit less cheerful, quite confident that somebody would arrange something for him. And somebody did. One of my mother's Bowdegrave cousins owned Minsham Old Hall and the few poor acres that had been left when the rest were sold for a sheep run. The house had stood empty for some time and was so old-fashioned and comfortless that nobody wanted it.

The sad thing was that there was just enough land to have supported us, had it been properly handled; and my brother Godfrey, most sternly sensible always, would have *tried*. The life we had led, flitting from place to place, had aged him; he belonged nowhere and had found his own company, often with working people who at thirteen are men. He would have looked after cows and pigs and tilled the few acres. But no! He must follow the pattern, go to be a page, then a squire, and finally a knight. I have no doubt that his life had been as full of humiliation as mine.

I had started my round at the age of twelve, going from cousin to aunt, from aunt to cousin-by-marriage, to learn manners, to learn dancing, to learn to play the lute, to learn to embroider. One day one of my powerful rich relatives was supposed to take a rich young man by the ear and say, "Marry this girl." But there was no man so rich that he did not look for a bride with a dowry. And also there was, at that time, a curious dying out in the old families, so that in many of them there were no sons, only daughters who thus became great heiresses. Once, at Beauclaire—I remember this so sharply—there was a little creature, Catharine Montsorrel, so ugly, so misshapen that I pitied her. But somewhere near Chester a man could get on a good horse and ride for three days around the boundaries of one of her properties, and out by the Welsh marches another man, on another good horse, could ride for six days. So she got married from Beauclaire and I did not. My failure was, in a way, the failure of the relative with whom I had stayed, and of course excuses must be made. I was sent home with the report that I had two fatal defects, a sharp tongue and a prim manner.

I will say for my mother that she never took these things seriously as most women would. Many another girl, sent home with such a character, would have been scolded, beaten, had the shame of her failure rubbed into her every day.

So now looking back, all in a moment, over Mother's life, and mine, so far, I felt kindly and weak towards her.

"If things had been different, they would have *been* different," I said. "But they are as they are. This man Reed is well-to-do and we owe him money. He said he would cancel the debt. That in itself is a thing to consider."

Mother clenched her little fist—she had beautiful, delicate hands which no amount of work could spoil—and beat upon the bed.

"You are not," she said fiercely, "to think of that. I said to your father . . . but for the debt he would never have dared. . . . You don't know the world, Anne. Poor we have been, but you have never been brought face to face—I mean to talk to, to be with—any man who hadn't . . . who wasn't . . ." She broke off, threw her hands about. "Chivalry," she said, snatching at the word like a drowning man at the straw in the proverb. "To know what good manners are—even if he doesn't always exercise them—that is the mark of a gentleman."

"Uncle Fortescue once dragged my aunt upstairs by the hair of her head, in the sight of all, and broke the jaw of the young squire who protested," I said quietly, as though speaking to myself. Mother blushed her quick bright blush.

"There was reason for that."

"Unmannerly just the same."

"That may be. But," said Mother, wagging a finger at me, "I'll warrant that none in that hall knew *why*, his real reason, I mean. And there is just the difference. He might pull her hair, but he did not besmirch her name as a common man in a rage would have done."

"I shall be careful," I said, getting back to the point, "to behave in such a manner as to give my common man, as you call him, no occasion either to pull my hair or besmirch my name."

"Marriage lasts a long time," said Mother dryly. "Suppose you never grow to like him, or tire of him, and he of you. Then where would you turn? To some blabbermouth apprentice who would boast when he was pot-valiant? Oh," she said, jumping from the bed and beginning to wave her arms, "these are not things to say to a young maid, yet they must be said. In a proper household such things are understood, arranged, there is constant change, comings and goings, blind eyes turned, allowances made."

"And ladies dragged upstairs by their hair."

Mother, like a skilled fencer, ceased her pressure at that point, and attacked from another angle.

"I can't see you as a nun at Ramsey. You may expect no favour from your aunt, if anything she will be harder on you than on the others out of her wish to be fair. You love your comforts, and are greedy, and vain. You have no vocation, which alone could make such a life bearable."

She had put into words what I had been thinking, and inwardly I wavered. But I said, "Add to my failings that I am proud. I cannot go to my Aunt Astallon again, and be looked over and passed by; and have them say, 'Let me see, how old are you now?' and have them nod and pull their mouths down. At least at Ramsey I should have no cause for shame."

"There's another thing," said Mother, flitting like a butterfly. "Think how it will sound, to send to all the family and say that you are to marry the son of a wool-man. Is that not shaming?"

"Not in the same way. Besides, why should they be told? Except when one of us is being foisted off on them they forget that we exist. We might starve to death for all they care. They're afraid to visit us for fear their hearts should be wrung. Aunt Astallon went to Walsingham, missing us by four miles, did she turn aside? No, she rode on and lodged at Sudbury. Uncle Bowdegrave visits Rushbrooke every year, when did he ever give a sign of being within riding distance?"

These were truths, facts, which my parents had steadily refused to recognise. Now, confronted with them, Mother seemed to shrink a little.

"Anne," she said, "you're very hard."

But it wasn't true. Seeing my point pierce her last defence, I was filled with pity and weakness. I really longed to cry out that I had not meant what I said, that I would go to my Aunt Astallon and try once more. But something held back the words. I was sick of pretending.

"I shall tell your father that you are set in your mind," Mother said.

Father, always three-quarters in favour of the match, rode off to Baildon to tell Master Reed his offer was being considered, but that, before any conclusion was reached, Mother wished to inspect the young man. Master Reed invited them both to supper. So the hem of the green and crimson gown had to be stitched back into place and the seams let out instead of taken in. Wearing it, and a very wide wired head-veil, she went off to Baildon and came back in a very curious state of mind.

I asked her the one question which troubled me most.

"Is he surly, like his father?"

Mother lifted off the headdress and ran her hands through her hair.

"He's not in the least like his father." To me that was pleasant news, but she said it regretfully.

My father fumbled in his pouch and brought out a little lump of pink, undercooked meat and offered it to Jess on her stand.

"If you married that boy, you'd have a very comfortable home," he said.

"If?" I asked.

Mother said sharply, "My mind is not yet decided. And when it is I shall take my time telling them so. *I'm* not one to fall on my face at the sight of a few silver cups, a glass window, and a great tapestry that still smells of the loom."

"It was well meant," Father said. "They wanted us to see that . . ." He cast a look about our comfortless hall and grinned. "Four main dishes, then gooseberries in a glazed coffer, and a syllabub that you could have turned upside down without spilling, it was so well whipped."

"I was ashamed of *you*," said Mother, "pocketing a piece as though you feared to be hungry on the way home!"

"I told the boy—what's his name, Richard—that it was for my hawk. He was knowledgeable, though he has never handled a bird. Said he had read a book."

"What did *you* think of him, Father?"

"A modest, amiable young man. And if he was some poor knight's son that had gone into the wine trade, your mother would think so too."

I suspected that they had argued all the way home.

"There's a difference between trading in wine and handling dirty old fleeces," Mother said.

"But the man was at pains to point out that the boy never soiled his hands. . . ."

"That I can well believe!" It was plain to me that something had happened to upset her and bring her to the brink of deciding against the match after all.

Presently Father went outside and I signed to Isabel to go to bed, which she did reluctantly. As soon as we were alone Mother got up and went over to the livery cupboard and began banging about in it. Our livery cupboard was never well provided at any time, and she couldn't be hungry, having come straight from a supper of four main courses, pie, and syllabub, so I could only guess that she wanted to keep her back to me. But why? After a minute I could bear it no more.

"You didn't like Richard Reed?"

"There's nothing about him to like or dislike. Truly, Anne, I'd be more at ease if you were . . . if it was a question of marrying the father, old as he is."

"Why?"

"He's a man. There's something about him. You could see that he was being civil, for the boy's sake; he wanted us to take to the idea and know you'd be . . . well looked after. But in his heart, he didn't care; he thinks he's doing *us* a favour!" This, which she should have mentioned with irritated scorn, she brought out as though it were admirable. "The boy's grown up in his shadow, pampered, made much of, never had to shift for himself. You'd have the upper hand of him in no time."

I thought what an astonishing thing to say—in that *complaining* manner!

"Would that be so bad?"

She flung something into the cupboard and turned round.

"Yes. No woman can be happy with a man she can master."

I suppose what I thought showed plain on my face.

"Ah, but we weren't always this way," she cried. "Not this way at all. Why, I've sat amongst the other women and looked down as Blanchfleur rode by, and he'd look up and I'd go hot and cold and almost choke with pride because I belonged to him and he was the strongest, boldest . . .'" She gave a little shiver and hugged herself with her arms. "You were nearly born on the road. We were at Rivington and he said, 'I'm off to Beauclaire in the morning.' Just like that, and I knew I'd be in the straw next day or the one after, and I knew that if I let him go alone there were plenty at Beauclaire that would be glad to see him ride in by himself. So I said, 'I'm coming too.' And he said, 'D'you think you'll hold together so far?' And I said, 'I shall hold together so long as I have to.' And I did. And he liked me the better for it. That was the time Lady Warwick threw him her glove—but he wore mine for all to see."

There was something—even after all those years—so triumphant in her voice that it made me feel as I sometimes did when trumpets blew. She spoke of what I understood; I had so often sat in the humble back seats of the Ladies' Gallery and watched the knights ride by, saluting the ladies who threw them favours. I'd dreamed of one day having a knight of my own. . . .

I put that thought away.

"Richard has been under his father's thumb," I said. "You shouldn't judge from one visit."

"It isn't in any way what I want for you, or what you should have. Anne, if you'll try once more. I'll persuade your father to sell Jess and you shall have a brand-new gown."

"I will marry Richard Reed and have two new gowns."

How long these arguments and this indecision would have lasted I do not know. My Uncle Bowdegrave, staying at Rushbrooke, helped to clinch the matter, by, for once, remembering his poor relatives and sending us a haunch of venison.

Mother looked at it calculatingly and said, "Now, if we were proceeding with this business, we could ask the Reeds to supper. It won't keep, so we must make up our minds."

"You know mine," I said.

"And mine." That was Father, speaking quite firmly.

"Well, only the Virgin knows when next I shall have meat in the house for five people. I think you're being a stubborn, hasty, foolish girl and I only hope you won't live to regret it."

So she capitulated and Richard and I met.

II

WITHIN a few minutes of our meeting I was certain that Mother's slighting remarks about Richard were due to prejudice, and perhaps a little to jealousy. He was such a very handsome young man, and so elegant, with a charming smile and the nicest manners in the world. I think my heart went out to him at once, just as I thought that if only he'd had breeding *how* Mother would have praised him, and said I was lucky. And what is breeding after all, largely a matter of money and land and staying in one place long enough to establish a name and a family; or pleasing the King and getting some honour conferred on you. I'll warrant that if Richard could have gone to Westminster, calling himself by some Norman French name and played his lute, he would have pleased the King so much that he would have been knighted straight-away.

Old Master Reed was lame of one leg and had grown crooked, as well as solid with the years; his face was weathered and deeply lined, he looked as though he had been too busy all his life to take much pleasure in anything. Beside his father Richard looked like a young larch side by side with a gnarled old oak.

The supper party was much easier and merrier than I had expected, largely, I think, because Father, when Mother was worrying about having only the one dish, had said, "There are times when wine counts for more than food."

"This is one of them—and we have no wine."

"I'll ride over to Ockley and borrow some."

"Don't say for what reason. Nothing is settled yet."

Sir Stephen Fennel, bless his heart, gave Father some good Rhenish, which made everyone cheerful and unembarrassed; even Mother so far relented as to behave as if Richard were a very eligible suitor who must be charmed. After supper she bade me fetch my lute and play a little. A little is what I played, just as I danced a little, played Nobbin a little, embroidered a little. I had no ear and no talent, but I had mastered four or five pleasing little tunes.

While I played Richard watched me, and I could see that he loved me. I remembered something I had forgotten—Father saying some words about

Richard having seen me and would look at no other girl. That had a smack of romance to it, like a minstrel's tales, and as I played I looked back at him under my lashes. Presently he rose and crossed the hall and sat down by my feet, and at the end of my last tune took the lute from me and said:

"Allow me now to play for you, Mistress Anne."

I had never, anywhere, heard anyone play like that. It wasn't just music, it was something more, like being under a spell, so that when it ended you sighed and your spirit settled back into your body again, a little painfully. You could have loved him just for the way he played the lute.

He ended his special music and gave us back our souls and then said, "Now, the tune that everyone knows. Will you sing?"

He struck up "The Pleasant Month of May," and we all began to sing. Under cover of it, Richard said to me, "I saw you once. I thought you were the most lovely lady in the world. Will they let you marry me?"

"They must. They shall. Or I will be a nun."

Afterwards, when more of the wine was being served with some little saffron cakes, Mother came to me and said, "Well. Are you still of the same mind? The old man is pestering your father for an answer."

I could hardly speak for the fullness of my heart. I had made my choice in a blind rage against the way the world had used me, and I had picked this jewel.

After that it was settled, and Mother began seizing every opportunity to send messages to every branch of the family. I could imagine, in all those distant places, relatives of all degrees putting their heads together and agreeing that at last my parents had come to their senses and done something suitable to their estate. In their relief they all sent me gifts of great generosity. Ironically, Mother's remark about my Aunt Astallon giving me a new gown proved to be prophecy, for she sent me enough of the best French velvet for a wedding dress; that inclined me to think that she had been dreading my next visit almost as much as I did. With the gifts came excuses for not making the journeys to bring the families to the wedding, and that was just as well; but the Fortescue cousin in whose household my brother Godfrey languished gave him permission to ride home—hoping no doubt that the wool chandler had a daughter. When Godfrey did arrive, he was leading a pretty grey palfrey, my present from that branch of the family.

The Reeds had no relatives at all, and Master Reed, talking over the wedding with Mother, said that he wanted nobody from Baildon at his son's wedding. But he professed himself willing to provide a feast, so the few guests we had—mainly friends of Father's, who came to see what the poor fellow could find to spread on his board—were vastly and pleasantly surprised.

Martin wore mulberry-coloured velvet, the tunic edged with fur, and the one thing that marred my day was to hear two old men, hawking friends of Father's, muttering about it.

"In my young days nobody less than a knight could wear miniver; and if he tried to it was ripped off and sold for the benefit of the poor."

"Times change."

"So they do, and not for the better."

I hated them for thinking the old days, when someone like Richard mustn't wear miniver fur even if he could afford it, were better than these more enlightened times.

After the feasting was done, Richard, his father, and I rode to Baildon. I was thankful that owing to our circumstances there could be no public bedding. During my various visits to my relatives I had assisted at these grossly indecent rites, and I knew that I should find them agonisingly embarrassing. Yet, when we reached the house which I had never yet seen, and stood uneasily in a small solar, most elegantly furnished, and drank a last stoup of wine from the silver cups which Mother had mentioned, I realised that the public bedding ceremony does serve a purpose. The lewd talk, the thrusting of fertility emblems upon the bride, all the jokes and the laughter and the ducking away from those who try to undress the newly married couple, help to break down the reserve between them, and once they are in bed, with the curtains closed, half the work is done.

If even Master Reed had been a little drunken and hearty and slapped Richard on the back and said, as I have heard fathers say, "Well, boy— to your work!" that would have helped. But he only looked at us, rather sadly, I thought, and raised his cup and said:

"I wish you happy." And when he had drunk his wine he went away; and we were two strangers, left alone.

Then Richard said, as though I were a visitor who had come a great distance, "I expect you are tired. Come."

He did take my hand, however, as we climbed the stairs, and still holding it he led me into a room far more comfortable than any I had ever slept in, for even at Beauclaire, being young and a poor relation, I had always shared one of the worst rooms. He pulled on my hand a little, so that we stood close, and he put his face to mine. We were cheek to cheek.

"You belong to me. I never dreamed it could happen." There was a

kind of exultation in his voice, but awe as well. I realised that he was as
nervous as I was myself.

"I belong to you and you belong to me," I said. "Are you happy?"

"So happy that I am frightened."

I thought that a strange thing to say, but very touching, too. I put up
my hand and pressed it against the other side of his head, forcing our
faces closer.

"There is nothing to be frightened about. And if there were, it is *I* who
should be frightened." I said that rallyingly.

He said, almost in a whisper, "I would never do anything to hurt you.
Never."

Was it, I wonder, the fear of hurting me that made him fail? He
loved me, I loved him, we were both sound and young. . . . But it was no
good.

It was an odd circumstance that I, who at Minsham had been so clear-
sighted, so contemptuous of all pretence, should change my nature with
my name, and wholeheartedly begin to play a game of make-believe.
I had not realised that I was so truly the daughter of my parents; here
was I, pretending that all was well, pretending that I was a properly
married woman, just as Mother always pretended that some day something would happen to restore our fortunes, and Father pretended he
was a landed gentleman. I discovered another thing about myself, too, I
was hotly passionate. There were times when I felt that out of my own
eagerness I could *make* it happen. This time! This time! I would think.
Now! Now! Poor Richard, groaning and sweating, as puzzled as I was
myself, would eventually fall asleep, and then I would cry, softly, secretly,
and rather ashamed. I would accuse myself of being ungrateful, too; for
apart from this one thing my new life was wonderful, better than I had
ever imagined life could be.

The sheer comfort we enjoyed was a lasting joy and an amazement.
People might laugh and sneer about merchants and their new money;
they knew how to live, how to build, and how to furnish. There was
more warmth and softness at the Old Vine than in Abhurst, Beauclaire,
and Rivington rolled into one. As for Minsham Old Hall, I was soon wondering how I had endured the stone floor, the unglazed windows, the
draughts that stirred your hair even as you sat by the hearth.

The Old Vine was really two houses, divided by a wide cobbled passage
which was entered by a doorway, big enough and high enough, when it
was fully open, to allow a pack pony, loaded, to trot in. On the right
of this passage was that part of the house which Master Reed had built
first and lived in when he was starting his business. Richard took me over

it and showed me how it had been. His father had had one room, his Uncle Tom the other, and there had been a kitchen for cooking and that was all. After some years, rooms had been built above all these apartments. One of them had been the room in which Richard had learned his lessons, he said.

Because I loved him, everything about him, back to when he was very young, was interesting to me, and when he pointed to the door and told me that, I was interested to see the room.

"The servants sleep there now. You don't want to look in there," he said.

"I think you hated your lessons," I said teasingly.

"No. After a week I liked my lessons, but I hated my master. Sometimes even now, I dream . . ."

"Oh, so do I. My Aunt Bowdegrave, teaching me to dance, and saying I had two left feet and would never find a husband . . ." I cut that off sharply and said, "I was ten years old." Something that I could never find a name for had made me withhold from Richard all the story of my humiliating youth. I wanted him to desire me, so I must always seem to have been desired. "Little she knew!" I said gaily.

"In those days I used to sleep here," Richard said, moving to the other door. "When Father made the office downstairs, Uncle Tom moved up. He's not my real uncle, but I still call him that. He was Father's partner once. He's bedridden now and a bit . . ." He tapped his head and made a face. "But if you'd like to see him."

"I want to see everything."

Richard opened the door and said, "Uncle Tom. I've brought you a visitor."

The old man in the bed must once have been big and stout, he had shrunken and the flesh hung on his bones in heavy folds. There was a musty, old-man smell in the room, and, added to it, another, even less pleasant, which, as I moved towards the bed, I knew came from a great, badly cured bearskin which lay across the foot of the bed.

Uncle Tom's eyes were bleary and his stare vague at first, but when I was near enough, something quickened in them and he grinned. I'd seen his like before, hobbling old dotards until they catch you behind the screen or in a lonely passage.

"A pretty one, too. Cure for sore eyes, you are, little mistress."

"Thank you," I said; and smiled and for fun bobbed him a curtsey.

"Aye, and better still, saucy."

"Anne is my wife," Richard said, a trifle stiffly I thought.

"Your wife, eh?" That seemed to take a little while to sink in. Then he said, "You're Lucky Dick; allust hev bin. Right from the first. Like your

dad. Well . . ." He looked me up and down, and I had a sudden, disconcerting certainty that he knew about us. This going over the house took
place on my second or third day there, and the thing was, naturally, still
raw and tender, in the forefront of my mind. "See you do right by her,"
Uncle Tom said. "Make the most of your chance while you can. You
shrivel and dry up afore you know where you are."

Richard took hold of my elbow and said, "Come along."

That was the old part of the house.

On the other side of the central passage the rooms were larger and
higher. There was the solar, with the window which looked out into a
garden, with a plot for herbs, and some fruit trees, and roses. Behind the
solar was a dining hall, where, every day, at dinner and supper, we and
several of the workmen and apprentices sat down together. Except that it
lacked a dais, it was like the hall of a great house. Richard, his father, and
I sat at a solid oak table which was never moved; the rest had trestles and
boards which could be set up or taken down according to the number of
places required. The food served here was good and plentiful and to me
delicious; but there were always other dishes, cakes, fruits, and sweetmeats,
in the livery cupboard of the solar.

Above the solar and dining hall were the bedrooms of the family.

Across the yard were stables and lofts, the sheds where wool was stored,
the "floors" where the fleeces were picked over. There was a smithy, a cow
byre, a pigsty and a hen roost, a round house for pigeons, and a pond.
Thirty years ago, Richard said, when his father had started, there had
been nothing at all, just a field full of old vine stumps. It seemed to me a
lot to have built up and set working in thirty years, but that was not all;
Master Reed had two ships on the sea, a warehouse in Amsterdam, and, of
course, the sheep run at Minsham. He would have been justified in being
very proud of his achievement, but I never saw him give any sign of being
so. Except that he loved Richard, was kind to me, and apparently faithful
to his old partner, he showed very few signs of any emotions; he was never
angry, he never laughed, he never seemed to be in a hurry, and he was
never ill. Richard said that he was a strict, but just employer. It took me a
little time to learn that his settled scowl and silence and sombre looks were
not due to ill-humour, and I was always disproportionately pleased if I
could coax a smile from him. I often felt a little sorry for him; he worked
so hard, every day, from dawn to dusk, just, it seemed, for the sake of
working; rather like an old horse at a millwheel or a well, which will go
round and round, plodding at the same pace, whether it is being driven
or not.

You might have imagined that a man who set such high store by work would have been a hard taskmaster to his son. Nothing was farther from the truth. Mother had said that Richard was under his father's thumb, but it was a most gentle, kindly thumb. "Leave that to me, boy," or "I'll see to it," were words constantly on his lips.

All through that first autumn of my married life, Richard and I just frivolled the time away. We took long rides, went to Bywater—where I saw the sea for the first time—and to Walsingham, and Colchester, Lavenham, Melford, Sudbury, and Clare. Summer died slowly that year, and in the fine warm weather the roads were busy with pilgrims and merchants and the people who made their living by amusing them. These last, the minstrels and tumblers and jugglers, had a fascination for Richard; he would watch them for hours, even make a special journey in the hope of catching up with some particularly pleasing performer again, and seemed actually to envy them. Once he said:

"Not to be tied to any place . . . don't you think that would be pleasant. I've often thought that I should like to take my lute and just set out."

"You play well enough. But it must be a hard life, especially in winter. And not being tied to any place means not belonging anywhere. I know. I spent my childhood moving from place to place. I hated it. I always had to leave something behind." I told him how, once, at Rivington, I had almost tamed a wild cat out of the woods; he was so pretty, striped tawny and grey, with tawny eyes. We must have stayed there for some time, because I had got him to the point where he would come when I called— if I waited long enough—and take meat from my hand, though he never would let me stroke him. At another place I had made a little garden; I'd planted gillyflower seeds and meant to make some gillyflower water and scent myself all over. We moved on when the little green plants were two inches high.

"Poor Anne," Richard said. "You've always wanted to settle. I've always wanted to get away."

"From what?"

"Ah. That I can't tell you. It's something that comes over me. I sit at the table sometimes and think here we are and here we shall be next year and next and next, and I feel as though I were stifling. Then I think: If only I could take my lute and go, gather a crowd and play and *play*."

For a moment he looked unlike himself, wild, altered, as though the wind were blowing through him, as though he could hear the music he dreamed of making. I felt left out, left behind.

"It's silly. I should hate it really, sleeping in a ditch or under a haystack."

"And rough company. And not enough to eat."

One place where we rode often, was of course, Minsham. Mother, on my first visit, had contented herself with asking was all well with me, and I told her everything was wonderfully well. The second and third time she asked no questions, but on the fourth, I remember it well, it was in October, and Richard had gone out to join Father and Isabel in beating the walnut tree, Mother said:

"You've not quickened yet?"

"Two months . . . no three . . . Three months is not long."

"No," she said. "No"; but her voice said the opposite. "But you should lose no time. You know what they say, and truly: For every year over sixteen there's an hour's labour with the first. You were sixteen last February. I bore my first a few weeks after my sixteenth birthday—they say women forget, but I remember it to this day, and I would not have you go through that *and* the extra hour. Get your first with all possible speed—the rest comes easy."

"It's not a thing I can order."

"You shouldn't ride so much. We are pleased to see you. . . . But unless compelled no married woman should set foot in stirrup for a year. It's like junket—it will never set if you keep stirring."

That evening, riding home, I was thoughtful. Once, on one of my visits, I had been present at a birth. One of my Aunt Astallon's attendants had had a clandestine love affair and had, up to the last moment, concealed her state, wearing a heavily pleated houppelande and joking about getting so fat. In the night, in the dormitory where six of us lay, her hour had come upon her, and nine hours later she was delivered. I could hear her screams still. And she was . . . how old? Getting on. Twenty-five perhaps. Yes, it worked out.

In the night, in the bed I said, "Are you afraid of hurting me? Is that it? Darling, pain now will spare me later. Hurt me. I want to be hurt."

But we ended, as we always had, with me comforting him, pretending, pretending. Never mind. Next time. All will be well.

I still rode—though the days drew in; but I made excuses not to ride Minsham way, and I did not have to face Mother again until Christmas, when, at Master Reed's invitation, she and Father and Isabel rode in to keep the feast with us. They stayed four days, and we had a right merry time, and I managed never to be alone with Mother long enough for her to ask me awkward questions. However, my father, who had remembered his first conversation with Richard—about hawks and hawking—had procured for him, as a Christmas gift, a young eyas tiercel which was to be trained, and eventually flown at Minsham.

"A lot of riding for you," Father said. "Because if you want him to answer your whistle, you must give him his beef as often as possible and whistle as you do it."

Mother gave me what she no doubt thought was a subtle, sly look, a grimace that would have been noticeable a street's width away. I nodded to show that I understood.

So the new year opened for me with a most embarrassing problem. Richard was riding out to Minsham twice a week, and always expected me, unless the weather was very foul, to go with him. And if I did, Mother would accuse me of stirring the junket. Under the strain of making silly excuses, either to one or the other, I became bad-tempered. His lute first, now his hawk I'd think to myself, he really never wanted a wife at all!

Once that thought had entered my head, I never completely got rid of it again. Richard had told me how he had first seen me—at the time when his father brought the blue cloth; how he had fallen in love with me then and dreamed of me ever since. When I heard that story first I thought it was romantic, now, looking at it in the light of later knowledge, I had a suspicion that perhaps he would have been content to let it *stay* a dream, just as he was content to dream about that other unlikely thing, being a wandering minstrel. He liked the idea of being in love, he liked my company, perhaps (may God forgive me the unkindness of this thought) the knowledge of my better birth and station added to the romantic idea; what he didn't want, and had no need of, was a real flesh-and-blood woman in his bed.

I rode out with him once during January at the time of the month when even Mother could not complain of my being in the saddle. Then, despite all his pleadings, I made excuses until the next time the moon ruled my blood. That time, as she greeted me, Mother said, "What, again!"

The ill-humour into which this remark threw me was not improved by the tone of her conversation throughout my visit. Had I been eating green apples? Where, I retorted, would I find green apples in February? Don't sit on grass. Lately, I snapped, there had been little temptation to do so.

"You are so irritable," she said, "that I wonder if you are not already pregnant and deceiving me. Is that so?"

I was tempted to nod and so end it, but I had no wish to complicate matters even more, so I shook my head. She then went on to tell me two more helpful things. I should steep a pound of red meat in water, let it soak overnight, then squeeze it and drink the juice. And I should borrow a shift or a petticoat from a woman lately brought to bed, wear it without washing it for a month, then return it to her with a present of a new garment, red in colour.

"What an old wives' tale!" I said.

"Old wives are usually mothers and their tales should be heeded," she replied.

That afternoon, as we rode home, it began to rain, and as soon as we arrived we went up to our room to throw off our wet clothes. Flinging my soaked hood on the floor, I said angrily, "It'll be a long time before I go to Minsham again!"

"Why, sweetheart? I thought you liked to go."

Suddenly everything boiled up in me.

"How can you be so stupid and blind," I shouted at him. Then I began to cry, and mixed up with the sobs and the blubberings it all came out, Mother's questions and admonitions, my evasions and pretences, my suspicions that he wanted a sweetheart but not a wife, everything, everything.

I had flung myself down on the bed, burrowing my face into the pillow, and when I had said *everything* I knew that I had said too much. I lifted my head a little and looked at him. I was frightened. He had the wild look on him and had gone as white as chalk. Now I had thrown away what I had had, a loving and pleasant companion, I thought.

He said, "I'll show you."

And there, amongst the wet clothes and the messed bedclothes, in the fading light of the February afternoon, I lost my virginity at last.

III

Now for me no more riding horseback; no green apples; no sitting on grass; retching and revolted, I gulped down pints of red meat juice, and when, early in June, one of the workmen's wives in the huts beyond the stables was brought to bed I borrowed her filthy petticoat and wore it, flea-ridden as it was and returned it, in July with a fine red woolsey cloak. It all availed me nothing; the August moon ruled me, this year as last.

All this was my private concern. Around me things moved on. Master Reed had taken another stride forward, and was building again. His new notion was to bring over some Flemish weavers to ply their craft in Baildon.

The Flemings were, at this time, an unhappy people, subject to this rule and that as the fortune of war decided. Richard had told me how, on one of his visits to the Low Countries, he had seen between three and four hundred people, men, women, and children, being herded along the roads, like animals being taken to market. Their ruler of the moment, the Emperor, or the King of France or the Duke of Burgundy—I was never clear on that point—had decided that one town was too full of people and another too empty, so they were arbitrarily chosen and made to move.

With such circumstances prevailing in their home country, Flemings were always willing to take service elsewhere. The best hired mercenaries were always Flemings, *routiers*, they were called. And the best craftsmen, the weavers, were unsettled too. Master Reed, who at set intervals made the voyage in one of his ships and visited his warehouse in Amsterdam, had engaged eight skilled men to come to Baildon and ply their craft.

A new building was reared, running out at an angle from the main house. The upper floor, very stoutly built to sustain the weight and thud of the looms, was to be the weaving shed; below it the weavers, all single young men, were to live. The weaving shed was a unique structure in that its walls were almost all window. The glass was very costly, but Master Reed was sure that within four years he would have reimbursed himself. There would be no duty to pay on the home-woven stuff, and he reckoned that he could sell it so cheaply that he would undercut everybody else.

"I began," he said once, "by doing smith work cheap. Then I offered cheap stabling. And when I went into the wool trade I was still cheap; I gave a little more for the raw fleeces and sold the baled wool for a little less. Now I hope to sell good cloth, *cheap*."

I think that was the longest speech I had ever heard him make.

The building was finished and the Flemings arrived in June—while I was wearing that horrible petticoat and trying to scratch myself without being noticed. And all through July and August, Master Reed and Richard were dealing with the problem of language. Master Reed had learned enough to make himself understood in Amsterdam; Richard knew rather more, he had been inland as far as Bruges and being young had a more pliable mind. But the Flemings were difficult; they worked very well and needed little instruction or guidance so long as they were at their looms, trouble began when they took their feet from the treadles. They made straight for the town then, and in the town they were foreigners, everything they did suspect and resented; this they could not, or would not understand, so fights took place for the most trivial reasons, or for no reason at all. They were woman-hungry, and since no respectable females would have anything to do with them they fell into the hands of whores and harpies who cheated and robbed them. It would all have been different and easier had Master Reed been popular in Baildon; but just as he hated all the townspeople, they hated him and took pleasure in dealing him a knock through the foreigners he had imported. Once they were all inside the town wall when the gates were locked for the night and then arrested for being vagrants. By the end of August, Master Reed was talking of finding someone capable of speaking to them in their own tongue and of controlling them.

"Some old *routier*," Richard said, "with a good hard hand. They'd understand that."

"And where would you find one, except on the road, a broken-down ne'er-do-well?" Master Reed said.

Anxious to be helpful, I said to Richard, "My father might know of one, or my brother. Mention it next time you are at Minsham."

He still rode out there two or three times a week, and I always sent a present of some kind, with some kind of excuse—we'd killed a pig and were glutted with pork, or this was a cake I'd made myself, or this was one of the first pieces of cloth from the Baildon loom. I did not go myself. Now that all was well between Richard and me I could send a downright frank message—"Tell Mother to remember the junket," I could say. And he could laugh.

Halfway through September he came back from Minsham with two pieces of news. One was that Isabel was to go to stay with Aunt Astallon, and the other was that as soon as she had gone Mother was coming to see me; she intended to stay two nights in Baildon at least.

"Is Father coming too?"

"No. Your mother only. She said she had business to do."

I sighed. What her business might be I could not guess; one thing was sure, she would find time to go into mine. Still, I braced myself. I was no longer playing at being married. Richard and I were *married* and in that assurance I felt I could face her.

She arrived riding the better horse of the two, the one Father usually rode, and when I had greeted her I asked, "What happened to Mag?"

"I'm going farther afield," she said mysteriously. "I was on my knees the other night, with my rosary in my hands, and the blessed Virgin herself put a thought into my mind."

I had a feeling that this concerned me, so I said, with levity, "That poor old Mag should be put to pasture?"

Dear Mother; she laughed.

"No. That we should go to St. Edmundsbury."

"What for?"

"Anne, you have now been married for more than a year. And you've been a good girl and followed my instructions. The time has come when nothing but a visit to St. Petronella can help us."

"St. Petronella. I never heard of her."

"Nor I, until I consulted the priest. Now there's a thing you never thought to do, I'll warrant." She looked at me gaily. "St. Petronella is the one for us. And how fortunate that she is so near."

We had the solar to ourselves; and while Mother refreshed herself she told me all that she had learned from the priest.

St. Petronella, in her lifetime, had been a fish-gutter at Talmont in France, and in a quarrel with a fellow-worker had been so slashed about the face that no man could look on her without a shudder. So her longing for children was never gratified, and when, after a long and holy life, she died and was beatified she gave special notice to the prayers of barren women.

About a hundred years before I was born a Franciscan friar found his way to St. Edmundsbury and was concerned by the number of lepers living in destitution outside the town. He wished to help them, but had no money, nothing but faith and his own resourcefulness. He made a Cross of elmwood and carried it, preaching and begging as he went, all the way to Le Mans where he laid it on St. Petronella's shrine amongst all the glittering votive and thanks-offering that covered it. He prayed that some virtue might pass into the wood. Then he carried it back and announced that virtue *had* passed into it. He set it up under an arch of rough stones and it had become a place of pilgrimage for childless women. As long as he lived he used the income of the shrine for the relief of lepers, and when he died the Abbey took over the shrine and built a little house for the lepers.

All this Mother told me as she drank some ale and ate cake in the solar. I listened and thanked her for her interest and concern for me. Once I had resented her questions and advice, but now it was different. Nevertheless, when she said:

"We'll go there, together, tomorrow," I protested.

"What excuse can we give?"

"Why excuse. You can give your real reason."

"It is a matter that is never mentioned, not even between Richard and me. As for his father . . ."

"Nonsense! To not mention a thing is not to say it does not exist. I'll warrant that Richard and his father have watched you with eyes as keen as mine, and been as greatly disappointed."

"Oh dear," I said.

"Never mind, we are doing all that we can. And the priest assured me that the Saint has worked some wondrous miracles."

I announced—brusquely because I was embarrassed—that on the morrow Mother and I intended to ride to St. Edmundsbury. Richard put out his hand and squeezed mine, understandingly. Master Reed looked at me sombrely out of his sad eyes and presently, when we chanced to be alone for a moment, said to me:

"Anne, I know the purpose of your journey, and I wish you well.

But . . ." He hesitated and then said jerkily, the words coming out of him in a rush, "Don't count too much upon it. Miracles . . ." He paused again and looked down at his lame leg and the thick-soled shoe. "They work in a queer twisted way," he said. "And I can't for the life of me see how what you're wanting could be other than straightforward. And I don't believe they can be that way. Miracles, I mean." He touched my shoulder and said, "Perhaps your faith is greater."

Next morning we set out, Mother and I, with a man to escort us. Richard wanted to come, but that I did not favour, why I could not say. I would not have taken the man, but Master Reed insisted; he was shocked to learn that Mother had ridden in from Minsham alone. His view of the open road was the view of the man who transports stuff of value from place to place and must ever be on guard against robbers.

There was no need to inquire the way to the shrine. Long before we reached it we found ourselves in the centre of a kind of fair, a fair devoted to the exploitation of childless women. It was so shameless that I wonder the Abbey allowed it. There were people selling charms, all guaranteed to bring fecundity; cakes made in the shape of babies; trinkets of bone or wood or stone, even of coral and ivory, all in the shape of babies. There were strings and strings of blue beads—blue being the Virgin's own colour and thus associated with motherhood. There were slatternly women with great broods of children—borrowed or hired, I suspect, lining the road and screaming that they would sell, for a penny, the secret of their fruitfulness. "Twopence, lady, and I'll put the good wish on you!" "Threepence, lady, and you shall be in pod by Michaelmas." I was ashamed and drew my veil close, and even Mother said:

"They overdo it somewhat."

Monks are cunning. After all that brash huckstering along the road, with the constant demand for pence breeding disbelief until you were ready to think of St. Petronella as just another fraud, out to rob you, you rode through a gateway where only petitioners and their attendants were allowed to pass. Inside was a kind of inn; rails to which horses could be hitched, a stone trough full of water, benches and tables where people could refresh themselves. The whole place was shaded by chestnut trees, from which, on this day, the great yellow fans of dead leaves fluttered gently and quietly to the ground.

On the far side of this enclosure was a gate in the wall. Through this the petitioner must go alone. The path beyond was paved and bordered on each side by a green hedge, neatly clipped, very thick, and an inch or two taller than a man. The path wound in curves so that at no time could I see more than a step or two ahead. I have never felt more lonely, more isolated from all other human beings. The contrast after the bustle and hurly-burly outside was complete. When I rounded the last curve there was the plain wooden Cross, under the rough stone arch, just as the Franciscan had set it up, more than a hundred years ago.

Offerings to this shrine were always in money—used for the relief of lepers and other purposes—so the shrine was quite bare, without even a flower. It was humble, and touching, and in some strange way far more believable and impressive than any other shrine I had ever seen. I went down on my knees and prayed that St. Petronella would use her influence, and intercede for me and give me a baby. Here, alone, in the quiet before this simple Cross, I could acknowledge the need which hitherto I had hidden even from myself. I thought about holding a baby in my arms, feeding it at my breast.

We rode home, and that evening at supper there was a new face halfway down the first trestle table; and because Mother was staying with us and sat at my usual place, I had a good view of the newcomer.

It is hard for me to describe this man, Denys the Routier, or Denys Rootyer as he came to be called. The most immediately noticeable thing about him was that he had only one eye; over the empty socket on the other side he wore a black leather patch, kept in position by a black string tied at the back of his head. His hair, roughly cut and inclined to be curly, was a pale sandy colour, many shades lighter than his weather-beaten skin; his one eye was brightly blue.

I was looking at him with interest because he was a stranger, and because of the black patch, when he turned his glance on me and immediately something happened inside me, as though something had given way and all my vitals had slipped. It was not unlike the first onset of sickness and I pressed my hand to my mouth and thought: Holy Mother! The miracle has happened and I have quickened. I looked at my plate, and although the dish was to my liking, specially made in honour of Mother, I knew that I could not take another mouthful.

Richard said, "The journey was too much for you. Come to bed. When you are rested I will bring you your supper."

"Fetch some wine; that will revive both our travellers," Master Reed said. So the wine came and I sat there holding the cup in my hands and turning it about, not daring to drink until my inside settled.

Mother and I answered questions about the journey.

Presently I said, "I see we have a new man."

"Ah yes." Master Reed turned to Mother and said, "Please tell Sir Godfrey that I am grateful and obliged to him for his good offices in finding so suitable a man."

"Oh, did Blanchfleur remember? He grows more and more forgetful

these days." She smiled as though describing a child's vagary. "Still, he
would remember a thing like that better than any simple errand I set him.
Which is the new man?" She craned her neck.

"The one with the patch over his eye," Richard said. "A good stout fellow, is he not?"

I looked again and saw that everyone else at the board was suddenly
diminished. The weavers were always somewhat pale, inclined to fleshi-
ness—that was a mark of their trade—but they were not all weavers at
the table. I glanced to right and left; Master Reed looked thick and
shapeless, Richard too fine-drawn, a pretty boy.

I told myself that it was because the new man wore no collar, his dark,
creased neck rose out of a collarless leather jerkin which fitted close to
his wide flat shoulders, and so he looked all of a piece, stripped of all
non-essentials, ready for action.

Mother was rippling on about *routiers;* their high reputation for loyalty
and courage, despite being mercenaries.

"But that is why," she explained. "Nobles and knights are forever
changing their causes for this reason and that, *routiers* fight for pay
and stick with the man who pays them." She lowered her voice a little.
"You must look to your maids, Master Reed; these old soldiers have a
way with women."

"Not old soldiers only," he said dryly. "I always choose old serving
wenches."

"Very wise."

I said, "I think I will go to bed now."

When I had been there a little while Richard came softly in, bringing
more wine and some food.

"Are you asleep?"

"No."

"Could you eat now?"

"No. I thank you all the same."

He put the things down and came and sat on the side of the bed.
"What really happened today?"

"Nothing really. . . ." I told him a little more about the way I had felt
by the bare, humble little shrine. Then I put my hands on either side of
his face and said, "I love you, I love you, I love you. You know that,
don't you?"

"Could I ever doubt it? I love you too."

Words, true words; but I need something more.

"Come in the bed with me, now."

He came to me eagerly, tenderly. He gave me all that he had. But
afterwards, in the dark, I lay alone again, and a voice, within my head,

yet distant as a star, asked, "Is this all?" I closed my mind to it, pushing against it, as one might push a door against an intruder. But it tried again; it asked, "How would this be, if done with the man with one eye?"

IV

MADNESS, we know, takes many forms; and this was mine. I never for one instant ceased to love Richard. There never was a moment, mad as I was, when to have saved Richard a pang of toothache I would not gladly have seen Denys the Routier hanged, drawn, and quartered. By all that is holy, I swear that this is true. The lust I felt for him was like a poison, swallowed unwittingly, doing its damage, taking possession of the whole sound body.

With Mother gone home I was back at my old place at the table, and could see him clearly only when he leaned forward or the man sitting next him leaned back. And after the first few days he was never there for the midday dinner and not to be counted upon at suppertime. In no time at all, talking to the Flemings in their own tongue, he had put the fear of God into them, and Master Reed, never one to waste anything, had begun to send him with the pack ponies as a kind of guard. So I never knew, when I entered the dining hall, whether his place would be filled or empty, and every evening, every evening for weeks, I vowed that this time I would not look. But I always did, sooner or later; and if his place was empty a kind of greyness would come over everything, my food would be tasteless. . . . Tomorrow, how many hours? Or perhaps, a long journey, the day after tomorrow. . . . It was like walking down a dark stone passage with a light at the far end. No, not a light, a dancing will-o'-the-wisp. For when the moment came and I looked and there he was, what then?

Oh, then, at some moment during the meal that one blue eye would look at me, and my inside would turn its now pleasurable somersault; the candlelight would brighten, the fire behind me throw out more heat, and I would know a moment of what I can only call timelessness. In that moment all kinds of things would rush together, reminding me of small pleasures I had known in the past and promising me a great pleasure to come—there'd be the cool scent of primroses, the warm scent of roses, the sound of trumpets, the feel of my Aunt Astallon's silk gown, the taste of strawberries, the colours of a sunset—all mixed up in one mad moment, meaning nothing, meaning everything. How can I explain it? It was as though every pleasant thing that I had ever felt in the past was a separate string to a lute, and his glance was the running of a hand over those strings, so that they all cried out together, in no tunable pattern.

I never spoke to him, never had occasion to go near him until one morning in the spring. It was March, I remember seeing the daffodils breaking yellow in the garden close, under the apple trees. Richard was riding out to Minsham, and I said I would go too. St. Petronella had failed me yet again, and I had spent the whole winter cooped in the house.

Martin's horse and my palfrey stood awaiting us, and nearby a string of pack ponies, laden with the new Baildon cloth, were lining up for the first stage of their journey to London. Denys stood with them. He came forward—one of Martin Reed's servants, civil, obliging—and helped me to mount. When he touched me my bones melted. In the two seconds before I was in the saddle it was all said. "I am yours, take me," my flesh said to his; and his said, "Would that I could."

"You look so pale," Martin said, turning his horse beside me. "Are you sure you should ride?"

"You know that it is only when I am pale with such good reason that I dare face my mother," I said crossly. And all the way to Minsham I thought about Denys. We would make a child, I thought, the moment we came together. We could defy the moon, the pale moon with its fluxes. . . .

After that I suppose it was merely a question of awaiting an opportunity.

April passed and May. I had grown thin, which was not becoming to me. One day, looking in the glass, I was horrified to see that after all I had inherited the Blanchfleur nose and would one day look exactly like an aunt I detested. Richard and his father put down my lack of appetite and uncertain temper to disappointment and were kinder than ever to me, which, because it made me feel ashamed, made matters worse.

June was always a busy month, with the new-cut fleeces pouring in from miles around, and often Richard would rise early, leaving me to slugabed. One morning he did so, and when I did go down I looked into the office, but he wasn't there, which was nothing unusual. Dinnertime came and the oak table was set with two places only.

"Where's Richard?" I asked.

"Gone to Bywater. We had word early this morning that *Sea Maid* had run into another ship and was damaged. He rode down to see what the damage was. He'll be back tomorrow." He set about his meal and then stopped. "I'm off myself to Kelvedon this minute. You'll be alone in the new part. Would you like Nancy or Meg to move over?"

"For fear of what?"

"Whatever it is women fear. Ghosties and goblins?" He gave me his painful, rare smile.

"Anything a kitchen wench could save me from I do not fear," I said.

Yet I had no intention of taking Denys into Richard's bed. I had no intention of doing anything. I did not even go into the hall for supper, to sit there alone, displaying my solitariness. I stayed close in the solar, thinking that he would think that I also had gone away. From the solar I went into the garden.

Every rose had its heart wide open; the languor of a summer evening weighed heavy on every leaf. I walked, lingered, walked on, unable to draw a full breath, my heart was so shaken.

Presently, between the rosebushes old Nancy came hobbling on her flat feet.

"Mistress," she began as soon as she saw me, "there's that Denys Rootyer at the back door. He say Master went off and never give him his orders for tomorrow. He say he ought to talk to you."

"Oh," I said, and struggled with my breath. Surely she must notice and wonder. "No orders were left with me. I know nothing."

"He seem to hev something in his mind. He just want somebody to say go ahead like. There ain't nobody else but you."

"I'll see him."

"Out here? Then you should hev a shawl. The dew's falling."

"Give him the shawl. That will save you a few steps."

"'Tain't everybody'd be thoughtful of an owd woman's feet," she said, pleased. "I give you good night, mistress."

Thinking no evil, thinking only of her bed, she plodded away. And presently, with his light, firm, soldier's tread, carrying my shawl over his arm, Denys came through the roses.

V

THERE followed some days during which, with a sense of bewilderment, I thought of Mother's words. I'd sit at the table and look at Richard, whom I loved, and then at Denys, whom I did not love, and I knew which of them gave me that feeling of triumph, of pride that had sounded in Mother's voice when she spoke of Father. How I envied her—and any other woman who could have that feeling lawfully, together *with* love. Those were days when I had only to see his great brown hand close on a piece of bread in the trencher to feel its touch on me again and wonder how, through all the years of my life, I could manage with what I had.

Those days were soon over. The July moon was a horned crescent, was a silver-gilt plate, grew gibbous and copper-coloured. It drew no response from my blood. To myself I said: I was right; I knew this would happen. To the others I said nothing. I waited until one morning towards the end of August, as soon as I set foot to the floor, I was deathly sick. Then I said to Richard:

"I think I am with child." And presently I was sure enough to send a message to my mother.

There was, naturally, great rejoicing. Even Master Reed threw off his melancholy air, and Richard's pride and pleasure cut me to the heart. I had other troubles too. One was shame and one was fear.

Now that the work was done and my womb was filling, all the lust went out of me, and all the madness, and I could see Denys for what he was—a great hunk of man flesh, a common hired soldier to whom I, Anne Blanchfleur, had submitted! There was the shame.

The fear lay in the thought that children tended to look like their parents. Suppose my child were born with that pale sandy hair and only one eye. How could I ever have been so crazy as not to have thought of that?

I studied Richard and his father. At a first glance they were unlike, Richard was much darker, much more lightly built, but the way the hair grew off their foreheads was the same, and they both had crooked little fingers on their left hands. True, Master Reed was lame and Richard had two good straight legs, but there were two schools of thought about such things. Some people held that anything that had happened to a man or woman by accident during his or her lifetime was not passed on to the offspring; other people claimed that anything that happened, even to having been frightened by a mouse, could leave a mark upon the child.

Mother rode in to see me and we had a long talk, all about such mysteries; I encouraged her and then wished I had not. She had a story of a pregnant woman who had longed for strawberries in December and who bore a child with a red strawberry mark on its left cheek.

"Whatever you long for, no matter how silly it sounds, speak out, Anne. Make them get it for you if possible."

I thought: I wonder how you would look if I told you that the one thing I long for is the assurance that a one-eyed man's child will not be born with one eye.

All this uneasiness of mind took its toll of my body. I think I suffered everything a pregnant woman can. They say that if you are sick at six weeks, at six months you'll be lively. They say that cramps beforehand are a sign of easy labour, you've had so much of your grue. They say that if your legs swell your face does not. I broke every one of the rules. I was sick at six weeks, and even sicker at six months; I had cramp;

my face swelled to the size of a bladder and my legs swelled till they
were as big as my waist ordinarily was; and in the end I was in labour
for two days and three nights.

Before the end I had my story ready. If I gave birth to a child with
one eye I was going to say that on the night when Richard and his father
were both away, Denys made an excuse to come to me in the garden,
and there raped me. Old Nancy would bear me out about the excuse, I
was in the garden, innocent as a lamb, and he did make that opportunity
to seek me out. Richard and his father would ask one dangerous question: Why had I not complained? To that I had a silly sentimental answer, silly enough to sound true. My father had found Denys for Master
Reed, and I didn't want him to think that Father had sent him a rogue.

My last sensible thought was of my story and how, if needs be, I must
stick to it. Then my agony began; and presently I didn't care if the
child were born with one eye or four, if only it would be born. I saw
Mother and screamed to her, "Help me!" and with tears on her face she
said, "You must be brave. You must help yourself. None other can."

I tried to be brave. I told myself that I was the daughter of one of the
boldest knights that ever rode in tourney, and of a woman who had set
out to ride from Rivington to Beauclaire, risking being brought to bed in
a ditch. But it went on too long. In the end I was screaming like a trapped
hare and I went on screaming until I had no voice left and could only
make harsh, weak cries. The pain abated and I floated away, and was
walking towards St. Petronella's shrine, but the solid green hedges were
all covered with open-hearted roses, drenching the air with scent. Just before the shrine Richard waited for me, but as I went near he turned into
Denys, holding a dark cloak with which he smothered me. I fought
against the weight of it and struggled up into the air and light again. The
priest was in the room.

I thought: I am dying. I wanted to say: I have a great sin to confess; I
have committed adultery. Had we been alone I might have said it, but
beyond the circle of the candlelight I saw other people—Mother, another
woman, several . . . Richard will hear about it, I thought, and be hurt,
and not revere my memory. No, sooner I would die unshriven and go
to Hell.

Hell was the Long Gallery at Abhurst, brightly lighted so that there
was no shadow into which one could retire. I stood alone and watched
four or five young men crowd about Catharine Montsorrel. My Aunt
Bowdegrave came and stood by me, showing her yellow teeth and saying
that with my sharp tongue and prim manner I should never find a
husband.

From there I slipped into a bottomless pit of darkness and lay there until someone above reached down with a grappling iron and hooked it into my body and hauled me up, screaming and struggling, and with each struggle the iron bit deeper into me, I was being cut in two. When I was severed what remained fell down upon the bed and the pain was over. I could hear a bustling and a soft clucking of tongues. Then I opened my eyes, and there was Mother, holding a baby, and the midwife with another.

"Twins," Mother said. "Boy and girl."

Twins were freaks; nobody expected them to be quite ordinary; if one, or both, lacked an eye, or even a limb, it would be no wonder. Holy Mother of God, you have dealt with me more gently than I deserve.

"Are they whole?" I whispered.

"Whole? They are beautiful."

Twins, Mother and the midwife agreed, are ordinarily smaller than other babies, but Walter and Maude were each as large as any single child; from this, and the abundance of hair on each of their heads, Mother deduced that I had carried them overlong and muddled my dates.

"Young women are so careless," she grumbled. "You told me March, and if they'd been born when they should, I might not have got to you in time."

They were not a bit like one another once the red, crumpled, newborn look had worn off. They were both born with black hair, but they shed it in the first weeks, and Walter's grew black again, Maude's reddish gold.

"The wrong way about," Mother said. "The boy should favour you, and the girl her father. As often happens."

"To our cost. My Blanchfleur nose! I would sooner have had yours."

Such trivial, cosy little conversations seemed to underline my sense of safety; as though I had forded a dangerous stream, been almost swept away, but struggled to safety and now could afford to talk about currents, deep waters, lost footholds. I was safe. I was lucky. I now had everything.

In a month I was up and about, fully restored to health, and, miracle of miracles, my waist was its normal size, I knew that by my dresses; my nose, now that the flesh was back on my face, took its proper place again, and I knew that I was prettier than ever.

There being two babies to feed, we were forced to engage a wet nurse —a thing not common in households of our degree, however rich—and when I proved to be a poor milch cow, while she had enough for four, she took on all that duty, and I was free to enjoy the summer and go riding with Richard again.

It was he who suggested that we should ride to St. Petronella's shrine and take a further present to show our gratitude. Something, and to this day I do not know exactly what it was, made me demur.

"I don't think that is customary. Women only go there to *ask.*"

"Then it's time somebody had manners enough to go and say thank you," he said, smiling.

I smiled too.

"I believe you have never been to St. Edmundsbury."

"That is so. We'll go, shall we?"

"You have to ride through the rowdiest kind of fair."

"I shall be with you. And this time you can look down your nose at all the spellbinders. I warrant none of *them* bore *two,* weighing a full stone between them."

To settle an argument between Mother and the midwife, Master Reed had carried the babies out and weighed them in the wool scales.

Having no argument, no reason for not riding that way, except a vague and mysterious feeling that it would be wiser not to, I gave way, and we set off on a fine warm morning.

Richard enjoyed himself enormously, especially when we reached the stalls. I was newly puzzled how anyone so gentle and fastidious and dignified should seem so much at ease in such surroundings. He bought gingerbread babies and charms of every kind, and a long string of blue beads which he slipped over my head, tangling it in my veil. Even the shaggy old harridan who so brazenly shouted "in pod"—only now she had changed her cry to "in pod by Lammas"—did not disgust him. He gave her fourpence and laughed when she promised us four lusty sons.

"Old fraud," he said as we moved on, "none of that gaggle of brats is hers, I'll warrant."

"Then why encourage her?"

"She must live. There's something about people who try to wring a living out of the world, with nothing but a slick tongue or a penny whistle, that appeals to me."

"I know. You might have been born at a fair, you seem so much at home."

"Then I could have played my lute."

"And dreamed of being the only son of a prosperous wool merchant, no doubt."

"No doubt at all."

We rode on and entered the enclosure. Richard slipped a gold piece into my hand, and I gave it to the monk by the inner gate. I set off briskly down the path, feeling the delight of moving freely and lightly again, and thinking that I had only to kneel and offer a few words of thanksgiving. But as I rounded one curve and then the next I found myself walking more and more slowly, while the distaste I felt for this apparently simple errand grew until it was terror. The day seemed to darken, and when I looked up at the sky I saw that a great purple cloud had reared up from the west and engulfed the sun.

I stood still and thought: I don't *have* to go any farther, no one will know. Stand here and count up to a hundred, twice, slowly. But that would be cowardly, and later I should despise myself. All my life I had heard a high price set on courage, and cowardice spoken of as rather worse than sin, and when I was a child, with my full share of childish fears, I had always schooled myself to overcome them. Now to be frightened of nothing, that was ridiculous. So I set myself in motion; walked on and reached the shrine which was in all respects just as before.

I went down on my knees and suddenly could think of nothing except the words Master Reed had said to me just before my first visit here. "Miracles . . . they work in a queer twisted way, and I can't for the life of me see how what you're wanting could be other than straightforward." But I could see, with sudden, clear sight, how my miracle had come about in, as he said, a queer, twisted way. Doubly twisted. First my madness, and then the fact that neither child bore any mark of its paternity. For let Mother say what she would about weight and crops of hair and muddled dates, I *knew*.

No doubt St. Petronella has been passionately thanked, even if the grateful petitioners did not make a journey to her shrine to do it, but she surely never was thanked, so passionately, so much from the heart, as I thanked her in that moment when I understood the extent of her miracle.

I went back to Richard and suggested that we should wait for a little, since that cloud threatened rain. We sat under the chestnut trees and ate and drank, and still the rain held off, and at last he said, "In summer it often clouds over without a drop falling." So we set off. When we were on the open road, far from any house, there was a fearful clap of thunder, and the heavens opened and down came the rain, mingled with hailstones as large as the blue beads I was wearing. I suggested sheltering under some trees nearby, but Richard said they were elms, dangerous at any time and doubly so in a storm, so we rode on, soon drenched and then shivering, for the day had turned cold as the hail fell.

Next day Richard was feverish and stayed in bed, hot and cold by turns, and coughing now and then. I made linseed poultices for his chest and rubbed him well with neat's-foot oil and beat honey and vinegar together for him to swallow, but the cough grew worse, and after the third night, when he had kept all our side of the house, save the babies, awake with it, Master Reed sent for the doctor. He had several remedies to try—one, the nature of which I concealed from Richard—was the liquor in which snails had been boiled, but nothing did any service until one morning he came along with a little horn full of a greenish-grey powder. One pinch of it, as much as one could take between finger and thumb, was to be dropped on top of a cup of warm milk or wine; just the one pinch and the dose was not to be repeated in less than twelve hours.

"It is," the doctor said, "a sovereign remedy, but it is also a powerful poison; taken in quantity, or too often, it could be fatal."

"I alone will administer it, and I will be very careful."

That night he slept, and sleep is itself a healer. In the morning his fever was lessened, his skin moist and cool to the touch. During the day the cough returned, but less violently, and so day by day he made progress. In most ways he was an easy patient, grateful and cheerful, but being held to the one room irked him; his only complaint was that the walls seemed to be closing in. We pushed the bed close to the window and propped him up so that he could look out and see the sky. And as soon as he was well enough—about three weeks after our unfortunate journey—he came down, leaning on his father's arm, into the solar.

That was a happy day, and as soon as he was settled in the window seat, overlooking the garden, I got out my sewing which I had neglected lately. I was making Mother a winter cloak, of our own Baildon cloth, the cloth which was to become so famous that men would speak of "my Baildon breeches," and women say, "I will wear my Baildon." The cloth itself was dove grey, there was an interlining of shredded-out lambs' wool, and a lining of red silk, the two last quilted together. It had a hood which could be pulled over the head or thrown back. It was, in fact, such a garment as Mother had never owned. Master Reed, immediately after our marriage, had done a generous thing, hired, for some absurdly high price, several of the acres which went with the house, to add to his sheep run, but none of the extra money found its way into Mother's wardrobe. Isabel went out into the world better equipped, and Mag, the old horse, had been replaced.

I was stitching away, when Richard said, "That is for your mother's birthday, isn't it?"

"Yes. The day after tomorrow and I still have this much of the lining to fix, and then the hood to stitch on." I held it out and showed him.

"It'll be ready. And I shall be ready to ride out and take it."

"I should no more dream of letting you ride out to Minsham the day after tomorrow than I should dream of . . . well . . . of throwing myself into the river."

"But I'm better."

"You're downstairs today for the first time. A fortnight hence will be time enough to talk about mounting a horse."

"I want to see Jason." That was his hawk.

"Then you must want," I said, stitching away.

"Uncle Tom once warned me that all high-nosed women were masterful and domineering!"

"How strange. Somebody once warned me that all black-haired men were obstinate and unreasonable."

He laughed and coughed.

"You sound like riding abroad the day after tomorrow."

"I shall."

"Then you'll go alone. I will not lend my countenance to such a thing."

Just then Master Reed entered the solar and Richard appealed to him to decide.

"You would be more than foolish. Just to visit a hawk."

"But Anne will want to see her mother."

"So she shall. Clement can ride with her and take out the tar and spend his day helping the shepherd."

Mother's birthday dawned clear and bright, and Richard woke feeling so much better that I had to repeat my threat that if he rode I would stay at home. His improvement and the fair morning sent my spirits soaring.

When I was ready to leave Master Reed came into the yard with me, carrying a small cask of wine.

"For your mother, with good wishes," he said, and muttered something about it being a balance for the tar barrel.

There in the yard stood a big brown horse, and my palfrey, and standing between them Denys.

I know my step faltered, for Master Reed said, "Forgotten something?"

I shook my head and went forward, wondering whether I could at this last moment say that I felt ill. A coward's trick, and disappointing for Mother. And perhaps, after all, Denys was only holding the horses; it was Clement—who understood sheep—who was supposed to spend the day at Minsham with the shepherd. I stood, all confused and uncertain, sweat breaking out on my forehead and upper lip and the palms of my hands, while the two men slung the wine cask.

There was still time to droop and dwindle and pretend a sudden pain. But I said to myself: Courage, courage.

Master Reed turned to me and said, "Up you get," and helped me into the saddle. I rode out through the covered way first and, once out of the gate, drove in my heel. My palfrey had never once been underfed or overburdened, or hard pressed, and during Richard's illness had stood in the stable cramming corn. "Let's see what you can do today," I said in its ear.

It did well. The road, heavy from the recent rainy spell, was in our favour; the brown horse was bigger, but Denys weighed all of twelve stone, and there were the two casks.

For eight of the ten miles I stayed ahead, then my beast slackened pace, and nothing I could do could make it recover speed. Out of nowhere there came to me the rhyme which Father had said to us, jogging us on his knee.

"This is the way the ladies ride, trippety, trip, trippety, trip. This is the way the farmers ride, bumpitty, thud, bumpitty, thud." And in the end, I thought, bumpitty thud will always catch up with trippety trip. How I longed for the horse in the end of the rhyme, "This is the way the gentlemen ride, gallop and trot, gallop and trot."

Denys came level with me and snatched at my rein.

"Did the brute bolt?" He pulled the rein savagely, so that my palfrey's head was wrenched round and we stood sideways across the road.

"Don't do that. I set the pace. I am anxious to arrive."

He said, and I shall always remember the curious simplicity and innocence that there was both in his voice and in his eye, "I wanted to talk to you. It's been a whole year, with never so much as a word."

I said nothing.

"This was our chance to fix something; to meet; to get together again," he said, as though explaining something to a stupid child. "I've been wanting you so badly, I wonder I haven't done something desperate, all these months. I wonder you never tried . . ."

He had no suspicion of the way I felt. I'd swung my horse about again so that it was facing the right way, and he brought his alongside, and put out his arm to touch me, but the tar barrel prevented him coming close enough.

"Come on, get down," he said in a thick, amorous voice.

I thought the quickest cut would be best. He had dropped my rein, so I set my palfrey going, and he came level, and I said, "What happened last June twelvemonth happened because I was mad. It must never happen again."

"Oh, come! What was so mad about it? And what harm did we do? I'd lay a year's pay you never had it so good—and nor did I. Things being so cursed difficult I tried to put you out of my mind, but I never could. And you'd say the same if you weren't trying to play coy with me. There's no need for that . . . and no time."

"I mean what I say. It's finished. Over and done with."

"It'll all come back. Women are often that way, after childbed. You'll see. This evening, eh? On our way back."

"Not then, or any other time," I said, trying to get another spurt of speed out of my horse.

He seemed genuinely puzzled. "What's got into you? What've I done? I'm just the same. You were starving for it—oh, I could tell. And I didn't do so badly by you. Two sound brats, with no lung rot."

Anger flared in me, but I mastered it, and said coolly, "You flatter yourself."

"Do I? Bedded for a year with a pretty boy that couldn't father a mouse —a woman like you! Think back to that night on the grass and look what you're missing." He followed this by a remark of such coarseness and familiarity as was not to be tolerated, even if it were deserved.

"At the next bend we shall be in sight of my father's house," I said. "Drop back and ride behind me as a servant should."

He laughed. "That's my lady! Like plums, the higher the sweeter, once you can reach them down." He hit my palfrey a sharp blow and it shot forward.

"That's the way," he cried, "let's ride in in style."

VI

FOR me the day was ruined. Mother was delighted with the cloak and the wine, pleased to see me, and avid to hear the last smallest detail about Walter and Maude, but I had to make a great effort to chat light-heartedly, and a greater one to do justice to the birthday dinner. I had to ride back to Baildon in Denys' company. The irony of the thought that little more than a year ago no prospect would have pleased me more only served to underline the horror of my present situation.

I have never known a day go so fast.

I gave Jason the gobbet of red meat which Richard had sent him, and listened absent-mindedly while Father explained that these last three weeks, during which Richard had not ridden out to Minsham at all, would make an excellent excuse for the fact that the young hawk would never accept him as his master.

"I've feared it all along," he said in his slow, fumbling way. "Twice a week . . . and let him be the only one ever to take the rufter off. I thought that might just do it. I was wrong and I was afraid the poor fellow would be disappointed, we can lay the blame now on these three weeks."

With some vague idea of handicapping Denys on the return journey

I said, "I can't think why you didn't let Richard have his hawk at the Old Vine in the first place. Shall we take it back with us this afternoon? I think that would please him."

"But who at the Old Vine understands falconry? That's just it. A tiercel isn't a lap dog, Anne. Maybe I was foolish . . . but he had shown some slight interest in hawking . . . I told you, that first time. And your mother thought . . ."

"Mother thought *what?*"

"That to get out, out of that office, into the air . . . Oh, I know twice a week isn't much, isn't enough, but it did make an excuse. And, as usual, your Mother was right, wasn't she? So the hawk wasn't wasted, though I daresay Richard will be a bit jealous that I can now handle his bird. Still, nobody can help being ill."

"May I carry Jason back with me this afternoon?"

"No. You can't handle him. . . . Isabel now, if it was Isabel, but you never cared for the sport. And you'd have no place—not so much as a perch. An unhandled hawk, especially one half trained like Jason'd go mad, or pine to death. No. When Richard is better, which God send will be soon, he must come out, and I'll fool them both. I'll stand close to him and whistle my whistle through *his*. We'll manage."

Alone with Mother again, I put on the drooping, dwindling look which I would have been wise to have put on in the yard hours before.

"You warned me about riding, but you had it all wrong. It is now that the jolting hurts me."

She looked concerned. "I thought you looked very wan when you came in. You had a hard time, you know, and it's not so long. Richard ill too, I daresay you've been up and down stairs and having broken nights."

"If my bed were aired," I said, "I would lie here tonight. Denys could tell them that I was just tired."

"The bed hasn't been slept in since Isabel went. But I could air it in an hour."

"Then I'll stay, and gladly."

Mother threw fresh wood on the fire and began to climb the stairs. "I'll help you," I said.

"You'll do nothing of the sort. I can handle that bed. It isn't like those great fat feather bundles you lie on at Baildon." She laughed. In a few seconds she came out of my old room with the bed—a poor thin thing indeed—folded over into a roll and held in her arms. She came down three stairs, then the inside edge of the roll loosened itself and fell lower than the rest; she stepped into it, as it were, missed her footing, almost righted herself, and could have, had that staircase had a handrail to clutch at, but it hadn't; she clutched at air and fell sideways onto the floor of the hall.

She was up in an instant, before I could get to her.

"Clumsy!" she said, and laughed.

"Are you hurt?"

"Not a bit." She went to the foot of the stairs where the mattress, now fully unfolded, lay, and picked it up and gave it a shake.

"Trip me, would you?" she said. "I'll roast you for that!"

We propped it up before the fire, and the amount of steam which rose from it proved its need for airing. Minsham Old Hall was very damp always, on the hottest day of summer you could write your name on the dewy moisture of the walls.

For supper we ate the remains of the birthday dinner and drank some more of the wine, and now we were truly merry. Denys had gone, with a black look for me over Mother's shoulder when she gave him his instructions at the door. Tomorrow Father was to ride in with me, and once in the house I should be safe. I'd never ride anywhere again until Richard was fit to ride with me.

Getting up from the supper table, Mother clapped her hand to her side and gave a little cry.

"I must have caught myself a clout without knowing it. A bruise, no more." But even her lips had gone white.

She was up in the morning, however, very cheerful, holding herself a mite stiffly and saying that forty-six was a bit old to go turning somersaults.

"I shall ride in myself next Wednesday to see those dear children," she said, as we parted. "Meanwhile, wish Richard good health for me and thank Master Reed for the wine."

I rode back to Baildon, thinking that I had managed very well.

Mother's birthday was on Thursday. I went home on Friday. Richard was better, but still taking his meals apart in the solar. I ate my supper with him, in the golden, slanting rays of the sinking sun. Master Reed, who had supped in the hall as usual, came into the room afterwards, looked into our wine cups, saw them full, and poured his own. Then he said, "Anne, Denys the Routier wants a word with you."

Whether I went red or white I cannot tell; I could only feel my whole face stiffen.

"With me? What about?"

"I don't know. He just asked if he could have a word with you."

I suppose it was my guilty conscience that made me think his manner a trifle more restrained than usual, his eye just a little suspicious . . . no . . . curious.

I turned and hurried, trying not to hurry, out of the solar.

The dining hall, on the eastern side of the house, was already dim and full of shadows. It smelt strongly of rabbit and onion stew, and even in that moment of extremity some part of my mind noted the curious fact that a dish of which one has not partaken always has a stronger odour than one which one has eaten. Richard and I, in the solar, had shared a cold capon.

Old Nancy stood in the doorway between the hall and the kitchen, watching Meg and Jane, helped by the two youngest apprentices, clear the tables. Denys leaned against the doorpost of the outer door, his back to the hall, looking out into the yard. The presence of four other—five other people gave me confidence. I walked towards him and said, "You wanted to speak with me."

He turned quickly, so that in the doorway we faced one another and he took hold of my hand. The action could not be seen by those inside in the hall because the bulk of my body was in their way. He fumbled with my hand for a second and then had me by the little finger, bending it down, pressing hard. There is no simple, quiet, secret action that can cause more sharp pain. Anyone who doubts this should try it on himself. Pressing ruthlessly on my finger he pulled me over the threshold. At the same time he hissed into my ear, "Call back and say your palfrey is lame and you are looking to it."

I leaned back, and, only just able to speak for the pain in my finger, said, "Nancy. Tell Master Richard I have gone out to look to my palfrey. It is lame, it seems."

"Now," he said, with a little more pressure on my finger, "come and look just how lame it is." He dragged me across the yard and to the fence of the pasture. "A pretty trick you played me yesterday. Now listen. Tomorrow is Saturday. In the afternoon they'll all go to their shooting at the Butts. I don't have to go. I've done my soldiering. I shall wait for you in the wool loft, the far end."

I said, and I could hear how thin my voice sounded, "Unless you let go my finger . . . I can give you no mind . . . I shall faint."

He let go then, but he put his arm around me and said, "You bring it on yourself, you're so tricky. It could have been yesterday, you silly little hussy," and he pushed his body against me. "Now it must wait till tomorrow, and I've waited so long. . . ."

"I can't. I can't. Even if I wanted to . . . my husband, his father . . . I can't just walk out of the house."

"Women always have two excuses—church and the dressmaker. Choose which you like, but I'm telling you, you had better come."

He let me go, and stooping tugged up a little tuft of grass with the soil clodded about its roots. He tossed it gently over the fence at my palfrey which was grazing amongst the other horses, a pale shadow amongst the darker ones. It started and moved away, one hoof hardly touching the ground, lame as a tinker's donkey.

"This time I made an excuse. If you fail me tomorrow I shall ask for you again, and again, and every excuse will be shakier than the one before. And I shall talk about you, in alehouses. . . ."

"You'll find yourself in trouble if you boast of rape."

He laughed, it seemed with real pleasure.

"I always knew a devil lurked behind that angel face of yours, my pretty! Rape indeed. Was your dress torn? Did you run screaming? Did you complain? Besides which, once I've set them all asking questions I shall make myself scarce, leaving you to find the answers."

Had I been innocent, I suppose that would hardly have been a threat at all. I remembered how my face had felt when Master Reed brought me Denys' message, I remembered the look I thought he had given me. My best weapon, a clear conscience, was snapped in my hand; I was not equipped to fight.

"I'll come," I said.

"And I'll set your horse to rights." He rested one hand on a post of the fence and vaulted lightly into the meadow.

I turned away and hurried towards the house. Master Reed stood at the back door looking out over the yard. I wondered how long he had been there, and whether, at that distance, he could have seen Denys lay hold of me.

"Anything amiss?" he said.

"My horse is very lame. Denys thinks it picked up a stone. He is dealing with it."

"How handy is he? He might worsen matters. I'd better . . ." He went, with his lurching yet rapid step, towards the pasture.

That night I hardly slept at all. It was easy enough to say: Come to the wool loft . . . two excuses . . . church and the dressmaker. I had never been one of those pious women, forever running to church at odd hours. Because of Master Reed's hatred of Baildon and all its folk, and because, living outside the town boundary we were free to choose, we went to Mass at the tiny church of Flaxham St. Giles, and usually went, the three of us together, to make our Confessions on Saturday, before supper in winter, after it in summer. Richard would think it very strange if I proposed going to church alone on Saturday afternoon. As for my dressmaker—who was a little hunchback—she always came to the house when I needed her; I wasn't even certain of where she lived. She was a relative of one of the pack-whackers, and when I had sewing to be done I simply asked him to ask his Aunt Margit to come.

To people who live more grandly, or more poorly, it may sound incredible that a grown woman should find it so difficult to absent herself, without rousing questions, for an hour on a Saturday afternoon. But always, when I wasn't with the children, I was in the solar, or the kitchen, or the garden, and with Richard just on the move again the whole thing was doubly difficult. If I said I would go and look in on the children, he would say he hadn't seen them lately and would come too; if I said I would see how my palfrey did, ten to one he would say that a stroll in the sun would do him good.

All this I had to worry out in the night, and to think that it wasn't just this Saturday . . . this kind of thing could go on and on.

In the end I pleaded the routine female excuse; I had a headache, I said, due to sleeping badly. That I had slept badly Richard knew was true. I said that after dinner I would go and lie down. Master Reed went into the garden, where some plums on two trees on the south wall should be ready for plucking, and Richard said:

"I shall go and do an hour's work in the office. Father hasn't complained, but the work must be mounting up."

That was better than I had hoped for; he might have offered to come and sit beside me and dabble my head with a vinegar cloth. I went into the children's room, brooded over them for a little while, and then stole out.

The yard was empty and quiet. No work was done at the Old Vine on Saturday afternoons; the young men went to practise their archery at the Butts on the west of the town; those whose age or some infirmity excused sought their own amusements. From the huts which we called Squatters Row, at the back of the stables, I could hear voices and the sound of a fiddle.

I felt extremely large and conspicuous as I made my way to the wool-shed, hugging the walls of each building I passed. I told myself that I had a perfect right to go out and see how my palfrey did. When I was level with the pasture fence I did step out of the buildings' shadow and stand, for a moment, staring. Then I cut back, through the two wool-picking sheds, where the sun cut in in golden, dust-filled rays, and then, at the end, up the ladder and into the wool store.

Denys was waiting for me. He took hold of me and kissed and pawed me for a minute or two like a madman. I pushed him away and said, "Wait. Wait. You want it to be good. . . . You said after childbed women were . . . And it is true. I think that is what ails me and I think a little wine would help." I held out the little leather wine bottle that I had brought.

"You don't need that," he said.

"Oh, I do, I do. Just give me time." I loosed the stopper and tilted the bottle to my lips, pretending to drink. "You know what is wrong with me, don't you? I was in labour two days and three nights. . . . A woman has to be pot-valiant to risk that again."

"You're over the worst. The next lot'll be as easy as shelling peas."

"I'm pot-valiant," I said, wishing to God I were. For when neither flesh nor spirit is desirous this is a sorry, sad business. He didn't think so; and, anxious to pleasure him, I made as good a pretence of sharing his joy as I could.

When he was spent he lolled back against the soft, greasy fleeces and sighed and smiled. After a minute he said, forestalling me by a count of ten, "Is any left in that bottle?"

I reached out and lifted and shook it.

"Not enough for both—but you're welcome to what there is. It heartened me."

"Rubbish. I heartened you. I told you everything would be all right. Didn't I? Didn't I?"

"Yes. And you were right."

He set the bottle to his lips and drank.

"I must go now," I said. "And I must take the bottle. It might be missed."

"Next Saturday. Here."

"Next Saturday. Here," I repeated. He tilted the bottle and then gave it back into my hand. "I had to force you. You see, I knew what was best for you. You're my beauty, my darling, and I don't know how I shall wait the week out. But I will." He burrowed his head into my breast and clutched at me with his hands. In one moment it would all begin again.

"I *must* go . . . or there'll be no next Saturday." He sighed and set me free.

I climbed down the ladder of the wool loft with the words "no next Saturday" still sounding inside my head. By the pasture fence I picked up a young apple that I had left there—how long before, half an hour, an hour? How long had the whole thing taken? I called my palfrey and it came, took the apple, and slobbered over my hand and sleeve.

I went back into the solar where Master Reed was laying plums on a dish.

"I couldn't sleep, so I went out to see how my horse fared. I gave it an apple," I said, "and look what a mess it has made of me. I must go and wash."

No next Saturday, I thought. There will be no next Saturday.

VII

THE next day being Sunday, Denys was not looked for and when he was found on Monday nobody could tell which day he had died, until one of the weavers said that he remembered seeing him come into the yard late on Saturday, very drunk. This—though it is unpleasant to think that in cases of felony some of the evidence given may be equally false —most admirably served my purpose, since it prevented the possibility, remote indeed, but lively in my mind at least, of anyone connecting Denys' death with my wandering around on the Saturday afternoon.

"He was probably not as sound as he looked," Master Reed said, and passed on to the matter of replacing him. Until that was done I knew I must be prepared to face hearing Denys' name now and again. I must keep my face smooth and secret, and show enough but not too much interest. Actually even that was spared me, though I would rather have been tested than excused the way I was. What happened was that within half an hour of the discovery of Denys' body, a hind, bumping and bouncing on Father's best horse, came to tell me that Mother was in bed.

"Very sick," he said she was, and anxious to see me.

Richard, who now had great faith in the doctor who had relieved his cough by night if not by day, insisted upon sending for him to ride out with me, but I was too anxious to be off. So he was to follow.

Mother was in bed, and as I set foot on the gallery I could hear the gasping rattle of her breath. Her brow and nose and chin were bone white, her cheeks dark purple with fever. Her eyes, dim with pain, were open, but she did not know me, even when I took her hot dry hand and spoke her name. Father was in the room, looking almost as ill and half crazed.

"What happened?" I asked him.

"Yesterday, no the day before, no, yesterday, she complained of pain in her side. I looked and it was bruised, very black and swollen. I made a poultice, a linseed poultice, and she said it eased her. Then she sickened and cried for you, but she was sensible then. It is only this morning . . ."

Suddenly the deep crisscross wrinkles below his eyes were wet. I envied him being able to cry. My need to cry scorched me. It was my fault that she had her fall, and if she died I'd have killed her as surely as I had killed . . .

"The doctor is riding close behind," I said. "He's . . . very clever. He'll do something."

"I hope to God . . ." Father said.

Mother went on fighting for breath. Every now and then a gobbet of thick yellow stuff, streaked with blood, bubbled from her mouth, and I wiped it away. Once, just after I had thus cleared her lips, she spoke, in a surprisingly bright, vigorous, *young* voice.

"I can hold together as long as I have to," she said, and then went back to that broken-winded breathing.

Father gave a sort of groan. "She said that to me . . . once before. The bravest . . ." he said, "braver than . . ."

And brought this low by her own daughter, a coward.

I thought of her courage, her unquenchable hopefulness which I had so much despised; I thought of her kindness to me every time I came back to Minsham, rejected and in what was tantamount to disgrace. It seemed to me at that moment that the only person on earth whom I truly loved was my mother.

I did not stand idle. All this time I was busy with what might be helpful. Remembering Richard and his cough, I propped her higher, to ease the breathing; I tried to make her drink something hot to wash the thick stuff from her throat; I wiped her face and hands with a cool cloth. Once, when I was doing that, she eyed me and said:

"I'll thank you, my lady, to take back this glove. Blanchfleur has no use for it!"

"Holy Mother of God," Father cried and dropped his head against the wall. "That that should trouble her now!" He banged his grizzled head against the wall several times and then went to the other side of the bed and cried:

"Maude. You know. You must know, there was never any other. Any good tourney man, it was the fashion to pursue him. Whose glove did I carry?"

But Mother had gone back to her fight for breath and minded neither of us.

Then the doctor arrived.

He looked at the bruise, just below her left breast, and said gravely, "Most unfortunate, the heart has been bruised; and the heart governs the melancholy humour. And the melancholy humour, left to run its course, can lead to death. However." He opened his bag and gave me some small objects, the seed cases of some plant, rounded at one end, pointed at the other.

"Make an infusion," he said. "Foxglove is a sovereign remedy for the heart."

But it was difficult to make her drink—as I had already discovered; the battle to breathe was too urgent, too closely pressed; most of the infusion was wasted.

She died just before sunset. The doctor, sadly disappointed by the result of his infusion, had gone; he had other patients waiting, he said, and he had done all he could. He had at last given an opiate, so that Mother seemed to sleep, though the battle for breath went on.

Just before sunset she woke, and returned to her senses. In a very weak fluffy voice she said my name.

"Anne."

"Here I am," I said. And my heart lifted. She knew me, she wasn't going to die. Some of the infusion, that sovereign heart remedy, had gone down and done its work; or the drugged sleep had helped to mend.

"Take good care of Blanchfleur," she whispered. Then her eyelids fluttered, the death rattle sounded in her throat, her mouth fell open, and she was dead.

I would gladly, and this is true, have lain down there on the floor by her bed and died too. On Saturday afternoon I had deliberately killed a man and been no more troubled than if I had crushed a fly which pestered me. But this was different. Remorse, perhaps the most terrible of all feelings, now had me in its mangling jaws. By accident, by a side blow, I had killed somebody who loved me and whom I loved. There is, and of this I am certain, no more terrible knowledge in the whole world. I should carry it with me until I died, and that seemed too much to face. I flung myself down on the floor beside the bed, and sobbed, in that dry, tearless way which brings no healing, and wished that I could die, just to be rid of the burden of guilt.

People don't—unless they are old and nearly ready for death anyway —die from the wishing. Presently I was aware of Father, sobbing and groaning away on his side of the bed. "Take good care of Blanchfleur," had been her last words to me; and taking care surely meant comforting him now. I got up and went round to him and sat on the bed's edge and lifted his head so that it lay in my lap. I tried to speak comforting words about Mother soon being with the Saints in Heaven, about the great reunion of all families which would one day take place there. But Father was also deep in this business of self-accusation; and unlike me he could accuse himself aloud. He blamed himself for a multitude of faults, ranging from never having made a proper home or clothing her suitably, to having given her cause for jealousy in the old days. On that score, at least, I could comfort him with what I knew was truth. I told him of the talk we had had before my marriage and of the pride and triumph in her voice as she spoke of his wearing her glove and rejecting the great lady's. As I spoke I remembered that during my time of madness I had looked at Denys' flat archer's shoulders and imagined myself sharing Mother's pride. So even that was spoiled and sullied, and my words which made Father feel better made me feel worse.

I turned at last, for relief, to material things. I had not eaten since breakfast, and most likely Father had not even broken his fast. I slipped downstairs in the dusk—seeing, as I did so, Mother's fatal stumble and fall—and looked into the buttery. There was precious little to eat, some bread and three pigeons, ready plucked but uncooked. Another pain stabbed me at the thought that had she felt well yesterday Mother would have cooked those birds. I turned away from them and took up the bread. And then I saw the little cask of wine which Master Reed had sent on Thursday for her birthday. Her birthday!

The wine, I thought, would help down the dry bread; so I drew a jugful, found two cups, cut the bread into slices, and set it all on the table in the hall. Then I lighted three candles, one for the table and one for the head and the foot of the bed, and carrying them went up to the room where Father was waiting.

"I will do what is to be done here, after," I said. "You come now and make shift to eat a little."

Moving like a very old man, he dragged out onto the gallery and at the stairhead looked down and said, "If I'd been half a man, I should have railed in those stairs. I always meant to, but I pretended to be busy with my hawks and other toys."

"It was an accident. Like your own. If you had not your mishap, you would never have been compelled to live here. Do not blame yourself overmuch."

Rather pity yourself, too, I thought. And that applied to me as well. We may make victims of one another but we are ourselves the victims of Fate, also. I had turned to Denys to seek what I could not find elsewhere.

We made some pretence, at first, of dipping our bread in the wine and eating, but we soon put that aside. We emptied the jug and I took a candle and refilled it. Father drank most and most quickly benefited. He began, in his slow bumbling way to talk of the past.

"You say she was proud of me, eh?" he began, and then went on to tell of triumphs here, there, and the other place, of doughty champions met and defeated, of noble horses he had ridden, of presents and compliments he had been given; and all so muddled that sometimes it sounded as though it was the horse which had complimented him and the gift which he had unseated. I thought of the body upstairs on the soiled bed and of what I must presently do, and wished that I could sink into a like soft confusion of mind. So I drank some more, and presently was eased. Father's stories ceased and he began to nod. I said, "Come to bed," and he was so fuddled that on the gallery he began to walk, of habit, towards his own room. I took him by the arm and turned him gently towards the other door, towards the bed upon which I had spent Thursday night. Then he remembered and whimpered a little.

In Mother's room I did what was to be done, all the more easily for being a little blurred in my mind. Then I set fresh candles and drew up a stool, intending to watch all night; but the wine got the better of me and in the end I lay down on the floor and slept.

Interval

I

ONE day—Lady Blanchfleur having then been in her grave for three months—Martin Reed said to his son, "Have you noticed the change in Anne?"

"I think her grief is easing—a little," Richard said carefully, and, turning his head away, coughed.

"She drinks too much wine," Martin said bluntly. "Last evening, and the one before, she was flown."

"I know. And a good thing too!" Answering his father's astonished look, he added, "If she goes to bed with wine in her she sleeps. Otherwise she wakes, screaming from nightmare, and then cries for hours."

"About her mother's death?"

"They were very close," Richard said. "You and I who never knew a mother's love cannot measure her loss."

"It is a loss many people sustain without resorting to wine—in such quantity."

Richard coloured. "If you grudge so simple a comfort . . ." he began angrily.

"I grudge nothing. You know that. I just do not care to see a woman the worse for—and reeking of—wine."

"What you call worse I call better; and as for the reek, it is my bed she shares."

"I'm not wishing to quarrel," Martin said and left the matter there.

Richard himself was puzzled. Once, in the night, sobbing against his shoulder, Anne had said, "It was my fault. I killed her." He had dragged out of her the story about a bed to be aired which had caused the fall. He had said, at the end of it:

"I can see how you feel, but you must not blame yourself too shrewdly. The bed was to be aired some day for Isabel. It could have happened then."

But she had insisted that it was all her fault. Presently, thinking to comfort her, he said that everybody had to die one day. And that was a mistake, for she flung herself from him and spoke in a wild way about killing and a sin.

"A sin, sweetheart, to wish to spend a night under your father's roof! Come now!"

That night he took a candle and went padding barefoot down the stairs to fetch the wine which seemed to comfort her; and from then on, until Martin mentioned the matter, it had been Richard who would fill her cup, twice, three times, from the livery cupboard in the solar. What harm could it do? She never woke bad-tempered or liverish as those who drank too much sometimes did. The wine eased her grief, just as the grey powder eased his cough in the night. Where was the difference? It was Richard himself who first gave her another and far more potent draught, "to try." It was neither French, Spanish nor Rhenish; it came from the Low Countries, where it was called brandewijn. Half a cup of it was as potent as three of any other kind.

One evening, some weeks after Martin's first protest, he came into the solar to bid Richard and Anne good night. It was almost bedtime and Richard had poured the brandewijn into a cup, given it into Anne's hand, and then, taking his lute, sat down at her feet on a cushion, playing a gentle, soothing tune. One candle was out, the other nearing its end, the fire sunk to a rose-hued glow. It should have been a pleasant, domestic scene, gratifying to the older man, but by some indefinable degree it missed so being and was something else, so that, even before he smelt the liquor, he was irritated; and when he did scent it and knew it for what it was, he spoke more sharply than ever before in Anne's experience.

"Brandewijn!" he said. "That is no drink for a lady."

She said, "How would you know?" Just the four words, with the faintest possible stress on the second, but the whole speech so insolent, so full of hurtful meaning, that for a second he was checked.

Then he said, "I should have said for a respectable married woman."

Richard asked, with a flippancy which annoyed Martin even more, "Must all pleasure be reserved for the disreputable and the unmarried?"

Anne laughed and reached out her hand and patted Richard's cheek.

Trollop! Martin thought suddenly, and then, because that was too harsh a thought, he said, "Maybe you know best. I'm old-fashioned."

From him it was a handsome apology for one word, not even spoken aloud.

He stumped up to bed, and, shedding his clothes, wondered—for he was a just man—why it had slid, that condemning word, so easily into his head? In his cool, undemonstrative way he had been fond of his daughter-in-law. Had been? *Was!* She was part of his achievement. A knight's daughter. And never, until this evening, when he had blurted out his rebuke, had she by word or deed lain any stress upon the difference in rank. Provoked, she had retorted, as any woman of spirit would. He bore her no grudge for that. And even had he done there was no reason, surely, why his resentment should put that word into his mind. And yet . . . and yet. Even as he accused himself of injustice, he recalled something so fleeting that he had sensed it rather than seen it, something so unlikely that he had pushed it away as nonsense and never thought of it again until now. Three months ago, one evening in the summer, he had stood by the back door of the house and looked out over the yard, towards the fence of the pasture. Anne and Denys Rootyer were standing close together, so close that they might have been touching; if they were they moved apart instantly, just as his eye lighted on them. No, he would never be sure, never admit to himself even, that they had stood closer than needs be. Nor would he admit that there was anything odd in the man's fetching Anne out in the twilight to look at her lame horse; though there again the obvious thing would have been to call a smith.

Why had he remembered it? Why think of it now?

Getting old, and fanciful. Sixty, he thought, and remembered the priest at Rede telling him that at twenty half his life's span had fled. Out in his reckoning there, Martin thought grimly: but for my leg I'm as good as I ever was, good for another twenty years. Unless I go awry in my wits! For suddenly, out of nowhere, another fantastic fancy had slipped into his brain. In June of last year, he and Richard had both been absent from home at the same time, and he'd offered that one of the maids should come across and sleep on this side of the house. What had she replied—that what a servant could save her from would never hurt her. And the twins had been born on St. Joseph's Day, March the nineteenth.

Here, alone in his own bedroom, he felt his face go red and hot, his heart beat so hard that it thudded inside his skull, exactly as though he had been caught out, publicly, in some misdemeanour. *How* was it possible that he should have entertained such a vile, shameful thought long enough to do the reckoning? Where could such a thought have come from, unless direct from the Devil?

He lay down in bed and blew out his candle. When next his business took him to Colchester he would buy Anne some trinket, something pretty and of value, a secret proof of his shame for allowing fantasy a place in his mind, even for a minute.

II

THE busy, happy years sped by. With Maude always just one pace ahead, the twins passed through all the fascinating stages of early childhood. When they were six years old an uninformed observer would have taken them for any brother and sister, the girl the elder by a year.

Richard's cough persisted, a little better in summer weather, a little worse in winter; his cheerfulness, his fixed refusal to regard himself as an invalid, screened, even from Martin and Anne, the stark fact that that was what he had become. He had ceased to ride abroad, never for the reason that he was not fit to do so, always because the weather was remarkably inclement, or there was too much work to do in the office, or the errand was something which Martin preferred to do himself. It was Anne who suggested that it was useless for him to ride with her on her regular visits of inspection to Minsham.

"He doesn't know," she said, speaking of her father, "whether we go or not. I only go to see that he is being cared for. I shan't stay an hour."

"I like to come with you. It's such a miserable business."

Sir Godfrey had sunk into apathy, prematurely senile, dirty, careless, almost witless, firm only on one point, he refused to leave his home.

"It's miserable," Anne agreed. "But why should we both suffer? You stay at home and then I shall be happy to return and find you cheerful."

She appeared to see nothing sinister in his acceptance. And when, one day when Maude was five years old and in boisterous play had all but pushed Richard from his feet, Anne said, "Maude, play a little less roughly if you please. Such behaviour is not becoming." The extreme fragility of Richard, which was then for a moment painfully plain, had escaped her.

On her own remorse-ridden grief time had worked its old healing magic and effected an almost complete cure. She no longer needed brandewijn to make her sleep; on Richard's good nights she slept well. Every now and then—often after she had been to Minsham—she would suffer a nightmare and wake, and be comforted by Richard and presently sleep again. But for Maude, Anne would, during the children's first six years of life, have been perfectly happy. As it was, she was like a person who has fallen

amongst thistles and afterwards carefully removed every tiny prickle except one, which breaks off and burrows down and cannot be plucked out;
it can be ignored most of the time, but is capable, nonetheless, at any
accidental pressure, of causing a sharp pain. There were days when
Maude was just a little girl, inclined to be headstrong and venturesome,
but easily ruled because she was so affectionate. Then a slanting ray of
light would strike the child's head where the babyish fairness was giving
way to bronze; or someone would remark Maude's size and strength,
by comparison with Walter, and Anne would be most sickeningly reminded. The mystery was that Walter gave the appearance of being
Richard's son; he had the dark, slender grace, the delicate structure of
bone, the slight air of defencelessness which called out all that was
maternal in Anne just as surely as something, unnameable, in Maude,
called forth dislike. The sense of guilt was thus kept alive, and occasionally exacerbated by a curious look which would cross Martin's face,
usually when Anne allowed her resentment to take the form of an over-
sharp rebuke to the little girl.

"I shall forbid you to play with the yard children if you bring their
manners indoors."

"How can you be such a hoyden? Look at your hands, your dress. Anyone would think you were a tinker's child."

Apart from putting in some mild defensive word on the child's behalf,
Martin never said anything, but he wore that oddly disconcerting look.

Richard had a warm partiality for his daughter, and one night,
in bed, at the end of a day in which Maude had incurred her mother's displeasure, said, "She's exactly like I used to be, at her age."

"You!" Anne sounded startled. "You were never like that, I am sure."

"But I was. I was the naughtiest boy in Suffolk, until Peter Priest took
me in hand. Always into mischief. Uncle Tom's bear . . . did I never
tell you?"

As usual he had come to bed first and then, a little later, Anne had
brought up the cup of milk, into which the pinch of grey powder was
sprinkled, and his voice was blurred by drowsiness as he recounted the
tale of his misdoings.

Anne remembered the old man, the stuffy room, the malodorous bearskin on the bed. Pert Tom had died during that time when she was too
much engrossed by her prolonged virginity to give the event much heed.

Lulled by the drowsiness of Richard's voice, she too fell asleep as soon
as the story was done.

She dreamed that she was in the Ladies' Dorter at Beauclaire, helping
to dress Maude, aged about sixteen, for the St. Barnabas Tourney. The
girl's dress, a crimson and green silk, was beautiful and her headdress

was a cloud of gauze. Anne looked at her with satisfaction and pride, thinking that with her looks and her clothes and her dower she was the equal of any young lady there. Then, under her eyes, Maude changed and became Denys. The wide archer's shoulders strained against the silk, the tough-looking red hair lifted the headdress. She said in an appalled whisper, "You can't go into the *Ladies'* Gallery." The dreadful creature said, "I must. You must take me. You can always say that I am your dressmaker!"

She screamed out her protest.

As on a score of similar occasions, Richard stirred and spoke. "Sweetheart. It's all right. I'm here." His voice was thick and when he had spoken he coughed.

She said, "I'm sorry I woke you. Just another horrible dream."

He did not, as usual, ask should he make a light; nor did he turn in the bed and put his arm about her, comfortingly. He made a coughing sound which ended in a choke, and then there was a gentle bubbling.

Jerked from dream horror to real fear, she said, "Richard."

He did not answer; and it was she who made the light and saw on the pillow the spreading pool of crimson.

III

For a while the shared sorrow brought Martin and Anne closer than they had ever been before; her grief was so intense, so shattering that his half doubt—it had never been more than that—vanished in a wave of shame. They could say, over and over again, how blind they must have been, and then, inconsistently, mention things that they had noticed. They could say that they should have been more careful, and follow that statement immediately by giving instances of how careful they had been.

Under this apparent unity of spirit there gaped, however, a great gulf. Martin, who thirty-five years earlier had cried over Kate, "She never had anything!" could now, in an attempt to comfort Anne, say:

"He had a short life, but he enjoyed it all. He never lacked anything; he had you, Anne, and the children. You must think of that. And think, too, how much better this way than after a lingering illness, knowing that death waits." That was, in truth, his own private dread.

"Oh yes," she said. "That last night, he was laughing, telling me how naughty he had been when he was a . . ." The words "little boy" would not be spoken. It was unbearable to think of a little boy growing into a man, stricken with lung rot and now dead.

The dreadful remorse, the guilt which had assailed her after her mother's death, was now returned, doubled. She remembered how once, during her madness, she had dared to think that his love for her was a dream, like his dream of being a wandering lute-player. She had lived to prove how wrong that thought was. Only a true, firm love could have helped her through the time after her mother's death.

Over and over again she remembered that the last words he ever spoke to her were words of comfort—because she had waked from a dream which only her guilt had made possible. She tore herself to pieces on the spiked thought that if she had not wakened him he might have stayed asleep, flat, and the lifeblood would have remained in him. So she was doubly guilty, twice over the murderer of those whom she had loved, those who had loved her.

One evening, three weeks after Richard's death, Anne and Martin were in the solar. He had forced himself to overcome his dislike of the room in order to keep her company. They had said all the old things and she had broken down again and wept bitterly. She ate almost nothing, he knew, and slept hardly at all. Often, waking from his light old man's slumbers, he had heard her walking about, up and down, up and down in her room.

This evening, at last, she sat down and snatched up a piece of sewing, but she did not work as a woman should. The needle stabbed in and out, like a weapon. Then she would pause, stare wild-eyed at the wall, and stab again.

He watched her. Her looks were all gone. She was worn down to the bone, and her skin was the colour of parchment. He recalled suddenly the pretty, soft-fleshed woman who in this very room had laughed and patted Richard's face with one hand and held a cup of brandewijn in the other.

He got up and limped to the livery cupboard, fumbled about and turned back to her, a cup in either hand.

"Richard," he said, and stopped because the mention of his son's name, like that, was still a pain. "Richard told me that when your mother died, Anne . . . this helped you to sleep. You see, you have the children. You must think of the children."

She had not, since Richard's death, been able to bear the sight or sound of them.

And from some deep, obscure desire for self-punishment she had, for three long weeks, avoided the palliative which, she knew, stood there waiting in the livery cupboard. She had proved its worth and knew that once accepted it could convince her that she was not to blame; that she had done what was best in the circumstances. One drink and she would be thinking of the joy Richard had taken in this proof of his virility; two and she would be making intimate little reckonings, remembering that on the night before he left for Bywater and on the night when he came back, Richard and she had lain together. Only the one night between. And he never knew. I never by word or gesture gave a sign or swerved from my outward allegiance. . . .

She took the cup and presently the feeble voice of her own reason raised a bold loud echo in the cavern of intoxication, calling that she was not to blame for everything, that circumstances had played a hand in what had happened, that she also was to be pitied a little.

Nothing, however, no amount of brandewijn, no amount of reasoning could make her look on Maude with anything but a carefully controlled loathing. She knew that as long as she lived the sight of her daughter would call to mind that dream, and with it all that came after. It became her fixed and relentless purpose to get the child out of the house.

Several times during the next months she mentioned, casually, the question of Walter's education. Martin was inclined to shuffle the matter off, there was plenty of time, he said; such matters needed much consideration.

Once Anne said, "I seem to remember Richard saying that he started his learning when he was six."

"I had Peter Priest ready to hand at that time," Martin said. "Also, Richard, to tell the truth, was more unruly than Walter. Walter can wait a year or so."

When next Anne mentioned the matter he said, "I bear it in mind. I keep my eyes and ears open for a suitable tutor for the boy."

She said, with a tinge of sharpness, "If you wait for another unfrocked priest, you may wait until Walter grows a beard."

"I'm not waiting for that. I'm looking for some clerk who could help me as well. I'm missing Richard sore on that side of the business."

The ache in his voice prevented her from speaking on the subject again for a long time.

The twins had their seventh birthday, and in the winter following it, on account of a piece of flagrant disobedience, a narrow escape from death which did give Anne ample reason to say, "That settles it. Walter must go to school."

"To school?"

"Yes. He needs the company of boys of his own age—and kind. Also he has some talent for music. The Choir School at the Abbey is just the place for him."

"Maybe," Martin said a little doubtfully. "If we could spare him."

"We should see him often; and they have holidays." She then spoke the words to which the months' old discussions about Walter's future had been a mere preliminary. "As for Maude, I think I shall send her to Beauclaire."

More startled than when she spoke of school for Walter, Martin said, "Where *you* were so unhappy yourself?"

"I was so poor, so ill-equipped. Still, even so, I learned everything that a gentlewoman should know."

"And that has been of use to you?"

"I learned how to conduct myself. I feel it my duty to see that my daughter has like advantages."

He said, "Maude could be dressed and fitted out. She will have a dower . . . but she might . . . suffer in other ways."

"Some pert jackanapes or spiteful girl, saying, 'Do I smell fleeces?' Is that what you mean?"

He nodded, a little angered by her instant perception.

"I'll tell you straight, Anne; I've no mind to see my good money go where it will be despised because I made it."

"No one in their senses would despise it. I said a pert jackanapes or a spiteful girl, didn't I?"

"I'm against it."

"Very well," she said, more meekly than he had expected. "Would you be against her going to the nuns at Clevely for a year or two?"

"Not against; but I see no good reason."

"Don't you? What about Walter? They've always done everything together, in fact in all their pranks Maude is the leader. Don't you think he would be hurt, and justly, if he were sent to school and Maude stayed here to be spoiled?"

"I hadn't thought of it that way. Yes, it might be so. I expect you know best."

"I'm their mother. So will you see about Walter entering the Choir School?"

"I will. There's no great haste, is there? I could bring the matter up when I go to pay my rent."

That ended the conversation abruptly. The rent of one red rose to be paid in June had always been a matter of joking with Richard, who had made, and set to a lively ballad tune, a comical song on the subject, all about a year when poor Master Reed could find only a white rose and was obliged to take it to the dyer's.

The twins had their eighth birthday in March, and in June Martin made application for a place in the Choir School for Walter. Dreading the time when he and Anne would find themselves alone in the house, he was delighted to be told that there would be no vacancy until Easter in the following year.

Making her own inquiries, Anne was much displeased to learn that, except in the case of girls who had lost both parents and were homeless, Clevely Priory did not open its doors to those under twelve years of age. Riding back from Clevely, she made up her mind that, when Walter went into the Choir School, Maude should go to Beauclaire despite anything Master Reed should say.

Part Four

MAUDE
REED'S
TALE

I

So long as my father was alive, I never noticed that my mother disliked me. We paired off naturally, when Walter sat in Mother's lap I sat on Father's knee; when Mother hugged Walter, Father hugged me, and though, even then, Mother was stricter to me than to Walter that was easily explained; I was much worse behaved.

Father died when Walter and I were six years old, too young to understand or to know what we had lost. Children are very self-centred; the sorrow in the house brushed against us but was soon forgotten. For a little while Mother seemed to want neither of us; then she changed and doted on Walter more fondly than ever. It was then that I noticed that she disliked me. She'd sit on the window seat or the settle and draw Walter to her, put her arm around him, smooth his hair with her fingers, and look at him with love. I would run over to join them, never—I was careful about that—never trying to push between them, trying only to take my place by her other side, hoping that she would put her free arm about me. She never did. She would jump up and busy herself, or push me away, telling me to go wash my hands or comb my hair, or send me to fetch something.

I could make her notice me, but only in a way which did me no good. If I behaved badly enough, she would give her full attention to scolding me; sometimes she beat me. Once, when Walter and I were seven, a very strange thing happened. It was in the winter and the horsepond had frozen solid and Walter and I had played on it for several days, old games which seemed new because we were playing them in the middle of the pond. Then one morning our grandfather came in and said there was a thaw and that we were on no account to set foot on the ice that day. However, Walter had left his hobbyhorse on the ice, and he said to me, "When the ice melts my hobby will fall into the water." He looked at me the way he always did when he wanted me to do something for him.

So I went to fetch the hobbyhorse and had it in my hand when the ice bent under me. I shot the hobby across the surface towards where Walter stood, and managed with my two hands to grip the edge of the hole and keep my head free. I yelled, and Walter, yelling, came towards me, and great cracks ran out under his feet; he went down, too, screaming like a pig having its throat cut. Men came running from the wool and weaving sheds, and we were pulled out.

Walter was blue in the face and very sick in his stomach; I was merely wet; so Mother beat me. She said I was bigger, girls should have more sense, and I went onto the ice first. I'd never had a beating like that, and I cried, saying I only went on to fetch Walter's hobbyhorse, but that didn't excuse me.

That night I woke to hear somebody crying and to feel a weight on me. I was frightened until I opened my eyes and saw a candle on the chest and Mother kneeling by my bedside with her arms spread out over me. She looked different, though where the change was I couldn't have said; and she smelt different. Ordinarily she smelt sweet from the little bags of lavender and rosemary that hung and lay amongst her clothes. Tonight she smelt of something sharp and sour. She was crying and saying jerky words, calling me poor Maude and saying she was unfair to me, with many other things which made no sense. I thought she meant that she had been unfair to beat me and not Walter. So I struggled up in the bed and put my arms round her neck and said:

"You didn't hurt me." I would have had a beating every day if it meant that she would put her arms over me and let me hug her. She went on mumbling about being unjust and I said, "I forgive you."

She gave a kind of squeal and pushed me off and jumped up, crying, "Holy Mother of God. That is all I lacked!" Then she went out of the room, walking in a funny way, bumping against the foot of the bed, and against the side of the doorway. She left the candle, and until it went out and I was in the dark I lay and wondered what was wrong in saying, "I forgive you." Perhaps it was a wrong thing for a child to say to her mother.

That must have been it; for next day she disliked me again.

We had another grandfather who lived in the country at Minsham and was too old, or too ill, to ride, so we had never seen him. He had a servant called Jacob, who used to come to the Old Vine every Friday and pick up some provisions and say, "Much as usual," when asked about his master's health. Mother sometimes rode out to visit her father, but as time went on she made more and more excuses not to do so.

One day, however, on a fine summer morning, she said, "You're eight years old now and able to make a longer ride. We'll go to Minsham today and you can meet your Grandfather Blanchfleur and your Uncle Godfrey who is staying there."

Walter and I had ponies which were much more like twins than we were, both brown with paler manes and tails. I called mine Browny; Walter, who was much more fanciful than I was, had named his Robin Hood, out of a story Father had told us.

Minsham Old Hall, we found when we reached it, was shaped like a barn, but built of stone, with very narrow window openings, unglazed. It stood in a yard, with no garden near it, just a tumble-down stable and a piece of pasture.

Inside it was even more desolate, and very cold, despite the sunshine outside and a fire on the wide hearth. In a chair sat an old man with grey hair and a beard, so overgrown that there was nothing else to his face except a loose wet mouth and eyes which had no life in them. I saw Mother brace herself, like she did once when a servant came screaming that there was a mouse in the meal-bag and Mother had to deal with it. She leaned down and kissed the old man, and then said to us:

"This is your Grandfather Blanchfleur."

Walter made his bow and I my curtsey, as we had been taught. Our grandfather seemed to take no notice of us at all, but he mumbled and I caught the word "Maude" quite clearly. I thought he meant me and, intending to be as brave as Mother, I moved forward, prepared to kiss him.

But Mother said, "It is not you he means. Go play in the yard."

As we went out she moved to the foot of the stairs and called up, "Godfrey!"

There was nothing to do or see in the yard; but Walter happened to say, "Grandfather is like Daft Jimmy." That was a poor witless creature who lived in the row of huts behind the stables at the Old Vine; *his* grandfather had been deaf and dumb, we were told, and Walter and I had invented a game in which we pretended to be thus afflicted and bound to make ourselves understood by signs. We played it now, until we were called in to dinner.

We were then introduced to our Uncle Godfrey, who was very handsome and finely dressed.

He greeted us by name, and very kindly, and—the first person ever to do so—seemed to notice me more than Walter.

"So this is Maude." He looked me over, and smiled, and said something about lovely curly hair. "A real Astallon," he said. "Ralph and his golden Eleanor have managed to breed two little fawn-coloured creatures. Isn't it odd?"

Our grandfather's chair had been turned so that he sat at the head of the table. He ate as we had been forbidden to do, sucking and slobbering at his food and wiping his fingers, now on the cloth and now on the front of his soiled robe. Walter gave me a kick under the table and a meaningful look, like when we played "Dummy." I kicked him back and made faces, trying to say, without words: Yes, and wouldn't we be in disgrace if we did it?

Over our heads the talk went to and fro between Mother and Uncle Godfrey.

He said, "You hated it so much."

"I went to Beauclaire with one pair of shoes. When my feet grew I had to curl up my toes, and they are crooked to this day. You hated being at cousin Fortescue's; you wanted to farm here. Do you remember that? Are you sorry now that you didn't?"

"Not now. You saved me, Anne. You sent me the money so that I could buy my knight's equipment, and I . . ."

Mother interrupted him.

"And that wasn't easy; it wasn't a cause that either of them would have understood or sympathised with, let me tell you. That was my dressmaker's money for two years, and it meant refurbishing old ones, turning and twisting. I say this to show that what I ask you isn't so outrageous."

"I know. I know." He looked about the cold room with its damp grey walls and smoke-blackened rafters. "Here, too, you have taken responsibility, while I, with your good destrier between my knees, rode in tourneys. Nothing that you asked of me in return would be too great."

"You see," Mother said, "when I made the suggestion he rejected it, flat." She put her hand down on the table. "For me to raise it again would . . . You may find this hard to believe, but they have a pride of their own, more stubborn and stiff-necked than ours. When they speak of 'my good money,' that is the same as 'my good name.' I told you what he said. But an invitation from you would allow me to open up the matter again." She looked at Walter and me, and said, "If you have finished, you may go back to play."

We played until we were called in to make our adieus. As we stood there, my Uncle Godfrey looked at the figure in the chair and said, "My God, Anne, what a way to end! I can just remember when he won the King's Cup at Windsor. If you ever pray for me, pray that I never stop a half-fatal blow."

Mother turned the colour of the heaped-up ashes on the hearth. She looked towards the stairs.

"He was all right," she said. "Flying his hawks, riding his old horse. Until Mother . . ." She broke off and shuddered.

My uncle took her by the arm and said, "Poor Anne, you had that too! I was in Poitou. You've borne it all."

"More than you will ever know. But this one thing. You will do it?"

On the way home she set such a pace that Walter and I on our ponies and the servant who attended us on his thickset solid horse had much ado to keep up with her.

Shortly after this visit Walter was told that after Easter in the next year he was going to the Choir School at Baildon. The idea disgusted him; the schoolboys lived monkish lives, slept on hard beds, ate horrible food, washed in cold water.

"I don't want to. Why must I?"

"Because you will be a merchant, with a great business to run. You must learn to read and write and reckon."

"I don't want to be a merchant," Walter said. "I want to be a minstrel . . . you know, walk about from place to place, playing the lute and singing."

Mother said, in a way in which I have never in all my life heard anybody say anything, "You want *what*, Walter?"

Confidently he repeated his statement. She snatched hold of him and kissed him.

"One day you'll know better. You wouldn't like to be poor. And at the Choir School you will learn all about music."

"Church music," he said. "Not the same thing at all. Besides, it isn't fair that I should go to school and Maude should stay at home."

Mother said, "Maude is not staying at home. When she is twelve she is going to the nuns at Clevely, but in the meantime she has received a very pleasant invitation. She is going to stay with your Uncle Godfrey, at Beauclaire."

For a moment that took the sharpest edge from Walter's dissatisfaction, but he was soon grumbling again. I, he said, should be leading a merry life with ordinary people, while he was shut up with monks. If anyone beat me I should have Uncle Godfrey to complain to, he would have no one.

When the arrangements were first made, "after next Easter" sounded a comfortably long time away; but the months sped past. When the details were fixed and Walter learned that I was to ride into Sussex on Browny, while he must leave Robin Hood at the Old Vine, he flung himself screaming on the floor, shouting that it was unfair. My grandfather came to see what the noise was about and said, in an uncertain manner:

"Anne, is it worth it? Perhaps we were hasty. I heard recently of a young clerk who might serve our purpose."

Mother simply said, "Walter is jealous because Maude is to take her pony. Imagine his state if she were staying at home!" She took Walter by the arm and jerked him to his feet, speaking more firmly than she usually did to him.

"Straight into bed with you, you naughty boy!"

He was still in bed, being given possets and mixtures to bring down his fever, when I left for Beauclaire.

My grandfather, always a man of few words, gave me a broad gold piece, and kissed me.

"I hope you'll be happy. You mustn't mind too much if you find things different there."

Mother came into the yard where one of the men, named Jack, was ready, with my little clothes chest fixed behind his saddle. She kissed me, and for a moment I clung to her, hoping even at this last moment for some sign of love. She loosed herself from me in the old familiar way.

At the end of the covered passage which led from our yard to the highway, I turned and looked back. Mother was staring after us and her face was just like Walter's when I had let him win a game. Whatever we played at I could always beat him if I tried, but now and then I would hold back and lose deliberately. Then he wore a satisfied look, a look that said, "Well, I managed that!"

I puzzled over it for a long time. Much later, when I learned that Walter never did go to the Choir School, but stayed at home and had his lessons there, I did understand all too well. I saw then exactly what Mother had managed; she had kept the child she loved and got rid of the one she disliked. At the time I could only wonder *why* she looked like that. All the same she had done me, all unwittingly, a good turn. Had she gazed after me with the slightest affection I should have broken down, for I still loved her then. As it was she sent me on my way exercising my head and not my heart, and that, in many of life's turning points, is an excellent thing.

II

WE approached Beauclaire from the east, at the end of a sunny afternoon, so that it stood up against the gold and rose of sunset's first display. I thought to myself: But this is a town, not a house; and my homesickness deepened.

A great castle of grey stone stood in the embrace of a wide moat which was spanned by two bridges, one directly in front of us, at the end of the road which we travelled, and the other to the side, at the right. The second bridge linked the castle, which was very old, with the house, much of which had been built within the last sixty or seventy years. The face which the house turned to the road was very handsome and large, but—as I was soon to learn—it was only one small part of the whole. It was built of brick at the bottom and above of timber and plaster, the plaster moulded into patterns. There were many windows and all glassed, but I could see no doorway at all.

We clattered over the drawbridge, through a gateway at its far end, and there turned sharply to the right and through a small deserted court-yard, then over the second bridge and into a larger yard full of bus-tle, several men mounted, and servants running about. We then passed through an archway and into a stable yard, where I thankfully dismounted.

Almost immediately there appeared a solemn-looking man, by his dress neither gentleman nor servant, to whom the man who had been sent to fetch me said, "I'm back and all's well, Master Sheldon."

Master Sheldon glanced at me as he might have done at any package or parcel that had been conveyed from one place to another, noted that I was all in one piece, and nodded his satisfaction.

"You made good speed," he said.

We should have made better had the servant had his way. I had dis-liked him from the start; he was one of those—a type then new to me—who are intensely servile when they must be, and make up for it by being insolent when they can. It was plain, at the moment of our meeting, that he despised me on account of my youth, and Jack because he was a plain unliveried servant. The new man wore green with the Astallon badge, a falcon, on his breast.

Jack helped me onto my pony, for the last time, and then dived into his pocket, brought out a little handkerchief, edged with pegged lace, and tucked it into my sleeve.

"It's to be hoped you 'on't need it, my little dear, but if you do you'll know where it is."

He then turned to the Astallon man and said, "You take good care of our little mistress; she've never been from home afore."

That remark, and the thought of parting with Jack, thickened my throat again. The Astallon man merely sniffed and looked down his nose in a way that said plainly he was taking no orders from servants.

I said, "Good-by, Jack. I shall see you at Christmas."

We rode in silence for some time. The man broke it to ask, in a burring voice which made it hard for me to understand his words, "Is that the best pace you can make?"

I thought I had not heard aright; Browny was, for his size, very speedy and he was trotting his best.

"What did you say?" I asked. He repeated the question.

"Yes, it is. Browny is only a pony, as you can see for yourself."

"We'll see," he said, and he lifted his whip and brought it down hard on the pony's rump.

Certainly since the two matched ponies had been given to Walter and me on our fifth birthday, Browny had never been struck like that; Grandfather Reed was softhearted towards all his horses and had given us a little homily about treating the ponies properly; and I loved Browny who was, anyway, quite willing to run as hard as he could without being beaten. Now, frightened and hurt, he broke into his little short-stepped rocking gallop for a minute or two, and then slowed down to a trot again.

I had a good enough reason of my own for not wanting him whacked into a gallop; I had been in the saddle two days and was very sore. I was only accustomed to taking short rides, or—as on our visit to Minsham—a long one with a rest in between. When Browny galloped, I bumped, and it hurt.

When the man came up to strike the pony a second time I cried, "Don't do that!" But he did, and we bumped forward as before. It happened twice more and Browny began to blow; so next time, just as he began to slow down, I pulled him to a standstill, clapped my hand to my eye, and let out a yell.

"There's a fly in my eye," I said.

The servant, close behind me, said, "Damnation!" and then, coming alongside, "Can't you get it out?"

I made a quick movement and snatched the whip, which he was holding in a slack hand just then, and I pulled the pony round a little so that my hand with the whip in it was as far as possible from the servant on the tall horse.

"Give me that whip," he said between his teeth. I was going to say: Not unless you promise not to hit my pony again! but what good would a churl's promise be? So I simply said:

"I shan't!"

There then followed, right out in the open road, a most unseemly scuffle. He pulled his horse round and made a grab for the whip, but I was ready and brought it down smartly on his wrist; he cursed and made another snatch, not this time at the whip, but at the top of my arm, which he seized and twisted. I was quite helpless then, and the only way to break his hold was to slip out of the saddle and stand in the road;

even so I dangled for a moment, held by his hand, before my weight carried me to the ground.

I was by this time thoroughly frightened; dismounting so hastily and carelessly had rubbed my sore bottom, and my arm had had a cruel twist, so I started to yell. I stood there, holding the whip behind me, my back pressed to Browny's heaving side, and I yelled as if I were being murdered.

"Give me that whip and get back on that pony," the servant said.

I yelled louder. He was in a rather awkward position; he could lift me back onto the pony, but to do that he must himself dismount, and when he did, I thought—some part of me quite calm for all the fright and the pain and the yelling—I would strike his horse, hard, so that it galloped off, and while he chased it I would jump back on Browny and ride in the other direction.

The road was far from being deserted. Two old women were herding along a great gaggle of geese and looked at us with interest, not untinged with amusement, but they were too busy with their charges to stop and ask questions. A man with a panniered donkey, waiting for the geese to pass the place where the horse and the pony narrowed the road, did speak.

"Whassa matter? Hurt yersel'?"

"Mind your own business," said the Astallon man, so fiercely that the man with the donkey quailed, smacked his beast with the flat of his hand, and passed on.

"My Lady will hear about this," the servant said to me.

"Aye, from *me!*" I said, and was straightway frightened again at the thought of some great lady listening to both our tales and believing *him*. So I yelled some more. But I kept my eye on the man and saw that he was going to dismount. I got ready, but just then along came some horsemen, riding fast. The first one cried:

"Make way, make way!" and the Astallon man, instead of dismounting, pulled in a little to the side of the road. The gentleman rode past, his companion followed, but he looked at us, the third gentleman passed. Then the second rider wheeled round and rode back. He was about the age of, and not unlike, my Uncle Godfrey.

"What is all this to-do?"

I said, "Oh, sir, please, please help me."

The Astallon man slipped from the saddle and put his hand to his forelock and began to speak rapidly . . . a sore task . . . sent to conduct the little lady . . . no will for the journey. . . .

I ran forward and took hold of the gentleman's foot in the stirrup.

"It isn't true. It's all lies. I was going willingly till he hit Browny."

The gentleman said, "If you would speak one at a time, I might make some sense of it." He leaned forward a little and studied the badge. "Astallon of Beauclaire?"

"That's right, sir. And sent to conduct . . ."

"Ladies first," said the gentleman. "Now, why do you stand here and make a noise like a hound in full cry?"

I told him in as few words as possible. "You can see I speak the truth," I said, and I pointed to the welts that had already risen on Browny's smooth rump.

"All right. Now you be quiet for a moment. You, tell me, was there any particular urgency about this journey?"

"I was told to make it with all possible speed, sir."

"All possible speed. Well, your master would know that so small a child would not be mounted on a saddle horse. All possible speed for that pony would be . . . let me see . . . three days. I shall pass close by Beauclaire, I'll turn aside and say that if you arrive earlier you have overdriven both pony and rider and should be beaten."

He turned to me with a smile and said, "A pleasant journey and a safe arrival, demoiselle. Would you like me to take that whip?"

I said, "Oh, I do thank you. Thank you. What is your name?"

"My name? Why, what is my name to you?"

"I shall mention it in my prayers every night as long as I live."

He laughed. "Then I shall be greatly in your debt. But I hope you will outlive all memory of me by fifty years. My name is John Fitz Arle. And what is yours?"

"Maude Reed."

"I wish you well. As for you, fellow, mind what I said."

(I put his name into my prayers that night, and I kept it there, for years and years, by rote and habit, long after I had forgotten what he looked like and everything about him, except that he had stood by me in a moment of great need.)

So I had won, but victory has its price. At inns one's accommodation and food depends very largely upon one's servant and his care for one's comfort. Jack had seen that I slept and ate well in Colchester, Chelmsford, and Brentwood. Now anything would do.

What I didn't know was that in all great establishments all the servants are forever trying to make their duties profitable. My escort had been given money for the journey. If he could have shortened it by a night—even if Browny had ended broken-winded—the price of a night's lodging for us and our mounts would have gone into his own pocket. This form of cheating was rife at Beauclaire, as it must be, I suppose, in any establishment too large to be sharply looked to by one person. Even over the

candles my Lord Astallon was swindled by his house steward, whose duty
it was to see that new candles were placed in every sconce and stand
every evening. The short ends were one of his perquisites, and, since
hundreds of candles were used every day, they would have amounted to
something. But he was not content. The new candles were put in place
and they were lighted; then some minion of the steward's would run
around, replacing them by the stubs of another evening. So the cry,
"Bring fresh candles," was constantly to be heard, together with complaints that candles these days lasted only half the time that they were
wont to do.

Even taking three days for the journey, thanks to my behaviour, I
think the man made some small profit for himself. I do not think that my
Uncle Godfrey, nor my cousin Astallon, would have wished me to lie in
the common sleeping room with tinkers and drovers; or to dine on boiled
goose-grass root three days in succession. Fortunately, as my homesickness
and misery grew, my appetite lessened. And as the appetite lessens so do
the spirits. It was a very miserable, quiet little girl who got stiffly down
from her pony's back, and saw him led away and thought: There goes
my last friend.

The servant indicated that I was to follow him, so on foot we went
through another archway and into a court with a well in its centre. An
old man was drawing up water in a bucket and tipping it into a barrel
which fitted into a frame with two wheels and shafts; a donkey stood
between the shafts and a boy stood by the donkey's head. This vast household used so much water that the old man worked at the well and the
barrel made journeys to and fro, all day long.

One side of this court was enclosed by a wing of the house itself, and
here was an entry, a deep, dark porch with an iron-studded door set
within it. As a sign of his displeasure with me the servant halted by this
door, instead of taking me in and handing me over.

"In there," he said, and walked away.

I stepped into the porch, feeling smaller than I had ever done in my
life, knowing how dwarfs feel in a world fitted to ordinary people. I stood
for a moment, gathering my breath and my courage, then I pulled off
my glove, and, making a fist, knocked on the door. It was, I soon saw, a
very thick door, and plenty of noise was being made on its farther side.
Nobody answered my knock. I beat on the door again and, when it stayed
closed, turned the great iron handle and pushed.

Immediately inside the door was a kind of small room, the door behind
me forming one wall of it, the other three made of finely carved screening
through which I could see. Our solar at the Old Vine was reckoned to be
a wonderful apartment, unmatched in the whole of Baildon, but this

room was three times as large and half as high again. Yet it seemed full, for the young ladies within were all wearing wide-spreading dresses and enormous headdresses. Four of them sat in a group, with a piece of embroidery spread over their laps, each stitching away at her own portion, and talking and laughing as they worked. One sat alone on a window seat, playing a lute, very softly and sweetly. Some others, at the end farthest from the hearth, stood at a table, throwing dice and making loud exclamatory noises; and three stood quite near the door, divided from me by the lacy woodwork of the screen.

I stood in the enclosure, like something in a cage, and looked about, then I pushed against each side in turn, and the left side proved to be a swing door. I walked into the room and went near to the three young ladies who were talking. One was telling some tale, making gestures as she did so.

". . . so I said, 'Oh, *is* that so? Then what about the evening of Holy Cross Day?' Could you have seen her face?"

One of the listeners said, "Oh, Ella, we swore never to mention that!"

"I was so much provoked. But listen! She then said, 'That is what comes of lending one's cloak!' And she tossed her head and turned. . . . God have mercy, where did *you* spring from?"

Tossing her head and imitating the turn, she had come face to face with me.

"I came by the door."

"And what do you want?"

"I've come to live here. My uncle arranged it."

"Who is your uncle?"

"Sir Godfrey Blanchfleur."

"Oh. Well, I don't think he is here now."

Perhaps she would have shown more concern, but one of the other girls tugged at her sleeve.

"Ella, go on! I must skip in just one minute. Lend her cloak, why, she wouldn't lend a pin!"

There was nothing to be hoped for from them, so I went farther into the room and from shyness approached the lady who sat alone, rather than another group.

All I had time to see, or wit to notice then, was that she was pretty, with a beautiful pale unblemished skin and hair so fair that it was almost silver.

I planted myself in front of her and said all in one shaky gulping sentence, "My name is Maude Reed and my uncle Sir Godfrey Blanchfleur invited me here, and now he is gone and I don't know what to do and I want to go to the privy very badly indeed!"

"Poor poppet!" she said, and laid the lute aside, jumped up and took my hand and hurried me through a doorway, into a passage, up some steps, down some steps, into another passage and so into a room where stood a row of big square boxes covered with black velvet. She threw open the lid of one of them and showed a gleaming copper pot, sunk in the black velvet of the inner frame.

"There you are," she said cheerfully.

Urgent as my need was, I waited for her to go. I was unused to the ways of the great. At home there was a privy, with a screen of bushes around it, and there was, of course, the night-pot under the bed in case of need, but I had not—at least since I could remember—used either with anyone watching.

While I stood, almost weeping with indecision, the door opened, and one of the young ladies who had been dicing hurried in. I knew her by her violet-coloured dress. She threw up her skirt and took the stool next to the one opened for me.

"Holy Virgin," she said, "that onion broth! It goes through me like a purge."

Encouraged, I sat down and did what I wanted.

My friend, so pale and slender, looking so far removed from such gross human needs, lifted her sleeve and held it before her nose.

"Catherine, what a stink! Little one, have you done?"

She took up a bell which stood on the ledge of a niche like an unglazed window set in one of the inner walls, and rang it vigorously.

"Now," she said, "if anyone knows about you, it will be Dame Margaret and I think she is in the Still Room. We'll find her. So you are Blanchfleur's niece; yes, you have his eyes."

In the passage we met an old woman carrying a bucket and a jar of sudsy water; she stood aside to let us pass. When the passage widened the young lady took my hand, asked me to tell her my name again, asked how old I was, was I homesick? Yes, so had she been, she said, when she first came to Beauclaire, but that soon passed; in the Children's Dorter there were several boys and girls, some about my age, and I should enjoy playing with them; and Dame Margery, who governed us, was not too strict, it was said.

I made bold to ask her her name.

"Melusine." It was one I had never heard before, and I repeated it to make sure I had it right.

"Yes, Melusine. I was named for a fairy lady in a French romance."

"You could be one," I said. "I thought just now . . ." But I could not tell her the thought I had had in the Stool Room.

"What did you think?"

"That you are beautiful."

She laughed.

"You have the Blanchfleur tongue, too."

But she sounded pleased.

When we had walked for what seemed to me a long, long way, she stopped and opened a door. It smelt as though the lid had been taken off a spice box. Behind the door was a smallish, cosy room, lined with shelves and cupboards, all the shelves full of jars and bottles and boxes. At a solid table in the middle of the room sat a stout, elderly woman with a plain linen head-piece, moving her hands about in a wooden trough, full of some dry-looking, sweet-smelling mixture. Ranged along the table were many bowls, some of silver, some of pottery, pewter, and wood.

"What have we here?" she asked, looking up.

"We have Maude Reed, who has come to live here."

"Why, yes, of course. They were warned at the entrance that she would arrive today or tomorrow, and should be taken to Dame Margery. What has happened?"

"She came to the Well Yard door, and Dame Margery has taken all the children blackberrying, or so I thought."

"You thought right—so tomorrow I shall be busy with the cordials. And this not off my hands yet! Very well, very well. They will be back very soon, it's nearly dark. She can stay with me."

Melusine smiled and left me. Dame Margaret asked if I were at ease, and if I needed to eat now or could wait until supper.

I said I could wait. So, having tossed the mixture again, she said I could help her to dish it out into the bowls.

It was just the kind of task most useful at the moment; it kept me busy and made me feel a little less lost and unwanted. When she saw that I was careful and neat-handed, she left it all to me. She took a cup and poured some dark rosy-red liquid into it and sat down, leisurely sipping. Between sips she asked me questions. At one point she snapped a finger and thumb and said:

"But of course. Your mother was Anne Blanchfleur. I remember her well." She looked at me with a new, close interest, up and down, noting my very shoes.

"Reed, you said? And your father is a wool merchant."

"No. My father is dead. My grandfather is a wool merchant, the biggest between London and Lincoln."

She made a little noise as though clearing her throat.

"Family ties are strong, for all that. Lucky for you, you are like your mother—in appearance, I mean."

"I'm not. My mother is very pretty, and I have red hair."

"It runs in this family. My Lord Astallon is red as a fox. As for pretti-ness, one day you may be pretty too if you learn not to glower."

The door opened, and another plain linen head-piece poked around its edge.

"Ha, Margaret! There is no linen, nor towels laid out for the Merlin Chamber, and my Lord Ashford just arriving."

"God be my judge!" cried Dame Margaret, jumping up. "It was tomorrow. I swear my Lady said tomorrow . . ." She trotted out of the room.

In the moment or so that the door had stood half open, the scent of roasted meat had come in and mingled with the spicy air of the room. I realised that I was, if not actually hungry, very empty. All through the journey my stomach had been full of misery, and the food at the inns, for the last three days, had been very unappetizing. Scratching up the last of the mixture of rose petals and lavender and bergamot heads out of the wooden trough and into the bowls, I began to think about supper. And that made me think of the Old Vine, of the bustle and chatter as the weavers and pack-whackers and smiths came trooping into the dining hall, my grandfather, quiet but kindly, taking his place at the end table, Mother beside him and Walter next to her. My place empty . . .

Here, at least, I was alone and could snivel a little; so I did, folding my arms on the table's edge and leaning my face on them. I snivelled until one of the candles went out. The Still Room was on the inner side of the house, with only one small window which looked out on a narrow court, so the candles had been lighted there early. Now one, and then another, guttered away. And I was afraid of the dark. Walter was too; but some-how he had managed to make his fear known, and when one day I con-fessed to Mother an equal dread of darkness she had said, "Copy cat! Just because Walter has this whim, so must you." So after that I had made light of it, sheltering behind Walter's need to have a light through all the hours of darkness. Now I was alone in a strange room, and where there had been six candles there were now four, and two were failing.

I went over and opened the door. The passage outside was quite brightly lighted. I walked along it, following my nose, which would, I thought, lead me to the food, the scent of which was now powerful. Soon the passage divided, one arm of it, narrow and dimly lighted, ran off to the left, the other, wider, very bright, led towards a set of stairs. I went that way, and at the stair head found myself in a room which was as much bigger than the one by the Well Yard door as that was compared with the solar at the Old Vine.

It was so magnificent, so unlike anything I had ever seen before, that for a moment I could forget that I was homesick, alone, hungry, and forgotten, and just stood staring. Every inch of the walls was covered with tapestry. At home we had one, and that was reckoned a marvel; here one joined onto the next, all the way round the great room. Ours at home was a scene from the Bible, Adam and Eve in the Garden of Eden, their nakedness screened by flowers and bushes, Eve offering Adam the fatal apple and the Serpent, coiled about a tree trunk and wearing a human face, watching the triumph of his wiliness. The tapestries in the Long Gallery at Beauclaire were pictures of stories which I had never heard; there was a knight on a great horse driving a lance into the body of a thing all covered with scales like a fish, but with a thick solid tail and claws like a bird and a head more like that of a horse than anything else. The knight wore a red cross on a white background on his breastplate. Every one of the woven pictures was concerned with knights. In one a knight lay on the ground, sorely wounded to judge by the blood that oozed over his shoulder from under the edge of his gorget, but he was blowing a great horn, and his enemies made a ring about him, waving their swords, aiming their pikes, while far off, on a distant hill, a gathering of knights seemed to be waiting and listening.

I walked all the way round, looking at the pictures and wishing that there were someone with me who could tell me the stories about them.

At the far end there was another high doorway, and I went through it and found myself in a smaller room, all hung with rose-pink draperies; and beyond that was another passage. There were many doors in it, and I opened them, one by one. Most of them opened onto darkness, and one, just opposite a candle sconce on the passage wall, gave me a fright, for it was full of suits of armour on their stands, and looked, at first glance, like men. That room smelt of the oil used on the harness, and of the vinegar which was mixed with the wood ash for polishing the metal.

By this time I could not even smell the food and knew I was lost. But just as I knew this I opened the door and found myself in the room into which, a lifetime ago, I had walked. There was the screen about the door, the table at which the ladies had diced, the piece of embroidery, and, on the window seat, Melusine's lute, just as she had flung it down. The candles were burning low here, too, but there were so many of them that the light still served. I walked over to the window seat and stood there, thinking that this was her place, and she was the only one who had been kind to me. I touched a string of the lute and it gave a little tunable twang.

There was a lute at home; it hung by a silk ribbon from a peg in the solar, and I had always wanted to handle it; but it had belonged to my father and was sacred. One day, however, Mother had reached it down and put it into my hands. "There you are," she said, "see what you can do."

All I could do, to start with, was to make a discordant noise. She sat and watched me, which was not helpful. I had, however, just begun to work it out, that when I touched this string such and such a sound came forth and when I touched this, another . . . and in a moment I felt sure I should have made a less distasteful noise when she jumped up, snatched the lute from me, and hung it back on its peg, saying:

"You have no art."

Now, left alone with a lute, I would have tried all the strings again and endeavoured to remember what I had learned in that one brief handling; but, as I reached the window seat where Melusine's lute lay, I could look out of the window and saw that the wall which ran out at right angles to the Well Yard Room was pierced with windows, all aglow, and as I looked a door opened and a man came out, holding something in his hand which he raised to his mouth and bit upon. So I went through the screen and out by the door and across the Well Yard and in through that opened door.

I was at the lowest end of the dining hall, from which all but a few servants and a tableful of pages had gone. At the other end was a low platform, with a table running across it, from side to side of the hall, and that table was edged with crimson velvet, heavily embroidered, a little like an altar cloth. Another vast table ran the whole length of the hall, and at the lower end there were others, set near the wall. Broken meats, half-eaten trenchers of bread soaked in gravy, spilled ale, gnawed bones, and apple cores littered the boards. Some men, each with a bucket, were going around sweeping everything from the tables, and behind each man came a boy with a filthy cloth which he drove—swish— across each surface as it was cleared.

The pages were eating heartily and talking and laughing at the same time. One looked up and saw me, nudged his neighbour, who looked and nudged his. They all stared but not one did more, and though some of the servants eyed me they said nothing. I walked along by the long central table, looking for something to eat. When I found it—it was a pigeon, all that was left of a dishful, to judge by the bones scattered round—I sat down, pulled the dish towards me, and began to eat. It was in that worst state, no longer hot, yet not quite cold, and I should have liked some bread with it; however, it took the edge from my hunger. As I ate I watched the clearing being done and thought how much more carefully we did things at the Old Vine, where the bones were collected separately and put onto the dung-heap where they softened down into manure, and all the soft waste went into the swill pail for the pigs. Nor would my mother, or for that matter Old Nancy, have allowed such filthy cloths as the boys were using anywhere within reach of our tables.

I crammed the last piece into my mouth just as the clearing man reached the place where I sat. I then walked down the hall again and out into the Well Yard and into the room where the ladies had been, hoping to find Melusine. There was no one there and the candles were almost dead.

I have known sharper grief, deeper misery, but never a feeling of more complete wretchedness, of being alone in a hostile world. Dame Margaret had spoken of my having been expected by the main entry; if I only knew where that was, I thought, I might find someone who would know me and tell me where to go. The idea of still being alone and lost when all the lights were dead and darkness everywhere filled me with panic.

Often, during the next few days, I looked back on my first evening at Beauclaire and thought how contradictory was its way of life. I truly believe that a homeless person, provided he or she were decently dressed, could have moved about in the house, eaten in the hall, slept in a corner, and gone unchallenged for a week, a month, maybe forever. Everyone would assume that the stranger belonged to some other department, or to some visitor's train. Yet, side by side with this, was the equally true fact that, once you *were* claimed and recognised and made part of the establishment, you could never for a moment get out of the place. There was somewhere where you must be, someone you must be with, something you must be doing from the moment you left your bed until you went back to it.

The household, which to me just then seemed so dreadfully disorganised, was, in fact, very closely and highly organised. All my misery was the result of having been sent to the wrong doorway.

Not daring to stay longer in the empty darkening room, I opened a door, found myself in a passage, and could hear some music and the sound of someone singing. The sounds seemed to come from the top of a flight of steps, so I climbed them and opened the door at the top and knew at once that I had solved one problem; I was no longer alone. The room was crowded with ladies and gentlemen, some ladies seated on benches and chairs with gentlemen around them, but most standing in groups. The music came from the other end of the apartment, and most of them were facing it, so had their backs to me.

I went in, like a pup looking for its master, hoping to find either Melusine or Dame Margaret. Here again, as I moved about people looked at me with a mild curiosity, but nobody asked *why* I was there. I was halfway up the room, at a point from which I could catch glimpses of the lute-player, and of a man with a harp and a boy with a wooden frame, the top bar hung with little bells, arranged in order of size, the smallest like a thimble, the largest as big as a cup, when I saw Melusine standing with a very fine young gentleman.

I had been moving diffidently, but at the sight of her I flung myself forward and took her hand.

"What!" she said. "You again. You should be abed."

"I know." I began to blurt out my woes, how Dame Margaret had left me and nobody had called me to supper and how I had been lost.

Faces began to turn in our direction; somebody said, "Hush!" The music ended with a loud sweep of the player's fingers across all the strings, and in the vibrating silence immediately following a sweet, high, languid voice called:

"What *is* all this ado?"

Holding me by the hand, Melusine led me towards where a lady sat on a bench with high, incurved ends, all gilded. The lady did look, indeed, like a statue of gold; her dress was yellow and so was her hair, and she wore it uncovered, pulled back from a high white forehead, and held in a net of gold, set with yellow stones where the strands crossed. Her face was like a statue's, too, carved into an expression of faintly shocked surprise, due to her eyebrows being shaved off and then painted on again, a full inch above their natural place.

Melusine let my hand fall and stepped back a pace and said in a stiff way, "Madam, this is Maude Reed."

"Maude Reed," she repeated the name, just as I had hours ago repeated Melusine's. She turned her head towards a man who stood behind the gilded bench. I remembered Dame Margaret's remark about the red hair. His was very red, quite different from mine. He leaned over and whispered in the lady's ear.

"Of course," she said, and turning back to me gave me a smile and said, "You are welcome."

I knew what to do and I meant to do it, to make her the best curtesy I had ever made, holding my skirt clear on each side and letting my head dip just at the right moment. And I did.

But the truth was that one of my reasons for misery and wanting to find Melusine was that I needed, once again, to visit the Stool Room; and my inside didn't know that I was making my duty to my mother's kin, Lord and Lady Astallon of Beauclaire, it thought I was attending to its needs. I felt the warm wetness run free, scouring my saddle-chafed thighs.

Forever disgraced, I thought, rising with the shamed blood scorching in my face. I cannot stay here. Tomorrow I must go home. And here they will remember me forever—Maude Reed the girl who made a curtsey and made water at the same time.

There was the little puddle; the moment I moved it would be seen by all, and, though I knew that I must move and that it would be seen, something made me try to defer the evil moment. I was like a person on his way to the tooth-puller's booth, lingering by every other booth that he passed.

"Madam," I said, "my mother sent you her loving greetings and her deep gratitude for taking me into your household."

"Your mother," she said, and again turned her head. My Lord again leaned forward and whispered into her ear.

"Your mother has trained you very prettily," said my Lady, turning back to me. "Now . . . You will join the Children's Dorter and be governed by Dame Margery, and I trust you will learn well."

Ignorant as I was, I recognised the tone of dismissal. But I still stood, guarding my shameful secret.

My Lord saved me. He made a sign to the musicians, who broke at once into a merry tune; and a slim young man with red cheeks came from behind the bench and bowed and extended his hand and said:

"Madam, I beg you, dance with me."

She smiled and stood up; and, since she could neither walk through me nor over me, I was bound to step aside.

Now, I thought, they will all see.

But her skirts were long and full and edged with fur. When she had passed there was nothing left to show that I had misbehaved myself. After a moment Melusine came to me and said, "I will take you to Dame Margery."

The young gentleman who had stood by her said, "When did you turn nursemaid? May I be your next charge?"

She said, "You do not expect to reach second childhood so soon, surely?"

Outside another door, which we reached after a long walk, Melusine halted, put her arm around me, and kissed me.

"Our paths may not cross again for many a long day," she said. "I hope you'll be happy."

I clung to her for a moment; then she put me gently away, and once we were inside the room, face to face with a dignified, solemn-looking lady, her manner was formal again.

"This is Maude Reed, Dame Margery," she said. "By some mistake she came in by the wrong door."

THE Children's Dorter at Beauclaire was really an establishment on its own. The actual Dorter was the chamber in which we all slept, boys and girls together, but separated by screens down the centre of the room; when people spoke of the Children's Dorter, however, they meant also the big room in which we worked and played, and took all our meals except the midday dinner, and very occasionally our supper.

There were eight of us at the time when I joined the Dorter; my Astallon cousins had two children of their own, a boy of nine, named Ralph, a girl of six, Constance. There was another girl of eight who bore about the same relationship to them as I did myself, she was a Fortescue—sent, after the fashion of the time, to be schooled in the house of a cousin, while, in her own home, other girls and boys were being trained; her name was Alison. There were two brothers, aged nine and seven, Henry and William Rancon, whose father had died by my cousin Astallon's side in the French Wars lately ended; and there was an eleven-year-old girl named Helen Beaufort, who was a relative—some believed an illegitimate daughter—of the great Cardinal. There was also a girl named Madge FitzHerbert who was a true half-wit; she understood very little, spoke indistinctly, and had protruding brown eyes which did not see very well. I never knew her to manage to thread her needle. She was there because her own mother was dead and her father, when he remarried, did not wish his new wife to see what manner of child he had bred already. He had some position at Court and was in high favour, especially with the Duke of Gloucester, the King's uncle. My cousins had accepted Madge as an inmate of their Children's Dorter in return for some favour which her father was able to do for them. My Lady Astallon had ambitions and was always craving to live in London and take what she called her "proper place in the world," but her husband preferred to stay at Beauclaire, with only short visits to his other estates, to attend to the management of his affairs and mind no will but his own. I've heard him say that the Duke of Gloucester was "riding for a fall," that when the tree fell the ivy fell too, and that for himself he would sooner rule on his own acres than be just one voice on the Privy Council of the King.

Our days were strictly ordered, but by no means tedious. We girls learned to sew and to embroider; not to spin, spinning was at that time out of fashion for the gently reared and the distaffs lay idle in a corner. We learned to dance, and to play various games without showing chagrin when we lost, or pleasure when we won. Self-control was a virtue highly rated by Dame Margery; she never, for example, minded how much, how often, or how viciously we quarrelled but we were not allowed to smack one another, or scream, or cry. The boys, when they fell out, were allowed to use violence on one another, but not in the house.

"Into the yard and settle it," Dame Margery would say; and the one who came back defeated had scant sympathy.

"You'll take harder knocks, if you live."

The boys, when they were ten years old, were removed from her care altogether—"And I want no one saying, when you get amongst men, that I have brought you up soft."

We girls, though treated differently, were disciplined too. We must learn to stand still, perfectly upright, without fidgeting or sighing for long stretches of time on end; we must always eat, without any sign of distaste, anything put before us. We must learn to govern even the workings of our bowels.

"Bless you, child," Dame Margery once said to Helen Beaufort, "in a few years' time, when you wait upon some great lady and are tiring her hair, will you drop the pins and cry, 'I must to stool!'? You will *not*. Go stand in that corner, place your hands on your head, and await my permission to go."

Unlikely as it sounds, impossible as it seemed to us at the time, her methods did work; bowels and bladders learned that they were not masters to be pandered to, but servants to be obedient.

In many ways we were fortunate in our mistress; she was a country-woman, who after some years in London had come back to the place that she loved, and she liked nothing better than to take us out, riding or afoot, naming us the wildflowers or the birds, warning us which berries were poisonous, letting us share, in a manner unusual in most households, the seasonal activities of the manor. On the day of my arrival the children had all been blackberrying; later we gathered mushrooms and hazelnuts. When the summer came, we were allowed—the girls demurely sunbonneted—to toss hay in the meadows, play amongst the stooks in the harvest fields. Once she took us all into the woods, carrying food with us, and let us make a fire and cook, tinker fashion. The meat was bitter with smoke on the outside and red raw within, but somehow it tasted different, and better than a dish similarly spoiled would have seemed eaten indoors.

My appreciation of our Dame did not come all at once. My first weeks at Beauclaire were very wretched. I made mistakes and was punished, I lost myself several times. When the boys teased me I fell into a rage, when Alison and Helen tried—as they did at first—to show themselves superior to me, I wept. So much that we did seemed to me useless, false, and hypocritical, and there was so much else that I did not understand.

This wool-merchant business, for example. Alison and Helen seemed to hold it against me that my grandfather was a wool merchant. At least here Helen, who was the older, always gave the lead and Alison followed her.

Once I cried, "And what's wrong with being a wool merchant?" and in fury took up the scissors and slashed into Helen's embroidery. Dame Margery punished me, and I yelled that it was not fair, I hadn't started the dispute.

"And do you expect fairness in this world, Maude? If so, you are going to be very sorely disappointed. Better learn now. Go stand in the corner and place your hands on top of your head."

I could learn, that was one blessing. I wasn't like poor Madge who could make the same mistake three times in one day. Next time Helen twitted me about the wool business I stayed calm. I didn't even look at her, I looked at the wall straight ahead and I said:

"My *father* was in the wool business too. And when I was born he did not call me his *niece!*"

Now for that I should have been whipped. But no! Dame Margery, a little later, said, "I am glad to see that you are learning to stand up for yourself in proper fashion."

Proper fashion, for young ladies, meant lashing out with hurtful words, not slashing with scissors.

Not long after that I performed, out of cowardice, an act of bravado which gave the boys a good opinion of me.

Every fine day, after the midday dinner, unless Dame Margery had something planned for us, we were allowed to go and play in what was called the Low Garden. In days long past, when Beauclaire consisted of the castle only, this garden had been the pleasance where, in times of peace, at least, the ladies could take the air. Since then new and better gardens had been made near the new house, but they were for the pleasure of grown-up people who did not wish to be disturbed by children's games. The Low Garden was now somewhat neglected, its grass tufty, its bushes overgrown, the walls surrounding it tumbled in some places. There was one stretch of wall, still quite sound, however, and one day the boys took a ladder into the garden, climbed by its help to the top of the wall and there strutted about like young cockerels, jeering at us girls who, they claimed, couldn't do what they were doing. They then began a game of taking turns to run the length of the wall and back.

My head for heights had never been put to the test, and I couldn't see why William, a month or so younger than I was, could do something which I could not, so in the end I called that it was now my turn; and I climbed the ladder and stood on the wall, which was about twelve inches

wide at the top, and which, on the garden side, dropped ten feet, and on
the outer side twice as much. The moment I stood on the wall and
looked down I realized the truth of their jeers, this was something no girl
could do, or should attempt. I also knew that to stand there, teetering, was
the worst thing I could do; only speed could save me. Trying not to look
at or think about the drop on either side, I walked briskly to the end of
the stretch of wall where it ran into the side of a solid square tower. I
turned and pressed my back against the blessed solidity of that tower and
knew that I should never have the courage to leave it and set out on the
return journey. My head was already spinning and my knees had turned
to melted wax. So I did the only thing there was to do; crying, "I'll wager
you daren't do *this!*" I jumped down into the garden. A sharp sickening
pain stabbed through my ankle, but Dame Margery's exhortations of self-
control bore fruit; I did not cry out, nor did I hobble, though my ankle
remained swollen and painful for many days, and will even now, in wet
weather, pain me.

Henry Rancon took up the challenge, climbed the wall, ran along, and
jumped as I had done. William said he couldn't jump because he would
jar a tooth that was already giving him trouble, and Ralph Astallon said
it was time we went back to the house.

After that, however, whenever they wanted a fourth for any game they
chose me rather than Helen, who was older and stronger.

So, bit by bit, I worked myself into place at Beauclaire, and before I
had thoroughly recovered from my homesickness Christmas was drawing
near. I expected to go home for Christmas, and I cherished a hope of being
allowed to stay there. After all, one of the reasons for sending me away
had been that it wouldn't be fair for Walter to go and for me to remain,
and Walter had remained; and another reason was that I should learn,
and I had taken care to learn all I could.

Advent came; the first Sunday in Advent, and then the second, and
nothing was said about my going back to Baildon for Christmas. It seemed
to me that it might be one of those things overlooked or gone awry—like
my arrival—so during that week I said to Dame Margery:

"Madam, I am supposed to go home for Christmas."

"Are you indeed?"

"No one has spoken of any arrangements yet."

"Heaven bless you, child, have patience. Your home is . . . how far
away?"

"Five days' ride."

"Then there is plenty of time."

Another Sunday came; and I reminded my Dame, and she said, "Maybe
I should make inquiries."

She must have done so, for next day, at dinner in the hall, my Lady Astallon sent for me and when I stood close said, "This notion about going home for Christmas. What put that into your little head?"

I asked myself, what? When there was talk of Walter going to the Choir School and of me going to Clevely, there had been mention of being home for Christmas; but he was now at home and I was here. It was I, bidding Jack farewell at Brentwood, who had said, "Home for Christmas."

"It was understood, madam," I said in a weak voice.

"Not by me. And not I think by your uncle. In any case, travel at this time of the year is undesirable; the inns so uncomfortable and the likelihood of being snowbound . . ."

She waved an elegant hand in dismissal, and I now knew better than to argue.

Next day, on my way out of the Hall after dinner, I was stopped by my Uncle Godfrey. He had, on and off, paid me some attention, for which I was very grateful. He had returned to Beauclaire four or five days after my arrival and had at once sought me out and asked how I fared. Now he said:

"This going back to Baildon for Christmas, Maude, would be very silly. Christmas here is kept in such style. People come from London to share in the festivities."

"But I expected to go home."

"There you are mistaken. Your mother was clear on that point. You stay here until you are twelve."

"And not go home at all?"

"Running to and fro," he said, "is vastly expensive and bothersome and unsettling. And all to what purpose?"

"I want to see my mother and Walter and my grandfather."

Something changed in his face, so that for a moment I feared that I had offended him. Then he took a lock of my hair between his fingers and twisted it, saying slowly, "You know, child, sooner or later you have to learn to do without people. It's best to learn young."

"But why? If it is a question of expense I still have the broad gold piece my grandfather gave me."

"You'd only make it harder for yourself. . . ."

Where the words or the thought came from, I do not know, but I heard myself saying, "My mother doesn't want me at home, does she?"

"She knows that you will do better here. And so, for that matter, do I. Who else looks to go home?"

"Alison, Alison Fortescue."

"Does she so? Well, for your ear alone, in that house Christmas is so meanly celebrated I'll wager she'll wish she'd stayed here. Many's the Christmas I've spent there and, believe me, even the plums in the pudding are counted out, one by one."

I wanted to shout that it was no matter to me whether there was one plum in the pudding or a thousand. Most of all I wanted to go and cry somewhere, alone, by myself. But the truth was that at Beauclaire there was no place to cry alone; once you were part of it you lived a public life, where every sigh or frown or tear was observed and remarked. At this moment, because my uncle had stopped me on my way out of the Hall, there were Constance and Helen, Alison and Madge waiting for me.

I walked slowly to join them, thinking that when I had said that Mother didn't want me home my uncle had not denied it. I remembered then what I had forgotten, the face she had worn as she watched me ride away. Something within me hardened. I thought: Well, if she does not want me, I don't want her. It wasn't true at first, but thinking it over and over made it become true. I still yearned for the smallness and friendliness of the Old Vine, for the kitchen where I was welcomed and given gingerbread men, for the yard full of men like Jack who would call me "Little Mistress" one minute and "Maude" the next. But, over that Christmastime, I began to be weaned.

That I had not been expected to go home was made very clear by the arrival, two days before Christmas, of gifts for me. From my grandfather—or so I imagined—another broad gold piece, from my mother a blue velvet hood, lined and bordered with fur. With these gifts was a square of parchment, bordered all down the left side with leaves and berries painted in green and red, and with words written in the remaining space. The letters were very black, except for a few which were gaily coloured.

I held it out to Dame Margery and learned, to my surprise, that she could not read. But she knew what it was.

"It is a Christmas Piece, to bring you good wishes. Carry it down to the Well Yard Room. Most like one of the young ladies can spell it out for you. If not, you must ask the Chaplain."

I was delighted to have a chance to go where I might see Melusine, for whom I still entertained a passion of gratitude and admiration. There was, rightly, a firm barrier fixed between the Children's Dorter and the Well Yard Room and the Ladies' Dorter, and I seldom saw her except at a distance. That morning I found her and she read me out what Walter had written. It said:

On this, the Birthday of Our Blessed
Lord, I send Greetings to my Dear
Sister and wish you Joy and God's
Blessing on you, from your Brother
Walter Reed.

Melusine read it for me three times, so that I could get it by heart. Then she asked how old was Walter, and when I told her that he was just my age she said, "He must be a clever scholar. It is nicely written and very even."

The Christmas Piece, bringing home almost as much as Walter to mind, made me homesick again. The pretty furred hood seemed a mockery, and when I returned to the Children's Dorter I gave it to Madge FitzHerbert, who had received no gifts at all.

The Christmas Piece I carried about with me all through the Twelve Days—which were kept, as my uncle had promised, with every possible gaiety.

While I was showing it to my Uncle Godfrey I said, "I would dearly like to read and write, too."

"You would *what?*"

I said it again.

"Then you must consult with Dame Margery."

"She cannot read. I had to ask the Lady Melusine to tell me the words."

"She has learning? Perhaps she could teach you. As I said, consult with your Dame."

Dame Margery showed more sympathy with my desire than I had dared to expect.

"You are to be a religious," she said thoughtfully, "and some learning might serve to advance you. I will speak to my Lady."

The answer, when it came, was typical of Beauclaire where the most prodigal extravagance ran side by side with sparing economy over trivial things. It seemed a pity for Melusine to waste her time teaching one child to read; who else would like to learn? Everyone else showed the utmost horror for the notion; I went round, pleading with one after another, even poor Madge. I argued that writing might be the one thing she *could* do, how could she know till she had tried. But she just giggled. In the end it was Henry Rancon, the least likely of all, who came to my aid. I thought of a good argument to use on him.

"At Easter you will move out of the Children's Dorter," I said, "and all your life will be changed. So you would have only a few lessons, and meanwhile I would do anything you asked. I would be your liege man."

Henry was always wanting somebody to be his faithful, unquestioning servant, and neither of the other boys was obliging.

"All right," he said. "I'll have lessons till Easter. Now you kneel down and put your hands between mine and swear to be my faithful liege and obey my every command."

That I did most gladly; and though Dame Margery said, "Wonders will never cease," when Henry professed his desire to learn to read and write, by Candlemas the lessons were arranged.

Tucked away in that same long passage where the suits of armour occupied a whole room, there was a small room in which some earlier Lord Astallon had gathered several books; there was a table, too, and a bench, and a slab of wood out of which sprouted three horns. One held the ink, the other the quills, and the third the sand for drying anything which was needed too hastily to permit the ink to dry of itself.

And here, on three afternoons of the week, in the space between our playtime and supper, Henry and I and Melusine met. On the first day, when I thanked her, most eagerly, for agreeing to teach us, she said:

"The saddle is on the other horse, Maude. To escape, even for an hour, from the everlasting chatter and bickering; to get out of that carp pond delights me."

Another time she said that it should be a law that every woman who was not a busy housewife should learn to read.

"If they could find stories in books, they would be less ready to make up tales about those they live amongst. And they would learn that their own small joys and troubles do not fill up the world."

I learned fast, partly because I wanted to and partly to please Melusine. Henry was content to learn how to write his name. Page after page he filled with "Henry Rancon. Henry Rancon," then "Sir Henry Rancon," or "Henry Rancon, Knight." He just lived for the moment when he should be a knight; he had the same feeling for my Uncle Godfrey—who was reckoned one of the best knights in England—as I had for Melusine; and I think one thing which resigned him to the tedium of the lessons was that, every now and then, and always unexpectedly, my uncle would look into the Book Room to see what progress I was making. My uncle, unlike most of his kind, spoke of learning with respect, and told Henry he was lucky to be taught.

"I never had the chance," he said. "At your age I was never in one place long enough."

"I could teach you now, Sir Godfrey," Melusine said.

"I am an old dog, too old for new tricks. But there are old tricks that I could teach *you!*"

"Of that I have no doubt," she said, and laughed.

It was towards the end of that February month that Henry made one of his demands upon me, in keeping with my vow. There had been some days of continuing snow, during which our afternoon playtime had been spent indoors, where tedium had led to squabbling and squabbling to punishment. Rheumy colds had afflicted us, too, and my cousin Ralph was still abed on one side of the screen, and Helen and Madge abed on the other side. Our Dame had her hands full and her temper was short.

On this day, however, the sun shone and the snow was melting fast, and as we came out of the Hall Henry said, "Come and play Hare and Hounds in the Maze."

The Maze at Beauclaire was a singular oddity. It was part of the old Low Garden, at least it formed one of its boundaries, but it was said to be older than the garden, older even than the castle. It was an intricate puzzle of narrow paths, crossing and turning back on themselves, bordered by clipped yew hedges as tall as a mounted man. In its very centre stood a block of black stone on a mound of grey ones. There was a story that in the very faraway past, when the people who lived in England were heathen, that stone was worshipped.

I had only penetrated deep into the Maze on one occasion; very soon after my arrival at Beauclaire, Helen Beaufort had mentioned, in Dame Margery's hearing, something about the Maze being the haunt of evil spirits, and Dame Margery had said:

"Rubbish. It is just a puzzle, laid out in the days when people could not walk far from the castle walls for fear of enemies, so they made the longest walk, and the most interesting, on the smallest possible space." And to prove that she believed what she said she had taken the lot of us, on a sunny autumn afternoon, and we had gone in and lost ourselves, and run this way and that, and shouted, and laughed and in the end come breathless to the black stone in the centre, and Dame Margery had said:

"You see. You have all lost your breath and wearied your legs as though you had run a mile. It is simply an exercise ground."

"Then what is the stone, madam?" Helen Beaufort asked.

"To mark the centre, so that people could know that they had arrived."

"It's a Rune Stone," Helen said in the stubborn way which she had mastered; not rude or ill-tempered, just a flat, unshakable way of stating something.

"And what might that mean?" Dame Margery asked.

"I don't know. I heard it spoken of as a Rune Stone."

"Meaning a marker, like a milestone," said Dame Margery. "Now, all take different paths and let's see who can be out first."

That night, in the Children's Dorter, after the light was out, Helen said to me, "A Rune Stone is not a marker, say what she may. Before I came to Beauclaire I lived at Greenwich and one was found there, and the priest had it hacked to pieces; he said it was evil."

There was no need for Dame Margery to tell us girls not to play in the Maze, we avoided it; but the boys often played a game of Hare and Hounds there, and certainly seemed to suffer no harm.

On this afternoon I said, "Oh, Henry, it's so cold and so sloppy underfoot."

"Running will warm you, and you can put on your thick shoes. Besides . . . you promised."

That was true, so I said meekly, "Can I be a Hound?" Hounds could run in company, the Hare must go alone.

"You are a Hound; with William. It is my turn to be Hare."

"I'll get my cloak and my thick shoes."

"We'll wait for you by the Maze," he said.

Alison and Constance were waiting for me, and as we went up the stairs I said, "I am going to play Hare and Hounds with William and Henry in the Maze. You come too."

"God's teeth," said Alison, who was fond of using grown-up expressions, "on a day like this? A cold thaw. I thank you, no!"

When we reached our room I went and stood before our Dame and said, "I am going to play with Henry and William."

I hoped that she, like Alison, might think a cold thaw a bad thing to brave. And that would let me out. But she only said that the fresh air would do me good, so long as I kept moving. So I fetched my cloak and looked for my thick shoes, and they had been taken away to be greased. So the bell must be rung and by the time it had been answered and the servant had been despatched for them, and had brought them, the brightness of the day had gone. In the Maze, I thought, it would soon be dusk.

However, I was sworn. So I ran out and joined the boys, who were waiting impatiently.

The rules were that the Hare started first, while the Hounds stood still and counted the fingers of both hands twice over. The Hare, as he ran, also counted twenty and when he had done cried, "Hee, hee, hee, you can't catch me!"

The Hounds then replied, "Woof, woof, woof."

Henry ran into the Maze and presently made his call. William and I ran in, crying, "Woof." It was already—for me, unpleasantly—nearly dusk between the high hedges, so I stayed close to William; at one place where two paths met he said:

"You take one, I'll go the other way." But William was not, even in pretence, my liege lord, so I let him run along his path and then I followed. At intervals Henry made the Hare call, and we responded. Henry's voice seemed to come from a different direction each time.

Presently William, as he ran, drew away from me. I tried to keep up, and when I couldn't, gasped out a shameless, breathless appeal.

"Wait for me."

He threw back over his shoulder, "We're not supposed to stay together; it spoils the game."

At the next turn I found that I had lost him, one path went left, one right, and so far as I could see along either he was not there. This was the moment that I had dreaded ever since Henry had issued his command. I stopped running and stood still. I needn't play any more; I could always say that I had tried to find them and failed. Had I had any sense at all, I thought, I should have fallen behind and turned back minutes ago, before I was far into the Maze.

Just before I turned I heard Henry's call far away to the left, and William's answering cry, to the right it seemed. To show that I hadn't given up too easily I cried, "Woof, woof, woof," too, but there was something about the sound of my voice that I didn't like, it sounded lost and frightened, less like a hound than a little bleating lamb.

I turned rightabout and began to walk, hoping that by going in that direction and keeping on long enough I must emerge at the entry. As I walked, I could hear Henry and William calling and counter-calling; once Henry sounded close at hand, and I hoped the next turn would reveal him. It did not. Nor the entry. And the dusk was deepening every second. To be alone in the Maze in the dark would be as bad as being in the Long Gallery at midnight on the sixth of November, when a long-dead Anne Astallon, whose husband had killed her in a fit of rage, was said to walk, weeping and wringing her hands.

I stood still and shouted, with all my strength, "Henry! Henry." There was no answer, and I thought, of course, he wouldn't answer, he'd think I was cheating in the game. One call though—if he heard it, he was bound to answer, being my liege lord, as I his man.

"À moi, Rancon! Aide! Aide!"

When that brought no response I knew I was out of earshot. I began to whimper and run any way, without trying to stick to one direction, and presently I found myself at the intersection of four paths and there was the big black stone.

I crossed myself and said, "God between me and all harm." I remembered what Dame Margery had said and tried to believe that it was placed there only to mark the centre; but Helen's words were much more powerful. It was still just light enough for me to see the chisel marks on the stone, deep in places, in others worn almost smooth.

I was extremely frightened, but with just sense enough left to know that what I feared was being alone in the dark, and that at such a place and such an hour even the most homely thing—a porridge bowl—could seem sinister. I didn't even know what "Rune" meant, so what happened next was not due to my imagination.

First I went to back away, into the mouth of the path by which I had come; and I found that I couldn't move. It was like one of those horrid nightmares when something pursues you and your feet are too heavy to run. My eyes were fixed on the stone, and I stood as fixed as it was. Then, in it, just level with my eyes, a light appeared, as though a small window had opened, with candles in the room within. The golden glow was faint at first, but it strengthened as I stared; and then out of the lighted square a face looked at me.

I did not, at that time, know what a cardinal looked like, the nearest I had been to one was when I listened to speculations about Helen's paternity, so I did not know what I was seeing. It was the face of the man that held my attention, not from any remarkable feature, but because his eyes, dark under heavy brows, looked straight at me in a very compelling, forceful way, as though he were using his will to beat mine down. I had no glimmer of a notion what he wanted of me, but I knew that whatever it was it was important to me; I knew also that I must not give in. As I thought that the face disappeared, the square glowed faintly for a moment and was gone.

By this time I was beyond fright. I knew I was about to die. I couldn't draw breath. It was as though an iron hand were clenched round my throat. Fighting against it, just to pull in breath once more took all my strength and I was failing, just about to die when the most beautiful sound in all the world reached my ears; a human voice, calling in its homely Sussex speech:

"Stay right where you be, little lady. I'm coming for ye."

The iron hand fell away, and I drew in breath with the sound of a cloth being ripped. I began to shake all over.

"Could ye give us a call for a bit of a guide?"

I tried, but my tongue was dry flannel between my chattering teeth.

"Now, now," the voice said, a trifle crossly, "'tis no use pretending, or hiding from me. The game's over now. You give us a shout!"

I tried and had just enough breath to make a small mew, like a kitten.

"Hi there! Can ye hear me?"

I managed to cry, "Hi!" and then, at the next try, "I'm by the stone."

"Stand still then."

In no time at all he was with me, a little bent gnome of a man, carrying a lantern. He put my fear—I was shaking still—down to the fact that I had been lost.

"That need never worrit you. We watch. We count 'em in and we count 'em out. Come on, now follow me."

As we walked he told me that once, long ago, when his own father was "just a little gaffer," some young people had gone into the Maze during the Christmas revels, and all come out but a young lady who was not missed until next day, and was dead when found.

"I should have died, too, if you hadn't found me."

"Oh no! 'Tisn't freezing tonight. Yon was a hard frost."

"I should have died of fear."

"There's naught to be feart of. There's two of us, and one is always on the watch."

"I didn't know that."

"No. We don't make much of ourselves. People don't like to think they're overlooked."

I don't think I was any more pious than the next child. I performed my duties and observed the Holy Days of Obligation and the fast days, but I seldom thought about religion. Now, however, I thought: That is like God, watching our comings and goings, Himself unseen but ready to help in time of need.

From that thought it was only a short step to be wondering whether the face I had seen in the Rune Stone was not really a heavenly vision and that what the man had been trying to convey to me was not to be frightened. The French girl, Jehan the Maid, had put visions and voices from Heaven in the forefront of everyone's mind. And *she*, I remembered, had been burned for a witch.

Dame Margery, who had not, I think, noticed my absence because she was so busy with the three sick children, scolded me for giving her needless anxiety, and set me yards of hemming to do for a punishment. William and Henry said I had spoiled the game, they thought I had given up too soon. I said to Henry, "I gave you the Cry of Extremity and you did not aid me, that cancels all vows."

I never mentioned my vision to anyone; and perhaps for that reason thought about it the more. Walter and I were born on St. Joseph's Day, and I thought it possible that the face I had seen had been of the Saint. After that I had a special devotion to St. Joseph, and when, around Eastertide, a seller of statues and medallions came round I broke into one of my gold pieces and bought a medallion of St. Joseph and fastened it to one of the cords of my velvet purse.

V

WHEN the next Christmas came round I did not expect to go home and felt no sorrow about it. The love which I had felt for my mother was now firmly fixed upon Melusine, who was just as pretty, and just as sweet-scented, and who never pushed me away. When Henry moved, with my cousin Ralph, out of the Children's Dorter at Easter, he gave up his lessons, as I had known he would, but, as was the way at Beauclaire, a custom once established went on and on, and it would not surprise me if, in that house, one lady went on opening the Book Room and spending three evenings in it every week, with or without a pupil until the Wars of the Roses brought all those great houses to ruin.

For ruined they are, I have lived to see things change, and those great rambling houses where three hundred people would sit down to supper every evening, where any traveller of noble rank was welcomed like a brother, where everyone above the rank of knight had his own cook, and bloody battles—sometimes fatal—would be waged in the kitchens over who should use this hearth, this spit, they are gone. The Wars between the Red Rose of Lancaster and the White Rose of York are blamed for the change, but I sometimes think they were bound to end, those great establishments, out of their own unwieldiness and waste. And perhaps because, under all the glitter and splendour, there was something rotten, something that made human beings of small account, and wealth of too much.

Helen Beaufort was older than I, and had already left the Children's Dorter and joined the Ladies'. This had two results for me. Although Helen welcomed the change and thought herself greatly superior to me now, she was lonely at first, and would seize opportunities to talk and tell me bits of gossip which I should not otherwise have heard. And, with her going, I became the eldest in the Dorter, entrusted with certain duties and responsibilities, and allowed, in return, certain small privileges. The one I valued most was to be allowed now and then, to go and read in the Book Room after supper. Whenever I had that permission, I would tell Melusine and sometimes she would say that if she could slip away, too, she would come and join me.

One evening she *had* managed it and we were sitting close together on the bench, both reading from the same book, which was what I liked to do because it gave an excuse to press close to her. The writing of the book was poor and difficult to read, but the story was so interesting that we read on, taking turns to read a piece.

All at once the door flew open, and when we looked up, startled, it was to see Ella and two other young ladies with expressions of smiling mischief slowly changing to astonishment on their faces.

One of them, Millibrand, said, "Holy Mother of God! It *is* true. She *reads*."

Melusine said, "What did you think I was doing?" Her voice was cool, but her face was red-hot.

"We couldn't believe it," Phillipa said, gazing round the small room. "There is a Welsh minstrel in the Long Gallery. To miss him, in order to brood over a book that smells of mould . . ." She turned up her eyes, begging Heaven to witness the unlikelihood.

"To miss him, in order to spy on me seems even poorer exchange," Melusine said.

"Ah, but . . ." Ella began. Millibrand pulled her by the arm.

"We are missing the music. Come along."

They ran away, laughing and rustling their dresses.

I got up and closed the door which they had left open. As I sat down again, Melusine put her arm around me and gave me a quick hug.

"My good angel!" she said.

"Why?"

"Oh . . . well, if you had not been here they would have dragged me off with them."

Now that I was learning something which I enjoyed, and seeing so much of Melusine, and had lost all trace of homesickness, I was happy at Beauclaire, and my eleventh birthday, bringing with it the thought that the coming summer would be my last, saddened me. I began wondering whether it would be possible for me to stay and in the end join the ladies in the Well Yard Room, instead of being uprooted again and going to Clevely. It was plain to me that I wasn't wanted at home, and so long as I stayed away I couldn't see that it mattered to anyone but me where I was. Walter and I had now become competitive about our writing and sent letters to one another twice or three times a year; I would write to him, I thought, early in the summer, perhaps at Whitsun, and ask him to ask Mother if I might remain at Beauclaire. Walter was to me, now, hardly a memory; I had changed so much in these three years, I knew he must have, too; he had become somebody whose writing remained much neater and more stylish than mine, try how I would.

With the summer, life at Beauclaire always became very gay; besides the big Tournament, regularly held on St. Barnabas' Day, there were several smaller ones, and there were many unplanned entertainments, too; wandering players would come and perform their mysteries, jugglers their tricks, sword-swallowers and fire-eaters their seeming miracles. Most of these delights we children were allowed to share, increasingly so as we grew older. There had at one time been talk of two young children coming into the Dorter, but Dame Margery had argued against it; Constance was now "getting off her hands," she said, and she herself too old to start all over again. So in that summer of my eleventh year, when even Constance could stay up late without yawning or falling asleep where she sat, we had more fun than ever before.

One day in June—I remember that the garlands and banners from our Tournament were still up—there was a bear-baiting. We children took our places, at the back of the Ladies' Stand. I saw Helen Beaufort sit with the grownups, and reminded myself that I had not yet written that letter to Walter. It again seemed unfair, and unnecessary, that next year I should go to Clevely, and should have borne all Dame Margery's training for nothing.

I'd watched bear-baiting before and never been squeamish about it, but on this evening something happened to me. I stopped being Maude Reed, a spectator up in the stands, and entered into the feelings of the bear. I may be wrong, but I think learning to read had had an effect on me. When you read you must get out of your own skin and into the skin of the people you are reading about, that is the only way to enjoy it.

They'd cut the bear's nose, both to make him savage and to let the dogs smell blood to make them savage, and I began by having a pain in my nose; then, as the fight went on, pains went all over me, particularly low down in my body where I had never had a pain before, and between my thighs. I sighed and shifted about on the seat, and Dame Margery looked at me reprovingly.

It was a remarkably good bear; dog after dog it dealt with. Now and again, when a dog was clawed or crushed or bitten, my feelings went that way for a moment or two, but in the main I was with the bear, I was the bear.

Everybody became excited. The ladies, who must in all circumstances remain well behaved, smiled and clapped their hands and made little murmuring or squeaking sounds; the gentlemen were more noisy, wagering money on whether a dog would "score" or not, a "score" meaning a bite which held while one could count up to five; they shouted, and laughed, and yelled the counts aloud and groaned when a dog they had backed was shaken off too soon.

Presently, even from where we sat we could smell the blood.

Then somebody called, "Try two dogs at once." So they did and the bear dealt with them gallantly and cleverly.

The dogs—some were strays that had been collected and kept for such an occasion, or young hounds which had something wrong with them which made them of no value in their proper sphere—were let loose from one end of the Tourney Ground, and presently, from that end there was a cry.

"Only one dog left, my Lords and Ladies."

Then it'll soon be over, I thought; and despite all his wounds the bear will have won.

But somebody shouted, "Blind the bear!" and somebody else called for pepper.

After all that, to have pepper thrown in his eyes.

I knew then that I was going to be sick. I was surprised. The pain in my body hadn't been anything like the belly-ache which often ends in sickness. Nevertheless, I was going to be sick. I pressed my hands over my mouth and made for the stairs which led down from the stand. I was near them, and did not have to push past Dame Margery. I just blundered down and to the back of the stand and then I was sick.

I couldn't go back. Never willingly would I watch a bear-baiting again. I didn't much want to go into the house, either. It would be deserted. Some other entertainment was to follow the baiting, tumblers or mummers were to perform by torchlight. I'd walk about for a little while, I thought, and then, when the poor wretched bear had been taken away, and sand spread over the blood patches, creep back into my place.

From the Tourney Ground the nearest pleasant place for walking was the old Low Garden, so I went there, not minding being alone there, partly because being alone out-of-doors was never quite so uncomfortable to me as being alone within walls, and partly because somewhere, at the far end of the Low Garden, there was the Maze and nearby, keeping his watch, would be one of the old men. I didn't go near the Maze, though, I stayed on a path edged by ancient rosebushes, so long unclipped that they were almost wild again, but covered with a profusion of flowers, pale pink, striped with deeper colour, and very fragrant. In the mild evening air they shed their scent, and I breathed it in gladly after the reek of blood and terror in the Tourney Ground.

I walked up and down the path, and every time I turned I could see, at the other side of the overgrown garden, the tall blackish-green hedge which walled in the Maze; and one time, as I turned and looked that way, I saw two figures standing just inside the entry of it. At first my only feeling was of surprise because I had imagined that everybody was at the bear-baiting. As I looked, wondering who they were, and wondering also why they had avoided the entertainment, whether they had at one time been sickened, too, they moved together and so stood in a long embrace.

By this time, from my reading, from talks with Melusine, from gossiping with Helen, and from merely being alive and not stone-deaf, I had picked up all there was to know about the relationship between men and women. I knew exactly why this pair had been in the Maze rather than at the baiting, and I wondered whether they knew about the constant guard. Then I remembered that the old man had asked me to call out so that he could know my whereabouts, and thought with some relief that that showed that he could not see clean into the Maze, he could only watch the entry.

The man of this pair, whom I did not recognize, broke from the woman's arms and walked briskly away in a direction which would take him to the stable yard. The woman stood still for a moment or two and then took a path which would eventually meet, in a corner, the one upon which I stood. She had hardly taken four steps before I recognised her; it was Melusine. I knew by the way she walked. Recognition had been slow because she was wearing a new dress, scarlet, a colour she never wore, and a narrow, steeple headdress instead of a wide, horned one.

My first impulse was to run and meet her, then I thought better of it. This had been a secret rendezvous, she might be displeased to know that it had been—at the end—overlooked. So instead of running to meet her where the paths joined, I drew back, and then, when she had passed, followed her. If she went into the house, then I could go into the house too. A little time in her company would be far more delightful to me than the best entertainment in the world.

At the end of the path she turned towards the house, not towards the Tourney Ground, and I followed her, keeping my distance all the time. I reached the Well Yard and was inside the deep porch when my Uncle Godfrey's voice hailed me.

"The baiting—is it over?"

I told him no, I had come in because I felt slightly unwell. He laid one of his hard hands against my neck, just under the ear, held it there a moment and said, "No fever."

He smiled and said he hoped I should feel better soon. That emboldened me to ask why he was not at the Tourney Ground and he said that he had been watching poultices applied to the leg of his destrier, Tristram, which had suffered a slight injury in the Tournament.

"Will he be better in time for the Dover Meeting?"

"It's to be hoped so," he said, and we parted. I was inside the Well Yard Room before my mind took notice of the fact that the man who had stood with Melusine just inside the Maze had worn a yellow doublet, and that my uncle was wearing that colour.

I knew by this time that my uncle was a knight without any land or other source of income, and that this was an unenviable thing to be. He had, more than once, tried to marry an heiress whose parents or guardians, in their turn, were looking out for a husband with money, and his efforts in this direction were now so bruited abroad that parents or guardians of heiresses looked at him a bit askance. That is what I mean when I say that the whole society of which Beauclaire was a sample was too much concerned with money. My Uncle Godfrey was handsome, kind, good-humoured, and acknowledged to be one of the best knights—some said the very best—in all the South of England. He was a man whom any girl could have been pleased and proud to marry, but he had no money, he could not be seriously considered. On the other hand, he was extremely popular with the ladies. In a strange, entirely false, stilted way it was the fashion, just then, for any married woman who was not positively repulsive in appearance to have a string of adorers who pretended to be in love with her. Perhaps pretended is a harsh word, some of them did, perhaps, cherish a hopeless passion; now and again perhaps a lady would slip from virtue, but it was rare; as a general rule the ladies wore their lovers and flaunted them as they wore and flaunted their jewels. Before a Tournament, for example, there was a competition amongst the ladies to count how many knights begged the honour of wearing their favours, just as fierce as the competition presently to be waged in the lists. There was a secret and very subtle game to be played with colours. A knight might ask a lady for a favour, a glove, a scarf, a sleeve to wear in the next event; he might be refused because her favour was already given; he would find out from her body servant what colour of gown she intended to wear, and then he would ride out on the day wearing somewhere about him that same colour. In this custom lay the origin of the ladies' hatred for having a gown the same colour as another's. There was another variation of the game, too. The ladies would go to great lengths and show much ingenuity in showing their preferences; my uncle's name being Blanchfleur, their task was easy, and at many a Meeting I have seen a dozen women wearing a white flower as a sign that they wished him well and had faith in his prowess. Officially my Uncle Godfrey "belonged" to my Lady Astallon, he was her kin by marriage, he was part of her husband's household, and she was very beautiful in the manner most admired just then, unreal, inhuman, with her shaved eyebrows and her hair plucked out all about her forehead to make her brow look high and the hairline as even as though it had been painted.

I thought of all this as I went into the Well Yard Room, and found it empty. I went on to the Stool Room, Melusine was not there, but she had been, just before me, I could smell her gillyflower-water fragrance through the faint, stored-up stink of the place. As I rang the bell I wondered had she gone into the Book Room. But when I reached the door it was locked. I turned back and, at the place where two passages joined, saw two old women; one had the bucket and jug of her occupation, the other carried a mug wrapped in a piece of flannel.

"Traipse, traipse, traipse," said the stool-emptier, bitterly, "all day long. And my feet as tender as the bird of your eye."

"But on the level," said the other. "Them stairs are my undoing. And I'll swear there's such a call for ginger, some of 'em must come round twice a month."

"Who is it this time?"

"The Lady Melusine. It ain't so long since ladies kept quiet about it, and danced the higher and laughed the louder so nobody should know, but *now!* No, we must lay abed and cosset our bellies with hot ginger twice a day."

"I'd swop with you."

"And after a week of the stairs you'd be glad to swop back."

I was close to them now, and I said, "I'm going up. Shall I take it?"

"Young ladies ain't allowed in the Ladies' Dorter."

"No one would know. I'd just put it in."

She looked at me with the suspicion of her kind; nobody ever did anything for nothing.

"Don't you go sipping at it. It's medicine, turn you black in the face if you drunk it without needing it."

But she handed it over.

I went upstairs slowly and carefully, pondering over why Melusine and my uncle must meet in secret. So far as I could see—quite apart from the fact that they were my two favourite people—they were well matched. Melusine was not a great heiress, she had a very modest dower, the freeholds of some properties in London, the rent of which was paid punctually four times a year and as punctually expended on new dresses or pieces of finery. Neither she nor my uncle was married, or betrothed to anyone else; her income, added to that he won in prize money, would keep them; she certainly wouldn't need a new dress if she lived to be a hundred.

I had reached the Ladies' Dorter, a room I had never, in all my time at Beauclaire, entered before. It was very large; the walls were painted and all the beds had hangings, some of plain silk, some embroidered with the family emblems of the owner. Great chests stood by the side and at the foot of each bed, and in the centre of the room was a table with several looking glasses on it. The room smelt of women, of musk, and violet and gillyflower and lavender, of linen fresh from the washing, of velvet, and under all of human flesh. My not-yet-settled stomach moved uneasily.

Melusine's bed was on the far side of the door; it had plain blue hangings. She had undressed and was lying flat with her bare arms exposed, her hands linked behind her head. She raised herself a little when I entered, and then, seeing me, sat up straight.

"Maude! What are you doing here? You know it is forbidden."

"Except for two old women we are alone in the house. So I brought your ginger."

"Why aren't you at the baiting?"

"I was sick."

"Poor sweet," she said, instantly sympathetic. "Look, you drink that posset. There's nothing more comforting to the stomach."

"I'm better now. It's for you."

The ends of her lips curved upwards in what was almost, but not quite a smile; it was a look I knew and generally accompanied some words of gentle mockery.

"It would be wasted on me. Drink it quickly and then run along. If you are found here . . ."

"Nobody will come yet. There is an entertainment by torchlight and it isn't nearly dark."

"Sit here and drink it then. Sit on the bed." She patted the place and then lay back, linking her hands behind her head again.

"Are you sure you don't want it?"

"That is one thing I am sure of." So I sat down and began to unwrap the flannel from the mug, saying, "The servant said that one sip would turn me black in the face."

"Why did she send you with it?" I explained that I had not been sent, I had offered to carry it.

She accepted—as I realised afterwards—this evidence of my devotion, plumbing its depths by the simple question, "How did you know it was for me?"

And I said, "She said so, besides I saw you come in."

"You saw me come in?" She was upright in the bed again. "Where have you been, Maude? *In the Low Garden?*"

I nodded.

"Then you saw us?"

I nodded again, stricken to think how I had given myself away.

She reached out and took hold of my arm; I could feel the heat of her hand through my sleeve.

"That's a secret. It must be kept, Maude, until the end of July. Do you understand? Will you promise?"

"Anything you said was a secret, Melusine, I would keep to myself, even on the rack."

"My poor dear child, you've never seen a rack! And it isn't *so* serious. Just till the end of July."

"And then you will be married?"

She nodded.

"Where will you live?"

"On his manor at Minsham."

I thought of that cold, bare hall, with the damp dew on the stone walls, the unrailed stairs, the bleak bedchambers above, and of that poor drooling old man, my Grandfather Blanchfleur.

"Oh no!" I said. "Couldn't you stay here?"

She said sharply, "No!" And then in an ordinary voice, "I forgot that you knew Minsham. Tell me about it."

I described it as well as I could. I also mentioned my grandfather. Melusine looked surprised and said she had never heard of him.

"He may be dead," I said. "I last saw him before I came here, and then he was almost dead."

"The house," she said, "it could be made comfortable—if money was spent on it?"

I pictured Minsham furnished with some of the comforts of the Old Vine, some of the elegance of Beauclaire.

"Oh yes."

"They'll soon be back," Melusine said, "you had better go. We'll talk tomorrow. And remember, this is between us."

I repeated the words which were traditional in the Children's Dorter for the making of any very special promise.

> "Else
> May my liver and lights die in me,
> May Old Scrat fly away with me."

Melusine laughed and said, "Oh, the memories that recalls! A most solemn oath."

I was in my bed and almost asleep when a thought jerked me wide awake again. If my Uncle Godfrey and Melusine were married and went to live at Minsham, perhaps I could go there too. That would be even better than staying at Beauclaire. Thanks be to St. Joseph, I thought, that I hadn't written my request to Walter. I wouldn't write now until the end of July when I could convey the news in any case, and, if I had persuaded Melusine to agree, beg to go to Minsham instead of to Clevely.

She was easily persuaded; she was, I think, genuinely fond of me, and as she said she would lack company, because my uncle would be away a great deal. I asked again couldn't she stay at Beauclaire, and I cannot remember whether it was then or another time that she told me what lay behind the secrecy and the need to leave Beauclaire once the truth was out. My Lady Astallon, Melusine said, would be furiously angry.

"But why? Uncle Godfrey is bound to get married some day."

"She sees no need for it. And if he did she would like to do the choosing for him, somebody he couldn't care for. You see . . ." She checked herself. "I shouldn't speak of such things to you, Maude. Here in this room I forget how young you are."

I would show her, I thought, that young as I was I fully understood the situation.

"He is her lover *in fact?* They bed together?"

"They *did.*"

"Would she have minded his marrying Alys Courtney? There was talk of that, wasn't there?"

"Alys Courtney was very rich. That would have been understandable. She was plain, too. Our marriage will be a very different thing. He loves me, and that my Lady will find hard to accept."

"I see," I said; and I did, though not very clearly.

Another time when we were talking—for we now talked far more than we read in the Book Room—I asked her how long she and my Uncle Godfrey had been in love.

"He with me, or I with him? He with me only lately, a year maybe; I with him, oh, years, ever since I moved into the Well Yard Room. The first thing I noticed about you, poppet, was that your eyes were like his."

I remembered how she had said, "You have his eyes," and that simple statement which had pleased me when it was made, because it gave me a feeling of belonging somewhere, now hurt because I loved her and was afraid that all her kindness to me had been on account of that likeness and not for myself.

"A year, eh?" I said, fumbling about amongst the thoughts in my head. "Then how would you have felt had he married Alys Courtney?"

"How you harp on her! There was nothing in it. My Lady tried to match them, that is true. But Godfrey *loved* me and so nothing came of it."

That was not the way I had heard it; the failure of the match between my Uncle Godfrey and the Courtney heiress had been reported to me by Helen Beaufort, and she had said that he was willing, eager, the Courtney family reluctant. But then, Helen had a spiteful tongue and would gladly deal me a slap through my uncle. And Helen, naturally, did not know the truth.

In another of these most exciting conversations I learned why the end of July was so important.

"He'll come riding back from Dover with that great prize in his hand, and then the announcement will be made. In the Hall? Is that the way it will be? Oh, I hope I shall be there," I said.

"Hope that he wins the prize! It will be all that we shall have to live on until my rents come in at Michaelmas. I've been such an improvident, prodigal fool. On Lady Day I had the price of as good a destrier as ever wore harness, and I frittered it away on a new dress and a brooch to go with it, and a ring for *him*. How was I to know that Tristram would take a wound?"

"Tristram. What has the horse to do with it?"

Melusine made her right hand into a fist and ground it in the palm of her left hand.

"This waiting," she said. "He must joust at Dover, and he must win. And his horse is unsound. My Lady Astallon has promised to mount him —a Great Horse from Flanders—so well trained, they say, that if you mounted a sack of flour on him, with a lance fixed, he could unseat his man. Godfrey, with such a horse, could not fail."

"He won again here," I said, "and on Tristram, wounded as he was."

"He'll win at Dover; a silver cup filled with gold pieces."

We counted the days to the end of July. I wanted to write my letter to Walter, asking him to ask Mother if I could go and live at Minsham, but of course I must not do that yet, for to do so would betray the secret.

In our counting of the days we reached the place where we could say, "Only twenty days more."

VI

EARLIER in the summer, in June when the people assembled for our St. Barnabas Tourney, some of them had brought rumours that this year the plague was worse than usual in London. Lord Astallon had seized upon this fact gleefully, and said in the Hall, loud enough to be heard from end to end of the High Table, "There you are! Was I not right to refuse Bowdegrave's invitation to spend the summer in his London house?"

Lady Astallon said discontentedly, "Your cousin Bowdegrave is now with the King at Windsor, which is full as healthful as this."

"I doubt it," said her husband.

And he was right. This year the plague reached Windsor, and amongst its victims were Madge FitzHerbert's father, his wife, and the child of their marriage, a boy of five years old. All in a moment Madge changed from being a half idiot, kept in the Children's Dorter because she was too stupid and ugly to be promoted to the Well Yard Room, into that most covetable piece of property—an heiress.

It was Helen Beaufort, who now knew everything—and who was quite pale and venomous with jealousy—who explained all this to me. Unmarried girls who had great fortunes were always taken into wardship by some man who administered their estates, and arranged a marriage for them, and out of both procedures made some pickings for himself. This was so well known and accepted a rule that the wardship of an heiress would be given away as a reward for service to the King.

"The King," said Helen, "is probably at this moment looking around to decide who shall have the privilege of being that ninny's guardian."

"My cousin Astallon should have it," I said. "She has lived under his roof all these years; as far as I can see nobody else has minded whether she had enough to eat or not, or anything to wear." It was a fact that any garment more than was strictly necessary which poor Madge possessed had been given to her by me, for I had passed on to her every thing my mother had sent me in the way of a present.

"Astallon," said Helen, "will never be thought of. He is not near the King, nor has he done him any service."

"Then it's very unfair."

"The whole thing is unfair," said Helen bitterly. "They'll probably marry her to an earl!"

"That couldn't happen. She still can't thread a needle, for all her riches," I said.

"If Astallon knew his business," said Helen in her most adult manner, and probably repeating something she had overheard, "he'd betroth her quickly to Ralph, or to Henry Rancon, and so keep control for himself."

Madge's new status, and her future, though a matter of interest to me, was not very near my heart, and as soon as Helen and I parted I half forgot about it, and went back to thinking about my own future, with Uncle Godfrey and Melusine at Minsham. However, on the evening of the next day I learned that Madge's future was very much my concern, and that Helen's gossiping prophecies had been wrong in only one respect. My cousin Astallon had taken the one way open to him to make use of Madge's fortune for the family good, but he hadn't chosen Ralph or Henry as a husband for the heiress; he had chosen his kinsman, Sir Godfrey Blanchfleur.

Before supper in the Great Hall, in full sight of the whole assembly, up stood the Beauclaire Chaplain, silly Madge, and my uncle, and the betrothal vows were made. Madge repeated her words in her thick flannelly voice, without any sign of understanding; my uncle pushed a ring on her finger and kissed her on the brow. And all over the Hall people got to their feet and raised their wine cups or their ale mugs and wished the happy couple well.

For a moment or two I was too stunned to think. When I did my first thought was a thoroughly selfish one. Now I should never go to Minsham! Immediately I thought of Melusine. If I was stunned and shocked, what, in God's name, was she feeling? I turned my head cautiously and looked along to where she sat. In my heart I saluted her. Men may win honour in battle and prizes and praise in tourneys, but women have their own kind of courage. You could never have guessed that the scene on the dais meant more to Melusine than to Ella or Phillipa or any other of the ladies. She was laughing and raising her cup.

All through the meal—and it was a festive one, with several extra dishes—Melusine's behaviour was so ordinary that in the end it deceived me. I thought to myself that this was just another trick—like getting the Great Horse of Flanders out of Lady Astallon. My uncle had gone through the act of betrothal in order to further some scheme of Lord Astallon's: now, if they sent from Windsor to take Madge into wardship, she need not go, she was betrothed. Then afterwards, when it was all forgotten, the betrothal could be annulled, and my uncle and Melusine be married after all.

That must be it, I thought; and Melusine knew. How else could she laugh and talk as though nothing had happened? I gripped onto this thought because it was the only comfort in my desolation, and soon I came to full belief and felt better.

However, next morning, in the Chapel, the Chaplain called the banns —for the second time, he said. And as soon as we were all back in the Children's Dorter my Lady Astallon came there, a thing rare in the extreme; she brought with her a sewing woman who carried a roll of rich tawny-coloured silk. Madge stood there like an ugly doll while the sewing woman measured her, and my Lady and Dame Margery conversed in voices too low for us to hear. Then the silk was spread out on the table and slashed into by the shears; the sewing woman treated the lovely stuff as though it were the coarsest, cheapest homespun. When the gown was cut out Lady Astallon said something that Alison and Constance and I *did* hear, all too clearly. We were to spend the day sewing the long seams of the skirt while the ladies in the Well Yard Room did the more skilled work on the bodice and the sewing woman managed the trickiest part of all, the long, falling sleeves. The wedding was going to be solemnised next day and the dress must be ready.

So it *was* going to happen.

Sewing was the worst occupation for me just then, since it left my whole mind free to brood over my misery, and Melusine's. Presently I thought: Nothing goes right for me! And all in a moment the tawny stuff and my needle and thread wavered and blurred; one tear, then another splashed onto the silk, making dark, star-shaped blotches. Dame Margery, who was watching, quickly thrust her plump white hand between me and the work and made the sign of the Cross.

"Tears on a wedding gown," she said in a shocked voice, "the worst possible luck, God and all the Saints guard against it! What ails *you*, Maude Reed, to behave so unseemly?"

I said the first thing that occurred to me.

"This is my morning for lessons; and I do not like to sew."

"And you dare show me this rebellious spirit, after I have governed you for three years? Shame on you," she said, and dealt me a clout on the ear. Her hand, for all its plump white velvet look, could deal a shrewd blow. "Get into the corner and put your hands on your head until you can control yourself."

She sat down in my place and began to stitch.

In the corner, gazing at the blank wall, I thought about Melusine. I had ceased crying, it is almost impossible to cry with your hands linked above your head; and presently I was able to say—without turning from the corner:

"Madam. I am now controlled."

"Then you may return to your work."

"The Lady Melusine," I said.

"What of her?"

"She will be awaiting me in the Book Room."

"I doubt that. She will be sewing too."

"She goes to the Book Room early. . . ."

"Then run along and tell her that you are sewing and she should be. And waste no time. You are to be back by the time I reach here." She measured off a tiny length of seam.

I held my skirt high and galloped in the most unseemly way to the Book Room, but it was locked. I thought she might have locked herself in, so I knocked on the door and called that it was I, Maude. There was no sound from within. I then turned and ran to the Well Yard Room, which was like running from the Old Vine into Baildon town; only two of the young ladies were there, sewing diligently on the tawny silk. One said that Melusine was in the Book Room, the other said she was in attendance upon Lady Astallon. Just as I was leaving three others, Ella amongst them, came rustling in and I asked them if they knew where Melusine was. Nobody knew; and I had already been away much longer than I had been given leave for; so I had no choice but to go back and sew on that hateful tawny silk. I looked forward to the dinner hour; somehow I would make an opportunity to speak to Melusine then, no matter what trouble I brought down on myself.

But Melusine was not in the Hall for dinner; several other young ladies were absent, Helen Beaufort amongst them. Word went round that my Lady had suddenly decided that she had nothing fit to wear for a wedding, and that they were sewing at full speed on a new, wonderful cloth-of-silver gown.

My Lady having decided to make the wedding properly festive (and from my talk with Melusine I could see that this was, to her, the most welcome match in the world), the Chapel was to be hung with wreaths, the symbol of unity. So first thing in the morning we were all sent out in search of flowers. We children were to confine our search to the Low Garden, which yielded very little, the first flood of flowers was over, the big daisies which grew in the long grass were withering, and the poppies which had taken their place were useless for wreaths as they shed their petals too easily. There were a few roses on the bushes and a few heads of blue bugloss and that was all. Then Alison said that she had seen, on the banks of the moat, a great bush of honeysuckle.

"Honeysuckle smells sweet, and it isn't prickly and it weaves well," she said.

So the four of us—Madge of course was indoors, being washed and made ready—went off to find the bush. Alison had seen it when she went to the bear-baiting, and it certainly was a big, lush-growing bush but it was on the outer bank of the moat and to reach it our shortest way would be across the drawbridge, upon which we were expressly forbidden ever to set foot. William said:

"Who will know? And even if they did nothing would happen today. It's a *wedding!*"

Alison was in favour of venturing, because the bush was her find, and I didn't care one way or the other, and Constance always did what we did. So we ran across the bridge and set about the bush, pulling off great flowery strands, some of them a yard long. And I thought with what joy I should be gathering flowers and making the wreaths were Melusine to be the bride, and what a sorry mockery it was now.

Then we heard men's voices shouting from the inward end of the bridge, and looked up guiltily, thinking that they were calling us. But they were not. They were looking and pointing down into the water of the moat.

"One of them's dropped something," William said. "Look, they're bringing a rope and grapple. Here, you have these. . . ." He pushed all his flowers into my arms, and went scampering off to watch something he hoped would be exciting.

I laid the bundle of leaves and flowers that he had given me aside and went on, dully and methodically gathering more, until I heard Alison, just beside me, let out a kind of hissing breath. I looked at her and saw that she was staring bridgewards, so I looked that way and saw Melusine brought up from the water.

The hooks had taken her by the middle and she hung in a curve, very gracefully, almost as a girl might hang from a man's arm in a more than ordinarily roisterous dance. At one end of the curve hung her scarlet dress, at the other her silver-gilt hair, both a little darkened by the water and that was all; and as they pulled her up the water fell from her hair and from her skirts, in sparkling, sun-touched drops. The thought shot into my head and out again: Even *so*, she is lovely.

Then I began to cry. Clutching the latest-gathered sprays of honeysuckle and crying wildly, I ran back to the bridge and crossed it. By that time they had laid her flat on the grey stone pavement, and they tried to prevent me going near, but I pushed past and looked down on her. I noticed then, and later took comfort from the fact, that she looked most peacefully happy; her eyes were closed and her lips were almost, not quite, but almost smiling. My own raucous, gasping sobs seemed an intrusion upon that peacefulness, but I could not stop them.

One of the men took hold of me and told me in a rough, kind voice not to distress myself. Alison came up beside me, and Constance; they stared, shocked but quiet.

"Come on now," one of the men said, "you must go in. Rightly you shouldn't have been there, you know. What's your Dame about this morning?"

Alison and Constance had gathered up all the flowers; they were loaded. Alison said, "Come along, Maude, we still have the wreaths to make, you know."

Across the bodice of Melusine's scarlet dress the green slimy strands of water weed lay, soiling, out of place. I laid my strands of honeysuckle over them, thinking: Wedding wreath! and sobbing more and more noisily.

More and more people had come running; there was quite a crowd. Alison said in my ear the most damning of all Dame Margery's rebukes, "Maude, you are making an exhibition of yourself!"

I knew that, but there was no help for it. I went on crying. One of the men picked me up and carried me into the house.

Dame Margery was kind at first. She petted and patted me and gave me something soothing to drink; then, when I continued to cry, she lost patience, shook me, finally slapped me and forbade me to attend the wedding. So I lay on my bed and wept for Melusine, while silly Madge became my aunt-by-marriage.

I knew that crying was useless; all it did was make my head ache more and more; I tried to stop, but I couldn't. Even when every tear was squeezed out of me and I was as dry as sawdust inside, I still went on making the hiccuping noise.

Dame Margery came back from the wedding feast, and, finding me still crying, gave me another drink, a poppy-smelling one, which sent me to sleep. But the moment I was awake I was crying again.

They began to treat me—perhaps rightly—as though I had gone out of my wits. I was moved out of the Children's Dorter and lodged in a small room alone. Dame Margery seemed most concerned because I could eat nothing; she was convinced that if I would only *try*, I could do so. Once she seized my nose and held it until, in order to draw breath, I was forced to open my mouth; instantly she popped in a spoonful of something she had ready at hand. It was a dish of fresh raspberries sprinkled with crushed sugar which was a rare luxury, even at Beauclaire. For me that mouthful had the very taste of misery and I have never eaten raspberries again, nor indeed any sweet thing at all.

Finally, as though in desperation, they fetched the Chaplain to me.

Remembering that he had taken the betrothal vows and called the banns, and officiated at that farce of a marriage ceremony, I had nothing to say to *him*, and lay on the bed, with my face turned towards the wall, crying and hiccuping, my mind closed to his talk until he said:

"I am surprised. I was given to understand that there was an affection between you and Melusine Talboys."

"There was," I said, without realising that I was speaking at last. "She was my friend, the one person who was kind to me when I came here, frightened and alone."

"Then you owe her a debt which you should begin immediately to repay."

He now had my attention. I cried, "But she's dead, she's dead. I can never repay her now."

"Her body is dead. But her soul—and that surely was the source of her kindness to you—is still alive and more in need of help from you, from us all, than ever before. If you had seen her cast herself into the water, would you have stood in a safe place and wrung your hands and wept, or would you have tried to save her?"

"I *would* have saved her."

The arrogance of that remark he deplored with a small sigh and went on, "Her state of mind no one can know, therefore no one can say that she died finally impenitent; she *did* die unshriven and her last act on this earth was the sin of self-destruction. She will be long in Purgatory, I fear, poor child. But her time there could be shortened, and her way out of it eased, by *you*, by your faithful and unremitting prayers. The scales of God's justice are finely balanced, and against the sum of all her sins and her final awful wrongdoing, prayers inspired by love and gratitude would weigh heavy."

I gave a great gulp and said, "I will pray."

"Ah," he said, in a pouncing, triumphant voice, almost as though he had said, "I've *got* you!" "Ah, but are you in a state to pray effectively? This unrestrained grief—as though you were a heathen for whom physical death was the end of all things—this refusal to eat or sleep, as though you, too, were bent on self-destruction, do these make for a claim to God's ear?" He gave another small sigh. "You're very young. I will try to put it plainer. Suppose your friend Melusine had deeply offended Lady Astallon and was to be punished, quite rightly, but you wished to plead for some mitigation, would you, do you think, serve any purpose by rushing into the Bower, crying loudly, your clothes in disarray, your whole manner distraught? Answer me."

"No."

"Very well, then. If you believe, as you must believe, being a Christian, that Melusine is not that poor dead body, but a living and immortal soul, at this moment suffering the cleansing pains of Purgatory, you will get up from that bed, wash and tidy yourself, and eat some plain, nourishing dish. You may have small appetite for it, but our appetites should at all times be under our control. Tell yourself that you eat in order to gain strength because your strength is needed. When you have done these things, come into the Chapel. I shall be waiting for you there."

Later in my life, when I often heard priests discussed critically and designated "good" or "bad," I would remember the Chaplain at Beauclaire. He was, so far as anyone could judge from outward signs, a worldly man, he lived luxuriously, he did Lord Astallon's bidding quite unquestioningly (as in that hasty marriage between my uncle and silly Madge), he was fond of fine clothes, addicted to hunting, not in fact a "good" priest. But, and this I do believe, ordination to the priesthood does convey some power, some authority outside the layman's understanding. And those upon whom that power has been conferred carry it, as a man may carry a lantern. He may keep the horn clean and clear so that the light is always visible, or he may let it grow smoky and smeary so that you might not know that the light was there. It is there, however, and in a moment of emergency it can be produced. So now the Chaplain, without saying anything which was new to me, without even being persuasive in his talk, had altered everything. I no longer saw Melusine as they lifted her from the water, dripping and dead. I saw *her*, as alive and real as she had ever been, suffering the physical pain and the spiritual misery of Purgatory, but knowing that it was only for a season, hopeful, not lost, not despairing.

The effect of this was not only to assuage my sorrow; it altered my whole attitude towards life. I no longer wished to remain at Beauclaire, and as that summer passed into autumn, and the autumn into winter, I began more firmly every day to look forward to going to Clevely and joining the nuns. I made no hasty decision about becoming a nun myself; in that mood of religious mysticism which followed my talk with the Chaplain I doubted my own worthiness to make such a decision. When I thought of Clevely I thought of it as a quiet place, with no distractions, where I could spend hours on my knees praying for Melusine without seeming odd or making myself conspicuous. At the age of twelve, having seen only one of the world's many aspects, I was prepared to retire from it.

VII

I LEFT Beauclaire soon after my twelfth birthday. With one exception nobody seemed sorry to see me go. Madge might have been, but she was gone already, making with my Uncle Godfrey a tour of all her estates and hereditaments. The exception to the general indifference was, most startlingly, Henry Rancon, to whom I had hardly spoken a word since he had left the Children's Dorter and become a page.

I had seen him, of course, in the Hall and about the courtyards and I had noticed, in an idle kind of way, that since leaving Dame Margery's rule his appearance had not improved. He was never very clean and he was often bruised, or scratched or scarred in some way. He'd grown very rapidly, too, and, however often he was given a new outfit of the Astallon green, his clothes seemed too small.

On my last afternoon at Beauclaire I was sorting out my possessions and packing what I had decided to take with me in the same little chest which I had brought from the Old Vine. I discarded whatever seemed to me, in my limited knowledge, to be unsuited to life in a nunnery. Nuns, I believed, were vowed to a life of poverty and non-possessiveness, and a girl who went to live with them would need very little.

The other children were in the Low Garden, it being a fine afternoon, and Dame Margery, having seen me employed, took a little nap and then went out to gossip with one of her cronies. When she returned she had Henry Rancon with her. She said, with one of her smiles which were secretive and sly and knowledgeable:

"Maude, Henry wishes to bid you Godspeed. He has remembered some of the mannerliness I beat into him, it seems."

I had been taught manners, too, so I said, "That is very kind."

We stood and looked at one another across the little chest and the pile of discarded clothes. He wore the Astallon green—velvet for pages and they were supposed to change from their uniform when they went to the stables or out for their exercises, but Henry plainly hadn't bothered; his velvet was rubbed and spotted and he stank of sweat, horse and human. His hair had just been roughly clubbed and should have been washed. He had a long scratch down one cheek and a large scab on his chin.

He said, in a grudging, aggrieved way, "I didn't know that you were leaving until just now, after dinner."

He spoke as though he should have been informed, and I almost said: What is that to you? But I remembered my manners and said, "I leave tomorrow."

"Back to Baildon?"

"Fancy you remembering that! Yes, Baildon, but not to stay. I'm going to the nuns at Clevely."

"To a nunnery?"

"Yes. I should have gone there in the first place, but they wouldn't have me until I was twelve."

"You're not going to be a nun?"

I said, and it was true, "I don't even know that myself. I should like to be, but . . ."

"Don't," he said. He looked over to where Dame Margery had seated herself in the window, and scowled fiercely. He tried to speak softly, but his voice had just broken and he had no note between a gruff growl and a squeak. "Soon I'll be a squire. With any sort of arms I do well, none better. I'll be a squire, and very soon a knight. Maude, don't, I beg you, decide on being a nun until I'm a knight." He said all this in a squeak and then suddenly dropped to a deep manly voice. "You can't be a nun yet, and in four years I swear I'll have my spurs if I have to break my neck to get them. And ever since we used to play together I've always thought . . ." He broke off and glared at Dame Margery again, his face going a dark, unbecoming crimson. "When I'm a knight, I want you for my lady, and you can't be that if you're a nun."

I laughed, for the first time since Melusine's death.

"If I decide not to be a nun, Henry, somebody else might have the same notion."

He said furiously, "But I asked you first!" He tugged at one of his dirty fingers and pulled off a ring; it was of some base metal—lead I should think, from the weight of it—with a zigzag pattern in blue enamel running round it. Even to make it fit his own finger he had been obliged to wad it with a twist of thread, now worn black and greasy.

"Here you are," he said, groping for my hand and pushing the ring on to my finger, "I've spoken for you and done it properly, ring and all. You can bear witness to that, Dame."

Dame Margery laughed.

"It's a bit one-sided, but it'll do for now. Unless Maude cares to say something." I could tell from the way she spoke that she thought it silly child's play, as I did myself. And then all at once it seemed pathetic that the awkward, blushing boy should be the only one to be serious; and I remembered that it was Henry who had offered to learn to read, so that I could have lessons. I said gently:

"I can't promise anything, Henry. But if you like, I'll keep the ring to remember you by."

"Do that," he said. "So then, good-by, Maude."

He pushed his head forward and kissed me. Most surprisingly the lips in his rough battered face were as smooth and soft as silk.

Interval

I

THE gifts which Anne Reed had, in most cases, fashioned with her own hands and despatched to Maude at Beauclaire, and which had been passed on to Madge FitzHerbert, were not, in fact, such perfunctory and deceptive offerings as the girl imagined. Once Maude was out of sight, the pangs of memory and conscience eased, and Anne could think of, could speak of "my daughter" as any woman might.

When Maude's first letter arrived Anne said, with complacency to Martin, "Things have improved since my day; nobody bothered to teach us to write. And you will admit that she sounds happy."

(The letter had been written in the Book Room, with Melusine sitting nearby.)

It was presently possible for Anne to look back upon her own youth, and, with that selective memory common to all whom the years have damaged, to see those early days golden with sunshine, brightened by hope, lively with appreciation of any occasional joy. She was convinced that she, too, could have been happy at Beauclaire or any other of the places where she had sojourned so miserably, had she not been so wretchedly poor.

As the days went by she came to think of her daughter as a more fortunate version of herself, just as pretty and graceful, but well shod, elegantly clothed, moving against the background of the Long Gallery, the Great Hall, the Low Garden. One day, she assured herself, when she had persuaded Martin into the provision of a dowry, the elegant, eligible young man of good family for whom she herself had waited in vain would pay his court to Maude and all would be well.

Never once did she suspect that her attitude towards the child was that which most people, after the first burst of grief, held towards the dead. Gone away. In safekeeping. Happy now. Anne had never felt that way about her dead, and could not know that she had watched a little girl ride away on a brown pony with the finality with which other people see a coffin lowered into the earth. Anne's dead, Denys, her mother, Richard, were all her victims, to be thought of as little as possible, subjects of the occasional nightmare from which refuge must be sought in the wine cup.

She had Walter, whom she loved extravagantly, both for himself and for what she could see of Richard in him. Richard's dark hair and eyes, his delicate look, his skill with the lute. Even when, at an early age, Walter declared that he was never going to be a wool merchant, he was going to take his lute and wander the roads and play to admiring crowds, the statement roused in his mother much delight and little concern. Richard had cherished that dream, too. Walter was Richard's son. Upon that certainty she could rest, much of her guilt absolved. As a statement it was not to be taken seriously; he would know better when he was older.

Martin had found him a good tutor, a young man called Nicholas Freeman, who had been trained in the monks' school at Norwich and come very near taking his priest's orders, changed his mind, and worked for a time in the office of a leather merchant in Norwich.

At first Anne had attached little importance to him, minding only that he should teach Walter thoroughly and as gently as possible. Walter learned swiftly.

"It will help if I am a scrivener as well," he explained gravely. "I can play to please the people and myself, and then if any one wants a letter written or a copyright made, I can do it and so make sure of my bread."

To count he refused, absolutely; and when pressed twice ran away. He was soon recovered, a small boy carrying a lute was not difficult to trace and Martin's men knew the roads and were well mounted. He was beaten, sobbed tearlessly, worked himself into a fever and was cosseted, but still refused to learn to count.

"I know all I need to know. I am not going to be a wool merchant."

Nicholas Freeman, with time on his hands, began to take an active part in the business. Martin's lame leg grew stiffer as he aged and sometimes he found difficulty in mounting his horse. One morning Nicholas asked:

"Would you like me to go for you, sir?"

"You think there is no skill in fleece-buying? They'd sell you anything."

"My father has a sheep run. I helped him until I was nine. I know all the tricks."

"Go then. But bring back any maggoty polls and I'll knock their price off your wages."

The young man laughed.

"With the price of wool as it is, and my wages what they are, that would be to take a quart from a pintpot."

Anne thought that an impudent answer, but Martin laughed and said, "I've been doing that all my life, boy."

Little by little the young man worked his way into Martin's confidence, was allowed more responsibility, was moving, Anne felt, into the place that should be Walter's. On that eagerly awaited day when Walter should, as she termed it, "come to his senses" there would be Nicholas Freeman standing between him and his grandfather. Martin seemed to find him easy to talk to, and sometimes as they sat at table she would study them both. The young man wore, for a clerk, a very healthy look, as though his farmyard tan had survived the years in cloister and countinghouse; in a slightly saturnine way, he was handsome, with bright hazel eyes, brown hair, and excellent teeth. Beside him Martin's lined face looked old. Old, she would think, and he never spares himself. Suppose he died before Walter settled and knew anything of the business; we should depend upon this stranger, and he might cheat us, we are so ignorant.

Spurred by the fear of material loss, she began to take interest in the business, listening, asking questions, sometimes venturing a suggestion. Martin, after the initial surprise, took refuge behind the immemorial barrier, "Nothing for you to bother about, my dear," "You wouldn't understand if I did explain," and, "Leave all that to us."

With Nicholas she had no better luck; he was a vain young man and had from the first resented her manner towards him; he rebuffed her gleefully, saying, "Why not discuss this with Master Reed?" and once, "Master Reed engaged me and it is to him that I render account of my doings."

The years went by. The twins' twelfth birthday came. Walter showed no sign of change of heart, but so long as he was allowed to go his own way he was amiable and inoffensive. When she thought of Maude, Anne imagined her moving from the Children's Dorter into the Well Yard Room at Beauclaire and taking her place with the young ladies. Upon that thought Anne braced herself for the tussle with Martin concerning the dowry. If he remained obdurate, she had one other hope. Godfrey, now married to the FitzHerbert heiress, was extremely wealthy; he might do something for Maude; he should do, out of gratitude for what Anne had done for him, long ago.

She had entirely forgotten that she had ever intended to send Maude to the nunnery at Clevely. That had been a move in a secret game, won at the moment when a little girl rode through the archway on a brown pony.

But Maude had remembered that she was to leave Beauclaire when she was twelve; Dame Margery remembered it, too, and so did Lady Astallon. And one lovely April morning, on that same brown pony, now too small for her, Maude came riding home.

II

ON a sunny morning, about a fortnight after Maude's return, Martin Reed came down to breakfast with some of the pain lines eased from his face. He flexed his lame leg two or three times as he sat in his chair and said, with satisfaction, "This weather suits me. I shall ride out to the Minsham run today."

Two years before, the whole of Suffolk had been ravaged by sheep-tick fever, and in replenishing his flocks Martin had tried an experiment. He had brought—with great expense and labour—sheep from the Cotswolds, where, in the greater cold of the high hillsides, the animals which flourished were the ones with particularly thick fleeces. He had been resigned to the possibility of the sheep growing lighter wool once they were on pastures less exposed; but that had not happened in their first year. He was anxious now to see for himself what difference a second winter had made.

"Like to come with me, Maude?" he asked.

"Oh yes, I would," she said eagerly. Then doubt and uncertainty clouded her face. Since the moment when the Chaplain at Beauclaire had given her a new aim in life, she had made some advances of her own. Self-denial was good, as well as prayer; a thousand small sacrifices of comfort or pleasure might "count," if offered in the proper spirit against the pains which Melusine was suffering in Purgatory.

Perhaps, she thought, imagining the pleasure of riding out in the sunshine, she should retract that acceptance and go instead to church, kneel until she was dizzy, pray until she was tired. That would "count."

But her grandfather's face had brightened and he was already considering which horse she should ride. She hadn't the heart to withdraw. Presently, at Clevely, there would be time and opportunity to make everything right.

So they rode out together and for some time spoke little and of trivial things. He explained about the sheep from the hills. He said, in a disgruntled way, that he had last year asked Walter to ride out and see them and that Walter had said a sheep was a sheep and no more. Cuckoos were calling from every thicket and he described to her how, as a boy, bird's-nesting at Rede on a precious Good Friday holiday, he had seen a cuckoo throw a blackbird's egg from a nest and settle down to lay her own.

It was talk to interest any child, and over Maude's response there was the patina of Dame Margery's training—not enough to listen and be interested, one must *look* interested, give signs of pleasure, encourage the talker to go on. Unaware of this, Martin simply found his granddaughter most pleasingly responsive; he found himself telling her things that he had never told anyone, things he had once, long, long ago, planned to tell Stephen and Robin when they were old enough to listen to his tales.

Thinking of them, which he seldom did nowadays, made him feel very old. Sixty-six this year. Forty long years had passed since the priest at Rede had told a stalwart young man of twenty that half his life was already sped. A long life, and superficially dull, work and work and work again. Two great sorrows, some success, several disappointments. And now, towards the end of it, here he was, riding alongside his granddaughter and feeling, under natural affection, something more lively stir.

He broke the silence by saying abruptly, "You didn't mean what you said the other day about going to live with the nuns, did you?"

"Oh yes," she said, without any hesitation, "I meant it. I have to."

"What does that mean? Your mother? That was all some silly idea she got into her head when there was talk of sending Walter to school. She said it would be unfair to send him from home and keep you. But the nuns wouldn't have you then. So she wheedled me into letting you go to Beauclaire. Against my will, I may tell you. And now you're home, and if I have any say in the matter there'll you stay."

"I can't go without your permission. They ask five pounds a year for my keep. And I must take a bed and blankets, linen. But I should cost as much at home."

"Cost!" he said. "Cost. That is nothing to me. You stay home, Maude, and I'll show how little cost matters. I'll buy you a grey mare. I know where to go—a fellow at Flaxham breeds them and trains them to paces that suit a lady. They have manes and tails like floss silk. You shall have a grey mare, Maude, and silk dresses, and a gold ring, a ring with a blue stone to match your eyes."

She closed her eyes for a moment and prayed one of the simple, unorthodox prayers which had become almost a habit.

All this, God! You alone know how badly, at Beauclaire, I wanted a proper mount. The dresses, too, and a ring with a sapphire. I'll sacrifice them all for one hour of Melusine's sojourn in Purgatory. Please take it, God. It is mine to give. I could have it, and I refuse it.

She opened her eyes and said, "You are very kind. You help me more than you know. But I must go to Clevely."

"Why?"

It is his five pounds, she thought; his money pays for the bed, the blanket, and the linen. He has the right to know.

"It is all so sad. I'm afraid that if I speak of it, I shall cry."

"Your mother," he said, trying to be helpful. "You must mind this. Mothers tend to like their sons better than their daughters, and when the pair are twins it shows more. You mustn't mind her, Maude. Let her have Walter. You're my girl."

All this, God, too! Please count my grandfather's favour, which I am about to forgo, against one hour of Melusine's torment.

She said, "It has nothing to do with Mother. I know how she feels about me; and it must be very hard for a woman not to like her own daughter."

Dear God, that is tolerance. I learned that very hard, could that count too? Just a minute. Because it was so hard to learn. Please, of Thy mercy, just a minute.

"Then why?" Martin asked in a grating and impatient voice, "why do you say you must go and shut yourself away there. When I want you home."

A long and horrible story. Something which, in its entirety, she had never had to tell. The Chaplain had known the details.

"When I first arrived at Beauclaire," she began. And Martin tilted his head sideways, the better to listen. She told him everything. The story ran smoothly at first and then was broken, like a stream which in its course runs over rocks. When she came to the recountal of Melusine's body being taken from the water, she leaned forward over the pommel of her saddle and wept, and Martin, speaking for the first time since the story started, said:

"There, there, say no more, I understand." And he saw himself with his head pressed against the cold, smoke-blackened stone of the buttress of the Abbey wall, and then, falling prone, nursed in the lap of Old Agnes.

To love hard, he thought, that is in our blood. For that reason I struck through the red mist and hit my master; for the same reason I cherished that mountebank, Pert Tom, and Old Agnes. I paid it tribute when I brushed aside, as though it were a cobweb, the almost certain proof that Magda had witchcraft in her; and years later I pandered to Richard over the matter of his love for Anne Blanchfleur.

"But I must say more," Maude said, wiping her gloved hand across her face, "because how otherwise can you understand? The Chaplain . . ."

She told him of the interview with the Chaplain, of her restoration to life and hope, of the task which he had laid upon her.

Martin listened attentively, thinking at first, with deep irritation, that this was all the result of her going to Beauclaire, but presently his mood changed. He realised that when she spoke of Melusine she did so as one would speak of the living, that she had achieved what all Christians should, but rarely do, do, the power to look upon death as an incident, not as the end. He compared this with his own feeling in similar circumstances. Kate, Stephen, Robin, and then Richard, all, to him, irrevocably dead. And God non-existent. Brought face to face with a faith so simple and unquestioning, so urgent that this child was plainly prepared to govern her whole life according to its requirements he felt a thrill of almost superstitious awe. Not for him to oppose her decision. At the same time something in him rose in protest. When he spoke he did so slowly and carefully.

"You don't feel that you could pray, and be self-denying and all the rest of it, equally well at home? Nobody would interfere."

She shook her head.

"You see, that would be doing what I want. All the end of the time at Beauclaire I did want to go to Clevely. But since I have been back . . . Days like this," she said, looking around at the fresh young green of trees and meadows, all aglimmer in sunshine. "No, I know what I should do; and I hope that you will give me permission."

"I'm sorry you stumbled upon heartbreak so young," he said. "I was older when the blow fell on me. And I had no faith. You have that comfort. And if you're set on Clevely, you must go. Promise me one thing though. Don't think that going there means that you must be a nun."

"Oh, I'm not nearly good enough for that."

He ignored that. "It'll be some time before you have to make such a decision; I may be dead by that time, so I'll say my say now. It means having no husband, Maude. That may not matter; in most cases I think wanting a husband is something that wears off after a time. But it means no child and that's a different thing. Women, unless there's something very queer about them"—he remembered Magda—"need children, live through them. I've seen a woman, aye and she was hungry too, give her share of a poor meal to a child who had gobbled down his own. There's all kinds of love, my dear, but none to touch that. I wouldn't wish you to forgo it. That poor drowned girl was friend to you, and if you feel she's in Purgatory and your praying and fasting for a couple of years'll help, I've nothing against that. You mustn't make a life job of it."

I'm a clumsy old fool, he told himself. Maybe I've gone and put the idea into her head. With a return to his gruff manner he said, "There's Minsham Old Hall. You want to see your Grandfather Blanchfleur?"

"Not today," she said, averting her eyes, so that she should not see the place about which she and Melusine had held those long, happy conversations, made so many plans. The memory revived her revulsion for money, money and the greed for it which had brought about the whole tragedy. And even her grandfather's kind offer of a grey mare with a mane like silk, of fine dresses and a gold ring—all to do with money. I will have none of it, she thought. Once again she thought kindly of Clevely, where she would be free of it all.

Part Five

NICHOLAS
FREEMAN'S
STORY

I

WHEN Maude Reed came home to her grandfather's house in the April of 1447, she was just twelve years old, and I was twenty-three: a full quarter century too young, one would have supposed, to be attracted by a girl of her age. And age was not my only safeguard; I am by nature un-sentimental and cynical; I was at the time happily provided with a mistress who suited me; and I had already, in the most practical and cold-blooded manner, made up my mind to marry Maude in about four years' time whatever she was like, even if she were the spitting image of her mother, whom I disliked.

Martin Reed himself put the idea into my mind. He was one of the least communicative people I ever had to do with, but even he, when in particularly low spirits or provoked, would seek some relief in talk. Several times, when Walter had annoyed him, he would speak of Maude, saying that twins were tricky things and the girl had been born with all the sense: saying that since Walter refused to have anything to do with the business, the one hope for it was for Maude to marry some decent, steady man, capable of running it.

Why should not I be that man? I was already, in addition to teaching Walter all he would consent to learn, keeping the accounts, and being trusted, day by day, with more of the practical side. As far as Master Reed could know, I was as steady as Baildon Tower; decent, too, for I had learned by experience; my new mistress lived some distance away, and was safely married. Her husband was a game warden whose duties, most con-veniently, took him abroad at a time when I was free of mine. In four years' time, I thought, I should be twenty-seven and ready to settle down; Maude would be sixteen, and, unless her grandfather and her mother changed their ways, she would have had little contact with men. The Reeds were singularly friendless people. In Baildon indeed Master Reed was hated, though farther afield he was held in respect as an honest man and just.

Not being a fool, I realised that my plan to marry my master's grand-daughter was very vague and vulnerable. When I joined the household at the Old Vine, the child was placed with one of Mistress Reed's noble relatives. Mistress Reed was highly connected, and had married the wool-master's son for money—by the cast of countenance she usually wore I judged that it had been a bad bargain, she had a very discontented look. She was mightily devoted to her son, and, I thought, to her daughter; she was always stitching away on some fine article of clothing to send to the girl at Beauclaire. And from a few words dropped here and there by Master Reed I gathered that the mother's ambition was that her daughter should marry back into the class to which she herself belonged. But there the matter of dower was paramount, and the old man was obstinate.

"I'm not laying out my good money as bait for some young popinjay," he told me once. "It wasn't by my wish that the girl ever left home. She was a merry little thing and I missed her sore."

I thought over that statement; Mistress Reed had had her way once; she might succeed again.

There was very little that I could do to influence events, so I did not worry. I made myself as indispensable to my master as I could, was civil to Mistress Reed and patient with Walter and lived comfortably for three years.

Then Maude Reed came home and I fell in love.

At the time it seemed unaccountable, even to me. Now that I am middle-aged and accustomed to wealth and power, I understand my young self better. I am a lover of, a collector of beautiful things, and to me for a thing to be beautiful it must have a touch of the exotic. Anything that is lovely and unusual either in workmanship or material is to me irresisti-ble; the moment I see it it makes an immediate impact and appeal, and I am not easy until it is mine.

Maude was Walter's twin and I had expected her to be like him; it was hardly necessary to make allowance for the difference in sex, for Walter's looks were girlish; he had a slim, seemingly boneless body, soft dark hair, and large dark eyes with long lashes.

My first sight of Maude, therefore, gave me a surprise. I looked, looked again, found myself unable to look away from her. And even now, after many years, I find it impossible to say exactly what it was that so charmed me. It was a face that *meant* something. Not pretty. Not young even. Already, at the age of twelve, her beauty was the beauty of the ageless, undamageable skull. It showed in her brow, in her cheekbones and jaw. Her eyes, which were very blue, were set back in hollows, and below the cheekbones her face was scooped out, too. Her nose was low between the eyes, and then jutted out, blunt-tipped and wide-nostrilled. The lips of her mouth were long and both flat and full, and on either side lines had already formed, lines of fortitude, or perhaps of humour, a little on the wry side. The hair which was revealed when she threw back her hood was a warm reddish brown, crisp and springy.

For the rest she was somewhat taller than Walter, and, though delicately made, not without bone; thin square shoulders, bony wrists, long, clear jointed fingers. No breasts yet; and as I stared, wondering at myself and seeking some reason for my interest and for feeling as I did, I suddenly bethought me of the carved and painted angels in the roof of the St. Mary Chapel in the Abbey. Her beauty, like theirs, was of angle and plane, not of curve, and, like theirs, it was sexless, and, despite what her grandfather had said about merriment, on the sombre side. I had always had a weakness for small, plump, smiling women.

She was noticeably ill-dressed in a gown that had been lengthened, not very skillfully, and was still too short, especially in the sleeves. Mistress Reed had every reason to start demanding where was this and that garment, recently despatched to Beauclaire. Maude said she had given the things away.

"In Heaven's name, *why?*"

"I had sufficient without them."

Mistress Reed gave her a look of intense exasperation and then asked, "What is that you have on your finger?"

"A ring," the girl said, clipping her other hand over the ornament protectively.

"Show me!"

She held out her hand unwillingly and withdrew it quickly. We had all seen the clumsy, ill-fashioned thing and the dark mark, like a bruise, which the base metal had left on her finger.

"Tawdry rubbish. I should have thought that after three years at Beauclaire you would have known better than to wear such trash. Where did you get it? At a fair?"

"It is keepsake; from a friend."

Mistress Reed, through her delicate, high-bridged nose, gave a sort of snort, and said, "The things I sent you . . . good sound things, you gave away!"

"Yes," Maude said.

They stood eyeing one another like wrestlers, each of whom has once thrown the other, and who now hesitate to try another fall. I saw that I had been wrong in thinking Mistress Reed devoted to both her children; she had no fondness for her daughter. And as Maude stood there, very straight, defiant, and yet oddly vulnerable, I was conscious of a wish to take her part, to protect her. It was a feeling quite new to me. But, after all, we have, every one of us, a weak point. The most hardened blasphemer has one name he holds holy, and once, in Norwich, I heard a triple murderer on his way to the gallows call to someone in the crowd, "Look after my owd dog!" Maude Reed was my weak point, the place where ordinary rules no longer held. I began to love her at that moment; but there should be another word for it; there should be several words to cover the widely diverse feelings for which we can only use the one word "love." I loved myself; I loved my amiable, cuddlesome Bessie; I loved Maude. Three very different uses of the word.

Maude had been home only a few days before I had an opportunity to serve her, to please her, and to put myself into her favour. She chanced to say that Walter wrote a much better script than she did herself. It was at table, where generally I was content merely to look at her.

"Who taught you?" I asked.

"One of Lady Astallon's ladies." I saw her eyes change colour, the black centre expanding until the blue was a mere rim. I had noticed before that light-eyed people, however strictly they rule their expressions, betray themselves thus. "Her name was Melusine," she said, and looked down.

Now Melusine is an unusual name, the name of a character in a French romance. Just the name it seemed to me, to slip into the mind of a young girl who, for purposes of concealment, tells an unpremeditated lie. That could be thought over later. I said smoothly:

"Ladies seldom have the advantage of being taught by a cloister-trained clerk. My teacher was a famous penman. If you like, demoiselle, I can show you, in a very short time, how to better your script."

At my use of the word "demoiselle," Mistress Reed and Master Reed both looked at me, the former with surprise and a touch of approval, the latter with one eyebrow cocked sardonically. It was a term of courtesy, used only towards young ladies of high birth, and not one to slip easily from the tongue of a clerk.

"That would be very kind," Maude said gravely. Then she smiled and her whole face was transfigured.

Mistress Reed, who liked me very little, could not forbear saying to me, "I should have thought you had enough to do, without taking on any more."

And to Maude, "You would be better employed with your needle. You write as well as you will ever need to."

"Not if I go to Clevely," Maude said.

For the first time since she had entered the house her mother looked at her kindly, almost lovingly.

"You wish to go to Clevely?"

Before Maude could answer Martin Reed brought his hand down on the table in a smack which made the platters jump.

"We'll have no talk of that," he said. "You're only just home. There's a whole long summer ahead. You stay here, learn to write, read if you want to, be a bit of company about the place. There's Walter, always on the fidget. I want no more of it." As though fearing an argument, he jumped up and limped away.

"If you wish to go to Clevely you shall," Mistress Reed said, looking at Maude and then quickly away again in the way she had. "I shall support you."

"If you do you're mad," Walter said. "Shut in, doing the same things, seeing the same people day after day. I'd rather be dead."

"Nobody," said Mistress Reed, in the soft fond voice which she kept for her son, "is suggesting that you should go to Clevely, Walter. We're talking about Maude."

"I came home to go to Clevely," Maude said. "It was all arranged, long ago, wasn't it? When I was twelve, they said. I thought it was settled."

"Of course, of course," Mistress Reed said hastily. "There was just the likelihood of your preferring to stay at Beauclaire. So the final negotiations were never . . . But it will be all right, I am sure."

I saw then how those lines, so out of place on either side of a young mouth, had been made. The girl knew, as well as I did, that her mother wanted her out of the house. How far that knowledge had influenced her decision to go into a nunnery as a lay boarder—which was all she could be at her age—I did not know, but, with that curious extra sight which infatuation lends, I could see with painful clarity that upon this matter of going to Clevely she was in two minds; half of her mind welcomed the idea, the other half rejected it.

I rejected it absolutely. I knew very well that dozens of girls every year went into convents as lay boarders; it was the fashion for girls of good birth to go and spend some time in the company of nuns most of whom were well bred, educated, capable of inculcating good manners, a smattering of learning, and a shrewd business sense in their charges. Most of the girls emerged little or none the worse for their cloistered years; a few became novices. Of that few, half—invariably well dowered—went on and took vows. An ordinary girl, going as a lay boarder, would have a likelihood of, say, one in twenty of becoming a professed nun.

But I wanted Maude here, in the Old Vine, here with me, susceptible, malleable. There was something about her, a kind of otherworldliness

that would make her very open to persuasion. I had been schooled by
monks; I knew how insidious mere atmosphere could be. I knew also
how greedy—not as individuals, but as a community—any professed
religious body could be. Maude Reed's dower would be a tempting bait.
Especially to Clevely, which was surely the poorest house in all England.

Walter had by this time given up even the pretence of taking lessons
from me, so when, at the time arranged, Maude came to the schoolroom
we were alone. I took a clean piece of parchment and across the top of it
wrote the alphabet in small letters and in capitals.

"There it is," I said, "and the secret is to make each letter sharp and
clear, with points rather than sprawling, circular strokes. And with the
capitals be sparing, write as though ink were gold—it is with gold that
the great penman wrote, you know—not to be wasted. You see, economy,
economy, and clarity is the result. You try now."

She was twice as teachable as Walter, though about writing he had
been eager and good. In no time at all she had mastered the better
style. Presently, looking up, she said in a defensive way:

"You mustn't judge the teacher by the pupil, you know, Master Freeman. Melusine wrote *beautifully*."

Anxious to ingratiate myself, I said, "Of that I am sure." I then asked,
as casually as I could, "You were fond of your teacher?"

For a moment I thought she was about to cry; but she set her mouth,
deepening the lines each side of it, and merely nodded her head.

There sprang into my mind a complete and feasible theory. There had
been a writing master at Beauclaire—I could see him, sly, meek, and ingratiating—and although he would not dare aspire to the affections of
one of the highborn young ladies, the woolmaster's granddaughter would
be within his range. Something had happened, discovery, scandal perhaps,
and so she had come home, a trifle broken-hearted and ready, with girlish
impetuosity, to fling herself into a nunnery. Or again, he, in his cunning,
might have suggested that, it being the safest place where a girl could wait
a year or two. Was it his ring that she wore?

The coarse, cheap thing was prominent on her hand as she wrote, and
presently I ventured to say, "I think your ring is very pretty."

With something of her grandfather's bluntness, she said, "Oh no. Nobody could think that! But I like it." Once again she put her other hand
over it and held it fast. At the same time her mouth took on such a tender
look that I detected, beneath that carved wooden-angel exterior, the
possibility of great sensuousness. With a quickening of my own blood I
thought: He kissed her when he gave her that trinket.

I bore him no ill-will; what has been done once is the more easily done again, even if it is falling in love with one's writing master. She was very young; he was far away and I was here on the spot.

Then I remembered that she was going to Clevely.

I let her write for a while; then I said, "You read as well as you write, I imagine."

"Tolerably well."

"It is a pity then that you will have small chance to practise either art at Clevely. It is a very poor house and the Ladies are few. They work in the fields and the dairy."

"How do you know that?"

"We buy their few poor polls of wool—or did, until they lost their sheep from the tick fever. I've seen the Ladies, their habits hitched up, working like hinds."

She said dreamily, "I like to read and write; therefore Clevely will be all the more suitable for my purpose."

"Your purpose?"

"Something I must do." As she spoke she reached out for the pen-rag and wiped the point of her quill clean; stood it in the stand; rose to her feet, and, after a few words of thanks to me for the lesson, walked away, very graceful and dignified.

I felt rebuffed, I tried to feel resentful, too, but the genuine feeling would not be evoked. For the first time in my life in connection with any female I was inclined to self-blame. I should not have dared presume, on so slight an acquaintance, to question her.

Master Reed continued obstinate about Clevely. Once, through a half-open door, I heard Mistress Reed ask, in a quiet, cutting tone, "Is it that you grudge the five pounds a year for her lodging?"

"You know better than that. I'm thinking of her happiness."

"It is her own choice."

"Of that I must make sure."

The weather warmed, and one day Maude and her grandfather went out together. When they returned he had somehow convinced himself that her desire to go the the nuns was genuine. I could see, by his glumness, that he had been convinced against his will; nevertheless, without further protest, the preparations for her leaving began to go forward.

I now began to be concerned, for the first time in my life, for another person's creature comfort. On my wool-buying visits to Clevely I had seen inside the house; the nuns had no Frater even, they ate at a table at one end of the kitchen, which had a floor made of trodden earth and walls of undressed stone, running with dampness. I had not seen the rest of their accommodation, but I imagined that it would be equally comfortless.

For a professed nun, vowed to poverty and self-denial, such surroundings might be, ethically, more right than the ease and luxuries that some communities enjoyed; but I hated to think of Maude in such a place.

I was silly enough to make one last effort to dissuade her. It was not planned, would indeed have been impossible to plan, for since the writing lesson which had ended so abruptly there had been no chance and no reason for us to have speech in private.

On this evening, just after supper, I was in the office, doing an extra hour's work. The weather had changed again and for the time of year it was bitterly cold, with a driving rain and a howling wind. Even for the sake of Bessie's embraces I was not prepared to ride three miles out and back again on such a night.

The door opened and I looked up crossly, expecting to see Mistress Reed, who had the annoying habit of coming into the office now and again when she knew her father-in-law was not there. She'd turn things over and ask questions—some of them, I admit, shrewd ones; and sometimes she would make suggestions which I would ignore and then in my own good time present as my own.

It was not Mistress Reed, however, it was Maude, who, from the threshold, said, "I thought my grandfather was here."

"He's gone to bed. In weather like this his leg troubles him."

"*We* trouble him too. I could see that at supper. So I thought . . ."

It was true that at the table Walter had once more referred to the time when he would travel the roads, playing his lute. Mistress Reed's expression had changed from discontent to piteousness, and the old man had looked first at Walter, then at Maude, and heaved one of his tremendous sighs. Disappointed in both his grandchildren.

I heard myself saying, without any of the respect or the desire to please that formerly I had used towards her, saying, in fact, quite roughly, "I'm sorry for your grandfather. Walter is past praying for; he was born with this bee in his bonnet. But the poor old man had hopes of you. Piety can be as selfish as anything else, and if you stayed at home and cheered your grandfather's last years Almighty God would probably count it more of a virtue than wearing your hands out in the Clevely dairy and your knees on the Chapel floor."

She looked at me with wide-eyed astonishment, as well she might. I was astonished at myself.

"I'm not trying to acquire virtue for *myself*. What made you think that?"

Master Reed, who had been in the office before supper, and who felt the cold, had lighted the fire; it had burned down now to a heap of ashes, fitfully glowing pink under a coating of grey. I had got to my feet when Maude opened the door; now I turned and threw two billets of dry wood onto the fire, and then, reaching past her, I closed the door.

"Come in and get warm, it's one of the last chances you'll have," I said, in that same brusque way. "I know what I'm talking about. I went to Clevely for their last lot of wool in the month of May, and Dame Clarice Gracey who acts as Treasuress still had chilblains to the elbow. *In May.* She had her sleeves rolled up while she weighed the wool."

Maude gave a little shudder, moved her hands together, twisting the ugly ring, and then moved towards the fire and sat down on the settle, holding her hands to the warmth.

"The worse it is, the better. Don't ask me why. There are some things that shouldn't be talked about. It makes them seem . . ." She paused. "It makes them seem less real, less important. Can you understand that? I have a reason for going to Clevely. I told it to my grandfather, because I thought he had the right to know, and because I wanted to speak of it . . . yes . . . there was that, too. And ever since," she turned her head from the fire at which she had been staring and looked into my face, "it hasn't seemed so real or so urgent. I've begun to wonder . . ." She paused again. "I believe that you could, if you wanted, talk a thing clean away, make it be nothing."

I had seated myself on the opposite settle, and now, leaning forward, I said, "Try. Tell me why you think you must go to Clevely. Maybe then you won't want to go."

"That is what I fear. Except that . . . there is this in it, the less I *want* to go the more it will count if I do."

"Count? Count against what? Come on," I said, "you can tell me. Another fortnight and the Bishop's hands laid on me and I should have been a priest, qualified to hear any confession and advise on any matter. Imagine that! So you see, you can tell me anything."

Like all women she went off at a tangent. They do it, not deliberately, or because they are incapable of sticking to one line of thought as any man who has been nagged can bear witness, they do it for the same reason that a partridge whose nest is in danger will go limping and flapping away, deluding the intruder into the hope that she can be taken by hand. It is a defensive measure.

"I did not know," Maude Reed said, "that you were almost a priest. What stopped you?" She spoke as though I were a runaway horse, grabbed by the reins.

I could hardly tell her what was my chief reason—that I knew myself unable to live celibate and should tire of pretending to be; my other reason was enough.

"I'm a farmer's son, with no family and no wealth to count on. For me the ladder to promotion was set very steep and lacked several rungs. Besides, I preferred the life of a layman; a priest should have a vocation."

She nodded gravely, and her hair changed colour where the firelight caught it.

"I know. Something—just a little thing it was, too—happened to me and made me think there was something in the world, after all. But there is a long time before I have to decide about a vocation."

"You make such a mystery of it all," I said brusquely, "talking about a purpose and what will count and other vagaries. You're far too young to take life so seriously. I'll tell you what I think. . . ."

"Yes?" She looked straight into my eyes.

"I think that at Beauclaire you had a bad attack of puppy love and something went wrong with it, so you go jumping into a convent like a scalt cat. It's very silly."

"I'm not jumping into a convent. I'm only going to live at Clevely for a time, as anyone might do."

Quite a lively temper, too, I found myself noting with approval. And another defensive tactic.

"I'll hazard a further guess," I said recklessly, "your bit of heartbreak at Beauclaire was concerned with your writing teacher—the one you call Melusine."

Dear me, that brought a result for which I was not prepared. She gave me a wild look and half rose, and then dropped back, laid her arms on the side of the settle, put her head down and began to cry.

I've heard dozens of women cry, with cause and without, and the most I have ever felt was a mild pity if they had what I considered good reason to weep, a testy impatience if I thought otherwise. Maude's tears seemed to come from my throat, her sobs to rend my chest.

I went down on my knees by the settle and put my arm round her and began to talk rubbish, saying that I meant no harm, that a little sentimental attachment was nothing to cry about, that I would sooner lose my right hand—what things people say in the endeavour to be persuasive!—than cause her a moment's pain. I reverted to childishness and referred to myself by the name that no one had used since I went, a boy of nine, to the monks' school at Norwich.

"Tell Nick," I pleaded, "tell Nick all about it."

She did too! Melusine and Uncle Godfrey and Madge FitzHerbert and how everything depended on money, and what an awful world this was. I kept my arm round those thin little shoulders and held her steady, and pulled out my sleeve and wiped her face on it. I hated all the three that she talked about because they had hurt her. The wench who'd lifted her skirt before the ring was on her finger was dead and beyond ill wishes; I wished a pox on the other two; and on all at the great house who had let such a situation develop, not seen what was afoot, and then, after the end of it, let this child carry her grief all sealed away in loneliness.

Presently, when she had cried herself out, I asked, "This is what you told your grandfather?"

"Yes. But I must not cry. I promised not to cry about it any more."

"Who made you promise such a daft thing?"

"The Chaplain."

Pox on him, too, I thought; a few good crying bouts and the wound would have begun to heal. She actually said, in a sad way, "There, now I've told you and it seems ever farther away."

"That is why miseries should be talked over, not bottled up."

I left her then and put another log on the fire and again sat down opposite.

"Now listen to me," I began. I raked through my mind for any scrap of comfort to offer her. Heresies I could have gone to the stake for poured from my lips. I told her that there wasn't a word of evidence of the existence of Purgatory in the Bible. That Christ never exhorted anybody to pray for the dead. That the descent into Hell mentioned in the Creed was a man-made myth. "On the Cross, to the dying thief, Christ said, 'Today you shall be with me in Paradise,' what could be plainer than that?"

My years of training for priesthood now served me, in reverse as it were; I was persuasive, logical, like a lawyer who can plead this side of a case or that, according to who hires his tongue.

The result was disappointing; she listened, but was not convinced. The point I thought most telling she countered with, "That man was only a thief; not a suicide."

"Your friend had been wronged," I said. And then I paused, remembering that I had wronged at least two women in precisely that same way, and never until this moment had a pang of conscience about it. "Nobody can judge in these matters. She may have been acting in a spirit of self-abnegation; if she was with child, and had a family who would have shared the disgrace. If you want to make a disputation about it, theft is forbidden in the Commandments, there is no mention of suicide there. And if you care to be strictly logical, Christ Himself was the outstanding suicide of all time; at any moment *he* could have called down an army of angels to rescue Him."

In my eagerness to comfort her I had gone too far, forgetting that I was talking to a child of twelve. I saw horror dawn and grow in her face and savoured the full irony of having done myself deep damage in her estimation, simply through pity. I stopped speaking.

She said, "Now I know where I have seen you before. It has bothered me, not being able to *quite* remember. In the Maze at Beauclaire."

"I never was there."

"Not you. Your image. In the Rune Stone."

It was my turn to stare. And it was my turn—I who have always been impatient of women who told long tales about their dreams, and sceptical of those who claimed to have had premonitions—to listen to the story of a supernatural experience, which had at least one redeeming feature of being comic. She described the man she had seen in her vision, and whom she claimed to be me, in full cardinal's wear! Maybe I had missed my mark after all.

"You were trying to convince me of something, just as you were just now. And I knew you were wrong, as I know it now. Though I am sure," she added with magnanimity, "you were trying to be kind. And I'm sorry to have made such a show of myself. The first thing we were supposed to learn at Beauclaire was self-control."

"Of which," I said, "as with many another thing, a certain amount is very good, and too much deadly poison. The one thing I wish for you—because it would mean happiness in the end—is that you shouldn't act hastily over this matter. It was a shock, and you've brooded over it in silence and the whole thing has grown out of all proportion. If you spent, say, just the one summer here, living an ordinary life and trying to keep your grandfather cheerful, I'm quite sure . . ."

She said, "You know what they say in Suffolk when temptation offers, 'Get you ahind me, Old Scrat!' I must say it to you." She smiled, with the tearmarks still damp on her face. "I know what I must do, and I am going to do it."

Master Reed could be stubborn, and Walter was obstinate past all reason, and she was of their blood. But there was something other than obstinacy, there was something almost piteous in her last words to me that evening.

"Besides, even if I wished to defer going it would be awkward; everything is prepared."

And that was true. Mistress Reed had brought her undoubted capacity for industry and organisation to bear upon getting Maude's clothes and household goods ready for Clevely with such effect that when, on St. Barnabas' Day, she left the Old Vine for the second time, two pack horses were needed to carry her gear.

I HAD never much cared for Mistress Reed, thinking her cold and proud, admirable only in her devotion to her children, and in that I was but half right. After seeing her with Maude I liked her less, and, because she had encouraged the girl to leave home, even hastened her going as far as possible, I began to detest her. Her punishment was on its way, however, and I sometimes wondered how far she had herself helped to fashion it. How could anyone account for Walter Reed, who was, of all the people I have ever known, the most peculiar?

His mother was ordinary enough; she had married beneath her, but when one compared the home from which she came with that to which she had come, that was understandable enough. She had never, I am certain, entertained a thought, or experienced an emotion uncommon to her kind. She preferred her son to her daughter, but then thousands of women do that, but conceal the fact, perhaps out of deference to their husbands, who usually have a fondness for their daughters and govern their sons strictly.

Walter's father, who had died young of the lung rot, was, by all accounts, ordinary, too. He was musical, and rather better educated than some merchants' sons, but everything that was remembered about him indicated that he had been industrious and businesslike and sensible.

Whence then Walter? How did two such ordinary human people ever breed that changeling child?

He cared for nothing but his music. He accepted his mother's adoration without the reciprocation of even the most tepid affection. He condescended to learn to read and write because those arts would, he thought, be useful to him when he was an itinerant musician. For music he had some talent; he could pick up the words of any song, however long it was, at one hearing, and from a fragment of a tune, hummed or whistled, he could reconstruct the whole. He also made good songs of his own. Mistress Reed up to a point encouraged him, often remarking that he had inherited his father's ability—that was how I learned that Richard Reed had been musical. Even when he talked of his future, although one could see that the thought of his leaving home cut her to the heart, she was curiously infirm of mind, saying oh there was a long time to go before he could think of that, saying when he was older he would have more sense, saying that his father had talked the same way and settled down to business in the end.

His grandfather's attitude towards the boy was equally uncertain; he was deeply disappointed, as any man who had built a great business out of nothing and then finds his heir scorns and repudiates it would be justified in being. But never once did he make an open protest or seem to realise that a child could be governed and controlled. In the first three years of my time at Baildon the harshest thing I ever heard him say to Walter about his wildcat plans was:

"All right, if you go, when the time comes, you go. Don't keep talking about it!" And even that order Walter disobeyed when he felt like it.

Twice in those three years Walter, after some row over his lessons, had run away and been brought back. Excused from learning to count—which in any case he was completely unable to do; he left home at last still counting on his fingers—he settled down until the summer which followed Maude's going to Clevely.

During that summer, in August, the height of the pilgrim season in Baildon, there was an incident, trivial but curious, which I remembered years after, when Walter's fate was decided.

He came in, on that warm, dusty evening, a little late for supper, his face flushed, his eyes fever-bright, and his whole manner that of one who moves in a trance. He sat down and, ignoring the food before him, told us that he had been playing his lute in the market place. Those who had listened had given him cakes and fruit and sweetmeats and a variety of small trinkets. He laid them out on the board; a little image of St. Christopher, a knife with a horn handle, a belt buckle, and a money pouch made of plaited straw.

"They had no money to spare," he said, "but those who had . . . Look!" He opened the pouch and spilled out six or seven shining farthings. "They liked it so much that they paid me! They paid me!" he said.

His grandfather looked at the coins as though they had been earned by blood, fraud, prostitution. Mistress Reed looked at them as though they were her death warrant. I simply stared, thinking: Well, if he can earn that much in an hour, he's cleverer than most; a good thatcher working from dawn to dusk earned a penny and a half in the day.

Mistress Reed spoke first. She said, "Of course they liked your playing, Walter. You play extremely well. I always said so. But you mustn't take all this," she pointed to the stuff on the table, "as proof that you can make a living playing the lute. You see, you are very young and rather small, so they think that it is *marvellous* that you should . . ."

"The Devil take your tongue," Walter cried. All the colour went out of his face, leaving it the colour that I had only seen before on a corpse. "That isn't true. They liked it, I tell you. No matter about me. When I sang of the death of Roland they wept. Great rough men. One man said, 'What magic is this? I have not shed a tear since my child died, and what is this Roland to me?' He said that with tears running down his face. And then you say it is because I am small."

He would have been weeping himself, had he been able, but he never could cry; he could sob and moan but I never saw him shed a tear.

His mother shrank back as though he had hit her across the face, but his grandfather leaned forward and said in a voice of controlled fury, "Never, in all my days, have I known a boy speak so insolently to his mother. She spoke for your good and she spoke the truth. So, in the market place a few fools praised you, and you come home calling on the Devil. You ask pardon this minute, or I'll give you what I should have years ago, a damned good hiding."

I watched, with great interest. When I first came to the Old Vine the boy's choosiness over what he would and would not learn had been attributed to my failure to manage him. Let them learn.

Walter looked defiantly at his grandfather, but the old man was not to be outfaced. Set in their myriad wrinkles, under the scowl-scarred brow, his grey eyes bore down, unflinching. Walter's stare flickered and wavered. He put out his hands and gathered all the things he had lain out for display, as though they were his defence and consolation. Across them he said:

"I ask your pardon, madam. But truly it was not because . . ."

"That will *do!*" Master Reed said.

There was a silence at the table, broken when Walter picked up his little silver coins and passed them lightly from hand to hand. Mistress Reed leaned forward and seemed to be about to speak, but though her lips moved and her throat jerked, no sound came. She lifted her cup and drank, set it down, and then, rather like a woman who has heard evil tidings, put her hand over her mouth and the lower part of her face. Her hands, I noticed for the first time, were like Maude's, very long and thin, the finger joints clearly marked.

I saw Master Reed give her a sidelong glance. I thought that this was where I, one of the company, yet not emotionally concerned, should make some tactful, impersonal remark which would smooth over the awkward moment. Before I could think of one Master Reed, in a casual way which contrasted sharply with his last manner of speech, said:

"It would serve you right, Walter, if nobody spoke to you for a week. But that would punish your mother more than you. You'd better ask her to say that she forgives you."

Walter said as meekly as possible, "Please forgive me, Mother."

Master Reed then seemed to be affected by madness. He hit the table with his hand and said more furiously than I had ever heard him speak even to a pack-whacker who had foundered two horses, "God's blood! Can't you just for once do what you're told?"

Mistress Reed again moved her lips and tried to protest, but the old man thundered on. "I said, *ask* her to say she forgives you. Do it, or I'll break your neck!"

By this time every eye in the dining hall was turned towards our table. Mistress Reed, ever mindful of formalities, moved a hand in a gesture very eloquent and graceful to draw Master Reed's attention to this fact. He shook his head like a horse tormented by flies and kept his eye on Walter, who, after a minute said:

"Mother, please say that you forgive me."

The words came from her like liquid from an upturned bottle. "I do, Walter, I do. I shouldn't have said what I did. Of course they liked your playing."

"Now mark this," Master Reed said, "when you lose your temper and say things like 'Devil take your tongue,' that is a plain invitation for the same ill wish to fall on you. You be mindful of what you say."

I admit that on the face of it it was no more than any man might say to any child, a mere paraphrase of the old adage about ill wishes coming home to roost: but the way he said it gave it weight and importance. It was almost as though he believed that Walter's angry words had affected his mother's speech; as though the grandfather believed that the boy had a power to ill-wish, and wanted to warn him, privily, against inflicting hurt.

Rubbish, I told myself, superstitious nonsense. The one power which Walter Reed possessed was that of making people think he played better than he did. In the main he was secretive about his music, shutting himself away in the solar and playing for hours alone. On those occasions when he would say, rather pompously, "Now I will play for you," I always reminded myself that I had been schooled at Norwich where the choir is famous, and had twice heard Blind Hob of Lincoln play for the Leather Merchants' Guild in that same city. But always, before the end, Walter would have me, and with all judgement suspended I would fall under the spell, too.

During the time immediately after Maude's departure, whenever I heard Walter play, I would ask myself whether both these children hadn't been born with a curious power to charm, Walter by his music, Maude by just being. Walter's charm ended when his lute was silent, but Maude's could survive her absence. I thought of her, not always sentimentally, sometimes critically, at almost every moment during the day when my mind was not actually engaged upon some immediate business. I would try to recall her face and succeed only partially, making a picture in my mind of a blur dominated by one overprominent feature, the way one does when someone tries to describe a person unknown. "He has a big nose," they say, and you see just a nose. So I would think in turn of her blue, deep-set eyes, the hollow in her cheek, the turn of her lip, or the way her hair grew. Then, at another, unexpected time, I could recall the whole of her, down to the nails on her fingers. I thought of her, at such times, much as a man on short commons would think of some favourite, flavoursome dish. I craved to see her, and when, one day early in December, Martin Reed said, "I take it Maude will come home for Christmas," I wanted to jump up and shake him by the hand, slap him on the back, give loud and obvious evidence of my approval.

"I take it Maude will come home for Christmas," he said.

Mistress Reed said in a doubtful voice, "I don't know about that. Nobody mentioned it. Would it be allowed?"

Forgetful of my place, I said, "Of course it would. Who could prevent it? She isn't a novice, or even a school child. She can come home when she wishes."

"So I should think," Master Reed said.

"I'm not so sure." Mistress Reed looked me in the eye and said, "You were schooled by monks; did you go home for Christmas?"

She'd heard me say—the cunning bitch—that I did not.

"My home was thirty miles from my school, madam; and in return for my lessons I sang in the Choir. I could not miss the Christmas Masses. The cases are hardly comparable." I almost added and it would have been true: Except that my brothers didn't want me home, any more than you want Maude.

"It shouldn't be too difficult to find out," Master Reed said in his dry way. "Nicholas can write a letter, which I will sign."

"But are you sure that it is wise to unsettle her so soon? . . ."

"Holy Virgin, you talk as though we wanted her there, Anne. She took this whim to go, but if she's outlived it there's nothing I'd like better than to unsettle her. Unsettle, that's fool's talk."

Mistress Reed said with cold dignity, "I'm remembering my own childhood, always on the move and longing for some settled place. That was all."

"Well, if you can't see the difference," he said angrily and snatched up his mug, drank from it, and set it down with a clang.

Later, in the office, he stamped about, bringing his good leg down heavily.

"I'm the customer, ain't I?" he demanded of me. "I pay five pounds a year for her to be there when I'd pay four times the amount to keep her at home. You can tell them that if you like. The whole thing was a mistake from beginning to end. She should never have gone to Beau-claire. Beware of women, my boy. You don't have to be in love with one for her to lead you by the nose and you don't notice till too late. Get your things and write. How do you address a prioress? You should know. Now I'll say what I want to say, and you wrap it up so she'll not think she's dealing with an ignorant old fellow."

My former visits to the nunnery had been made after the shearing season, when the sun was warm and the fields green; even then I had been struck by the dreariness of the place, set all alone, far from the high-way behind a barrier of trees. The House and the Chapel were both shaped like haystacks built of dark, dressed flint, the least cheerful of all building materials. They were linked by a kind of cloister, begun in stone and finished in wood; some of the pillars indeed were simply tree trunks, stripped of their branches but retaining their bark. Immedi-ately in front of the cloister was a little herb garden, at this season bleached and depleted, but as neat as a piece of embroidery. Everything at Clevely was as neat as it was bleak.

The only door in the House opened directly upon the kitchen, and there was no portress here. My old acquaintance, Dame Clarice, an-swered my knocking, told me that the Prioress was ill in her bed, and without ceremony opened the letter.

"This is for Maude to decide. You may ask her. Let me see, Tuesday. You'll find her in the dairy." She indicated a door immediately opposite the one at which we stood, and said, "At the end of the passage."

I stepped in, aware at once of the smell of a religious house. Ordinary people on their way home from church shake the incense odour off into the air; professed religious on their short cloistered walk carry it with them to mingle with the scent of boiled onions and stockfish and the por-ridge that burned very slightly in the pan. With this smell of my school-days in my nose and my heart jumping because I was, in a moment, going to see Maude again, I walked along the cold dim passage, feeling suddenly young and unsure of myself.

I could hear, before I reached the dairy door, the sound of girlish chat-ter, once a merry laugh, mingled with the clatter of pans and the swish of a scrubbing brush. Perhaps she was happy here, I thought, and per-versely took no joy in the thought.

There were three of them in the cold dairy, all wearing coarse sacking smocks over their clothes, wooden clogs on their feet, and linen hoods covering their hair. One was engaged in scrubbing the shelves, one, on her knees, was scrubbing the floor, the other was scouring a bucket. The three faces turned to me with looks of surprise, then the one who was kneeling scrambled to her feet and said, "Oh, Master Freeman, is anything wrong?"

Even as I assured her, I was thinking to myself: Name of God, yes! Wrong that she who had never been full-fleshed should have grown so much thinner; wrong that her hands should be so red and swollen, the nails broken short and grimed from the dirty water. I told her my errand, and for one unguarded moment pure pleasure lightened her face, only to go out again like a blown candle. She said in a wooden way:

"I thank my grandfather for so kind a thought; but I had best stay here."

"He is counting upon your presence. Would you ruin his Christmas, when in the course of nature he can have few more? Remember what I said to you about selfishness."

"And you remember what I said about Owd Scrat!"

I longed to pick her up in my arms and run with her, out of the place; to shake the obstinacy out of her. I could only use words, and I was choosing, out of my own hurt, the most wounding ones I could muster, when the bucket scourer came to my aid.

"Oh, Maude," she said, "please go home and bring us back some Christmas fare. Raisins," she said, in an ecstatic voice.

"Ham," said the other, and I swear that her teeth shone for a second like a hungry dog's. "Ham for me, Maude. Please. We'll do your work. You go home and bring us back some goodies."

"A fine impression we shall make upon Master Freeman," Maude said. "He'll think us entirely governed by our appetites."

I took note of the conventual "we." I said, "You see, demoiselle, at the cost of a very slight sacrifice of your own self-esteem, you could mightily please three people—these and your grandfather."

"Four," she said. "I should myself be pleased."

"Five then, for I also should be . . . delighted."

"I should have to ask leave."

"It is already given. Dame Clarice said that it was for you to decide."

"The words must have *choked* her," cried the girl who had asked for ham. She giggled and put her hand to her mouth.

"Not for twelve days, then. Four."

"Good Maude. Kind Maude. The sooner I shall have my raisins."

Maude made a gesture of impatience, and moved towards me and the door. We went out together, and she pulled the door closed and leaned against it.

"You must not misjudge," she said. "They are both orphans and have lived here for four years. We have enough to eat."

"That I beg leave to doubt. You've grown very thin."

"We eat with the nuns and they work far harder than we do."

"You and they, in there, are growing," I protested.

"Which we shouldn't do if we lacked sufficient nourishment."

"There's no arguing with you. Shall I fetch you on Christmas Eve?"

"If you have time to spare." She smiled at me, and I saw that her odd little face which so easily assumed an expression of melancholy could just as easily shape itself to merriment. Martin had mentioned that she was a merry, hoydenish little girl. I cursed once again the bad management, the ignorance, and false values that had brought her to *this*.

Yet there was no denying that six months at Clevely had done a good deal to lighten her misery of spirit. During those four days of Christmas when my eyes, whenever possible, were upon her, as though they could never look their fill, I noticed that the old haunted look of desperate unhappiness had gone, and been replaced by a serenity which had a beauty of its own. Life at Clevely might be harsh and comfortless—some of the things Maude let slip shocked even her mother—but it seemed to be spiritually satisfactory and I, watching every blown straw that betrayed the wind's direction, saw several ominous signs.

Mistress Reed, as before, grumbled about her daughter's clothing. Why was this one dress so much worn, had Maude donned it every day, and why, where were the others? She was little pleased to hear that Jill was wearing one and Avice the other. Even I, doting as I was, detected a certain priggishness in the way Maude said:

"At Clevely we have all things in common. Except shoes. Feet vary so much. But," she added as though in extenuation, "we share the clogs."

Mistress Reed said, with a tartness which I understood, "That calls up the three-legged race which children run."

Maude laughed. "So it does! I should have said that we wear any clogs which come to hand, or to foot."

I recalled how teachable she was; in six months she had mastered the art of Christian imperturbability, as one of my teachers had called it.

Then again, at the well-spread table, the question of convent food arose.

"When you go back," Master Reed said, "that is if you insist upon going back, I shall send some hams and salt beef, and good wheat flour."

Maude said, and, hate the word as any man of sense must, there is no other, *demurely*, "That would be very much appreciated. Dame Winifred Challis who often has sick poor people in the guest-room is mostly at her wit's end to find them tasty dishes."

"You mean you wouldn't eat what I sent?"

"Oh no. We all eat from the same dish. Even the Prioress."

"Going hungry is no virtue," Master Reed said. "Thousands of people live their whole lives without knowing the feel of a full belly. You're enjoying what you're eating now, aren't you?"

"Oh yes. Very much. But to eat like this every day would be gluttony."

How well I knew it, this prate about the deadly sins! It could have only two effects. Hearing it often enough the young must give in, accept that to enjoy a comfortable bed was sloth, to eat a good meal was gluttony, to think one independent thought was pride, and on and on, until in one day of ordinary living you could commit the whole seven, twice over. (Whoever named them did so cunningly. Murder, which comparatively few people are tempted to, is not among them, anger, which every man must feel, is.) The only other way for the young to take is plain rebellion, bouncing away in the other direction, as I myself had done. Was Maude capable of it? That only time could tell.

In the privacy of the office Master Reed loosed his complaints.

"I've worked very hard, and at times been ruthless to see my family secure and comfortable, now the one I care most for might as well be a scullion. Better. Scullions grow fat on the dripping." He scowled at me. "I always thought food was plentiful in such places. They hand it out. When I was first lamed I lived on what was given me at the Abbey Alms Gate."

"It varies," I said. "All religious are supposed to be vowed to poverty. Their interpretation of it varies, and some merely disregard it. I believe Clevely is genuinely poor. They never managed to replace their sheep and so lost what piteous income their wool brought in."

His scowl lifted.

"I'll give them some sheep. How many could they look after properly without unduly adding to their labours? Three dozen? Fifty?"

"They had eight, if I remember rightly, before. I don't know how much pasture they have."

"Ask when you take Maude back. I'll give them what they can take, of my good Cotswolds from Minsham. And I'll buy every handful of wool at top price. That should help them to feed those poor girls a bit better."

"It wouldn't benefit Maude in any way, sir. The sick poor might fatten. And you'd be putting the gyves on Maude tighter than ever. Once make Maude a supply line between you and Clevely, and next time you see her she'll be in novice garb. I know my monks, and nuns differ from them only in ways that have no effect on greed."

He said, "I think you're wrong, Nicholas. Oh, right about the persuasion, possibly, but wrong as to the result. My family is naturally perverse. I believe if they tried to coax her *into* a habit, she'd run home and turn Lollard."

"You say that because she resisted our persuasions." I saw one of his eyebrows twitch when I said "our." "Yes, I tried to talk her into waiting, at least. But we were arguing against something that she felt she should do; and we were only using words. They—if they do try to persuade her —will be arguing for what she feels she should do, and words will be the least of it. Inside every community there is an atmosphere, a kind of mental climate which is very difficult to withstand."

He gave one of his enormous sighs, and said, as he had once said when Walter was under discussion, "People do what they must, I suppose. But in this case," he scowled as he sought for the words he needed, "I never can feel that this is something that was in Maude and must out. It's been brought on from outside. If you knew what drove her to religion, you'd understand what I mean."

"She told me the whole story once. And sorry hearing I found it. *One* person had been kind to her in her loneliness, so she fixed on her the whole affection of a young and tender heart. And then the only word of real comfort she was given came from a priest. The result was inevitable."

There was a pause and I thought he was finished with the subject, but he said, "I failed her, too, perhaps. I thought of my own griefs—over which by this time, God knows, the grass should have grown. I envied her the certainty of her faith. I said as much. And I was wrong."

"As to that," I said, "I answered her with no faith, only with logic. It was a waste of breath."

He gave me one of his sharp looks.

"You seem to have a . . ." I thought by the way his lips shaped that he was going to say "a fondness," he amended it, "an interest in the girl."

I said boldly, "I am very fond of her, sir. Who could help it? Her looks are charming, her mind is lively, and even her obstinacy shows a good spirit."

He was pleased; it showed in the softening of his harsh old face. Then his eyes narrowed, as though he were regarding a bale of wool, assessing its weight and value.

"Her mother," he said slowly, "is often somewhat harsh towards her. You notice that?"

"Too often. I am tempted at times to forget my place and speak up in defence."

"Ah," he said, as though some question had been asked—not in words —and answered in the same fashion. "And you are now how old?"

"Twenty-four."

"You know the business; you are trustworthy and healthy, as handsome as a man needs to be. And twenty-four. Are your affections or interests engaged elsewhere?"

I told him, no, which was near enough to the truth as mattered.

"Then I'll tell you, Nicholas; if I could wish one wish it would be that in two years' time, or three, you and Maude would marry. I could die easy then."

I muttered some deprecating words about time being young yet, and being honoured by this proof of his confidence and liking. Never again did the matter come into the open; but the words had been said; and if justification of my action was needed, later on, there it lay.

III

THE next two years seem to me, when I look back, to have been as long as any other ten in my life. At Master Reed's insistence Maude came home at fairly frequent intervals, always for Christmas, for the birthday she shared with Walter, and again, either in August or September; between these visits time sagged and dragged.

I had always held that any man who suffered any avoidable trouble or pain was a fool, and after Maude had gone stubbornly back after that first Christmas visit I made great efforts to rid myself of my infatuation.

I tried a change of mistress. My Bessie was as cheerful and cuddlesome as ever and I was fond of her, but I had become increasingly aware of some lack in our relationship. It was a coupling of the flesh only—a business with which I had always hitherto been supremely content but which now seemed to fulfil only half my needs. I had only just determined to do something about this when an astonishing and unlooked-for piece of luck came my way. Mistress Reed's brother, Sir Godfrey Blanch-fleur, he who was responsible for all the trouble that had sent Maude to Clevely, came down to visit his mad, moribund old father at Minsham and was shocked by the conditions in which he found him. It chanced that on one of the manors he had gained by his marriage he had found some distant relative of his wife's family, a widow with two young sons, living on sufferance. He spent a little money on making Minsham Old Hall weathertight and slightly more comfortable and installed this lady, with three good servants, to rule the household.

Clemence Kentwoode, had she possessed the minimum of money or property, or even been childless, would not have remained a widow for a week; she was pretty, witty, and amorous. She had the smattering of learning, and the grace of manner common to her kind, and although, at first, the greater freedom and independence which life at Minsham offered pleased her, she was soon desperately lonely. For me it was an easy conquest, but as soon as the excitement of the advances, and the novelty of the affair had worn off, there I was, in no better case than before. Worst indeed, having proved the failure of any substitute, however delightful. I was still in love with a child, a sanctimonious, sentimental, stubborn child.

And then, suddenly it seemed, a child no more. It was the birthday visit when she and Walter were fourteen years of age. I went, as had now become customary, to escort her home on the afternoon of the twelfth of March, and the moment I saw her I noticed the change. The sexless, carved-angel look had vanished. Though the Clevely diet and her growth upwards had assured that no flesh should accumulate on her bones, from somewhere Nature had found material enough for little pointed breasts which pressed against the material of her plain grey bodice, pulling it taut. The child had become a woman, the joy-giver, the child-bearer.

For me that was a miserable holiday; she seemed to have turned shy, losing what frank and confident friendliness she had ever felt for me. Nor was I the only one to suffer. Master Reed had bought her, as a birthday present, a fine gold ring with an inset sapphire, a trinket both valuable and beautiful. At the sight of it she burst into tears in which my experienced ear detected unmistakable hysteria and, holding one hand over the ring she had brought from Beauclaire, sobbed out that at Clevely nobody was allowed to wear more than one ring.

Her grandfather, with what I considered admirable restraint, said, "Well, wear them turn and turn about, then!" She turned, and sobbing flung herself upon him, putting her hands about his neck and saying that he had always been so good to her and she did not wish to displease him. He patted her awkwardly, and said, rather as though soothing a frightened horse, "There there. There there. It's all right. Don't upset yourself. There there."

Mistress Reed, with a look of controlled loathing, said, "If this is cloister hysteria, we want none of it here."

And where, I wondered, in her restricted life had she heard of "cloister hysteria," that ease in the shedding of tears which, alongside its opposite, stoic fortitude, is reckoned a virtue by all those communities who must make virtues or sins out of every natural thing. Her words inevitably made me take Maude's part and I said:

"Sudden contrasts are very upsetting. At Clevely she has so little and here she has so much. I remember when I was at Norwich we were all, for some prank which no one would confess to, confined to Dorter and Frater for a week. Then we were let out, and in the grass a single daisy had flowered. We all wept at the sight of it as though we had received news of bereavement."

"That," Mistress Reed said with cold dignity, "is exactly what I mean. Cloister hysteria. We don't want it here."

Maude pulled herself free of her grandfather's patting hand.

"You mean you don't want *me* here. That is nothing new. You never did. I've known for years that the sight of me affronts you. Everything you've ever given me was a sop to your conscience. I know. And you need not worry about my bringing the cloister here. I shall not come here again. When I go back I shall begin my novitiate."

Martin Reed banged his hand on the table.

"Enough!" he said. "That's enough. In all my days I never heard such a to-do over nothing. You, my girl," he looked at Maude, "will never be a novice with my consent. Five good pounds a year I paid them for your keep, and never in all my dealings have I had worse value for money. That'll stop. Tell them that. If they take you in a veil, they take you bare. See how they like that. As for you," he swung round and faced Mistress Reed, "all the wench said was true. Out of the house, first to Beauclaire, then to the nunnery. Why, God alone knows." He reached out and snatched up the ring which had precipitated the scene, and tossed it towards me. "Take it," he said, "give it to your leman. She can sell it and buy one of her boys some bit of gear that'll set him on the road to knighthood." He spat out the word as though it were an obscenity and rushed on, "That's been the ruin of us all, pretensions, with nothing behind them, sacrificing decent sober hard-working people and silly little girls who love the first person to speak a kind word and fine gentlemen so fine they'll wed lunatics for the sake of their acres. . . ." He had, on the whole, been coherent up to that point, then he began to mutter and babble.

I jumped up and went to him and took him by the arm.

"Master Reed, you are unwell. Let me help you to your room."

His weight, greater than I had reckoned for, defied me. I said to Walter, who throughout the whole business had sat watching, detached and observant, "Give me a hand." He came forward unwillingly and took the old man's other arm. We got him to bed and sent for the doctor, who bled him and diagnosed a fit of the choleric humour. No meat, he said, and no wine for two days, and we were all to take care not to anger him; he advised, too, that during the two days of low diet the old man should remain in bed.

So next morning, speaking as usual, looking pale after his bleeding, Master Reed said, "Send Maude to me." My heart, which had been very low since those words about the novitiate, rose a little. He looked very pitiable, propped against his pillows, and she, I knew, was fond of him; maybe he could talk her round. But I found, when I went in search of her, that she had gone already, stealing out before breakfast and taking one of the yard boys with her to bring back her horse.

I began then to think seriously about my future. With Maude in a nunnery and Master Reed likely, according to the doctor, to fall down dead any time he was crossed, my prospects were not promising. It was too late now to begin insinuating myself into Mistress Reed's favour; in the event of my master's dying I should be out on my ear smartly.

Up to that time I had been completely honest in my dealings, which included handling considerable sums of money and negotiating even larger ones. But from that St. Joseph's Day I began to emulate the Unjust Steward in the Bible story, whom Our Lord Himself praised for his foresight rather than blamed for his dishonesty. I was very careful, never taking more in coin, or making as a false entry more than could, at a pinch, be regarded as a genuine mistake; and it was all the easier because after that birthday visit and Maude's running away my master began to decline, not only in body but in mind and spirit. He began to talk of Maude as though she were dead, and sometimes he would call her Kate, and then catch himself.

I said to him once, "You mustn't despair too soon. Every novice doesn't take vows by any means."

"Despair," he said. "It isn't that. It's acceptance. It all goes by rule and the rule laid down for me was that Walter the smith's son should never have anything."

Then he said, "Did I say Walter the smith's son? My memory plays tricks. I knew him as a boy. It's I who must lose all I gain."

"Oh, come," I said, "you've been very successful in business."

"Yes, I've got a good business." He said it as though he mocked himself and it.

When the time came round for the five pounds to be sent to Clevely he sent it meekly; and charged me to tell Maude that she had but to ask for anything more that she needed. That message I was not able to deliver since Maude was either not allowed or had herself chosen not to see me. Dame Clarice took the money and told me, kindly but firmly, that it was impossible for me to see Maude.

Before I got back to the highway I dismounted and lay in a field full of tall white marguerites. I threw myself from side to side, crushing the flowers, full of misery and self-pity and fury at my own folly. To have let romantic love get hold of me and wreck my happiness, fool, sick-minded fool! Gay Nicholas Freeman, over whom several women had cried, lying in a damp field, perilously near crying himself!

I resolved to throw off this weakness. Good-by to Maude Reed, I thought, when at last I rose up and brushed the grass and broken petals from my clothes. Being already halfway to Minsham, I would go on, and see Clemence and take full pleasure in the thing I had, instead of crying, like a baby, for what was out of reach.

IV

HALFWAY through the next month, July, any wrong which Mistress Reed had done her daughter, and through her Master Reed and me, was repaid tenfold.

Walter walked into the dining hall for the midday dinner carrying his lute and wearing his best clothes. His mother made some comment upon his attire, and he said, as casually as though he were announcing a visit to church or a nearby fair:

"I'm going to Walsingham. A party sets out this afternoon."

I knew, and so did his grandfather, that the hour had struck. Mistress Reed, ever blind to what she did not wish to see, spoke for a moment as though he were merely joining a pilgrimage. Did they go mounted or afoot? Were any of the party known to her by name?

His smooth, secret face took on for a moment the bony stubborn look that was his sister's.

"They're tumblers and jugglers, riffraff. We shall walk, from Walsingham to Lynn and then to Lincoln."

She could not be blind to that. She turned pale, and with trembling lips began to plead.

"Too young," she said. "You're too young, Walter. Wait just a year, one more year. I promise then that you shall go, if you want to, with my blessing."

"I'm as old as Maude, and she has chosen what she is to be."

"Girls are always older for their age. Besides, Maude is safe." She reached out and took him by the wrist. "Walter, I beg of you. The roads are full of dangers. Thieves," she said. "Cutthroats."

"The poor are safe enough. Thieves only set upon merchants with fat moneybags." He gave Master Reed a saucy, provocative glance.

"Don't be so sure," his grandfather retorted. "The only time I was set upon, beaten, and left for dead, I was in rags and hadn't a farthing to my name."

"There are plenty on the road who would kill you for your shoes," Mistress Reed said. She turned, still holding her son's wrist, and appealed

to the old man. "Forbid it," she said. "You are head of the family and
he is only a child. Forbid him to go."

He said harshly, "What would be the use?"

Walter jerked his wrist free.

"All this fuss," he said disgustedly. "It isn't even sudden. I've been saying for years what I would do. And now, I know, is the time."

As he said the last words he threw back his head, and the fine black
hair that was smoothly clubbed about his skull shifted and stirred, as
though, in that still place, a free wild wind blew on him.

"You must take some money," Master Reed said, "in case of sickness,
or other ill-fortune. It must be sewn into the lining of your jerkin."

"You're encouraging him," said Mistress Reed, beginning to cry. "I see
it . . . because I let Maude go, you . . . Walter . . . yes, I see. I'll
fetch her home, I promise. Make Walter stay here and I'll persuade
Maude."

Walter jumped up and grabbed his lute and looked ready to run.

"Wait," the old man said. "You must have the money and the names
of honest men I know in many towns, who would help in case of
trouble. I'd have done as much for her," he added inconsequently, "if
I had known."

"Nor is that all," cried Mistress Reed, checking her tears. "Walter, wait.
I never wholly believed—you see, your father talked the same way and he
never . . . no matter now—I never believed you would go, or so soon. I
would have done something about it. Don't waste your music on the
greasy gaping crowd, Walter. Make something of it. Go to Beauclaire or
Rivington, or to your Uncle Godfrey at Horsbury where you could be
heard by those who could advance you. Music like yours should be
played at Westminster or Windsor."

That was flattery. To do him justice, I will say that during the last
months his playing had improved and the spell which he could cast on
his hearers now had solid worth behind it. But Westminster and Windsor!

Walter said, "I would hate that way. To be taken up because this man
was my cousin or that one my uncle. Not for me! When I go to Windsor
or Westminster it will be as plain Walter Reed, the strolling player. *And
I shall go by invitation.*"

Since the day when I heard the fourteen-year-old grandson of a wool
merchant speak those words, I have mingled with the great; I have spoken
with crowned kings and stood in the presence of St. Peter's anointed
successor. I have never, anywhere at any time, heard anyone speak so
arrogantly.

Mistress Reed, her last card thrown and the game lost, said in a dull
voice, "Come, let me sew in your money."

"Wait," Walter said. He looked into the hall, where the weavers and yardmen and such pack-whackers as were home for dinner that day had their eyes and ears upon our table, even as they plied their knives and spoons. He climbed onto the bench where he had been sitting and took up his lute.

"I am going away for a little while," he said in the clear, confident voice of one already used to addressing a mob. "This is my farewell to you. It is called 'A Song at Parting.' I made it for this occasion."

He had based it on one of those old pagan tales which had managed to slip through the close net of censorship which the Church had tried to drop between the stories of the antique world and those of Christendom. In a light, pleasing voice, neither child's nor man's, he sang of the final leave-taking between Orpheus and Eurydice, when, he having broken the condition of her release from Hades, she must turn back into the shadow world.

I suppose everyone within hearing, the stolid Flemish weavers, the rough urchins who swept the stables, the brutal drivers of the pony teams, and the maids who came crowding into the doorway to the kitchen, had at some time known a parting from someone of whom they were fond. The song spoke direct to the memory. I sat there, thinking of Maude, that tender mouth never to be kissed, that slim, just nubile body doomed to sterile virginity. I felt my own eyes moisten. Mistress Reed broke down and put her face in her hands and sobbed without restraint. Everyone cried except Master Reed, who stared straight ahead of him, God knows at what ghosts.

Walter struck the last note; looked around with satisfaction and jumped down from the bench.

Perhaps his music had touched his own heart. He laid a hand on his mother's shoulder and said, "I'm not going for good. I shall be back one day."

Master Reed got heavily to his feet and said, "I'll go get the money. Show it to nobody, Walter, and don't speak of it. Keep it in case of need."

V

WALTER's departure had two results. Martin Reed now began to speak openly of me as his successor.

"It'll be in your hands," he said, speaking of the business. "Even if Walter comes home when he tires of the road, he'll know nothing. I want my daughter-in-law kept in comfort so long as she lives and I've always

helped keep her father who'll probably live to be a hundred. Then there's
Maude's dower. And I hope you'll get a family of your own. So you'll
need to keep busy."

The third time he spoke to me in this strain I said to him frankly,
"Unless, sir, you make a will and state clearly that it is your wish for me
to take charge of the business, all these plans will come to nothing. If
you die intestate, Walter is your heir, and his mother on the spot will be
his regent. Before you are in your grave—God forgive me for mentioning
such a thing—I shall have a month's wage and my quittance."

I spoke the more surely because, since Walter's going, the relationship
between Mistress Reed and myself had undergone a great change for the
worse; and for a reason which no one would credit.

She had attempted to assuage her melancholy over the loss of her son
in a way unusual to women; she took to drink. Openly, at the supper
table, she would drink three or four cups of wine in place of her usual
one; and secretly too. I've gone into the solar in an evening and found
her there, her hands idle on a piece of embroidery or plain sewing, and
the air reeking of brandewijn; I've seen the cup standing on the floor,
half, but not quite, hidden by her skirts. I've passed her on the stairs,
standing aside where they widened and turned to allow her to go by, and
smelled the same pungent odour, and she just come from her bedroom,
early in the day.

She was never noisy or truculent; indeed in her cups she became more
agreeable; the lines of her face would lift and soften. One realised, for
the first time that, if she married young as most girls do and quickened
soon after, she could still be just short of thirty. My Clemence was thirty-
two. Mistress Reed had always seemed at least ten years older. But
drunken, she lost something of her stiff, cool, self-contained look.

One evening, when Walter had been gone a month, I came in late,
from Minsham. I had no more reason for secrecy, for over the episode of
the ring on that fatal birthday morning Master Reed had betrayed that
he knew about my attachment. After that any errand of supervision of
the Minsham sheep run, where the sheep from the Cotswolds still flourished and produced their overweight in wool, would be undertaken in
the afternoon; then I would have supper with Clemence, make love, and
ride home.

It was now four months since Maude had gone back to Clevely without even a good-by, and my defences were building up. As I rode home
I had thought to myself that if I could persuade Martin Reed to put me
upon a sure footing, either now, or by will, which would take care of
the future, I might do far worse than marry Clemence. She had much
the same background as Mistress Reed and would be a match for her, I

thought. And though the two boys were imps straight from Hell—you could almost smell the brimstone on them—one thorough good beating apiece, which as their stepfather I should have the right to administer, would improve their manners if not their characters. I toyed with this thought, not enthusiastically, but rather with the resignation of someone making the most he could of the second best, all the way home, while on the warm night air the scent of honeysuckle and meadowsweet lay heavy.

I noticed as I came to the Old Vine that there was a light in the solar window. Mistress Reed, a bit drunken, had left the candles burning, I thought. When I'd stabled my horse I would go in and pinch them out.

When I re-entered the passage which ran clear through the house, the solar door was open and she was standing just inside. Her hair, which I had never before seen completely uncovered, hung loose to her shoulders, very curly and pretty, pale gold. She wore a blue velvet bedchamber robe, so ungirded that I could see her breasts. And they were pretty too. She was very drunk.

I was reminded of my first visit to a house of ill-fame. It stood in a narrow lane, just off Tombland, in Norwich; the girls had worn exactly that half-revealing, half-concealing garb, and that same air of deliberate welcome.

"You're very late," she said.

"Yes, I am. Would you like me to put out the candles for you?"

"No. Not yet. Come and talk to me for a little while." She put her hand on my arm and I went into the room with her. She moved towards the window, which stood wide on the garden. The lopsided moon which had lighted me home hung like a lantern, and the sweet night air, the breath of flowers and green things growing came in to mingle with the sharp scent of the brandewijn.

"I'm so lonely," she said. "Years and years and years with nobody to talk to."

She sat down on the window seat and would have pulled me down beside her, but I stiffened myself, and her hand, as I resisted, slid down from my arm to my hand. She twisted her fingers so that for a moment they were twined with mine, and she looked at me with as plain an invitation as any woman ever gave any man.

I thought very rapidly; a dozen thoughts in a breath's space. Ha, I thought, and I had believed that it was too late to work my way in with her. And I thought how amusing to see the trollop who had lived behind that screen of whalebone and good breeding. And I thought: You are the one who sent Maude to Beauclaire and therefore to Clevely and I will have no truck with you. Other thoughts I had too, of how long she had lived widowed, of things Clemence had murmured in moments of joy, of how it was better to live out your time as a maid than to be widowed since what you had never had you did not miss. Almost I could be sorry for her. But not quite. Besides, I had just come from Clemence and there was no desire in me. So I pulled my fingers free and said: "Madam, it is too late now for talk. I am for bed. I advise you to do the same."

She began to whimper, saying that she could not sleep; that once the brandewijn would assure her slumbers, but now no more.

"In the end there is nothing," she said. "Nothing left. Nothing at all."

I reached over her bowed head and closed the window and latched it. As I did so she half rose and pressed herself against me. I stepped back and said, "Madam, you are not quite yourself this evening. Come take my arm and I will help you upstairs." I left one candle burning and put out the rest.

Still whimpering, she said, "I *am* myself. Locked in, all alone with terrible things to remember." She looked at me with drunken cunning and with a change of tone said, "Ah, you would like to know, wouldn't you? And all I'll tell you is that God has taken away Walter, to punish me. So I'm all alone and even you won't be kind to me."

My surprise and mixed feelings had settled down now into simple disgust. I said briskly, "I am always civil to you, madam. Even now I am offering you my arm, and to light you upstairs."

She gave me a beaten look, but she put her hand in the crook of the arm I offered and moving unsteadily mounted the stairs. At the door of her own room she paused.

"They come and stand by the bed and look at me," she said in a complaining, confidential way. "They never did that before. I'm afraid." For a second I suspected that this was a cunning trick to get me into her bedchamber; but almost immediately her manner underwent another sudden change. "I shan't flinch," she said. "The blood of brave men runs in me. Let them do their worst."

She opened the door and marched in, as though meeting a challenge, and before I could give her the candle slammed the door in my face.

I went on to my bed thinking about Joseph and Potiphar's wife. As a character I had never much admired him, but now I saw the story from his viewpoint. I only hoped that when she woke, soreheaded and sober in the morning, she would have forgotten the whole episode. But her manner betrayed her. She had never been markedly pleasant to me, now she became even less so, always speaking to me in a cold, contemptuous way and taking trouble to make wounding remarks. She told me that I was going bald very early, and another time said that I was getting fat, unbecoming in a young man; she even hinted that my hose could do with a wash. One would have thought that I was the one who had made an attempt to seduce her.

That was why I spoke frankly to Master Reed of the need to make his will; but like all unlearned and self-made fellows he regarded the making of a will as tantamount to signing his death warrant.

"Yes," he said, "I will see about that." And did nothing.

For a boy who had evinced so little affection for his family while he lived in its bosom, Walter wrote very regularly and at some length. I suspect that some, at least, of his letters were written to advertise his skill and in the hope of drawing custom. He had plainly become one of the great fellowship of the open road, and at various times his letters were delivered to the Old Vine by tinkers, minstrels, pilgrims, friars, and merchants. Once even a gay young knight, with two squires in his train and his jousting armour on a pack horse, came jingling along to hand in a letter which Walter had written at Nottingham Castle.

"The boy played with such skill," he explained, "that I invited him to come with me to Colchester, where I join my Lord Delahaye who has a lively appreciation of talent. The young knave made mock of my offer, but said that if I went to Colchester I could deliver a letter for him. It has added some miles to my journey, but no matter; I have seen the nest that hatched so sweet a throstle."

Master Reed and I had just finished supervising the loading of one of the pony trains, and were on our way into the house.

"If you would be pleased to dismount and enter, sir," Martin said, "you would be welcome to the best I have to offer."

"I thank you, but I am already delayed."

"Run find your mistress," Master Reed said to me; and to the young knight, "One moment more, for charity. The boy's mother . . . it would ease her mind to speak with one who saw him so recently."

Mistress Reed came running out, and the knight doffed his feathered cap and answered with civility the questions she asked about how Walter looked, was he still well shod, and what kind of company he was in. He repeated the story of his offer to introduce Walter to Lord Delahaye, and Mistress Reed, already a little mazed with wine, drew herself up with great dignity and said:

"If Walter had wanted advancement in that way he could have gone to his cousin Astallon at Beauclaire."

The young knight said, "Madam, your son will never lack advancement. With his skill and effrontery he should go far."

If Walter's letters were to be believed, such offers, and some even more dazzling, were an everyday matter to him. His reply was always that to him confinement in a great house, even a palace, would be as irksome as in a small. He seemed more impressed by his smaller triumphs, "everybody wept," "some women came and kissed my hand," "a man gave me his last farthing."

Mistress Reed kept all the letters in a box of carved wood, spent hours brooding over them and fingering them, and constantly referred to them as proof that Walter was dutiful, that he remembered his home and family with affection and would most surely return.

Once when she said that, Master Reed said, mildly but with meaning, "We trust that he will. And it would be a pity if he found us in less good fettle than he left us."

That was the most pointed remark he ever made to her in my presence; but then, despite his lack of learning and his gruffness, he was not insensitive. Whether in private he remonstrated with her I do not know. To me, on one occasion, when her insobriety was such as no one could overlook, he said:

"Poor woman. She cannot face grief. When her mother died it was the same, and when Richard died. It is her refuge, as work has been mine." He thought for a second, sticking out his underlip. "At least she hurts nobody but herself," he said. "By my work I've ruined two men that I know of, and probably others."

I forgot Mistress Reed. I thought to myself: It is a bad sign when old men who have led successful lives begin to look back and reckon what damage they have done. It is a foreshadowing of the final reckoning which they are preparing to face.

Time went on; the seasons changed. My little secret hoard of coins grew, more swiftly as Martin Reed relaxed, bit by bit, the strictness of his supervision. Physical changes in those one sees several times every day escape one's observation; it was with surprise that one summer evening, coming suddenly upon Mistress Reed in the garden, with the level rays of the westering sun full upon her, I realised that she had grown fat and that puckers of loose skin hung like little bags beneath her eyes and under her jaw. She was drunk, as usual; and she was staring so fixedly at a place where the grass grew lush under an apple tree that I thought she had dropped something and was searching for it. She actually pressed one hand against the trunk of ths tree for support, and, thus balancing, bent over and with her other hand touched the grass.

I was going straight past her, but she heard my step on the path and straightened up, and, squeezing her eyes against the light of the sun, said, as though we had been for some time in converse:

"That is the *one* thing that is sure and certain, the one thing you can count on. God punishes every sin."

"So we are taught," I agreed, and made to pass on.

"But we don't believe it. That is where we make our mistake. And then it is so subtle. The punishment never comes either from the direction, or in the form that you expect. Bear that in mind. You plant a sin like a grain of wheat and you think punishment will come up, a full ear of wheat. For that you are prepared. But it isn't wheat that comes up; it's a damask rose, and you pluck it, and the thorns tear your flesh and the scent of it is poison. I know what I'm saying."

"I have no doubt of that, madam. Would you like my arm to assist you into the house? Then I must ask you to excuse me."

I went on into the house, thinking that here we were with another year almost half gone, Midsummer Eve again. And Master Reed still with his will not made, my future still very insecure, and Clemence growing a little, a very little, but still noticeably cooler. It was fifteen months since Maude had gone back to begin her novitiate, and though I had done my best to shut her out of mind, more than once, in the very act with Clemence, I had suddenly thought of her and gone impotent. That had frightened me; and Clemence, sympathetic the first time, had turned suspicious the second.

Leaving Mistress Reed, mauldin under the apple tree, I thought to myself: It hardly needs God to punish us; we somehow contrive to punish ourselves.

VI

THE news about Walter took a long time to reach us. A letter written in the April of 1451 arrived from Gloucester in June. It said he was well, and about to set out for Winchester. After that there was silence.

We should hear at Christmas, Master Reed said; yes, Mistress Reed echoed, we should certainly hear at Christmas. But the season came and went without a word. Mistress Reed burrowed more securely into her refuge, and the old man said, whether to comfort himself or her, that the absence of news might be a good sign. Probably in the autumn, faced with the discomforts of another winter, Walter had turned his face for home and therefore did not think to write.

Then, on a blustery March evening, my master and I were in the office when a servant girl, white of face and wide of eye, ran in and said that there was a creature asking for Master Reed at the yard door.

"If you mean a beggar, say so," Martin said, and prepared to lever himself out of his chair.

"I'll go," I said, and jumped up.

"If it's a letter or a message from Walter, bring the bearer in. A spoken word tells twice as much," Master Reed called after me.

The servant girl ran straight back to the kitchen instead of hanging about, as their habit is, to catch a word out of which to make a long story.

When I reached the door I realised that her use of the word "creature" had a frightful accuracy. There are the natural deformities to which the eye becomes accustomed, the squints, harelips, hunchbacks, mutilations due to accident or battle. But there is another sort, inflicted by unscrupulous showmen upon infant children. They take them when their bones are soft and pliable and shape them, as a gardener shapes a tree that is to be espaliered. Then, if the unfortunate child survives—few do—they have something truly unusual, something out of nature, for a sight of which, in a dim-lighted booth, the sensation seekers will hand over their pence.

This was one such, a striking example of the devilish art. His left arm had been trained to grow behind his head, so that he had two arms, one long and one short on the same side, and his head appeared to grow from under his arm, like those of a strange people mentioned in some traveller's tale.

In his armpit his head lay sideways, so that to look up he must turn his eyes almost out of their sockets.

"Are you Master Martin Reed?" he asked. His voice was muted.

"I'll take you to him," I said, sickened beyond being able even to ask his business. With my back to him as he pattered after me towards the office I managed to ask, "Is it anything concerning Walter Reed?"

"Yes. Yes. Bad news that I hate to tell. But I promised."

Outside the office door, which I had closed behind me because the wind was raging through the house, I said, "Wait here a moment." I went in.

"It is about Walter," I said, as gently as I could, "and bad news, he says. And the bearer, sir, is one of those freaks that they show at fairs—a shocking sight."

He drew a deep breath which lifted and straightened his heavy bowed shoulders.

"Let's know the worst," he said.

I admitted the poor creature, but did not go in myself. I went and sat on the stairs, near enough to be within call, telling myself that this was, after all, the proper thing to do. I was *not* one of the family, intimately as I lived with them; nevertheless, knowing the real reason for not going into the office, I knew that I was a deserter. Still, I was here if I was wanted. And in a minute, no more, the office door opened and Master

Reed, grey-faced but quite calm, came out, turned towards the kitchen, saw me, and stopped. He lifted a warning finger.

"Go and ask them to mull some ale," he said, almost in a whisper, "and bring it and some bread and meat to the office. Then go and bring down my sheepskin coat. The poor creature's starving and soaked to the skin."

The stout old cook and the two serving girls were in a huddle by the kitchen fire, sharing a horrified pleasure.

"Is it gone?" asked the girl who had answered the door.

"The master is asking for mulled ale and bread and meat, in the office; and look lively," I said.

"I ain't taking it in. Opening the door and seeing *that* stand there hev took ten years off my life already."

"Put the things outside the door of the office, then, and knock. And look sharp," I said.

As I went out of the kitchen I heard the girl say, "Use a crock we can smash, Kitty; if I'd to set my lips to cup *that'd* used, it'd turn my stomach."

I went and fetched the coat, and, not wishing to behave like a silly serving wench, went into the room, determined to conceal my aversion. The poor creature knelt, shivering, by the fire. Master Reed still sat at his table. I looked at him questioningly and he said:

"The boy's dead, Nicholas; in bad circumstances."

I mumbled that I was sorry, which was true, though my feeling was, in the main, pity for him.

He was a remarkable man; there is a great deal of talking—and some writing too—about the beauties of chivalry, of physical courage, hardihood in the face of danger, all of it very far removed in most people's estimation from an old wool merchant whose hand had never closed on a sword hilt; but that evening he was magnificent in his fortitude. He got up and took the coat from me and went over to the grotesque and said:

"Throw off your wet things and hug this about you. You'll soon be warm. Food and drink are coming." Then, as though resuming the conversation which my entry had interrupted, he said, "That kind of thing means a lot to women. She may well ask what infirmary. Can we answer?"

"There is a House of White Ladies nearby."

"We'll tell her that. The best of nursing, the kindest of attention. After all, the boy's father," he paused and swallowed, "was in his own bed, he had every care, and a physician, yet he died. She will believe, and feel that no one was to blame."

The serving girl tapped on the door. She had gone by the time I opened

it. I took in the cup and the platter and carried them to the freak, who
had wriggled out of his clothes and was wearing the coat as a cape. His
own jerkin, I noticed, with a fresh little thrill of distaste, had been made
for him; it had no sleeve on one side, two on the other. He snatched at
the things I offered, taking the mug in the hand nearest his face, the platter in the other.

Watching his ravenous attack upon the food, Master Reed said, "There's
plenty more. Ask if you want it." He then gave one of his great sighs and
set himself in motion. "I must break this to his mother. She might insist on
seeing you. You know what to say if she does."

"I know, master. Maybe I should've softened the tale for you. It never
entered my head."

"No, for me the truth was best. And I thank you for bringing it."

He indicated with a jerk of his head that I was to look after the freak
and went limping away. I pulled a chair into a position from which I
could look straight ahead of me without seeing the man who was still
stuffing his mouth like a man filling a sack in a hurry.

"What is the truth?" I asked.

"He died, alongside me in Winchester gaol. November, December, cruel
cold it was, the walls running with water and puddles on the floor. He
took a cold and then a cough and it killed him. Not but what that was a
mercy in a way; he'd have burned, otherwise. They'd got upwards of
twenty witnesses and that was too much to overlook even though he did
have friends in high places, and the Bishop himself was inclined to give
Walter the benefit of the doubt. He was so young, too, and had such a
nice way with him, enough to make anybody wonder. But twenty witnesses and more. No, that was too much. And in broad daylight too."

"What had he done?" I asked; though I knew all but the details of the
answer, for I remembered that summer evening, the hasty angry words,
the grandfather's warning.

The man by the fire crammed his mouth and chewed loudly.

"Mind, I wasn't there. I was in the gaol then—for stealing—but never
mind me. I only know what Walter said, and that wasn't much, till they
took his lute away he used to spend his time playing, only afterwards,
when he was sick and heartbroke did he talk. And of course when I was
turned loose I heard the talk. They're talking about it still in Winchester;
some feel a bit ill-done by to have missed the burning."

He chewed again and resumed his tale.

In Winchester there was always a fair on St. Luke's Day, and most
often it was a summer day crept into autumn. "St. Luke's little summer"
people called it. This year was no exception; the sun shone clear and
bright. There was a man who sold medicine, guaranteed to cure anything

from a winter cough to the stone, and he gathered his crowd about him by banging on a drum. Twice during the morning Walter's playing had stolen his crowd away before he had sold much, and about midday the man had approached Walter and protested. Walter had moved away, but the people had followed, and within an hour the medicine-seller had come to him again and suggested a partnership.

"They say—but of course afterwards people will say anything—they say he offered him a fourth share, Walter to play and gather the crowd and then break off in the middle of a tune and let the man cry his wares. And they say that then Walter went white with rage and said, 'Am I to play that you may gull fools? Devil take your pills and potions.' Fifty people claim to have heard him say that."

He broke the tale and I heard him chewing. I also heard, from the other side of the house, some wild, most lamentable crying. I pitied Master Reed from the bottom of my heart.

The story went on. Within five minutes, before in fact the medicine-seller could get back to his stall, a bullock, running amok from the nearby cattle market, crashed into it; became entangled; and stamping, rolling, tossing its head, smashed every pill to powder and broke to fragments the thing which had been the medicine-maker's greatest pride and treasure, a big flask of Venetian glass, half full of red liquid which he claimed to be the elixir of life—the other half had been, he said, poured into the pills.

"Well," the freak said in his soft voice, "that could have been accident, though they counted it uncanny that, except to that one stall, the beast did no damage and was easily taken. In itself that would never have damned him. But next day . . ."

Next day the medicine man, with nothing to sell and a damage to avenge, took his drum and followed Walter round, banging loudly and out of time, spoiling his music. At first only a few people, who cared neither one way nor the other found this amusing, but presently even those who wanted to hear the proper music gave way and found the situation rather comic, and laughed. Walter stopped playing. He took some coins from his pocket and threw them towards the man with the drum.

"Will that buy your silence?" he asked.

The man scooped up the money and said, "Aye"; then, as Walter began to play again, amended it to, "Aye, for two minutes," and banged on his drum. The crowd laughed. Walter said, and this was what twenty reliable people were prepared to swear to, "Then there's no help for it. Let your arm wither."

"And they say that it did. It fell limp and began to grow small. By evening it was dry and shrivelled as a twig. There it was, and no help for it. One day he was mixing medicine and banging his drum—the next helpless. And twenty people near enough to hear what the boy said. It was hopeless. The Church court had him first and they handed him over to the secular arm, and that meant the townspeople. And how they felt is shown by what happened to the bullock. They claimed that was no ordinary beast, but possessed of the Devil. They burned it alive, and those who hadn't tasted meat in six weeks or seven forbore to touch a shred of it, though it lay there, open to all."

How much to believe; how much to discount? I sat there and wondered.

At last I said, "The boy himself; did he think he was guilty?"

"How can I answer that? In the beginning I thought he was a thief, like me. In the end, when they'd taken away his lute and he was miserable and talked more, he said . . . Yes, once he said that to feel strongly enough was to have power. I do remember that. I remember because I said that it was not so, because I felt strongly the wish to be shaped like other people; and he said what was done was done. And then he said that he wished . . . No, he said, 'If I had the power they say I have, I'd wish one wish for myself, to be out of this, and free, in the open, with my lute in my hand.' And he had half of his wish, for presently he coughed and choked on the blood and died, and they did put his lute in the grave with him. Or so I am told."

He went on with his supper, and we sat in silence until Master Reed came in, looking like a man who had just been released from the rack. But his most immediate concern was to find a place for the deformed man to sleep. When that was settled and I ventured to offer a few words of sympathy, he looked at me steadily and said:

"Poor child. With such promise too. But the two things sprang from the same root. And I knew it. That made me less firm than I should have been. Poor Walter." He sighed again. "Maude should be here," he said. "Her mother'll need her, and I need her. I've not been firm enough in the past, but over this I shall be firm. Maude must come home."

VII

FROM the way in which Mistress Reed had behaved since Walter's departure, and the wild cries with which she had received the news of his death, I expected the following days to be made hideous by the manifestations of her grief and by her efforts to escape it. I looked ahead and imagined that life at the Old Vine, never very cheerful of late, would become dreary in the extreme. For the first time I began to wonder whether there might not be something unlucky about the house itself, or about the family. I knew I was a long way from being the carefree, cheerful, philandering fellow who had come there to teach Walter his letters. However, I soon shrugged that thought aside as nonsense. I pitied Master Reed, and his daughter-in-law too, but Walter's death had not harmed me; my future indeed looked brighter and more certain. And, I thought to myself, although Walter was buried, far away in Winchester, there would surely be a Requiem Mass for him, and surely Maude would be bound to attend, and perhaps she would feel some pity for her grandfather and decide to come home and gladden his last years. It was a frail hope, but I clung to it.

I kept well way from the house all the morning, and at twelve o'clock went in for my dinner. The square family table was unoccupied. The men assembling at the long tables were quieter than usual, and the serving girls, running round with bowls of meaty broth, had an air of suppressed excitement. The news about Walter had spread, I thought. The door behind me, the one which led into the main part of the house, opened, and Master Reed, instead of entering, stood in the opening and beckoned me to join him.

"Come here," he said, and stumped away up the stairs and to the door of Mistress Reed's room. His face wore a strange expression, something only just short of pleasure as he opened the door and said, "What do you make of that?"

It was as though he were showing me something which, after long labour, he had made, or, after long waiting, had at last achieved.

Mistress Reed sat on the edge of her bed, dressed as far as her petticoat; she held a comb in her hand and was slowly almost sensuously passing it through the length of her hair. She acknowledged our presence by the open door by turning her head; there was no interest, no recognition, no expression at all in her face. The lines which discontent, grief, and anxiety had graved had all been wiped away, leaving a blank placidity. It was the face of a half-finished statue whose maker has not yet decided whether it shall portray joy or sorrow.

Having once looked our way, she looked away again and resumed her slow combing. Master Reed gently closed the door and said, "She has been like that all morning. Pray God she stays so."

"Amen to that," I said. "Her father did."

"Aye. That's the way it takes them. He turned simple when his wife died." He pondered for a second. "It's not much of a life, but better than being crazed with grief; and easier for everybody else. I must set one of the wenches to mind her."

In one way Mistress Reed was more fortunate than her sire; if the materials were put in her lap, or by her side, she would stitch away, contentedly, for hours. She no longer made anything, just worked away on long hems and seams, or did embroidery stitches without any design or pattern. One of the serving girls, glad of the easy task, devoted all her time to her.

On the third or fourth day Master Reed said, "We need a girl to take Phyllis' place in the kitchen. And who has time to see to that? Not you. Not I. This house lacks a mistress. Maude should come home, now. She must come home."

"The question is, will she?"

"Properly tackled, I think so. For one thing a house without a mistress is as tempting to any woman worth her salt as a ship without a captain to a sailor. For another, it offers her a chance to do something that would *count*, as she calls it. To come home and look after the sick woman who, all these years, was never fair to her, is to return good for evil, surely. Yes, that'll appeal to Maude. I'll go to Clevely tomorrow."

It rained in the night, and though the morning was fine a biting wind blew and the heavy black clouds rushing across the sky threatened more rain or even snow. I was in the weaving shed, settling some petty dispute, when I looked through the wide window and saw Master Reed emerge from the house; so muffled in clothes as to be shapeless and wearing a woollen cap pulled over his ears and brow. Remembering how he had held close to the house all winter, and thinking of the inclement weather, I went down and said unwillingly, because I doubted the outcome of the errand and felt that if it failed he would blame me:

"Let me go, sir."

"No. You mean kindly, but you don't have enough authority. Today I'm going to have it out. My mind is made up, and when my mind is set I mostly get my way."

I realised, with a faint start of surprise, that that was true. Mild and quiet as he was, this whole great business with its many aspects ran smoothly under his absolute authority; only within doors, with his family, did anything displeasing to him continue for longer than it took for him to notice it. He had given in to Maude's whim, Walter's waywardness, Mistress Reed's insobriety, not from weakness, but from kindness of heart.

Well, I thought, all power go with you. I helped him into his saddle, and then stared at the evidence of his confidence in himself, another horse, saddled with Maude's own saddle, and wearing a leading rein was led out. Master Reed took the rein, said, "Come up, then," and they trotted out of the yard.

When I went in to dinner one of the maids was thumping about in Maude's room, making it ready.

And faith, we are told, can remove mountains.

While we were at dinner there was a short sharp shower; but immediately after, just as I was leaving the house, the sun came out. I stood for a moment beside a lilac bush which had thrust a branch over the garden fence; it shimmered with buds, wetly green. Somewhere in the depths of the garden a bird was singing with passionate joy and the golden light lay everywhere like a blessing. I was suddenly certain that Maude would come home that afternoon, and that everything would be well. Anticipation ran, with the tickling thrill of a finger touch, all the way from my thighs to my throat.

Half an hour later it was snowing lightly, and when, in the premature twilight, my master rode home, alone, he was furred all over with white, even his eyebrows bore their little load.

I had imagined, from the length of his absence, that Maude had packed her goods, and that the return journey had been made with laden slowness. But the led horse's saddle was empty except for the snow.

Master Reed replied to my unspoken comment, "I went on to Minsham and took a look at the sheep. Had to do something to settle my mind."

He dismounted stiffly, and, instead of pushing away my proffered arm, took it and leaned on it heavily.

"It's been a bad day, my boy. And a fine fool I made of myself, as you shall hear."

I had made a good fire in the office, and a pint of well-spiced ale in a pewter mug waited on the hearth. I'd had the poker in and out of the heart of the fire for the last two hours, and now I pushed it home again. By the time I had helped him to shuffle off his wrappings it was glowing red, and I plunged it into the ale.

"That'll warm you, sir," I said, handing him the steaming brew.

"It's cooling I need. Feel that if you doubt me." He reached out his free hand and touched mine. "You'll understand, if I can bring myself to tell you."

My curiosity was lively; but the hand he had laid on mine was unnaturally hot and I remembered what the doctor had said about the danger of his being upset. I said as soothingly as possible, "I can see for myself that you are disappointed. Beyond that you can tell me as much or as little as you like."

"That's right! Now you begin to talk to me as though I were a baby. That's all I need after the day I've had."

He sipped his ale and I saw the sweat break out on his forehead. He pulled at the neck of his jerkin, exposing his stringy throat. Another thought struck me.

"Mistress Maude . . . she is well, I hope."

"How can I know? I tell you I never even . . . But I'd best begin at the beginning."

Clevely had altered; he'd spotted the change as soon as the place came in sight. Upwards of fifty ewes gathered in a field for lambing, with a shepherd and a boy in charge; another man in the houseyard, and not a nun to be seen anywhere. And the old kitchen door was now fenced off and a new one made at the far end of the house, with a deep porch in front of it and a portress to answer the bell. He'd asked for the Prioress, which was mere courtesy, since everyone knew that she was now bed-fast; but it was not our old friend Dame Clarice Gracey who came into the cold little room where he was bidden to wait; it was a new nun, young, not more than thirty, who said she was the Prioress, so favouri-tism must have been at work to set her so high at that age.

He explained the situation and asked to see Maude. The Prioress, in a manner as smooth as cream, commiserated with him on the loss of his grandson and the indisposition of his daughter-in-law, but said that it was impossible for him to see Maude.

"Nicholas," he said, leaning forward a little, "when she said that it was like being hit over the heart. I thought she'd taken the veil without a word to us and I might never set eyes on her again. Come to my senses just too late, I thought, and for the rest of her days the poor silly child will come and go, eat or fast, sit or stand according to the word of this high-handed, mim-voiced bitch. And that roused my blood. I said even a nun was allowed to see her grandfather; I said she could stand by and hear every word that was spoken: I told her they weren't an enclosed order and if she didn't let me see Maude I'd complain to the Bishop. She wouldn't be ruffled; she said Maude was still a novice, free to see me or anybody else she'd a mind to, but I couldn't talk to her today because she wasn't at Clevely."

He hadn't believed that. He thought the Prioress quick-witted enough to have guessed what he wanted of Maude; and he thought of his five pounds a year; and he thought that maybe the Prioress had already seen that Maude was in two minds about the matter. So he as good as called her a liar to her face and accused her of not daring to let him talk to his granddaughter.

"So then, Nicholas, she said, 'Daren't is a strange word to use to me. What have I to fear? That you remove her from this house? I assure you I could fill her place ten times over and with girls well dowered.' Dowered is a word I hate the sound of. Before she could toddle it was dower, dower, dower. Hearing the word then, on top of all else, maddened me. I said, 'Then, if you've nothing to fear, why daren't you let me see her?'

And she said, 'If you suspect me of hiding her in this house, search it. It is unusual to make a man free of the house, but if it will set your mind at rest, you may have my permission to go anywhere and conduct your search.' And I thought to myself: There's been ample time for that woman at the door to carry warning and have the girl hidden somewhere. So I said, 'I thank you, madam. That I will do.' And I did."

He drained the mug and set it aside and began to twist his hands together. He had big hands, calloused and seamed with ingrained dirt which no amount of scouring would ever remove; but they were oddly skillful; he could splice a broken thread on a loom as neatly and delicately as any of the weavers who made the care of their hands an excuse for never handling a tool. Now he moved his hands as if he were trying to wrench out his fingers one by one.

"I went everywhere, not once only, twice, three times, turning back in my tracks in case they had Maude on the move. My boy, if she'd been the size of a bobbin I couldn't have missed her. Dorter, storeroom, chapel, cellar, everywhere. And it all so poor; I swear our bed in Squatters Row was softer and warmer than any in that house; and as for their storeroom, it was pitiable, braxy mutton and weevilly flour such as I wouldn't offer any seaman of mine to eat. And in the end, back I was in the little cold room and she waiting for me, saying, 'And now will you perhaps accuse me of spiriting the girl away?' Then she said she'd tell me what she would have at first if I had asked her. According to her, the singing at Clevely is an offence to the ear and an insult to God, so Maude and one other—the only ones that can carry a tune—are sent to Ramsey to learn better and come back and teach the rest."

"Enough to make any man angry," I said. "But why blame yourself? Your suspicion might have been correct. You acted rightly."

He moved one eyebrow.

"You think so? I felt all in the wrong. And I apologised. She took advantage of that. She talked about Clevely, all the improvements that must be made; how in the past it had not been a nunnery in the real sense of the word, just a place where women lived and worked together and went to Chapel when the milking was done or the butter made. She's going to alter all that; and her great need is money. Five pounds a year, she was good enough to say, was generous enough when Maude lodged there and worked to earn her keep, but since then, as I, a businessman should know, money had lost some value and the noble was worth but six shillings nowadays. She talked to me like a huckster. What did I propose to do for Maude when she took her vows? And there's Maude thinking that all the world outside has gone awry through love of money. And me, that always called a dower a bait for knaves. I'd have done better,

Nicholas, to have sent her to Beauclaire with the promise of a dower on a tag about her neck. A knave would at least have seen that the bed he had to share was soft and warm."

"What did you promise?"

"Nothing. I'm not that much of a fool. I tell you, we bargained like a couple of stockfishmongers. I said I wanted Maude to come home and see the state her mother was in, and I wanted one last good talk. Then, I said, if I could be sure that her mind was made up and no hope for it, I'd give a dowry they'd talk about for years. And so I will, but I must be sure first. She said that was fair enough and Maude will come home as soon as she's back from Ramsey."

"When will that be?"

"Oh, that depends on the singing." His voice took on a sardonic note and then changed. "And she did say one other thing, whether to set much store by it or not, I don't know. She said the visit to Ramsey would do Maude good, aside from the music, to let her see a properly conducted house, because that was how Clevely would be in future and discipline must be accepted meekly. That sounded to me a bit . . . but there, they have such a way of wrapping things up, half the time they mean something other than you'd think."

He shuddered suddenly and held out his hands to the fire.

In the morning he woke with a cold, of which he made light; the Minsham shepherd, he said, had a much worse one the day before and was out in the snow making a lambing pen. Giving this as an excuse for not keeping to his bed, he sneezed through the day, saying after each bout of sneezing, "There, that cleared it." He went to bed early with hot brick to his feet and a basin of onion gruel inside him. He'd budged many a cold with such simple remedies.

This one refused to be budged. It resisted even the curative measure of a day in bed, and by the third day had settled on his chest. He drew his breath with a wheeze and a rattle, and spoke with a hoarse croak. But he held that it was nothing but a cold, he'd had many worse. A linseed poultice was what he needed; surely to goodness somebody in the kitchen could make a linseed plaster.

The cook made it; and also a concoction of honey, vinegar, horehound, and cinnamon, upon whose virtue she was prepared to stake her own.

I took upon myself the application of the poultices, since, with Phyllis minding Mistress Reed, they were shorthanded in the kitchen. When I put it on hot that evening for the last time and settled him for the night, he seemed easier, and still most resolutely cheerful. But his cough, a rattling, ineffective effort to clear the clogged rheum from his chest, kept me awake most of the night. Three times I made a fresh plaster, plied him with the mixture, warmed a cup of milk.

"I shall get the physician to you in the morning," I said. He made no protest. Surprised and a little frightened by this, I thought that perhaps I should fetch the priest, too.

I wished that that could have been done in a more casual, less ominous way. But the Old Vine was not a house where the priest was a visitor; we had nothing to do with Baildon, our parish was Flaxham St. Giles, and the church and the priest's house were three miles away. Sir Andrew, the priest there, was elderly. To send for him was to hint that things were in a bad way.

I might have spared myself these cogitations, for in the grey dawn of the fourth day, when my master roused from an uneasy, restless doze, he stared at me for a moment as though he did not recognise me and then said, his voice more hoarse and weak than ever:

"It's beat me, my boy. I want the priest. Make my confession and my will at the same time."

"Sir Andrew?"

"Yes. Send a good horse . . . pillion."

"I will. But you mustn't lose heart, you know. You've got a stubborn cold and you can't throw it off as you did when you were younger. I'll get the doctor to you, too."

He wheezed out something about a waste of time, and something I didn't quite catch, about a hawthorn tree. Then he coughed and hawked and spoke more clearly for a moment.

"You mustn't fret. I've had my day; and it's a long time since Kate went."

That name, as much as anything, convinced me that he was dying; dying men look back over their lives, they say, back to their very beginnings. And Kate, whoever she was, must have belonged to his youth; I had never heard anyone mention her, though in the yard there were one or two who claimed to remember his wife, "a queer body" who'd never settled down in Baildon, but gone to her own people and then come back to have her baby and died when it was born. Her name was not Kate, I'd heard it, once, I think, and it was outlandish.

The thought that Martin, my master, was about to die fell on my mind and clove it in halves, like an axe coming down on a billet of wood. On one side there was all concern for *my* future. He had no heir except a girl in a convent; I understood the business, he trusted me, and liked me. Surely I must be provided for. But he had spoken of giving Maude a dower which would be talked of for years; and if he thought he was dying it would matter very little to him whether she stayed at Clevely or not.

Blood, when the test comes, is thicker than water, and I could well imagine him saying that it was all to go to Maude.

On the other side of my mind there was no material consideration at all. I just realised how much I held him in respect and esteem, how much, whatever happened, I should miss him, quiet, solid, and sensible. True I deceived him a little and robbed him a little, sometimes railed at him in my mind for being slow and stubborn and old-fashioned and fussy over details, but I knew his worth; and although his honesty had not made me honest, and his kindness had not made me kind, he had shown me a standard against which I myself, and any other man I ever met, would measure very small.

Having sent for the priest and the doctor and seen the work in the yard begun, I went in and carried up a new poultice and then a piece of clean parchment, the quill, and the inkhorn. I looked down at these and thought: Instruments of Fate. A few scratches one way or another and a whole future is settled and sealed. I was tempted to remind him that to leave a fortune to Maude would be to make sure that she stayed in Clevely for life. Without saying much he had limned that new Prioress for me; she would be capable of settling, in the way she wanted it, the shilly-shallying mind of any girl so richly dowered. When it came to the point, however, I found that the words would not be said. Instead of speaking I fluffed up his pillows, and then went and fetched my own to add to his, so that he was propped almost upright, and seemed to find relief so.

"You're very good to me," he croaked.

"I'll remind you of those words at Lady Day," I said lightly. I drew my wage then.

He saw the joke and smiled. But he said, "I've seen my last Lady Day."

A pang ran through me, for him, for myself, for all poor people who must, in the end, face the unknown dark. Kings, nobles, clerks, and swine-herds, all laid level at last, the songs sung, the good meals eaten, the kisses forgotten and done with. A great hunger for life took me. I decided, all in a moment, that I wouldn't darken another day of my life by hankering for anything; if he doesn't leave me a farthing, I thought, I'll still be alive, and young, capable of enjoying myself.

The priest arrived, red-faced from his ride in the wind, carrying a bag of embroidered linen.

"I am sorry indeed to find you thus," he began. Master Reed dismissed me with a glance and I went out, closing the door.

The woman who cooked for us all caught me on my way out of the house. What, she asked plaintively, should she do about dinner, and sup-per moreover; it was four days since anybody had given her an order and she'd managed as best she could, with bits of this and that, but now she was at the end. With the mistress gone silly and the master taken to his bed, whom could she ask but me. "Thass all very sad, but when they come in, all them great hearty men, they ain't to be put off with sorrowful words and titbits."

That, I knew, would be the last thing that he would wish. His attitude towards food was extraordinary; very abstemious himself, he was always careful to see that his table was spread with good food and plentiful. Yet the waste of a crumb worried him. I had often noted this incongruity and concluded that he was a man who, in his time, had gone hungry and knew the value of food.

And now, once again, my severed mind bothered me. By the time dinner was on the table . . . Oh, let us not think of that! Dying can be a long business. They'll come in hungry; and this is one of the days in their lives, in my life; all of us being rushed along by uncheckable time towards the moment when food will concern, will please us no more.

"You say you've been on the makeshift," I said. "To put it even, what is the thing they like best?"

"Salt beef and dumplings." She was beautifully certain about that. "But that'll mean opening a new cask of beef. You say I am to do that?"

"Yes. Open a new . . ." I broke off, hearing overhead the imperative banging of the stick which I had placed by Master Reed's bedside so that he could summon attention.

"Cask," I said, "and plenty of dumplings." I took the stairs two at a time.

It was the priest who had done the banging. When I entered he stood there, the stick in his hand. He gave me a sidelong, curiously shamefaced look and then looked down at the carved knob of the stick.

"My hands," he said. "All knotted with old age and stiffness. It's as much as I can do to write my name nowadays."

And probably, I thought swiftly, as much as he could do at any time. In some places and in some circumstances very little learning was demanded of a man anxious to take orders. And that little, unpractised for thirty or forty years in a country parish, would shrivel to nothing.

Master Reed, coughing and hawking, said, "You do the scribing, Nicholas."

The priest threw me another look, faintly hostile. I knew how he felt; there was no real need, in his opinion, to have the will written down. Dozens of men every year disposed of their property by word of mouth—a nuncupative will as it was called—and when it came to the attesting of such unwritten testaments there was no word that carried so much weight as a priest's. I accuse Sir Andrew of nothing when I say that, had I not been there with my ready pen, he could have called two gaping oafs from kitchen or yard, listened to Martin Reed's wheezing expression of his last wishes, and later on very easily proved that on his deathbed the wool merchant had turned very pious and left most of his goods to Holy Church. That had been done a thousand times and would be again. The number of Chantries in the country, served by idle, self-indulgent priests who could not even remember the names of those for whom they were to sing Masses, and by whose bounty they lived, proves that.

In this case, here I was, seating myself sideways, awkwardly against the chest where I had set the writing things, leaving the table for the cloth, the wafer, and the wine of the ritual.

Master Reed, in a voice that sounded like an ungreased wheel in the distance, said, "First I want every man who's worked for me five years or more to have three shillings and fourpence; those less long, twenty pence."

Before I could set down a word the priest said, "A written will should be properly made. That is no way to begin. You commend your soul to Almighty God and then say that you are of good mind and memory."

"You can both see. I'm short of breath. We'll get the main things down. Trim it up afterwards." Master Reed signed to me to write, which I did hastily.

His habitual economy of words now served him well; the sentences, though barely audible, were brief and clear. Calling me his "faithful servant and good friend," he left me the premises, the goodwill, tools, and instruments which would enable me to carry on his business as wool merchant, weaver, and smith. His two ships and his flocks were not included in this bequest, but he left me twenty pounds in cash for immediate expenses. Out of the profits of the business I was to pay, each year, three pounds to Sir Godfrey Blanchfleur, the elder, and ten to Anne Reed, widow of Richard Reed deceased, so long as they should live.

It was easy enough to keep pace with his dictation because of his frequent pauses to cough and gather breath. Having written that I looked at him, hoping to convey my gratitude in a glance, but he was staring ahead, frowning. He drew a rattling breath and went on.

Everything else of which he was possessed, the house, his ships, his cash money, the sheep run at Minsham and the flocks; two house properties in Baildon Saltgate, the Great Field at Horringer, the freehold of the God Spare Mariners inn at Bywater, were to go to his dearly beloved granddaughter, Maude Reed. . . .

The name emerged in such an inconclusive way that for a second or two I was certain that he was going to add some conditional phrase. Holding the pen suspended, I looked at him again and as I did so a bout of coughing racked him. When it was done, he said:

"That's all."

Slowly I placed the full stop which would hold Maude in the nunnery. There was a little silence, broken by the priest's rasping voice, saying with genuine horror, "Such a will a heathen might make. No mention of Holy Church, of alms or charity or so much as a Mass for your sinful soul. My son, I bid you think again. For your own sake."

"What do you want me to say?"

"I," Sir Andrew's voice conveyed his affront, "I want nothing, except to ease your passage through Purgatory and give you credit at the Last Judgement. You, Martin Reed, like the young man who came to Our Lord, are a man of great possessions. I would not have you, like him, go sorrowful away when all the reckoning is made. And of this will I say that a Saracen who had never taken the Body and Blood of Christ upon his tongue might leave it behind."

Master Reed had sunk a little farther back into his pile of pillows and half closed his eyes.

"Sir Andrew," I began, in an expostulatory voice.

"Be silent!" he said. "You were brought in to write and well you have done it. I have his soul to care for. Martin, for your own sake, make a gift to the Church, one of your many properties. One-third to buy Masses for your soul; one-third for the poor; and one-third to be used at the priest's discretion. At Flaxham we have no bell." He added the final words with a disarming simplicity.

"Then let it be the Minsham sheep run, that being nearest to you."

"I will see that the Masses are faithfully said."

I scratched the sheep run out of the list of properties that were to be Maude's, and thought how the Prioress would grudge it, could she but know. I added the bequest to those already written, with details of its disposal. Then a thought struck me.

"You have not named those who should execute your will, sir."

"You," he said, wearily. "And Sir Andrew, here, if he is willing."

"Right readily. And the bell, Martin, shall bear your name, with some reminder. 'Pray for the soul of Martin Reed, whenever you my tongue shall heed' or something like that."

"I thank you," Martin Reed said, but he looked at me as he spoke, and one of his eyebrows lifted as I had seen it do when Mistress Reed spoke with extra haughtiness, or Walter made some unusually extravagant statement. And I thought to myself: This is not the way he would have willed it on the afternoon when he came back from Clevely. I put the quill into the inkhorn and tipped it a little, so that a thin black stream ran from corner to corner of the written sheet.

"Now look what I have done," I said. "I am very sorry. The chest is awkward to write at. Shall I now make a fair copy?"

"Yes," said Sir Andrew firmly. "And in the rewriting make a proper beginning. Write, 'In the name of Almighty God, Amen.' And then go on, 'I, Martin Reed, being of good mind and memory, make my testament in this wise.' Can you bear that in mind? And first mention the gift to Flaxham Church, it will look better there than tagged on at the end."

I looked again at my master. Save for two small dusky red patches over the cheekbones, his face was the colour of a candle; his eyes were half closed.

"In all else, sir, this is as you wish?"

"Make a fair copy, Nicholas; while I make my peace with God."

I bent down and lifted one of his big, work-worn hands and put my lips to it. I fumbled in my mind for some words—not my own—with which to refute the priest's attitude, and found them, spoke them haltingly. "'What more can a man do than love mercy, do justice, and walk humbly before his God?' That you have always done, and God will know His own, sir."

I picked up the writing things and went from the room as the priest settled his stole.

Downstairs in the office I rewrote the will in a neat clear script, setting it down as I had been bidden, until I came to the point where, leaving Maude's name hanging in the air, Master Reed had paused. There I wrote in what I genuinely believed he would himself have added at any other time: "on condition that she abandon all intention of becoming a nun." He had wanted Maude to come home and marry and have children; those few added words would give her the chance to do so at least.

Then I thought, nobody would make such a condition without providing against its non-acceptance. So I added that if Maude insisted upon becoming a professed religious all her portion was to go to Flaxham Church. It hurt me to dispose so lightly of such a fortune, but the priest had just shown me that, like many people who do not rely upon the written word, he had an excellent memory. That final sentence would blur his memory and stop his mouth. It also, in a curious way, cleared my conscience.

Two witnesses who had no interest in the will were needed. I fetched two men who were waiting in the forge. They made their crosses and I wrote their names below.

By midday Martin Reed was peacefully unconscious, and in that state he died, just before dawn on the following morning.

Interval

What he found so hard to stomach was that in the end he brought about his own undoing; was punished for behaving well; sustained a hurt which would last a lifetime simply because he had shown a delicate consideration for another person's feelings and exercised self-restraint.

That he had, perhaps, challenged Fate by being too certain, somewhat arrogant, a trifle smug, never once occurred to him.

He had been right, surely, not to make an instant proposal of marriage when Maude, at last, came back to the Old Vine. She had suffered enough emotional strain, returning to Clevely, after three days of hard travel, to learn that her grandfather was dead and buried, and, while that grief was still raw, coming home to learn of Walter's death and to be confronted by her idiot mother.

At Clevely the Prioress had lost no time in producing an aged copy of the Bull Periculoso of Pope Boniface VIII.

"Here it is, clearly set down in black and white, in the vulgar tongue for the benefit of the unlearned," she said. "A rule made one hundred and fifty years ago, which has been disregarded by the heads of many Houses with consequent disorder and ruin. Read it."

It was a piece of stiff parchment which had been kept tightly rolled for many years. Under the prioress's white, well-kept hands it opened a little and then tried to spring back into its roll.

"Take hold of it. It has no teeth! There. . . ."

Maude read a sentence about forbidding, on pain of excommunication, any nun or sister to go outside the bounds of a monastery. She looked up with a puzzled frown. She and Dame Lucy had been *sent* to Ramsey.

"There," said the Prioress, and the finger jabbed down upon the next sentence. "Read it aloud."

"Item," Maude read, "let no one be received as nun or sister until we have enquired more fully into the resources of the House."

"It could hardly be clearer," the cool voice said. "A convent is not, as so many people suppose, a refuge for the indigent. The terms of your grandfather's will ensure that if you stay here you will have nothing. Not even the miserable five pounds a year that has hitherto been paid, and which he as good as promised me should be increased. Old men in their dotage," she said savagely, "change their minds with every wind. And the Flaxham priest, naturally, had an eye to his own advantage."

Maude took her hands from the document, folded them in front of her in the approved manner, and stood silent. There was nothing to say. She knew, in her heart, that her grandfather, although he had allowed her to live at Clevely, had done so against his will; and that had she become a nun it would have been with his disapproval. She had often wondered, during the last year, whether he had not known her better than she knew herself; and since the installation of the new Prioress her uncertainty and lack of contentment had grown daily. Now, after the long and wearing indecision, the choice had been made for her.

"There is no need to tell you," the Prioress said, "that this is a House virtually without resources. What I brought to it is already spent and not half of what is needful is yet done. If, in the circumstances, I allowed you to stay here, I should act in direct disobedience to this Papal Bull, and should myself deserve to be removed."

She spoke as though she were repudiating some plea, refuting an argument. Maude wondered how often this scene would be reenacted; upon how many women who were sure of their vocation, and who perhaps had no resources, even sequestrated ones like her own, this Papal Bull would be used like an axe. For herself it did not matter. She drew a long breath, lifted her head and said clearly:

"Madam, I am not asking you to keep me."

She never guessed that a little humility at this point, a few tears, some pleading words would have persuaded the Prioress to disregard Boniface VIII's express command. She never guessed that she had been sent to Ramsey to make a study of the music, not because she had a better ear than most of the others but because the Prioress hoped that the idea of improving the Clevely singing would forge another link, give her an aim and a purpose. Maude had taken less kindly than anyone except Dame Clarice, who was so old that she counted for little, to the new regime at Clevely, and Maude was, in fact, exactly the type of woman whom the Prioress wished to rule; educated, well connected on one side, at least, sensible, and rich.

Rich no longer. The Prioress's disappointment was commensurate with her hopes, which had ridden high after her interview with old Martin Reed; and since he was beyond her reproaches she expended her anger upon Maude.

"I don't *mind*," Maude told Nicholas in one of their many talks. "I wasn't sure; I don't think I ever was sure, and Grandfather knew it. I think that is why he made that condition. As a test. All the same," she frowned, and on her smooth white forehead the ghost of Martin's double horseshoe cicatrice appeared, "I was *shocked*. In the old days money never mattered at Clevely."

"Then it was," he said lightly, "the only place on earth where it did not; and now there is none. Money always matters."

"Not to Walter. He was the one person who never minded about it."

He was tempted to retort sharply that even so it was money, some infinitesimally small sum of it, that had led to Walter's premature death. But he had seen that same darkening of the eyes as had once accompanied any mention of Melusine, and, as on former occasions, all his impulse was to comfort and console. So he took her hand and told her gently that she must not grieve for Walter; Walter's life, short as it was, had held as much happiness as most people know in sixty years; he had always done exactly what he wanted, and nothing that he did not; he had loved nothing and nobody but his music, and that love had never failed him.

He could, even thus early, have gone on to speak of other forms of love, confessed his own. But he refrained.

Opportunities to step smoothly from the impersonal to the intimate abounded, seemed indeed to thrust themselves upon him. She spoke once, in an astonished way, of the fact that her grandfather had named no guardian.

"I expected to be somebody's ward, like poor Madge FitzHerbert," she said. "And when I left Clevely I made up my mind that nobody was going to marry me for my possessions."

He realised that the omission had been an oversight; in his hasty rewriting of the will the matter of Maude's age had never entered his mind. He could not now say what was true, that Martin, in the making of his will, had visualised her under the guardianship and management of the Prioress of Clevely.

"Your mother is still living," he pointed out, "and I am here to look after everything for you. You need no guardian. And the notion of being married for your money is an absurdity. You are no Madge FitzHerbert. You are beautiful."

Her face coloured and the pace of his heartbeat quickened. Now? Why not? So easy. You are beautiful and lovable and I love you; to marry you has been my one desire since the moment I saw you almost four years ago.

But he left it where it was. A compliment, accepted with a blush.

There had always been, at the core of his feeling for her, an element of the worshipful, novel to him in his experience of women, and therefore oddly enjoyable. There was also in his attitude something resembling that of the gourmet who, before setting about some particularly succulent dish, eyes it with pleasure, sniffs its savour with gloating. Some part of his restraint was also not far removed from fear. She was so innocently friendly; a word spoken too soon, some betraying gesture made before he had succeeded in endearing himself to her, might ruin all. He had come so far, waited so long, worked so cunningly, that in the end nothing but perfection would suffice.

He behaved—as he saw, looking back—in lunatic fashion. Not content with a dumb wooing, fetching and carrying, acting in all but the ultimate assertion of rights, like an elderly man with a lovely and capricious mistress, he went to other lengths. He broke with Clemence, promising her a pension of five pounds a year and bearing first her reproachful tears and then her vituperative anger with the utmost detachment, as though suddenly a wall of glass had reared itself between her and him. He rode home from Minsham whistling, and on the next day took himself into the confessional at St. Mary's Church, and, for some moderate penance and a contribution to the Poor Box, was absolved from all his sins of fornication.

Young men, on the eve of knighthood, made similar confessions, and washed themselves thoroughly and then kept vigil in churches all through the night. That thought occurred to him as he left the church, raising his eyes to the carved angels in the roof, the angels of whom Maude, at the age of twelve, had reminded him. A carving, once made, he thought, was finished, could never grow or change. *His* angel, while losing nothing that could deserve reverence, had developed all the qualities which would enable a man to say truly, "With my body I thee worship." It occurred to him that on the night before his marriage he would keep vigil in this church, under the angel roof.

So he stepped out into the greenish April dusk at almost the same moment as a young man, thoroughly washed, confessed, and absolved, went into the chapel of the Knights Hospitallers, at Dunwich, to keep his pre-knighting vigil.

The days lengthened; the trees shook out their young green; daisies and cowslips and lady's smocks gemmed the meadows. There had never been so sweet a spring as this one through which they rode, on her business, on his, or something which concerned them both. It was a matter for laughter that *his* pack ponies on their comings and goings must use *her* front door and trot through the very heart of *her* house. And his certainty that he had done right, that he had carried out both Martin's wish and Maude's was proved beyond all doubt on the day when Sir Andrew, riding a bony mule, came into the Old Vine and, with the air of doing Maude a favour, said that if she cared to return to Clevely and take vows she could. Flaxham Church, out of what would then fall into its hands, would endow her handsomely. The Prioress, upon whom he had called, was very anxious, he said, to have Maude back, providing her return was in accord with the Bull Periculoso. If she saw his real purpose, Maude gave no sign of such awareness, but thanked him heartily and said she had no wish to return to Clevely.

"There are other houses," he suggested.

"None where I am needed as I am here. I look after my mother."

He argued at some length, and then, finding her immovable, made a peevish complaint about the wording of the will.

"It was made hastily and badly."

"You were present at its making, Sir Andrew," Maude said mildly.

"Yes; and I said at the time that it was such a will as a heathen might make. And I had my mind set upon persuading your grandfather on another point, so that that condition slipped in without my noticing. Also I had a cold in my head and at such times I am a little hard of hearing. Of one thing I am *sure*, and that is that it was never your grandfather's intention to so make his will that you should renounce your vocation."

"I think it was his intention to prove to me that I had no vocation."

"Then why did you contemplate the religious life?"

She frowned thoughtfully.

"I was trying to run away from certain things in this world that I was unwilling to face."

"And have they changed?"

It was impossible to explain how the balance had been adjusted, Clevely, under the new regime, another lost illusion, and the Old Vine, free of her mother's dislike, no longer a place to flee from. She said simply, "The change has been in me."

Some hot and hasty words about the uncertainty of purpose, the halting faith, the self-indulgence of this new generation, formed in his mind, but stopped short behind his teeth. She was his parishioner, and a wealthy one; it would serve him ill to alienate her. He had already ordered the new bell; there was that much gained; and now, to test her attitude he said:

"I find that I made your grandfather a rash promise. I also was hasty that morning. The bell will cost more than I thought and I shall not be able to afford the engraving which was to remind all those who heard its voice to pray for his soul."

She said eagerly that she would pay for that.

When he left, disappointed in his main objective, he looked forward to a future rich in little extortions. She had not taken advantage of his offer, but he was sure that in her heart she had appreciated it. She was convent-schooled and would be amenable. He remembered a proverb, current amongst the homely members of his flock—there were more ways of catching a cony than by chasing it, shouting.

Nicholas Freeman decided to declare himself on May the third, which at the Old Vine had always been the date of a humble, rather curious little family festival, known as "Sparrowgrass Day."

At the end of the garden, beyond the rosebushes and the apple trees and the herb plot, was a bed of asparagus, twenty years old. Richard had brought the first crowns back from one of his trips to Flanders; they had spread and flourished to such an extent that each year, at the height of its bearing, the bed gave at least two cuttings of such plenty that every man and boy in the dining hall could have ten or twelve green spikes as a vegetable with his supper dish. Martin Reed had convinced himself that the plant had medicinal qualities, it cleansed the blood. Earlier in the season, when the first shoots were ready for cutting but not in such number that they would "go round," the asparagus presented a problem to a master of Martin Reed's nature; the square family table in the hall was always served with exactly the same food as any other. Luxuries were enjoyed later, in privacy. A cooked vegetable, however, could not be served after supper, casually from the livery cupboard; nor could the first, succulent green growth be wasted. So, for some years, in the last days of April, or the early ones of May, Martin and Richard, and later Anne and then the children, had observed Sparrowgrass Day, and had supper served at the table in the solar. Then someone had observed that it was on May the third that Martin had first approached Anne's father about her marrying Richard, and so the little feast day was fixed. Other delicacies, such as fresh fish hurried up from Bywater, were added to the table, and always jugs of good wine.

This year Nicholas intended to keep the festival and, because Maude's birthday had fallen during the days of mourning for her grandfather and gone unmarked, it could be a celebration of her birthday too. He had ridden into Colchester and bought her a present from the goldsmith's there. It was a reliquary pendant, hung on a thin gold chain. The pendant was a flat, slim oblong of gold which, upon pressure on a spring, opened into a triptych of pictures, beautifully worked in enamel, the centre picture showing the Crucifixion, the one to the left the Annunciation, and the one on the right Christ's Ascension. When closed it measured an inch and a half by two, and was a masterpiece of delicate workmanship. It had cost every penny of his filchings and three pounds of his cash legacy.

He planned it all to the last detail. Mistress Reed could go to bed and eat—in the disgustingly slovenly way she had lately developed—her dish of asparagus there. He and Maude would sit in the solar, at a table with a good linen cloth, set near the window to catch the evening light. There would certainly be, to start with at least, the sadness inseparable from any family anniversary after a bereavement, and he would exert himself to talk as entertainingly as possible. The servant would serve the asparagus, and then the fish, and go, leaving the sweetmeats on the cupboard. When they were alone he would remind Maude of her forgotten birthday and produce his gift. After it had been admired he would fix the chain about her neck, drop his hands to her shoulders, turn her towards him, and kiss her.

All this planning gave him the same half-incredulous pleasure as he had felt through the waiting time. He, Nick Freeman, whose approach to women had always been so forthright, setting a scene, preparing the very words he would say. It was amazing, but it was wonderful; he loved her, never having loved any woman before, therefore it must all be as different as he could make it.

The very day was exactly as he would have had it could he have ordered it as he had ordered the clothes he intended to wear that evening; a warm, fair day, full of the first scents of summer. The little pink monthly rose, always the first to come into bloom was covered with half-open buds; the lilacs were in heavy flower. A bowl of the roses, he thought, closely massed together in the centre of the table, between the silver candlesticks. Giving this order to the maid whom he had taken into his confidence, an odd thought occurred to him—it was almost as though he were a priest, arranging an altar! The thought provoked a smile, which still lingered in the corners of his mouth and in his eyes as he went on to have a word with Phyllis. Mistress Reed to be out of the solar and into bed by six o'clock.

Then, so that the whole thing might be a surprise to Maude, he sought her out with the suggestion that in the afternoon they should ride together. There was a clip of wool he wanted to inspect at Marly.

"I've never been there," Maude said.

"You turn off at Flaxham and ride alongside the river. It is a pretty ride, especially now, with the hawthorns coming into bud."

Before they left he took out his new clothes and laid them on the bed. Never in all his life had he had such clothes because always every garment he had bought, even for best, had ahead of it years of servile office wear. His new tunic and hose were garments for a young, prosperous merchant, garments that Maude's own father might have worn, a tawny yellow, slashed with buff, colours carefully chosen to enhance his dark good looks, and the easy cut of the tunic calculated to conceal the hint of threatening stoutness. He laid the pendant beside the clothes, ready to slip into his pouch when he changed.

They exchanged casual, unimportant remarks as they rode, until, in the distance, they could see the double arch of the ancient stone bridge, with its image perfectly reflected in the water below. On either bank of the river were the hawthorns covered with bright green leaves, just un-curling, and clusters of buds a little less white than the flowers into which presently they would break. Somewhere on the other side of the river a cuckoo called, and another answered.

Maude gave a great sigh which called her grandfather to Nicholas' mind.

"Beautiful!" she said. "So beautiful. And when I think how nearly I missed it all." The ecstatic note in her voice gave way to a kind of grating impatience. "Oh, I know that the summer will pass and the bloom will fade and the leaves will fall, whereas the spiritual things, the devotion and the duties and the joys go on, unchanging whatever the season . . . and when one is old. I *know* that. In my mind. But my heart was never convinced. It would not be. I prayed and prayed for some sign, for some proof that what I knew I should do was the thing that was right for me. And nothing happened. Then, when the sign came, it pointed the other way."

They had halted their horses who, after nuzzling one another, dropped their heads and strained towards the green grass.

"I warned you," he said. And she took that, not as a reproach, but as proof that he knew what she was talking about. That was what made him so delightful a companion; he did not need everything explained and underlined.

"I know. But when you are young what do you know about yourself? I mean . . . a dim-witted person might, for the best of reasons, wish to be a scholar, and try and try, and he would learn *something*; then one day he might be sent to feed pigs and realise that feeding pigs was what God meant him to do. You know why I went to Clevely; I told you. And for a long time it seemed right. Being cold and tired and hungry, salting the butter away in casks with the salt getting into the cracks of my hands was all helping, I thought. I offered my little sufferings so that Melusine . . . And then, all at once it was no good for me any more. Nothing I did was a gift; it was a tax, wrenched from me."

"I could see that," he said.

"There was one time when I was afraid I might go mad. Shall I tell you what I thought? I thought that if this went on much longer, I should begin to hate Melusine. I thought she should never have done . . . never have got herself into such a situation in the first place; or, having let it happen, she should have married one of those silly young men who were always following her around. Wasn't that shocking? The one person who had been kind to me. The person who had taught me to read and write. To think such shameful things."

"Thoughts walk in uninvited," he said.

She turned to him with a look of bright relief.

"That *is* true, isn't it? I was in the Chapel, at the end of a twenty-four-hour fast. I was making a Novena. And that thought, as you say, walked in. And after that it all seemed such a waste. But I went on praying, and in the end there was a sign—the Bull Periculoso!"

"May Heaven reward Pope Boniface VIII," he said lightly. But one day, or rather one night, one night very soon, when they lay spent with loving, breathless with loving, when she had tasted to the full all the joy she had so nearly missed, he would tell her to whom she owed it. The story of how the long-dead Pope had had a little help from a humble living clerk would be worth telling.

The thought of being in bed with her, of her hair spread loose on the pillow, of the way he would handle and teach that virgin innocence moved him so much that once again he was astonished. He might have been a boy again, virgin himself, excited by the prospect of his first experience in the art of love.

"I think we should move on," he said. "We mustn't be late for supper. I have a surprise for you."

They rode towards the bridge, she trying to extract from him some details about the surprise, he refusing to tell her, and both finding cause for laughter in this simple business because they were happy and it was a day for laughter.

How well, he thought, he had chosen his time. Her return to the world had combined with the natural resiliency of youth to enable her to throw off her sorrows. She was whole now, and happy, and his for the taking.

Presently he had another notion, as farfetched as the earlier comparison of a supper table with an altar. They were already, he thought, like a married couple. The proposal, the acceptance, the ceremony would be nothing but formalities. The real bonds of affection and common interest and good companionship were already forged.

He looked back upon how he had come to Baildon, having been thrown out of the leather merchant's house in disgrace; upon how, before ever he had set eyes upon her, he had decided that to marry his master's granddaughter would be a desirable thing to do. How seldom in this life did one's desires and one's material advantages run alongside. How profoundly, how miraculously lucky he had been.

He fell silent and rode for some time indulging in those gloating, self-congratulatory thoughts which ignorant heathen everywhere and at all times have regarded as dangerous, likely to provoke the gods to jealousy and wrath.

The road by which he and Maude, at the end of their ride, approached the Old Vine, ran steeply downhill, and the road itself had been made, immemorial years ago, by heavily laden horses who, to ease the incline, had struggled not straight forward but from left to right and then from right to left. It had three sharp bends; and three times, riding downhill, one could catch, and then lose again, the sight of the house, the weaving sheds and stables, lying at the bottom of the slope, with, just beyond, the wall and south gate of Baildon.

On this afternoon, as the view came first into sight, they could see two horsemen ride through the gateway; both men, one riding a tall horse, the other a heavier animal which bore, beside its rider, a sizable bundle behind the saddle. They saw so much, and then the road turned and a clump of elms blocked out the view.

When they could next look down the riders had almost reached the house and were visible in some detail. The one on the tall horse was young, his tanned face dark against his straw-coloured hair; the other man was older, and the bundle behind him, by its awkward angular shapes and the fact that it was enclosed in a soft, yellowish bag of goatskin, could be identified as a suit of armour packed for transit. Two squires on their way to join their master. The view was obscured again.

The road ran out on to the level and made its last turn. The two riders had halted by the great door of the Old Vine. The younger was studying the house, looking it over, up and down, from side to side. Perhaps because he was conscious of the new clothes lying spread upon his bed, Nicholas observed, between one blink of the eyelid and the next, the shabbiness of the scuffed, rubbed, greasy leather jerkin worn by this young man. At the same time, not to be missed, was some indefinable hint of quality; in the way he sat in his saddle, in the turn of his head, as he looked the house over. This quality was oddly reflected in his mount; rawboned and rough-coated, it yet bore the stamp of breeding.

Nicholas looked at Maude and was about to say: It seems we have visitors; for the young man, making a sign with his hand which his companion interpreted as an order to wait where he was, turned his horse and rode into the great door of the house. There was no time to make the remark, for Maude brought her hand down in a slap on her horse's rump and it shot forward. Nicholas caught one glimpse of a face he had never seen before, transformed, almost idiotic with joyful surprise.

His own horse, without urging, hurried after its companion, and they clattered into the yard nose to tail.

The young man was in the act of dismounting, his eyes fixed on the back of the house in the same keen earnest scrutiny to which he had subjected the front.

He reached the ground and then, hearing the clatter of hoofs, turned about. Maude threw herself out of the saddle and cried, "Henry!" Her face was red as a rose from chin to brow and his turned even darker.

He said in a gruff, embarrassed way, "I told you I should come."

It was not what he had intended to say, nor the tone in which he had intended to speak. And just behind Maude a man, too old to be her twin brother, a neat good-looking man, was just dismounting.

Too full of sudden fear to mind his manners, he seized Maude's hands and pulled off both her gloves. Only one ring, and that the one which he had pushed onto that finger more than four years ago.

"You've worn it . . . all this time?"

She nodded, and laughed, and said, "It's still too big."

Satisfied, he remembered what, through four hard years, he had kept in mind, as part of his goal. Still holding her hand, he went on one knee and lifted her fingers to his lips.

"Sir Henry Rancon," he said, so thickly that he seemed about to choke, "now and forever at your service, demoiselle."

"Last time," she said, "it was the other way round. You remember? Stand up, Sir Henry, and let me look at you."

He had changed very little, except to grow; the shabby old jerkin was much too small. An old scar ran from one eyebrow to the edge of his badly cropped, dusty hair, and a newer one, hardly healed, showed just below the line of his jaw. She remembered the surprising softness of his lips and wondered . . . And was then aware that Nicholas had come to stand beside her. She turned to him, and, with a smile that haunted him to the end of his life, dealt him his mortal wound.

"This was the surprise! Oh, Master Freeman, how did you guess?"

They had been on Christian name terms for at least a month.

Sometimes, during his almost meteoric rise to the upper ranks in the clerical hierarchy—for with money behind him, celibacy willingly embraced, and ruthless ambition as his motive power, nothing could stop him—he would ponder the irony of it all. Occasionally such musings ended with disconcerting thoughts about puppets and the strings they danced on, thoughts unsuitable in a churchman, tacitly dedicated to the theory of man's free will.

He suffered one such moment when, thirty years later, he was presented with his cardinal's hat. He recalled then, as though it had been something he had dreamed, Maude's story of the Rune Stone at Beauclaire. That was easily to be dismissed as girlish fancy. Less easy to ignore was the memory of old Martin Reed saying mildly, out of his garnered experience, "People do what they must."